The Bygone Wars:
Book 2

All the Wars of Heaven

by

Scott J. Robinson

All characters and events portrayed
in this book are fictional,
and any resemblance to
real people or incidents is coincidental
(and, let's face it, unlikely).

ISBN: 978-0-9943355-3-1

For more information visit
www.tengama.com

This book is
dedicated to

Bayli, Noah
and Kace

All the Wars of Heaven

-oOo-

Earlier

TUKI FAZED OUT OF THE TRANCE, letting it slowly slip away. Sounds and scents, colors and sensations followed one after the other like sand draining through his fingers, but the trailing edges of the vision clung to his consciousness like never before. For a moment, it was hard to separate the *here* from *there*, to separate the *now* from *then*. He drew in a deep breath, trying to calm his swirling thoughts. He felt a terrible sense of foreboding. When he opened his eyes, even that was gone, leaving him naked in the heat of the desert with just the memories. He blinked rapidly.

The warm wind touched his dark skin. Sand set it to tingling.

The day had drifted on, farther than he imagined. The shadow in which he sat had pushed its ragged edge several meters closer to the shattered, sand-choked well in the center of the square.

"I have travelled far," Tuki said to the glass ewer as he took it up in his hand. He knew he should not judge, but he would never have thought that such a plain item, made by humans, would be able to take him so far. When he had first found the ewer, buried beneath the sand in the corner of a desert-drowned house, he had thought it would hold no life within its flawed form. But life it had contained, and what a life!

He wondered what long dead human had possessed enough skill to produce such a wonderful Eye. And he wondered what journey he had made. Obviously it was a journey of many kilometers, for no such hills were in the desert and he had never heard of anything like the strange snaking creature he had seen. But had he also travelled in time? Had he witnessed what was, or what will be? Or had he watched the meteor's destruction of the silver trail as it happened? And what of the other creatures— the three legged ones and those with the hard, colorful shells who rode the strange bats? There were too many questions to be answered by one young male, alone in the desert.

Later

"WHENEVER YOU'RE READY, FLINT," Keeble muttered.

"Ready for what? You want us to attack them?"

"No. Just get us out of here."

"You want me to come up with a plan?"

"Yes."

"Well..."

"Let's just run then?" Keeble liked simple plans—unlike the bloody hurgon. They couldn't go back the way they'd come. They were closer to a door on the other side of the platform. "Over there and up the stairs."

"On three then."

Keeble hadn't known Flint could count to three.

"One... Two... Three."

They turned and ran.

Behind them, the hurgon fired their weapons. Keeble felt a tickle against his shoulder. The hairs on his arm stood on end. He cursed as he bounded up the stairs behind Suldon.

There were shouted warnings and screams from behind. There were what could only be flung insults. But the firing of the weapons continued. Safely off the platform, Keeble stopped to look at his shoulder. The material of his shirt had been burned away. A ragged black hole showed red skin beneath.

"Whistler, that was close."

"So what do we do now?" Sandy asked. She had a burn on her hip. It didn't look good to Keeble but the trollop didn't seem worried.

Another troop of P'targa soldiers rushed past, weapons at the ready. They charged down into the train station, firing as they went. Two died before they'd gone more than a couple of steps.

Keeble swallowed. Nina moved up the stairs and leaned against the wall. She stared at her hands and didn't say anything. And Flint went the other way, taking a peek around the corner. And a second later the troll dashed out onto the platform, grabbed a weapon from a fallen P'targa and came back again.

"Don't do that, Flint," Keeble said. "That's an order."

The troll shrugged. "They was busy." He gave the weapon to Sandy. It was a glove, not an entire sleeve, but looked to be the same as the weapons attached to the armor.

"That may be, but they'd stop to shoot a hakan if they had the chance."

"Maybe."

"What *were* they doing?"

"Shooting. Dying."

"Who was doing which?"

Flint gave it some thought. "Everyone was doing both."

1: Clockwork

PING HAD USED THE PORTALS to step between worlds twice, but the thought still made her heart race. Sitting in the starship, hands gripping the arms of her chair, she wondered if flying between universes would be the same. Those who had done it before— Kim, Meledrin, Tuki, and Keeble— didn't seem worried at all, though they did seem to be concentrating on their tasks with unusual ferocity. She glanced at the alien, Cuto, but she could tell nothing at all about what the creature was thinking. Shuddering, Ping quickly turned away.

When the tasks were completed, a shifting mist of silver night materialized before the ship. Ping closed one eye and held her breath. She winced at they passed through. But, as when she passed between worlds, nothing interesting seemed to happen. The lights turned off, but they'd been told that that would happen. The subtle, all-but-unnoticed vibrations of the ship ceased but they'd been told about that too. But, in general, everything seemed to go on as usual. Time continued to advance as it always had.

"If something goes wrong…" Scree said into the silence that gathered beneath the dome.

Kim nodded distractedly. "If something goes wrong, there will be absolutely nothing we can do. So there really isn't any point waiting here." She sighed. "In fact, if there's an emergency, I think I'd rather die in ignorance."

After another three and a half minutes, Tuki rose from his seat. "I will go and speak with the moai," he said, collecting a lantern from a locker. Moments later, he was gone.

"Why do things not work?" Ping asked quietly, unsure if anyone would hear.

Kim answered from her seat raised up high at the rear of the room. "We don't know the particulars. But apparently no advanced machinery will work in this universe."

"So, things like the monsters'…" She glanced at Cuto, thought the creature could not understand her. "Like the aliens' armor? And electricity?"

"Exactly. You know about electricity?"

Ping shrugged. "A little bit. Not really. Nobody really knows very much." She looked around the ship, as if all the lights and equipment were still working. "Nobody from Tiandi knows very much."

"I think that's about the level the dwarves are at."

Ping nodded, but wondered why they were going to the dwarf home world to find more crew members if the dwarves we no more advanced than her own people. And why did they not have a full crew anyway?

There were questions she could easily get the answers to, but Ping stayed silent, staring out at the strange universe. She might have stayed where she was for the entire six hours, simply because she was unwilling to see how much the lanterns really illuminated the dark, unknown of the ship, but Keeble told Kim that he was going to have a look at the clocks.

There are clocks on the ship? Ping assumed the dwarf wasn't talking about simple grandfather clocks used to tell the crew if it was time for breakfast. She unbuckled her belt and watched him head for the stairs, but Cuto was already following close behind. She glanced up at Kim. "Is the… Is Cuto really your friend?"

Kim gave it some thought, then shrugged. "All the evidence so far says yes, though I'm not sure if Cuto really knows what will happen when the chips are down."

"Pardon?"

Kim sighed. "Yes. I think Cuto is on our side."

Her desire to see the clock out weighed her fear of both the alien and the dwarf. "I will go with them."

Ping collected a lantern and hurried down the first flight of stairs. There was no light visible on the next level, but a soft glow was coming from the next stairway. She went down and down some more. She was so used to the descent that she almost missed when Keeble and Cuto finally exited. Ping found them in a large room with two workstations in the middle and several more around the walls. There were also cabinets and storage boxes in every available space.

When Ping arrived the dwarf already had a drawer open and was pulling out books and folders. She stopped near the door, chewing her fingernail and watching nervously.

The alien said something and Keeble looked up.

"What are you doing?" the dwarf asked shortly.

"I was hoping to watch you fix the clock." She took a step forward but glanced at Cuto and stopped.

"Well, you can't help."

Ping didn't say anything. She hadn't really expected to be allowed to help. And she didn't know if she would be able to anyway as everything on the ship seemed so far ahead of anything she had seen before. But she stayed where she was, watching Keeble and Cuto as they poured over the books.

"It's only losing a second every hour," Keeble muttered, "it can't be that hard to fix."

Ping almost said something, but remained silent at the last moment. Keeble looked up anyway and saw her standing with her mouth still open.

"What?"

Ping shrugged. If a clock was losing time it could be one of a thousand things. A regular clock, anyway. She didn't know about the ones on starships.

"If you don't have anything to say then don't stand there looking like you're going to say something."

Cuto did say something, waving his arms about.

Keeble grunted in reply. "I doubt we'll get if fixed anyway," he said before sighing and, after three seconds of head scratching thought, waving a hesitant reply.

More arm waving from Cuto, more head scratching from Keeble. Then a halting verbal and visual reply all at once. "I know but *she's* standing there. I can't concentrate."

"I could help," Ping said.

Keeble laughed. "What do *you* know about clocks?"

"I was a member of a clock making club. I was working on the Elephant Tower clock. But they were just normal clocks, with gears and levers and..."

"You were a clock maker?"

Pip nodded. "I was an apprentice."

"You were only an apprentice?"

Ping nodded, chewing on her thumbnail. Keeble shook his head and went back to looking through his books and files. After three and a half minutes Keeble sighed and slammed shut his book.

"There's two clocks and both of them are faulty."

"There are two?"

"Everything has a backup. There's two gravity drives and two Ohoga engines."

"What are the clocks used for?"

"They are a backup for the electronic clocks, I think, but more importantly, they are timers. They count down when we are in this universe to open the gate so we can leave."

"Electronic clocks?" Ping had no idea what they might be.

"They're working fine, as far as I know. Our main problem with fixing the regular clocks is that the computers don't work in this universe so it will be very difficult to diagnose the problem. We may have to wait, in the end."

"Right." Ping nodded and moved further into the room. She kept a close eye on Cuto but the alien made no threatening moves. "And both of the clocks are faulty?"

"The one we're using is losing time and the other one is completely buggered. I think it's jammed."

"Which one are you going to fix?"

Keeble shrugged. "I'm going to try to diagnose the one that's still running. I won't be able to fix it until we get back to our universe, seeing it's being used while we're here, but maybe I can find the problem..."

Ping didn't think that was the best plan. It must have shown on her face.

"What's wrong with that?" he asked angrily.

"The other one will be easier to diagnose and it could actually be fixed. And, the one that is losing time can still be used but if something happens to it..."

"Easier?"

"Big problems are easier to find. They are more obvious."

"But not necessarily easier to fix."

"But you can't fix the one that's being used anyway."

Cuto said something, obviously asking what was being said and Keeble spent four minutes and forty-seven seconds translating. When he was done Cuto replied and Keeble shook his head and went back to his books. It was five minutes before he spoke this time, but it was only to himself. Or perhaps to Cuto. "It could be anywhere," he muttered.

"Disconnect something in the middle," Ping said, "then turn it on and see if it is still jammed."

The dwarf and the alien both looked up.

"And what if it is?"

"Then disconnect another bit in the section that's jammed and see what happens then. You can narrow down the problem a long way."

"I knew that." But he went back to looking through the books. Cuto looked from Keeble to Ping and back again before also turning his attention to the books.

"Why is he here?" Ping asked Keeble.

The dwarf looked over his shoulder.

"We rescued Cuto from a prison on Earth. He's been trying to help us stop the war." Keeble shook his head. "Except Cuto isn't a he. The hurgon don't have different genders, apparently. That's what Meledrin says, anyway, if you want to believe her."

Keeble obviously did believe her, even if he didn't want to admit it.

"Well, how do they..."

Keeble gave her a shocked look. "I don't know and I don't want to know. I'm certainly not going to ask."

"Sorry, I—"

"Well, don't. If you're going to stand there asking stupid questions like a woman you can go somewhere else."

Ping fell silent and stayed where she was while Keeble spent another ten and a quarter minutes searching through the books and files. Cuto watched over his shoulder and the two of them talked in the sign language before Keeble finally looked up at Ping again. He pursed his lips.

"I'm going to disconnect something," he said. And with a grunt of disgust he got to his feet, found a toolbox, and stumped from the room with Cuto close behind.

Ping didn't hesitate this time, hurrying to keep up. On the floor above, Cuto started working on an access panel with a screwdriver that seemed tiny in his— its— huge hand. The monster worked with strength, but it seemed to be an inexorable strength unlike Scree's explosive one.

Soon Cuto and Keeble ducked through into the interior of the clock and started clattering around.

It was four and a half minutes before Ping worked up the courage to poke her head through the hole to look around. She stared. Even perfectly still it was the most intricate, amazing clock she had ever seen. Snapping her mouth shut she looked around for Keeble and Cuto but could not see them anywhere. She climbed into the clock and looked around some more, touching the closest cog, running her finger along the smooth, square edge. She followed from one cog to the next, then along a sprocket to a spring. She followed trails of force and compression, slowly walking deeper into the clock. It was above her and all around her, larger and more complicated by far than any clock she had ever seen, but still just a clock. She could see how it worked— at least, she could see how parts of it worked.

When she stumbled across Cuto and Keeble she immediately saw that the part they were working on would not help. "Ummm..."

"What? You shouldn't be in here."

"Disconnecting that won't help."

"Of course it will."

Ping chewed on her thumbnail.

Keeble sighed. "Everything looks the same in here. Gears and springs and... It all looks the same."

"You don't look at individual parts. You look at groups, and each one is as different as people."

"Which one then?"

Ping looked around, cataloguing parts and sections in her mind, and pointed to a cog attached to a coiled spring. "That one there."

"Are you sure?"

She nodded, paused, nodded again and watched as Keeble looked at Cuto. The two of them waved their arms for one minute and a twelve seconds then took their tools and moved to the cog Ping had indicated. Six minutes later, she was watching again, standing on her toes so she could peer over Keeble's shoulder, as the dwarf shifted the lever that would reengage the clock with the main spring. They turned the see the first half of the clock stuttered once then, slowly and smoothly, begin to move.

Ping could not help but marvel. It was just gears and levers and pulleys and springs, turning and pushing and pulling, but to her the movements seemed almost to be a dance, the waltz of time, with each little piece playing its part in a whole that was much greater than the sum of the parts. She did a little dance herself and clapped her hands. "Isn't it marvelous? I've never seen anything like it." And yet it was just a clock, and as she watched more and more of the design made sense to her. It was still beyond her skills to completely decipher without seeing schematics or looking further, but more and more of the pieces were falling into place in her mind.

Keeble grunted. "Yeah, wonderful." He scratched his beard and looked about. "So now we know the problem is after the break, right?"

"Right."

He grunted again. "But look at everything that isn't moving. There's still thousands of bits that it could be."

"So we reconnect the cog and disconnect something further on."

"This could take hours."

As far as Ping knew they had hours. "What else are we going to do?" she asked.

"We? I'm the one fixing this. Me and Cuto. You're just... A consultant."

Ping didn't think Keeble liked women very much. Or perhaps it was just her, though he hardly knew her at all. But now that she had spent some time with him he didn't scare her— he was like a grumpy hamster, chittering away but not really threatening at all.

The dwarf went to refit the gear and Ping followed behind with Cuto. "If you don't know much about clocks, who is supposed to fix them? Where is the rest of the crew?"

"Rest of the crew? We're it. Me, Kim, Meledrin and Tuki. We've only been in the ship for a few hours."

"What? But..?"

"We were trying to escape from some Americans and found a whole heap of ships in a hangar. Then we had to get them working and Kim had to learn how to fly."

"But how do you expect to fight the—" she looked at Cuto— "The aliens?"

Keeble shrugged. "We don't want to fight the hurgon. So Kim says anyway— Cuto here seems friendly enough. It's those other aliens that are the problem and I don't think all the ships in the world are going to help." He paused for a moment, seeming to realize what he was saying. He sighed. "It's either try or go land somewhere and wait around like a startled rabbit to see what happens." Job done, Keeble looked around. "Which bit next."

Ping looked too and pointed. The dwarf set to work.

Perhaps the Hakahei fighting this new threat would be like me fighting the hurgon, Ping thought. She didn't have a hope until Scree came along. And now Scree had found a whole pack of trolls. Perhaps they would be enough. She had escaped one threat, leaving her home and her people behind, only to find herself in a battle against something much worse.

Five minutes later, Ping winced when the dwarf turned the clock on a second time and the huge machine screeched a complaint.

2: Interesting Thoughts

SCREE SIGHED.

Six hours. He was suddenly aware of time like he never had been before. He wondered how Ping felt— she knew time better than she knew anything. Did that make her more or less affected by its tricks? She had already left, trailing after Keeble as he went to fix something or other. Scree couldn't decide if that was going to go. Keeble obviously didn't like women and Ping had no reason to be too keen on men at the moment either.

They'd work it out.

The other trolls were still in their seats but starting to get restless.

Scree could see the moment getting closer. He thought he'd be able to guess the exact moment when...

"Is there somethin' we can do?" one of them asked.

Up in her seat Kim gave the matter some though. "There's a garden down stairs— it's all dirt at the moment but you could play football or something."

Scree had no idea what football was and doubted the others did either, but they'd work out something.

"That'll do."

Scree was supposed to be in charge of the trolls and should probably get to know them and make sure they weren't going to go around breaking things and killing people because they were bored. But he also wanted to find out something about Kim— what sort of leader was she going to be and was she worth following? And he also wanted to find out about what was going on.

"Six hours," he said out loud after Kim had given the others directions to the garden. It didn't sound any better that way.

One lantern in the middle of the floor throwing long shadows away from the flotilla of lanterns standing nearby. Darkness crouched in the corners and behind the consoles.

Kim sat back and put her feet up. "You'll get used to it."

"I gots no real problem with waiting. It just seems strange sitting around for alls that time, doings nothing, and waiting to get somewhere. If I wants to get somewheres I normally just runs."

Scree watched Kim and guessed she was about to make a joke. "You *could* run if you like. Round and round the gardens. Or there's a passage that runs around the outside of level 3 that's probably made for running."

He grunted. "I didn't say I *liked* running."

"There's the gym as well."

"The what?"

"Gym. Gymnasium. It's a room with machines that help you exercise."

Scree tried to work out what she meant.

"Machines for exercising? What's wrong with just doing stuff?"

"Well, you could be on the ship for weeks at a time..."

It all seemed a bit strange. But Scree supposed his whole life was a bit strange now.

"So, that second ship that turned up..."

Kim sighed and nodded. "They're the ones we have to worry about. If we had enough ships in space we could win a war against the hurgon easy enough. I think. But the multeese? I'm not sure if there are enough ships anywhere to beat *them*."

"So how many ships is there?"

And now she looked a bit embarrassed. "At the moment we're it."

Scree raised his eyebrows.

"I know. The extra skyglass will get us another ship into space but that may well be the grand total of our fleet."

"So the hurgon *are* a problem, then."

"Well, yes, but we really need them if we are to have any hope against the multeese. We need them to be the rest of our fleet."

"You could have told me that before I got on the ship." Though it wouldn't have made any difference. Not for him anyway.

"You didn't leave me a lot of time to think."

"The best answer is always the best answer, no matter how long you get to think." Scree sat back and put his feet up as well. "And what about you? How did you end up here? This ain't like no army I've ever seen"

Kim laughed. "How can you tell? I used to be in the army but this one's a private venture. I was just in the wrong place at the wrong time. Then some people pissed me off and here I am."

"That's just about how I get through life."

"Tell me about it."

Scree guessed that was a figure of speech and she didn't actually want to hear about his life. "Let's go look at these exercise machines."

Scree collected one of the lanterns and fiddled with it for a moment before it burst into life. The light wasn't as bright as it was in the other universe; he wasn't sure what that meant.

The room Kim led him to was on Level 3. She showed him how to use the different machines though she wasn't sure of some of them herself. There were simple things like weights for lifting, right up to a moving platform for running on. Most of them had little screens that needed electricity to operate, but they could all be used in the dark of the strange universe as well.

After he'd been shown all the machines, Scree made his way to the metal bar with the weights on each end. Kim had told him about the two ways the lifting was done so, planting his feet, he hoisted the weights up onto his chest and then above his head. After a moment he put it back down.

"That was a bit easy for you," Kim said. "How much is on there?"

Scree shrugged as Kim bent to look at the weights. The writing meant nothing, apparently, so she hefted another one that was in a rack nearby. Then she went back to have a look at the bar.

"That's..." she looked up. "I reckon that's about 200 kilos."

"Is thats a lot?"

"I think the world record for the clean and jerk is..." She cocked her head as if trying to rattle a number from a seldom-used corner of her brain, "Well the Australian Army record was about 240 or 250 kilos. I think."

"Let's put some mores on there then." He watched as Kim did just that. "How much nows?"

"Two twenty. Maybe."

Scree lifted that as well without too much effort. He could tell Kim was impressed and asked for some more.

"Two forty," she said when she was done.

He succeeded again, but with a grunt of effort and a quiver in his arms. "Agains." He stretched.

"I'm not sure if that's safe. Lifters normally rest for a while between each go."

Scree got a weight and added it onto one end himself. When he was done Kim was still looking at him. After a moment, she put the same amount on the other end.

"260 kilos. Don't hurt yourself, Scree. Just drop it if you have to, the floor'll handle it."

Taking a deep breath, Scree set his feet again. He knew he'd have to work this time.

With another deep breath he lifted and got the bar onto his chest. He was forced to crouch for a moment before surging to his feet. He paused again, not sure if he could go any further.

"You have to get the bar above your head," Kim said, "but that doesn't mean you can't make it easier by getting your body lower instead of getting the weights higher." She showed him how to do it.

It seemed reasonable, so he did it and slowly rose to his full height with the weights above his head. His arms quivered again, but he held his position for a few seconds before letting go and jumping clear. The weights clattered to the floor and Scree bent over, shaking his arms but grinning fiercely.

"Rest might haves been good," he said.

"I think a lot of athletes would start to worry if you decided to hang around on Earth. There are men who make a living from lifting weights like these. That's all they do. Training to lift, and lifting."

"Maybes they should gets out and do some living instead. Who wants to do that alls day?"

"I don't know. But I think you should rest before you do any living."

As Scree went to sit down, Kim removed her jumper and went to one of the machines. She was lean and muscled and looked good. In a few minutes she was sweating up a storm and Scree was glad he'd lifted the weights. He was happy to just sit and watch.

"So, you was in the army? How long ago was that?"

"A few years now. I was a pilot."

"A what?"

"A pilot. They fly planes and helicopters."

Scree shrugged. He didn't exactly know what planes or helicopters were but he got the idea. "You still fit."

She glanced over at him as she ran, faltering slightly when she saw him looking.

"I got into martial arts in the army. I still do it pretty seriously. A girl can never be to careful."

"What's martial arts."

"Fighting. Hand to hand stuff."

"Show me some."

Kim laughed and this time it was Scree getting looked over. "Scree, I haven't seen you fight, but I reckon you could beat the shit out of me any day you liked."

"Maybe, but a guy can never be too careful."

"So, fighting *is* your thing?"

Scree shrugged. "I guess so. Never really done anything else."

Kim nodded slowly. "All right then."

"What's that supposed to mean."

"Nothing. It's just..." She slowed and stepped off the machine. "All the vehicles around here have very large seats."

"What?"

"Vehicles. Like the Lander you flew back on Kiva."

Scree nodded. "Yeah. So?"

"Well, the only people who would really fit them properly are you and Tuki."

Scree couldn't follow where she was heading and said so.

"Well, I've got to say I can't really imagine Tuki or any of the moai I've met— all ten of them— being all that confident behind the wheel, even after a lot of training. You, on the other hand..."

Scree still had no idea what she was saying.

Kim sighed. "One of the vehicles on the ship is a fork lift— a Loader— for loading stuff in the hold."

"Right."

She sighed again as she started to wipe sweat from her arms with her jumper. "So, I don't think the trolls were just here for the shooting and the killing. If you were supposed to be here at all, that is."

"We's in charge of the hold as well? Making sure it's all tidy and organized?"

Kim nodded.

That was an interesting thought.

-oOo-

In the garden, the trolls were playing by the light of a half dozen lanterns. They were using something tied up with string as a ball, passing it amongst themselves. There were two teams, and the only goal was to keep the ball away from the opposition for as long as possible. There were no rules. It was a game Scree had played often enough himself.

He watched as Cliff was smashed by a pair of opponents and lost the ball. He was on his feet in an instant and in pursuit.

They were typical trolls, cursing and swearing but taking every pounding in good humor. The trouble was, planning wasn't really a part of any game they played. And it wasn't with life either. They worried about the present and that was about it. Not so long ago Scree was the same, but he knew that in the ship that would be a bad thing.

Scree watched for several minutes then stood and took a deep breath. He was going to take a gamble that could ruin everything right away.

"Hey," he shouted during a lull in the action, bringing the game to a sudden stop. "Why youse playing with all these lanterns?"

"What ya mean?" Gorge asked. He was the oldest, ancient for a troll. His head was bald, but he sported a full beard. "We got lanterns so we can see."

"Well, why don't youse use your night-eyes?"

"What you talkin' bout?"

Scree breathed a silent sigh of relief. An ancient troll had come to the Redworm Pack when Scree was barely more than a boy and shown them how to use their night eyes. In all the years since, roaming around a lot of the world, they hadn't found anyone else who knew anything about it. "Your night-eyes. There's plenty of lights coming in through them windows."

"There ain't no light," Bones said. "What's he talking about? There ain't enough light to see."

"Course there is, you just gots to know hows to see it."

"And you know?"

"Course. Wouldn't be telling youse abouts it otherwise."

"Show show us."

"Well, turn off all them lanterns"

While Bones, River and Shardy collected the lanterns, Scree closed his eyes and dug down in the corner of his mind to turn on his night-eyes.

"All them lights off?"

"Yep."

Scree opened his eyes and looked at the group in front of him, all standing silently and looking in his general direction.

"Somes of you go left and somes of you goes right. I'll tell you who is wheres."

The group split in two, bumping past each other in the darkness, cursing loudly. Five went one way and fifteen the other. Scree listed the names but nobody was convinced by his success.

"Chasm, hold up some fingers then."

Scree watched as the trollop flicked her long hair out of the way and held up four fingers.

"Four?"

The trollop nodded. "Yep. He's right."

Scree thought they might be more impressed by the fact he could count than by his ability to see in the dark. "Told you. There's plenty of light in heres, you just gots to know how to look."

"So, how does we look then?" Cliff moved to the front of the group of fifteen, pushing his way through.

"There's a spots in your mind," he said, "ways down low at the back. And if you nudges it just rights, you can see. It's easy really, but it's just abouts finding the right spot." He remembered the trouble he'd had trying to control the radio in his mind, but there'd been nobody there to help.

It turned out that it wasn't that difficult after all. Talus had it in no time. "Got," he said with a nervous laugh. He was the youngest of them all— barely sixteen summers— and not much more than six feet tall. "Everything's all red, but can see." Talus laughed some more. "Down back on left, it is."

"Hey, I got it, too." Gulch said in his deep baritone.

Soon all of them could see and were wandering around touching each other and throwing the ball in the darkness.

"How you know 'bout this?" Cliff asked eventually.

Scree shrugged. "Just do. And there's more."

"More?"

The others quickly returned to the conversation.

"Yep. If youse nudge the other side of your minds, youse will be able to hear stuff."

"I can hears stuff now," Cairn said, blinking his one eye.

"Yeah?" Scree sniffed. "Huh. Just like you can see things, I suppose?"

Stone had the first success this time. "I hear somethin'. But it ain't very interestin'."

"Sounds a bits like rain?"

"Yeah."

"Well, nears that same spot theres another spot that lets you change the rains."

Scree started talking in his head and saw a smile cross Stone's face a few moments later.

<*I can hear.*>

<Good. Weren't hard.>

The game was a whole new thing when both teams could speak to each other in their minds at different levels. Teamwork became a simple thing. It became important, and that was a good thing.

Scree grunted as he watched.

-oOo-

Sherindel didn't look any different to Kiva from space. Forests and oceans, mountains and deserts. Admittedly, there were less of the deserts than on Kiva, but drop him in the middle of somewhere and Scree didn't know that he'd be able to tell the difference without stars. Keeble and Ping had adjusted the clocks in the break between jumps, and this meant Tuki, with his three apprentices watching over his shoulder, got them closer to the planet than would have been possible before. Scree wasn't really sure how that worked, or what half of it even meant, but it wasn't his job to know.

Now, they couldn't go any closer without annoying the hurgon who waited there in their living ships.

"So, where's we going?" Scree looked at Kim.

Kim turned to look at Tuki. "Is the skyglass showing any gates, Tuki? They were blue crosses."

"Two, Kim. They are hardly more than a thousand kilometers apart."

An image came up in dome and Kim cocked her head to one side to look. "Keeble? Anything look familiar?"

Keeble shrugged. "Mount Elgara. I hardly ever went outside remember."

"Mel?"

Meledrin turned away from the globe hanging in the air at the top of the dome. "I could not say for sure. Daraneen Forest is many hundreds of kilometers across.

The Daydawn River is the largest in the forest and... I do not know. I have not been far from Grovely."

Kim shook her head in disgust. "Well that gate to the north is on bit of a peninsular, by the looks. It probably isn't wide enough." She cocked her head the other way as she examined the other cross. "There's a forest and mountains. Can the two of you narrow it down a little bit, at least?"

Another shrug from Keeble and Scree had to agree with Kim's frustration.

"Right," Kim said. "Northern hemisphere or southern?"

"Excuse me?" Meledrin asked.

"Sherindel is a big ball that spins—"

"I know that, thank you—"

"So are you to the north of the half way point of the ball or to the south?"

"I do not know."

"Winter or summer when you left?"

"Spring."

The woman looked from the world below out towards the sun. "Doesn't really bloody help," she muttered. "How far north were you? "Mild winters? Snow?"

"Mild winters."

"An ocean?"

"I have not seen, but there was one to the west."

"And the east?"

"Forest. And then mountains."

"I went north to get there, I think," Keeble added. "So there are mountains to the south as well."

"And oceans to the south of you, Keeble?"

"No. Not for a long way, at least."

Kim turned back to examine the world in the dome over head. There was only half of it there because only half of it could be seen. A blue spot marked their own position in space, and red dots showed the living alien ships, the kil'ini. Tuki had said there were a hundred and ten of them.

"I don't think it's the second one either," Kim said. "Lets find the last one." She got the ship moving, skirting around the world. "Can you make the image of the planet larger please, Tuki?"

He could and he did. Scree examined the half world. "What this about spring and winter and stuff?" he asked.

Kim explained exactly how seasons worked and Scree wondered how the humans on Earth had worked all of that stuff out. He wondered how they really *knew*.

He was watching out the window and saw a spot that looked likely. "Hows about there?"

Kim stopped the ship. "Well, that's where the last cross is on the skyglass." She wiggled a finger in her ear as she compared the image above with the world below. "Looks more likely than the other two."

And of course, that was where one of the larger masses of monster were. "Meledrin went through a gate froms here to Earth, right? So the humans mights be down there, fighting the monsters. And so that's wheres all the monsters would be."

Kim nodded. "So now all we have to do is get down to the ground."

"Can one of the Landers work from all the way up here?" Keeble asked.

"Maybe." Kim shook her head. "I wouldn't want to try right now though. It'd be a relatively slow trip and that thing is not very well armed or armored."

"So we's going down in this one again?"

Kim gave an uncertain nod. "Yes. How much fuel do we have?"

Scree didn't know what that was but Keeble checked.

"We have about half a tank left. So we have used about three eights in all our travels. Not much at all really."

Kim laughed for a moment. "Except in galactic terms we've only just driven down to the corner shop and then across to pick up the kids from school."

"What?"

"Never mind."

"Wells, we could goes down somewhere else and then go across to wheres we wants to go once we past the monsters," Scree suggested.

"But the flying around once we're down there will be the thing that uses all our fuel."

Inaki cleared his throat nervously. "Excuse me, mo'min."

It looked as if the moai expected to have his head bitten off.

"Yes, Inaki, what is it?"

"What is fuel, mo'min?"

Kim explained fuel, using a fire as an analogy. It all sounded a bit strange but Scree didn't have much choice but to believe her.

"I says we go straight through," Scree said. "I can clear the way—"

"I don't want to kill them, Scree."

"I knows. None of them will die if they gets out of our way."

"It's not just that. They aren't our enemies—"

"Well theys should stop trying to kill us then, I thinks."

"We need them to trust us, and that won't happen if we keep killing them."

"You the boss."

She grunted. "Where's Cuto? Someone get Cuto up here please."

"Yep," Scree nodded. "I's on it."

Scree used the radio in his mind, asking the other trolls to send the alien up if they know where it was."

"Well, are you going?"

"Under control." He tapped the side of his head.

"Oh."

Cuto arrived a few minutes later with some trolls close behind. The alien went to Meledrin's console and started talking.

"They do not believe us," Meledrin said eventually.

"Course theys don't." Scree didn't know why they'd even bothered.

Cliff looked around. "Who don't 'lieve us?"

"There's more aliens, Cuto's people, out there watching the planet," Kim explained. "They won't let us through without a fight."

"We get t' fight?"

"Sorry, Cliff, but no." Kim flicked some switches and started the ship moving forward. "We're going to do what we did last time. Race through as quickly as possible."

Scree smiled. He told his companions to move back and switched on his seat.

"Scree, we're not—"

"I knows. You just drive, let me worry abouts not shooting thems."

The woman sighed. "You guys might want to sit down."

Scree looked at some of the other trolls. "Go get in the other seats. Don't shoot the aliens though."

Gorge, Stone, Flint and Shardy raced for the stairs while Cuto went to crouch behind a chair and grab the rail at the back.

3: Different Angles

KEEBLE CHECKED THE SYSTEMS, though they couldn't have changed since last time he checked. Everything, except batteries, was in the green. It'd be another half an hour at full speed before they were charged properly.

Then, with nothing else to do, he turned his attention to the view-port. The world spun below them. Mountains and forests, oceans and deserts that the dwarves knew nothing about. They had once, long ago, but now turned inwards more and more each year. If he'd had any choice, Keeble wouldn't have left the mountains of his home either.

He watched the world below and wondered what riches the other mountains held, until the kil'ini finally started moving. Five were coming towards them. Others were covering the holes they'd left, like humans playing football. And it seemed that Kim was going to do her best to ignore them all. They were traveling about a kilometer a second and it wasn't as if their ship was built for dodging.

The living ships started to fire. Scree turned on the shields, forcing Keeble to look away so he could check the power levels. When he looked back, the troll was firing. The others must have been as well, but they were just shooting at the missiles again, instead of the aliens.

It was a strange group that Keeble found himself a part of, but it was Scree that surprised him most. It was obvious after only a few hours that he was the one most qualified and best equipped to lead them all, yet he sat back and let Kim, a woman, tell him what to do.

Keeble sighed and decided that it might be a good idea to help. "There's another type of gun, Scree," he said.

"So?" The troll continued to fire.

"So the one you're using requires ammunition. The other one is called a beamer— it's just a type of light and only needs power in the batteries."

"Yeah?"

"Yeah." Keeble told him how to change weapons and apparently he told the others.

The trolls only needed to hit the spitballs once with a beamer to get the desired effect. At first it was an easy task, and Keeble watched dozens of the alien projectiles explode in the first couple of minutes. But more kept coming and they couldn't stop them all. The sphere that surrounded Scree's seat moved constantly, spinning this way and that as he targeted— Keeble didn't know how he could concentrate on two sights with so much accuracy.

Keeble shook his head. *And Scree chooses to follow a woman.* He hoped the troll would come to his senses.

When the first of the enemies' missiles escaped the cross fire and hit the shields the energy levels dropped. His heart started to race though they were safe for a while yet. More missiles got through.

"Where are all the other trolls?" Keeble asked.

One of the other trolls, Sandy, answered, hair-beads clacking as she turned to look over her shoulder. "They is on Level 3, in the mess."

"Right." Keeble turned off all the lights below level 3 and re-routed the power into the shields.

The ship raced between the first pair of aliens and they had a few seconds of respite as the two creatures feared injuring each other. A few seconds later they were in the clear and quickly out-raced the weapons. There was a second line of defense, but they were passed quickly as well with the trolls continuing their defensive fire. Keeble started to relax, slumping back in his chair as Kim reversed the thrust and started to slow them down.

Keeble tapped his metal arm on the edge of his console in time to the fluctuating read-outs. Hull temperature was climbing steadily, though the shields took up a lot of the heat. Power in the batteries was dropping rapidly. He almost pointed that out to Kim, but there was really nothing she could do anyway, beyond what she was already doing.

Cliff, the biggest of the trolls, with a scar from his missing ear all the way down his neck, stood up and walked to the view port, compensating for the juddering movement of the ship as if he'd been doing it all his life. "There's somethin' on fire out there," he said.

"Don't worry about it," Kim replied through gritted teeth, as if she was physically involved in the effort to slow the ship. Keeble decided that if she could see his panel she might be at least a little bit worried.

"Don't worry?" From the look of Cliff's smile, he was starting to like her.

"It's just the air."

"T' air's on fire?"

Finally they slowed beyond some threshold and things started returning to normal. The shields sank through red to orange then yellow. The hull temperature dropped as rapidly.

"Batteries nearly charged," Keeble said after checking the information three times. They'd been a long way off a short while ago. "Must have something to do with the heat— it must have dropped below a manageable level."

"What about everything else?"

"Bit late to be asking that now." But he checked on the damaged hull and life support systems.

"Oh."

Once he knew they weren't going to die soon, Keeble turned his attention to the three dimensional map in the hollow of the floor. There were still a long way up but the detail was amazing. That curve of mountains. That spot where four valleys met. "I think that's the spot. Over in the corner there."

The map scrolled, probably Tuki's doing.

"No, the other corner. Yes, there. See those four valleys?"

"Are you sure?"

"I've never seen it from this angle so it's hard to tell. But I think so."

"Mel?"

Keeble laughed and the elf ignored the laughter and question both.

Kim shook her head. "Good enough. So do I land in the valleys somewhere?"

"Where they meet is open and flat. It might be the safest place."

"Right you are, then."

"You knows," Scree had his seat facing the sky, "there weren't many of them monsters above the moai when you landed on Kiva; maybes we drew the aliens to them."

Keeble hadn't thought of that. "And maybe we'll draw them to the dwarves."

Kim pointed to the map. "I think it's a bit late for that. Look."

On the map, thick columns of smoke were visible all around the four valleys. As they drew closer they could see that trees and earth had been scorched. Closer still they could see dead bats with the metal canisters cracked open. Dwarves and monsters alike littered the ground for kilometers. There were no living creatures in sight.

Kim set the ship down in a clear spot a kilometer from the meeting place of the valleys.

They sat in silence, examining the images Tuki put into the floor well. The trolls were probably thinking tactically. Keeble wasn't thinking much at all. He was stunned by the obvious ferocity of the battle that had taken place.

Kim broke the silence. "Use the door on Level 10," she said. "I think I got close enough to the cliff that you should be able to just jump out."

"What's the plan?" Keeble asked, pulling his attention away from the images and gathering his thoughts. He turned off the shields, seeing Scree seemed to have forgotten about them, and checked for damage.

Kim shrugged. "You're going to go and see if you can find some volunteers."

"That's it?" Keeble hook his head. "I just hop out and go find some dwarves?"

"You aren't going on your own." She paused and looked across at Scree. She pursed her lips. "Scree is going to decide how much help you need and who that help will be. If you want details, you'll have to ask him."

Keeble turned to Scree and the big man was smiling.

"I'm in charge?"

Kim didn't look sure, but nodded anyway. "Yes you are, Scree. Unless you know of someone better suited to the job."

"Huh!"

"Just don't disappoint me."

Keeble expected the troll to jump out of his seat and rush off to find a weapon— he seemed like that kind of man— but he stayed where he was and gave the matter some thought.

"Well, the *Hakahei* is the most important thing, so we haves to decide how many peoples we want to leave here as protection."

"Well... Five should do it, I think," Kim said. "Shouldn't it? I doubt the aliens' handgun thingies can do the ship any damage. And even dropping an incendiary bomb from a bird should be harmless enough. Maybe. If we do get into any trouble there are the ship's guns."

"Five it is then."

"Maybe you should divide the trolls into four troops."

"What? Why?"

"Easier to control. You don't have to waste time dividing the troops in the heat of battle, you can tell the leader of the troop what you want, and they can organize the details."

That obviously wasn't the way trolls normally fought. Keeble imagined they'd normally decide to thump some people then walk up in one big group and just do it.

Kim continued. "So, you're now a major, Scree. Pick four sergeants and give them some men. Women. Whatever. Then leave one troop here and take the rest."

"And what's it that we's looking for, exactly?"

Keeble answered him. "At the very least, we need a Singer who has a Song of Doing. A couple more dwarves in general would be good to help with maintenance." It had taken he, Ping and Cuto over three hours to fix the problem with the clock, and that was after they'd had worked out what the problem was. The engines were going to take a lot more effort.

"We actually need a couple of everything," Kim said. "The Americans will need some dwarves as well. They'll say they can fix the stuff themselves, but they'll be wrong."

Keeble smiled. At least she could admit *that*.

Kim looked around. "Come on people, what are you all waiting for?"

Keeble unstrapped his belt with a sneer and headed for the lift.

"Sees you on Level 10, Keeble, near the door."

"Right. Don't take too long. The longer we sit here—"

"I knows that."

Keeble wondered if he needed to take anything. One of the rubber suits with some small air tanks would probably be good, so he could survive in the smoke, unless he came upon an enemy he couldn't see. A weapon might have been handy, but his axe was long gone. Well, as Kim had pointed out, that was Scree's area of expertise.

He took the lift to the engineering level to retrieve the suit he'd used earlier then continued to the lowest level of the ship. Levels 9 and 10 were both cargo holds, large open spaces filled with a vast amount of... Keeble didn't know what was in most of the boxes. Possibly, after more than fifty thousand years there wasn't much at all. Kim had been looking in some of them but hadn't said anything about what she found.

While he waited for his escort, he went to the nearest box and tried to open it. There were handles near one corner that would allow one entire panel to be opened like a door, but the lowest of the three was stuck in the locked position and the highest was just out of his reach.

Fifteen minutes later, Keeble was going to find some tools and something to stand on when the trolls finally arrived. Apparently they'd used the time to get changed into their own suits, and they all filled them with much precision than Keeble. They weren't like the ones Keeble had seen everywhere else. These seemed to come with armoring of some kind and were adorned with a number of pockets. Scree had changed as well and seemed very pleased with himself.

"Like our new clothes? Got 'em from that rooms with the extra weapons' seats. None in your size though."

"You'll just have to make sure you jump in front of any bullets then."

Scree's suit was completely black but the others were adorned with a slash of one of four colors— red, blue, green and yellow. The four troops, Keeble guessed. They all carried weapons and he was pleased when Scree threw an extra one in his direction. He juggled one handed for a moment, before steadying it with his metal hand. "How does it work?"

"This bits here is like the power switch. And you press this bits here to make it work."

"How did you test these on the ship? You didn't fire at the hull, did you?"

Scree looked insulted. "Just don't point it at anybodys you don't wants to kill. And take one of these as well."

Keeble took the second item offered, one of the little radios to wrap around his head.

"Hello, can you hear me?" Keeble said.

He could hear Scree's reply even though the troll didn't move his mouth. <*Gots you. And remembers, you only have to think the words, Keeble. You there, Kim?*>

<*Loud and clear. And Scree, don't leave any of our people behind.*>

Keeble thought that was a strange thing to say but Scree either took it in his stride or ignored it. "Right. We ready?"

The trolls nodded, though it was obvious that Gorge and Red Troop had been given the relatively safe task of staying behind to guard the ship. They didn't look all that happy, but Scree was in charge and apparently they were listening for now.

"Rights. Keeble, where's we going when we gets out?"

"We're going to the right," Keeble said, but it all depended on what they saw once the door was open. They might not be able to get to the ground at all— a woman had parked the ship, after all. It was about a kilometer to the Swallow Gate, and quite a climb. The River Gate was at the base of the valley but was four and a half kilometers in the other direction.

"Let's go."

Keeble opened the huge doors as the trolls arrayed themselves in defensive position.

"Green and Yellow, goes."

Keeble stayed out of the way, watching as Stone and Chasm led their troops out onto the mountainside. The ledge Kim had parked beside was about a meter lower than the floor and a meter away— the trolls had no problems negotiating the gap. They split up and headed for cover.

<*Nobody here,*> Stone said from behind a rock on the far side of the trail. The troll looked like he'd been carrying out similar tasks all his life.

"Let's go."

Keeble followed Scree out the door, surrounded by Blue Troop. He landed awkwardly, rolling his ankle. He gritted his teeth and said nothing.

<*Be ready fors us, Gorge. We mights be in a hurry. This ways, Keeble?*>

"Yes." The line of the mountains curved the right way, making the ledge near the Swallow Gate visible. Keeble pointed it out to Scree.

It seemed Stone had won some type of contest earlier. His troop took the dangerous point position again. Chip— tall and lean for a troll, like he was built for running— was sent even further ahead to check the path. The other groups followed behind, moving quickly. Keeble had trouble keeping up. He kept his short legs pumping and was soon breathing heavily. His ankle ached ferociously. Dwarves were built for sprinting, not endurance, but it seemed Scree and his companions didn't differentiate between the two. Keeble kept a tight grip on his weapon even as he wondered if there was any point. If the trolls needed *his* help then they were in all sorts of trouble. But he said nothing about the pace of their journey or the pointlessness of his weapon. He hoped the trickier parts of the trail would slow the trolls down.

At the first difficult section, where a rockslide had covered a switchback turn, the trolls scrambled past like mountain goats, hardly slowing.

"Almost feels like home," somebody said. Keeble thought it might have been Sergeant Chasm, with long hair and a missing front tooth.

Somebody else laughed. Keeble didn't know who.

"Somebody'll probably be tryin' to kill kill us soon, *then* it'll be like home."

They weren't attacked, but they did come across the remains of a battle. A dozen dwarves were lying dead by the side of the trail. They'd obviously sought a defensive position in a gully, but it hadn't done them any good. The aliens' electrical guns had fried most, but one was missing an arm, another was split open from navel to neck. The ground was dark with death.

Keeble stopped despite Scree's protest. He stood in the middle of the trail, staring, trying to catch his breath. The stench was almost overpowering— it caught at the back of his throat and made him gag.

A dozen dwarves and only two dead aliens, colorful armor cracked open. The breaking open of the armor had probably been done after the battle had passed.

Peak blinked his one good eye. "A couple of days ago," the troll said.

Keeble didn't know how Peak knew, but he wasn't about to argue. He'd thought that going back to Tab Cavern wouldn't affect him at all. Coming in on the ship he'd thought that the war would not affect him, beyond making it harder to find the people he needed. These were the people who had cast him out, after all. They had turned their backs on him when he obviously *could* sing a Song of Being. He owed them nothing. But the bodies lying in the gully proved otherwise. The dwarves were his people and the aliens were killing them for no good reason. He clenched his gun tighter, felt his hand trembling on the handle. He turned away from the bodies but no matter where he looked he could still taste death with every breath.

He would *not* cry in front of the trolls. He cleared his throat. "Come on."

He ran behind Scree, wondering if Milo and Ari and all his other friends were still alive, wondering if he would stumble over their bodies somewhere. Or would Ari still be in her bunker, where she was required to stay?

Keeble laughed at that though. If any dwife would leave her bunker without permission, it would be Ari.

Around the next corner Keeble stumbled on the haft of a broken dindo and was steadied from behind by strong hands. He turned and saw... Flint, with bald head and drooping moustache.

"Watch the path, little man."

Keeble grunted and ran on. He smelled the site of the next battle before he saw it and kept his eyes resolutely ahead. He kept his attention on where he was placing his feet.

By the time they reached the Swallow Gate, Keeble was struggling again. He would've gone on though, unwilling to admit any weakness to the trolls, but Scree saved him the bother. He called a halt beneath the overhang and pulled a small water bottle from one of his many pockets. Green Troop were already out of sight down the passage.

<*Trouble ahead.*>

Keeble didn't know who'd spoken. It didn't matter. He knew enough about trolls to know that if one said there was trouble, it would probably be serious.

<*Whats?*>

<*Don't know sure. Passages dark until now. Now open cavern and light. Movement inside, but can't see from here.*>

<*Can you get closer, Talus?*> Stone asked.

Scree overruled Stone's question. <*Don't bothers. Not till the rest of us is there. Is there other doors, does you know?*>

<*Don't know.*>

Keeble cleared his throat. "I know the layout of all the caves. When I know which cavern it is, I'll be able to tell you."

"Goods. Come on then."

There was only one passage for a long way. Normally, it would never have been dark, but nobody had replaced the burnt out torches. Keeble bustled along in the midst of the trolls. Flint's hand was on his shoulder again, guiding him through the darkness.

Keeble felt things brushing against his legs. He didn't know what they were but he imagined dwarves reaching for him with cold stiff hands, seeking help he couldn't give. He swallowed and blinked away tears and hoped the trolls couldn't see *everything.*

4: Wanderer

THEY PASSED THROUGH THE FIRST three intersections without slowing. At the fourth, they stopped. There was light now, enough to see two dead dwarves and burn marks on the walls. Keeble cleared his throat and looked for Stone.

The Green leader was waiting down a side passage, just out of sight. The other four members of the troop were scouting further along the passages. To the left, they'd go eight hundred and forty two meters before they found anything at all, and that would be nothing more than a hole in the floor. He wondered if he should warn them about that. To the right was storage— a maze of little rooms filled with a hundred years of outdated clutter that nobody wanted to throw out.

Stone pointed down the main passage. <*Fifty meters. Big room.*>

Keeble tried to remember to talk in his head. <That's Pablus' Room. There's only one other way into it from here, and that's a vent down that way.> Toward the storerooms. A vent that many a dwarf boy had crawled through in the years since it had been drilled. No troll was likely to fit.

<*How bigs?*> Scree asked.

<Not big enough.>

<*What abouts for you?*>

Keeble shrugged. <Maybe. But what would I do in there?>

<*Get the attention of whoever's in the room.*>

Keeble didn't mind the idea of being a distraction but he complained anyway. <It isn't my job to do dangerous things, remember.>

<*Be safer in there once we gets started.*>

<Kim said she doesn't want you to kill anyone, remember?>

Scree laughed. <*Since when have you been worried about what Kim said?*>

Since when indeed? But Scree was continuing.

<*Anyways, if we don't haves a choice, then we don't haves a choice.*>

<Right then.>

The light from Pablus' Room was enough for him to see by and he made his way to the vent. Talus was standing in the shadows of a doorway nearby, waiting to help.

While Keeble was struggling into the hole with Talus pushing him from behind, the other scout went by, returning to join the group for the fight.

Scree was talking. <*These guns is different to the monster gun, but I still reckons the best place to attack them will be on their backs. That's where they keeps air for breathing in space. If youse can't hit the back, then I reckons the face is the next best spot.*>

It was many years since Keeble had been in the vent and it was a tight fit. He grunted as he hauled himself further in.

"You right?" Talus asked in an audible whisper.

"Yes." He started dragging himself forward, thinking he was making enough noise to be heard all the way to Tab Cavern. While he crawled, Keeble listened as Scree outlined a fairly open plan in his ear. It didn't involve much more than spreading out and finding cover.

<*Is we ready?*>

A chorus of yeses.

Keeble grunted. <I'm almost there. I'll give you a description when I arrive.>

<*Right.*>

Near the end of the vent, Keeble stopped to catch his breath.

His previous experiences of fighting, few and far between that they were, had been nothing like this. Normally, he was with a group of companions on patrol and the battle came at them unexpectedly. There were groups of brigands, normally humans, sometimes dwarves, who wandered through the mountains looking for anything that would keep them going for another few days. Patrols were sent out to discourage them. The brigands were always in small groups and badly equipped. Hardly a danger at all. And there was never any time for thought. He didn't know how the trolls could stand this cold, calculated waiting. If the whole plan didn't revolve around him he would have stayed where he was and let the experts sort it out.

Finally, Keeble pulled himself to the end of the vent and looked out into the room. It was thirteen meters, twenty-two centimeters in diameter, though not quite circular. Below his position was a small fire with six hurgon crouching around it watching a pot full of something that didn't look very nice. Their empty armor was a few meters away. Other than that, there were a score of others, half of them suited up and facing the door through which the trolls would come, the others playing a strange game against the far wall.

Keeble gave the trolls a description of the situation, trying to think of all the information that might be useful. There were some wooden boxes piled near the passage to Swallow Gate. There was a promontory of rock sticking out from the western wall.

<*How manys other doors is there?*>

<Two. It's a fair way from here to the next rooms.>

<*Right. Here we goes then. You shoots the back of one of the armored guys. They'll takes a while to turn and target you so you should have plenty of time. But make sure you get out of the way. We wants to get more dwarves, not lose the one we gots.*>

<Right.>

Keeble sighted along the barrel of the weapon, took a deep breath, and pulled the trigger.

Nothing happened. He cursed under his breath before remembering the power button. He fumbled with the switch. The click it made seemed unnaturally loud in the vent. He paused, eyeing the enemy warily, ready to get out of the way. Eventually he rested the gun on his mechanical hand, aimed and fired.

The gun bucked slightly in his hand, affecting his aim. The noise it made was a soft clang, like the rhythm-keeping tap of a blacksmith's hammer against the anvil between true blows. He zeroed in on the back of his chosen monster, adjusted for the kick, and fired again. He saw the projectile hit the target with no result. He fired a few more times. It wasn't until the eighth shot that anything happened. A spectacular ball of fire filled the room. One of the unarmored hurgon was beating at burning clothes. None of the others in the armor had been affected, and they were turning to look in his direction.

Keeble scuttled back from the opening as quickly as he could. "I hit him eight times," he said out loud between gasps for breath. If the trolls wanted that final piece of information, they made no sign. They were too busy shouting and firing.

When the battle was in full swing, Keeble crawled forward again to look.

The monsters' weapons gave off sizzles of electricity. Most of the trolls were out of sight behind the boxes, popping into the open every now and then to fire. It was always a different troll, always a long way from the last, to keep the monsters guessing. Those of the enemy who were not in armor were already dead. Most hadn't had a chance to move, being struck down around the fire or in the midst of their game. Several suits of armor were just blackened shells lying on the floor.

But the trolls could no longer attack the armored creatures' backs. They were concentrating on the faceplates as Scree suggested, but weren't meeting with much success.

After watching the darting trolls for a moment, Keeble realized he was in the best position and brought his own gun to bear on the back of an alien. He hesitated before letting of a series of quick shots. Nobody noticed. Nothing happened.

One of the other monsters suddenly stopped moving. Keeble assumed its faceplate was breached.

He concentrated on his own shooting, firing a few more rounds. An explosion sent out shards of pink and green shrapnel.

Keeble shimmied back into the vent.

Then next time he emerged it was all over. "Somebody want to help me down?" he asked. "It'll take for ever to go out the other way."

Cliff, the tallest of them all, made his way over to the vent. It was too high even for him, so two of his troop brought over one of the boxes they'd hid behind earlier.

A minute later, Keeble was looking closely at some armor with Scree and Stone. There wasn't a lot to see.

"Let's see what happens."

Everybody stood back and Keeble fired one shot at the chest of a still-standing suite of armor. The bullet sank into the armor and stayed there. Fine cracks ran away from it.

"Every shot must weaken it until one finally gets through." He bent to look closer. "I thought it was metal, but obviously not."

Scree shrugged. "Doesn't matters, really. Comes on. We should keep going. Where to now?"

Keeble pointed and this time it was Chasm's Yellow Troop— closest to the door— that led the way.

Tab Cavern was almost a kilometer away, down deep in the mountain they'd just climbed. The passage curved this way and that, and there were many intersections with lesser passages leading away. Keeble listened to the chatter in his head as Yellow Troop decided who was going where and reported back on what they found. Keeble told them that all they had to do was follow the main passage, but they wanted to check everything out. They were having fun.

Keeble gritted his teeth and kept walking.

It shouldn't have been fun. Tunnels had collapsed. Storerooms and bunkers had been ransacked. There were descriptions of battles and dead dwarfs running though his head like commentary on a football match. The hurgon were way ahead on the scoreboard.

At the final intersection before Tab Cavern, the five members of Yellow Troop waited beside the still form of an armored alien. The faceplate had been broken and the face beyond was bloody.

<*What's in this next rooms?*>

Keeble looked down the passage, though he already knew what was there. "The next room is Tab Cavern, the main room of the entire complex. There are one hundred and five entry points on nine different levels. The room itself is on two levels. We'll come out on the upper level, which is six meters, forty two centimeters above the lower section."

"How bigs is the upper bits?"

"Twelve meters and eighty one centimeters from the door to the edge of the lip. The lower section is a rough circle about forty three and a half meters in diameter."

"Right. Talus, go and sees what you cans see. Don't gets caught— and watch out for that extra eighty one centimeters."

"If you don't like the details of my report, just say so." Keeble said. "I don't know how important those things might be."

Scree smiled and shook his head. "Don't do nothing different, Keeble."

Talus scurried forward, crouched low, moving silently.

<*Nothing top level, boss. More boxes. Lots boxes. Big mess.*>

<*Can you gets to the lip?*>

<*I'm there. And... Festerin' cats. There's lots of 'em, boss. I can't count, but there's lots. Some got armor, some not. They eatin', drinkin', playin'.*>

<*What else?*>

<*They got prison. Bars across door and guards. Looks like dwarfs inside.*>

<Which door?> Keeble asked.

<*Ummm... Right next to a big rock that looks like a tit.*>

Keeble nodded. The Hollow Room. It was just a small room, nine and a half meters across. There was no other door in. He passed on the information.

Scree called the scout back.

"We could just just go there," somebody said out loud.

Scree shook his head. "We coulds probably gets there no worries, getting outs again would be the problem. We needs another diversion. Keeble, can we get around opposite that room and up high real quick?"

"Yes. But..."

"Hows?"

"Why do you want a diversion?"

"So we cans get out alive."

"The best way out is through the cell."

"But you saids there was only one entrance."

Keeble was going to explain about Singing but decided it would be easier to just show them. "Well, there's a kind of secret entrance as well." The fact that there were prisoners in the room at all told him there were no Singers, but whoever was in there might have information.

"Why isn't them dwarves using the secret entrance?"

"Not everyone knows about it. It's a secret."

"Right. Can't we just go in by the secret entrance?"

"It's too far."

Scree shrugged. "All right. Let's have a looks then."

The 'lots' reported by Talus hadn't prepared Keeble. There were at least a hundred and fifty of the aliens making a mess of the cavern. There were a dozen campfires, using the remains of what had once been a market for fuel. There were ranks of armor on one side, waiting for their occupants.

<*Right. I says we just run and get there, by the time they reacts we'll be right.*>

<*But we got to get out remember,*> Peak said.

<*Just gets down there and gets in the cell.*>

<*In the cell?*>

Scree looked at Peak and the one eyed troll shrugged. <*You the boss.*>

Before anyone could say anything else, Scree broke cover. He led the trolls down the ramp to the main floor. Most of the aliens didn't see them as they hurried around the wall toward the cell. They fired as they went, concentrated fire on the faceplates of the guards. With the concentrated fire they broke through. Scree shifted aim immediately but Keeble kept his eyes on the barred door.

By the time he got there, the occupants had already opened the lock and were coming out. It'd only been the guards keeping them in. At first it was old dwarves who hurried out, then women started coming. Keeble swore under his breath.

"Everyone, back inside." He grabbed the arm of a passing oldster and turned him around. "Back inside."

"But..."

"You'll die out here."

As if to prove the point, the oldster did die, cut down by a sizzle of energy. The trolls killed the attacker before he could kill anyone else. The outermost of the fleeing dwarves seemed to get the point.

"Back inside," Keeble yelled. "Inside. Back." He swore. Dwarves kept coming out as the first group was trying to get back in.

He swore again when he saw who was holding the door open.

"Ari?"

"Keeble?" The dwife stared at him for a moment then turned her attention back to the fleeing prisoners.

Dwives and children and old men were the only ones in the room. No workers at all.

A dozen dwarves had not gotten the message. They had broken out into the cavern and were heading for various exits.

"What's happening, Keeble?" Ari asked, looking bewildered.

<*Let 'em run,*> Scree said to the other trolls. <*We chase 'em and we all die.*>

"We need to get everyone back inside," Keeble shouted. He watched as Ari finally stopped herding. Her long hair was hanging loose and the bottom of her stiff, linen skirt had been torn away revealing her ankles. It was an atrocious display that Keeble could live with in elves but... It was nice to see a friendly, dwarvish face again.

"But why?"

"Because we'll die out here. Everyone back inside," Keeble yelled again and finally it started to happen.

<*Get in there and get it happening, Keeble.*>

"Right."

The room was quickly filling again as dwarves rushed back inside. It would have been bad enough with just the dwarves, but with the trolls as well...

Chasm was the last in and she was shouting at the top of her voice for somebody to get them out of there.

Keeble had already started. He hummed the foundations of his Song. Normally he would have carefully checked every little piece, but there was no time. He built up the Song with a wordless, dancing cadence and finally he sealed the joints with a series of clicks. When it was all there, filling the chamber, he changed it slightly to include a deep breath. Then he strengthened it again and, without whittling it down, he pushed the song into the chamber's far wall.

"I'm done," he said softly. The dwarves in the room were silent. The trolls were shouting. "Let's go, quickly."

As one, the dwarves surged into the hollow space in the wall that his Song had created, taking most of the trolls with them. Only Scree and Chasm remained in the room.

Keeble heard Chasm swear. Scree was staring open mouthed, but he took the big trollop's arm and dragged her into the wall. Keeble closed the gap behind them. There was another room fifteen meters distant. Even if it wasn't empty, they'd have the element of surprise on their side. Concentrating hard, Keeble led the way.

He could feel the stone on his skin, like mist. Ari was clinging to his arm with shaking hands. "They caught us by surprise," she whispered.

Keeble was sure she wouldn't normally have been nervous about being in the stone, but she was clinging to his *mechanical* arm. That would make it painfully obvious that he shouldn't be able to Sing at all.

"They had us trapped in the caves, divided."

Keeble concentrated on his Song, refining it as he went, checking the joints he should have checked earlier, strengthening it.

"We were with a group that broke out yesterday morning, but they found us. Most got away."

Ari's trembling grip distracted him. They were in public. Keeble could see a boy with part of her skirt wrapped around his head as a bandage.

"I don't know where the others are," Ari said.

Keeble brought everyone out into Tabin Cabin and gratefully let his Song collapse. Sweat coated his entire body. He could hardly breathe.

5: A Slight Problem

SCREE BREATHED A SIGH OF RELIEF when he stepped out of the stone into a real room. He was even more grateful when he saw Keeble. The dwarf didn't look good. He didn't waste time finding out what had just happened though.

"Wheres are we?"

"Under the mountain," Keeble said, shaking himself as if trying to wake up.

Scree was about to complain but decided the answer meant as much as anything else. "Who's in charge thens?"

Scree watched as Keeble looked around. Apparently the dwarf couldn't decide for himself, so he asked in his own language.

For a moment there was no reaction then one old man and another pointed at the woman standing by Keeble's side. Both she and Keeble looked stunned and shook their heads. The four involved in the disagreement then began a heated discussion that might have gone forever if Scree hadn't interrupted. "Stinking cats, Keeble, is she in charge or nots?"

"No, she isn't."

"Then who is?"

Keeble shrugged as he looked around. He seemed to pick a dwarf at random. "Him."

The old man mightn't have been able to understand the words, but he understood enough. He shook his head before he too pointed at the woman by Keeble's side.

Scree knew Keeble's opinion of women, but didn't have time to argue. "She's it, Keeble. Now find out her name and asks her where everyone else is."

"Her name is Ari, and she already told me. She doesn't know. A large group tried to escape yesterday afternoon. Most got away but this group was recaptured. The others are outside the mountain somewhere."

"Cat gut." Scree shook his head. "How far does we chase?"

He tried to get in contact with the ship in his head, but the radio wouldn't work. He swore. He could still hear the trolls who'd come with him, but the ship wasn't answering. He'd follow for now and ask Kim when he got the chance.

"How does we gets out then? We wants to go where the others went."

"Well, I can find out where they went, and I can tell you what would normally be the quickest way, but now..."

Scree shrugged. "She leads then."

"No." Keeble looked shocked. "I'll lead."

"She'll leads. You'll stands near me and translate. Rights?"

"I won't."

"Then I'll leaves you in a corner. You done a good jobs on the ship so fars, but we gots a job you can't do. We needs to find somebody who cans do it."

"Very well." He didn't look very happy about it. He stared coldly at the woman. "She'll lead and I'll translate."

Scree smiled. He knew Keeble wouldn't be able to leave the ship when there were still things to be fixed, even if it meant following a woman. "Right. Let's go thens."

Not a lot of translation was needed, in the end. The woman seemed to know where the main concentrations of monsters were— or maybe the most likely places they'd be— and led the group creeping along passages. She looked nervous and muttered constantly to herself, but didn't lead them astray. Trolls and escapees seemed happy enough to follow. Only Keeble looked annoyed.

"Old men ain't allowed to work either, is they?" Scree asked Keeble.

"What?"

"Dwarf men sit at home and do nothing, don't they, once they gets to a certain age."

"Yes. It wouldn't be safe, otherwise. How did you know?"

Scree smiled. "These old men is willing to follow a woman. They knows what it's like."

Keeble grunted.

"I would've though a wanderer would know what it's like too." Scree smiled.

Half an hour after they'd started, the dwife motioned the small precession to a halt.

"The Largin Gate is just ahead," Keeble whispered.

Scree sent Cliff and the Blue Troop forward, listening in his head as they reported back then took down the two monsters that guarded the final room.

"Let's go."

Largin Gate led out into a short slice in the side of the mountain. High glassy walls loomed over the path until it opened out into a wide, steep sided valley. There, they found a trail a headless cat could've followed. The fleeing dwarves had left a path down to the tree line, and probably all the way through the forest. Scree guessed there were about three hundred of them, and that they had about half a kilo of bushcraft between them. All he needed to know was if they were to follow.

He tried the radio again. <Meledrin, you theres?>

There was no reply.

<Meledrin—>

<*I am present, Scree. Are you returning?*>

<No. Slight problems.>

<*What is it?*>

<Nobody who cans help us under the mountains. Theys all gone norths.>

<*How is it that you know that?*>

<Cause there is *some* heres. The ones who couldn't run quick enough. So does we chase the others, or forget about it and get back to the ship?>

<*I do not know. I shall query Kim.*>

That was all he'd wanted in the first place.

<*Scree, what's going on?*> Kim asked a minute later.

<None of those Singers here. All gone north or dead.>

<*Shit.*>

<We chasing?>

<*How far are they?*>

<Left yesterday afternoons.>

<*Shit.*>

<Chase in the ship?>

<*We're pretty well hidden in this valley and haven't been bothered at all yet. If we fly out into the open we could bring all sorts of attention.*>

<We chase on foots for a while then. We thinks about it again later.>

<*Ok, then. Keep in touch.*>

<Right.>

Scree examined their surroundings. He examined the dwarves huddled just outside the cave entrance and decided his team would never catch anyone if they tagged along. But if he left them on their own they'd likely not live long at all. Keeble might have been the only one in the group with a magical song, but the others could probably learn to fix things like he did if they couldn't find anyone else.

"Cliff, you stays with the dwarves and come along as quick as you cans. The rest of us is going to trys to catch the first groups."

"What about me?" Keeble asked.

"You can come if you cans keep up. But we won'ts be waiting."

"I think I'll stay with Cliff."

"Good." He checked to make sure the Green and Yellow Troops were ready, though they always would be. "Let's goes."

There was a worn game trail leading northwards and the trampled path made by the escaping dwarves more or less followed. It looked like they'd been moving quickly but the trolls could move quicker. They could run all day without getting tired. It was getting on towards noon and Scree guessed they'd catch the stragglers, the oldest and the youngest, before midnight even though they'd had nearly a full day's start.

He started to run and the others followed.

-oOo-

"What's that?" Scree slowed to a walk and cocked his head to listen. There was something. <Stone, what you hearings?>

<Don't know. Something.>

<Checks it out. Be careful thoughs.>

<Already checking.>

The main pack continued forward at a walk. For the last half hour they'd been following the edge of a wide, steep-sided gully. The dwarves had moved along the bottom but Scree didn't like the ambush options if his troops were down there as well. The thick forest hid most of the sky and threw the world into permanent gloom though they were still well short of dusk. It would hide the opposition as well.

<Fight.>

<Whats? Who?>

<Aliens, dwarves and humans.>

<Screeching cats. Come ons>

Scree led the way forward at a full run. He leapt over obstacles, ducked low hanging branches, swerved and dodged as he readied his gun. He didn't know who was fighting who exactly, but he needed those dwarves alive. When he stopped on the edge of the gully and looked out over the fight, he quickly worked out what was happening.

The hurgon were in control. There were only about eighty dwarves left, but humans and elves had joined them. The humans wore off-green uniforms that would help them blend with their surroundings and carried weapons like the Ravens from near the first gate. There were about twenty all up and a similar number of elves. A lot of elves were using human weapons as well.

Scree thought he'd better make everyone knew whose side he was on. He gave a battle cry then started firing into the backs of the nearest aliens.

The humans had taken up a defensive position against the opposite wall of the gully where a few slight humps in the ground offered some cover, though seeing they were professional soldiers, Scree wondered what they were doing down there in the first place. He stayed where he was at the top of the slope and fired. The troops arrived and started to let loose.

The explosion of the first monster certainly got everyone's attention. The humans gave a ragged shout to encourage their flagging companions.

Scree fired a few more shots then tried to think of a plan. They could just keep firing, but the weapon he was using fired bullets and would run out sooner or later. There were fifty or sixty hurgon down in the gully. Giant bats circled overhead probably carrying more of the aliens and waiting for the call to join the battle.

Down in the gully, there were a few exploded alien suits of armor, but the trolls' allies were falling faster.

"Youse keep firing, I'm going down there."

He jumped down into the gully and raced towards the battle. He knew the monsters wouldn't be quick enough to follow him with their weapons, but if one was already pointing in the right direction as he went past... He paused to set his shoulder into the back of a blue and green suit of armor. With a heave he toppled it onto the ground. Then he was running again. The air crackled nearby as a monster set off a shot. Missed.

Scree ran in crazy, dodging lines and dived over a low, protective mound at the far side of the gully. The defenders watched him silently as he tried to catch his breath. He saw a human with a patch on the shoulder of his uniform and crawled quickly to his side.

The human said something and smiled, but Scree couldn't understand. He shrugged. But he saw what he was after clipped to the man's belt. He grabbed the radio and pulled it free. The human complained about that but Scree held up a stalling finger. He found the switch that turned it on easy enough, but it took time to work out how to change the level of the sounds.

<Kim? Mel?>

<Yeah, Scree. How's it going out there?>

<Not good. Under attack. Found humans and dwarves and elves.>

The human by his side was trying to get his attention, but it wasn't about anything important. He was just trying to communicate in general.

<Just keeps talking. Kim, I got a radio here.>

<What? The dwarves own the highest technology on this planet, Scree, and they don't have radios. What the hell are you talking about?>

Scree adjusted the level control on the radio until he could hear Kim chattering. The soldier grabbed the radio from Scree and spoke into it.

<Right, Kim, talks to this human for me. Tells him we gots to get out of here now. We can kills all the monsters, but probably not before they kill all the dwarves.>

As Kim and the soldier spoke, Meledrin translated quietly in Scree's head.

<Who are you?>

<Captain Dominic Thorpe, Special Air Services.>

<British SAS? Jeeze louise. Well, Major Scree, that's the big guy by your side, says you have to get out of there right now. He says the trolls will live and the aliens, will die, but not before a lot of others are dead.>

<We'd love to get out of here, but—>

<Kim, tells him that they have to just run. The monsters is too slow to follow.>

Kim passed on the message and Scree listened to Meledrin's translation of the reply.

<We'd love to, but most of these folks've been running since yesterday and haven't got a lot left in them. And besides that, we ran in the past and more bats came down on top of us.>

<Tells him they got to, Kim. But I think we'll need the *Hakahei* very soon.> Another couple of monsters exploded as the trolls continued to fire.

<*Scree I don't know if that's a good idea.*>

<No choice.>

<*Right. But how the hell do you get into the ship?*>

<You find a clearing. We heads there. You is on the ground withs the Lander waiting for us.>

<*Sounds easy.*>

<Is. We is on the other side of the mountain, almost directly north.>

<*Right.*> Kim said something in her own language and the soldier replied. <*The Captain says he has something to signal with, Scree. I'll find you.*>

<Right. Does it quick then. We'll start heading south and signal in a couple of minutes. Tells the Captain the plan.>

At the end of his conversation with Kim, the soldier shook his head. Then he gave a resigned shrug and started shouting to his charges. He received a groan of protest in reply but the humans started getting the locals organized. Using hand signals, Scree told the Captain that he'd draw the enemy fire and the others had to make the most of the chance. He didn't think he'd be in much danger. He was quick, the aliens were slow. Easy.

When it appeared everyone was ready, Scree broke from cover and ran north. After a few meters he zagged across towards the far side of the gully. The aliens couldn't hit him, but a good portion of them tried to track his movement, swiveling slowly. It wouldn't be long before the trees gave him cover.

A tree exploded not far away, sending down a shower of branches. Scree dodged. Too late. A branch hit his shoulder. It took a long gouge of flesh and knocked him to the ground. He cursed as he struggled to his feet and stumbled onwards. His arm hung uselessly at his side. Not broken but might as well be for all the good it would do him in the short term. A sizzle of energy grazed past his other shoulder, melting the suit and cooking the skin beneath. Scree fell to the ground and stayed there. He breathed deeply, gritting his teeth against the pain in both his shoulders. He tried to look dead.

A few minutes later he raised his head and looked around. There was nobody nearby. He rolled carefully onto his back. Both arms were an agony. Blood pumped from one, the other burned.

Trying to ignore the pain, Scree sat up slowly.

<*Scree, you right?*> Gem asked.

<Livings.>

<*Where you?*>

<Fifty meters north of fight. Middle of gully.>

But the fight seemed to be evaporating, for the moment. The refugees had run, scurrying southwards as quickly as they could, and the monsters had set off in slow pursuit. They had no chance of keeping up, but others would arrive soon.

<*I see you. Comin'.*>

He saw Gem running towards him. The young trollop from Yellow Troop came across the ground in a low crouch, gun slung over her shoulder to keep her hands free. She winced when she saw his wounds. Scree clamped a hand over the gash, hurting his other arm in the process.

"Stinking cats guts."

Scree didn't know if it was he or Gem who swore.

Kim's voice erupted in Scree's head. <*What's going on?*>

<*Scree hurt, boss,*> Gem said, standing and looking.

<*Shit. Is he all right?*>

<*Good as dead, boss. Loosin' blood by the bucket load.*>

<*Shit, shit. I see the smoke signal.*>

Scree could see it as well, red smoke drifting up through the trees.

<*Where you landin', boss? I's comin back.*>

<*Okay, there's a clearing about three hundred and fifty meters to the south east of the signal. I'll be putting down there. Don't bother coming back if you don't have Scree.*>

<*What?*>

<*Bring Scree back.*>

<*Don't know if he'll make it.*>

<*Well, we aren't leaving without him, dead or alive.*>

<*Right.*>

Scree couldn't think about much other than keeping a hand clamped around his bleeding shoulder, but Gem swore under her breath and got him on his feet. She supported him as they made their way to the eastern wall of the gully.

Stone had taken charge of the rest of the troops and the refugees. <*We see ship. On our way.*>

<*Where you at, Gem?*> Chasm asked. <*Gulch on his way.*>

Gem gave their position. <*What about Blues?*>

<*They seen the smoke. They comin' too, but a while yet. Them old timers slowin' 'em down.*>

Scree saw Gulch above them on the side of the gully, his shock of red hair obvious amongst the greenery.

"Minced cats. This gunna hurt, Scree. All cliffs along here, hey."

Gem directed Scree up a slight slope to the base of the low dirt wall. Scree knew what was needed of him and released his injured arm so he could reach up. Gulch took his blood-covered hand and hauled him upwards. Both his arms seemed to explode with pain. Gem pushed from below.

And Scree remembered nothing more.

6: One Task

PING STOOD QUIETLY, one shaking hand hovering over the button that would close the door, the other working reflexively at the material of her torn breeches. Behind her, forty dwarves and elves were sitting in the cargo hold. Those who were able were seeing to injured companions. The canyons of freight and boxes hid much of the activity.

Ping returned her attention to the world outside. In the clearing below, the third load of passengers were climbing aboard the Lander. Some were stumbling with fatigue, some were being carried. Human soldiers and trolls were crouched around the edge of the clearing. They looked out into the forest with studied calm, weapons raised to their shoulders.

The hurgon had not arrived yet, but they wouldn't be far away. The huge bats were circling closer.

The Lander rose unsteadily into the air. Ten seconds later it lurched in through the doorway, wobbling dangerously. Ping stepped back to avoid being hit. Passengers immediately stumbled out amongst those already there. Some sank to the floor at the first possible moment, others stood, dazed and confused. A third group set about trying to help where they could. Even they did not seem more than half there.

A horrendous screech of pain and fear snapped her attention back outside. One of the bats had approached the ship but was now struggling to get away. A burst of fire on its flank halted its progress and it tumbled to the ground. Two seconds later another of the creatures suffered the same fate. The bat demolished a large section of the forest just a hundred meters beyond the edge of the clearing.

The trolls were using the ship's guns enjoying the chance to finally join in the fun. Did Kim know? Ping decided she wouldn't tell.

The Lander struggled into the air again and moved slowly out the door. It dropped a couple of meters before Kim took control of the descent. The next trip would almost complete the process, leaving only a few of the soldiers to watch for the return of Scree and his helpers. Ping didn't have access to a radio, but she longed to know where they were. There were also the other group to think about, making their slower way from the caves where the dwarves had lived. Without a radio, Ping knew nothing of their location either. She stood near the door and watched the clearing and the sky and tried to see beneath the forest canopy.

After dropping off the next load, Kim climbed from the Lander and made her way to Ping's side.

"Gem and Gulch are about a hundred meters away with Scree," she said, wiping sweat from he eyes. She looked out at the forest as well, as if she'd be able to see the troll.

"What about the others?"

"What..? Oh. They'll be a while yet. They're about ten kilometers away and slowing every step, apparently. We'll go and get them in the ship when Scree arrives."

"Why not use the Lander?"

"Well, I—"

"There may not be anywhere to land the ship."

"Shit." Kim stood staring out the door for long seconds. "But if the birds attack the Lander out there..."

"The trolls can protect you with the guns."

As if to prove the point another bat flew too close to the ship for the liking of Red Troop so someone shot it down with three well-aimed volleys.

"Right then. I suppose." Kim used her radio to ask the trolls to cover her and twenty-five seconds later the Lander was gone from sight, around the curve of the hull and to the south.

And now Ping knew nothing. There were dozens of strangers behind her that could have used her help, but her task was to watch the door and close it if the need arose. The human soldiers down in the clearing were looking nervous but kept their attention fixed outwards. The bats were not coming close, but the hurgon that pursued them must be closing in by the minute while the only means of reaching the safety of the cargo hold had just flown away. The trolls were watchful, but not worried.

As Ping watched, the men below became even more tense. They all turned in one direction, aiming their weapons into the trees. Chasm and the other trolls suddenly looked a bit more serious as well.

Ten seconds later some of the humans and trolls started firing their weapons into the trees. Ping couldn't see what they were firing at but it was only a few seconds before something in the trees exploded. Soon, everyone was firing. There were more explosions. Over to one side a hurgon emerged from the trees. Then another and another.

Ping bit her thumbnail and got ready to close the door. Her shaking hand hovered.

A human shouted and fell to the ground. Two seconds later, the trolls in the ship started to use their weapons as well. At first they used the light weapons but quickly learned the other weapons worked better. Each bullet punched a hole through armor and knocked the alien from its feet.

Another human screamed and fell to the ground. Another. The shots from the ship stopped and there was ten seconds of tense stillness.

The leader of the humans asked a question and an elf gave a halting translation. "Long must wait?"

The was a pause before a troll replied. "Kim just getting to the others now. And Gem just about here. Don't shoot nothing now."

Forty seconds later Scree and his two helpers emerged from the trees.

Ping wiped tears away from her eyes. It wasn't obvious if the troll was dead or merely unconscious. She didn't know which she would prefer.

Gulch and Gem lowered him carefully to the ground and one of the humans hurried to examine his wounds. He removed his pack, brought forth a small green box and started to work.

Kim had given Ping her wristwatch. She watched the hands ticking slowly around the dial though she could count the time well enough in her head. Outside, bats occasionally drifted close, as if testing to see if whoever was in control of the guns was still alert. Little did they realize that the trolls would *always* be alert. Trolls and humans occasionally fired into the trees, targeting aliens Ping couldn't see.

Ping wanted to see where Kim was. Could the guns protect her from ten kilometers away? What happened if there were already hurgon on the ground near Cliff and the following dwarves?

She was startled when Kim finally returned. The Lander buzzed around the side of the ship, overshooting the doorway. After a brief pause it slowly reversed. The doors were open at the back. Cliff and his troop were hanging out over thin air— one foot and one hand all that kept them in touch. At least *they* were having fun. Two score dwarves huddled beyond them. They were sitting on each other's laps, standing shoulder to shoulder in the aisle.

When Kim had gone back past the door and started to come forward, Ping could see her swearing. She slapped away thick, inquisitive hands as the three dwarves packed into the seat beside her tried to press buttons. The vehicle thumped down onto the deck and the passengers climbed out. Kim worked at the controls to go pick up those still on the ground.

It took forever to load Scree carefully onto the Lander and for everyone else to climb aboard. A minute later the small craft was in the hold and Ping completed her one and only task— she hit the button to close the outer door. She watched as the door slid all the way from the ceiling down to the floor though she didn't know what she'd do if it didn't work.

Kim swung herself out of the Lander and had a quick look around. As she started to hurry towards the lift she said, "A couple dozen bats are circling," as if she could still see out the door. "Hurgon are on the ground and kil'ini are starting to move into position above us."

Even if Ping had thought to reply, Kim was already gone, racing toward the lift.

Ping examined the ragged group littering the floor of the hold. The injured were being tended to— by elves and humans mainly. Most of those not involved in either side of that process were sitting on the floor, looking as if they were quite happy to stay there for the foreseeable future. Only the trolls looked as if they were ready for more action.

"Wha' we do now?"

It was a strange group, overall. Trolls in their special, colored suits, humans in their grays and greens designed to blend with the forest, all others in rags.

"Hey. Wha' we do now?"

Ping realized that Cliff was speaking to her. The big troll was standing nearby, forcing her to take a step back. All the trolls were looking in her direction. They reminded her of Scree. They made her nervous.

"What? I..."

"Wha' we supposed t' do?" He scratched at the place where his ear had once been. "Can't stand here all day."

Ping didn't know what to say. He was asking her? How was she to know? She was about to say as much, to point out that she had been on the ship no longer than the trolls, but stopped. For a long time she had been trying to find some way in which she might help Scree. But he had been so competent that all she could do most of the time was tag along and slow him down. The rest of the trolls seemed just as competent, but they were asking her questions, they needed her help. There was something she could do to prove she could be useful, not just to the trolls but to everyone on the ship.

Ping took a deep breath and tried to think. It wasn't easy with the trolls watching her and the others spread around on the floor like the wreckage of a flood.

The little hospital was on Level 3, but there was hardly room for everyone there. There were lots of beds on Level 2 though. "Ummm... Perhaps we should... try to get everyone up to Level 2."

"Right. Need... Somethin' t' carry hurt people." Cliff smiled, as if the idea of carrying the injured was a strange concept.

"We could just carry them," Bones suggested, looking at Ping. "They ain't that heavy. We could carry them for sure. No problems I reckon." He looked at one of his companions. "We could carry them, couldn't we?"

"You can't just lug injured people around." Ping looked around. How would you move injured people? "Stretchers," she said. *Obviously*. "They will be in the hospital on Level 3. Do you know where that is?"

"Yeah," Flint said. He had a crooked nose and a big bushy moustache that dribbled down past his chin. "That take all day, though."

That was obvious too. There wouldn't be that many stretchers and it was a long way to walk with them. If the trolls were so smart why didn't they come up with the ideas?

Ping tried to think. "Well, how can we carry..." The boxes in the hold were big and machines were used to carry them. A Loader could carry half a dozen elves, or maybe ten dwarves.

"Wha'?" Cliff asked.

But she wasn't sure. She cleared her throat and looked around. All the trolls were still watching her. "Who wants to learn how to drive?" Would Kim want the trolls driving the Loaders? It didn't matter. Kim wasn't here to tell them one way or the other.

"What?"

"This way." She beckoned the troll to follow, and the rest of Blue Troop came along. She almost had to run to stay ahead of their long strides. Through a large set of doors they found more huge boxes and, on the far side of the hold, two Loaders lined up side by side.

"Two of you need to learn to drive them. The rest of you need to find something, boards or something, to lay over the..." she gestured... "the front bits."

Ping watched Cliff stare doubtfully at the Loaders for a moment, before motioning to Bones and Quartz to climb in and start learning. The rest went searching.

Ping studied a Loader's controls for several minutes with the two trolls looking over her shoulder. Bones was about the same age as Ping and talked more than any of the other trolls.

"Should be fun to drive," he said. Apparently he also had trouble staying still—he bounced about on the spot. "All them other ones up in the hangar work the same way, you think? They the same?"

Ping shrugged. "I'm not sure," she replied absently.

"Maybe I'll go see later."

"Hmmm..." Ping tried to concentrate. She had watched Scree fly the little ship on Kiva and then watched Kim flying the *Hakahei*. She knew enough to make some suggestions.

"Hop in," Ping said.

Both trolls leapt into the Loaders. Ping stood with Bones and showed him some of the controls. The troll hunched over as he concentrated.

"They ain't moving at all." Bones moved the joystick that Ping thought was for steering and pushed the...'go' lever. He squirmed on his seat and moved the controls the other way. "How do we get them to move? They ain't doing anything."

"We must need power." Ping started looking.

Bones looked as well. He stabbed a button at random, then paused. His finger wavered over his next button of choice as he waited to see if there was any action. He stabbed again. Tense pause...

Finally, the Loader rose a small way off the ground. The troll laughed and offered Ping a smile. "Huh, now getting somewhere." Two lights, one front and one on the back, were flashing. "Be carryin' people in no time."

While Ping showed Quartz which button would get her started, Bones moved his Loader around the relatively small space available. He concentrated fiercely, still hunched forward, hands gripping the controls tightly. His lips moved constantly.

It was only three minutes before the two trolls were dancing the vehicles around, humming past close to each other. They didn't go very fast but sometimes found themselves stuck in difficult spot. They would stop to consider, play with the controls, and start dancing again.

Cliff and his followers returned fifteen minutes later. They had commandeered Ruby, a young trollop from Green Troop, and between them lugged two large pieces of metal whose true purpose escaped Ping. That didn't worry her— she couldn't imagine what half the things in the ship were used for. All that mattered was that they suited current requirements. With the new platforms sitting securely on the front of the Loaders, Bones and Quartz headed slowly toward the refugees.

When the first load was moving to the freight elevator, Ping wondered what she should do next. The humans were still looking after the wounded, walking along beside the mechanized stretchers. Trolls were organizing the next load. Trolls were herding those who were healthy enough to walk on their own. Only one Loader would fit on the lift per trip, but some upright passengers would fit as well. Lift 4 also went all the way up to the top of the ship— a few people could fit in there.

So Ping stood and watched as the trolls chivvied people into action. The dwarves grumbled all the way, and the elvish women obviously didn't like taking orders from the men, but most did so anyway, with put upon looks and much sighing.

It took three trips to ferry the wounded upstairs. Ping walked along beside the last load with Green Troop and the last of the healthy dwarves. The leader of the humans, Captain Thorpe, was already upstairs. The last elves had long ago decided that sitting in a cargo hold was beneath their dignity and gone up.

The first freight lift only went up one floor, to the Level 9 hold. From there, they had to make their way to the other side of the ship to find the next one. It took them all the way to Level 3 in a smooth steady climb. Ping wanted to go one level higher, but that was the lift's limit.

"This lift is slow," Bones said while he fidgeted in his seat. "You'd think they'd make it quicker. The Loader could go quicker if... you know... it could go up and down. Slow, slow, slow."

Ping sighed quietly. Flint, standing nearby, tugged on the end of his moustache and tried not to smile. Nobody else could understand.

The hallways on Level 3 were relatively narrow and seemed over-crowded. People were lying on the floor or leaning against the walls. There was the passage that went all the way around the outside of the ship but they ignored that, as if comforted by the confined spaces.

A lot of them would normally be expected to die, but Ping had seen a dozen machines that she did not understand in the little hospital. She had to wonder what the humans could do to treat the wounded that neither she nor the others would think possible.

Those with more serious injuries were being left where they were on the floor. They were easier to keep an eye on there, Ping supposed. And perhaps it was easier to get them to the hospital from there as well. Some humans emerged from one of the smaller lifts. They had a stretcher and used it to take an elf with a broken and splinted leg to the floor above.

The organization and treatment of patients continued without help from Ping. She gave a slight smile, letting herself think, for a second at least, that she had organized the operation so well that it could now run without her. But the human soldiers were the main reason. Their leader kept them moving, kept them focused, with casual efficiency. He never shouted. He never really explained anything. A few words was all it took.

Ping decided she had earned her smile. Captain Thopre may be in charge up here, but she had gotten everyone out of the Hold. It had been her plan and her instructions that had started the process. She had been useful and that was something to be proud of amongst all these older, more experienced people.

When two soldiers came from the hospital with a stretcher, Thorpe was with them. The tall, thin man in the red hat examined the options lying on the floor and pointed to Scree, lying still and unconscious not far away. Ping wondered what that meant. Was the troll in a lot of pain? Did he *feel* the gash on his shoulder?

He would live though. He had to live. Would the other trolls listen to Kim without Scree around? Would they be as capable as Scree? Would they exhibit his best qualities or his worst.

Ping wiped tears from her eyes again as she watched the soldiers carry Scree towards the hospital. They had to step over resting dwarves to get there. They had to push past indignant elves. Those not injured were still milling around, getting in the way, disrupting the flow of those who had tasks to perform.

Ping looked at Stone but the troll didn't seem inclined to do anything. She sniffed and cleared her throat— her job hadn't been completed yet.

"Hello everyone," she said. Nobody took any notice. Most couldn't understand anyway. Or probably hear either. Keeble was sitting on the floor nearby. "Keeble, can you get everyone into the dining hall, please? Those that don't need help."

"I thought you were in charge. Now you want me to do the work for you?"

Ping just stared, not quite sure how to reply to that. Did she have any right to ask Keeble to do anything? Probably not. She swallowed and started to turn away.

Apparently, Stone had other ideas. "They not understand her, Keeble. Just do what she ask."

"I don't have to take orders from her?"

"Don't think of it as an order if you wants. Think of it as a sensible suggestion. Everyone is getting in the way here. Some of your friends could die if them humans get distracted." He shook his head in wonder, watching as another patient was carried away.

Keeble wound the gears on his mechanical arm in and out. "They aren't my friends."

"Do it anyway."

"Why are you following her orders?"

"I'll follow any good sensible suggestions I gets, Keeble. Good way to stay alive. Now do it."

The dwarf sighed but rose slowly to his feet.

7: Manual Operations

WHEN KEEBLE TRIED TO GET EVERYONE MOVING, they wouldn't listen. Elves were elves and weren't about to listen to *any* dwarf and the dwarves deliberately avoided meeting his eye. Obviously, someone had recognized him as a Wanderer and the word had spread. None of them would listen now. With a shake of his head, he went into the mess by himself to sit down at a table.

A few minutes later, others started to enter— not at his bidding, of course, but simply because they wanted to. Dwarves and elves wandered in the door, singly and in groups, liked the look of the place and decided to stay. Elves only sat with elves. Dwarves only sat with dwarves. At first, not even the latter would sit at Keeble's table. Soon though, the others were full, or occupied by elves, and they had no choice. And just because they sat near him, didn't mean they had to talk to him. Ari sat next to him, as silent as the others.

Keeble wound the gears on his arm. They needed oiling. They were in a bad state of disrepair all together.

For a long time it seemed nothing else would happen. Dwarves sat grumbling. Elves sat silently. A pair of trollops from Yellow Troop, Gem and Pool, stood by the door, as if to stop anyone from escaping. Apparently they weren't going to do anything else. Keeble supposed that maybe he should say something, but nobody would listen to him. Where was... Ping? Maybe she had gone to the bridge to help there. That was more important than talking to this lot. He sneered. What would *she* do, anyway? So Keeble stayed silent and in his seat. And in all his days could never have imagined what happened next.

Ari's chair scraped back and the dwife rose nervously to her feet. She cleared her throat. She twisted the stiff material of her horribly shortened dress in her hands. "Ummm... Everyone..."

There were shocked gasps and shouts of outrage from the dwarves. For Ari to stand up uninvited and draw attention to herself was unthinkable, even here, even in a situation that none of them had faced before. Keeble blushed despite himself.

But Ari would not be silenced, though she was blushing herself and hung her head for a moment. "I will stand here until I am heard," she said softly. It was doubtful anyone beyond those closest heard anything at all. The word spread, however, and the talk in the room slowly dropped to an angry murmur.

Then it appeared the dwife did not know what to say. Finally, she raised her head and spoke. "The world is a different place," she said.

Angry shouts in reply. She was heckled despite the fact nobody could really argue with what she'd said. Keeble had never really thought of it like that himself. He'd thought that his journey to Earth and Nexis had affected only him, but now he realized he was wrong and it had taken a woman to point it out.

"It *is* different. Keeble was called Wanderer because he failed the Rock Singing test, but he proved he could Sing when he helped us escape from Tab Cavern. He has come back from the dead— how can any dwarf here pretend the world has not changed?"

"Nothing has changed, woman," someone shouted.

"Then perhaps we should change."

Keeble narrowed his eyes and wound the gears in and out. In and out. Was she right? Or was it just dwife chatter? Either way, Keeble could see that, if nothing else, the looks in the eyes of the other dwives had changed. In and out. He could do with some coffee.

But Ari hadn't finished. "We are the Wanderers now," she said. "We have no family or friends. We are in Keeble's home. We must look to him to tell us what to do."

She quickly sat down and stared at the top of the stainless steel table.

Nobody said anything. What could you say when somebody said that your world was no longer what it had once been? Well, it was easy to say something when that somebody was wrong, but when you could think of no arguments against them... Keeble decided the men could probably all think of a dozen reasons to leave things the way they'd been, but they were not logical reasons a dwarf would say out loud. And the dwives? They were the ones who started to talk first, whispering to each other and stealing glances at those around them.

Keeble didn't know what he wanted to believe. If Ari was wrong, then he was a Wanderer still and would have no friends among the dwarves. If she was right... The women had already decided she was, and nothing anyone could say now would convince them otherwise. There could be trouble. The last dwife revolt had been almost a hundred years ago and did not end nicely.

Gem and Pool still stood by the door, not talking, hardly moving. They were women, but cool and confident. Pool was the older of the two, with a crosshatch of scars on her cheek and her long black hair pulled back in a ponytail. She wore a look of indifference that suggested she didn't care one way or the other what task she was given. But what orders had she been given? To stand there with Gem?

What was happening on the bridge?

Keeble suddenly wondered why he was even there when he should be upstairs, or trying to fix the engines. He'd taken the straps of the radio away from his head earlier. He quickly replaced it so he could listen. The others in the room looked at him strangely when, seemingly, he started talking to himself. If they wanted to know, they'd just have to ask, though his position as Wanderer might be firming by the moment as he chatted away. And of course they had to decide if talking to him was admitting that he *wasn't* a Wanderer? And if he was no longer a Wanderer...

"Kim?"

<*Yeah, Keeble?*>

"What's happening?" He couldn't get used to the idea of talking in his head.

<*Batteries hit full charge a minute ago, apparently. And we hit top speed in... Sixteen minutes.*>

"We're in space?" He hadn't realized, though he could remember the fluctuations in gravity as the ship's systems adjusted to the changing conditions. "Sixteen minutes until the jump? And how long is the jump?"

<*We're going three jumps of just under fourteen hours. About 84.5 light-years. Plus about two hours between jumps for charging.*>

"When am I supposed to get the engines aligned? I think the batteries will charge quicker once I've done that."

<*No time at the moment. When we get to Nexis, maybe. You can ask for volunteers from the dwarves to help.*>

"I don't know if they'll want to help me."

<*Why not? Oh, the Wanderer thing, right? Well, just get some lanterns organized then, and tell them all what's happening.*>

He turned to look at the trolls guarding the door before remembering they were actually trollops. But apparently they'd already heard the instructions. Gem nodded at Keeble's unspoken order and sauntered out, looking to see if she could get some lanterns.

Taking a deep breath, trying to ignore the look of recognition in the trollop's eyes, Keeble rose to his feet. The noise in the room died away. "Soon it's going to be dark," he said. A few of the dwarves looked at the ceiling lights, as if wondering what would go wrong. None of them looked at Keeble's face, pretending that the voice was coming from nowhere. "This ship can travel between the stars, but to do that it needs to do something that takes a lot of power so there isn't enough power to run the lights." It was easier than explaining everything. "There isn't enough power to run anything at all. It'll be dark for nearly fourteen hours."

There were groans from some of the listeners, though Keeble thought it was a bit funny, coming mainly from people who'd lived in caves all of their lives. He didn't bother looking at the elves. He knew how they'd be reacting— they wouldn't be reacting at all. Like the dwarves, the elves sat mainly in two groups, men and women, but looked as calm as they might have done eating breakfast.

"There are lanterns, so we won't have to actually sit in the dark, but there isn't a lot we can do while we wait. There are some games..." He didn't know how to play any of them, and the dwarves might well be insulted by the idea of playing games. "And there are books, for those who can read the language." None of them could read the language... "We could also have some language lessons, so everyone can understand what the others are saying."

"Why do we care what the elves say?" a dwarf shouted.

That was just stupid, they could already understand the elves. For a moment Keeble wondered if he was like that, only thinking when he knew the thoughts would lead to the conclusion he wanted.

Keeble asked, "What about what the Captain says?"

"Who is the captain?" Keeble recognized the dwarf who spoke. It was Tasko, a Singer.

"Her name is Kim, she is—"

"A woman? A woman is guiding this ship?" Tasko's face was flushing as red as his hair.

Keeble nodded. It was strange— he did not like the idea of Ari speaking to the group, but he was apparently willing to follow Kim. He kept telling himself she'd get them all killed, but he still did as she said. And they were still alive. And Ping had helped him repair the clock. He sneered. It was more accurate to say that he'd helped her. A month ago he would have shuddered at the thought of such a thing.

"When we've finished with the language, I can teach you something of how this ship works."

"You know how it works?" Makar this time, old and gruff and weathered by too many years outside the mountain collecting hides.

Keeble was slightly embarrassed. They were thinking of him as a Wanderer, as someone who could know nothing. But he *did* know things, just nowhere near as much as he would have liked. "I know some. I know enough to keep us moving as long as nothing serious goes wrong."

And with the thought of something serious going wrong... The hole in the hull. "Tasko, can you feel the ship? Are there any other Singers here?"

Eight men raised their hands. "And Kaper and Deis are with the wounded."

"Can you feel the ship?"

"What?" Tasko hadn't moved. He was eyeing Keeble suspiciously.

"Tell me if you can feel the hull."

Tasko got a far away look and started to softly Sing his Song. "There's nothing," he said. "It isn't stone."

"It's stone," Keeble said. "Apparently most of the ship is made of stone, just nothing like we've ever known."

"I tell you—"

"It *is* stone." So he still couldn't fix the hole, then.

<*Damn... Out of the frying pan...*> Kim's voice in Keeble's ear shocked him. <*Hold on, everyone, we're jumping now.*>

He fumbled for the talk button on his radio. "What? Why?" Everyone was looking at him.

<*We've got company.*>

"Yes but—"

"*Hold on.*"

Keeble asked no more. "Everyone, we're about to jump, get ready." Why was it 'jumping'? It was nothing like jumping.

There was nothing he could feel, but Keeble knew as they approached the gate. He could tell that the other Singers felt it as well. It was written on their faces— the power of it, the *depth.*

Just before the ship's power cut out, Keeble heard Kim's voice, soft in his ear as if she were talking to herself...

<*Holy shit. What have I—*>

The lights went out. All the newcomers shifted nervously before trolls started returning with lanterns. Gem with a handful, then dark skinned Sandy and one-eyed Peak. A lantern was placed on each table. And others were left, unlit, near the door.

"We'll start to teach you how to speak the language of Rongo," Keeble said. If the dwarves weren't kept busy they'd be pulling the ship apart in a matter of minutes.

But Keeble didn't care about talking— he just wanted to go to the bridge to find out what was wrong.

-oOo-

"What's the problem?" He lifted his lantern a little higher, as if it would show more than the scattering of lanterns already there.

Kim sighed. She looked haggard, a decade older than when he'd left the ship with the trolls. Tuki was the only other person on the bridge and he hardly looked any better.

"I learned a very important lesson," Kim said. She leaned back in her seat and covered her face with her hands.

Keeble smiled. *About time.* "And what lesson is that?"

"Don't set the timer until we're about to jump. Not until we're ready."

"Why?"

She took a deep breath. "Because we were only going 2.3 kilometers a second when we went through the gate. The timer was ready for our full jump."

"Fourteen hours?"

"Yes."

That didn't sound good. "So, how far will we travel? How fast will we be going when we come back out?"

Kim cleared her throat and wouldn't look at him. "Not very."

"You're saying we may not get out at all?"

"We won't. We'll stop in about 3 hours."

Keeble slumped down on the bottom step. "What do I tell everyone?"

Kim sighed again. "Tell them what you want. There's nothing we can do."

"There might be."

"Like what?" Kim snapped. "We're screwed."

"How long will our air last?"

"You tell me?"

Keeble nodded. *Yes, that's my area.* "The timer can be set for almost two days, so there must be enough air for that, but we have more people than the ship is designed for and who knows the condition of the systems..." He nodded again. "But they'll have allowed some room for error. Say 85 people at four days." There were about twice that many people on the ship. Keeble looked up at Kim. "Two days. Maybe."

Kim was slumped in the chair, already defeated.

"I'll get some dwarves together and you can tell them what's happening."

"There's no point—"

"So you'll just sit there and die?" Keeble shouldn't have been surprised, watching womanly nature finally reassert itself, but he was. He gave a grunt of disgust at the thought. "I'll get some dwarves. You can tell them. You were the one who got us here after all."

Keeble took his lantern and made his way back down stairs.

-oOo-

Keeble looked around the mess hall. Dwarves, humans, trolls, dwives and elves. Ping was there too. They all looked back at him. He hadn't bothered to get Kim. He could tell them as well as she. In fact, in the case of dwarves, he could probably do it better.

"You mean we is stuck in this place?" River asked. The trollop was leaning against the wall, EVA suite half unzipped. She didn't look happy.

"At this stage, yes, but if anyone has any ideas..."

For a long time nobody said anything and Keeble couldn't work out if they were trying to solve the problem or imagining their deaths.

Ari was the first to react, nervously raising her hand. "The ship is full of air under pressure. Could we use that to push ourselves forward more, like a jet?"

Keeble stared for a moment. The idea wouldn't work, but it wasn't *completely* stupid. One of the others beat him to the explanation. Dogar's words were harsh, but Keeble could tell that he would have voiced the idea himself had he thought of it.

"No way that will work, dwife. This ship is several thousand ton so there isn't enough air to move us significantly. And if there *was* enough air for that, then when we got back to our universe we'd have no power plus no air and no momentum. We'd be stranded there long enough to die."

"This is what we get for leaving a woman in charge," someone shouted.

"We all knew," Dogar added. "We should have done—"

"We knew for about a minute before she made the mistake, Dogar. We had no chance. Keeble should have—"

"The line of reasoning is stupid," Keeble said. "Without Kim you'd all be dead on Sherindel."

Ari cleared her throat. "Could we turn off the timer then set it for a shorter time?"

Would that work? Keeble turned to look at Ping.

"There isn't enough power," Ping said, barely loud enough for everyone to hear. "Or time. The clocks are mechanical, but the timer is *set* electronically. We need to turn the ship's power on to be able to adjust the timer... If we had more time we might be able to work out how to change the settings manually, but the clocks are larger than this room." She sighed. "No time."

Keeble shrugged. "And anyway, the gates are different. I have no idea where we might end up if we went through the out-bound gate while we are in this universe, and no idea where we would end up if we went through the inbound gate after that."

Ari slumped slightly. "It could not be any worse than here, surely."

She was right, little good that it did. They'd only have had enough power for one gate but after they'd arrived wherever it was that they were going they could have thought things through again. But it didn't matter...

"If we have no chance of getting back as things are now," Ari said, the only one coming up with idea again, "should we not turn off the timer?"

"Why?"

"Well, we have one battery full of power, but if we allow the gate to open pointlessly..."

"We just went through why it can't be adjusted, dwife," someone said coldly.

Ping looked up. "We don't have to adjust it. All we have to do it disconnect it from the Ohoga engines."

Keeble decided to remain silent and wait for somebody else to say something. But apparently they had the same idea. "Somebody answer her," Keeble said eventually.

Dogar had spoken to the dwife before, so all of the dwarves turned to him to speak again.

He grunted in disgust. "That is a good idea, dwife."

"Then why don't you go up to the bridge to tell Kim, Dogar?"

"I'm a Gang Boss, Wanderer, I don't run errands."

"And I am a Wanderer, so I don't do anything at all." Keeble stared until the older dwarf left the room, grumbling all the way.

When Dogar had gone, another dwife nervously raised her hand. "Why do we need to worry about the clocks at all?" Ness said nervously when Keeble nodded. "Surely the Ohoga engine can be activated manually."

Keeble didn't say anything— nobody did. He scratched his head. "That could work. Ping, how long do we have?"

The woman looked up. "Just over two hours until we stop moving."

Keeble grunted. The computers weren't working. None of the other dwarves could read the language yet. And there were a few hundred manuals that he would have to search to find what he was after.

"Can you read, Ping?"

"A little."

"Come on then." He hurried from the room and the woman rose to follow.

"Where are you going?" a dwarf shouted.

"We've got two hours to find out how to use the Ohoga Engine manually," Keeble shouted back over his shoulder. "Everyone stay here."

There was a mad rush towards the door but, after letting Ping through, Pool and Gem moved to block the way. Keeble heard one dwarf hit the floor and the others quickly decided that getting past mere women might not be as easy as they thought.

In the Engineering Bay, Keeble immediately started pulling manuals from boxes and cabinets. He tried to remain calm and do things in an organized manner but there were so many manuals and not enough time. Many were on specific systems and machines and could be discarded immediately. Water Recyclers, Fuel Still, Lifts, Intercoms. But within five minutes he had a pile of twenty volumes relating to the Ohoga Engines in one way or another. Then there were the ones that referred to things he didn't know about at all. They might be useful, though probably not.

"You keep sorting," Keeble said. "Anything that mentions Ohoga Engines here. Other stuff there. Unknowns there." He looked at the piles still to be sorted. "I'll start looking through these to see what I can see." He picked up the first manual that mentioned 'Ohoga' in the title and flipped to the index. He scanned the titles quickly but discovered he was hardly taking notice of what they said.

"Do it properly," he muttered. "No use going quick if I miss what I'm after." He took a deep breath and made himself slow down.

"Do you require assistance? Pool said something about you reading?"

Keeble looked up and saw Meledrin standing in the doorway. He almost told her to go away— how could an elf help?— but he bit his tongue. Meledrin, though she was both a woman and an elf, could help. He grunted and motioned her towards the most likely pile. "We are looking for something, anything, about operating the Ohoga Engines manually. Just look through the index and see if you can see anything mentioned. Or something that might be related."

Meledrin nodded and took a seat close to the pile and started to read.

"Can the other elves read yet?"

Meledrin shook her head. "We have barely started with talking, Keeble. No thought has yet been given to reading."

"Perhaps you should..."

"It will not happen quickly enough to help."

Keeble nodded and returned his attention to the books.

There was a manual clock on the wall and Keeble looked up every two minutes only to discover that ten minutes had passed. The words before him were starting to blur— both before and after he read them. He struggled to distinguish the shapes of the letters on the smooth, shiny pages. And he found himself reading sentences three times trying to coax meaning from amongst the common, easily understandable words. An entire manual on how to adjust the Mazad Dublo settings. Another on how to recalibrate the Fitsal Sensors. But what did all that mean?

He flipped pages and threw the latest manual in disgust. He stretched his back and checked the clock. Fifteen minutes to go.

Fifteen minutes? But it had been three quarters of an hour just a couple of minutes ago.

He looked around at all the books that still had to be checked. He grabbed one and... Take a deep breath. Clear the mind. Rest for just a second.

"Anything," he asked Meledrin and Ping. He wondered if he sounded as empty as he felt.

Ping sighed and shook her head.

Meledrin had been through twice as many books as Keeble and Ping together but she shook her head as well. "No. I..." She held up a hand as if Keeble had been the one speaking. "Perhaps this." She handed the file to Keeble.

He scanned the page she had been reading. "There's a switch," he said. "There's a switch."

"What?" Ping went to read over his shoulder. "Where?"

Keeble was still reading. But unfortunately the book wasn't about the switch, so it didn't tell him where it was. It gave him the name though. Putting the file down on the floor he started searching through the files he'd already checked. He scrabbled through the pile on the floor, sliding books and files aside. He knew he'd seen something earlier but could not remember exactly where.

Then he found the book he was after and had to find the page.

"Where, Keeble?"

"Shut up. I'm looking."

"Five minutes, Keeble."

Then he had it. It was just a switch. He worked out the position and the quickest way to get there. Grabbed a toolbox, raced for the stairs. He tried to pull out the tool for removing wall panels as he ran but his mechanical hand made it impossible. When he reached the panel he dropped the box and pulled open the lid. His hand was sweating. He wiped it on his EVA suit, which didn't help at all. Shuffling through the toolbox for the tool. He had the panel off minute later. It clattered to the floor and he was through the hatch. Then he was racing through the engine, leaping equipment, ducking pipes as he headed for the switch. And he was there. He pulled the lever and nothing at all happened. He reached out to push the lever back the other direction when he noticed a humming sound. He stood, hand poised over the lever, while the sound grew. Then suddenly it stopped.

"Keeble?" Ping's voice drifted through the machinery. "Keeble? Are you there? What happened?"

Keeble looked around but nothing seemed to have changed. "I don't know." But he knew it hadn't worked. If it had worked they would be back in the real universe by now. The lights would be on. Machines would be starting up. Kim would be on the radio asking what had happened.

It hadn't worked. Keeble sat down where he was, head in his hands, and wondered what they were going to do now.

8: Fun to Be Had

SCREE WAS AWAKE IN AN INSTANT. He sat up, alert, until he realized exactly where he was— the hallway outside the medical bay. It was littered with injured people: elves, dwarves and humans. The soldiers, in their mottled green, were tending to them, working in the light of the lanterns. Through the open Library door, Scree saw a couple of elves reading.

There were voices coming from the mess hall. Raised voices. Arguments. It seemed to be dwarves, from the sound of it, but whoever it was spoke their own language.

Scree started to stand.

"Hey there, buddy. No rush. We aren't going anywhere."

Scree turned and saw Captain Thorpe hurrying to his side.

"I feels fine."

"Maybe, but you lost a lot of blood. You should be careful."

"Been hurts worse before with nobody to look after me."

"I find that hard to believe."

Scree shrugged, wincing as his shoulders complained loudly. He shifted the focus of the conversation. "Youse speaking my language."

Thorpe nodded. "It's surprisingly easy to learn. I don't know how long we've been here, but it couldn't be much more than a day."

"Where is we?"

Thorpe looked away for a moment. "We're in the other universe."

Scree narrowed his eyes. "We dead?"

Thorpe shook his head, nodded. "All but, apparently. We stopped before we went through the exit gate."

"Bleeding cats." Scree started to rise again, but Thorpe laid a hand on his arm.

"Just stay there. They can live without you."

"You means they can die without me. I'm nots dying without a fight."

"There isn't a lot to fight here, Scree."

"Always something to fight." It sounded as if the dwarves in the other room agreed with that sentiment.

"Just give yourself a few minutes then. A few minutes won't matter."

Scree relented, though only because he wanted to ask a question. "So, whats happened back on Sherindel? Where was you going?" He leaned back against the wall. "And what was you doing down in that damn gully."

The Captain sighed and sat down as well. "The whole troop was through the gate thing about half an hour after Kim led us there. We were only lightly armed, but we were able to help the elves to an extent. Trouble was, there were just too many of the aliens."

"They called hurgon."

"How do you know that?"

"There's one around here somewhere. He ain't too sure around all us people though."

"You... Why didn't anyone say?"

"Nothings to do with you, I suppose." Scree shrugged painfully. "Cuto's friendly enough if you can understand what the hell he's sayings."

"Friendly? But..." Thorpe seemed to think better of arguing. He shook his head as if clearing it. "Anyway, we held the area for a while, an hour or something, then we were overwhelmed and forced to run. We were already a couple of kilometers from the gate when support came through. With heavier weapons our men were holding the gate easy enough, but we were still being harried. That was... I don't know... a few days ago now.

"We'd been lying low, but the dwarves went past us obviously needing help. So we helped..." He removed his red beret and slapped it against his knee... "and brought down more of the aliens. We thought the caves were the safest bet, even if they were occupied already... That's where you came in."

Scree nodded. "We just wanted some dwarves."

"What for?"

"Apparently dwarves can fix just abouts anything if you gives them a few minutes to think abouts it. We had one of them, but we needed some more. And there's some other people on Earth who have some ships that'll probably need fixed."

"Someone on Earth? Who?"

"Don' know much about it. I ain't been around here from the start. But apparently Kim found this ship in a hangar somewhere and there lots of others there as well."

"Kim *found* this?"

Scree carefully pushed himself to his feet and Thorpe didn't try to stop him. His shoulders hurt so much he had to grit his teeth, but it was nothing he couldn't handle. His right shoulder was bandaged heavily. The left, the one that had been fried, more lightly so. He examined the remains of his EVA suit. It had been damaged when he was injured then cut away completely later. He'd had it barely a day and he needed a new one. He wondered how many there were to spare.

Scree made his way around to the stairs, moving past sleeping patients. Thorpe followed.

Keeble and Tuki were the only people on the bridge. They both sat silently, staring out the front window. Neither even moved when Scree entered.

The colored mist was outside. It was red and blue— and a sickening purple somewhere between— that swirled ever so slowly. There was something else out there as well— the silvery sheen of a gateway hanging motionless in front of the ship.

"Why's that there?"

Keeble's head snapped around. "What?"

"What's the gate doing?"

"Nothing."

"I can sees that."

Thorpe cleared his throat. "Keeble tried to open the gate while the ship was still moving but was too late, by about a minute. So now it's just hanging there." He checked the timekeeper on his wrist, though Scree doubted it worked. "It's been there for four hours."

"Where's Kim?"

Scree watched Keeble looking around, as if only just realizing the woman wasn't there. "Don't know."

So he asked in his mind if any of the trolls knew where she was. Those who answered didn't know, so he got them to start looking.

"What we doings about this?"

Tuki shrugged. "There is nothing we can do."

"Who says?"

The moai pointed at Keeble.

Scree shook his head. "Keeble go and take charge in the mess. Get the dwarves thinking."

"It won't do any good."

"I don't cares. Do it anyways."

"But—"

"Keeble..."

"Who put you in charge? I've been on the ship longer than you."

Scree didn't even bother answering that. He just stared.

"All right. All right. We've been discussing it for hours, but I'll go back down there again."

"Good."

When the dwarf had slumped from the room Thorpe gave a bark of laughter. "You do have a way of motivating people."

"I don't intend to sits around here and wait to die." He looked around. "We needs to find Kim."

"She said she needed to rest," Tuki said.

"Right. Why don't you goes and rest as wells? Nothing you cans do here."

"But I..."

"Go somewheres else, Tuki. Goes and talk to your friends or somethings."

"Very well."

"Now what?" Thorpe looked around the bridge, as if someone else might need ordering around.

"Don't knows." Scree wanted to know where Kim was. She should've been the one shouting at people, getting them to do things. Or at least telling people nicely and getting someone else, like himself, to do the shouting. She wanted to rest... "Follows me."

The Captain's cabin on level one could be entered by two different doors. Scree tried the outer door but it was locked, so he made his way through the captain's office to the second door. With Thorpe standing behind him in the office, lantern held aloft, most of the room was in shadow, but Scree saw movement on the bed and waved the human closer.

Kim rolled over, arm up to shade her eyes. "Go away."

Scree smiled. "Goods. You still knows how to tell peoples what to do."

"Shouting at people is easy."

"So why don't you gets out here and do it?"

"What's the use? I got us all killed." She rolled back over and hid her face in the shadows.

"We ain't dead yet. We cans give up, or we can fight and I always fights. I thoughts you did too."

"You don't know me."

"Obviously."

Scree stood there looking at the curve of her hip, the thin strip of tanned flesh revealed at her waist. He couldn't think of anything else to say. His usual means of motivation was to thump people, or to threaten them. He didn't want to thump Kim, which surprised him. He'd never known a time when he was unwilling to thump a person. He grunted at the thought.

"Spending too long with Ping," he mumbled.

"Pardon?"

He turned to look at Thorpe. "Nothings."

So, he couldn't thump her, and he doubted threatening would work seeing she was already expecting to die. He might have stood there till the day he died, which was not to be too far away, by all accounts, had not a voice in his head disturbed him.

<Scree, we got problems.> Flint sounded calm enough, as if his dinner wasn't cooked exactly right.

<Whats?>

<Gorge, Gem, Cairn, Crunch, River and Talus ain't happy.>

<What you means?>

<They says if they is gunna die they might as well have some fun before they do.>

<What sort of fun?> Scree didn't care if they had fun amongst themselves. Though if that was what they had in mind it wasn't likely anyone else would've heard about it. He grunted again. A month ago he probably would have joined them.

<They is talking about elves at the moments.>

<Wheres?>

<Theys in the dirt room.>

"Come ons, Thorpe. Lets go."

"Where to now?"

Scree examined the weapon sheathed at the man's waist. "How does that gun of yours work?"

"What?"

"How does it works?"

"Uhhh... Well, basically, very basically, when you pull the trigger it releases a hammer that hits on the bullet shell, which creates an explosion that propels the bullet forward. Why?"

"No electricity or nothings?"

"No. Why?"

"We might needs it."

"What? Why?"

-oOo-

Scree made his way down to Level 3 where he collected a group of volunteers. The human soldiers all came, plus some male elves and a large group of dwarves. Apparently their discussions were not getting them anywhere and they needed a break.

From there they went down again, a rowdy mob clomping down the stairs.

Scree got them into some type of order as they headed for Level 5. Humans with the good weapons first. Dwarves second, and elves, a couple of them armed with bows, third. He considered putting the dwarves first, seeing there were too many of them anyway. Hopefully though, only the threat of Thorpe and his men would be needed.

As soon as he stepped out of the narrow passage and into the main section of the dirt room, Scree knew he'd arrived just in time. There were two groups of trolls there. Both had found themselves weapons; pipes, machetes, lumps of wood tied to the end of ropes; but there the similarities finished. The group led by Flint stood quietly together, watching the second group. The others were flailing about, thumping at the ground and walls, working themselves into a frenzy.

"Stinking cats."

"What manner of place is this?" Suldon, a young male elf with silver hair and bow held negligently in his hand, shook his head in wonder. "It is a garden."

"That's what I thought," Scree replied. "But why'd they wants a garden on a ship?"

"I know that if I were to spend long periods of time on this ship I would be much happier with a garden to wander in."

"Buts would you be willing to waste all that water to keeps it going?"

A young dwarf with sandy hair spoke up. "Actually, a garden could help save water and air. You see the trees are needed to—"

"Yeah, wells we don't have time for this right now." Scree went to join Flint, Sandy and Gulch. Not ten meters away the six others whacked at the ship.

"How longs they been going?"

"Couple minutes."

That wasn't too bad, though if they kept going for much longer... Scree picked the most likely leader of the group. "Yo, Gorge, what youse doing?"

Gorge struck the wall a couple of more times before turning to look. "What it look like?"

"It looks like youse looking for troubles."

The older troll showed his teeth in what was supposed to be a smile. "Won't be no trouble."

"Might be. Why don't youse have your fun rights here?"

The others stopped their thumping to join Gorge.

"More fun to be had elsewhere."

"No, there ain't. No fun at all outside this room right now. The boss said so."

"Well," Crunch said, "maybe the boss don't know where t' look. I intend t' show her. Maybe I show her personally— she got us in this mess after all."

"She did. And she'll get us outs, as well."

Crunch looked at Cairn and they both laughed. "You know where she is? Or she still playing at hide and seek?"

"She thinking. And that's the problem with you lot. You don't think."

"We thinking," Gem said with a smile. "Thinking about how we gunna have some fun."

"Hows about after that? Whats you gunna do then?"

"We gunna die, like everyone else."

"We got lots of smarts peoples on this ship. We ain't dead yet. Even Flint knows that. He probably reckons we gunna die, but—"

"We just trolls doing what's best for trolls, Scree. Same as ever."

"What's best for trolls for the next five minutes, maybe. But what about after that? What's best for you trolls tomorrow? And the day after that?"

"Ain't gunna be a tomorrow."

Flint shook his head. "How you know that? As long as there's a chance I'm gunna see if it works.

"Flint's thinking abouts the future, not just about now."

"You two startin' to sound like humans."

Scree laughed. "Maybe we is. And that ain't a bad thing, 'cause humans ain't stupid."

"You gunna live in a town soon."

"I already is. This ship. I worked out what a town is recently. It's a place to keep useful peoples you might need later. And a home is a place to keeps useful things. That ain't so stupid, when you thinks about it." He laughed again, but continued to stare coldly at the other trolls. "But youse ain't thinking, is you. Youse all just normal trolls." He paused. "Actually, you ain't even normal trolls. Normal trolls don't give up. They fights to the end, no matter what. You have this fun, and you giving ups."

"You reckon we can get out?" Talus no longer held his piece of pipe like he wanted to use it. He wasn't looking at Scree though. He was looking at Sandy, standing by Flint's side.

The young trollop scratched her head, as if she was really giving the matter some thought. The beads plaited into her hair clattered. Eventually she shrugged. "Won't find out if we kills everyone who might help. Or even if we just scares 'em."

Talus nodded slowly. "But scaring and killing people is fun."

Sandy ducked her head and scratched at ground with her foot. "Well, yeah, but so's havin' friends."

Scree spoke to Flint in his head. <What's all that abouts?>

<Couple of the younger trollops has been talking with Ping and Ari and other dwarf women. Seems they like it.>

Scree smiled and shook his head slightly. <Who'd have thunk.> He'd grown up with older trolls telling him that all other people just naturally wanted to see trolls dead. He hadn't been able to argue, because just about everyone he saw tried to kill him or wanted someone else to do it. And he'd wanted to kill them back. Respect was a funny thing.

He spoke out loud. "Why don't you come over here, Talus. We all dies soon enough, no need to hurry things along."

Gorge grunted. "What make ya think you gunna kill us, Scree? There's only..." His brow furrowed. "There's more of us. The rest of them is looking for the boss."

Scree looked over his shoulder. "I thought you could count a bit, Gorge. There's lots of us."

Gorge laughed. "But they's just humans and dwarves and... elves." He said the last with a particularly vicious sneer.

"They's enough. You know what a bow is, right? You gunna out run one of them?" He looked over is shoulder again. "You dwarves spread out a bit. The rest of you— if they attacks, make sure you kill them. They pissed off now, if we wounds them they just get even more pissed off." He had a sneer of his own for Gorge.

The dwarves did as they were told. They weren't big, but they were solid and looked fierce in their own way. The elves didn't look fierce. They looked like elves always did, as far as Scree could tell.

"You comings over here or what Talus?"

The young troll had been edging away from the others and was already a couple of meters to the side. He nodded and dashed across to stand between Flint and Sandy.

Scree smiled at Gorge. "Now there's even less of youse."

Gorge shrugged. "Won't make any difference."

"No, it won'ts. Now puts down the stuff."

"I'll put this down after I've had some funs."

"What about youse lot? If I beats him is I in charge again?"

"Maybe."

"Maybes? How abouts it then, Gorge?" He wouldn't be able to resist. "You ands me."

"Yeah. You and me."

Scree smiled and loosened his shoulders. It hurt. He winced at the pain.

"I'm keeping this club."

"You saw me break Bluff's neck— if you thinks the club'll help then you can keeps it."

Captain Thorpe touched his arm. "Is this a good idea? You shouldn't be risking yourself."

"No risk. Gorge is big and old and slow." He made sure the other troll could hear. Gorge's anger was building at the delay, and Scree's advantage grew with every moment.

"And you were half dead a few hours ago," Thorpe replied.

"Don't start worrying until I'm... three quarters dead. Watch the rest of thems though."

"Right." He didn't look happy.

Finally, Gorge'd had enough and attacked. He was slow for a troll, but by most other standards that was pretty quick.

Scree brushed aside the bigger man's attack and struck at the back of his elbow. And Gorge flicked his club, a lazy attack that managed to save his own elbow.

Scree grunted when his injured shoulder was struck but let momentum swing him around. He struck Gorge's ribcage with his elbow, kept spinning and was behind him. He danced in and hit him once, twice in the kidneys. Gorge grunted and squirmed away. Scree let him go. He took the opportunity to flex his shoulders. They hurt like a stomped cat but he tried not to show it. There was blood on one of the bandages.

"The human taught me that fighting, you know." Scree smiled. He could see he was about one insult away from getting Gorge to do something really stupid. Normally when trolls fought they weren't thinking enough to notice stuff like that. "I should go gets the boss and let her thump you." One more. "But nah, you don't send the boss to clean rats from the sewer."

Gorge charged forward, swinging his club in a fierce backhand swipe. Scree ducked easily. From low down he gave a left-hand uppercut to the other troll's groin. Gorge slumped forward slightly, momentarily. Surging up to his full height, Scree hit him under the chin. Gorge's head snapped back. Bones broke. The troll stayed on his feet for a moment, dead, before toppling backwards.

Hearing a rush of feet behind him, Scree turned quickly. But all he saw was the four remaining mutineers running away, dashing for the safety of the shadows.

"What are youse doing," he said over his shoulder. "Shoots them."

Half a dozen arrows whistled over his head.

Cairn took two in the back. Another took River in the leg, but she hobbled on. Crunch turned at the last moment and slapped one away from his chest and winced as another grazed his hip. Gem stumbled and fell. She twitched and squirmed for a moment before dying.

A moment later River and Crunch disappeared into the tunnel that led to the other side of the garden.

"Pissing cats." Scree tried to remember the layout of the room. Without power there was no way out on the other side of this level. Scree looked up, though, to the half level above. "Flint— take Talus, three elves and a couple of humans up to the next level. There's two doors— you's got to stop them from getting out the far one into the workshop."

"Right." He'd organized his pack and was gone in seconds, scrambling up the cliff to the floor above.

"What about the rest of us," Thorpe asked.

Scree was glad the man hadn't objected to the commandeering of his men. "There's another doors straight up there, and the steps behind us. We's going to spread out a couple of lamps down here, then go straight up there. We can watch the door and the stairs from there."

"Right."

"Would be all over if you'd used your weapons."

"We tried. They didn't work."

"What? Why not?"

Thorpe shrugged. "The hammer's fell but... Nothing."

Scree didn't know exactly what that meant.

"When we finish here we'll have to see what we can find out."

Scree shrugged as well. "Let's go then."

The whole group started to climb, but Scree stopped the first dwarf in line. "Not you dwarves. Youse got to go back up stairs and help work out how to gets us out of here."

"We want to help here."

"We can handle this, but we needs everyone we can spare thinking of how to gets us out of here."

"Right then. Let's go lads." The dwarf led the way towards the stairs.

Scree was halfway up the cliff when he had a sudden thought. *There's one person we haven't thought to asks.*

He started to climb back down. "Thorpe, you's in charge up there. Make sure you kills them trolls this time."

"Where are you going?"

"Going to help with the thinking." He laughed at the absurdity of that and headed quickly towards the stairs.

9: Cliffs of Knowledge

MELEDRIN LOST HER COMPOSURE FOR A MOMENT when Scree opened the door and burst into her room. She schooled her face to calmness as she waved her hands in the ceremony of *Lesser Changing.*

"Have you no manners, Scree?" Though he had proven on more than one occasion in just a short period of time that he did not. "It is customary to knock before entering someone else's quarters."

The big man shrugged. "But then theys'll know you's there."

"That is the point. You have no need to sneak up on people who are your companions. I could have been..." she was going to say 'unclothed', but blushed at merely the thought. "I could have been talking privately with someone."

"This is more important."

"It may well be, but you can inform me of that when I inquire as to who is without."

"What?" He shook his head. "Looks, there is one person on this ships who knows more about the gates than anyone, and we ain't asked him how to get out of here."

"Keeble is—"

"Not Keeble. The monster. Cuto."

Meledrin was about to instruct Scree on the bad manners of interruption but decided that the troll's idea earned him some leniency, this time. Scree was a strange man, even for a man. He did not care what others thought of him, and he did not think he was very smart, so he was not afraid to think about things in ways that nobody else would. He was quite a bit smarter than he gave himself credit for.

"You are correct," Meledrin said eventually. "I shall go and speak with him."

"Should we tells Kim?"

"Yes. Are we aware of her location?"

"She was in the Captain's cabin a while ago, buts now?" Scree shrugged again.

"Let us try there in the first instance." Meledrin led the way to the stairs and to the ship's Administration Level. Kim was lying on the bed in the Captain's cabin staring at the ceiling.

Though the door was open and Kim had seen her approaching, Meledrin knocked anyway, with a pointed glance towards Scree. He seemed to ignore her, of course, though he would have noticed.

"Go away," Kim said. "Go bug someone else."

"It is our intention to 'bug' someone else," Meledrin informed her, "but we require your assistance."

"Let me assure you, Mel, both you and Scree can bug people plenty well enough on your own."

Meledrin thought to ask that her full name be used, but decided it was probably much too late. "Perhaps we can, Kim, but we need your assistance in other areas."

"What areas are those?"

"Your ability to make leaps of logic." Meledrin said. Scree was good at that, but Kim was able to make the leaps from higher cliffs of knowledge. "We... Scree... thought that we should ask Cuto about any means of escaping from this universe.

Kim grunted in disgust. "He isn't already helping?"

"Cuto is not—"

"I know. He isn't a male. Whatever. Why hasn't Cuto been helping?"

"I believe Cuto is uncomfortable in the presence of the hakan strangers. Will you assist?"

"No. You can still manage on your own."

In the past, Kim's stubbornness had been an asset— she would not give up until she received the desired result— but in this instance it was working against them. Meledrin sighed and did not know what else to say. Apparently Scree was of the opinion that he did.

"You's in charge, Kim."

"So, I'm ordering you to do it on your own then."

"So you wants us running up here annoying you every few minutes with questions?"

"Like what? He can either get us out or not. Nothing I can do about it."

"Plenty you can do."

Kim didn't say anything. She rolled over and stared at the wall.

"Well, if you's just going to lie there and sulk then I'm taking command."

"Good." She didn't look at them. "You're welcome to it."

"Right, then I'm ordering you to comes with us."

"Ha. You really think that'll work?"

It was obvious to Meledrin that the strategy would be unsuccessful.

"Well, thinks of it this way. You can walk down there as our boss. You can walk down there cause I ordered you to. Or you can be carried down there by half a dozen trolls." Scree smiled. "Thems the only choices you got, Kim."

Meledrin almost said that she would not allow Kim to be carried anywhere by the trolls, but managed to hold her tongue.

Kim sat up. "You wouldn't." Kim would know Scree was serious and that the other trolls would probably do as he said, but there was no possibility she would allow such a thing to happen.

Scree just smiled.

"Jesus. Bloody troll." Kim climbed to her feet and pushed them out the door before her. "Come on then, let's get this over with so I can go back to sleeping."

"Yes, boss."

Kim sighed. "Get me another elf, Scree. One that'd like to stay on the ship when the others leave."

One moment she was assuming they would not successfully escape from the universe, the next she was formulating plans for when they did.

Meledrin shook her head. "I am able to perform any translation duties you require, Kim," she said, incensed that the woman would think otherwise. "Nobody else knows the hurgon language."

"I know they don't, and what if something happens to you? What if you need to sleep when somebody else wants to talk? We need other language specialists around here, Mel."

"Very well."

"I wasn't asking for your permission."

It seemed Kim was once more throwing herself fully into her role as Captain. The woman was as bad as Scree. Meledrin waved a *Lesser Changing* to calm herself. "Well, Scree, are you going?"

"Chasm getting someone." He smiled and tapped his temple. "Radio in head's not a machine. Mutineers are dead, bys the way. Two elves and a human was injured."

"Mutineers?" Kim asked, saving Meledrin the bother. "What mutineers?"

"Six trolls, but theys taken care of now. Should we throw them outside, do you think?"

"I don't know. Christ. Mutineers?"

Scree shrugged. "Cuto's in his cabin."

A woman was standing by the alien's cabin door when they arrived. Meledrin shook her head and turned to her companions. "Kim, Penisari cannot do this. She has no authority."

"No authority to what? We aren't on Sherindel any more, Toto, all your old rules count for nothing now."

Toto? 'Mel' was bad enough, but to start calling her something else entirely. Meledrin took a grip on her anger with another *Lesser Changing* and returned to matters at hand. "But she was not given any responsibilities for a reason. She neglected duties and—"

"From what I can tell, Mel, it's men who do just about all the work for you anyway. Did she forget to bless her tree in the morning or something?"

Meledrin scowled. Kim was being facetious, she knew, but was not far from the truth. "Let us go."

They knocked on the door and entered to find Cuto looking at the pieces of a small machine spread about on a bed. The alien spoke rapidly and Meledrin had trouble following.

After a moment of sorting words she translated. "Cuto says the machine is only a book reader and..."

Kim waved the translation away. "Cuto can pull stuff apart if he likes, as long as it doesn't affect the working of the ship. He isn't a prisoner."

Meledrin translated and the alien gave a quick nod, which was a hakan gesture.

"*We wish to talk with Cuto about important matters,*" Meledrin said then.

The alien turned and planted each foot on the deck in turn with two solid thumps. It seemed to Meledrin that Scree would not be able to shift the alien if it did not wish to be shifted.

Meledrin took one of the two chairs, while Kim took the other. Penisari glanced at Scree but seemed to decide, correctly in this instance, that the troll would rather stand. So she carefully shifted parts of the dismantled machine and sat on the bed. She was only a couple of years Meledrin's junior, but seemed much younger. She clasped her hands before her and examined the floor.

Kim cleared her throat. "Penisari... Peni, you just listen and try to learn the language. Mel, see what you can find out."

Meledrin explained their current predicament to the alien. She wanted to dispense with the spoken words but persevered.

"*Is there any way to escape?*" Cuto asked.

"*We were hoping you could help,*" Meledrin said. "*Do the kil'ini use this universe to travel between the stars? How is it done?*"

'*The kil'ini can but do not. And Cuto does not know how it is done,*" the alien said. "*Nobody does.*"

"*What is meant?*"

"*How does Meledrin breathe?*"

"*Meledrin does not know,*" Meledrin said, "*it is just done.*"

"*Then how could Meledrin expect the kil'ini to know. Kil'ini do it and that is all there is to know.*"

Meledrin translated for Kim. She could see Penisari working through the words, trying to make the links, trying to weed the adjectives from amongst the nouns, trying to sift the adverbs form the verbs. Meledrin did not envy her the difficult task, but was not about to assist— not even to point out the lack of pronouns.

Kim sighed and shook her head. It took Meledrin a moment to realize that the sigh was directed at her.

"I don't want to know the actual mechanics of it, Mel. I just want to know how they make it happen."

"I do not understand the difference."

"We don't know how the Ohoga Engines work, but we know how to *make* them work. Do the kil'ini tear the space-time continuum with their tentacles? Do they fart? Do they sing a song to make a gate like Keeble reckons this ship does? And seeing they aren't mechanical, would they be able to survive and maneuver and... whatever... in this universe?"

"I shall ask."

"Good idea." Kim was shaking her head.

Meledrin asked Cuto and listened carefully to the response.

-oOo-

Meledrin examined the bridge from her seat and wondered how Kim had decided who should be present. There were obvious choices, such as the dwarves, but some of the trolls did not even appear to be listening to the conversation.

Ping cleared her throat. "So," she said, looking around nervously. "If we can get a message out of this universe and into our own universe, and if one of the kil'ini happens to hear it, and it wants to help... then it will be able to survive long enough, and maneuver long enough, to save us?"

Meledrin watched as Kim looked at Cuto for a moment and nodded.

"Well, that sounds easy then." Ping slumped back in her chair.

Cuto did not appear concerned one way or the other though it was still hard for Meledrin to gage any but the most ostentatious body language from the alien. Many of those in the room, the *hakans*, sitting in the seats surrounding the viewing pit did not appear concerned either. Most sat and stared out at the swirling mist of the universe— and the gate still hanging just out of reach— as if the answer to their problems might be out there. They were resigned to their fate. The panic had come earlier.

Drago, long beard in plaits, hands laced across his stomach, cleared his throat as if about to offer his thoughts. He shifted in his seat and subsided into silence.

"How long do we have?" Suldon asked. Why the saveigni was present was beyond Meledrin. He could not even control the fidgeting of his hands.

Nobody replied.

"Keeble?" Kim asked eventually.

The dwarf shrugged. "Maybe two days."

"If there were plants in the garden..." Suldon said.

It had all been stated previously. If there were plants in the garden they could live for much longer, but unless someone knew of some way to grow 50 thousand year old seeds into plants in a few hours it was wasted breath. And they did not have enough breaths to waste.

Ping sighed. "If we could get into the other universe, and could get a message to someone, and they were willing to help... would they be able to get here quick enough anyway?"

"What do you mean?"

"Well, where are we? In the real universe— in our universe— where are we? Are we within two days of rescue?"

Meledrin swallowed noisily and hoped nobody would notice. According to Kim the universe was such a large place. Meledrin could not help but think that Ping had struck at the heart of the problem. She turned to look at Tuki and saw that the moai was already working on the problem and struggling. He turned and called to Okalani. She hurried to his side. They consulted, apparently juggling the huge numbers in their heads.

"Traveling at approximately 2.3 miles per second when we passed through the gate we would have traveled slightly less than half a light year from Sherindel."

Kim laughed bitterly. "Does anyone know how fast radio waves travel? It'll probably take a few decades, or more, for our signal to go half a light year."

Meledrin glared when Penisari spoke to Cuto. She was about to say something to remind Penisari of her place, but paused to listen to the alien's reply.

A moment later, Penisari translated for everyone else. "Cuto states that it would be a matter of a few hours for a kil'ini to arrive here, and that, had we the right equipment, we could get a message to them in almost no time at all." She glanced towards Meledrin as if checking the accuracy of her translation.

Meledrin nodded in reply.

Keeble was the first, barely, to ask the question. "What equipment? Can we make it here?"

Another conversation between Penisari and Cuto. Meledrin was too stunned, and gripping too tightly to hope, to object.

"Cuto states that the kil'ini know of a method to send short messages across the galaxy almost instantaneously. They have shown the hurgon how to do much the same with machines, though the power involved normally makes the exercise futile when they can simply ask the kil'ini to send the message for them."

"Ask if it will show us how to make one of the machines?"

"Cuto can but is not sure if it will do any good."

"But you said—"

"We do not just need Cuto to help us, we need someone to come and rescue us."

Suldon interrupted, speaking directly to Cuto. Meledrin gasped but again, she paused to listen, then started to translate as the conversation continued. "'It is obvious that there is much that hakans could learn from hurgon,' Suldon says, 'and our people have never been ones to waste such opportunities. Trade of both knowledge and goods would be much more beneficial than war.'"

It was quickly obvious to Meledrin that Suldon had found the one thing for which the hurgon might be able to take a risk. Kim saw it as well, for she sat up straighter and seemed ready to jump down from her seat to shake the alien.

"Cuto suggests that the T'Loop might be willing to negotiate for exclusive contracts with hakans," Suldon said.

Though Meledrin had understood the alien she still felt her heart flutter with hope when Suldon translated.

10: Simple Machines

PING SIGHED WITH RELIEF and slumped back in her chair. Half the people in the room did likewise.

Kim scratched at her head and sucked on her teeth. "Ummm... Okay." She leaned forward, elbows on knees. "I can't guarantee something like exclusive contracts— I may not be involved in the talks— but if the T'Loop help us they'll obviously be looked upon favorably. I guarantee to try, but I can't offer any more."

Suldon and Cuto spoke again and everyone else hung on every word, though there were only a couple who could actually understand. The two of them seemed to be haggling, and enjoying it immensely.

On at least a dozen occasions, the young elf seemed to stumble over words. He looked to Meledrin and she would, seemingly reluctantly, offer assistance. She didn't try to take over though, which Ping thought was a bit unusual. And she didn't know if it was a good thing of a bad thing.

"Cuto says that without a firm agreement—" Meledrin said at one stage, but apparently nothing else was important enough to be passed on.

"Warder," Suldon said eventually. "I... We..." With a glance to Meledrin, "have told Cuto that we can offer the T'Loop family no agreements on tariffs or contracts— or anything else— but that we may be able to enter into a partnership— his family with... our... company." He looked around. "I hope that meets with your approval. Cuto is interested in the idea but the entire situation is unusual. There are no 'Daughters' present but he trusts you and will take your word."

Ping wondered if it would make any difference. Would he know enough details to explain how the kil'ini 'radio' worked. And if Keeble understood how it worked, would the required parts be lying around so he could make one? And would they have enough power? And...

"Suldon, thank Cuto for his trust and... I don't know, tell him we're pleased to be working with his family and look forward to making a lot of money. Or something. You seem to have worked everything else out, so make up something now as well."

"Kim..." Meledrin said.

"Shut up, Mel. Suldon got us this far; I certainly trust him enough to say something as simple as that."

Ping smiled slightly at Meledrin's shocked expression, but Kim was continuing.

"Keeble, talk to Cuto and see what you can come up with."

Keeble nodded and, calling the names of several dwarves, strode towards the door. "Come on Suldon, let's go to the workshop."

Suldon and the alien followed the group of dwarves and Ping followed them. A moment later Ari was by her side. They collected lanterns and made their way towards Level 4.

-oOo-

"We might be able to make it," Ping said, "but what about power?" She and Ari stood on the outside of the group, but they hadn't been chased away while the men tinkered with the beginnings of the machine. The problem of power was a question they'd all been avoiding.

"Ummm..." Ari said. Nobody turned to look at her. She continued anyway. "All of those vehicles in the hangar have batteries, don't they?"

Two of the vehicles in question were partly dismantled at the far end of the workshop. Parts had been stripped from them to use in the radio— the ansible.

"Not nearly enough power," Keeble said.

But Ping wasn't sure how much power the machine would use, and wasn't sure anyone else did either. They didn't need to speak across the galaxy. And perhaps the hurgon couldn't store very much power, so what was a little bit on the ship would be a lot to them. Ping said all of this and received no reply.

"We still have to get into the other universe," Makar said.

Apparently Ari had been giving that some thought as well. "The door of the hangar faces close enough to forward," she said, "so if we push one of the little ships out..."

"So, we throw a Lander hard enough to reach the gate..." Keeble nodded slowly. "Right, that's for you two to work out."

Ping gaped. Several of the male dwarves did the same. One of them went to say something, but Keeble turned to look at him.

"Think of it this way if you want, Makar— they can stay here and annoy us as we try to use bits of string and old washers to make the most advance machine ever made by dwarves, or they can go off and do something that's relatively easy."

The other dwarf grunted. Ari was standing and smiling stupidly. Ping grabbed her hand and led her out into the hangar before someone changed Keeble's mind.

Like all dwarves, Ari started logically and out loud. "We have no power, so that leaves simple machines or brute force," she said.

"Or both," Ping offered.

"Right."

"So... wheels."

Ari nodded. "And a ramp."

"Right. We put some wheels onto one of the vehicles then set it at the top of a ramp and get the trolls to push."

Ari smiled. "Easy."

"Have we got anything to make a ramp out of?"

"Umm..."

"Let's get some help."

Ping didn't know why they bothered asking any of the male dwarves. They all said they'd never work with women, and stayed firmly put in their chairs. They'd do their bit by sitting in the semi-darkness trying to conserve oxygen. Many dwives were reluctant to go as well— worried about the reaction of the men and worried about taking on any responsibility— but half an hour later they had some volunteers and were working on the problem.

"I found some spare wheels in the store room." Ari appeared carrying two of the items in question. They were hardly fifty centimeters in diameter and came with hard rubber tires. "There's more in there."

"How many do we need?" Ping looked at one of the vehicles, but she didn't know how to begin working out how strong the wheels were or how heavy the vehicles were.

"Another two should do it," Ari said, dumping the ones she already had onto the floor. "They're very robust."

"How do we attach them?"

"We weld."

"What?"

"Weld. Heat metal until it liquefies and use it as a glue. There's a thing in there that looks like it's made for the job."

"Oh."

"And the ramp?"

One of the other dwives raised her hand nervously.

"Yes, Dido?"

"If we make the ramp out of two long metal rails, like the railing off the stairs, we can remove the tires from the wheels and make them like train wheels."

Ping didn't know what a train was, in any language, but the others were all smiling and nodding. "That sounds great." She smiled at Ari and the dwife smiled back. "Can any of you weld?"

But of course they couldn't— it wasn't allowed. Men would have to be asked again.

"Let's worry about that when the time comes," Ping said. "Let's get everything ready first, just to be sure we have what we need."

"So, what do we need?" Kesi was shorter than everyone else, but broad and solid. It looked like she hadn't had an easy day in her life, despite the fact that dwives hardly ever left the bunkers where they lived and were generally forbidden to do anything other than cook.

"We need rails off the stairs," Ping said.

"And some way to raise one end of the ramp," Ari added.

One of the dwives raised her hand.

"Yes, Nina."

"I will go and look at the rails, if you like," she said quietly, as if fearing her offer would be rejected and she would have to go back upstairs.

Ping smiled. "Tess and I will help. Aria and the others can see to the other bit."

Ping headed for the airlock. First they'd get some tools, then they'd see what they could see.

"Is it true you are in charge of looking after the clock?" Tess asked, when they had collected a box of tools from the workshop and retreated beyond the hearing of the dwarves. The young dwife pulled her plaited hair over her shoulder and was studying the leather thong that held the ends together.

Ping wasn't sure about that. Nobody had said. "I don't think so. I helped Keeble but... I was only an apprentice clockmaker in Shadon."

"You were an apprentice?" Tess made if sound as if an apprentice clockmaker was next in line to a king. "My younger brother was an apprentice boilermaker in Tab cavern..." She paused for a moment and studied her plait even harder. "I remember the day Jobber found out— he said it was the best day of his life. My father threw a party for him and I was allowed out of the maiden bunker for the whole day."

Ping wondered if it was the best day of Tess' life as well. "Maybe you could be an apprentice clockmaker on the ship," Ping said, before she had even wondered whether it would be allowed. The look on the dwife's face made it impossible for her to take it back.

"But what will Keeble say? What will the other dwarves say?"

Ping didn't know any of that. "It doesn't matter," she said. "It is up to Kim."

Tess obviously didn't care. Perhaps the offer was enough.

Ping turned to Nina and saw that she was intensely studying a spanner in the top of the toolbox. "Maybe you could be one as well, Nina. If I *am* in charge then I don't think any dwarves would work with me. We'll have to check with Kim."

"Of course."

The offer was enough for her as well.

The two dwives might have smiled all day, but they'd reached the stairs and needed to get to work.

"Do you think these rails will be strong enough?" Ping asked, trying to give one a shake. It was ten centimeters wide and five deep but seemed solid. It didn't budge under Ping's rough treatment.

"I think so," Tess said. "There's only one way to find out." She threw her plait back over her shoulder and bent down to see how the rail was held onto the brace. "Spanner," she said, holding out her hand.

"What size?" asked Nina.

"I'm not sure, really," Tess admitted. "It's about two centimeters, but what is that in the ship's measurements?"

Ping laughed and shook her head. "It doesn't matter what they call it, as long as it's the right size. Give her a two-centimeter spanner, Nina. Find another for me."

"What are you doing?"

Ping almost fell off the step. She turned and saw a dwarf standing in the doorway. She cleared her throat. "We're removing the rail."

"Why?"

"Who are you?" She didn't want to make trouble, but wasn't going to let a dwarf spoil her good mood— she mightn't have that many left. The two dwives were staring resolutely at their shoes.

"I'm Topper. Keeble sent me to check up on you."

Topper was only young and had his cheeks shaven, leaving a long brown beard on just his chin.

"What did you do to get punished?"

He didn't answer right away, as if trying to decide if he was being teased. "Nothing. I'm a Singer, so I have experience leading Work Gangs, and I'm young enough that the others think I can be bossed around."

Ping smiled. "You showed them, didn't you?"

He clenched his jaw tightly, biting back on some words. "Why are you removing the rail?" he asked eventually.

"We're going to make a ramp."

"A ramp?" He nodded slowly. "I'll tell Keeble what you're doing."

"Topper?"

"What?"

"Can you weld?"

"Of course I can weld."

"Well, none of us women know how. Would you... do it for us?" Ping had been going to ask if he would teach them how it was done, but he probably wouldn't have agreed to that.

He hesitated again, finger tapping against the doorjamb. "There's some welding equipment in the workshop. I'll get it, though it probably won't work without power." It was more than most dwarves would have done.

"Then how will we do it?"

"The old fashioned way, I suppose."

"Thank you."

11: Lightning

KIM WAS LYING ON THE BED, unable to sleep. How could she sleep? She felt empty inside.

She had spent half her life shouting at authority figures, telling them when they were wrong, what they should have done, and how they should be out of a job. School teachers, university lecturers, army officers. But she had a feeling none of them had ever stuffed up as much as she had.

She knew nothing about anything but thought she could save the universe by commandeering a space ship and gallivanting around the place without so much as reading the instruction manual. And all she'd done was get a whole heap of people killed.

She wondered if it was too late to say sorry. To the people stuck in the ship with her, but also all those she'd railed against in the past. Perhaps Major Williams should be at the top of the list.

Kim recognized Scree's footsteps out in the Captain's office and quickly sat up, trying to straighten her badly crumpled clothes and tangled hair. The troll knocked, though the door was open and he must have heard her preparing herself.

"You not sulking again, is you?" He looked at her warily.

"No. Just resting. I haven't slept in... It seems like days." It felt like days since the grand plan had been put into motion, though it was barely twenty hours.

"Well, no time to rest now. Ping and Keeble thinks they'd just about ready."

"They are?"

"Yes."

"Oh."

"What? You wants them to take their time?"

Of course she didn't. She wanted to be out of this cold, sickening place as quickly as possible, but people had to risk their lives to try to get the message across and Kim could guess who each of those people were going to be. Her own name wasn't on the list. She examined Scree's face— bald head, strong jaw, sharp blue eyes and boyish grin. He was about to throw himself out into the universe in a metal box and all he could do was smile about it. He really didn't care about anyone else's thoughts on the matter. Not that it really mattered— if the plan didn't work everyone would be dead soon enough. And the odds of the plan succeeding were very slim.

They couldn't test the 'ansible', they couldn't know if they had enough power, they couldn't know if the aliens would hear, and couldn't know if they'd come, or if they'd help. There were so many things that could happen.

Kim didn't want anyone to go out into the swirling mist in a stupid little Lander. If they didn't reach the gate then they'd be stuck out there, in full view, until the air ran out. And nobody would be able to do a thing.

But that was it, she supposed. All those leaders she complained about in the past had to live with the knowledge of killing people, or sending them out to die. Perhaps everything they ever did was in reaction to that. Or to the possibility. Kim sighed.

Scree would be going. Scree, Keeble, Cuto and Suldon, probably. Kim sighed. Scree was the one who'd held everything together.

"You'll be going?"

"Of course." He smiled some more. "And you'll be staying." It wasn't a question.

"Of course. Who else can sit around here and keep the peace while we wait to die?" She could think of a few people who could do that. Captain Thorpe was the obvious choice. The Troop leaders. They'd have as much to do with the last few hours on the ship as she did. "Be careful, Scree."

Scree laughed at that. "Hows am I supposed to do that? Sit carefully in the seat while we waits to go through the gate? Sit carefully in the seat while we waits to see if the thing works? Sit carefully while we waits for them aliens to come get us?"

"Then why are you going? You should stay here. You just said that you'd be all but useless there. Keeble can work the ansible. Cuto can talk to his family. Suldon can make sure he says what he's supposed to say..." She didn't want Keeble or Suldon to go either— she liked them. She even liked Cuto.

"I won't be useless. I'll drives. I'll keeps an eye on Cuto. I'll be in charge, separate to the other stuffs going on and trying to thinks of what you'd do. You wants Keeble making the decisions if some woman alien comes over the radio to talk to him?"

"There are no 'female' hurgon."

He gave her a look.

"No, I don't want Keeble in charge."

"Rights. Then I gots to go."

"Either you or me."

"Yep, and you ain't going."

"Why not?"

"'Cause I said."

"What about Captain Thorpe then?" Kim said.

"He's just visiting. You goings to put a refugee in charge? A human, soldier refugee?"

"No."

"Rights. Then I gots to go."

"Of course you do." She didn't know why she'd tried to talk him out of it. He was the best person for the job. "So they're almost ready?"

"So Keeble says."

"We'd better go and have a look then."

"Right."

Kim rose to her feet, quickly pulling on her shoes as she headed for the door. Scree was at the outer door of the office when she exited the sleeping quarters. "Scree."

He turned to look, leaning against the doorjamb. "Yeah."

"Be careful."

"I'm always careful."

Kim laughed. In his own way he probably was, but it was a kind of edge of your seat carefulness seen in action-buddy movies— careful while making sure the action kept coming. If the Lander got stuck in this universe, he was sure to find a way to live. Or he'd look good dying.

Kim cleared her throat and followed the troll to the stairs and down towards the hangar.

When they arrived, Kim watched as Scree talked with Flint. No doubt he was asking the other troll to keep an eye on her. Flint tugged on his moustache and looked in her direction. She shook her head and sighed.

Flint should've been made leader of one of the Troops, he was smarter than most of the other trolls and had taken readily to the idea of life on the ship— every time Kim saw him he was speaking with someone new. And she'd overheard him talking to some of the trolls as well, nudging them ever more towards accepting the *Hakahei* as their new way of life. Scree had once said that trolls normally went through life doing what was best for themselves. Perhaps some of them were finally learning that there was more to life than immediate, *physical* wellbeing.

"We're ready, I think."

Kim jumped and turned to look a Keeble. She followed his gaze to the Lander and the ramp that would help it on its way. A large group of people was gathered around the construction.

Male dwarves were examining the work done by the women. One was hitting at a weld with a small hammer. Another was pulling at one of the two rails that held the Lander as if hoping it would collapse.

"You sure?"

"No. How about a test run?"

"Ha ha. Very funny. You did roll the Lander up onto the ramp though, right?"

"Of course."

"And it was smooth and... everything."

"No, it was horrible, but you know us dwarves— near enough is good enough."

"So, Ping and the dwives did a good job then?" Kim didn't realize the trap she'd set until it had already been sprung.

Keeble grunted. "Topper did most of the welding. But yes, the dwives did a good job. Doesn't mean I have to like it. And doesn't mean that three men and a small dog couldn't have done better."

"Give them time, Keeble." Kim smiled. "Soon they'll be as good as the men. And seeing Ping is in charge of the clock it's something you'll have to get used to."

"She can't be in charge."

Kim sighed and shook her head. "She knows clocks better than you, Keeble."

"She was only an apprentice clock-maker."

"Look, we'll talk about it when you get back."

Keeble didn't say anything, as if mulling over the horrible thought. Or perhaps he knew it was unlikely either way. If they survived this whole mess then he probably knew that Ping had the job no matter how much talking he did.

"And what about the ansible?" Kim asked. "Will it work?"

"I don't know. A lot of the words didn't translate. In a lot of cases we knew what Cuto was saying but still had no hope of accurately duplicating what he was describing. So we just had to invent something that might do the same thing. It's very rough, but as close as we're ever going to get in here." He looked uncomfortable, as if he'd repeated his comment from earlier— close enough is good enough— without the sarcasm.

"How embarrassing for you all."

"If it doesn't work then nobody will know. If it does, wonderful. Power could still be one of the main problems."

"How does it work?"

"Sort of the same principle as their weapons."

"Huh?"

"The weapons attached to their armor— I'm sure that CIA officer explained to you— they align a line of particles in the air and fire electricity along it, basically."

"Basically?"

"I could explain it—"

"Don't bother."

"That's what I thought. Well, what the ansible does is align quarks—"

"Quarks?"

"Ummm... yes. They're the smallest piece of matter possible.... I don't understand completely. Neither does Cuto. Something about stamping the message on the quarks of a neutron then letting the power of the diffracting electron shift the message outwards to the next electron. And the kil'ini can see all that, apparently."

"Keeble... What? I only have high school physics and that was about ten years ago."

"That's more than I have. I read some basic books and talked to some pilots..."

"The upshot is?"

"If we can get the lightning to work then it will give us enough power for about five seconds of message, I think. But we don't know if we've got enough power to build up the lightning. We've collected all the batteries we could find but—"

Kim was still stuck on 'lightning'. "Whoa. Wait a sec. Lightening? The ansible is powered by lightning?"

"Yes. Something about separating the electrons from the somethings... I'll have to get some more books on physics I think. You humans are a long way ahead of dwarves. Anyway, all the particles in the universe are linked sub-atomically and so..."

"So it can get there almost instantly?"

Keeble nodded, showing his usual reluctance when he wasn't 100 percent sure. "Yes."

"As long as *you* understand."

Obviously he didn't. The dwarf glared and made his way to where Cuto and Suldon waited by the ansible. It was a strange contraption, hardly what Kim expected from what was this universe's first lightning-powered-faster-than-light radio. There were pipes and valves and chambers that might've had something to do with some kind of gas, plus wires and circuits and... Kim didn't know what else there was. It looked a complete mess, like something a child would use as a make-believe engine for his make-believe car.

"That can't possibly work," Kim muttered.

"I beg your pardon?"

Kim was surprised again. "Jesus." She turned to look at Meledrin. "Nothing. I... Do you think it'll work?"

Meledrin shrugged her thin shoulders. "I do not know. Though I believe we should pretend it will work. Plan for that, because all other plans are useless."

"I don't know. Maybe..."

Meledrin raise an expressive eyebrow.

"You know, we could..."

"Where will you get the power for this?"

"I don't know. Gravity is a type of energy and... Jesus." Kim looked for Keeble, but he was no longer where he'd been. The ansible was gone as well. She spotted him by the Lander, examining the wheels while a handful of dwarves tried to get the machine into the back. "Keeble."

He didn't hear.

Meledrin answered instead. "Kim, what is it?"

Kim ignored her and rushed over to Keeble's side.

"Keeble."

"What?"

"There may be some more electricity."

"Where?"

"In the floor. There must be some machines still working to make gravity, otherwise without centrifugal force we'd all be floating around in here."

Keeble shook his head and pointed to where several dwarves were working at a refitting a floor panel. "Already thought of that. Doesn't work. It isn't real gravity and it's just stored in a kind of electronic sponge that releases it slowly. Stay in the ship in this universe too long and you'll start to loose weight."

"Shit. God damn it." Kim sighed and looked around. "Well, I guess we need everything in this room either made secure or moved out. There'll be a lot of air trying to get out of here very soon." And what a waste of air it was going to be. How many hours would that shorten their stay? Could they pump it to another room? Possibly, but all the other rooms were full of air as well. *Shit.* "Scree, whoever's going to push that thing has to be in EVA suits. And the crew."

"Yeps." He sent trolls running. They were already in the suits, but needed the breathing apparatus.

Soon everyone seemed to be doing something, except Kim, who stood and watched.

Trolls were loading the ansible into the back of the Lander. Dwarves were ready to attach the mess of equipment to the half dozen batteries already inside.

"All we can do is try."

"Yes."

"Listen, Keeble, I am sorry for getting you into this mess. Sorry for getting everyone into it."

The dwarf shrugged. "The only people who don't make mistakes are the ones who aren't trying." Imminent death seemed to have mellowed him.

"Thank you."

He shrugged again.

"Be careful."

"I want to live, Kim. There is so much more to find out. Even just on this ship."

"If we get out of this I'll let you pull this thing apart piece by piece."

He smiled and grunted all at once. "No, you won't. But thanks for the offer."

"I will, just not all at the same time."

"We'd better go."

"Yes."

Scree, Cuto and Suldon were waiting by the Lander.

"What we want is a ruck, behind this Lander," Keeble was saying to the trolls. "We want as much speed as possible."

"What we want first," Kim said to the two of them, "is for everyone not involved in this operation out of here."

"That means you too, Kim."

Kim looked at Scree and nodded. "I know..."

But the troll wasn't paying attention. He was smiling over her shoulder and shaking his head. When Kim turned to look she almost laughed out loud. Meledrin was dressed in an EVA suit, slim figure hardly making a bulge. She was having little luck trying to shove her wealth of copper colored hear into the hood.

"Mel, what are you doing?"

"I will be going with Scree and Keeble."

"What? You... Suldon can..."

"Yes, he can. But so can I. I can do the task, but if we are unsuccessful then Suldon will be more use to you here than I will."

"Are you sure, Mel? This will be..."

"Difficult? What is so difficult about listening to Cuto to make sure he says what we need him to say? What will Suldon do that I cannot do if the hurgon cheats us, which is unlikely anyway? We have a couple of seconds at most. All any elf will be doing is passing the news onto Scree so he can take out his frustration."

"Mel, I—"

"Is there any reason I should not go?"

"Well, no. But what would Palsamon think of this?"

"What does it matter what he thinks?"

Kim shook her head. "If you love him, then it matters. You once asked me what love is, Mel— love makes it impossible to think of yourself without thinking of someone else in the same heartbeat. It means always wondering what that person would think before coming to a decision. Sometimes what the other person thinks makes no difference, but it's the wondering that counts."

Scree watched from nearby.

"Then I do not love him," Meledrin said. "And if he were to counsel against my going, it would show that he does not love me."

Kim nodded. Perhaps Meledrin knew more about it than she let on. "All right then." She felt like wringing the elf's neck anyway. "Who's opening the door?"

From among the ruck of trolls, Gulch and Creek volunteered.

"Right, just open the door a little bit at first to let the air out a bit slower." Kim nodded and looked around. She knew she was running out of reasons to stall. "Everyone who's pushing, riding or opening, into position. Everyone else into the airlock."

Gulch and Peak moved to the door. Kim followed the crew to the rear of the Lander. They'd be sealed inside before the door was opened to give them a little bit more air.

"Be careful," Kim said, "though I don't really know how you can do that. If something happens and you don't make it through the gate we'll try to get you back but... An emergency grappling cable or something... Perhaps we should tie one to you now?"

Keeble shook his head. "The drag could make us go anywhere. Leave it. Worry about that if the time comes. It won't make any difference."

"Right. Good luck."

"There's nothing more we can do, Kim," Scree said. "There's nothing more *you* can do."

"I know. But..."

"Get out or we'll be here all day. Where's the bloody elf?"

Kim turned and saw Meledrin standing near the door with Gulch. She was staring out a window. "Mel?"

Perhaps she was having second thoughts, though that would be a first, and those thoughts wouldn't show externally. Kim sighed and turned back to Scree.

"Be careful."

The big man smiled slightly in reply and pushed her towards the door.

Kim didn't look back until she was in the air lock and a troll was winding the handle to close the door. Scree was stalking across the hangar to Meledrin's side while Keeble checked over the ungainly makeshift spacesuit the dwarves had made for Cuto. Kim wondered if she would see any of them again.

12: All of Space

MELEDRIN DID NOT WANT to be thrown out into the nothing, but if there was a chance of dying in her own universe, she knew what she would chose every day. The swirling mists outside nauseated her— just the thought of them. And the stillness on the ship. Every noise seemed to be deadened, every breath stale and lifeless. The cold clarity of space made her nervous, but she would go through anything for one more glimpse of starlight.

Finally, she *did* wonder what Palsamon might think. She wondered what he was doing. She liked the way he looked when he slept. Back on Sherindel she had lain awake many a night watching his face. Though she was sure he was completely honest with her, she thought that while he slept he was truly open, not just telling the truth, but the *whole* truth.

"I do not know what he would say." It was such a strange situation that she could not even begin to guess.

"Whats?"

Meledrin jumped. She had not heard Scree walking up behind her. "Nothing." She smoothed at her EVA suit, as if it could be any smoother.

"Right. We's all ready. Let's get in the Lander."

Meledrin noticed that Kim and the non-participants had already left— the airlock on the far side of the hangar was almost completely closed. Everyone else was fitting masks and breathers. Cuto's EVA suit was a rough, dwarvish alteration of a dwarf-sized suit with a clear plastic bucket for a helmet. She fingered her own breathing apparatus as she watched, but did not put it on. Everyone was moving quietly, slowly, as if at a religious ceremony or in the presence of a dying friend. Even the trolls, congregating near the back of the Lander, seemed to be taken by the mood. Keeble stumped forward slowly to check the angle of the ramp one more time then turned and went back again.

While this last activity continued, Meledrin turned back to look out the small view port near the door's controls. Swirling tendrils of mist were licking at the glass, testing it as if alive, exploring. She wondered if she had made the right decision.

She muttered a *Lesser Action* and stepped closer to the glass, examining the mist as if its secret might be revealed. She saw nothing more but her unease grew with each passing moment. The mist was hypnotic, beckoning her into the cold, unknowable darkness.

"You should get in the Lander," Gulch said from nearby.

He was barely audible from behind his breather mask but Meledrin was still surprised by his voice. She gave a small nod but still didn't move. She wished she had not volunteered for this assignment and considered fleeing back to the airlock to locate Suldon. But before she had a chance to do anything, Scree grabbed her by the arm and started to draw her towards the Lander.

Meledrin refused to be dragged like a reluctant child. She shook off the big man's grip. He turned to look at her, face twisted into a smile, and she motioned him on while smoothing her clothes once more. The troll should not have touched her, but threats and indignation were unlikely to affect him in any way.

Keeble was already in the front passenger's seat, and Scree climbed into the driver's seat, so Meledrin was forced to endure Flint's assistance as she climbed in the back of the Lander with Cuto and the equipment. There was scarcely room. She slipped carefully past the pile of batteries and found herself a seat behind Scree. A troll slammed the back door shut and checked the seals. He waved at the back window, faceless in his mask, and gave the thumbs up as if that might settle her nerves. She flicked her fingers in a nervous Changing and took a deep breath. She tried Greater Action as well, but neither seemed to help.

The trolls are probably enjoying every moment of this. They are worse than dwarves with a new tool.

When the head disappeared from the window a moment later, Meledrin thought her heart would stop beating. The silence deepened. She looked out the front window in time to see Gulch and Creek starting to open the huge outer door. They did not open it very far, no more than a few centimeters.

For a long while nothing more happened and Meledrin dared to hope that Kim had called off the foolish mission.

But then the two trolls started to work at the wheel again, opening the door further. The mist licked at the edge of the door, feeling, seeking, testing.

When the door was all the way open Keeble looked at the angle of the ramp once more, leaning forward in his seat and muttering to himself. He gave the thumbs up and settled down.

The Lander moved forward as the trolls began to push.

It tilted forward, gathering speed. Meledrin looked out the rear window again as the vehicle moved lower and the trolls came into view. When the small vehicle moved off the ramp, thumping down onto the floor, Meledrin gripped the seat tighter and closed her eyes. Nobody was going to be looking at her. She hoped.

They flew clear of the ship completely and might as well not have been moving at all. She could feel nothing. She opened her eyes and looked around. The Lander had not fallen apart. All the evidence suggested they were still alive.

But it was difficult to tell if the Lander was still in motion. They were still in the other universe and shimmering disc of the gate filled most of the forward view so it just seemed to hang there, motionless. Meledrin could have gone to the rear window to view the *Hakahei* as it would be a better reference, but she was loath to move at all. She stayed where she was and waited to see what would happen.

Time seemed to stretch. The universe slowed.

And Meledrin thought she could feel the moment when the Lander finally stopped. If Scree kicked out the front window he could have almost reached out and touched the Ohoga Gate. They could have leapt out of the craft and into the other universe. But it would do them no good. Without the Lander there was no ansible. Without the ansible there was no help. And without help there was no hope.

If she was alone she may well have cried. She waved a slow, listless *Greater Changing*. After a moment of thought she sighed and waved a *Greater Ending*. Was there anything else? *Supreme Ending? Ultimate Ending? Final Ending?*

She slumped back in the seat, exhausted by the tension of the last couple of days.

Oh, for the forests of Sherindel. To see Palsamon's face one more time.

She looked at the two men in the front of the Lander, strange companions for an elf over a few short days that felt like a lifetime. They were not bad, as far as men went. Both intelligent and resourceful in their own way...

"Squished kittens," Scree said fiercely. "I could..."

If he said any more Meledrin did not hear for outside the rear window of the Lander a craft appeared, shouldering aside the mist.

It took Meledrin a moment to realize that it actually *was* a craft. It was huge, dwarfing the *Hakahei.* It was like a cliff as it came abreast of them, a mountain slowly drifting forward. Windows, marks on the hull, mounted equipment and bulges. They all streamed by silently, trailing mist behind.

Meledrin had no doubt that this was a ship belonging to the multeese, the aliens that had chased them near Sherindel, the one that had forced Kim into prematurely activating the Ohoga Gate. This was the alien that Kim wished to defeat.

The multeese were probably laughing, if such cold creatures knew how to do such a thing.

The craft seemed to just keep going. Meledrin gaped. It was staggering. It was unbelievable. So much so that Meledrin thought she was imagining the whole thing. But Keeble and Scree were watching as well.

Though the troll was not staring at the craft, merely looking. Not scared, merely curious. Keeble was talking in a long string of babble that might well have been a foreign language for all Meledrin could understand. Mass to force ratio. Habhod equations. Dispersion.

"They's goin' slow," Scree said.

Keeble nodded. "Maybe they wanted to have a look at us."

"Why?" Meledrin asked. Though from all evidence the multeese enjoyed watching the squirming of what it considered lesser creatures.

"Does seem a bits pointless when they could squish us any time they want."

"Except now, apparently," Keeble said still watching. "Maybe their ship doesn't work here either."

The craft was approximately twenty kilometers long, according to Tuki, and yet it was going to pass them in less than a minute. It was hardly the last thing she wanted to see before she died. Scree agreed.

"This ain't any way to die," the troll said.

"Don't give up yet," Keeble said.

"What you talking abouts?"

"Wait." Keeble grabbed Scree's arm. It was not a clutch of fear or goodbye. It was one of hope.

"Wait for what? We ain't going nowhere."

Scree was right. They were completely motionless. Stuck. Meledrin had seen it some time ago. And the way Cuto was slumped in the seat suggested the alien did as well. It was only Keeble.

And as soon as she had decided that Keeble was slipping towards his quiet insanity once more, as soon as she opened her mouth to... Meledrin felt the Lander move. It inched forward until its nose was touching the gate. Then, in a sudden rush, as the alien ship was finally past them and sailing away, the Lander was flung through the gate and into the other universe.

Meledrin stared, willing each breath into her lungs, concentrating on each beat of her heart. They had been motionless. She was sure. And yet they had moved quicker than they had moved for their entire short journey. What had happened? In the front seat Scree and Keeble were shouting with joy, filling the Lander with the sounds of life. Scree was punching the air. Keeble was jumping about on his seat.

Meledrin didn't move. She barely even noticed the spinning of the ship as she tried to gather her thoughts.

"Yes," Keeble shouted.

When she looked again, the dwarf was doing a jig in his seat.

"Yes. Yes. Yes."

He slapped Scree on the shoulder and he big man smiled in response, looking slightly bemused.

Meledrin drew in a deep breath and waved a shaking-fingered *Greater Changing*. "What happened? We had ceased to move."

It took a while for Keeble to calm down and answer. "Turbulence, woman. Slip streams."

"What?"

"Quiet now. I'm not sure how much air is in these bottles. We need it for talking to Cuto's family. Scree, get us pointed in the right direction. Use as little power as possible."

"Won't take much." Scree fired up the ship and stopped their wild cartwheeling. While he worked on pointing them towards Sherindel, from directions supplied by Tuki, Keeble climbed into the rear of the craft and started to work with the ansible. After a few minutes of inactivity Cuto started to help. Meledrin translated as the two of them worked. It was not long before they were ready.

"Right." Keeble sat back on his haunches in the confined space and looked at Meledrin. "Tell Cuto that he'll have a couple of seconds of talking at most. He needs to get his family to this spot as quickly as possible."

"I am aware, Keeble. I will tell him."

"There's more. After we fire this thing up there are no second chances. It'll use every bit of power we have. We won't have any lights. The oxygen circulation system won't work. Nothing. We might have a few hours of air. And then a few more hours in our suit breather packs."

"Yes." She had known all that but it was different with Keeble telling her in such a serious tone.

"After we send the message we'll have about ten hours I think. At most. Even if the hurgon come, we may be dead."

"Yes." *Must he continue belaboring the point?*

"So we have to conserve air. We send the message and then everyone sits and doesn't move. When breathing gets hard we'll put on the breathers. And we try to go to sleep. And that's it. No talking. No moving. We sit."

"Yes."

"Then tell Cuto."

Meledrin did.

"*Keeble should leave the oxygen tanks off most of the time,*" Cuto said after he'd heard the plan. "*When it becomes hard to breathe, the breathers are used while the bad air is vented, then the tanks are opened to let in fresh air. That will help a little.*"

"*Very well.*" Meledrin passed on the information.

Keeble nodded his acknowledgment then turned to Scree. "We right, Scree?"

"Yeps."

"Right then. The most important couple of seconds of our lives." He nodded to Cuto.

Meledrin held her breath, as if that little bit of extra oxygen in the cabin might help. Cuto positioned himself, took a deep breath of Meledrin's saved oxygen, and hit a button on the ansible.

The light in the cabin flickered for a second as the hurgon spoke quickly. Then the light was gone and all was silent.

"What did he say?" Scree asked quietly.

Meledrin breathed. "He first said two words I do not know and then some numbers."

"Ask him what the words were," Keeble said.

Meledrin thought of pointing out that they were not supposed to waste oxygen by speaking, but did not. She asked. She was too tired and distracted to voice any disagreements.

"*Cuto. What were those two words? Meledrin does not know them.*"

He looked up. "*The first was a family password— one that will need to be changed now that it has been blurted across the galaxy.*"

"*We can hope that it was anyway,*" she replied. "*Hopefully someone heard.*"

"*The other was a code requesting emergency assistance. The rest was coded coordinates. Or close enough for a kil'ini to find this place.*"

"*Meledrin hopes it is enough.*"

"*So does Cuto.*"

Meledrin translated the conversation and Keeble nodded his approval. "Good. We should sit down and be quiet now."

"Very well."

But the dwarf did not move. Meledrin blushed as he looked her up and down.

"What is it you are wanting?" she asked.

"Your legs are longer than mine. There's more room in the front."

"So? I..." She realized he was offering her the more comfortable seat. She gaped for a moment. It was a kindness she did not expect from a dwarf, especially here at the end of the world. "Thank you, Keeble. That is most kind."

Keeble grunted in response as Meledrin climbed through the gap and into the front seat. She watched the dwarf for a moment as he turned off the oxygen supply, as Cuto had suggested.

Then they settled down to wait with, seemingly, all of space spread before them and all of time behind.

13: Dirty Air

PING WONDERED WHY HER HEART WAS POUNDING. Was it for the interminable minutes the Lander had hung before the Ohoga Gate? Was it because the multeese ship had sailed silently past them in the mist? Or was it because, after the huge vessel had passed, the Hakahei had been drawn forward, towards the gate. The Lander had passed through, taken to the other universe, but they had been spun off into the nothing. Or maybe her heart was pounding because the Hakahei was spinning still, moving further away from the location of the gate and the Lander by the moment.

The trolls and elves were the only ones who seemed to have reacted differently. The elves acted as if they saw twenty-kilometer long spacecraft every other day. The trolls were suitably impressed but still spent the two and a half minutes of the ships' alignment looking for weaknesses in the enemy. Apparently they didn't see any.

"Flint," Ping said eventually. "Can you talk to Scree?"

The troll cocked his head to one side and went glassy eyed for several seconds, concentrating intensely. Then he shook his head. "It was worth a try."

So, Scree and his companions were gone and there was nothing anyone could do to help. To Ping it now felt as if they were waiting to die. She had done that before, after the hurgon had attacked Shadon, and it did not seem any easier this time.

"Now what?" Flint chewed on his moustache and looked around as if hoping the Jugglers of Jilin would appear to entertain him.

Kim joined them. "Now we wait."

"Wonderful." Ping said. *Waiting to die.*

"Yes. No vigorous activity either, Flint. Make sure the trolls don't go playing football or anything. We don't know how long our oxygen is going to last as it is."

Flint grunted in disgust.

"Is walking too vigorous?" Ping asked.

"Probably. Why?"

Ping shrugged and looked down at her old leather shoes. "I wanted to look at the clocks some more. They are amazing."

Kim shrugged as well. "You like clocks that much?"

"Yes. They make me... They make sense, if you know how to look. They bring order."

"I try to avoid them personally. Too long in the army, probably."

"I could look all day."

"Well, not today, sorry. If you go off to do your thing, everyone else will want to do their thing as well, then everyone's running around doing something."

Ping nodded and looked up at a vent in the ceiling that normally dispensed cool, filtered air. "The air is already starting to taste bad," she said.

"I thought that too." Kim looked as well. "I was hoping I was imagining things."

"Maybe you're both imaging it," Flint suggested.

"Maybe." Kim smiled.

Ping continued to examine the vent. "Keeble said there are air cleaners."

"Yes? So? They won't work without power."

"I know. But perhaps we can take filters out of them and... I don't know.... force air through them manually."

Kim was nodding slowly. "It could work. It won't be great but..."

"Anything is better than nothing?"

"Exactly. I'll allow *that* activity. See what you can work out then. Get some dwarves to help."

"Me?"

"Who else?" Kim laughed. "You don't think I'd put one of them in charge, do you?"

"But I'm just a clock making apprentice."

"Not now, you aren't. Now you're a Lieutenant in charge of the ship's clocks and whatever else I decide. You're an officer."

"But... I don't know if I want to be an officer."

"Yeah, great isn't it. Don't let those dwarves boss you around."

Ping nodded but wasn't really sure that it was a good idea at all.

Kim was still talking. "Look, if you don't want to stay on the ship or anything, that's fine, but I really don't want to let any dwarves loose in here without someone watching them. All right?"

"Yes." Though Ping wasn't sure. And she wasn't sure what she wanted to do after all this was over. She found it hard to believe she would actually have any choices at all.

"We have air breathers everywhere to go with the EVA suites." Kim added, turning to Flint. "Can you organize to get those collected and stashed somewhere handy for later on? And we'd better make sure we don't use too many lamps."

The lanterns were everywhere in the passage, burning up the oxygen. Ping nodded but wasn't paying attention. She was thinking of dirty air and dwarves and wasn't quite sure which she dreaded more. Collecting a lantern she marched away with as much purpose as she could and, as expected, immediately attracted the attention of several dwarves. Most people on the ship had been inactive for a long time and some of the dwarves obviously decided they'd had enough of that. So much so that they were willing to trail along behind a woman. A group of five followed close on her heels, not talking to her, but merely—coincidentally—going in the same direction. Ari and the rest of the dwife ramp-making crew followed as well, hanging well back behind the men.

Ping didn't say anything. Let them ask if they wanted to know.

When she reached the Engineering level, where the water and air recyclers were located—two of each—Ping did not know which machine might be which. But she remembered an access panel at the back of the cabin she'd chosen as her own and thought that might be a good place to start.

"This is my cabin," she said when the dwarves started to follow her through the door. "I'm going to have a sleep."

"You are *not* going to sleep," Mintar said. "You are up to something and we need to keep an eye on you."

Ping tried to keep her eyes on Mintar. "You could try asking."

The dwarves looked at one another. Ari, standing on her toes, trying to see from the back of the group, was the one who asked. "What are you doing?"

"There are two air recyclers on this level," Ping said, trying to sound confident. "They probably have filters and pumps that are usually run automatically. I thought that perhaps we could rig some to run manually, with somebody working the pump or something."

One of the dwarves shook his head. "I thought of that hours ago."

"You did not Drago," Makar said. "I have never heard you keep quiet about a three quarters *stupid* idea, let alone a good one." He seemed to realize that in making the remark to his friend he had also complimented Ping's idea. And Ping was a woman. Makar swore and tugged at his plaited grey beard.

"It *is* a good idea, isn't it? We just have to get it to work."

"Well, don't just stand there then. Let's go and look."

"Right, but this *is* my cabin, so don't touch anything." Not that there was much in there. She kept her clockmaker's toolkit fastened to her belt at all times. The only other things she owned were the tattered clothes she was wearing, which Scree had found for her on her home world of Tiandi. How long ago was that? It seemed a lifetime but was actually less than two weeks.

The panel at the back of the room came away after a couple of seconds of work. The lamplight streaming through the opening revealed a large room full of machinery and shadows.

"Let's not all waste time wondering around on each other's heels. Somebody should go and get a full tool kit."

Nobody moved. The men were looking at the women, as if suddenly expecting them to do something after years of expecting them to stay at home and do nothing. The women were staring back, determined to avoid being cast as the gofers of the group.

Taking a deep breath, Ping picked one of the men at random. It was weather-beaten Dogar. "You, Dogar, get a toolkit from the Engineering department or you can all go back up to Level 3 and sit on your hands."

The Engineering department was barely five meters away, but the dwarf didn't move. "You can't tell me what to do."

Ping took a deep breath. Normally she would agree, she was only an apprentice, after all, but Kim had put her in charge for a reason. And, from the little Ping knew about dwarves, it seemed like a very good reason. She could see Ari and the other dwives watching her silently. They were probably more qualified to give orders, but *that* was never going to happen. *So it's up to me.* Kim was relying on her, to both fix an air recycler and keep the dwarves under control. She took a deep breath. "If we get back to our own universe.... when we get back... we'll be dropping all the dwarves and elves on a planet under the protection of some humans." Apparently. That's what Kim had said.

A couple of the dwarves grunted.

"We'll be asking some of you if you would like to stay on the *Hakahei* as part of the crew."

More grunts.

"Which of you would like to stay?"

Nobody said anything, but it was obvious they all wanted to stay. They were as intrigued and excited by the ship as Keeble was. As much as Ping was herself.

"Right," she said, "well Kim, a woman, is in charge. Do you think she'll choose for you to stay on board if you won't take orders?"

"Well, why don't you send one of the dwives?"

"Because I'm sending you."

"I won't do it."

"Then go back upstairs."

"You can't make me."

"Ari, you know Flint?" Ping liked Flint. He was the only troll who had a smile that wouldn't send children and maidens running for the hills. And he'd been there when Ping was promoted.

The dwife nodded nervously.

"Can you go upstairs and ask him to send somebody down to... escort this dwarf back upstairs?"

"Ummm... yes."

"Good." She gave a nod that she hoped looked authoritative. "By the time the escort arrives there may be a couple of others going as well."

"Very well."

Before Ari had taken two steps the Dogar's shoulders slumped. "All right. I'll get your tool box."

"Thank you. Just leave it on the floor here when you have it. We don't want to drag it around too far until we know where we're going."

Ari smiled, but Ping could only sigh with relief. Now that she had them thinking about the idea of taking orders from her, she needed to show them that she wasn't a tyrant and would listen. For one thing, they'd know a lot more about most of the things than she did. Ping almost decided it was absurd for her to order the dwarves around—they instinctively knew how to fix things, how to build things. But in the last few days Kim had shown that knowing how to do things had nothing to do with knowing what needed to be done. The experts were there to come up with answers to the leaders' questions.

She cleared her throat and looked around at the dwarves for a moment. "If anyone sees anything—or thinks of anything—say so straight away, no matter how silly you think the idea might be," Ping said to them. "That silly idea might help somebody think of a better idea. And we need all the help we can get."

With another deep breath, which didn't help as much as it should, Ping climbed through into the room and a line of dwarves followed.

They wandered around for five minutes, shining lanterns into corners and holding them high to illuminate the machines.

"I think this is a water recycler," Drago said.

Ping wandered over to his side, as did a few other dwarves.

"Why do you say that?" Makar asked.

"There's sand in here," the dwarf indicated a large metal cylinder he'd been examining. There was a lid on the floor near his feet. "Sand wouldn't help with filtering air—no air I've ever seen anyway."

Ping nodded.

"There's a door down in the back corner," Topper said. "We should look through there."

The door led to another large room and more strange machinery. It was tied in knots with large loops of pipe that disappeared into walls and ceiling and floor. It looked promising.

"I'll see if I can..." Makar looked at Ping, lips pursed. He cleared his throat and looked at his companions. "How about I take a look and see what's in there?" He pointed to a metal tank that went almost to the ceiling and had one pipe entering—or exiting—the top and another at floor level. There were several similar set-ups surrounding a mass of equipment in the center of the room.

Ping smiled and nodded and the dwarf set off.

"I'll need tools," he said when he'd climbed to the top. "A spanner and a hex-driver."

Ping looked at the rest of the group. Dogar sighed and started to move back towards where he'd left the tools, but Ping shook her head. To show she was not biased she motioned to Dido. The dwife rushed off. Everyone else started to spread out to see what they could see.

Ping stayed where she was and watched. The arrival of the tools brought a new purpose to the activity.

"Water," Makar said when he'd removed the panel.

"What?"

"It's full of water."

Ping climbed up beside him to look. "Maybe this is for water recycling then."

"I don't think so."

"Why not."

"See the way this pipe goes in, starting up above the water level like that?"

Ping nodded.

"If you blow air in through there, it goes through the water, then will get forced out that other pipe by pressure. There are two other pipes on the other side there that go to that main tank in the center of the room. Probably to make sure there's always fresh water."

Ping thought about it. "So they filter the air through water?"

"I think so."

"Would that be enough?"

"Not close. But it would certainly help. There's a lot more equipment to look at yet."

Ping sighed. She hadn't expected it to be easy but—

"I think I found the main pump."

Ping looked around and hurried over when Topper gestured. He was really gesturing to the other dwarves, but Ping went anyway before someone else could take charge.

Topper had removed a panel from the side of a machine to reveal the workings. Ping didn't know how he knew it was a pump, but nobody disputed his claim.

"Can we work it manually somehow?"

For the next five minutes, the dwarves argued back and forth, pointing and prodding and rebuilding the entire machine with their words. Eventually Topper, first among equals seeing he'd made the original discovery, answered.

"Give us an hour and access to that workshop upstairs and we can do it."

"How many people?" Ping asked next. She was trying to think logically, which was what the dwarves would do. She was also trying to get them to make all the decisions so all she had to do was give the orders.

Topper looked around. He looked at the pump. He looked up as if he could see the workshop above. His beard waggled back and forth as he added in his head. "Four of us."

"Four of you can have the pump running manually in one hour?"

"Yes."

"You're in charge, Topper. Take Dogar, Ari, Tess and Kesi..."

"But..." He looked shocked by the thought.

"You worked on the ramp with the dwives, didn't you?" Perhaps he'd only done that because nobody else was watching.

He looked at the other dwarves. "Yes, but—"

"Did the dwives do a good job on the ramp?"

"Yes, but—"

"Very well, then. Drago—"

"All right," Topper said, holding up a forestalling hand, "but I'm in charge?"

Every little step counted. "Yes. But remember the dwives are extra pairs of hands and fresh viewpoints. Don't waste them." Ping gave another sigh. She'd passed a test as much as Topper.

Ping had a smile for Ari as the group broke away to start planning. The rest of the dwarves were waiting.

"What about us?"

"Well..."

"You don't know, do you?"

"I *do* know." And she did. Or she thought she did. "What we need to do is close the hangar door and take the dirty air out of the garden and put it in the hangar."

The men looked at her. One of them nodded. "But we'll need two pumps for that."

"Why?"

"Because there's already gas of some kind in the hangar—from this stupid universe—and cleaning it won't help make it breathable. And because of that, there's no room for our air."

"So we need to empty the hangar?"

"Yes."

"So we need a pump to pump that gas outside?"

"Yes."

"So we need two pumps..."

"If we're going to fill the hangar, yes. But we can just take the air out of the garden and put it back in. It won't be as efficient as what you want, because we may be cleaning the same air several times before we're done, but it'll work."

Ping chewed on her bottom lip. "Right then. That will do. But the point now is that we need to get the air out of the garden, into the pump we fix, then back into the garden. So we need to know which of these pipes is best and which of these pumps are best."

Drago smiled—freedom from the woman. "So we go to the garden, find the vents, and follow them to a pump?"

Ping nodded, eventually, but fell back onto her earlier premise. "You dwarves are the experts in this case. How about I just tell you what needs to be done and let you decide how best to do it." She smiled and none of the men seemed to have any problems with her line of reasoning.

"Sounds reasonable."

"But..."

"What?"

"Well, I'm in charge, so can you let me know what you're going to do before you do it? That way nothing is your fault and I know what I am putting my name to."

Drago laughed. "We can do that, if we must."

Ping nodded. "Good. I promise not to interfere with the details. And tell Topper what's happening so he doesn't start altering a pump prematurely."

14: Family Business

MELEDRIN WAS DRIFTING TOWARDS SLEEP AGAIN. She roused herself, shifting in the seat that had ceased being comfortable well before Keeble had purged the stale air for the first time. That process had been repeated twice more but the air had eventually run out completely. Meledrin came to the conclusion that her breather was starting to fail as well.

The expanse of stars was ingrained on her memory from hours of sitting and looking. She thought she knew the position of each of them like Tuki might, though their significance eluded her. And after all that time they were no more attractive than the shifting mist of the other universe. The company of Palsamon had never looked so wonderful, the company of any elves, with conversation and shared remembrances. Instead, she had chosen to spend her last few hours with as mixed a group of people as she could ever find. Not people, even.

Cuto could barely speak with Scree or Keeble, though they were all learning more all the time, so the alien's sad ramblings, about his family and his world of Hulgorn, had been for Meledrin alone. She had listened quietly, not replying because it was not required of her, but wondering how a creature so removed from her own people could be so similar. And yet Keeble and Scree were so different.

"But perhaps they are not so different after all," she said softly. "Perhaps they are so similar that the minor differences seem so great." There was a saying amongst the elves—The closer you stand to the tree, the more of the mountain it hides. There were several meanings already associated with the saying—most of them to do with avoiding dwarves—but Meledrin wondered if perhaps she had found another.

She blinked when she realized she was looking at a new star. She had imagined such a thing so many times over the last few hours and was now reluctant to say anything. She waited, breath held. She tried to wipe at her aching eyes, but the mask made it impossible.

The star grew brighter. She signed a *Beginning*.

"Scree." She touched the troll's arm with a quivering hand and gave no thought to the fact that she was doing so. It was hard to rouse him, but eventually he came awake.

"What is its?"

"Look there. The star..."

The troll looked, but seemed as unsure as she.

"Do you think it is becoming brighter?"

"Maybes?" He too, tried to rub at his eyes. "Yo, Keeble." He reached around behind his seat and thumped the dwarf on the leg.

Soon Keeble and Cuto were staring out into space as well.

We are all wardens waiting for the first seed of the season to fall from the Ohoga Tree, Meledrin thought, leaning forward as if that might help her see. And they all watched the light falling towards them.

Perhaps Cuto could see better than anyone else, or perhaps it knew in some other way, but the alien was the first to let excitement bubble to the surface. It shook Meledrin's seat in a lumpy fist and slapped Keeble on the knee.

"It is Cuto's family," the alien said in its throaty voice. *"That is a kil'ini."*

"How does Cuto know?"

But Cuto didn't answer and the star continued to grow.

Several minutes later it was obvious to everyone that it was not a star. Several minutes after that a kil'ini came to a stop a short distance away.

"That is Lisa'lee'la," Cuto said. *"Lisa'lee'la is in partnership with one of Cuto's Aunts and Uncles. A fine kil'ini."*

"What will Lisa'lee'la do?" Meledrin asked.

"Watch at first, suspecting a trap."

Meledrin translated for Scree and Keeble.

"We're running out of air," Keeble said. "We don't have time to sit here waiting."

"We can't do nothing else," Scree told him. "So sits down and don't get excited."

"Don't get excited? How can I not?"

"It won't helps. Mel, ask Cuto how good the kil'ini can see. If he comes and sits up here, will it be able to recognize him?"

Meledrin asked. "Cuto says yes. But they still may suspect a trap."

"Well, that's better than nothing."

Meledrin shifted aside slightly while Scree slid between the two seats into the rear compartment and motioned Cuto forward. The alien nodded and moved as quickly as the confined space allowed. It crouched on the front seat and waved its arms in the kil'ini sign language.

Then they all watched and waited. Scree and Keeble were gripping the backs of the front seats, heads close together as they examined the strange creature before them.

To Meledrin it felt as if half an hour passed before something else happened, but it could not have been so long. She watched as the creature reached out with a long tentacle. The tentacle stopped before it came within fifty meters.

"Lisa'lee'la is just being cautious," Cuto explained. *"A little bit at a time."*

Several minutes later the tentacle came closer and carefully wrapped around the Lander. And then, again, the kil'ini waited.

"A little bit at a time." It seemed that Cuto wished to jump for joy but was afraid any such movements might be interpreted the wrong way. The alien squirmed on the seat.

When the kil'ini finally started to draw the Lander closer, the hurgon leaned forward even as Meledrin was leaning back. The window of the small craft was brought up close to a large, dark eye that examined them all closely with a cold, unblinking gaze. They were shifted to another eye.

"Kil'ini see differently with each eye," Cuto waved arms in the air, still conversing with the kil'ini. *"And each eye has been connected to different systems inside."*

"You mean that the hurgon don't just ride inside the kil'ini and go where they are taken?"

"Once, but not any more. Hurgon have many systems like humans have, all linked into the kil'ini. Aunt Meenu will be looking at Cuto and Meledrin right now."

"Really?" Meledrin reflexively reached up to straighten her hair, but her head was covered by the EVA suit's mask and hood. If they did not realize she and her companions were wearing protective clothing they may be mistaken for some strange grub-like creatures. Thankfully, Cuto's makeshift suit left the alien's face in view behind a clear, plastic faceplate.

"What is happening now?" They were moving again.

"Lisa'lee'la is going to eat us."

Meledrin gasped, but Cuto did not appear to be worried. The alien was jumping about excitedly.

"The kil'ini is going to eat us," Meledrin told Scree and Keeble. "That is a good thing, I believe. I can think of no other way that we might gain access to the inside. No other way I would prefer, that is."

Scree turned to look in her direction. She could not see his face. "Did you just make a joke, Meledrin? I don't believe it."

Meledrin was not sure she believed it herself. Could the simple truth be a joke? She knew she felt like smiling, but doubted that had anything to do with humor. They were several minutes away from certain life or certain death. She would take either of those situations over the suspended agony of the previous few hours.

An orifice opened at the front of the huge creature and the Lander was fed carefully inside.

"Cuto and the hakans must wait a short while," Cuto said softly. *"It takes time for the kil'ini to seal properly and then fill with air."*

The Lander floated weightlessly in the center of a chamber almost a hundred meters across. The walls were dark and rubbery. The orifice they had entered through was throbbing slightly. Meledrin imagined muscles working beneath the surface, tightening slowly. Light came from all around.

When a hole opened at the other end of the chamber, Cuto fumbled with the manual controls on the Lander door and pushed it open. He ripped off his helmet and had an alien smile for everyone.

"It has been done." The alien jumped around, showing more animation than any time previously.

"Keeble," Meledrin said. "Do you think it is safe for us to breathe this air?"

"He can breathe ours, can't he?" Scree replied.

"But perhaps he is more robust than us in that respect."

Scree was already taking off his mask. Meledrin watched, suddenly nervous.

"If we can't breathe we's dead anyways." He took a deep breath while Meledrin held hers. "Don't taste too good, but neither did the stuff in here."

"You want to stop him?" Keeble asked, pointing as Cuto climbed out through the open hatch.

"What for? We's at their mercy now. A hostage won't help us."

The hurgon pushed off from the side of the Lander and flew towards a wall. At various places around the room eyes on stalks moved to watch the alien's progress. Pairs of tentacles below each one were waving conversations, though to who, Meledrin could not say.

Keeble grunted and watched as Cuto clutched at a lump on the wall and stopped. "If you're sure."

"I'm sures."

"All right then. Well, are *you* going to get out?"

"Me? Nopes. Meledrin is going first."

"Me?" Meledrin pulled off her mask and carefully tested the air. Scree was correct—it did taste horrible, but did not seem harmful. "Why am I alighting first?" She shook free her coppery hair and combed her fingers through it. It would take a week to get out the tangles.

"You want them to see me first?" Scree asked. "Besides, you the communicator."

"Yes, I am."

Meledrin suddenly wished she were still back in the other universe. Suldon seemed to adapt to change much more readily than she. He thought on his feet while she was loath to step beyond the bounds of tradition. But then, perhaps, in this situation, decorum and calm was what was needed, not quick thinking. She took a deep breath and climbed out into the kil'ini.

The lack of up and down made Meledrin feel ill, as did the entire concept of floating in mid-air. Cuto did not seem worried. Neither did Scree as he came out into the open. Meledrin was pleased to see that at least Keeble clutched at the open Lander hatch as if afraid of losing his balance.

Five hurgon appeared at the small, puckered door. Four were dressed in brown uniforms and armed with large bulky weapons that fitted over their arms. The final hurgon, also armed, was bare-chested and wore loose-fitting, purple pantaloons.

The weapons were not just weapons, if they were at all. The aliens pointed the machines behind them and fired small bursts of energy that allowed them to maneuver in the zero gravity. One hurgon stopped by Cuto, who had been excitedly conducting an arm waving conversation since exiting the Lander. Another stayed near the door and the third moved ten meters further around the wall. The other two continued forward.

Meledrin flinched, despite her best efforts, when the weapon arms were pointed in her direction but the hurgon fired the engines and came to a smooth stop just three meters away. Scree scowled.

"Greetings," Meledrin said when it became apparent the others were not going to speak. She attempted a bow and started to rotate slowly. She increased the problem when she started to flap her hands in a moment of panic. Too late, she remembered the aliens might interpret a flapping of hands as laugher. They certainly did not look pleased. She stilled her hands and tried to think.

Scree came to the rescue. Anchoring himself to the front of the Lander, he reached out and oriented her correctly. Meledrin did not look at the troll, though he had touched her without warning, and tried to repair her fraying dignity.

"Greetings," she said again, coughing and grumbling through the word. *"This one is called Meledrin. Please, excuse Meledrin for not constantly attempting the appropriate Ini Rituals. Meledrin's awkwardness in zero gravity has been witnessed. Also, understanding of the Rituals are limited. No disrespect is meant to hurgon or kil'ini."* Without the rituals, the kil'ini, which could not hear, would be unable to follow the conversation, but that could not be helped.

The colorfully dressed hurgon grunted and removed its arm from the weapon sleeve. *"Would Meledrin object if Kato,"* it said, gesturing to its companion, *"translated into the Ini Rituals?"*

"No objection would be made."

Kato, the interpreter, slipped its arm from its weapon as well and proceeded to gesticulate wildly, apparently bringing the kil'ini up to date on the conversation so far.

"This one is Guvi. Does Guvi speak to the leader?"

Meledrin considered the question, turning to regard Scree. Nothing had ever been made official—why would it be in such a small group—but Kim obviously saw Scree as her second in command even though he had not been on board the Hakahei as long as others. Meledrin decided she did not desire the position herself, but wished there was a woman who could take it on.

"No, Meledrin is not the leader," she said eventually. *"The leader is currently trapped in the other universe that hakans use for interstellar travel."*

The hurgon grunted.

"And of the hakans who are present, Scree," she motioned towards her companion, *"is in charge. May Meledrin inquire as to your position?"*

"Guvi is a second cousin—the highest ranking military officer on board."

"Greetings Guvi."

"What is it the hakans want?"

"Our leader wishes for Lisa'lee'la to pass through to the other universe and bring back the stranded construct and the hakans on board."

"Why would Lisa'lee'la do that?"

Meledrin saw Cuto suddenly go still in the background, pausing halfway through a gesture. Meledrin licked her lips. Perhaps Cuto should have thought to warn her of hurgon politics and laws. Perhaps she should have thought to ask. She tried to think.

"Is Guvi a member of the T'loop family? Or is Guvi a member of a military force assigned to Lisa'lee'la by outside parties?" The alien's wording had not made that clear, perhaps deliberately so.

"We don't have all day, Meledrin," Scree said softly. She nodded slightly in reply.

"That is not Meledrin's concern."

"So Guvi is not a member of the T'loop family? Then it is Meledrin's concern, for certain agreements have been reached that are not for public dissection."

Cuto was vigorously waving his arms once more.

Guvi stared. *"Hurgon are at war with hakans. All things are the concern of the Multicracy."*

"Meledrin is not from a military construct. These hakans are not a part of the war."

"That is yet to be decided. Guvi can—"

"Second Cousin."

Everyone turned to see another hurgon entering the room. Guvi scowled.

"What is it, Meenu?" Guvi did not complete the Ini rituals, and neither did his interpreter. Apparently they did not feel that their conversation should be for public dissection either. The newcomer did wave its arms though, and Cuto translated the Second Cousin's words for the kil'ini.

Meenu shifted its hands in a fashion that Meledrin knew to be a smile. Though why the kil'ini could not see a smile was beyond her.

"Guvi knows the charter very well. Multicracy personnel cannot interfere in family business, even in times of war."

"This is not family business."

"Of course it is, Guvi. Lisa'lee'la travelled here in response to a T'loop coded message in which emergency assistance was requested. It was not a Multicracy code. It was not for general listening."

"The detour was allowed on the understanding that it was a military matter."

"No contracts were drawn. No verbal agreement was reached."

"That is irrelevant, Aunt. These hakans are now officially prisoners of the Multicracy. If this is not liked, Meenu can take it up with the Cousin Commander when Lisa'lee'la rejoins the fleet."

"Well, Meenu does not like it. Be assured, Guvi, that official complaints will be registered."

"As Meenu wishes." Guvi smiled and motioned for the guards to come forward.

15: Greater Good

MELEDRIN DRIFTED SILENTLY. Scree was doing enough talking for all of them.

"We was close," he said for the tenth time as he floated back across the room. "We made the ansible thing, we got through to this universe, we got the kil'ini to come find us. And now Kim and everyone else has to die because the hurgon don't *want* to helps." He grabbed onto one of the room's tentacles and stared into the nearby eye for a moment as if contemplating blinding it.

Keeble didn't say anything either.

Meledrin knew that Scree would soon be moving again.

"I should've ripped out that Guvi's throat while I had the chance." And there he went.

They had not been in the cell for more than five minutes when the door opened again. It was neither Guvi nor its cohorts who floated inside though. Luckily for the newcomer Scree was across the other side of the room and floating free at the time or it might well have died before getting the chance to utter a single word.

"Aunt and Uncle have sent Weri to speak with the hakans," the hurgon said. It did not complete the Ini Rituals.

Meledrin held up a hand to stop Scree as he crossed towards her. "Wait, Scree, Weri is from the T'loop." The hurgon cowered back as Scree continued across the room. It held its ground until the last moment before pushing off from the 'floor' to find a safe vantage. Scree did not follow when he reached the wall.

"What does Aunt Meenu want?" Meledrin asked.

"Weri is the T'loop Daughter Legat on this kil'ini. The Aunt has sent me to discuss terms away from the ears of the Multicracy."

"If action is not taken now then all terms will be pointless, because Aunt Kim will be dead."

"Will the terms not hold for all Meledrin's family?"

"Meledrin's family is only on one ship, Weri. An entire family is dying in the other universe."

"Oh. Cuto said that, but Aunt Meenu and Uncle Leeni did not believe."

"Hakans are very different to hurgon, Weri."

"Weri is learning that."

"There is something else Weri should learn. Current hakans are also very different from those who once attacked Hulgorn. Those people no longer exist."

"But barely 500 cycles have passed."

"For us, 500 Hulgorn cycles is a very long time. Hakan civilizations have died and been reborn again since then."

"But..."

"It is true. Meledrin knew nothing of this war until hurgon attacked. Hakans do not want this war. Hakans want peace with the hurgon."

"Weri cannot negotiate that. Not even the Aunt can negotiate that. Meledrin must speak with the Multicracy."

"Then do not negotiate it. Negotiate the rescue of the Hakahei *and Aunt Kim will speak with the Mutlticracy later. But Aunt Kim is dying right now. Meledrin's family is dying."*

Weri nodded. *"But if Meledrin's family is not a trading family, what can be offered the T'loop?"*

"All the Hakahei *family can offer is its friendship. And pledges that the T'loop will always come first in any dealings with the families, though not with the hurgon as a whole."*

"What is meant?"

"The T'loop can be offered better deals and special consideration, but no action will be taken that will be bad for the hurgon people, just because it is good for the T'loop."

Weri thought about that then waved its arms crazily. Meledrin followed most of what was being said. She was not supposed to. The two tentacles that Scree had used as an anchor earlier moved quickly in response.

Eventually, the hurgon turned back to Meledrin.

"The Aunt wishes to know who makes the decision on what is good for the hurgon?"

"That would be a matter for..."

"There are situations that hakans cannot understand."

"Meledrin is not sure."

"This other one is in charge? Ask."

Meledrin nodded. "Scree, I have told Weri that we will not agree to do things for the T'loop family, as part of our agreement, if those things are against the hurgon people as a whole. She wishes to know how we will decide what is good or bad for the hurgon people."

Meledrin was incensed when Scree laughed.

"What is so amusing?"

"How would we knows what is good or bad for the hurgons? All we could do is ask them."

"I believe there may be immediate issues of concern."

"You means them military guys on this ship?"

"Correct. I believe the T'loop family is planning some sort of revolt against the military forces."

"Wells... Just have a bit in the agreement that says we can gets out any time we like if we thinks the greater good of the hurgon has been affected by these T'Loop and the hurgon will be the ones who tells us that."

Meledrin thought about that. And again she wished she had let Suldon come on this mission. He had been the one who had realized the importance Cuto placed upon trading and taken advantage of it. Meledrin could translate easily, but she could not think in the manner that was needed. She was embarrassed by the fact that Scree knew what needed to be done and she did not. Perhaps that was why Kim had made him second in command.

"I will tell Weri."

-oOo-

According to Weri, there were 54 great hurgon families and 207 minor families living on 15 worlds across 9 solar systems. There were also citadels carved into a score of asteroids. It was over 100 light years from one side of hurgon-controlled space to the other. The closest that any of these places ever came to any of the old hakan worlds was 64 light-years.

Meledrin understood the distance, if only vaguely, and so did not know why the hurgon could not just leave them in peace. That was explained to her as well.

When Hulgorn had been attacked all those years ago the great families had just been starting to emerge. When the hakans had retreated, the Great Families had continued to prosper as the hurgon moved out into space, using their wealth to gain more wealth.

One of the minor families was angered at missing out on this surge and shifted its focus. Instead of trading as the others were, the Fen'dai had turned to mediation. As a supposedly disinterested third party they resolved disputes between the other families. The venture's success made them vital to the smooth running of the growing civilization. They formed the Multicracy, a council controlled by the Fen'dai. They strengthened their hold by insisting on assigning a political officer, a Cousin, to each family ship. Cousins were supposed to do nothing more than watch and report on any breaches of the council's laws, but to do this they needed access to all of the families' records.

The records should have remained confidential, but the Fen'dai made a secret agreement with another minor family and started passing on information. With these two families working together, one from the inside and one from the out, they were able to grow their power immeasurably. In doing so they broke a contract—the worst crime imaginable to a hurgon—but by the time anyone realized, it was too late. The Fen'dai and the Multicracy were the foundation upon which the hurgon civilization stood and it was more trouble than it was worth to change.

But Meledrin understood that at least one family had finally had enough. The T'Loop intended to free themselves of the Fen'dai yoke and once more be true masters of their own affairs.

Meledrin passed on the story to Scree and translated his reply—*"This is the truth?"*

"Yes. Of course."

The troll thought for a moment then nodded. Meledrin returned her attention to the hurgon.

"Very well. Uncle Scree agrees to the contract. At this point. But at the first opportunity Uncle Scree and Aunt Kim will consult other families in the specifics of what Weri has told us."

"Weri does not think—"

"Weri has no choice. The T'loop have no choice," Meledrin cut in before she realized. She blushed slightly. *"Hakans wish to stop this war. For any hakans to be acting in league with a renegade family would be harmful to the cause."*

"The T'loop are fighting against the current laws of the hurgon but the laws do not necessarily reflect popular opinion or the greater good. Who can say if hakan opinion of the greater good coincides with T'loop? The two peoples are very different."

"Not so different, Weri. Trust will necessarily be reciprocated."

The hurgon nodded. *"Can Weri draw up a contract?"*

"Weri can. But neither Meledrin nor Uncle Scree can sign it."

"But..."

"Your language cannot be read by any hakans at this time, Weri. None will sign a contract that cannot be read or understood."

"Then what..?"

"Trust."

Weri did the hurgon equivalent of a nod before quickly leaving the room.

"They is running out of time over there, Meledrin."

She turned to look at Scree. It seemed that Keeble was on the edge of saying something as well, but he restrained himself.

"I am aware of that, Scree, but this is not an easy process. The T'loop family must start a revolution before they can help us and they need to know that hakans will be on their side when it comes to the fighting."

"I thought we was trying to stops a war. Kim won't be happy if you just goes and starts another."

Meledrin decided that Scree was not truly worried either way. He would fight anyone in order to stay alive. All the hurgon. Half of them. Or the mysterious aliens in the flying mountain. The opponents in the game made no real difference to him.

Aunt Meenu entered, floating slowly through the door as if considering the intricacies of the verbal contract about to be entered.

The hurgon looked up. *"How does Meenu know that Meledrin will ensure that commitments are honored?"*

"How does Meledrin know that Meenu will honor commitments in return?"

"After Lisa'lee'la has rescued Aunt Kim and the construct, what does Meledrin really care?"

"Meledrin cares greatly. The Hakahei is currently the only hakan construct capable of leaving the ground. Hurgon will soon wipe out all hakans unless the war is stopped. And stopping the war will give hurgon somebody new to trade with. An end to the war is in everyone's best interest. And if the war ends it is in the best interest of Meledrin's family to have a head-start in any negotiations."

"No hurgon has entered into an agreement such as this without several binding contacts—noting every particular—since before Hulgorn was first attacked."

"This is a very unusual situation, Meenu. But if two families cannot trust, how will entire worlds ever trust? We must start somewhere. Aunt Kim can introduce the T'loop to the leaders of the hakan worlds so contracts can be negotiated with them. There can also be treaties that would strengthen the T'loop position against the Fen'dai."

"Very well." But Meenu did not look sure. *"Very well."* It waved its arms for the kil'ini to see then floated silently in the air and said no more.

They waited for a long time until the two tentacles on the wall waved a vigorous reply.

"Come. It is time to return to where Meledrin and the Uncle were found."

"What of the Fen'dai?"

"They have been contained. On a single kil'ini it is a simple thing—the kil'ini has final control of everything after all. But the Fen'dai have kil'ini of their own that agree with the hurgon universe in its current form."

Meenu pushed towards the door with practiced ease and motioned for the others to follow.

"Come, Scree, Keeble," Meledrin said, "we are going to rescue our companions."

"What abouts them soldiers?" Scree asked.

"They are already taken care of."

"Oh." His disappointment was obvious.

"Do not fret, I am certain there will be people you can thump at some future juncture."

Meledrin had trouble moving through the passages. She tried to copy Meenu but could not get the knack. Scree was having no problems at all, and even Keeble was doing well. Meledrin bounced from wall to wall as they moved 'upwards' and towards the front of the kil'ini.

"How long until crossing to the other universe is possible?" Meledrin asked as she almost collided with a hurgon waiting in a doorway.

"It will be just a short while until Lisa'lee'la returns to the place where Meledrin was found. The crossing will take place at that time. The kil'ini regained full strength just moments ago."

"And the Kil'ini will not be harmed in the other universe?"

"Not as long as Lisa'lee'la does not have to remain there for more than a short period."

"Hurgon do not normally go to the same universe as hakan ships?"

"No. There are more accommodating universes. The one the kil'ini take the hurgon to is full of oxygen. In this way the Kil'ini can avoid the need to find planets that offer sustenance to the hurgon."

They eventually arrived at the door to what appeared to be the bridge. A dozen hurgon occupied seats at a strange array of consoles that appeared to have grown from the flesh of the kil'ini, even though Cuto said that systems had been added.

"Careful—there is gravity in the room. Come down to the floor."

Though Meledrin had been warned, she was still surprised when she moved across the threshold and suddenly felt her weight dropped back onto her legs. She stumbled for a moment, only to be held upright by Scree.

"How are they going to do it?" Keeble asked. The dwarf had already wondered past Meenu and was examining a softly glowing screen past a hurgon's shoulder.

"Meenu, how will the task be accomplished?"

"The kil'ini will enter the other universe, take the construct into the same chamber as the minor construct was taken, then return here. A few minutes only, though a wait will be required while the poisoned air is expelled."

Scree asked to be taken to the chamber as soon as he heard the translation and was out the door before anyone could say 'yes' or 'no'. Meledrin watched as Cuto, unobserved until then, hurried to follow the troll. Scree did not need to be shown the way, though he may not have known the best way, but an escort was needed in any case.

"How many kil'ini fly with the hurgon, Meenu?"

"Thousands. And there are more all the time. It takes much time for a kil'ini to reach maturity but then each lives for many hurgon generations.

"Do all kil'ini fly with hurgon? Or do some choose not to?"

"Some remain separate, but often will talk when contact is made, giving news from all parts of the galaxy."

Meledrin watched on a large screen as the starscape disappeared to be replaced by swirling mist. There was no gate. Nothing seemed to change, and yet one moment they were in one universe, and the next in another. The hakans may have been more technically advanced but, to Meledrin, it seemed that the combination of hurgon and kil'ini was limited only by their dreams.

"The Hakahei *is not present,"* Meenu said.

Meledrin thought of the multeese ship and the turbulence that had eventually drawn the Lander through the Ohoga Gate. *"The construct may have moved slightly,"* she replied. *Slightly?* She had no idea how far it might have moved. Or in which direction. Between them, Scree and Keeble might have been able to deduce something but...

"Lisa'lee'la has found the construct. It will be a few minutes more."

16: Until We Know

TUKI WAS STARTING TO DRIFT OFF TO SLEEP. He had done nothing for so long and yet was so exhausted he could hardly move.

A clatter disturbed him and he roused himself to look around. He was sitting in one of the moai sized chairs facing the stage on Level 2. Dwarves and trolls were all around him—on the floor and slumped in chairs. Most of the elves had taken up positions near the front of the stage. They sat like they lived, quiet and proper.

"Everybody up." Tuki looked around again and saw Captain Thorpe standing near the stairs. The soldier slapped his hand against the wall as if his voice was not loud enough on its own. "Everybody up. Time to move again."

Tuki grunted. He did not want to move. They had already gone from Level 2 to the garden, to the hold and back to Level 2. The dwarves and Ping seemed to think it would help somehow—something to do with the filters—but it all just seemed like a waste of time.

"Move it." Captain Thorpe moved around the room, nudging people, trying to get them moving.

Tuki stayed where he was. Captain Thorpe had no authority. Kim was in charge on the ship and unless—

Kim came out of a cabin and looked around. "Come on people, you heard the man. Let's move." She sounded no more enthusiastic than Tuki felt, but she was on her feet and moving.

Tuki sighed out a bitter, biting breath and pushed himself to his feet. His legs and arms felt leaden. His head spun.

Kim walked past close by and had a small smile for him. "How are you feeling?"

"Not very well. I just want to sleep."

"You can do it down stairs. Not here. Go on."

But he stayed where he was and looked around. He listened as Kim and Captain Thorpe spoke.

"How are we doing?" Kim asked.

"Not good." The soldier was starting to look ragged. "Ping and her crew say that—judging on the last couple of efforts and the deterioration of the air quality—this is it."

"Shit. What did we get out of the Garden last time? Four hours?"

"Yes."

"And three hours up here?"

"A little less, I think."

"So an hour then?"

"That's what Ping said. Topper and Drago say less." The Captain turned to look at the room's inhabitants again. "Everybody up," he shouted. "I want everyone down in the garden in five minutes. Move it." The trolls started to rouse. "Flint, Stone, lets get them moving."

"It there any point?"

Kim answered him. "We won't know that until we know."

"What about the breathers?"

"They're in the garden. There aren't enough of them for everyone and most are at least half empty."

Tuki made his way to the stairs behind a trollop and a pair of staggering dwarves and started down. Halfway down a dwife gripped his arm.

"Thank you, Tuki."

It was Kesi. She moved so slowly that Tuki wondered if they would ever make it down to the garden.

"I thought you were supporting me," Tuki said.

The dwife smiled up at him and patted his hand. She had seemed old and worn beyond her years when Tuki had first seen her. She had improved somewhat in the company of Ping and the trollops, seeming to come to life, but now she was more pale and shrunken than ever. Tuki wondered if he was shrinking too. Would he be the size of a dwarf by the time they reached the garden.

Okalani and Aka'mu were behind them, staggering and stumbling downwards.

"Heaven is not like I expected, Tuki," Okalani said quietly into the wheezing, thick-tongued silence. The look on her face was as bitter as the air.

"It is exactly as Kim said it would be, Okalani," Aka'mu replied. "We were given the chance to look into our hearts."

Perhaps they had, but Tuki wanted to keep looking for a good while longer yet. "We are not dead yet," Tuki said, though the defiance sounded weak, even to him.

The trollop leading the way looked back over the heads of the dwarves. The lantern she was carrying swung crazily above her, making the shadows dance on floor and walls. Her name was Ruby and she was only a couple of years older than Tuki, though the experience written in her sharp blue eyes suggested otherwise. Her shoulder length red hair, tied in two pigtails, was molten in the shifting light. "We ain't dead, are we, Tuki-boy? Scree's a stubborn bugger and that Keeble's even worse." She ran her fingers along the wall to keep her balance as she continued to descend. "Scree won't let us die 'cause that means he lost the game. He *don't* like losing. And Keeble won't let us die 'cause that means there was something he couldn't fix."

"But maybe it cannot be fixed," Okalani said.

"Bet it can," Ruby smiled. "I bet all the gold I got that we'll live through this."

"But I have no gold."

Ruby shrugged. "Don't worry about it. I don't intend to pay if I lose either."

It took a moment for Tuki to work through that in his mind and the realization must have shown on his face. Ruby winked, smiled some more and stopped to open the door that led out of the stairwell and onto Level 4. Tuki smiled himself and held Kesi's hand.

In the workshop on Level 4, Topper was stopping people. He held a lamp above his head as well. It showed his haggard face and bleary eyes—he seemed to have aged even more than Kesi. "Every time we open the door we're going to let air out," he said softly. "So we want to open it as little as possible. We'll wait until everyone's here, then move through quickly. All right?"

Tuki did not have the energy to argue, though he doubted 'quickly' would be an option. He nodded and leant against the wall. Ruby had taken up a similar position nearby.

"Do you really think we will live, Ruby?" Tuki asked quietly. He did not know if anyone else was listening, but he was beyond caring what others wanted to hear.

Ruby nodded. "Yeah. There's no point believing otherwise."

"But they have been gone so long."

"Did you expect them to get back in five minutes?"

Tuki shook his head.

"Did you expect them to get back in an hour?"

He shook his head again.

"Didn't expect them to get back quick at all?"

"No."

"Then why is you surprised they're taking so long?"

"But we are running out of time."

Sandy, sitting on the floor nearby, dark skin almost blending with the shadows, gave a short bark of laughter. She shook her head and the colored beads plaited into her hair rattled. "Runnin' out of time is a way of life with trolls, Tuki. Just means you ain't runnin' quick enough, or you're runnin' in the wrong direction."

"Or maybe you aren't supposed to be runnin' at all," Ruby said. "Maybe you're supposed to stand and fight."

"I don't have the energy to fight," Tuki said.

Ruby shrugged. "You don't have to. Scree and Keeble is doing it for us."

Tuki had the energy for another slight smile. "You don't think Meledrin will fight?"

Both of the trollops laughed for a moment. "The elf'll fight in her own way," Sandy said through a clatter of still-swinging beads. She leaned back against the wall and stretched her legs out in front. "Scree and Keeble'll kick and bite and scratch and swear all the way to the end. Mel'll try to talk the universe into seein' things her way."

"And be mighty pissed off when she don't do no good."

Tuki nodded. Each breath was a struggle. Each blink seemed to take a lifetime.

The room was continuing to fill with people. The walking dead gathering for one last gasp of air.

"Why are you here?" Tuki asked when the silence stretched on.

"'Cause Kim said—"

"No," he held up a hand to stop Sandy from going any further. "Why didn't you stay on Kiva and… thump people and... whatever? Why do you do what Kim says?"

The trollop gave the question some thought. "Trolls has always been about doin' what's best for trolls, Tuki. On Kiva, durin' the last few years, that meant findin' a good pack that was runnin' in your direction..." She obviously wanted to say more, but was not sure what.

Ruby took up the explanation. "But maybe trolls on their own is never going to be a good pack. And maybe, down there, we could *never* run in the right direction. And we could *never* run quick enough." She sighed. "Ever feel like you're running but ain't getting anywhere?"

Tuki thought of his own life on Kiva, in a village where his only goals had been to get married to Keala and to see her smile. "Yes," he said.

Ruby nodded and touched Tuki's hand for a moment. "Well, now we're all running to *somewhere*, Tuki, and even if we ain't going to get there, we're still making progress."

It was a while before Kim came down the stairs and, with Shardy's help, turned the wheel that closed the big airlock door. Several elves had already fallen asleep and it took a while to rouse them. Even in their exhaustion, dwarves volunteered to kick them until they woke, but Suldon and Penisari shook them and called their names until they were all on their feet.

When everyone was ready one of the trolls, Crystal, opened the door into the garden and everyone went through as quick as they were able. The door slid slowly shut behind them.

Tuki wondered if it was all really worth it. What chance was there that every little crazy part of their completely crazy plan would work? The odds were... He tried to work out what the odds might be as he stood at the top of the cliff in the garden and looked out the huge windows at the sickening puce mist. He could not think properly, though his head no longer spun quite like it had.

Kesi sat down where she was and laid back in the dust. For a moment Tuki was worried for her, but she was breathing steadily and color seemed to be returning to her face. She smiled at Tuki. He nodded back. But he did not sit down with her. Instead, he moved along the edge of the cliff until he came to the stairs, then made his way down into the main area of the garden.

He was pleased to see that the *Hakahei* had stopped spinning. The wild tumbling had made him ill last time they'd been in the garden. He felt bad enough as it was without adding that to his misery.

He wandered aimlessly for a while, kicking up dust with his big feet, and trying to ignore the window. He imagined he was in the desert on Kiva again and cursing the day he had seen the kil'ini in the sky and thought it was a shooting star. That event had started his adventure, sending him off to places he had never imagined.

But kicking up dust and making it harder to breathe was not going to help anyone. With a sigh, he sat down near the tunnel that led through to the other half of the garden. With his back against the cliff, he could look out the windows at the universe and wish for some stars to guide him home.

Not far away, half covered in dust, was a small glass plate. It was well made and covered in an engraved leaf pattern. He wondered how long it had been sitting there, unnoticed. For a moment he thought of leaving it there, sleeping in the dust like he would surely be soon enough. But he reached out and picked up the plate. For a while he turned it over in his hands, running his fingers over the leaves, then he sent his mind into the glass searching its depths for any stories that had been trapped within its multitude of prisms.

He leaned back and smiled as the plate told him of the garden. There were trees and flowers and grass. There was a waterfall tumbling down one of the cliffs into a small rock pool. There was an elf pruning a tree. Here was a dwarf digging a hole for a new plant. And up on top of the cliff, others were resting or talking quietly. And outside the windows there was starlight. A thousand stars shining in the blackness of space.

Tuki reluctantly pulled his mind away from the glass lest he decide to stay there forever. His friends were in the real world, and he would sit with them in the dust. So he held the plate in his hands, feeling it, while he stared out the window longing for starlight. He was once again disturbed by a clatter and watched, surprised, as a panel hinged away from the wall close by and revealed Ping's face. The little woman smiled slightly.

"This is it," she said, looking behind her. She crawled out into the open, rose to her feet and dusted off her clothing—as if she was not going to be sitting in the dirt with everyone else very soon. She looked exhausted, as did the eight dwarves who emerged behind her.

One of the dwarves grumbled, as dwarves were want to do. "I think it would've been quicker to go by the stairs.

"Probably," Ping replied, "but it wouldn't have been as much fun." She did not look like she had been having fun at all. "Hello, Tuki."

"Hello, Ping. So, there is no more air?"

She shrugged. "We may be able to get some more, but... I don't know. That is for Kim to decided, I suppose. It gets harder to do the work every time and the results are not as good." Ping picked up one of the breathing masks and little air bottles that were lying in the dust nearby. Tuki had not even noticed it. "There are these as well."

Tuki nodded. "If the Goddess is watching, She will help us." But could Poti watch from a different universe?

The dwarves that emerged from the access passage stayed in a group, as if the experience of working together over the last few hours had formed a bond between them. Even the dwives sat down in the dust. They were the only ones who looked like they were enjoying the conversation, but Tuki could imagine how he would have felt to be thought of as equal amongst the women of Danyon Ford.

He watched as they nervously took part in the talk, as if expecting to be rebuked for just speaking. It seemed the male dwarves were surprised themselves when the rebuke was not offered. Other dwarves were watching from nearby, the women in jealousy, the men angrily. But none interfered.

"My mind keeps drifting," Ping said in a lull in the conversation. "How about a Song from the Singers?"

"I only became a Singer the day before the monsters—the aliens—came," Topper said, as if that was a reason for him not to Sing.

"Sing for us. The times I have heard Keeble it seems to clear away the cobwebs."

Topper nodded slightly, then started to Sing his Song. To Tuki it just sounded like a lot of strange sounds put together. As it built, though, he could feel the power of it. He could feel it washing through him and around him.

He laid his head back against the wall. He no longer felt like sleeping but was relaxed and calm. He took a bottle of water when Inaki offered it, had a sip then passed it on to a Ping.

After a while, a second dwarf joined his voice to Topper's. The Songs they Sang were completely different, but still the two of them merged together perfectly and floated like fairy-dust in the garden.

Time seemed to stop, but this time it was not a bad thing. Tuki looked around at everyone. People sat talking quietly as the Song calmed them and a stillness descended. They were resigned to what was happening, hoping still for life, but prepared if things were otherwise. Even the trolls waited to see what would happen. It was only when he looked back to Ping and her work-crew that he saw anything different.

Topper and Drago were still singing, sitting back with their eyes closed and smiling slightly. Tasko was Singing as well. He had risen to his feet and was tracing patterns on the wall of the ship.

"I can feel it," the dwarf said around his Song. "I can feel the wall. And it's like nothing I've ever felt before."

Ping stood and went closer. Others were turning to look, a moment of interest in the still garden. So they all saw when Tasko took a scoop out of the wall with his hand and held it up in the pale light. He smiled around his Song.

Ping was gaping. "But Keeble said..."

Tuki might have gaped as well, but he was really not surprised by anything any more.

Tasko smiled some more. "As soon as I started to Sing, I could feel it." He was carefully putting the piece of wall back in place, smoothing down the edges. Soon it was indistinguishable from the rest.

Topper was shaking his head, setting his long, narrow beard to waggling. "I still feel nothing," he said, still Singing. He rose to his feet and touched the wall.

"Well... I don't know," Ping said, now apparently thinking she had to come up with all the ideas.

Tess wanted to prove otherwise. "Perhaps it is to do with safety," the dwife said. "Perhaps they do not want just one person to be able to make changes to the hull."

"So..." Topper was still feeling the wall, making indentations with his fingers then smoothing them out. "They make sure you need three Singers to effect the hull so nobody can scuttle the ship?"

Tess shrugged, suddenly unsure. "Maybe."

Ping was scratching her head. Tuki watched it all disinterestedly. What would it matter if they could not get back to their own universe?

"Everyone stop Singing," Ping said. "Then Drago and Tasko start first. Topper, you last."

They did as they were told, and it was not long before Topper's hand had disappeared into the hull. His was a Song of Being, the same as Keeble's.

"What if we are in a battle and the hull is damaged?" Tuki asked. "What if we only have two Singers left alive?"

"Well..." Ping said.

But Topper was nodding. "And to repair a split, like the one I understand is down stairs, would take a long time with only a Song of Doing. We would have to dig everything out all the way to the outer surface, and then build it back again—with someone on the outside, for the first bit at least. With both Songs available, we could merely mold the insubstantial stone to fill the crack."

But Tuki really could not understand any of that. He sat with his back against the cliff and looked out at the swirling mist. Only... There was something else out there.

He squinted, as if that might make a difference. He rose to his feet.

The rough green shape of a kil'ini was floating about a kilometer away. It was upside down—or the *Hakahei* was—and its tail was towards the ship, but it was slowly turning to face them. Tuki pointed but others were already turning to follow his gaze. The quiet babble of conversation rose sharply.

Tuki smiled and drew in a deep breath without worrying about the consequences.

"Why did we ever doubt?" he said to nobody in particular. Like Ruby said, if there was a way to live then, between them, Scree and Keeble would find it. Tuki looked for Ruby in the crowd and smiled at her before turning to watch as the kil'ini came closer. A huge mouth opened on the front, gaping wider by the moment. The creature swallowed the ship like a child swallowing a grape.

Tuki sat down and cried.

17: Rescue

KIM WATCHED FROM THE UPPER LEVEL of the garden as the alien creature came closer. It had four large eyes, each on a stalk as long as the *Hakahei* was tall. Each moved independently of the others, twisting this way and that like the long feelers that writhed in the swirling mist. Kim had never seen anything so beautiful.

She was surprised when the creature started to open what appeared to be a mouth, with the obvious intention of swallowing them. But if that was what was going to work best, she really didn't care. And if it actually intended to eat them... Well, she didn't particularly care about that either. Dead was dead, after all.

After staring and smiling like an idiot while the kil'ini approached, mouth ever wider, Kim burst into motion. She raced along the wall, gasping for breath, pushing past people, until she came to the small airlock that gave access to the hangar. Once there, she had to wait. She gripped the wheel that would open the door. She fidgeted. She chewed on her bottom lip. She looked around to share her excitement with her companions. She fidgeted some more.

Outside, the kil'ini was upon them and merely continued to sail forward. It swallowed them whole, without slowing. Kim found herself dividing her glance between the view of the hangar and the view of the interior of the creature's mouth. Neither seemed to change for a long time.

Finally, she saw movement and almost cheered when she saw the unmistakable figure of Scree hanging onto a rough green wall, obviously in zero gravity, a few meters from the open hangar door. After a moment, he pushed off and sailed for the *Hakahei*. Crossing the threshold, the ship's artificial gravity, still leaking slowly from the floor, plucked him out of the air. He landed in a messy heap, so un-troll-like. Kim gasped, but he was quickly on his feet.

She started to open the door, felt the muscles in her arm tense to turn the wheel to break the seal, but Scree was wearing a breather. She resisted.

"Don't open the door," she shouted hoping that someone around the other side of the garden could hear her. They didn't want to release their hard won oxygen until someone told them it was safe. They didn't want to die this close to salvation. They didn't want to die.

Kim pounded on the small glass window, trying to get Scree's attention. He didn't see and strode to the larger airlock that would give him access to the stairwell. Or perhaps to the workshop and the door on the other side of the garden.

"Don't open this door," Kim repeated to those grouped behind her. She pushed her way through the crowd, back the way she'd come. There was a large area with nobody in it. Everyone was packed around the doors like people trying to get into a concert.

The eastern door was still closed. Kim made her way slowly through the packed people, sidling through, and found Chasm and Thorpe at the front. Words had obviously been exchanged for some members of the waiting crowd, mainly dwarves, were glowering at the two of them.

"What's going on?" Thorpe asked.

"Scree was wearing a breather. It's a huge chamber the *Hakahei*'s in, so it must take them a while to purge the bad air and get oxygen in here. Or something." She pushed between the two of them and put her face up against the glass of the window. "You didn't see him?"

"No."

It seemed a lifetime before the troll returned. When he did come into view, his breather and mask had been removed. They'd been replaced by a worried expression. Kim started to work at the wheel to open the door. Chasm took over and Kim used her own hands for waving and pounding on the window instead. Scree saw her and the relief on his face was obvious. He raced to the door and started to help get it open. He was grinning like a schoolboy with a new bike and Kim knew how he felt. She'd never been so pleased to see anyone in her life.

Before the door was all the way open Kim slipped through and threw herself at him. He caught her but didn't seem to know what to do after that. Kim supposed he might not be used to the idea of people being happy to see him but she didn't care. She held him and laughed and cried all at the same time.

Eventually she decided that it might not be a good idea for the Captain to been seen hugging the leader of the marines and crying on his shoulder. She loosened her grip and felt herself lowered to the floor.

"Hello, Scree," she said, wiping at her eyes and trying to get control of herself. Well, she was the Captain, she could sniffle like a girl if she wanted. "It's good to see you again."

The big man nodded, looking slightly bemused. "Yeah. I kinda worked thats out. Hows we doing?"

Kim looked back through the door at the people crowding there. "We're doing good. We're all doing good."

Scree smiled again. "Huh."

"So when do we go back to the other universe?" Kim wiped her eyes again. "How long do we have to wait?"

"Probably already there. Don't have to waits at all and you doesn't know when you goes through."

People finally started to come through the door, pushing past Kim and Scree and taking in deep breaths. The air wasn't great, but it was better than they'd tasted for quite a while.

Ceiling lights started to glow softly. Somewhere, a fan started to hum.

"So what did you have to sell to get us out?"

"Nothing yet, but it ain't that simple, anyways."

"Ummm... What?"

"The hurgon are havings a few problems themselves, from the little bit that Meledrin told me. Theys kinda started a rebellion on this kil'ini."

Kim groaned. Surely things were confused enough as they were without getting factional fighting involved as well. She took a deep breath. "So are we sure these are the good guys?"

"Ask Mel, but I don' know if she knows for sure. How could she?"

"Right. I supposed we'd better go see what the hell's going on." Taking a deep breath, Kim wiped at her face again and smoothed at her hair. "How do I look?"

Scree looked slightly confused by the question and shrugged. "You looks great."

"Yeah, right. I probably looked like I've just gotten out of bed." *But maybe that's how he likes his women to look.*

Clearing her throat and blushing, Kim moved past Scree and headed for the airlock. Out in the hangar, a small group of 'people' waited near the main door. Meledrin stood at the front. Keeble was on one side, grinning crookedly, a hurgon was on the other. Cuto was among a group of 5 standing behind. After an apparent moment of indecision, Keeble hurried across the hangar to join Kim.

"Hello, Kim. Good to see we weren't late. We were starting to worry."

Kim smiled slightly. "I'd gone past worry, Keeble. You did a great job. Everyone did."

Kim took a deep breath and turned back to the aliens—the first *official* contact. She looked behind. "Scree, Ping, Keeble, come with me. Stone, don't do anything threatening, but make it obvious you and the other trolls are guards who can do harm if needed." She thought that was it but changed her mind. "Captain Thorpe, I suppose you should come as well. In fact, do you want to run things?" She really wanted somebody else to take over. She couldn't think. She needed to sleep. Proper sleep.

"No, Kim, neither of us can speak for Earth. So you just speak for yourself. I *will* come along though."

"Bastard," Kim said.

The Captain smiled. "Why don't you ask for a chance to rest and consult with Meledrin before you do anything."

"Do we have time? This war is still going on. People are dying. And those other bastards are out there somewhere looking for someone to squash."

"So why don't you see if you can get a lift to Nexis? That's where you want to go, right?"

"Yes."

"That's where human officials can be found, right?"

"If you want the USA doing the talking."

"They're as good as anyone else."

"Well, yes, if we have to choose *one*. I'd rather we had the United Nations or something."

"You want the UN to organize something? I thought you were in a hurry. And the only interpreters are right here anyway."

Kim nodded. "Right."

"Right. So ask for a lift to Nexis and have a rest. Talk to Meledrin and see what she can tell you. We don't have a *lot* of time, but there's no need to rush the most important event in recorded human history."

Kim took a deep breath. "Right."

Stone had already started to organize the guards. A pair of trolls were on either side of the small hurgon gathering, right back at the wall. Another five were standing in a row near Kim. The hurgon were looking nervous, but their escape route had not been blocked.

The official party fell into step behind Kim as she crossed the hangar.

"Aunt Meenu, of the T'loop family, and kil'ini Lisa'lee'la send greetings," Meledrin translated almost before Kim had come to a halt.

"Greetings back," Kim said, hoping Meledrin did not translate literally. "And we thank everyone for rescuing us."

Kim watched as the hurgon waved its hands around a bit and spoke rapidly in reply.

"Aunt Meenu accepts your thanks, but asks why warriors have been stationed in the hangar."

Kim looked at Stone and the rest of the trolls. "We're just making sure this is a rescue and not a capture and making it clear that if it's actually the latter then this is still our ship and we won't give it up easily."

"They rescued you, Kim. I was—"

"Humans can lie, Mel, perhaps hurgon can too. Don't add a commentary, just translate. Though you don't have to do it word for word."

Meledrin sniffed. "Very well." And she spoke to the hurgon.

"Aunt Meenu respects your right to protect your vessel, but says that no warrior will be allowed outside."

"Tell Aunt Meenu that at this stage we'd all prefer to stay on the ship." Kim had thought of Cuto as male, but she could see no different between Cuto and this Aunt.

Though perhaps Meledrin had some trouble with the translating and 'Aunt' was the closest she could come up with. Though Suldon had used the word 'Daughter' earlier as if it was a title. She decided it didn't matter, as long as all the elves translated things in the same way.

"Aunt Meenu asks, 'If that is the case, what will Aunt Kim be doing?'"

"If Meenu wishes to stop the war between hakans and hurgon then the quickest way to get that process in motion would be for the kil'ini to take us to Nexis where we can all start talking with the Americans."

"Aunt Meenu says that they can go to Nexis, but what will happen after arrival is not certain. This kil'ini has been assigned to watch Sherindel, so if it is seen to be somewhere else, the Fen'dai officers assigned to Lisa'lee'la will be asked by their family to explain."

"And that means what, exactly?"

"The Fen'dai family members currently on this ship are being held captive."

"Right. What?" She thought about it for a moment. "This ship is owned by the T'loop family, right? So who are the Fen'dai?"

"This kil'ini is working with the T'loop family, correct. The Fen'dai are members of another family who travel with all other families to keep track of their dealing and act as mediators in all disputes."

"Right. So..." But it could take all day to work it out and that shouldn't be done standing in the hangar. "Look, tell Auntie Meenu—"

"Aunt Meenu."

"Whatever. Tell Meenu we can't make guarantees. I recommend we either go to Nexis or Earth—with Nexis being the preference—because we can't do anything stuck out here in the middle of nowhere."

Meledrin talked with the hurgon for a long time and Kim started to wonder if they were getting anywhere. Eventually the elf turned to speak with Kim again. "Aunt Meenu says that Lisa'lee'la shall go to Nexis. It tried to explain how long that would take, but I believe we may need Tuki's skills to do the arithmetic. In the mean time, Lisa'lee'la will send a coded ansible message to other T'loop kil'ini around Nexis to appraise them of the situation. The T'loop family members there will be able to work out a course of action before we arrive."

Kim wasn't sure she liked that all that much—letting the aliens come up with a plan in a situation she knew nothing about—but it was obvious she had no choice.

"Thank Auntie Meenu for her trouble and tell her that we would be pleased if she would come back... later... to discuss matters further. But for now we need to rest and try to work out what the hell's going on." Kim smiled wanly. She needed sleep but didn't think she'd be getting any in the near future.

18: Repairs

KEEBLE SAT ALONE AND CHEWED THE DRY, tasteless food. It was horrible stuff and didn't get any better with familiarity. What he really wanted was some coffee. Just the smell of a good strong mug would have made him feel better. He sighed and took a sip of water.

When he looked up he noticed Topper, Drago and a small group of dwarves sitting at another table. They seemed to have formed some sort of bond while he was off saving them all with Scree and Meledrin. They were staring at him. Keeble stared back. They weren't eating and hadn't been for some time.

Eventually, after a hushed discussion, Topper rose to his feet and crossed the mess. The young Singer stood across from Keeble for a long time, not saying anything, tugging at his chin-beard.

Keeble crunched through some more food and washed it down with a sip of water. "What is it?" he asked, tired of waiting.

"We know how to fix the hull," Topper said. He looked back over his shoulder, as if wondering if that was what his companions had really wanted him to say.

Keeble stared at him. "What do you mean you know how to fix the hull?"

Topper stood and tugged on his beard until Keeble was ready to grab him and shake the answer out.

"When you said the hull was stone," Topper said, "we didn't believe you. Now we do. We can feel it."

"Who felt it? When?"

"The *third* Singer can feel it."

"What?"

Topper beckoned for him to follow. Keeble pushed back his chair so hard it clattered onto its back. Okalani and Aka'mu looked up from another table. A small group of trolls didn't stir from their conversation.

As they walked out into the ship-circling passage, Topper started to Sing his Song. Tasko started as well. Keeble watched suspiciously.

"Sing, Keeble," Topper said.

Still suspicious, Keeble started his Song. And almost immediately, everything else was forgotten. He could feel the stone of the wall and it was like nothing he'd ever felt. The patterns of its structure were so tightly woven they were almost non-existent.

He laughed. "Of course. It just takes more power." It was obvious, really. He sank his good hand into the wall up to the elbow.

"Do you want to fix the hole now?" Topper asked around his Song.

"You want my help?" Keeble looked from Topper to Tasko and back again. "There are other Singers. You could ask them."

Tasko nodded. "We could but..."

"They never offered to help before, when you were gone," Drago said. "They sat up here and did nothing while we worked to keep everyone alive."

Topper nodded as well. "A Wanderer who works is worth more than them any day."

Keeble smiled. "Well, let's go and fix the hull then. Can't leave it as it is."

"Right," Topper said. "And then we can fix the air recycler as well."

"What's wrong with it?" The air recycler had been fine when he left.

"We had to pull it apart to make a manual filter."

"That was a good idea. Who thought of that?"

Tasko cleared his throat and looked from one of his companions to the other. "Ping came up with the idea. One of us would have thought of it eventually."

Keeble grunted. "Did it make any difference?"

Drago shook his head while Tasko said, "I don't really think so."

But Topper waited till they were all done. "We would be dead now if it hadn't worked," he said. "And the dwives came up with a few good ideas for the filter." He seemed reluctant to say that, even after his praise of a moment before. "Well, a couple of ideas."

"You let them help you with something that important?"

"Ping made me. And, you know, they... They came up with some good ideas."

Tasko nodded. "She did make him."

Keeble shook his head. He'd been forced to accept Ping's strange ways, but had been hoping the extra dwarves would help cure her of those—she should not be allowed to fix things. But he went away for a couple of hours and she showed them she could be useful.

"Well come on," Keeble said, "let's go fix the hole before Ping comes up with a plan for it." They didn't need any equipment. The four of them could fix the hole without much trouble at all.

Keeble went down to the Level 8 access panel then he started crawling through the ducts with the others close behind.

In the tank, Keeble showed them the circular section of boilerplate glued to the wall.

"Very shoddy job," Drago said, shaking his head in disgust.

Keeble cleared his throat and wound the gears on his hand.

"You did this?" It looked as if Tasko was having second thoughts about working with a Wanderer.

"I didn't have a lot of time or equipment," Keeble said defensively. "There was only me and Cuto, remember."

Drago shook his head again. "Let's get this done then. And the sooner the better."

Topper and Drago Sang the foundation of the enterprise while Keeble combined his Song of Being to Tasko's Song of Doing. As soon as they focused the magic onto the wall, the boilerplate clattered to the floor. Together, the four dwarves walked into the misty stone to start filling the gap.

With the four songs echoing around in the empty fuel tank, they were able to work at the mist, shifting it here and there quite easily.

They hardly spoke, working as a team, concentrating on the work. Keeble almost felt he was back at home again, working on the passage from Tab Cavern to Goolar's Well. Or building a vent duct between rooms. Or...

But he shook his head as he smoothed over the last of the joins. "It never felt like this," he said.

"What?"

Keeble stepped away from the wall and examined the work. He smiled and nodded, running mental fingers along the mist, testing the depths for any weakness. When he found no problems he called the others away from the wall and let his Song drift away to nothing. Topper and Tasko stopped Singing as well, falling silent after just a couple of notes. Drago started to wind his Song down slowly, removing first one layer than the next.

"You realize all the work we used to do at Tab Cavern never really had a purpose?" Keeble continued to look at the hull as he listened to the remains of Drago's Song.

"Of course it had a purpose," Topper said.

"The population wasn't really growing, so we didn't need all those extra rooms. The Goolar's Well passage was going to cut five minutes off the journey, but who ever went to the well anyway?"

"Yes but..."

"How long had Ferdan been working on his flying machine?"

Tasko shrugged as he bent to pick up the useless piece of boilerplate. "Ten years," he said. "I worked with him for a while."

"Who was going to fly it?" Keeble asked. "Where were they going to fly?" Dwarves rarely left the city beneath the mountain. They traded with the humans—goods for food, but otherwise most stayed in the caves and kept to themselves.

"That doesn't mean the flying machine was pointless. Just the knowledge is worth having."

"On its own it isn't, Tasko. Not on its own."

Nobody replied to that. They stood listening as Drago finally let the last notes of his Song fall away.

"What will women ever know," he said, "until they can feel that?"

Tasko nodded, but Keeble was not so sure. Perhaps knowing a Song was like knowing anything. It was not the knowing that really mattered at all. It was what you did with the knowledge. Dwarves had their Song's but where did that get them? In Tab Cavern in recent years they'd started going around in circles. They'd reached the extremities of the solid rock so most new passages inevitably started to curve back on themselves. They'd run out of mountain but didn't think to step out under the sky and see if there were other mountains to be found. There were other dwarvish cities on Sherindel, but Tab Cavern had lost contact with most of them a long time ago.

Kim had more power than could be found in a Song, he decided. He cursed her every decision and called her a fool of a woman, even as he was doing as she asked. Scree had power. He had survived a hard life through his own wit and strength. They both did what they did on their own, without the assistance of 'magic'. And people were willing to follow them because of the way they spoke and the way they looked you in the eye.

With a grunt, Keeble turned and started heading for the hatch. "How about we go and have a look at those clocks. Bet Ping has not got them fixed yet."

-oOo-

Keeble cursed as he entered the engineering bay. Ping was looking at a computer. Ari and Dosa were looking over her shoulder as if they could read.

"What is that word?" Ari asked of the other woman, before realizing that Keeble was there. She blushed.

Ping, concentrating on the screen, didn't know the dwarves had entered. "'Calculations'," she said. "If we didn't have the computer, we would need Tuki to work it out though." She worked at the keyboard, biting her lip in concentration.

Keeble cleared his throat.

"Keeble. Ummm... Hi." Ping gave a tight smile.

"You shouldn't be in here," Keeble said, though he knew there were several legitimate ways she could argue about that. The dwives though... what excuse did they have? "What are you doing?"

"We're trying to work out how to fix the clocks." She pushed hair away from her face and quickly looked back at the screen. Ari did as well, avoiding his gaze. Dosa was sidling slowly towards the door.

"It's about time. How is Tuki supposed to do his job properly if the clocks aren't working?" That was not quite fair either but Ping and Ari both blushed.

"Well... Dosa thought... We think it might be a missing tooth on the second actuator cog."

Keeble turned his gaze upon the dwife and she stopped moving. All the dwarves were looking at her. "Dosa thought that? Why?"

Ping didn't reply. Keeble could see how she was manipulating everyone. Perhaps she wasn't doing it consciously, but it was happening. She was letting the dwives show that they were capable of making a contribution. She was *forcing* them to speak and be heard.

Keeble wanted to stop that happening, but by the time he thought of something to say it was too late.

Dosa started to explain her deduction. "The two clocks keep up perfectly for almost one full revolution of the actuator. I didn't know what it was called..." She was hardly audible. "But then the high one seems to pause for just a second, as if a tooth is missing, before tension and friction finally push it on."

"A second?" Drago asked.

Dosa looked to Ping, then answered again. "Yes, but with one of those seconds each revolution—each minute—it soon adds up."

Topper was nodding. "It's only a guess at the moment though, right? We'd have to look to be sure."

Keeble cursed him silently.

Ping nodded. "We'll need your help."

Keeble cursed Ping as well. Join the two groups together and let the men feel they are the experts and that the women are just trying to learn.

"Well, let's look then," Topper said. He looked from Keeble to Ping and back again.

"Why don't *you* look," Keeble said.

Topper nodded slowly. "All right then. Dosa and Tasko can help."

Keeble was about to say no but gave a curt nod instead. It was possible the dwife was right after all, and the sooner the problem was found and fixed the better. "I'll stay here with Ping and see if we can find anything else."

"Where's the best access for the high clock?"

"I know," Dosa said, before suddenly looking nervous again. "Ummm... I know the way."

Keeble grunted and watched as the three of them left. He muttered to himself, cutting off when Ping turned to look in his direction. "What else can we look for?" he asked, trying to appear as if he knew what he was looking at.

Ping shrugged slightly. "I'm not sure. I've not gone into the system very far yet. There's a lot of stuff I don't understand."

"I thought you were the expert."

"I am but... We didn't have clocks this advanced on Tiandi. With the clock in Elephant Tower I could stand back and see all the parts and just know how things worked. But here..." She sighed. "There are so many little pieces and lots of them do things I don't understand."

"Right. So you're moving deeper into the system? Part by part?"

"Yes. But it's hard to see anything a part at a time. And hard with the whole thing at once."

"There's probably a way to see different sized sections of the clock." Keeble nudged her off the chair. "Here, let me look." He had it worked out in no time and turned to look at Ping.

"Right." She was nodding slowly. "I thought there might be something like that but..."

Rising to his feet, Keeble cursed *himself*. He'd fallen for the very trick he'd noted Ping using earlier. He was acting like she was a trainee, explaining things to her, feeling important and knowledgeable. In itself, being seen as superior to any of the women wasn't a bad thing, but he was teaching her, which would never have been allowed in Tab Cavern.

He turned quickly when Topper and his small crew returned. "Well?"

"She was right. Half a tooth is missing on the second gear wheel. We were there for the completion of the rotation—you can see how it doesn't grip straight away."

"Excellent. Easy to fix then."

Dosa looked at her feet.

Tasko shook his head. "Actually..."

Topper grunted. "A couple of hours to do the job. We'll have to pull out the... I am not sure what it is..."

"The dilaton commutator?" Ping offered. "It says here." She pointed to the screen.

Topper looked over her shoulder. "That's the bit all right. And to pull that out we have to pull out half the gears in the actuator. And to pull out some of those..."

Keeble grunted and looked around the room. He spied a toolbox and crossed to it. "Let's go and take a look then, shall we." But he didn't pick the box up. The women were going to be coming one way or the other it seemed, so perhaps they just needed to be given the longest apprenticeships in dwarvish history... "Ari, bring that."

Keeble climbed the stairs to Level 5. There was a pair of young dwarves, a couple of years Keeble's junior, coming down the stairs.

"We were wondering where you went," one of them said. He had spiky hair and a short beard.

"We've been working."

"More work? Can we help?"

Keeble turned to look at Tasko, waiting on the stairs behind. "Bargle and Hoodek both helped with the... with the recycler."

Keeble sighed. He had totally forgotten about the dismantled air recycler. They all had. The other dwarves looked just as embarrassed as he felt. "Tasko and Drago, take these two and get the recycler back together."

"We're on it." The four of them went down, sidling past the clock repairers on the narrow stairs. Keeble finished climbing to Level 5 and followed Dosa to the clock entrance.

-oOo-

Keeble watched as Ari entered the mess and made her way to the food dispensers on the wall. When she had collected three packets of food she stood and looked around the room.

Keeble looked away but she came and sat down at his table. There were plenty of other places she could eat.

"What do you want?" Keeble asked.

For a moment it looked as if Ari might get up and leave. "We used to eat together all the time."

"It's different now. Things have changed. You've changed."

Ari shook her head. "No, I haven't. The world has changed, not me. I wanted to work before, I wanted to have friends and do interesting things. Now the world is a place where I can."

"Well, maybe I don't like the world."

"Well, maybe the world doesn't care," Ari said. She sounded angry but didn't look up. "We used to talk all the time, Keeble. But it was always about you. About what you had done and what your friends had done and... I was just a piece of furniture that responded to your conversations slightly better than the table." Finally she looked up. "Well, now I'm going to talk back. If you don't like it, you'd better change seats."

"You can't tell me what to do."

"No. But at least now I'm allowed to tell you what I think." She looked back down at her food, tearing open a packet and spilling half of it onto the table. "At least now I'm allowed to think."

Keeble grunted. But Ari had always been thinking. That was one of the reasons he had liked her. When he went home after his shift finished she always had ideas. He cleared his throat. "You remember one time you told me how to improve the design for the donatel stove?"

"You said it was a silly idea."

"I told Bavil. He made some adjustments and..." He watched as Ari gave a small smile then turned her attention to cleaning the mess off the table. "I told him it was my idea." Keeble looked at the mess on the table too. He was saved from having to explain when Cuto stepped up beside the table. *"Greetings, Cuto,"* Keeble signed carefully.

"Greetings, Keeble,"

"What is Cuto doing here?"

"Cuto was hoping to help with repairs."

Keeble shrugged. *"All major repairs were recently finished. There are only small jobs remaining."*

Cuto nodded and Keeble smiled. Nodding was not a gesture the aliens normally used. "*That is good,*" Cuto said. But the disappointment was obvious.

"You could help with one of the small jobs."

"Not if the help is not required."

"I think Meledrin is doing something in the gardens. Cuto might be able to talk to her."

"Cuto thanks Keeble and will talk to Meledrin."

Keeble watched as the alien left then turned back to Ari. But he still didn't know what to say. "I'm going to find something to do," he said. "You should..." He cleared his throat and watched her hands still working at the mess on the table. "I'll probably be back here in a couple of hours to get a drink." He glanced at her face then hurried from the mess.

19: Solitude

MELEDRIN DISCOVERED A SEAT in the storeroom and placed it in the middle of the garden. She sat, eyes closed, and let her mind drift. She sat for some time, surrounded by the dry, still air and the dust. Like the room, she was silent and empty.

After more than half an hour of stillness, she stirred and looked around. She could already see how it might be. A row of trees hiding the main the main walls, perhaps. Creeper vines on the cliffs up to the higher levels. Ferns in the tunnel leading through to the other side. It would be a place of calm amidst the bustle and hard-edged certainty of the rest of the ship. Meledrin decided she would not be able to remain on the ship if the room was not used for its intended purpose.

She sighed. It would be some time before anything would be done, she imagined, so at present it would have to suffice in its current condition.

The sound of a door opening disturbed her and she turned to see Cuto standing in the dust, looking around curiously.

"Greetings, Cuto," she signed. *"Are you well?"*

"Greetings, Meledrin. Cuto is well, thank you." The alien signed as well and didn't bother with the words at all. It looked around again. *"Keeble stated that Meledrin might be working in the garden."*

Meledrin sighed again. *"Meledrin wishes she was able to do some labor here, Cuto. Unfortunately supplies are required before that is possible."*

"Then what is Meledrin doing?"

"Merely sitting and enjoying a moment of quiet, Cuto." Meledrin looked around again. *"It is not such an inviting place at the present time, but given the chance Meledrin and the other elves will turn this into a place of peace and beauty."*

Cuto looked confused. *"To sit in?"*

"Yes. If that is what is desired. To wander. To read."

"But where are all the other hakans?"

Meledrin looked around. It was unusual for there to be no other people at all in the gardens, but that was hardly a reason for concern or suspicion. *"Meledrin is unsure. But the solitude was welcome."*

The alien looked even more confused. *"Solitude is welcome?"*

"Of course." Meledrin thought it strange that a being from a planet filled to the brim with people would not see solitude as a gift beyond imagining. But, if finding solitude might require a mission of great effort why would one even give the idea thought. *"Cuto never spends time alone?"*

"No." Cuto shook his head. *"There is only family."*

Meledrin did not know how to reply to that. She tried to gather her thoughts. *"But Cuto is an individual. Cuto has conscious thoughts and free will. How can Cuto not matter?"*

Apparently Cuto did not have an answer to that. The alien stood and stared at Meledrin as if giving the matter thought for the very first time. *"Without family, Cuto has nothing."*

"Without Cuto and others there is no family. A family is nothing more than a group of individuals. And it is the differences, the individuality, that makes families strong, for if one family member cannot solve a dilemma, perhaps another can."

"Cuto is not sure."

"Perhaps a lack of diversity is the reason your culture had stagnated." Meledrin regretted the words as soon as she said them. And she wasn't even sure if she were correct. Kim seemed to think the hurgon were mired in their history, but she had been wrong as often as not.

"Cuto will think on this."

It appeared that the alien was going to do it on the spot. It crouched slightly, as if settling in, then ceased to move. Meledrin watched for several minutes, waiting for some sign of life, but none was evident. The slow, vacant stare unsettled Meledrin and suddenly her spot of peace and quiet was not as welcoming as it had been. Leaving her seat where it was, Meledrin walked through the tunnel around to the far side of the garden.

The second side was much the same as the first. Dust and stillness. Except Suldon was sitting on the top level, legs hanging down over the cliff.

"Greetings, Meledrin," the young saveigni said.

"Greetings, Suldon."

"Are you imagining what type of garden this might be? Where the trees might stand? What flowers might be at their feet?"

"I have been, though that was not truly my purpose in coming here. I just wanted to sit and not be surrounded by the cold stone and metal and... And whatever else this ship is constructed from. I wanted to feel the earth beneath my feet again—dry lifeless earth though it is."

The saveigni nodded. "Dry and lifeless it might be, but there is something about it. The age, perhaps? It has been sitting her for millennia, waiting for something to happen."

Meledrin looked around though she did not feel the same. "Perhaps."

"You seem troubled."

For a moment, Meledrin thought of offering a denial. "You are perceptive," she said eventually. "I was speaking with Cuto just a moment ago and pointed out what we hakans would see as a flaw in hurgon society and culture." She sighed. "I believe I was wrong to do so, but Cuto now seems to be thinking on the matter and I am unsure if any good can truly come of it."

"If the flaw was pointed out without malice and in a polite manner I cannot see that it is a bad thing. If Cuto is thinking on the matter then it seems that no offence was taken. I would not concern yourself."

"Perhaps you are correct." But she was still unsure. She spoke with Suldon for a few minutes more, until the saveigni begged his leave and made his way towards the upper levels of the ship.

Meledrin climbed higher as well, but only to the upper level of the garden. Once there, she moved back to the other side of the ship and looked down on the spot where Cuto stood. It appeared that the alien had not moved at all. Like its society, perhaps it would stand there until the current situation was resolved and only then move on to something else. Perhaps the hurgon were waiting for the war to end before they moved on to their next phase of existence. And until then they would tread the same path over and over again. For five minutes she watched before she too made her way towards the upper levels of the ship.

-oOo-

Meledrin returned to the garden some time later and Cuto still stood in the same spot. She went to stand in front of the alien. It did not notice her.

"Are you well, Cuto?" she eventually asked out loud.

Finally, the alien stirred. *"Yes, Meledrin, Cuto is well. Cuto has given much thought to what Meledrin said but has not been able to come up with an answer."*

"It is not easy to question all that is known. And perhaps I am wrong, Cuto. Just amongst the hakan peoples there is such diversity in cultures and ideas. This proves that there is no one right way. Different lives suit different peoples."

"Perhaps. But perhaps living a different life does not make it correct."

Meledrin sighed. *"Meledrin does not know the answers, Cuto. Perhaps there are no answers."*

"Cuto will think on it some more later. When Cuto spoke to Keeble before Keeble said there were small jobs that needed to be done. Does Meledrin know it those jobs remain incomplete?"

"Meledrin does not know."

"Cuto will find Keeble to ask."

"Meledrin will accompany Cuto."

Meledrin walked by the alien's side as it made its way to the stairs and up to the Engineering Bay. There were five dwarves there. They all looked up for a moment then four of them went back to their work as if the alien was just another member of the crew.

Keeble smiled and started signing. "*Greetings, Cuto. Much work has been completed since we last spoke.*" He pointed to a list on his computer screen. Over half the items had been crossed out. "*The hakans are making progress.*"

Cuto nodded and examined the list as well, as if it could read what was written there. "*Are there any tasks that Cuto can complete?*"

"*Well like I said before, you can help with any, I suppose...*"

"*Cuto would like to work alone.*"

Keeble glanced at Meledrin.

"I believe it would be a good idea to allow Cuto the opportunity, Keeble," she said in Rongo.

"Why's that?"

"Cuto is questioning his reality."

"What?"

"Cuto is giving thought to the way hurgon society works."

"That's a good thing, is it?"

Meledrin winced. "I am unsure, Keeble." From the little she knew, she decided there were many problems with hurgon society, but who was she to judge? The alien civilization had outlived the hakan one by a considerable amount of time.

"That doesn't help. And what if he can't fix... Whatever it is he tries to fix."

"The hurgon have no gender—" Meledrin stopped when Keeble glared at her. "When the task has been completed, appoint a dwarf to carry out an assessment."

"Right. Of course. I suppose that won't take any longer than actually fixing it." He checked his list for a moment. "*Is Cuto sure?*" Keeble signed.

The alien didn't look sure. "*Cuto has much to think on. All hurgon have choices to make at this time, perhaps time in solitude will make the choices easier.*"

"*What are the hurgon thinking about?*"

"*It is soon the time of seeding. Cuto must decide between symbo and givtar. Or neither. It is Cuto's first time choosing and Cuto is conflicted.*"

"*What does that mean?*"

"*It is a time that affects all hurgon. It is a time of great opportunity.*"

Keeble shook his head and gave up. "*So you want to work alone?*"

Cuto nodded.

"Keeble, I think it would be beneficial if Cuto worked in a location that was well away from other individuals."

Keeble started checking his list again. "*Cuto, one of the doors in the hold isn't working.*" He brought up a map to show the alien the location. "*There's a tool box over there."* He glanced at the screen again as if wondering if there was anything else to say. *"Let me know when Cuto is done."*

The alien nodded. It collected the tools and left.

"I think you have done a good thing, Keeble."

"What's so special about fixing a door?"

"The fixing of the door means nothing, in itself. But Cuto is working alone. I believe this is almost unheard of for hurgon."

"That's crazy. Even for dwarves, that's crazy."

Meledrin raised her eyebrows. "Indeed."

-oOo-

Meledrin switched on the radio so Kim could talk to the Americans but then had nothing to do as she guided the ship towards the ground.

It seemed a lifetime ago that they fled Nexis. The Americans in the hangar and then the hurgon and finally, the multeese. Running, ever running but not seeming to make any progress. Mother Meenu was aboard the *Hakahei* but that was only progress if some type of agreement could be reached with the authorities on Earth. Otherwise it was more running around in circles with no hope of an ending.

Meledrin sighed and watched as the mountain came closer. She was unsure how Kim knew it was the correct one—as far as Meledrin was concerned there were half a dozen that all looked more or less the same. But finally Tuki was able to adjust a camera and the landing area outside the door became visible. Kim took the *Hakahei* down to the area indicated by the Americans. She set the ship down with a jolt then sat silently in her seat. Everyone turned to look at her.

"Now whats?" Scree asked eventually.

"Now we save the world," Kim said. "The worlds." But she sat there and didn't outline any plans.

Scree sighed. "So what do we need to do? And what do we need to avoid doing?"

Apparently Kim was learning from the dwarves—she nodded and started to think out loud.

20: Knowing a Bit

SCREE CHECKED EVERYONE WAS READY. Red troop didn't exist any more—Gorge's rebellion had seen to that. The last two members, Shardy and Sandy, had been put into other troops to make up for the losses there. Fifteen people weren't enough, as far as Scree was concerned. Three troops weren't enough. But they were good people—any troll who could sit and do nothing on the ship while they waited to die was good people—so it would have to do.

Stone and Green Troop were waiting in the airlock. Keeble wound the gears on his hand, and Suldon checked the weapon he'd been given as if he knew what he was doing.

With a nod to them all, Scree hit the button to open the door.

The area in front of the hanger on Nexis was designed for landing ships. Kim had found a spot where a cliff reached the door on Level 3, and landed the ship. But it was about six meters to the stone, according to Tuki's hurried calculations and Scree wasn't going to argue. *Radii* and *circumferences* had been mentioned... He trusted the lad to get it right and had sent trolls to find something to bridge the gap.

But the Americans had been doing some testing of their own. Before the door was all the way open, a gangplank extended from the cliff and touched gently against the hull. It didn't meet perfectly, but that was probably Kim's fault, not the Americans'.

A few meters away, a small group of soldiers waited. The leader was a tall thin man with close-cropped red hair and a scar on his cheek. There were three others with him, standing just behind, weapons slung over their shoulders.

Scree led the way, stopping in front of them.

The leader said something as he waved swirling dust away from his face. Scree couldn't understand anything, but Suldon's voice in his mind translated.

<*Good afternoon. I'm Lieutenant Nathan Jones of the United States Air Force... We weren't sure you'd really return.*>

Scree didn't say anything.

<*I believe he is awaiting a reply of some kind.*>

<Lets him wait.>

After the initial inspection Scree ignored the humans and examined the surrounding area. The stone shelf of the main platform. Other shelves—on a few different levels for different sized ships—around the outside. A dozen other men were visible, most near the huge door to the hanger.

Eventually Scree turned to look at Jones. "We're going to opens the door to a ship. That's all we's doings. And while we're doing that, you'll take Palsamon to our ship. Right?"

Suldon started to translate, though Scree, knowing a bit about elves, doubted it would be word for word. He didn't let him finish anyway.

"Don't translates," he said out loud.

Suldon stuttered to a stop. Nobody said anything.

Eventually Lieutenant Jones started to look annoyed. "Why not allow him translate," he asked in halting Rongo.

Scree smiled. "Cause if you don't understands this language when it takes only a few hours to learn, then I ain't goings to help you."

Then man scowled. "I can speak but not good."

"Don't matter what you've got to say at the moment anyway. I've told you what's going to happen." Scree smiled some more.

"I don't know I allow you do anything, sir. Commanding officer told me get skyglass then report."

"I'm sures he did." Scree was having fun—he had all the power and could probably get anything he wanted. "*My* commanding officer told me to open a ship and bring back Palsamon, that's all."

Jones didn't look happy.

Scree checked his weapon then walked across to the hangar door. Green Troop, Suldon and Keeble were close behind. He stopped at the door. There were heaps of ships and just about every one had a group of humans around it, working at getting in. Nobody seemed to be having any luck.

"Which ship does you wants?" Scree asked Jones. But if Scree knew a little bit about elves, then he knew a little bit about humans too... He headed toward the biggest of the ships before the man could reply. The Lieutenant probably didn't know anyway and would have to ask someone else.

The ship Scree chose was right down in the back corner. It looked exactly the same as the *Hakahei*, only twice the size. The humans were certainly impressed by it—they covered it like flies on a rotten cat.

"Tell thems all to get off. We wants nobody anywhere near the ship."

Jones had a sour look that might have impressed some people. Scree waited. The Lieutenant made his protests with brow wrinkling effort, but Scree didn't reply. He ignored the man some more. Eventually, Jones got the point and ordered the men down.

Someone else countermanded the order.

Another soldier was striding across the hangar like a man with a purpose. There were a handful of others being drawn along in his wake. A wave of salutes followed. Scree sighed.

Lieutenant Jones and the newcomer spoke quickly. Neither seemed very happy.

"Jones tells me you won't hand over the skyglass?" the newcomer said eventually. "I thought we had a deal."

"Who is you, exactly?"

"Where is Miss McLean?"

"Who is you?"

"If you don't—"

Scree turned and looked at the far wall.

"I'm Major Williams. I'm in charge here."

Scree turned back to face the man. He smiled. "Great. I'm Scree and here's how it is—"

"Lieutenant Jones already told me what you intend to do. But I want to know where the skyglass is."

"Where do you think it is?"

"Do you have it?"

Scree looked down as if he might be hiding something in his rubberized EVA suit. Apparently Williams didn't have a sense of humor but managed to control himself with an effort.

"We gots you a skyglass," Scree finally relented. "It's on our ship."

"Why aren't giving it to us now?"

Scree shrugged, though he knew the answer. "You'll have to ask Kim. Like I said to this guy, I'm just doing what she told me to do. So, you gets all them people off the ship, and we'll opens the door for you. Then we will goes back to the *Hakahei*, with Palsamon."

"Where's Miss McLean?"

"She's organizing things for later."

"What's happening later?"

"She'll be introducing you to your crews and stuffs."

"Our crew? For our ship? We'll be supplying our own crew, as Miss McLean well knows."

A shrug. "Talks to her about it. But, of course, it don't matter one way or another if you can't gets into the ship."

Finally the Major gestured angrily to Jones. "Palsamon is recovering well. I will have him escorted to the dock." And he stormed off with his followers.

"Where's we going in, Keeble?" Scree asked as the last of the Americans scrambled down from the scaffolds surrounding the ship.

The dwarf looked. "There."

"And comings out?"

"Over there."

"Rights." Scree examined the two points, trying to fix them in his mind.

A precarious looking scaffold had already been arranged at the exit door, but something had to be moved to the entry point.

Scree got the Americans to do the dragging and the grunting. He stood with his arms folded and smiled at Jones occasionally. A crowd gathered to watch.

When the new scaffold was in place, Scree told Keeble to lead the way and told the rest of his group to head up to the exit.

"How you going get in?" Jones asked. "We worked that panel almost entire day with no luck."

"You just watch and learns why you'll be using the crew that Kim's organized." Scree started to climb. <Stone, you just makes sure you keeps that door clear.>

Stone grunted, as if offended by the very idea of not completing his job properly. Scree laughed in reply. A week ago neither of them would've cared one way or the other.

Keeble was already Singing his Song. Scree could hear the strange sounds hanging in the air around him. He could feel them. By the time they reached the top of the scaffold and the panel there, the dwarf was ready. He shifted the sounds subtly, then climbed into the hull and disappeared. Scree turned to wave at Jones and the other Americans. He smiled at their stunned expressions and climbed in after Keeble.

"Tight fit in here," he said.

"It's an air lock," the dwarf replied as he shifted the focus of his Song and moved through another wall.

When Scree joined him, the dwarf was shining a torch around, revealing a narrow, low, dust coated maintenance passage. "Wasn't made for trolls. Don't know why you had to come anyway."

"You do so. To make sure you don't get lost or don't decide to hangs around and fix something."

Keeble smiled. "I might stay."

"No you won't. You don't wants to be working for the Americans."

"Bet they don't put a woman in charge."

"Maybe not, but I don't think their boss will be as good as Kim—she don't interfere in what you doing, does she? Tells you what she wants then goes away?"

"Yes. But I'm in charge of the Engineering department."

"Think them Americans will put you in charge of anything?"

"No."

"Right. Admit it, you don't think Kim's too bad anyways."

"Maybe not." He shrugged and smiled slightly. "Don't like her as much as you though."

Scree stared at him. "Let's get moving. No time to sits here talking."

Keeble laughed and turned to crawl towards the center of the ship. "Where should I go then, Mr Expert?"

"Just get us out of these damn passages. Worry about the rest after that."

"Right then."

It was a few minutes before Scree poked his head out into a hallway and looked around. "Where is we?"

"I thought it was your job to know that."

"Nope. Just my job to gets us where we're going. Big difference."

"Well, if this is the same as our ship only twice as large then this level would be water and fuel tanks, like our Level 8 is."

"Well, that ain't it."

"No. So who knows then? Let's just get out of here."

Scree looked around, but one direction down the hall looked the same as the next. He pictured the position of the other door in his head, but that was meaningless until they found some stairs. And they knew enough to know that there'd be stairs somewhere. While Scree thought, Keeble went to open a door.

"It is a refectory," the dwarf said after getting it open just a crack and peering through. "It's huge though. Four times the size of our own."

"Let's gets out of here."

Scree picked a direction and set off. It was easy to find a set of stairs but he was having trouble judging the floors. He got off a level too early and, after wondering through a couple of doors, found himself in a hangar that took up at least half the level. He recognized some of the vehicles there, Landers and Miners, but there were also a dozen craft that looked a whole lot meaner than anything on the Hakahei. He wanted to look, but Keeble pushed past to see what the hold up was.

"Wrong floor? Whistler's Mother. I could have picked the wrong floor. No use sending you along for that." He turned around and went back the way he'd come. Keeble seemed to be enjoying himself now. Scree cursed and followed.

The next floor seemed about right. Scree stalked through the hallways, trying to find the outer edge of the ship. A half open door show a room with a dozen weapons control chairs. Again, Scree wanted to stop and look but knew it'd do him no good. The next room was completely empty except for a small box full of the shiny cubes that Kim said were like books.

"Must be getting close," Keeble said, backing out of the room.

"This way."

They continued along the passage. It twisted and turned, as if people were supposed to get lost in there. There were doors every few meters to divide the ship into smaller and smaller sections. "This must be a fighting ship," Scree said as he passed through another door.

"Why do you say that?"

"'Cause there was all thems weapons chairs. And all these doors."

"What do doors have to do with anything? If the enemy gets in the ship it's a bit late to be worrying about locking the doors."

"We gots the same sorts of doors on the *Hakahei*, just not as many. They not to stop people, they to stop air in case the ship gets a hole."

"So?"

"So with all these doors they obviously think there's a lot more chance of getting a hole..."

"Right. Of course." The dwarf examined the next door they passed, as if it was suddenly completely different.

Scree was glad when he found the outside of the ship and the right door. There was no passage leading all the way around here, just a big room designed for defense. There were people sized nooks in the wall and barricades. Not an easy room to pass through if someone wanted to stop you.

Scree started to work at the handle to open the door.

Once somebody outside started to help, pushing against the edge of the stubborn door, they were done quickly. Scree slipped outside.

Major Williams was back and stood with Jones at the bottom of the stairs, watching as Scree sauntered down. A few score of men and women were behind the officers, keen to get inside and have a look.

"Do we get the skyglass now?" Williams asked.

"Calm down," Scree said, from the bottom step. "Once we gets back to our ship Kim will be coming to speak with you."

"Speak with us?"

"Yeps." Scree could see the humans eyeing the open door above, wanting to get in.

"And she will have the skyglass?"

"Nope. If you have a problem with that, talk to her about it. You's going to have plenty to keep you busy, anyways." Though they couldn't because he was still standing in the way. Trolls were on the steps behind him, humans were waiting to get on. Finally he moved and the stairs were cleared. The Americans rushed on, setting the whole scaffold to shaking with the thunder of their steps.

21: Sunshine

KIM STEPPED OFF THE GANGPLANK and stopped where Scree had stopped an hour earlier. There were two dozen people behind her waiting for a signal. Kim wasn't the one giving the signal. Pool, her personal bodyguard for the day, scanned the area, eyes narrowed in concentration. The trollop was about thirty years old, with roughly trimmed short hair and hawk-like nose. She looked as mean and competent as any of the males.

Kim ignored the activity behind her and concentrated on the group in front. She tried to remember the symbols of American military officers but it had all been so long ago. If she could get close enough to read the badge... Kim heard Pool give the all-clear in the radio stuck on her temple and looked back as the rest of the group exited the ship. A stranger bunch there had never been. Rowdy male dwarves, dwives like school leavers turning up for their first day of work. Two meek moai—even the usually haughty Okalani—and six elves who might have been out for an afternoon stroll in the gardens. The four remaining members of yellow troop looked like professional soldiers, calm, alert and deadly. Kim took a couple of steps forward. The trollop bodyguard went with her.

"Miss McLean?"

"Major Williams." She didn't need the badge. "Nice to meet you."

"I'm sure."

"Now, don't be like that."

"We aren't in the mood for being nice."

"Well, if you aren't nice to me things could get a little bit complicated."

"And why's that?"

"This is Pool, Major. She's a troll. And she likes me." Kim turned to look at the troll. "Well, I think she likes me. Do you like me, Pool?"

Pool didn't answer. She grunted and kept looking for signs of trouble.

"Anyway, the point is, she'll hurt anyone that she thinks is some type of threat. So, please, *do* be nice." The rest of Yellow Troop weren't far behind either. Five pure bred trolls with advanced weapons would make a mess of a much larger number of Americans. Even highly trained Americans.

"I have nearly a thousand men in this area, Miss McLean—do you really think I could not have you in custody in a moment if that was what I wanted." There were half a dozen armed men just a step behind him.

Kim smiled. "It *is* what you want, Major, and yet here I am, standing around in the sunshine as if I own the place." She smiled some more. "Did General Hilliard pass on all the information? If so, then you'll know elves and dwarves and moai are basically human. We're all from one race and have been genetically engineered in one way or another."

"The General told me something but—"

"If the story he told you is hard to believe then it's probably true. I'm pretty sure trolls are human as well, and their job was to kill people. They're very good at their job. They like it. I have sixteen trolls and I have a big shiny space ship... We both know you wouldn't stand a chance." Kim stole a glance over her shoulder. The ship was not all that shiny really, and not all that big, but... "I also have something you want." That was the clincher. "How about I introduce you to your crew, then show you how to work the ship?"

"Humans may not be engineered to travel in space, but we can learn anything. We don't need your crew. Just give us the skyglass and let us decide how to use it."

"Back on Earth, Hilliard was trying to work the skyglass," Kim said. "He had a computer talking to it in the right language—this one—but nothing was happening. Want to know why? Because it takes more than talking the right language or holding your tongue right. It takes an extra piece in your brain. A piece that Tuki and all other moai have."

The Major examined the people behind Kim. "Well, I see the moai, but I don't see the skyglass."

"Funny that."

Major Williams sighed. "Wouldn't that be easier to show us how to use the ship with the skyglass plugged into it?"

"Of course. What would be harder would be for me to get back to the *Hakahei* afterwards."

"Miss McLean, I give you my word—"

"Just like Hilliard gave his word to Tuki?"

"I was not—"

"Of course you weren't." Kim shook her head. "This is the way it'll be done. I'll go onto your ship with all these people and show you how it works. Some of these people will stay behind and the rest of us will return to the Hakahei. Then about a hundred refugees will come off my ship and Captain Thorpe of the SAS will give you the skyglass. There will also need to be a meeting, but we'll talk about that later."

"You have the SAS on your ship?"

"About twenty Brits. They were the first through the gate in England. They had a bit of trouble and couldn't get back when the gate was retaken."

"Of course, they're all welcome."

"Good. And the rest of the day's itinerary?"

"If I don't like it?"

"Then I'll get back on the *Hakahei* and wait to see how many seconds it takes you to change your mind."

The answer was inevitable. "The ship is this way, Miss McLean."

"That's what I thought." Kim walked to the huge hangar door and across to ship Scree and Keeble had opened earlier. American service personnel were coming and going with all types of equipment. Kim wondered if any of them—people or equipment—would be any use.

"That was a Marine officer," Kim said, pointing to the ramrod back of a soldier. So maybe the sixteen trolls couldn't handle all one thousand of them, but the Americans still wouldn't get onto the *Hakahei* without the permission of those on board.

"The air force doesn't have a lot of ground troops and we've taken a beach head on what may be a hostile world. The regular army will be here soon enough too, I imagine." He didn't look impressed by the idea.

"Afraid somebody is going to steal your thunder, Major." Kim smiled. She'd have to think about curbing her attitude, but she was a space privateer now and they were supposed to be witty and daring. And besides that, it might well be all that was keeping her sane.

Kim stopped at the bottom of the scaffold on the outside of the ship and looked upwards. Without power to the ship, there were far too many stairs to climb after only a couple of hours of sleep in a few stressful days.

"Jesus, Major, you couldn't have picked something smaller, could you?"

Williams didn't reply and Kim started to climb the stairs. She went up ten levels on the outside of the ship with Pool by her side. The Major and his retinue were on her heals and her own retinue brought up the rear. Service personnel were coming the other way in a steady stream, all looking as if they were being pulled from both ends. There was probably a growing logjam coming up as well, all being slowed by Kim's labored progress.

Kim had a slight reprieve after passing through the airlock and into the ship. She got to walk almost thirty meters on flat ground, following a line of rough red arrows spray-painted on the floor. But the arrows led to more stairs and she had to climb another eleven floors.

"Are the lifts that unreliable that they need these stairs?" someone asked from close behind. Kim didn't turn to see who it was and she didn't answer.

After finally climbing the spiral stairs to the bridge, Kim sat down on the next set of stairs leading up to the communications seat. She looked around while she tried to catch her breath.

The first thing she noticed was that the room wasn't all that much larger than her own bridge. Other than that, there was one obvious difference she could spot straight away. There was a seat located behind and slightly above the pilot's chair.

Kim looked at Major Williams' growing impatience and found the energy to smile. "It'll be a while yet before you're going anywhere I think, Major."

"At the rate you're moving, yes."

"All right, then. Help me up." After a moment, Williams took her outstretched hand and pulled her to her feet.

She turned and went eight steps up to the communications level and up another three. There was a middle-aged man sitting in the pilot's seat and staring at the controls as if deciding which one to play with next. He wasn't wearing a uniform and had a clipboard by his side. There was a blank sheet on paper on the clipboard. Kim shooed him out of the seat, sat down, and looked around again.

"Stop pressing buttons, you lot. You won't get it going."

"Ma'am, we—"

"What did you ever learn about a video recorder by pressing the buttons when it was off?"

Someone said, "Well, you might learn how to turn it on."

"Okay, which smart-arse said that?" She looked around, but the smart-arse was right. "Don't let me catch you making me look like an idiot again." She got a bit of a laugh and it looked like the first bit of levity they'd had for a while. Most of the people relaxed slightly. Most stopped pressing buttons.

Kim sighed. She needed to sleep.

Again, the controls arrayed around her were pretty much what she expected. There were a few added extras but not a lot. "Who'll be driving this thing?"

The man who'd been in the seat nodded. "That would be me, ma'am, at the moment. Though I imagine I'll have others to do it for me soon enough."

"Why you?"

"Ten years on submarines. This is my first commission."

"Congratulations. I'm Kim."

"I gathered that. I'm Commander Ryan Fallons."

"Well, Ryan, what do you think of joining the air force?" That may have been why he had no uniform—an emergency posting.

He shrugged. "I'm sure there'll be a space corps or something invented within the next few days. Otherwise, two days of it in a very strange situation... Hard to say, ma'am."

"Well, it's only going to get stranger. So, here's how it goes." Kim explained the workings of the ship as best she could. The Commander made notes as she went, asking pointed questions for clarification on several occasions and sticking notes to some of the controls. She also explained the basics of the Ohoga engines. Aka'mu and Okalani had been briefed thoroughly on the subject and would act as the experts until people picked up on the idea.

Everyone else in the room silently watched proceedings.

"That's it?" Fallons examined the controls again when Kim indicated that she was finished.

"It's as much as I know. Our ship is a lot smaller and doesn't have all the controls. According to the computer it's a scout ship, I would think this is a war ship, though hopefully a small one."

"Why do you say that?"

"Why do I say I hope it's small? Or why a war ship?"

"Both."

"Well, if this is as big as we can find, then I reckon we're all dead, Commander. And I think it's a warship because Scree said there are lots of weapons chairs down below."

"So... What else do I need to know?"

"Where are the engineers? Mechanics? Whoever's supposed to fix this thing and keep it running?"

Major Williams cleared his throat. "Most are down looking at the engine."

"Which one?"

"Pardon?"

"There are two different types of 'engines'. Plus there are two clocks. Do they have an idea what they're looking at? It's easier to start on the computers. Do you know where the Engineering Bay is?"

"I believe so."

"Well, that'll be the place to start—once you get power. That will be the Engineering console over there, when you're right. There'll be another down stairs though. How about radio operators? Communications?"

"Here, ma'am."

"Right, well, that's the navigation console you're looking at, guys. Communications is there."

"Oh."

They looked embarrassed, though Kim couldn't imagine why. They couldn't hope to work out much at all without power or without thinking about who might be using the controls.

"We've got another present for you as well. While the men moved to the other controls, Kim tried to think of the names of the elves. Meledrin had spoken to them more than anyone else though and Kim was bad with names at the best of times... "The elves will show you the basics up here but you'll also have to send some engineers across to the *Hakahei* to talk to the dwarves about the ansible. Beyond that you'll all have to learn together."

Fallons was looking confused. "They'll learn together?"

"Commander," Kim said with a smile, "all of these people here, except for the big muscly ones with guns, are going to be a part of your crew."

Fallons looked at the Major, but wasn't getting any assistance. "Ma'am, I'm sorry but the United States—"

"The US has never been in a situation like this before, so there's no precedence, Commander. Elves can learn to speak any language as quickly as you learned to speak this one. They can learn to read as quickly. It's what they do. If you met an alien, just how were you going to ask them if they're friend or foe?"

"Well, if they shoot at us—"

"And the moai will be better navigators than anyone on earth. The dwarves? Well, they've already proven their usefulness. We wouldn't be inside without them, would we?"

"That was..."

"Exactly. They can tell you all about it. We only have one clock expert, though, and you can't have her, but some of the dwarves have been talking to her none stop for about two days so they know more than anyone else about the clock on this ship.

"These things are surprisingly easy to drive, Commander, but only because the right crews are available. Sort of. No offence, but I don't think a bunch of Americans... a bunch of earthlings from any country... would get very far."

"That's it then?"

"That, as you say, is it. I could give you the basics of all of the systems, but there are people here who already know a lot more than me and will know even more as soon as they are given free rein to have a look and tinker."

"Tinker?" Fallons examined the dwarves and came to the only possible conclusion. "But... they look like they just stepped out of the 19th century. What would they know about space ships?"

"Talk to the CIA and General Hilliard at Area 51. You need these people, Commander. Just keep them as consultants at the start, if you want, but I can guarantee that situation won't last long. Don't tell me you don't have the room."

"Okay then. But just because *I* agree doesn't mean the people who matter will."

"Major?"

"Miss Mclean, I really don't think—"

"Major, I brought you a skyglass—"

"Did you?"

"Yes, I did. Do you really think we'd go to all that trouble just to sabotage you by giving you a crew that'll screw things up? Just keep them on the ship and talk to them. You'll find out just how useful they are."

The Major sighed. "I can't give the orders, but my recommendation will have substantial weight."

"Good. Then try. You won't regret it." She looked at the console to see if she'd forgotten anything. "And that's it from me, I think."

Fallons looked as well. "So... I just learned how to fly an interstellar spacecraft in ten minutes? Something doesn't quite seem right there, but I can't seem to put my finger on it." With a shake of his head he examined his notes again.

"It's surprisingly easy, once you get the hang of it. You'll just have to get up there and drive around a bit. At least there's not a lot to run into."

"Except aliens."

"Yes, about that... You might want to come with the Major and I for a bit of a chat."

"Might I?"

"Yes."

"What chat is this, Miss McLean? Does it involve the skyglass?"

"As in—does it involve me giving it to you? No, it doesn't. You'll get the skyglass Major, but there are more important things to talk about now. How long would it take to get a representative of the US government here?"

"About an hour. The Secretary of Defense has been in Macchu Pichu since yesterday morning, local time."

"Then get him. And set up a secure meeting room."

"Miss McLean—"

"Have I disappointed you yet, Major?" And she cut him off before he could even start... "Except for the fact that you don't yet have a skyglass?"

"These people can learn nothing without power to the ship."

He was right too, but Kim had been expecting this argument. "Well, I can give you the skyglass now, Major, but only if the secure meeting room I was talking about is on the *Hakahei.* That means you, Commander Fallons and the Secretary of Defense come aboard unarmed."

The Major looked her up and down, as if judging what she might do if she got all of those men onto the ship.

"If I wanted you all dead I'd have let the aliens do it."

He nodded slowly. "The marines will want a representative or two in on these discussions, I imagine."

"I dare say they will, and I'm sure they'll be big and muscly and capable of handling themselves, right?"

"Most marines are."

Kim smiled. "I'll arrange for some extra seats. And while you're on board, I'll have some people see to the loading of those things you promised."

"I have some organizing to do."

"Sure. Commander, would you like to escort me out of here?"

"Of course."

Standing on the bottom step, below the communications console, Kim looked around at the crew. It was a group that looked normal to her now. She couldn't imagine working with just humans. She would see the other races in normal humans. Ping was almost oriental. Meledrin was Nordic and Keeble, South American. If they could get over their differences and recognize the similarities they'd make it work. The real question was, would it do them any good? The image of the huge alien ship gliding silently past the in other universe scared her even now.

She sighed. "Good luck, everyone."

22: Salvation

STANDING IN THE *HAKAHEI'S* AIRLOCK two hours later, Kim felt she should've been in a dress-uniform. Scree and Ping were lined up beside her as part of the welcoming committee, both looking slightly uncomfortable in their official roles.

"Scree, relax," Kim said. "None of you trolls have to be soldiers—anytime—you just have to get the job done."

"Yeah, but..." He'd found a new EVA suit—Kim wished he'd get some real clothes.

"If you want to slouch, I am sure you can do it without breaking your concentration."

He grunted, but did relax a little

Eight men were crossing the platform in front of the hangar. General Hilliard was walking beside an older man who could only be the Secretary. Then came Ryan Fallons and Major Williams. Four others, who'd obviously been brought along as protection, flanked that group. Two dozen others had stopped by the door.

The outer door of the *Hakahei* was already open and guarded by five trolls. Two were on the platform outside, one right near the door—apparently to make sure nobody climbed the cliff from below—and two more at the back of the airlock. That was Cliff and Blue Troop. Yellow Troop were upstairs with Meledrin. Green was standing by, ready to hand over the skyglass and start the loading of the supplies. They would finally have some real food.

"Miss McLean," Hilliard said when he stepped into the airlock.

"General Hilliard. How nice to see you again."

He laughed. "I'm sure. Is all this really necessary?" He motioned back to the guards.

Kim shrugged. "Don't ask me. Ask Scree. He's in charge of that kind of thing. He pretends to listen to me occasionally."

"General." Scree held out his hand to be shaken and Kim gave him a backhanded slap across the ribs. It hurt her hand and he hardly seemed to notice. She wished he'd stop being so serious.

"Scree?" He reached out and gripped his hand.

Kim broke in when she noticed the strain in the General's eyes and the silent battle going on in the handshake. Hilliard was a big man but getting on in years—he didn't stand a chance in that encounter.

"And this is Ping. Her people are called zorigami and seemed to be closely related to dwarves. She likes to fix things as well—clocks mainly."

Kim hit Scree again and he released the General's hand.

Hilliard nodded and wrung his hand. At least he didn't try to hide what he was doing. "You already know the Major and Commander, obviously, but this is Craig Hayes, the United States Secretary of Defense."

"Mr. Secretary. How are you?"

"I'm fine, thank you, Kim. And if you'd please call me Craig."

"So a politician at heart then?"

He laughed a rich warm laugh that Kim immediately liked. "Afraid so. Too long out of the army to keep all that formality going."

"Not sure if that's a good thing or a bad thing, Craig," Kim said with a smile. "A politician or a soldier? Neither is high on my list of people to hang out with at parties."

General Hilliard interrupted this time. "This is Colonel Peter Harris and Sergeant Tim McCree of the United States Marine Corp."

"Gentlemen."

"And Corporal Dwight Marsella and Private Mick Dunning of the Air Force Ravens."

"Don't I know you from somewhere, Mick?" Kim looked the huge black man up and down.

"Possibly, ma'am. I believe you knocked me unconscious when you were leaving Area 51."

"You weren't acting? Well, I wouldn't worry about it too much. I wouldn't have even hit you if I thought you were allowed to fight back."

"Miss McLean. Perhaps we should get started? I don't know why you wanted us here exactly, but every moment is bringing us closer to disaster."

"Or closer to salvation, General. Captain Jones will be given the skyglass in a couple of minutes. If you'll follow me, please."

"You aren't going to check us for weapons?"

Kim looked Colonel Harris up and down—he wasn't wearing any weapons in plain sight—and shrugged.

Kim led the way upstairs to the boardroom on Level 1. She paused before she went through the door though. "If any of you gentlemen *do* have weapons you may want to keep a tighter-than-usual hold on yourself about now. You do anything that is even a little bit threatening and you'll get hurt." She opened the door and went in.

Inside, there was a small console with controls near the door, one long, fixed table and a dozen fixed chairs. Meledrin and Captain Thorpe sat in two of the chairs. Meenu and Cuto, more comfortable on their feet, were standing at the end of the table. Five trolls stood around the outside.

The first Americans through the door—Dunning and Craig Hayes—froze and stared. They were nudged aside by those coming along behind who also stopped to stare.

The Secretary of Defense was the first to recover. Kim was impressed. After just a moment of gaping, he strode forward until he was a meter from the aliens. Then he seemed at a loss. His normal response would have been to shake hands or bow, but without knowing the customs of those he was meeting...

In the end he bowed slightly and introduced himself. "Hello," he said. "Greetings. My name is Craig Hayes. It is an honor."

He watched the alien, waiting for a response, but turned quickly to Meledrin as she translated. He was looking at the alien again when it started to talk and did not look away again for the rest of the conversation.

"Aunt Meenu, of the T'loop family, returns greetings." Meledrin said, translating the alien's words exactly.

"You could have warned us," General Hilliard muttered to Kim.

"I could've, but you might not have come. Or you might have insisted on bringing more weapons than you did. I had to get you here."

"What the hell's going on?"

"You'll find out." Kim turned back to the other conversation, which was still going. For a moment she wondered what they could be talking about. How do you go about making small talk with an alien? But Hayes and Meenu were exchanging ranks and serial numbers, or something similar, with Meledrin translating a couple of words in arrears.

"The aliens don't think we're going to *surrender*, do they?"

"No, General."

"Are *they* going to surrender?"

"You wish. No. The T'loop, one of the Great Families, are offering an allegiance. But that's probably not quite as good as it sounds at this stage, because in about six hours, give or take, the T'loop are going to be in a lot of trouble."

"Why?"

"Come on, let's sit down."

Craig took the hint and left off with the chitchat. Meledrin went around the table doing introductions.

"Mr. Hayes," she said when she was done and had spent a moment listening to the alien. "Meenu wishes to know if the information given by Kim is correct. Do the hakans—that's us—know nothing of the war that was started 500 sun cycles ago?"

"That is about 50000 of our years, Sir," Kim said. "Back when the ship crashed as Roswell."

"Ummm..." Hayes laid his hands on the table and gave the question some thought. Kim liked him even more—he took time to answer what appeared to be a simple question. "I can't speak for the other hakan worlds, but our world, Earth, knows nothing."

Hayes continued. "Our oldest recorded history does not reach back that far. We were surprised and terrified when the hurgon attacked our world."

"Can Mister Hayes prove any of this?" Meledrin translated.

"No, I can't. But even if we did know of that long-ago-war, now is what matters, and we do not want the war to start again."

"It is too late. It has already restarted."

"Yes, I know. But... It can get worse yet."

Kim gave a quiet bark of laughter. Yes, it could get worse, because a couple of minutes earlier, Stone had given the skyglass to an American somewhere and the battle ship in the hangar was probably coming to life as they spoke.

Hayes continued. "And Kim has said that there is an enemy worse than any we have ever faced. Is this true?"

The man could not know much about the multeese. Kim had given a hurried warning when she'd first fled Nexis, but that was all. Perhaps Major Williams had somebody watch the battle overhead. Either way, Hayes was probably just trying to demonstrate that humans and hurgon had something in common.

Meenu remained silent for a long time. *"Yes, it is true. The kil'ini of one Great Family were completely destroyed. Hurgon thought it was a hakan construct."*

Hayes shook his head. "We have barely a dozen craft that can fly in space. None are as large as the one we are in now."

"So you cannot help the hurgon against it?"

Hayes shrugged. "There are more craft in the hangar here, but we have no skill in their use, and are only able to use one anyway."

"Then what is the use?"

"We will help where we can, Aunt Meenu," Hayes said. "We will do what we must. That is the nature of friendship. It is the beginning of trust."

Hilliard cleared his throat. "Let's get to the point, Sir. Can Auntie Meenu stop the attacks against Earth?"

Meenu looked at the General, an unreadable expression on its face, then turned to Meledrin for a translation. Meledrin looked at Kim.

"Do it. We don't want them to think we're hiding anything."

Meledrin nodded and asked the General's question though she already knew the answer.

"Meenu cannot stop the battles in the short term. Control is only over 16 Kil'ini of the 2019 Kil'ini in the flock. And before one rotation of this planet is completed, the T'loop Family will be called outlaw."

"What? This conference isn't sanctioned by the hurgon government?" Hayes turned to look at Kim. "Miss McLean, did you get us into a conference with a rebel faction before seeing if the proper authorities are willing to talk?"

Kim nodded slowly. She could see how that might look bad. She smiled slightly. "Come on, sir, you've seen all the movies—the rebels are always the good guys."

The Secretary of Defense didn't appreciate the joke. "How can we really know who's who here? How can they prove it to us?"

"Okay, look, maybe you're right, but you have no idea what we had to go through to set this up. There's no way the others are going to talk to us—the only reason these ones are talking is because Cuto, the alien you had imprisoned, is one of them. We had to start somewhere."

Meledrin translated all of that for the aliens, apparently taking Kim's order to the extreme.

"Meenu states that the T'loop family will do what they must," Meledrin said.

"Shit. All right then. Let's hear the story."

"The Fen'dai are the family that have held the hurgon together since hakans and hurgon last met. Fen'dai are amongst every family, watching each contract as it is sealed, ensuring they are not broken. But the Fen'dai have something to gain with each contract. They have power and knowledge that they share with another family in exchange for wealth. Together the Fen'dai and G'nayli have grown rich. That was before. At this time, when hurgon should be spreading to new worlds and growing great with knowledge and peace, Fen'dai are the glue that hold the hurgon back."

Hayes sat back in his chair and drummed his finger on the table. "So, these Fen'dai are supposed to be inside each family to keep the peace and make sure everything runs smoothly? But they're really just spies?"

"Mister Hayes has spoken correctly."

"And what's going to happen in a day that's going to cause so much trouble?"

"The Fen'dai officers on the T'loop ship in this vicinity will fail to report in."

"They're dead?"

"Incorrect. The Fen'dai officers are detained."

"Christ. So this rebellion is already unstoppable?"

"Yes. The Fen'dai know that hakans were on a kil'ini. The true nature of events will be deduced."

Hayes sighed. "Well, it looks like we've thrown our lot in with the T'loop family for now. In the future, Miss McLean, I'd appreciate it if you would consult somebody first when you make decisions that effect the entire human race."

That annoyed Kim. She stared at Hayes coldly—a look General Hilliard probably recognized. "And tell me this, *Sir*, if I'd asked you, what would you have done? If I'd asked the President, what would he have done? I have just as much right to make that decision as he does, and I can't imagine he'd have gone to the UN for advice first." But perhaps, when she had made the decision, she'd not really made a decision at all. What choices did she have at the time? That annoyed her even more. "If it wasn't for me Hilliard would be torturing Tuki right now to get information about the skyglass—and getting absolutely nowhere."

Colonel Harris cleared his throat. He wasn't an administrator so had taken no part in proceedings so far but obviously considered the first part of the conversation over. Teams had been picked, even if nobody was happy with them. The time of the kick-off had been decided. What happened on the field was his domain. "So what happens when the Fen'dai don't make their reports at the end of the day?" he asked.

"The Fen'dai will ask the T'loop what has happened."

"And if they don't like the answers?"

"The Fen'dai have a flock of their own. Kil'ini will be sent to investigate. The T'loop Family will be outlawed."

"And what happens then?"

Meenu sat silently for a long time. *"Meenu does not know. Other outlawed families have been hunted and exterminated, but a Great Family has never been in that position before. Some Families will align with the Fen'dai because the current system has seen them prosper. Most will stand well clear. Some will see this as an opportunity to break free."*

Harris shook his head. "In other words we don't know shit."

"Best things to do first" Scree said, "is warn as many friendlies as possible. Does Meenu know of any other families that the T'loop can trust?"

"There are four Great Families and seven Minor Families allied closely with the T'loop. They can be trusted."

"Well thens, they has to be warned as soon as possible."

"It may already be too late for all of this. Three Families patrol the space around this world. Two are friends and must have seen this ship coming down to the planet. The third family is unknown. The Kan'ota kil'ini were on the far side of the world so secrecy may have been maintained, but Lisa'lee'la cannot know."

Scree shrugged. "Then why don't the T'loop take their friends and go to find out?"

There was a slight pause after Meledrin translated for the hurgon. Aunt Meenu looked from face to face, then she spoke.

"The T'loop will send a message to all allies to meet at, Atlantis, the world you call Earth. That world is more heavily populated and in the greatest danger. The T'loop will end the fighting there, and speak more fully about a course of action against the Fen'dai."

Kim nodded and smiled. "Cool."

Meenu spoke again. *"Kim, if you permit, Lisa'lee'la will carry your construct as it was carried previously. This will be safer—as it will avoid confusion—and much quicker."*

"Ummm... No, I think we'll just fly ourselves, thanks. We'll have everything running better than ever soon."

"There are many kil'ini and many families unknown to Kim. Meenu would prefer Kim was kept safe until negotiations are concluded. And Meenu would like to start the talks with the hakan leaders as soon as possible. That cannot be started without the assistance of Meledrin or Penisari and Lisa'lee'la will arrive long before the Hakahei."

"Oh, yeah. Right. Ummm... Of course, then. Let's get this all over with as soon as possible."

The meeting broke up quickly after that. The aliens were led from the room and their escort of cousins brought from one of the offices. The trolls herded them all downstairs.

General Hilliard stood in the hall outside the meeting room and watched them go. "Will you allow us to put men on your ship, Miss McLean?"

"Why?"

"To have a look at the kil'ini, if nothing else. But also to get a feel for..." He waved vaguely at the sky.

"For the ways of the universe?"

"Something like that yes."

Kim smiled. "Sure. You can put your political officers on our ship."

"Don't start that again."

"Maximum of four. We're leaving as soon as we can." Nobody argued with her. She would've argued with the General for the fun of it. He probably would've been disappointed if she hadn't. It worried her that they were taking her so seriously though, as if she knew what she was doing.

23: A Special Word

TUKI, STANDING NEAR THE AIRLOCK, watched through the long window as five Americans crossed the platform towards the ship. He was surprised to realize that he knew most of them. Sergeant Tim Mcree and Mick Dunning had come onto the ship earlier with the Secretary of Defense. Airman Ben Dongoske—the first Earthling Tuki had ever spoken to—was also there. The three of them, plus a woman, had bags slung over their shoulders. The other was Major Williams, obviously coming to see them off. Outside, Chip and Crystal, guarding the end of the gangplank, stopped the Americans from boarding the ship.

One of the soldiers looked Chip up and down, as if wondering if he could force his way past. "I'm Sergeant Tim McCree." The man saluted but looked as if he knew the trolls wouldn't be impressed. "Your Captain has given us permission to come aboard."

Chip shrugged and scratched at his eyebrow with a crooked thumb. "Maybe. But she say not yet."

"What's going on here?" Major Williams said. "It's been agreed—"

Kim came out of an elevator and Tuki straightened, as if she would complain that he was slouching or eavesdropping on the conversation.

"Hey, Tuki," she said as she strode past and went into the airlock.

Tuki shuffled his feet. He was so close to the airlock he might as well have gone in there, but he stayed where he was.

"Miss McLean, what's going on?" Major Williams asked.

"Major, the men..." Kim raised her eyebrows and looked at the group... "and woman, will be allowed on in a moment, but first I want to make sure some things are clear."

The Major sighed. "What things?"

Tuki smiled slightly. It was obvious Major Williams expected Kim to list some terrible conditions.

"This may not be a military vessel, but we still need to have rules—and we need to know those rules will be obeyed. So, these personnel will have to agree to abide by my commands, no matter what."

"Miss McLean, we can't—"

"Then *I* can't, Major. For Christ's sake, would you just let anyone wonder around one of your bases? I'm not going to ask them to commit treason or anything like that. I just need everyone to know where they stand."

Tim Mcree spoke up again. "Ma'am, I can't allow myself to be put under the command of—"

"Think of it this way, Sergeant. If I *were* to let you onto this ship without us all knowing exactly what your position on it is—which I wouldn't—then when the time came for things to be done, you'd be locked away in your cabin for your own safety. That's what happens to visitors. You'd sit and cool your heels, and we'd come and tell you all about it later. Maybe. Of course, we'd be under no obligation to tell you anything at all."

It was obvious to Tuki that Tim McCree didn't like the sound of that. None of the American's did.

Airman Dongoske cleared his throat. "And where would we stand, otherwise?"

Kim had a smile for him. "How's your head?" She had hit him on the head when they were escaping from Area 51.

"Fine, thank you."

"Good. The four of you would be forming a fourth Marine troop on board. Captain Thorpe and Paul Manning of the British SAS have chosen to stay with us. Captain Thorpe will be in charge of the new troop. You, Sergeant McCree, will be his 2IC. All of you will answer to Scree and myself, without question, though I'm not prone to giving orders of a military nature when there are lots of people around with more experience. And while they probably won't give you orders either, you'll all listen carefully and respectfully to anything said by Ping, Keeble, Meledrin and Tuki, who are officers on this ship."

Tuki almost choked. He was an officer? After leaving Kiva, Kim had told him he was Lieutenant but he had not really known what that was. Who would listen to him anyway?

"Of course, I don't expect it to make any difference—we're only going to Earth—but still."

"And if we don't agree to this?"

"Then wait for the next ride. Major, you'll give the order, though I don't know how much that'll mean to the Marines. Then each of you will give me your word, which will hopefully mean a lot." Kim smiled some more. "You'll be treated the same as everyone else on board. There are ditches to dig in here, but the elves are looking forward to doing that themselves and the dwarves love to work in any situation. Ping and the dwives have volunteered for kitchen patrol. Dwarves will be cleaning. It seems when we were engineered, everything was considered."

Major Williams looked to his countrymen and they all nodded, one by one. "Very well. I am placing you all under the command of Kim McLean. A posting that will end only when ordered by a ranking officer from any of the US Armed services."

They all gave their word.

"Thank you, everyone. Welcome aboard."

Tim McCree came on board first. The sergeant was a short, solid man with a flat face and flat haircut. "This is Private Amy Mcree, my sister," he said as the others followed him into the airlock. She was taller and had her hair cut a little longer. She did not look any less capable. "And I believe you already know Airman Dongoske and Brick Dunning."

"We have met, though that's the first time I've heard that name 'Brick' used. And you, Sergeant, can we call you Tim?"

"Of course, Ma'am."

"Good. And I'm Kim. And the big guy skulking around the corner there is Tuki."

Tuki blushed as they all came closer.

Kim smiled. "Don't be fooled by his size, he's the sweetest person on board."

Tim held out his hand and Tuki stared at it for a second before thinking to shake it like the humans liked to do. The man's hand was small in his own, but strong and firm. "Pleased to meet you, Tuki." His smile was friendly, showing a long row of slightly crooked teeth.

"Thank you."

Amy and Brick shook his hand as well, but Airman Dongoske hung back, waiting until the others had moved on.

"Hello, Tuki."

"Hello, Airman."

"Call me Ben."

Tuki nodded, but said nothing. What was there to say?

"I wanted to apologize for what happened before. Back at the base. I wanted the General to keep his word. I asked him to, but..."

Tuki nodded again. "I do not think that what you did was good, Airman... Ben... but I think I understand. You had to do what the General told you to do."

"Yes, but—"

"And the General?" Tuki looked at his hands. "The General had to make hard decisions in strange circumstances."

Dongoske smiled and nodded. "Thank you, Tuki. I just wish Kim understood as well."

"Kim does understand, Ben." Tuki didn't think there were too many things Kim didn't understand. "Leading is about closing your eyes and jumping because someone has to go first. It is about sending your friends to die." Tuki thought of the card games Kim had taught him. "It is about playing poker when there is nobody to tell you the rules."

"Yes, I suppose it is."

"So, you volunteered to come on our ship so you could apologize?"

The Airman laughed. "I've been working on the apology for a while. I insisted that General Hilliard start making sure everyone involved in the operation knew how to speak Shoshone. I set up the classes and suggested they bring in some people from the other services, just in case. It's just that this opportunity to apologize directly came up and I thought I'd take it." He started to follow where his companions had gone, though they were long gone and could be anywhere. "I volunteered for this mission for a chance to go into space. How could I not? Huh. I think just about everyone in the armed services volunteered, but the fact that I've been speaking this language all my life got me over the line."

In the halls and the mess, good-byes were being said. Refugees had their meager belongings in hand and were getting ready to disembark. Trolls were stationed to make sure those who were supposed to leave did so. Some, especially amongst the dwarves, wanted to stay where they were.

Keeble and Ping had been allowed to select 16 refugees to work in engineering and clock maintenance—a large portion of them had to be dwives, despite Keeble's grumbling. And Meledrin chose four elves: her husband Palsamon, Suldon, Bethalin, Penisari and Tamidilin, to work with her in the gardens and in communications.

Seeing Okalani and Aka'mu had been assigned to the American vessel Tuki and Inaki were the only two moai left on the Hakahei. Tuki had been told to pick two people for the navigation department as well. He had not known who to choose and stood dumbly for several minutes, looking from face to face in the common room. Finally Palsamon stated that he would like the job. Meledrin had protested but in the end chose Bethalin to take his place in her own group. Then a young elf woman named Lisarea volunteered as well. They would not be able to use the skyglass directly, but once it was plugged in the console controls gave full access.

Looking at the refugees, Tuki realized he was in charge of the three other members of the navigation department whose members included a married man much older than himself and a woman. He swallowed and wondered what he could do to stop being a Lieutenant.

Including sixteen trolls and seven humans, that made a total of fifty people living on the ship with a total of 36 bedrooms. Most rooms had between two and four beds but some also had one bed large enough for two people. Tuki wondered who would volunteer to share.

That meant they had only—Tuki added in his head—59 percent of a total crew. Kim wanted no more.

In the hallway, dwarvish refugees lined the wall. They grumbled that if they were to be kicked off would they be done with it already. Elves stood quietly, seemingly unperturbed.

Ruby was the nearest of the troll guards. Tuki turned to her, no longer blushing at the way her breasts pushed at the EVA suit and almost poked out through the unzipped gap at the front. She smiled at him and shifted slightly so her breasts moved beneath her clothes. Tuki did blush then and quickly averted his eyes. Her smile grew.

"Why is everyone still here?" Tuki asked her, examining his hands.

"Americans reckon they aren't ready yet. That lot couldn't organize a BBQ in a farmyard."

"We like everything to be organized," Ben replied. "We have to sort out medicals and a lot of stuff that you don't understand."

"That other lot, the crew, went out before."

"But we didn't—"

Tuki interrupted before an argument could develop. "Ruby, do you know where Kim went with the humans?" He wondered if he was not really an officer after all, keeping things under control.

Ruby shrugged. "To the stairs. After that..." She shrugged again. "Let me check."

She went blank for a moment—a look that Tuki knew meant she was adjusting the radio in her head.

Dongoske was looking the troll up and down. "What's she checking?"

"She is asking the others where Kim went."

"Ummm... Which others?"

"The trolls."

"Right." He cleared his throat. "And how's she doing that, exactly?"

Tuki had not been with the trolls for very long at all, but they had been through so much in that time that all the quirks were commonplace already. "They have a radio in their head. They can talk to each other and constructed radios."

"Bullshit? You're kidding me, right?"

"No."

"Tuki, Scree says they went up to Level 2 to talk to Thorpe and get some rooms organized."

"Thank you, Ruby."

The troll smiled a crooked smile in reply.

Tuki led the way to the stairs, as Dongoske looked back over his shoulder. "Quite a young woman there."

Stone, coming down the stairs, grunted. "Too much woman for you, I reckon, skinny. You might want to look at an elf."

Tuki heard Dongoske snap his mouth shut, as if biting back a reply. The Airman was not skinny compared to most humans at all, being squat and solid, but compared to a troll... Tuki kept going, stopping any reply that his companion might eventually have made.

Kim stood with the other humans in the open space upstairs. Along with Scree, they were watching as people chose rooms.

There were sixteen beds in four rooms near the engineering bay, so everyone knew where the dwarves would be sleeping. Being communal people, they were happy to have friends living with them. Elves were the opposite, preferring to spend time alone if possible. Though they did not appear to rush, they moved quickly to the rooms with only two beds. The trolls did not seem to care one way or the other, perhaps realizing the room would be used for sleeping and not a lot more. Or perhaps they intended to change rooms every night, sharing with this troll one night and that troll the next. Tuki had heard from others how they never settled for long in one spot.

Seeing there was not a full crew, some people might have gotten rooms on their own. Lots of people merely went to the rooms they had already been using.

"You lot had better get to it," Kim was saying, though the humans stayed where they were. "Hey, Tuki. Ben."

The Americans, including Ben, finally moved out to find rooms. Tuki stayed where he was, listening as Kim talked with Scree.

"How's the loading going?"

"Almost done. Still don't see why we needs a garden though. Could do lots with that space."

Kim sighed as if they had been through this before. "There are lots of reasons, Scree, but just keep this one in mind—the elves will probably spend most of their spare time in the gardens. It'll keep them out of your hair." With a laugh, she reached up and rubbed at his bald scalp.

"I should thumps you for that," Scree said, but he was smiling as well.

"Yeah? You wouldn't have the guts."

Tuki gasped as Scree, lightning quick, slapped Kim across the buttocks.

Kim gaped for a moment. "Oh boy, are you asking for it." She tried to hit him, a full-blooded blow that would have knocked Tuki off his feet. Scree knocked her fist aside and suddenly they were fighting.

To Tuki, it appeared deadly serious. They were concentrating fiercely and moving almost quicker than he could follow but when the trolls of Blue Troop came running they cheered and urged the combatants on. They were not at all worried. Even the humans, when they quickly returned, smiled and viewed it all with nothing more than professional interest.

Tuki moved quickly away, wondering if he would ever understand the other races.

Tuki had already chosen his room. It was one of the larger ones on the northwest side of the ship, with a wide bed and more room to move. It was almost as large as the house of the mo'min back in Danyon Ford and much larger than he thought he would ever need. He reached out his arms and turned a full circle without touching the walls. Kim had insisted he take it and for a while he had wondered if he was meant to share with someone. But everyone else had been told that the large rooms were already taken and they should choose elsewhere.

"This your room, Tuki-boy?"

Tuki spun again and saw Ruby leaning against the doorframe. Her EVA suit was still partially unzipped. She still smiled. Tuki nodded in reply.

"It's big," she said, echoing his thoughts. "I reckon the room I'm sharing with Crystal and Sandy is plenty big enough though. Kim says we have to keep our own rooms clean."

"Yes. I'm used to sharing a bunk-room with a dozen other go'gan." It was not until he had left his home that he realized things might be otherwise.

"What's a go'gan?"

"An unmarried male."

"You got a special word for that?" She entered the room—sauntering around a full, slow lap—before coming to stop. She was not far from Tuki. Then she took a step closer. She was so close that Tuki thought of Keala and the few times they had kissed. He looked down at his hands. Ruby, as if guessing what he was thinking and suddenly becoming as embarrassed as he, quickly stepped away. She sat on one of the room's two chairs and leaned back to put her feet on the other. "This is nice though. Could get used to it."

"It will feel strange, I think. But Kim said I must."

"She's right. You're one of the leaders and people have got to be reminded of that."

There it was again, talk of Tuki being a leader when he was just a go'gan. "People don't listen to me."

"Yes they does. Or they will, if you says something. You is really quiet, not like any of the trolls I'm used to."

"Yes, but if they listen will they do what I say?"

"You don't have to give orders. Who you going to order anyway, when Kim and Scree do enough ordering for everyone. All you got to do is tell people what you think, tell them the way it is. At first anyway. And when they start seeing that you got the right ideas, they'll start listening. Giving orders ain't far from there. What if..."

Tuki looked up at her as she trailed away to silence. She was watching him, but looked away.

"What?"

"Well, if you want to talk to somebody, let me know and I'll come here and sit in your comfy chairs," she smiled, "and you can tell me your ideas, and I'll tell you what I think."

"Why would you want to do that?"

She shrugged, but then spoke. "Maybe I want to hear your ideas. Maybe I just want to talk to someone other than the same old trolls all the time."

"What about Ping and Ari, you used to talk to them all the time."

"Well, look, if you don't want to talk, just say so." She rose quickly to her feet and went straight out the door.

Tuki thought to call her back, but the words died in his throat. What would he say?

24: Working

KEEBLE CHECKED HIS READOUTS, moving from screen to screen.

"What are you smiling at, Keeble?" Kim asked.

"There are only ten faults left on the ship."

Kim sighed. "I heard you the last five times you told me."

"Don't blame me. You asked."

That just seemed to annoy her more.

"What's your problem? The engineering department did well and I'm happy about it."

She shrugged. "It's not that. I just... Something."

"This is not the opportune time for concern," Meledrin said, looking up from her own controls. "Aunt Meenu and Lisa'lee'la are awaiting our arrival."

"Yeah, yeah. I know." Kim glanced at Cuto and Keeble turned to look as well.

The alien had helped with the repairs as much as any of the dwarves, seeming to throw himself into the work like never before. He was tireless and as strong as any of the trolls. He didn't talk very much though. Normally Keeble would have found that distracting but he had worked with the alien for a while now, right from when they first entered the ship, and was getting used to his strange ways.

"Come on then," Kim said. "Let's do this. Keeble?"

One last check. "Good to go."

"Mel?"

The elf looked up at her." Yes?"

"Anything I should know?"

"I have heard nothing to suggest we cannot or should not take flight at this time."

"Thanks. Tuki?"

Scree cut in. "Just fly the damn ship. Someone'll shout if there's a problem."

"Scree there's certain things—"

"There's certain things you does when you's stalling. Either fly the damn ship or tell us we's staying here."

Keeble smiled as Kim glared at the troll.

"We flyin' or what?"

Kim's top lip twitched as she reached for her controls. She hit the button for the microphone. "Prepare for lift-off," she said without looking away. "We're about to take off." She released the button, spun the steering ball, then sat back. "We ready?" And she pushed the thrust lever to send the ship shooting into the air.

Keeble grunted , waiting for the ship to adjust the gravity. "Was that necessary?" Nobody answered.

It was only a few minutes before they were in space. The Kim spent a few more minutes bringing them to a complete halt. Meledrin got co-ordinates over the radio and Tuki found the right kil'ini amongst all the others.

"Are you sure?" Kim asked.

Tuki nodded but Kim turned to look at Cuto anyway and waved her arms in the ini rituals. And the alien confirmed what Tuki had said. So Kim spun the steering ball and got the ship moving again. As they approached the kil'ini the creature spun to face them and opened its mouth. Cuto waved his arms about some more and Meledrin quickly translated. A moment later Kim did as instructed and brought the ship to a halt.

They waited while the kil'ini reached out for them with a long, rough tentacle.

"Not sure I'll ever get used to being eaten," Keeble said. But then it was done and it wasn't really all that bad at all. "So, I'm guessing we wait now?"

Kim node. "I imagine Meenu will send someone to talk with us."

"Well, there are still some repairs to do. I'm not going to sit here—it might take the hurgon a week to get here." It took a while just for the chamber to be filled with air.

Keeble slipped out of his seat and headed for the lift. He wasn't in a hurry. This was one of the times he liked best. If all the jobs were done he'd get bored. If there were too many to do if felt as if you would never end.

There were already a lot of dwarves in the engineering bay. The all stood there, looking slightly uncomfortable, as they waited for someone to tell them what to do. Keeble sat in the chair at the main computer and smiled. No so long ago he'd been a Wanderer and now he was in charge.

"Well, don't just sit there," Dogar said. "Let's get working."

Keeble nodded and checked the list of required repairs. There probably wouldn't be enough for everyone, but after 50 thousand years every part of the ship would need stripping down and cleaning if nothing else. The first thing he needed to work out was which job he wanted. Nothing on the list was all that exciting, but he remembered the half dismantled vehicles in the workshop.

So he started delegating tasks. He was halfway through before he remembered the dwives. He had to give them the simple tasks, like fixing the jammed door in the hold. Either that or pair them with someone else. All the dwarves had agreed to treat the dwives with respect and treat them as equals. But he knew, at this stage, there were some who would treat them more equally than others. He sighed and started again.

None of them could read more than a few words yet so if they had any problems the manuals were useless to them. "None of this stuff is urgent, so if you have any problems ask someone else for help." Some nodded, some grumbled, but they all set about completing their tasks. Keeble started to make notes about who was doing what—they could complete the paperwork later—and when he looked up, discovered that only Ari remained.

"What would you like me to do, Keeble?" She looked at her boots.

Keeble cleared his throat. "I was going to have a look at one of the vehicles in the workshop."

"Right. Do we want to look at some manuals?"

He shook his head. "Let's just go have a look first."

Hoodek and Dosa were already in the workshop looking for something-or-other but Keeble ignored them and went to the vehicle. He was pretty sure the first one was used for defense—or attacking, perhaps, if the trolls were involved—and the other looked like it might be used for collecting hydrogen from space. He wasn't sure of either one, but figured he'd find out in the next few hours.

"Let's start with this one," he said, pointing to the fuel gatherer. It was probably more important. He did a lap trying to take it all in at once. Then went and had a look in the troll sized cockpit. Then he stood back to look at it all again. And he didn't really know all that much more than when he'd started. So he went around to the back to have a look at the parts that had been removed and into the hole they'd been removed from. They were definitely going to need a manual.

"Perhaps it's already been fixed," Ari said. "Maybe they just hadn't gotten around to putting it back together.

Keeble nodded. "That's doesn't really help us though." He would have to assume it wasn't fixed. It wouldn't take that long to put it back together so why would the previous repairers—most likely dwarves—not just do it? "We'll need a basic tool kit and one of those electronic testing kits."

He wasn't sure that they were electronics—the colored boards didn't look much like the electronics the humans used—but he still thought of them that way. "We'll have to work out how to fix them soon." There were replacement parts galore in storerooms and in the hold but that didn't mean they would last forever. "Come on."

Cuto was in the engineering bay, looking a bit lost. *"Have you come to help again, Cuto?"*

"Yes."

Keeble tried to think of who was doing what. *"Keeble is unsure if anyone really needs help..."* He pulled at his beard and glanced across at Ari for a moment. He sighed. *"Perhaps you can just help Ari and Keeble."*

Cuto looked at Ari for a moment too. *"Are there any tasks Cuto could complete unassisted?"*

"All the jobs are gone, really." Keeble said. But he remembered what Meledrin had said about the hurgon working alone. *"Maybe I can find something."* After a while he asked Cuto if he would be happy to just do some cleaning and tidying.

When Keeble and Ari went past the hangar a few minutes later the alien was already working through a pile of crates in a corner to see what he could see.

Back in the workshop Keeble sat down with the parts in front of him and started to read the manual. The main problem was, he didn't even know if they'd found the part that was causing the problem. "I think we'll just have to start by checking these bits on the floor." So Ari got the testing equipment and started touching the probes to the nodes.

Keeble sat back for a moment to watch. "My father didn't like you very much," Keeble said after a minute of sitting. Ari looked up and he realized that it might not have sounded very nice. He cleared his throat. "Well, it wasn't about liking. He didn't approve."

Ari had finished on the first circuit board and Keeble set it to one side.

"I didn't know that," Air replied.

"How would you?" When any visitors came to the bunker Ari had been treated as not much more than a piece of furniture. A piece of furniture that could cook.

"What did I do wrong?"

Keeble shrugged. "You didn't really do anything wrong. But I talked about you, and the things you said. The ideas you had." He shrugged again. "Everyone knew how smart you were. They thought you didn't respect me. And they thought I was too lenient on you, letting you do and say the things you did, even if it was only at home."

"I didn't know I wasn't allowed to be smart."

"You weren't allowed to be anything, Ari."

Ari handed him the second part and they sat in silence while she worked on the next.

"Why do dwarves ask dwives to move out of the maiden bunker?"

"Because we..."

"Did you ask me because you wanted *me* to live in your bunker? Or was I just the first dwife you saw in the maiden bunker that day."

"Of course I asked you in particular."

"Then I was allowed to be *something* because something made you choose me."

"I suppose."

"But after you chose me you didn't want me to be anything?"

Keeble took the next part. "I never said that."

"Not to me. But what did you say to your father? And what do you say to people now?"

Another shrug.

Ari gave a sigh and put down the final colored board. "This one is fine too." But she looked at the testing equipment and then at the open panels on the vehicle. "It would help if we actually knew what was wrong. Maybe we need to put it back together."

"We can't put it back together. We'll just have to keep trying." Keeble got the regular tool kit and started pulling apart something that looked like it might be a pump.

It was Ari's turn to watch. "Did you know that Topper likes Ping?"

"What? No, he doesn't."

"Yes, he does. Maybe he doesn't realize it yet, but he does."

Keeble grunted. It looked to him as if Ping had found strength while in Scree's company and it wouldn't be easy for Topper. Looking at Ari, Keeble kept working on the pump.

25: Stars

TUKI STARED AT THE LOADER for a long time. It was clamped to the floor in the Level 3 airlock, ready for action. He could work out how to undo the clamps, that was easy enough, but as for the action? He had no idea.

"What ya looking at?"

Every time Tuki looked at one of the young trolls, they seemed to be slouching. Talus was the youngest of them—a couple of years younger than Tuki even—and he took the slouch to all new levels.

"The Loader."

Tuki watched as Talus turned to look at the machine as well, as if he might have missed some interesting fact about it. "Why?"

"I was wondering how to move it."

"Why?"

"Well, Kim says this hallway is a running track. And that wall on the other side of the Loader looks like a door, so if I could move it, I could run all the way around."

"Right. You could just run around through the passages."

"I thought of that. But it doesn't seem right. I would have to slow down to go around the corners and I could run into people in the halls."

"Most sensible people would get out of your way. You bloody big."

"Yes but..." It didn't seem right.

"I could move it for ya."

"You could?"

"Sure. You the boss."

With that, the troll moved forward and worked at the clamps. After that he sat in the seat and examined the controls.

"Do you know how to drive?"

Talus nodded emphatically. "Well, kinda. I got showed a bit when we was rescuing them elves, but..."

Tuki would have been frozen by such lack of knowledge, but Talus shrugged and hit a button. The Loader rose off the floor. When the troll did something else he seemed slightly surprised by the result but recovered quickly. "You open the door and I'll park in the hall round the corner."

"Pardon?"

"Open the door."

Tuki found a button by the lockers on the back wall and pressed it. Half the door started to retract into the ceiling, the other half into the floor. Before the sections completely disappeared, Talus had the loader out of the airlock. Directly outside was the freight elevator. It led down past the hangars and garden all the way to highest of the two holds. Talus did not go down though. He turned into the branching passage and pulled up against the wall there, opposite the kitchen's storeroom.

"Huh." He climbed down from the Loader, looking at the floor. "There's clamps out here too." But he had not parked in exactly the right place, so had to climb back on and try again.

"Thank you, Talus."

"Yeah."

But the troll was concentrating so Tuki started to run.

The ship was inside the mouth of the kil'ini so there were no stars outside to look at but the action of running still cleared Tuki's mind immediately. He could imagine he was in the desert again. He noticed for the first time that the floor of the passage was soft, unlike the floor in the rest of the ship. There were marks on the outer walls, below the long, curving windows. One dot every quarter, he thought, counting the steps between marks. He found himself back at the starting point.

Talus jogged by his side for a while. "Why ya running?"

"There is nothing else to do." But that was not true. Almost everyone else had found something productive to do. Elves were teaching people to read or working in the garden. The dwarves had all been repairing things earlier but now they were doing all sorts of things. Keeble was in the kitchen trying to make coffee. Other were cleaning and tinkering. Scree was down in the cargo hold with Gulch, Shardy and Peak, cleaning up after Stone's hurried packing. The humans and the rest of the trolls were examining weapons and armor and talking about things Tuki didn't understand. Even Inaki was busy showing the two apprentice navigators the basics of the skyglass. Perhaps that should have been Tuki's job, but he wanted to run.

Talus was still by his side. "Why would ya want to run though? I reckon doing nothing's much more fun."

"I think better when I run," Tuki said, watching as he approached the next dot on the wall then passed it by.

"Fair enough. If ya want to think." They completed another lap and Talus stopped near the airlock. "Let me know when ya get there."

Tuki nodded and increased his pace. He had spoken the truth—he did think better when he ran. His thoughts swirled in the wake of his passing and then fell into place behind, moving forward with the rhythm of his steps.

His first thought as he ran, was that trolls were not shy. No troll was shy, ever, as far as he could tell. With no fear or ego, as appeared to be the case, how could they be?

"So if Ruby was not being shy, what caused her to rush away after getting so close?" Tuki wondered aloud.

"Ruby? Shy?" Talus laughed.

Tuki had completed another lap without realizing. Talus had found something to drink and was sitting with Bones beside the clamped Loader.

"That's three laps, Tuki. You set a record that everyone else can try to beat."

Tuki kept on running, around the curve of the ship, past the dots on the wall, one by one. He wondered how high the troll could actually count.

Talus was right though, it was laughable to think Ruby was shy. But what else could it be? He did another three laps before giving up on that line of thinking. Next was something equally as strange—the idea of himself as a leader.

-oOo-

"What are you doing, Tuki?" Kim asked. Meledrin was standing by her side.

"I am running, Kim." Tuki smiled as he went past. Bones and Talus had moved on long ago.

"Yes, I see that. Well, how about you stop?" She had to shout around the bend as Tuki continued to move.

"All right." But he would do one more lap. He had been counting in base eight, so that one extra lap would complete his fourth full set.

When he reached the airlock again, Kim was waiting with her hands on her hips. "You can keep going if you like, but I thought you might like to come and see a bit of the kil'ini."

Tuki looked up the hall, as if there might be something just out of sight around the bend that could snag his interest. Then he looked out the window at the grey green flesh of the kil'ini, as if there might be something out *there* that could snag his interest. "If you wish."

"Up to you, buddy."

"I will come."

"Good, come on then."

First came the problem of weightlessness. Tuki had watched people, trolls and dwarves mostly, throw themselves out into the nothing of the huge kil'ini chamber as they played games or inspected various systems on the ship, but it was a different thing to do it himself. The internal door of the chamber was out of sight around the curve of the ship so Kim and Meledrin both launched themselves at a wall. Once there, they gripped knobs of flesh, realigned themselves and launched again. Neither seemed as confident as others Tuki had seen, but showed no concern.

Still, he could not do it himself for a long time. He stood looking at the point where they had disappeared behind the bulk of the ship.

"Come on, Tuki. Haven't got all day."

Who says we don't, Tuki thought in reply to the shout. *Where else were we going to go?* But he didn't say it out loud.

"Come on. It's easy."

Easy for her to say. Tuki was somebody who liked solid ground under his feet and sky overhead. *Or sky all around is acceptable as well,* he decided, having become used to the idea of travelling between worlds.

"Hey, Tuki. What you doing? Want to play chess?"

"Umm... Ruby. Hello." Tuki gripped the edge of the door, as if he might float away while he was not concentrating. As if Ruby might try to drag him away. "I cannot, thank you. I am going with Kim and Meledrin."

The trollop looked around. "Where is they?"

Tuki pointed vaguely, though he knew the exact direction of the puckered door where they waited.

"You scared to jump?"

"No."

"Don't let me hold you up then. Kim's likely to go on without you."

Tuki turned to look out the door again. He could feel Ruby watching him.

"Just go nice and smooth, Tuki. You'll be right."

Tuki closed his eyes and stepped out into the nothing. He pushed off slightly and felt himself float. When he opened his eyes and saw that he was moving lazily towards the wall. He realized almost immediately that he would not make it. Like the space ship in the other universe, he would float in perfect stillness for all time. Kim and Meledrin were watching. Would they come to his rescue?

But they were not needed. Ruby had seen his plight and followed him out. His smile at her arrival was short lived. She came right up near him and stopped. They were face to face, and Tuki felt sure that the full length of her body was touching him. For one heart beat, two, she stayed where she was and Tuki could taste her breath, then she gently pushed away with a hand on his chest.

"Now we are both stuck," he said.

She smiled as if that was the whole idea but said, "No, we aren't." Twisting about slowly, the trollop put both her feet in the center of Tuki's chest and smiled some more. "Ready?"

Tuki nodded. *Ready for what?*

But before the thought had fully formed Ruby 'jumped'. She leapt off Tuki's chest and the force of the action shifted them both. Tuki moved towards the wall, Ruby towards the ship. She smiled as she somersaulted through the air. "Will I see you when you get back?"

"Of course." But he did not know if that was exactly what she meant. "Thank you, Ruby."

"You're welcome."

Once he reached the wall, Tuki took a moment to get his bearings again, then, with a deep breath, launched himself towards Kim and Meledrin. Overcompensating for his last effort, he pushed too hard.

He knew that straight away, as he had known his problem earlier. Kim knew as well. Tuki watched as she shook her head and come out to meet him. They met in mid air and Kim grabbed at his arm. Her force and weight slowed him considerably, but hardly enough. Kim grunted when they hit the wall.

"I am sorry, Kim."

"No. That's fine." Her eyes were watering. Her voice came out as a breathless croak. "Takes a bit of getting used to."

"That's not..."

"Come on, let's keep going." Kim motioned to a hurgon escort to lead the way. No translation was needed.

The rest of the journey was not too bad. They moved through passages that meant a wall was always within reach and no forceful maneuvers were required but Tuki was sure that, because of his clumsiness, the journey took longer than it should have. He had wondered what there would be to look at inside the kil'ini, but the wonders were never ending. There were hurgon, if nothing else. They wore clothes as bright as their armor and moved with distracted precision. They all seemed to be reading something, or talking to someone, or thinking of something vitally important as they moved about, but they never collided. They moved past each other as if in a dance. They only slowed when they saw Tuki and his companions, bumbling novices, ricocheting towards them. They moved aside and watched them pass without saying a word.

The halls were all different colors. Some seemed to have blood pulsing just below the surface. Some walls breathed. There were paired tentacles everywhere that the kil'ini constantly used to talk with the hurgon. And everywhere there were eyes watching him—near each pair of tentacles, in each intersection, in each small chamber, in each bend of the hall. There was not one place that could not be seen in the gaze of the shifting, purple eyes-on-stalks.

"Watch out for the gravity in this room, Tuki," Kim said when they reached their destination.

He watched her hook her toes under the edge of the floor and step across the threshold. He tried to mimic her, and almost succeeded. His knee buckled slightly with the sudden onset of weight, but he remained upright and extricated his toes so he could go in further.

The bridge of the ship was nothing like that of the *Hakahei.* There were no windows and no chairs. The only thing that might have been controls were more of the tentacles.

On what appeared to be a large piece of flat bone at one end of the room, Tuki saw a picture drawn in light. As well as stars, other kil'ini were visible in the picture and Tuki knew enough to know that, even for them, there was an up and a down. There were a dozen of the creatures and they were all orientated in the same way, top down in the image. So, unless the kil'ini he was in was travelling upside down then the image was upside down.

Tuki said nothing as he continued to look. He half listened to the conversation between Meenu and Kim, with Meledrin in the middle.

"Why has Kim come here?" the hurgon asked.

"I want to know what's going on, is all. I like to keep track."

The other hurgon in the room seemed to pause in their tasks. The ever-waving tentacles went still for a second. Then everything was back to normal and Tuki wondered if he had seen anything at all.

"There have been difficulties."

"Oh? Nothing major, I hope."

"A kil'ini travelling in the flock has become injured. The flock has been slowed."

The star pattern being projected onto the bone was worrying Tuki. He almost had the answer, he was sure, when something else intruded onto the image.

He gasped and everyone turned to look at him, except for the hurgon whose job it was to watch the image. All the tentacles around the room were waving madly.

Everyone started to speak at once. Meenu seemed to be having two conversations, one with words and the other with gestures.

"The other has come," Meledrin said, though whether it was her own thought or the translation of what someone else was saying, Tuki didn't know.

The huge spaceship that had chased them from Nexis and sailed ominously past while they were stranded in the other universe had returned. It sailed across the starscape and the camera followed to keep it in view.

The alien fired its weapons. Each one of the projectiles struck true, and it took only a couple, at most, to split each kil'ini asunder, spilling hurgon and equipment into space. Everywhere Tuki looked, the creatures were dying or winking out of existence—there one second, gone the next.

"We are about to shift to another universe," Meledrin said softly, eyes riveted to the screen.

And then they were gone. The screen showed nothing but black. Or perhaps it showed nothing at all.

"Meenu says we should return to our ship," Meledrin said. "It will be some time before we arrive at Earth."

"Okay, then," Kim said, "but tell her to keep us informed of any developments. And tell her we hope that her family hasn't suffered too many losses today." She stared at the black screen as if she could still see the huge alien ship and the half dozen kil'ini it had killed in just a few moments.

Tuki stared as well. The ship had appeared right amongst the kil'ini with an accuracy he would have found impossible to replicate. Power was something to fear. But power coupled with precision?

-oOo-

Tuki waited so long that he was about to turn and walk away when the door slid open and Ruby looked out at him.

"Tuki." She smiled and pushed the door open a bit more. Tuki looked past her and saw Sandy sitting at the table with a radio or something similar plugged in her ear.

"I am not disturbing you, am I?"

"No, course not. We just never had a door before, so it took a while to work out what the banging was all about."

"Oh, right." He was ready to retreat anyway. The reason for his visit seemed silly now. And he was probably wrong.

"You wanna come in? We only got two chairs though." She had a worried look on her face. "I think someone stole our other one."

"Ummm... No, thank you."

"What you want then? You wanna go for a run?"

Tuki smiled. "You like to run?"

Ruby shrugged. "Sometimes."

"Oh. Maybe some other time."

"Sure. What then?"

"Well, I wanted to talk to somebody about something, and you said..."

"Yeah, I did, didn't I? You don't wanna come in though? You wanna talk here at the door?"

"I don't know. It is silly, anyway."

"What is?"

"Well... It's just... I think we are going in the wrong direction." He shook his head. "But it is just silly."

"Why? Not why's it silly—why you think we going in the wrong direction."

"I saw the stars outside when I went with Kim. There was a screen and..."

"You never been in this part of space?"

He shook his head.

"You get a chance to look proper like?"

He shook his head again.

"So you don't know where we is going?"

A shrug.

"And did you tell Kim?"

"No."

"Why not?"

"Because I have never been in this part of space, and I did not get a good chance to look, and... I don't know."

"Stars is your thing, right?"

He nodded. "I guess so."

"Then you got to tell her."

"But what if I am wrong?"

"Look, Tuki, that ain't your problem. What you got to do is tell Kim what you think. And tell her that you ain't exactly sure." Ruby came out of the room, grabbed Tuki by the hand and started to draw him down the hall. "You let Kim worry about what happens after that. It ain't our concern until she says it is."

"But what if I am wrong?"

"Like I said, you say you ain't sure. You look on your skyglass thingy to see what you can find out. You investigate. You ask Inaki for help. But only after you tell Kim so she can start thinking about the problem as well."

Tuki allowed himself to be dragged upstairs to the administration level.

Investigate in the skyglass? Why hadn't he thought of that?

He didn't need Ruby to drag him, but her hand was surprisingly soft in his.

26: Waiting

SCREE WAS STRAPPING HIMSELF into his weapons seat before Tuki finished the story. And he knew that this time not even Kim could come up with a reason why he shouldn't thump some aliens.

Knowing that, he waited for her to tell him to stop. And he knew that he would, for long enough to listen at least.

"Don't, Scree," she said with a sigh.

Scree, hand on the button that would turn on his chair, turned to look at her.

"We have no idea where we are. We don't even know what universe we're in—we have no idea how to get back."

"Keeble could works it out."

Keeble wasn't even on the bridge. Topper, sitting in the Engineering chair, shook his head. "From what I understand," he said, "we would need to be able to hear the sound made by the gates to be able to duplicate them."

Scree sniffed. "Kim said there ain't no noise in space."

"Not the *sound.* The magical 'sound'."

"Oh." He'd known that but wasn't thinking straight. *Still a troll after all.* "And you didn't hear nothing when we went through?"

Topper shook his head.

"But don't we know the sound of the gate used to get us back to our universe anyway? You heard that one."

"Yes, but perhaps the sound doesn't dictate where we go, but how far we go to get to the other universe. Or something. We really have no idea at this stage."

Scree unbuckled his belt. "Flaming cats. How abouts I take some guys and go wring some necks then. Theys sure to tell us what we want."

"No, Scree." Kim sat back and put her head in her hands, as if it was all becoming too much. Again.

"Course not." As he climbed back out of the seat he noticed Ruby watching him, looking him up and down as if seeing him for the first time. Scree hadn't had sex in days, but the attention didn't even raise his interest—not that sex was on her mind either. "So what does we do?"

"We wait. Tuki finds out where we're going, if he can—at least there's power in this universe. Or he tells us where we are whenever we get where we're going."

"Maybe we're there already," Ping said quietly. "How would we know?"

Palsamon was sitting in the navigation seat—he'd been studying the controls earlier—and set to work, looking as if he knew what he was doing. That didn't last long. He centered the view on the skyglass but then obviously wasn't sure what to do next.

Tuki nodded. "You were going right. You need to move out now though."

Palsamon went back to work.

Scree paced.

"There is nothing to see," Palsamon said.

"There is a lot to see," Tuki said in reply. "See that—it is telling us of the found objects. The computer just cannot recognize anything."

"Still in the other universe then," Kim said, half to herself. "Could we start making maps of other universes though?"

Scree's pacing took him beside Tuki, and he could see him nodding slowly. The lad suddenly began giving instructions but Palsamon was soon left behind and moved out of the way so Tuki could do the work himself.

"You can make more maps on there?" Scree asked.

Tuki kept working but nodded vaguely. "I think so. There are whole sections of the skyglass that have been left blank. A large portion of it."

Scree watched as Tuki worked steadily. He pushed buttons carefully as if worried he'd break them, and fiddled with controls. Finally, he sat back.

"I need a name, Kim."

"What? You already have a name."

"No, for the universe. I found a menu that asked if I wanted to start a new map. I said yes, and it wants me to name it."

"Ok. Umm... Well, you pick one."

"But what if the people who live here already have a name for their universe?"

"Then we'll change it over later. But for now... Just pick."

"Very well then. I will name it... I will name it Danyon," he said and smiled. "Because a little while ago that village was my whole universe. So now it can be a real universe."

"That's a good name, Tuki."

"It's wonderful," Scree said with a grunt. "But now what does we do?"

"We wait."

"Great." That was all they *ever* seemed to do.

-oOo-

"Scree?"

A month ago Scree would have woken in an instant and been ready to kill. A month ago he probably wouldn't have been asleep at all.

"Meledrin used to bawl me out for not knocking," he said. Quartz was standing in the doorway of his cabin.

"I knocked. You mustn't've heard."

Scree grunted in disgust. A month ago the trollop wouldn't have gotten within a dozen meters without him *smelling* her. "What's happening?"

Quartz shrugged. "Nothing. You tell me."

"Nothing's happening," he said.

She came into the room, shutting the door behind her. "You wanna do nothing?" she asked. "Or you wanna do *something*?"

Scree rolled onto his back to look at her. She was slender, for a troll, and tall. She had large breasts and if she moved the zipper on her EVA suit one centimeter lower...

She smiled and licked her teeth as she sat down on the end of the big double bed. "All the trollops say you ain't been ruttin' with them since that first day with Crystal, so I was thinking maybe..."

Scree gave the idea some thought, but the fact that he had to think about it at all gave him the answer. "Nah, thanks anyway, Quartz."

She sneered and rezipped her zipper. "Maybe I should send Gulch or Cliff in here. They more your thing?"

"Maybe I just don't like you."

"What's likin' got to do with it?" But she started to smile and rose to her feet. "You got your eye on the boss, don't ya? Huh. Ruby said that but I didn't believe."

"What does Ruby know about anything?"

"She seeing lots of stuff recently. Got a head on her shoulders, that girl. Might be smarter'n you even."

"If she was that smart she wouldn't go around tellin' you all this cat pissing stuff."

"Boss won't go for the likes of you. She'll get herself that pretty young elf Suldon, I reckon."

"You don't know nothing about the boss then." But he was worried she was right, and it must've shown on his face. Quart laughed as she left the room.

Sex is easy, Scree thought. *No wonder humans have all those wars when they got all this other crap in their lives.* He lay back down and stared at the ceiling.

When somebody approached his room a few minutes later, he was ready. It was a human. A man. Thorpe probably.

Who ever it was knocked.

"Yeah."

Thorpe opened the door and stuck his head in. "We're there."

"Where?" Scree sat up in the bed, yawning and stretching. He thought that maybe the bed had something to do with his newfound ability to sleep. Never before had he slept on anything so comfortable.

"Somewhere." He pushed the door the rest of the way open. "We're a couple of thousand kilometers out from a planet."

"Kil'ini?"

"Everywhere."

"Come on then."

The bridge was full of people. Too many people. Kim was trying to get them back down stairs but wasn't having any luck. There were two trolls. Apparently they weren't keen to use force and Kim wasn't telling them anything.

Scree looked at the nearest person. It was Meledrin standing and staring out the window. Not a good choice. Next to her was a dwarf. Scree strode across, grabbed the dwarf, and threw him into the nearest crowd of people. That got their attention.

The victim quickly untangled himself and stood, ready to fight, until he saw who'd done the throwing.

"Two choices," Scree said. "Sit down in the chairs and buckle up or get out."

Nobody moved.

"If I haves to send a troll to make the decision for you, they won't be helping youse to your seats." Scree smiled nicely at his audience while Peak and Chasm cracked their knuckles.

Finally they started to move, slowly filling the seats surrounding the viewing well. While they arranged themselves, Scree strode around to the front. "And in future, you should obey Kim's orders like your lives depends on it..." He smiled some more... "'Cause maybe they does."

Up the back, Meledrin was still standing.

"Why you still there?" Scree asked. "Sit down."

The elf sniffed but didn't argue. She didn't sit in one of the gallery seats either. Quite predictably, she asked Penisari to get out of the Communications chair so she could sit down there.

Kim shook her head before Meledrin had finished the sentence. "How about you just sit down there somewhere, Mel. Peni is on duty now."

Scree watched as Meledrin thought of protesting, but eventually she sniffed again and found herself a seat. Maybe the thought of a troll manhandling her towards the elevator helped.

"Why are you not sitting down, Scree? And why are they not?" She motioned to Chasm and Peak.

"I ain't sitting, 'cause I am giving the orders. And they ain't sitting cause they guarding."

With a glance at the weapons control chair, Scree wondered if he should sit down. But he looked up at the image in the dome. Even if they could get out of the mouth of the kil'ini, which wasn't certain, there were too many others outside. Way too many.

"And now we waits," he said.

-oOo-

Two hurgon floated in front of the window. Scree watched them silently. Most of the other spectators had left long ago, leaving only half a dozen other than those on duty.

A voice in Scree's head told him that ten more hurgon, including Aunt Meenu, were waiting near the Level 3 airlock. A message came over the intercom a few seconds later.

"*Meenu wants to talk to the boss,*" Stone said.

Penisari quickly adjusted the controls so Kim could talk to the air lock. Kim could have done it herself, but the elves could do it quicker.

"Stone, tell Meenu to shove it up her arse."

There was a moment of silence. "Suldon says that he don't know exactly what that's supposed to mean, but he ain't gonna say it. And he don't know if the hurgon have the right word anyway."

"Well, just tell Meenu I don't want to talk."

"Right then."

Scree waited for the reply. He was getting good at waiting.

Suldon's voice, calm and clear, came over the radio, as if he was reporting on the weather. "Meenu says that if we prove to be more trouble than we are worth then the kil'ini will be asked to crush us."

"And tell Meenu we'll go down shooting."

That was the stuff Scree liked to hear, though he doubted it would come to that.

Suldon again: "Shooting while inside the kil'ini mouth would not help in any way, for there would be a reflexive clamping of muscles that would crush us all the quicker."

Kim shook her head and muttered quietly, "Of course there would." She stabbed at the speaker button. "Ok then. I'm coming. But tell the bitch that I just got out of the shower, so I may be a while."

"Pardon? You want me to..."

"Just tell Meenu to wait."

"Very well."

Scree followed Kim down stairs. He called in his mind for Blue Troop to meet them on Level 3. But Kim didn't go there immediately. He found himself standing at the door to the Captain's cabin as she sat on the corner of the bed.

"I just keep getting us into more and more trouble, don't I?"

Scree thought about that then shook his head. "Trouble's when you can't get out of it. We gotten out of everything so far."

"What if we don't get out of this one though? We're surrounded by enemies, millions—trillions—of kilometers from help."

"So they our enemies now?"

Kim shrugged. "Maybe. I don't know. Well, yes, obviously. We made a deal and they broke it. They obviously weren't ever interested in a treaty."

"What if they was but decided we couldn't really help them after all. Us people with two ships between seven worlds."

"What?"

"What if the T'Loop story was true? Just that they thinks they've now come up with a better plan?" Scree took a step into the room, then hesitated. After a moment he went and sat on the bed next to her.

"What will that give us?"

"It means there'll be others out there willing to help if we makes the same offer to them that we made to the T'Loop."

Kim nodded slowly. "Right," as if she wanted to be convinced.

"T'Loop is a 'great family'. They already gots it pretty good, really. What about all them minor families who ain't getting anywhere? We got heaps of allies to choose from now."

"We've just got to find them."

"Right." Scree smiled. "If Meenu wants us to go down to the planet, I says we do it. Then we see what we can see."

Kim nodded again. "Let's go then." She didn't sound sure but got to her feet.

The hurgon still floated outside the open airlock. If Scree had to guess he'd have said they were angry, moving and fidgeting as they were, but maybe that meant something else for them.

He stood beside Kim, toes hanging out over nothing, while Meenu made her greetings. Kim said nothing in reply for a long time. The hurgon started to fidget some more. Suldon was hardly any better. Finally, Kim spoke.

"What happened to our agreement?"

"It would not have been beneficial to the T'loop."

"Yes, it would."

"In the long term, perhaps, but without short term benefit, the long term may never be reached."

"What?"

"The T'loop need assistance now."

"And you think we'll help you now?"

"That is not for you to decide. Kim's agreement is not needed in this. Assistance will be given simply because hakans are in T'loop custody."

"And if we don't like being in custody?"

"Kim should do what must be done. Meenu will also do what must be done."

"Do we help you if we're dead?"

"No. But you do not want to die."

Kim's shoulders slumped minutely and Scree wondered if she was acting. He felt like pointing out that, if she *was* acting, subtlety might not help—the hurgon probably couldn't read hakan body language.

"So what do we do?"

'Hakahei *shall follow a guide light down to Hulgorn. That is all for the moment. There are thousands of kil'ini outside.* Hakahei *cannot kill them all.*"

Kim took a deep breath. "Ok then. Let's get this over with."

27: Worst Case

PING SAT IN THE FRONT ROW with Ari and Tess, watching Kim and Scree talk quietly as they waited for the rest of the crew to arrive. They had talked to the hurgon only recently—Ping tried to gauge how things had gone. Scree looked like he was having fun, which probably meant things were going to get interesting. Kim's worried expression did nothing to ease the concern. Ping gripped Ari's hand but found no comfort from the contact.

"All rights everyone, listen up." Scree held up his arms for quiet, then stepped away to allow Kim to speak.

"We're now prisoners of the T'loop family and will be landing on Hulgorn, as they've instructed. It seems our assistance was not going to help enough, or soon enough, so they came up with another plan."

Several of the trolls and dwarves let everyone know what they thought about that, and what should be done, but Kim waited for them to fall silent.

Ping found herself gripping Tess's hand as well.

"For now we're going to do as they say, because it suits our purposes, as much as we can have any in this situation. We're not going to fight back now, or cause any trouble at all, until we can see exactly where we stand."

Ping wondered if Scree had agreed to this plan of action. Or inaction. Once, she'd thought she could tell what he was thinking because there were only a couple of thoughts to choose from. Now she didn't know what she was thinking herself half the time.

"What are we going to do, do you think?" Ari whispered, squeezing Ping's hand.

"I don't know. Scree and Kim will come up with something."

"And if they don't?"

"Then somebody else will." Ping didn't know who though, seeing nobody knew anything of the world they were heading towards. But then, nobody had known anything else a couple of weeks ago either.

"So," Kim continued, "everyone just keep your head down, but be ready to act if we should need it."

Ping thought Kim was looking for something inspirational to say, like all the great leaders from the tales. But apparently nothing came to her.

"All the officers to the bridge, the rest of you get strapped in."

Ping stayed where she was until Tess gave her a nudge and motioned toward the lift.

"What?"

"The bridge."

"Oh, yes."

Apparently, a lot of people thought the best place to get strapped in was on the bridge. The 30 seats were already full when Ping arrived and more people were standing around as if a vacancy might present itself. Scree soon made it clear what he thought of that idea and the unlucky losers headed for the lift.

Ping took her seat beside Keeble and wondered what she was supposed to do next. Surely her skills wouldn't be needed. Neither would Keeble's, in the short journey they were about to undertake. She checked the read-outs for the two clocks. They were synchronized exactly. What else could she do?

"Let's do this," Kim said as she started the engines. "And don't shoot anything once we get out there, Scree."

Scree grunted in disgust and Ping smiled slightly. Not too long ago the troll would've been insulted by the idea that he *wouldn't* kill any of the enemy, now he was insulted by the opposite.

"Do we have enough fuel to get down and back up again, Keeble?" Kim asked.

Ping checked the gauges.

"There's enough for a while yet," Keeble said.

Ping knew all the minor tanks were full of the ingredients the Americans had supplied.

"We'll run out of hydrogen before anything else," Keeble continued.

"We'll worry about that once we get away from here."

"That's the way," Keeble said sarcastically, "worry about it when the time comes."

Ping shook her head. "Shut up, Keeble," she said softly. "We can't get any hydrogen now, so why complain about it?"

He stared at her but didn't reply. Scree was staring as well. Ping blushed and checked her clocks.

The kil'ini opened its 'mouth' and Kim carefully maneuvered out into space.

Ping felt her own mouth gaping and closed it with a clacking of teeth. There were kil'ini everywhere, and each one seemed to have at least one eyestalk pointed in their direction. Some of the creatures were huge while others were hardly larger than the Hakahei. These smaller ones were clumped in groups that darted this way and that like shoals of fish. Each creature had at least three tentacles and they were waving furiously as if carrying out multiple conversations in their strange sign language.

Out in the open, Kim paused. The world was visible, a large grey smudge not far away, but to weave their way amongst the kil'ini would take all day. But, as if on some prearranged signal, the creatures started to move, clearing a path.

"All righty then," Kim said.

Still, Kim made many fine adjustments to follow the curving path that was being offered. While Kim concentrated on working the controls, Ping watched the gauntlet of creatures. Each one was different and would be quite easy to recognize once you got to know them. Their eyes, huge and colorful, watched with piercing intelligence. Eyestalks swiveled to follow the *Hakahei*'s progress. And all the while, tentacles continued to wave.

"There are so many," Ping said. She didn't know how they were supposed to escape once they got down to the planet. With all these creatures above them they couldn't sneak away. And to convince all of them that their departure was a good idea was unlikely.

"That just means theys easier to hit," Scree said, keeping one of the kil'ini locked in his sights.

Hulgorn, the hurgon home world, was growing in the view-port. Ping turned to look at that, as if it was more reassuring. It was a dull, grey place. Dark, roiling clouds covered most of it.

"Do we know where we're going?" Ping didn't want to go down there at all. It looked a horrid place.

"Apparently some type of guide-light will start shining soon. We just follow it in."

Keeble grunted. "If any light can get though those cloud."

"Well, we'll just go down until we're under the cloud."

As ping worried and chewed on her lip, Kim started to head directly towards the planet. She spun the ship so the bridge was pointing away, and went slowly in. A view of the clouds appeared in the dome.

Finally, a light did find a way through the clouds, coming in acutely from the ship's west. Kim changed direction, working carefully at the controls, riding the beam of light down towards the ground.

They finally broke through the cloud cover and Ping gasped. As far as the eye could see, even from high up, was a vast, strange city. The clouds were not rain clouds at all, or not completely. It was smoke, spewing from thousands of huge chimneys and as many smaller, unrecognizable buildings.

"Is there a fire?" Scree asked.

"I wish," Kim replied quietly.

Concrete and bricks and iron as far as the eye could see. Ping wanted to look away, but found it impossible. She did not know if she had ever seen anything so horrible.

It didn't look any better as they got closer. There didn't seem to be any trees at all. Buildings everywhere. No color. No relief.

Ten minutes later, Kim set the ship down in a large square, thumping awkwardly down onto the cobbles, and Ping went to the window to look. She could see three sides of the square and huge, drab buildings closed each in. One rose higher than the ship, a grey brick structure that showed only three windows and a single door in its length. A dozen streams of smoke drifted sluggishly upwards. Lights showed movement in the windows but the square remained quiet.

"Now what do we do?" Ping asked. But she already knew the answer to that. They waited. "Are we supposed to be friends of the T'loop family? Or are they just showing off the fact that they captured us?"

"I'm not sure," Kim replied. "But we certainly won't be acting too friendly. We don't want there to be any confusion should potential allies be snooping around."

Keeble grunted. "And how do we tell if the next allies are better than the last lot?"

"Well, theys can't be much worse."

"That's *very* comforting."

"Isn't it though," Kim said.

Ping returned to her seat and looked up at the view in the dome. Meledrin was switching between cameras. The ship was completely surrounded by buildings. The one behind them was the highest of them all. Dozens of windows glowed brightly. There were many doors as well. One reached from the ground almost to the fourth story and others were meters above the ground. Kidol, the giant birds, seemed to be coming and going from the roof in a steady stream as if a great many hurgon were being ferried in.

"What's our plan?" Ping asked eventually,

"We don't have one. We'll just see what happens."

"Yes, but... We have to have some sort of plan in case *nothing* happens. In case we can't get allies or... Or if our allies want to know what we plan."

"I don't know—" Kim said.

"Then think of something," Scree broke in. "Ping's right. We need a fall back plan, just in case."

"Okay. Jeeze." Kim played with the thrust directional ball, spinning it on its stand. She didn't say anything.

Scree grunted. "Everybody out," he said. He got out of his chair and started to shoo everyone out of the gallery. "You stay," he said to Captain Thorpe. "And you four." Palsamon, Stone, Flint and Topper sat back down.

"How come they get to stay?" If not for the beard and gruff voice, the dwarf who said it might have been a miffed child. "I've been a Singer longer than Topper."

"Once you can talk to a woman without nearly choking on the words you might get to stay too. Now move your stumpy legs out of here."

"Why am I here," Palsamon asked when the room had cleared of stragglers.

"An old head might think of things," Scree said.

"I have less experience at all of this than anyone else."

"That might help too," Ping offered. *She* didn't know where to start.

Apparently Topper did. "We need to know what we have, firstly."

Keeble was nodding but Scree looked lost already. "We got whatever is on this ship."

"At the moment," Topper said, "but for how long? If the hurgon wanted to get on board, could they? I understand that the kil'ini can damage the ship, but can they do it from space? On Sherindel the hurgon had those suits of armor and simple explosives. Is that the best they can come up with, or do they have better weapons back here?"

Ping smiled. Topper didn't really know where to start at all but, like all the dwarves, he thought better out loud and in company. If somebody just started talking, others would usually follow.

"They're fighting a war; why would they keep their best weapons at home?" Kim asked.

"Because they can't fit them on the kil'ini or those bats?" Keeble offered. "Because the batteries to run them won't fit?"

Scree was nodding slowly. "I think we gots to assume that they don't have better weapons. Or at least they don't have ones that can get them into the ship."

Meledrin raised an eyebrow. "And why do we have to assume that?" She was scanning the radio frequencies, searching for anything.

"Because if they can gets into the ship easily then we got nothing."

Ping didn't agree. "But if we assume that they can't get in here then what happens if they do? Perhaps we should assume that they can so we'll be ready for it."

"She's right, Scree," Kim said. "We plan for the worst."

"Well, the worst would be ifs we are all taken off here and put in cells."

Topper nodded. "So anything that might be useful to us—weapons, food, lamps—we put them somewhere where they won't be taken or destroyed. Down in the hold, maybe. Or in the Grav Field ducting."

"Rights. Somewhere where we can get to it quickly."

"And the hummers," Ping said.

"What, we hide them?"

"Sort of. We make sure that they don't give away their secrets without need. And we make sure that, if we are split in two groups, we have one sort of hummer in each group, just in case."

"The trollop is good." Flint smiled. Ping blushed slightly while the troll, smoothing down his moustache, continued. "And that would mean that we keep the radios in our head a secret as well."

"Cuto already knows," Meledrin said, "about both the radios and the Singing."

"Then we hope he doesn't think of mentioning it to anyone."

"Whatever we are to do," Meledrin said, "we need to decide quickly."

Ping looked up at the image floating overhead. A group of hurgon, some armored, others wearing what might have been ceremonial robes, were walking across the huge, rough cobbles of the square.

"Shit. Okay. Ping, you're in charge of getting stuff hidden. Chasm and Topper will help. Meledrin, you're going to keep scanning the radio to see what you can find out." She drummed her fingers on her console. "Tuki, you're going to protect the skyglass."

"Me? But—"

"We'll split Blue Troop—three stay with Tuki, two come with me. Stone, tell Cliff he can start a war if needs be, but make sure the hurgon don't get the skyglass."

"Course."

"Get them to try to restrain themselves though."

The troll merely nodded.

"Meledrin, you're in charge."

"Very well."

It didn't look as if the elf was worried one way or the other, but Ping wondered how Meledrin would've reacted if Keeble was left in charge. Probably she would not take advantage of her position anyway, being happy enough to have the title.

"What about the rest of us?" Keeble asked.

"A group will be going out there with me to see what we can find out."

"Who will that be?"

-oOo-

Ping stood by the door on Level 9 as Peak piloted the Lander down to the ground. She stayed where she was, watching silently. After touching down, the Lander's passengers—ten in all—climbed out and confronted the hurgon. Ping couldn't hear what they said, for the world was alive with all manner of clattering and banging, hissing and scraping. And it smelled as bad as it looked and sounded. Each breath stung the back of her throat. Her eyes watered.

She might well have stayed there all day but Gulch pulled her back from the door when Peak returned the empty Lander to the hold. Nearby, Chasm pressed the button that closed the door and they were left in relative quite.

"Stone says we supposed to be moving stuff?"

Ping didn't reply. *Typical of a troll*, she thought. Their friends outside were already forgotten. It wasn't Chasm's job to watch them, so she didn't. She got on with other things. Ping wondered how they could be so single minded in all the things they did.

Chasm sighed at the lack of response. "What we moving? Where to?"

Ping shook her head to dispel the last vestiges of the outside world and looked around, as if the answer might be among the packing crates. Quite possibly it would be—she was in charge of that part of the operation, after all. "Useful things," she said.

"Oh, good. That's all right then."

Ping tried to get herself thinking straight. The only way she could help Kim was to make sure everything she had to do was done. "We have to pretend the hurgon can get into the ship any time they please, so we need a hidden supply of food and weapons and... stuff."

28: Grey and Forlorn

KEEBLE SNIFFED AT THE AIR but the only smell he could distinguish was that of bird shit. The kidol seemed to be one of the main forms of transport so that was hardly a surprise. He could see their dark shapes crossing the sky in never ending lines. He watched them for a moment before turning to look at his more immediate surroundings.

Out in the open, and without the benefit of magnifying cameras, the square was huge. So, not all that immediate at all.

"Half a kilometer to a side?" Keeble asked softly.

Tasko nodded in reply.

The buildings were larger than they'd looked as well. The main one could've housed the entire population of Tab cavern with room to spare.

But Suldon had finished translating the greetings, occasionally glancing at Tamidilin to make sure the other elf agreed, and things were getting started.

"Have any weapons been brought?" the hurgon leader asked, eyeing the trolls up and down.

Kim smiled for a while in reply. "Maybe."

"The T'loop family has offered no harm."

"And we haven't threatened to use a weapon."

"The T'loop wish for cooperation."

"Well, you should've thought of that before you kidnapped us."

"The Hakahei *voluntarily entered Lisa'lee'la to be transported."*

"Yes, but not to here. We were supposed to be going to Earth."

"No such contract was entered in to."

"We had a verbal agreement."

"Verbal agreements are worth nothing."

"We'll keep that in mind in our future dealings."

"Will Kim come?"

"What for?"

"To speak of matters further."

"This is a nice spot."

"Air toxicity is high today—long term comfort cannot be assured."

Keeble looked around, wondering if what she said was true. The air was thick with smoke or haze that didn't taste good, but was it any worse than going to places-unknown with the enemy? He knew Scree, Sandy and Flint didn't have weapons—where would they hide them in the EVA suits—but that wouldn't stop them from getting violent if they felt the need. If they stayed here, support was within reach if required. The three trolls seemed to be having the same thoughts. They didn't look exactly nervous, but it was obvious they didn't like the chances of keeping everyone safe if they went somewhere else. The beads in Sandy's hair clattered quietly as she constantly scanned their surroundings, eyes narrowed in concentration.

"We'll go with you," Kim said eventually.

"Very good. Follow, please."

Keeble hung about at the rear of the group with the other dwarves; Tasko, Bargle and Nina. Bargle was only young but as keen as a cold wind. Nina was... Keeble shook his head. He hadn't even bothered waiting for Kim to tell him he needed to choose a dwife in the group, he'd just done it. Nina was quiet and dependable and knew her place. She wore a stiff linen dress down to the ground and a scarf tied over her head.

"You two keep your eyes peeled for anything that looks interesting," he said. Tasko would know what to do. "Any little hint of technology might be enough to give us ideas."

"Will do."

"Yes, Keeble."

The wall of the huge building was rough and dirty with all kinds of crazy lines, but the main door was fitted perfectly and opened without a sound. The lines inside were hardly any straighter, but the overall construction was still impressive.

A huge hall, twenty-five meters wide and fifty long, confronted them. Carved colonnades down either side seemed to be holding back all manner of strange equipment—stone assemblages, metal constructs, timber frames. Some were simple designs and Keeble could immediately discern the point. Those he dismissed. Others he could not begin to fathom.

Nina was muttering to herself. Tasko had stopped to look at something and had to be herded forward by a hurgon guard.

Bargle was almost laughing. "A stone crulingas," he said, before the guard was nudging him forward as well.

Keeble looked, and the lad was right, but why would they even have bothered? He continued to look at the paraphernalia as he went, but it was all either beyond him or beneath him.

"What do you make of that?" Tasko asked, pointing to an array of metal rods.

"I have no idea."

Kim might've known what some of the things were, but she wasn't even looking. Keeble grunted and continued forward as slowly as he was allowed.

There was a strange bicycle with three wheels and chunky, rusting gears. There was a blue, glass cube. There was a big, curved bow with brown fletched arrows.

At the end of the hall, a door swung silently open to reveal a shorter, narrower passage. There was a set of stairs leading into each wall and half a dozen more doors. They were led straight on. Through the next door, a small group of aliens had gathered beside what appeared to be a steam powered train. It was a huge, hulking affair of boilerplate, iron and huge rusting bolts. Smoke dribbled slowly from the smokestack, filling the upper half of the room with an impenetrable fug. The ceiling might have been vaulted like the last, or just barely out of Flint's reach.

"Where are they taking us?" Keeble asked Kim.

Kim didn't know. She looked to Suldon and the elf asked. He listened impassively to the hurgon's reply. "Deeba says we are currently standing in Lakeena Hub, one of the main transportation centers of the city. Twenty-three train lines, twelve canals, twenty major highways and five skyrail glides all meet within five kilometers of this place. There are also twenty courtyards, such as the one where we landed, that were designed to hold construct-spacecraft."

"What spacecraft?" Keeble asked. "I didn't think they had any."

Suldon spoke to the hurgon again. "Currently the hurgon have no ships that can make landfall, but the Fen'dai have, with the help of kil'ini, been assembling ships in space that they hope will one day have the capability. Deeba does not think very highly of these craft."

Keeble eyed the steam train. "They've made spacecraft?" he asked.

"Apparently."

The hurgon were motioning them all towards the train. They held their ground when Kim baulked at the invitation. "How about you just answer the original question, Suldon," she said. "Where the hell are they taking us?"

Either the elf had forgotten the answer, or had never actually been told. He spoke to Deeba again. "We are being taken to the central compound of the T'loop family. It is not far."

Keeble didn't know why Kim hesitated. With a shake of his head, he strode onto the train. There were no seats but wooden boxes had been arranged in rows for the occasion. He sat down near a window and tried to get comfortable.

"Keeble, what are you doing?" Kim asked when she sat down by his side.

"What does it look like?"

Everyone else had come aboard and were finding boxes to sit on.

"But what if I—"

"What if you didn't want to get on the train?" Keeble said with a sneer. "What else were you going to do? Maybe apologize and go back to the ship? Or we could sit on the floor out there and wait for the world to collapse?"

"That isn't the point."

"It never is. There's always another point that people can't see."

The train started to move away and Keeble discovered he was facing backwards. "Some decisions have already been made, Kim. Don't fight them." He spun about on his box to face the other way.

For more than fifteen minutes the train moved between rough brick walls, so there wasn't anything to see anyway. Eventually they broke out into the clear. Or what passed for clear on Hulgorn. It wasn't immediately obvious if it was night or day. Grey light seeped around corners to give everything an eerie hue. One building looked much like the next, old and surely large beyond need and sensible architecture.

Watching through the soot smeared window, Keeble was reminded of the bars in Tab cavern where all the old dwarves gathered to sit with their ale and their bitter, lonely silence. Buildings leaned tiredly against each other, grey and forlorn. Every second structure had smoke streaming from one orifice or another. Crumbling fences protected doors that were not worth the effort. There were probably a million stories to tell, but nobody really wanted to talk or to listen.

The train grumbled past a fallen building. The iron frame still stood in some places, the bones of a rotting carcass.

"Meledrin would hate this place," Keeble muttered. He hated it as well.

A crane, sitting on the one visible patch of bare ground, was frozen in its moment of glory, a huge section of wall overflowing its rusting bucket. Excavation equipment, hulking beasts, loitered in the rubble nearby. It all seemed to have been there a very long time.

A line of lights slid by overhead and Keeble craned his neck to look.

"Did you see that?" Keeble asked when the lights were gone from sight.

"I did," Nina said, ducking her head to examine a crease in her dress. "Perhaps it was one of the 'skyrails' the hurgon mentioned."

"Perhaps." But if it was then the 'glide' that held it aloft had been invisible.

Keeble looked at the sky again and when he looked back down, they were in another place entirely. The buildings here were smaller, though still as high. They packed them in, shoulder to shoulder, along the side of the railway. Construction was still slightly haphazard, as if a secondary concern, and the soot-grey color scheme still dominated. There was no color beyond the diffracted light in ancient, rippled windows. No trees, no paint, no small patch of cleanliness. There was no moon overhead, just filtered greyness.

"This place is dead," Keeble said. He turned to look at Kim, who sat silently by his side. She was staring out at the world in horror.

-oOo-

Keeble stared glumly as they huffed along the edge of a huge quarry, carved out of the middle of the city. What was the use of all the industry and work if it didn't look good, or feel good? He'd recently said that the task was the point of what dwarves did. But he now knew that was only half true. The task was important, but so was the end result. It might not be vital to the world, but it still had to add something, even if it was merely beauty.

The quarry disappeared into the gloom, replaced by more buildings that might have been the same ones they'd passed half an hour ago. Keeble wished for just one to be set apart from the others.

Apparently, Hulgorn the city covered almost a third of Hulgorn the world. The buildings dipped their crumbling toes into the oceans and swamps and rivers, creeping a little further out every year.

"Deeba does not seem to care about the world at all," Tamidilin said softly. The elf was sitting with Suldon and Nina. "The world means nothing, beyond being property to be bought and sold if the need arises and the profits are high enough. It's not as if their affection is for the hurgon people if what Cuto says is correct. They only care for their family."

Tamidilin shook her head. "There are 54 great families, if I have the math right, and 207 lesser families." She looked at Suldon, as if he might be better at the math than she. Which was possible. "Some of those minor families are subsidiaries of the Greats, bought out or locked into contracts. And there are thousands of clans that are 'worthless', scrabbling in the footsteps of others just to make it through each day."

"Wonderful," Kim said, "we find ourselves amidst a loving, caring race. We shouldn't have any problem at all convincing them to help us when they won't even help their own people."

"We do not appeal to their kind hearts, Kim," Suldon replied. "We appeal to their greed."

"And what happens if we can't pay up?"

Keeble beat Suldon to one of Kim's favorite lines. "Worry about that when the time comes."

Kim shook her head but gave a slight laugh. The train rattled on.

Eventually they pulled in at a large, brightly lit station and turned away from the main track onto a small siding, as if preparing to stay for a while.

When they exited the carriage, Keeble could see that more care had been taken in the construction of this building. Most of the lines were square, corners and trims were finished, but it still seemed to be done with a complete lack of imagination. A row of squat, plain columns supported the roof. Grey floor tiles butted shoulders so tightly that they were all but indistinguishable from each other.

"One focus tile every now and then is all it needs," Bargle muttered. "It would make so much difference." Bargle had not even finished his apprenticeship, and he could see it.

"We are to go this way." Suldon pointed towards a door.

Half a dozen armored hurgon stood guard, swiveling noisily from side to side as they scanned for trouble. Keeble wondered how long it would take Scree, Flint and Sandy to kill them all, or at least make it so they weren't a threat.

Beyond the door were half a dozen more guards in more of the same armor—mustard yellow with a cross on the front. They stood in embrasures, cloaked in shadows that made them appear more dangerous than they probably were. They did look sinister and evil though, which probably *wasn't* a trick of the light.

"The square where the *Hakahei* is currently located is on the edge of the T'loop Compound. We are now near the center," Suldon translated for Deeba. "It is the sixteenth largest compound in area, and the twenty-eighth in population. Over 10,000 family members live here permanently. Deeba seems very proud of that—an average sized family, but a powerful and rich one. They own much of Lapenti—though minor families are contracted to do most of the work on that world—and have compounds on two more worlds."

Beyond the guards, the hall seemed to go on forever. Doors, labeled with incomprehensible writing, were randomly spaced on each side. There were no windows. There were no decorations.

"We are being taken to see the Grandmother and Grandfather," Tamidilin said, as if she expected nothing else.

One door led to a huge elevator. The entire group fitted in and hardly seemed to fill one corner. A hurgon manipulated a lever the size of Scree's leg and the room started to climb, clanking and rattling as if there were a dozen rusty cogs about to fall away. Keeble thought it might have been quicker, and safer, to use the stairs.

The lift eventually shuddered to a halt, hissing like one of the hurgon suits of armor.

The room they entered was a stark contrast to the ones they'd seen before. The stone walls were covered with bright, narrative tapestries—peaceful idyll, the coming of the hakans, kil'ini reaching down from the sky, views of space. The ceiling was a low lattice of stained timber interwoven with colored strips of cloth, while the floor was covered in thick, luxurious carpet. A red stripe down the center of the room led twenty-seven meters to a raised platform.

Keeble stopped when the rest of the group did, just outside the lift, between two stylized plants formed from cold, polished iron. A hundred hurgon turned to look, almost as one. To Keeble, the hurgon did not look like nobles attending a ball or a royal presentation. They looked like a council of war. And, as Deeba led the group forward again, Keeble had the distinct impression that hakans would always be the enemy. Fifty thousand years of grudge didn't go away in a couple of days for these people.

Keeble shifted slightly, nudging Nina out of the way, so he could see past the front of their little procession. On the platform ahead, two wrinkly old hurgon were leaning back against T-shaped objects—it was the closest Keeble had seen any of them come to sitting. They wore yellow and red robes, with soft hats that flopped down near their shoulders. The Grandmother and Grandfather didn't look all that impressive.

"Meledrin says we got trouble," Scree said without breaking stride. He managed to sneer at the nearest aliens at the same time.

Keeble thought that went without saying. Kim kept getting them into trouble and Scree just kept following, possibly because he thought her trouble was more fun than the trouble he'd get into on his own. But he wondered how Meledrin knew.

"What sort of trouble?" Kim asked.

"About a thousand hurgon in the square arounds the *Hakahei*, all looking likes they want to get in."

Keeble grunted. *The* ship *has problems. Oh.*

"Shit."

"She wants to know whats she should do."

"How the hell should I know? Tell her to get a council together if she must."

Scree shook his head. "You think Meledrin is in my head asking for advice about how to tell people what to do? She don't know what to do because she don't know our situation. Does she let them in so we ain't killed? Or does she tell them to go skin a cat."

"I take it you're paraphrasing?"

"What?"

Kim sighed. "Tell her to hold the ship for now. We'll let her know if anything changes."

"You're the boss."

"And just why is that? I keep forgetting."

Over the next couple of minutes, Keeble discovered that he rather liked having Suldon translating everything just a few words behind the conversation. It allowed him to take in what was being said without actually feeling involved.

He didn't know exactly why he had been brought along on this little jaunt, but it certainly wasn't to take part in conversations such as this.

Eventually Kim stopped talking to the Grandparents. Deeba motioned her back towards the lift. Kim hesitated for a moment, examining the Grandmother, before nodding and going where she was directed. If Keeble had been paying more attention, he might've known what was going on, but all he could do was follow. In the lift he asked. Suldon answered.

"Grandfather Cinda is going to see if an emergency meeting of the Great Council can be called so Kim can address them."

"Don't see that happening," Tasko said, though he had been paying no more attention than Keeble.

Suldon nodded agreement. "I believe that Kim is of the same opinion. But at the moment we can do naught but comply."

The elevator didn't descend all the way to the ground before it stopped and the doors rattled open. Scree led the way out, checking all around before allowing anyone else to exit. The hurgon didn't like that much, but Keeble doubted any of them would call Scree to order.

"Where are we going again?" Kim asked their guide.

"Rooms available for the hakans until a meeting can be arranged," came the translation.

It was obvious why Kim had asked. They found themselves at the junction of two long, drab hallways. The floors were bare stone with rutted paths worn down the center. The walls were rough and bare. The doors—Keeble could only see two from where he stood—were no better.

The hurgon said something and beckoned for them to follow.

"It wants us to follow," Suldon said.

Keeble grunted and fell into step behind Kim and the two elves. Scree was out the front, with Flint and Sandy bringing up the rear.

"Deeba apologizes and says that the rooms are very small," Suldon said.

Four guards broke from the trailing group and hurried forward to open four different doors. Kim was already shaking her head. "We'll stay together."

Suldon quickly translated. "Deeba says that will not be possible, the rooms are too small to comfortably accommodate ten people."

"Well, I guess we'll have to be uncomfortable then."

"Deeba will not allow it, Kim."

"Well..." Kim crossed her arms. Keeble knew the look—she was getting stubborn.

But Tasko had moved to one of the walls and was standing with his hand against it.

"It doesn't matter very much, where they put us. We'll be able to leave whenever we want."

"What?"

"The walls are real stone—solid stone. Keeble can Sing his way out whenever he wants. I could too, I suppose."

"But the guards. He won't be able to cross the hall."

Keeble nodded and was looking from one side of the hall to the other. "Two rooms on each side... Just make sure the trolls are on my side—or at least two of them are. I can let them out and they can worry about the guards."

Kim chewed on her bottom lip. "You're sure?"

"Yes."

"Shit. Ok then, let's do it." She examined the group. "Scree in my cell so I can talk to the others. Flint and Sandy with Keeble. And we won't take no for an answer on this one. The rest of you guys go where you like." She sighed. "Come on then."

29: Murmurings

THERE MAY NOT HAVE BEEN BARS on the door but Kim decided it was definitely a cell. She sat on a cupboard and stared at the ceiling.

"How long do we wait, do you think?" She looked at both Scree and Bargle, her cellmates, but it was Scree's answer she wanted to hear. Bargle seemed unsure as to how he had actually ended up locked in with the two of them.

"How long does we wait for what?"

"To see if they really are going to get us a meeting with the council."

Scree laughed. "We go as soon as we is ready."

"But—"

"There ain't going to be no meeting. If they wanted a meeting then we would've gone to Earth."

Kim sighed. He was right, of course, but she *wanted* the meeting. She didn't want to keep fighting. "What if—"

"If these T'Loop let us out into the real world where we can talk with anyone then they risk their advantage in this whole game. We might get away. We might find some friends elsewheres. They keep us hidden and they can show us off to demonstrate their power, or maybe they'll say we're their allies and we's coming back to get their enemies."

He was right. He was right. She knew he was. "So what do we do?"

"We finds someone who want to change the rules of the game, not just improve their position in the current ones."

"And how do we do that?"

Scree shrugged. "Ideas is up to you. I just—"

Kim laughed. "You just thump people, I know. But for a guy who just thumps people, you come up with a lot of ideas yourself."

Bargle cleared his throat and Kim turned to look. "Yes?"

"These hurgon have radios, right?"

"Right."

"So they might be talking to each other on the radio. And we might be able to get an idea about who's pissed off if we listened in."

Kim smiled. "Right. Well done, Bargle."

He smiled at the praise and continued. "So, we get the elf witch to start listening in."

"The elf witch? Meledrin? Should I tell her you said that?"

Bargle shrugged. "Why should I care?"

"Scree..." But it seemed Bargle *did* care. He looked slightly shocked, as if thinking Kim was going to get Scree to pass on the information. "Scree, get Meledrin to start listening in. Then let's get the hell out of Dodge."

"Whats?"

"Tell Mel then get Keeble to bust us out of here."

"Right." He went blank for a moment. "Sandy wants to know, do we want them hurgon to think we's still locked up?"

"Umm... can we do that? Yeah, sure we do. Why not." It might be good for amusement value, if nothing else.

The wait seemed interminable, especially seeing Kim couldn't work out what the plan actually was.

"Are we going or what?" Keeble asked a few minutes later. The dwarf's head, covered in grey dust, had appeared in the middle of the floor. He rested his elbows on solid ground and dusted at his beard. It was a very disconcerting sight though she could see the magical hole now she knew it was there.

"Someone could have fallen through that, Keeble."

He was smiling broadly as he Sang—the air was thick with the sounds. "I told Scree what was happening," he Sang.

"And just how did you know where the center of the room was?"

"For Whistler's sake, woman, I can measure."

"Keeble..." Scree said.

The dwarf sighed. "Yes, be polite, I know. You're as bad as Flint."

Nobody moved.

"So are we going?" Keeble looked at Kim.

"Of course."

"Good. I'm standing on a table and a box here—it isn't all that stable."

"We'll just lower ourselves down and someone down there can make sure we don't fall."

"Right you are." The dwarf's head disappeared.

Bargle was closest and after a moment of hesitation, he slipped down into the floor.

Scree motioned for Kim to go next. She crawled carefully back and down into the hole while Scree kept guard and held onto her arm. She was lying on her stomach, legs hardly visible, when two strong hands grabbed her around the waist and helped guide her feet down to the box. As Keeble has said, it wasn't stable, but the hands kept her steady.

Kim ducked into the clear air of the lower room and Sandy smiled at her.

"Right?" the trollop asked.

Kim nodded.

Scree came down next and didn't need any help. "We right?" he asked. It was a question for everyone, but Kim felt his eyes on her.

"Of course." She drew a picture on the table. A dirty grey powder covered almost everything. "They should hire a cleaner." He was still watching.

"One more group," Keeble Sang. "I'll get them."

"You two go with him."

The dwarf shifted the focus of his song and used it to punch a hole through the wall. A rain of mortar settled to the floor.

Flint and Sandy disappeared through the wall with Keeble between them.

"Now what do we do?" Kim asked nobody in particular as she leaned back against the timber wall—it was probably worth a fortune. "Where do we go? Who do we talk to?"

Nobody had an answer.

"Does Meledrin have anything to report?"

A pause while Scree asked.

"Meledrin ain't there, Peni is. She says there are 'murmurings', but doesn't know where froms or who bys."

"Shit." Kim drummed her fingers against the edge of the table. What was there to think about? "Ok. Tell her to keep working on it. And she can talk to them if it helps."

"What are we going to do?" Nina asked, while the troll relayed the information.

"We'll just play it by ear."

"Pardon?"

"We'll make it up as we go along."

"Oh. Dwarves don't like that very much."

"Yeah, neither do elves, but it's the thing that both humans and trolls do pretty well."

Keeble stepped back through the wall with his enlarged party. Tasko and Suldon nodded greetings.

Elves and dwarves were so similar in so many ways that it just made their differences more compelling. Neither race ad-lib very well, but they still took everything in their stride, though for different reasons. Elves handled changing circumstances because it would appear undignified to complain or scream or run around pulling their hair out. Dwarves handled it because the pressure just bounced off them as they rampaged through life oblivious to most things except whatever they had set their mind on. They concentrated on the small things while the big things carried on without them.

Kim wished she was in their situation. Dealing with changing circumstances meant first acknowledging them, then grabbing them by the scruff of the neck.

"So, we're looking for dissidents," she said. "They'll probably be poorer hurgon from smaller families."

"Let's get out of here first," Scree said, "and then see what we can find."

"Right. You're up then, Scree. Lead on."

"How about we see if we can go straight down?"

Kim nodded and Keeble started his Song again, waving people away from a spot in the center of the room. Scree and Flint chose Suldon to check the room below. They grabbed his ankles and lowered him into the floor.

"All clear," Suldon said when he was hauled back up. He straightened his hair. "It seems to be a library."

"How fars to the floor."

The elf gestured upwards. "I believe the room is the same height as this one."

"Nothing below us?"

"There is not."

"Right." And without further ado, Scree stepped into the hole and fell through to the level below. He didn't make a sound. Sandy went a moment later, hair beads clacking.

Kim, watching the hole, waited tensely for them to return. She jumped when Sandy's head reappeared. "We've got two tables under here now. I'm standing."

"Right, go dwarves."

Nina went first, creeping towards the edge of the hole and then lowering herself carefully. Sandy helped the dwife, though when their turn came, the other dwarves brushed her offered assistance aside.

When Kim eventually climbed down from the tables in the library she looked around in wonder. There were row after row of books, thousands of them from floor to ceiling. Most were the size of the thick, chunky encyclopedias she knew from home. She pulled one of the nearest down and opened the huge stamped-leather cover. The writing was as chunky as the book, made up of boxes with strategically placed dots. She didn't know where to begin. That wasn't her job though. She put the book back on the shelf and found a couple of small ones, hardly larger than a normal paperback, though still heavy with patterned leather.

She gave one to each of the elves. "Take these. You may be able to work something out from them."

Tamidilin dubiously looked at the one she had been given. "Perhaps," she said, "though with a context—"

Kim shook her head. "Yeah, I know, without a context it's hard, but we have to start somewhere, right?" They should have gotten Cuto to teach them how to read. *That* would have been the place to start.

Scree was at a door. He had it open a crack and was peering out. "Where to now?"

Kim looked at Keeble.

"This is the ground floor," the dwarf said.

"How do you know?"

"There's solid rock below us."

"Do we want to tunnel the rest of the way out then?"

Keeble shook his head. "The stone on this planet is very dense. It is tiring for me to Sing it. We can continue to go through the walls if needs be but..."

Kim nodded. "All right then. Let's use more ordinary means for now and save your Singing for an emergency. We don't want to have to carry you around."

Suldon nodded. "I am more concerned about being trapped within the stone."

"There's that too."

They moved quickly and quietly and didn't meet anyone until they'd made their way back to the train station. Kim didn't know whether Flint was deliberately heading in that direction or if it was just an accident. They congregated in a small storeroom to plan their next move.

"I think we should steal the train," Bargle said, dreamy look on his face. Keeble and Tasko both nodded agreement.

"Don't be stupid guys," Kim replied. "It's a train. It's stuck on track. They'll be able to follow us. In fact they can make us go where they want because they control the switches." All three of them looked slightly sheepish.

"There are lots of hurgon out there," Scree said, motioning to the door and the train station beyond.

"Well, Keeble, do you know how far it is to the outside?"

The dwarf shrugged. "I can sense one more wall beyond this one. There may be others, but I can't tell."

Kim looked around, hoping to find an obvious answer. As usual, she wasn't having any luck. "So you can Sing some more?"

"Yes."

"Let's do that then." Just keep moving.

The trolls moved barrels and boxes to clear the wall, then Keeble did his thing.

Kim watched as a peg hammered into the other side of the wall found itself without support. The peg—and the cloak that was hanging on it—fell to the floor and the three hurgon in the room slowly looked around. The trolls raced through the hole and clobbered them before they could investigate. Scree had the door to the platform locked before Keeble stepped through the wall.

"Next," Keeble said, without even slowing. Flint and Sandy were ready.

30: The Wrong Way

MELEDRIN SWITCHED OFF THE CAMERA when Kim and her small party disappeared through the door and wondered which tasks she should undertake next. After a moment she switched the camera back on, in case her companions were to return, then sat and looked around again.

Stone was reclining in the gallery with his feet resting on the seat in front. From all appearances he had settled in for the day.

"What is it that your troop is doing, Stone?"

He did not turn to look. "They're guarding. One at each compass point looking out the windows."

"And what is it that you are doing?"

"Co-ordinating."

Meledrin studied the troll's back, as if the muscles and the EVA suit would somehow reveal if he were being facetious. "Are you aware of the method for controlling the cameras from Scree's chair?"

"I can control that from there?"

"Of course. You can do nothing with the picture in the dome, the well, or in other screens as Kim, Tuki and I can, but you can control what is on Scree's screen."

"Show me."

It was a simple process that the troll learned quickly enough and he began switching between the various views as if the hurgon were going to sneak up on them that very moment.

"Can I see the cameras inside the ship too?"

"There are no cameras inside."

"Yes there is. I saw them. Thorpe told me what they were."

Meledrin was about to shake her head but restrained herself. If Stone said he had seen a camera then he probably had. "I am unsure. I will check." She returned to her seat. She had checked all the buttons on her console and knew what they all did so... But one of the buttons had changed the view on her screen to simple blackness. She had thought a camera was broken—though she had neglected to mention this fact to a dwarf. She pressed the button again, and was given the same view as before. This time, she checked the small readout that told her what camera she was looking through. Tool Storage—Level 7. With a sniff, she pressed the buttons that changed the camera view. There were more cameras inside the ship than out.

"There is a button located near the camera controls."

"There's lots of buttons."

Meledrin describe the appropriate one.

"Yeah, I got it."

So she explained how it worked.

"Right then."

"Why do you wish to see inside anyway?"

"Why not? I can make sure nobody is causing any trouble."

Meledrin flicked through some of the pictures. The camera in the library showed Palsamon sitting at a desk with a book open in front of him. He looked to have recovered, physically, from his injuries. In fact, Meledrin thought he looked as good as he had for a long time. It seemed so long since they had spoken in private...

Meledrin changed cameras again, moving quickly though the views available. Bethalin was still working on a computer with the trolls as they attempted to organize the hold. Penisari was in the garden, working with Lisarea. They had not yet planted anything and were working to loosen and fertilize the cold, grey soil.

After a moment of studying the controls, Meledrin remembered how to target specific areas of the ship with the intercom.

She spoke into the microphone. "Penisari."

Down in the garden, the other elf looked up from her work, leaving a smear of dirt as she wiped at her cheek.

"Can you please come to the bridge?"

Meledrin watched as Penisari left her hoe against the wall and walked toward the door. Several minutes later she stepped out from the lift and made her way to the Communications platform.

"Yes, Meledrin?" she said, looking as if she thought she had done something wrong.

"I am leaving you in charge here."

"Thank you."

"It is not such a wonderful chore." Meledrin wondered if she would have left Penisari in charge if it was. "All you will be doing is waiting for a message from Scree."

"I can also study the controls?"

"Of course. As long as it does not interfere with your main task in any way."

"Of course."

"Very well then. Contact me if I am required."

Meledrin did not wait for an answer.

When she reached the library it was as if Palsamon had not moved. His head was still bowed over the pages, almost perfectly still, as he read. Meledrin watched for a long time, standing in the doorway. She knew from experience that Palsamon could remain like this for hours, lost in a book. He turned a page with his long index finger then went still again.

"What is it that you are reading?"

He looked up, showing no surprise at all. "It is a story that revolves around a woman trying to solve a murder. It is set on Sherindel. Our world was once very different, or so it would seem."

"Our world is so different now compared to just a short time ago." Meledrin wondered how many elves remained on Sherindel. Their communities were isolated and none could have supported others in the first few days of the attack. None of them could have joined their resources, poor though those resource might have been for fending off attacks.

Apparently Palsamon was thinking the same thing. "Perhaps we will find elves on other worlds."

"Perhaps. Or perhaps those who were crowded onto this ship are all that is left of our people."

Meledrin moved to sit opposite Palsamon, her hands resting on the cold metal surface of the table. "Read some of the story to me."

Palsamon looked at her, then nodded slightly. He leafed back through the book a small way. "*The gate opened of its own accord as Tapnuin approached and he paused. He had been told he could not leave until the Inspector had given his permission—the security system should have been programmed accordingly. Was this a test? Or did it mean he was allowed to venture beyond the wall once more?*

"Tapnuin moved closer to the gate and then, quickly, moved through. Outside the garden, the street was quiet. Where earlier there had been flitters parked nose to tail along the curb, now there were just two vehicles, sitting under trees though the shade had long since moved on.

"Across the travel lane, the four story structure of the metaguval building thrust mightily from the trees. Elsewhere, lights were blinking into life, but not there."

As Palsamon continued to read, Meledrin closed her eyes. Her companion's voice was deep and strong. She was unsure if it was the quiet passion of his reading or the words themselves that brought the pictures to life in Meledrin's mind. There were buildings as large as the whole of Grovely, with gardens growing inside. There were vehicles that hummed along almost silently, apparently without all the fumes of the current human vehicles. There were tens of thousands of people all living in the city that seemed to have grown out of the forest.

"What is the city called, Palsamon? Is it named?"

"It is called Calanendra."

Meledrin gasped. "Truly?"

"Yes."

A hundred kilometers to the north of Grovely there was a plain known as Calanendra. It was said that a thousand different trees grew there—ones that could be found nowhere else. It was said that the banks of the Daydawn River were strangely uniform. "Do you think..?"

Palsamon shrugged. "Who can say for sure, though I suppose there must be some connection."

Because of the strangeness of the place and the thousand different tales that were told about it, hardly any elves visited Calanendra. Again, it seemed that Palsamon was following her thoughts.

"We consider ourselves a worldly people, and yet we shy away from places of ill omen. Perhaps if we had been less absorbed in our own small doings we might have discovered our own space craft millennia ago and been flying between the stars."

"But..."

"Perhaps if we talked to the dwarves long enough for them to learn some of our legends then they might have gone to Calanendra to look for themselves. They would surely have found anything worth finding. But instead, we looked at our trees and read our flowery poetry."

"What is wrong with elvish poetry?" Meledrin snapped. But she knew she was reacting to her own feelings of unease.

"It is all about *us*. We write about inconsequential things while the whole world lives and moves around us."

"Nothing is inconsequential."

Palsamon sighed. "You know what I mean. We have our own little world and do not look beyond it."

"The dwarves are no better. They have all their machines and... whatever else... but most remain unused beneath their mountains."

"Why must we always compare ourselves to somebody else? We should not judge ourselves by the standards other people set for themselves."

"Then by which standards should we then judge ourselves?"

"By our own. We think we are a worldly, intelligent people, and yet female elves have treated men like second class citizens for as long as can be remembered."

"Yes, but—"

"You were more liberal in that regard than most, Meledrin, and yet now you still cannot accept the fact that men are as capable as women."

"But how can—"

"Have you not seen enough proof in the last weeks?"

Meledrin was shocked into silence. She wondered how Palsamon dared to interrupt her. Twice. But by the time she had thought of a suitable remonstration, she had also had a chance to think about what he had said.

Palsamon continued. "Even now, you judge Penisari by the standards of Grovely. She missed one Morning Ceremony ten years ago because she was sick, but nothing she does will ever redeem her in your eyes."

"She put the Ohoga Tree at risk."

"Do you *really* believe that? Do you really believe a tree that has stood for millennia will die because of one forgotten ceremony?"

Meledrin sniffed, changing tack. "Penisari is on the bridge even now, monitoring the communications equipment."

"Really?" Palsamon laughed. "And would she be there if you expected any significant activity? Even now, I expect you would still be up there if you didn't wish to talk with me."

"I do not wish to speak with you," Meledrin said quietly. "I am on my way down to the gardens."

Palsamon shrugged. "My point still stands. There is something you would rather be doing, so you pass the onerous task on to somebody else."

"I am the leader. I can order people to do as I wish."

"Do you see either Kim or Scree giving the boring, dangerous or possibly pointless tasks to others? Leading is about more than telling people what to do, Meledrin."

-oOo-

Meledrin examined the work that had been completed by Penisari and Lisarea. They had fertilized the soil on one side of the garden's lower section. It seemed that Lisarea was ready to commence the next section. The woman was dragging a half-full bag towards the tunnel to the other side.

But Meledrin wanted to get a sense of the task moving forward. Working with soil was all very fine, but it was about the plants ultimately.

"Lisarea, we will..." Meledrin paused. *More than giving orders?* "I think we should continue to work on this section for now, Lisarea. Let us get some planting done here so we have *some* plants."

Lisarea hesitated for a moment and Meledrin realized that her last comments could be taken as orders. She sighed. "You do not agree?"

"It is just... Ping and Topper seem to believe the fertilized soil must be watered first. Something to do with breaking down the components of the fertilizer."

"Well, we can water here now and..." Meledrin looked around, as if there might be buckets lying somewhere with which they could carry water. At the same moment she realized it would take many buckets and would be a labor-intensive task she also realized that Lisarea was once again looking uncomfortable. "You do not agree, again?"

"Topper said that there is a watering system in this room. Water falls from the ceiling like rain."

"Ahhh..." Of course. Carrying buckets of water would not be required on the ship.

"We could turn the system on now, but it would mean working in the mud and 'rain'."

"No, you are correct. That is ridiculous. Let us proceed with the fertilization of the other side."

"Yes, Meledrin." Lisarea bent to the heavy bag once more and started to drag it through the dirt.

Meledrin walked almost all the way to the tunnel before stopping to look back. With another sigh she went back to assist.

"What are you two doing?"

Meledrin had not even bent to lift the bag. She dusted non-existent dirt away from her hands and turned to see a young dwarf watching them. Meledrin did not know his name. "We are fertilizing the soil. What are you doing sneaking around in here? Are there no tasks for you to complete elsewhere?"

"I wasn't sneaking," the dwarf seemed offended by the accusation. "Nobody would make any noise walking on this dirt. And I just finished a task—I tidied the garden storage shed and catalogued the contents."

"Very well. Do you have the list?"

The dwarf offered her a pile of paper he was holding.

Meledrin perused the list. There was nothing very exciting on it. Garden tools—as was to be expected in the garden storage shed, she supposed. "I believe there are small hand held computers that can be used instead of sheets of paper," she said.

"Well, nobody told me."

He was offended again, as if anything could be taken the wrong way.

Meledrin had merely brought the computers to the dwarf's attention so he could use one next time and complete his task more efficiently—something all dwarves were keen to do. But he immediately thought she was criticizing. How could dwarves and elves ever hope to get along when the dwarves took umbrage at everything?

Meledrin looked at the list again. It was very long, taking up the best part of four pages. It was written in neat, dark writing with columns clearly marked and categorized. "Right hand garden gloves, 3. 2 wearing thin. Left hand gloves, 5." She raised an eyebrow.

The dwarf shrugged. "All the gardeners must have been right handed.

"Hoes, 4 (including two in use in the garden)." Meledrin scanned the garden and spotted two hoes leaning against the wall. "2 with damaged handles."

"We won't need to replace the whole hoe," the dwarf explained, "Just the handles."

Meledrin leafed through the pages. She looked at Lisarea, still standing by the fertilizer, and then back to the dwarf. "There is a barrow?"

He nodded. "It was right down the back, buried beneath some sacks."

Meledrin smoothed the front of her dress, reclaimed soon after she had returned from the rescue mission.

The list was detailed and could be put to good use by the elves in the garden and by whomever was in charge of resupply. It was a very good list, but the first thing Meledrin had thought to say was that it could have been better.

She cleared her throat before realizing what she was doing. "What is your name?"

"Hoodek."

"Hoodek, I apologize."

He narrowed his eyes suspiciously.

Meledrin continued. "I did not mean to suggest you had done a poor job. It seems to me you have completed your task admirably."

Hoodek tugged at his beard, a universal sign that a dwarf was working on a problem of some complexity. "Thank you," he said.

"Hoodek, perhaps..." Meledrin handed the pages back to him. "Do you enjoy gardening?" she asked.

The dwarf looked around. "I don't know. I've never done it."

"There is much work to be done here..."

"So you want dwarves to come down here and carry things for you?"

"No, I..." Meledrin looked at Lisarea and the bag of fertilizer. "We elves can complete the work—we *will* complete the work—" as if she was convincing herself, "but the garden is not just here for us. It is here for everyone."

He obviously didn't believe her. He shook his head, turned, and started to walk away.

"Hoodek?"

"What?"

"Dwarves are ugly and loud and uncouth—"

"Why thank you," he said sarcastically. He started to walk again.

Meledrin sighed. What was she trying to say? Was an insult the best way to start saying it? Why was it that in the presence of a dwarf she had suddenly lost her command of language? "Hoodek, what I mean is... That is all elves have ever seen in the past—that is all we have ever looked for. Like dwarves have seen us as boring and aloof."

"And ugly."

Meledrin gave a slight smile. "And ugly, too, apparently."

Hoodek grunted.

"So, I was merely going to suggest that it is time we started looking for something else. Especially in here, where to do otherwise would be sheer folly. I will not order you, or anyone else, to assist in the garden. However, let it be known that the assistance of dwarves would be greatly appreciated. The assistance of anyone would."

Hoodek watched her as if still not trusting. Eventually he nodded. "I have to give this to Ping," he said, waving the list. He turned and walked away.

"What are you looking at?" Meledrin asked Lisarea.

The younger elf snapped her mouth shut, "Nothing," and bent to the bag of fertilizer once more.

"Perhaps we should find the barrow," Meledrin suggested.

31: Lay of the Land

"WE'VE BEEN SPOTTED," Scree said.

"Where?"

He was already pointing but shifted a bit so Kim could squint into the darkness along his arm. He could hear her breathing right near his ear. The others weren't far away, waiting quietly.

"I can't..." Kim cocked her head to one side. "You mean in that window half way up the wall?"

"Yep. There's somebody in armor. They probably see us clear as day."

"We should keep moving then."

Scree grunted. They could keep moving all night, but unless they had a destination it wouldn't help. He and Flint had been leading back toward the ship—for all they knew, their yet-to-be-found allies might be in that direction—but he didn't like pointless wandering.

<Are you there, Scree?> Penisari's voice was thin and crackling, barely audible.

<Where else would I be, Peni>? Scree answered the elf silently. <Do you think I left my head behind somewheres?>

<*Of course not.*>

<Have you founds anything out?>

<*There is a great deal of radio conversation between the hurgon. I have monitored one ongoing exchange in which five hurgon have iterated how unhappy they are with the situations faced by their families. They have been forced to virtually sell themselves into slavery to one of the Great Families because of exorbitant interest rates.*>

<Sounds promising.> Not that Scree knew what 'interest rates' were. <Any names?>

<*Only one. P'targa.*>

<Don't happen to know where they is, do you?>

<*No, they do not speak of anything like that. They seem to be attempting to remain anonymous. I think that single name slipped out in error.*>

<Right then. We'll see whats we can find out. You keep listening though.>

<*Of course.*>

"Scree, are we going or what? I think someone's coming."

Scree looked across the vacant patch of ground. Beyond a pile of cracked and crumbling bricks, still barely out of the far building, four hurgon were carefully negotiating the rough ground. They were dressed in colorful cloth pants but held large, mean looking weapons.

Scree pointed along the wall. "That way," he said. Nobody but Kim would be able to hear, but Flint was in his mind, so it didn't matter. "We'll get into that buildings there then see what we cans see."

Flint went along the base of the wall and the others followed in his wake, dwarves, elves and Kim, clattering over rubble and stumbling through clinging fingers of wide bladed grass. The hurgon continued the implacable chase but were too far away to use their weapons.

<*There's all sorts of chatter on the radio, Scree.*> Flint said a minute later. <*Suldon thinks them hurgon are calling for help, though I don't know I said all them weird words right.*> There was a pause. <*We may have company when we get to the building.*>

<No choice. Go see whats you can see.>

Flint didn't reply, but Scree saw him race ahead, leaving Sandy to lead.

<*Can't see nothing,*> he said a moment later. <*Looks deserted.*>

<Make sure it stays that way.>

<*On it.*>

When Scree arrived at the door he found Sandy inside, crouched in the first room. Her dark skin made her almost impossible to see.

"Where's Flint?"

Sandy pointed upwards.

Scree nodded. "We'll wait here for a bit."

Flint came back a few minutes later, slipping into the room like a ghost. "I reckon if we get up to the roof we'll move a whole heap quicker," he said as he looked over Scree's shoulder to check the steady progress of their pursuers. "Looks like we can go just about anywhere without touching the ground.

"Let's do it," Kim said. "Where the hell are we going though?"

"We's looking for a minor family called the P'targa."

"Who says?"

"Peni."

"Okay, where are they?"

"No idea."

"Right, that narrows it down then," Kim said. "Maybe the first thing we can do is look for a train station or something. They may have a map or something so we can get the lay of the land."

Scree nodded and motioned for Flint to lead on.

On the roof, they stopped again. There were irregularly spaced lights creating pools of shadow. Sitting in the lee of a timber and brick wall they scanned the sky, looking for one of the sky trains they'd seen earlier. None of the tracks were visible but, after a few minutes, a twitching light passed rapidly across the tops of the buildings a couple of kilometers away.

Flint was already climbing up a rusting ladder to the next rooftop, following the light. Sandy went next, stopping at the top to urge everyone else up.

They quickly crossed the tops of a few more buildings. Pipes, big and small, snaked across the concrete and stone plains. Some joined together or met at strange looking machines that chugged noisily and belched out steam or smoke. Some disappeared into the small buildings that dotted the roof. Some disappeared into the roof.

They slipped silently past hurgon, darting from shadow to shadow or crawling on all fours. Hurgon stood on other buildings as well, maybe choosing to spend a few minutes in the quiet of the rooftop world. Scree wondered if they were avoiding the hurgon they wanted to talk to. Were they skirting past the P'targa family while they searched for a map?

They had no trouble for nearly half an hour.

Eventually, they were brought to a halt by a wall that towered over them.

Flint and Sandy, scouting to either side, returned while the elves and dwarves were still catching their breath.

"Ten meter gap that way," Sandy said, motioning over her shoulder. "About two hundred meters back to anything else. But it looks like the gap is a moat or something. It goes around the corner and keeps going, like they knew we was coming and wanted to stop us." She motioned forward, in the general direction of their journey. "The sky train thing is about a hundred meters that way."

Scree cursed and walked back a bit but Kim was nodding vaguely. "Maybe we're moving from one family's compound to another," she said. "They have the moat to make sure the only way in or out is through this building." She tapped the roof beneath her.

Scree didn't particularly care for the why. All he knew was that they had to keep moving forward. He stepped away from the wall and craned his neck to see the top.

"Keeble?" Kim said.

"I'll check."

Scree cursed again. Why climb the wall when they could go through it?

Keeble started to Sing and the magic built in the air. "It's about fifty centimeters thick," the dwarf said, laying his hand against the stone. His hand disappeared and Keeble followed. He was back a moment later, still singing. "There is a huge hall, we're about twenty meters above the floor. No way down."

"How about straights down?" Scree asked.

"Maybe. It's about a meter thick. Someone lower me down."

Scree and Flint each took one of the dwarf's feet and held him upside down. When they felt the tone of his Song change, they started to lower him. It was just a moment before he started to twitch and they hauled him back up. His Song ended abruptly.

Keeble cleared his throat. "A slight problem," he said. "It's a guardroom down there. There's about twenty of the ugly bastards hanging around doing all sorts of strange things." He cleared his throat again. "Well, they were. Now they're all rushing around looking for weapons, I imagine, because they saw me."

Scree looked quickly around. There was a small shed on the roof about fifty meters away. Probably the stairs.

"How big was the guard room," Flint asked. "Where was the main door?"

Keeble paced away from the group. "There is a wall here," he said, "with a door in the corner here." He went quickly across the other side of the group. "The other wall is here, and a door."

"And that way?"

"Ten meters. With a door."

Scree grunted. "Let's just pick one of the sides and go then. We're wasting time."

Keeble stood indecisively for a moment as he started to Sing, then pointed at a patch of roof. "Here."

Scree and Flint upended the dwarf again and lowered him.

"A bit lower," Keeble called around his Song. "Right, now let go."

Scree and Flint looked at each other, shrugged, and released the dwarf's feet. A couple of seconds later, Keeble's head appeared.

"It's a store room. I'm standing on a pile of crates. It's directly below the hole, so just lower yourselves in." He gestured back the way they'd come. "And you might want to hurry up about it."

There were three armored hurgon stomping across the roof towards them, arms already raised, and a dozen others in black breeches, all with weapons.

"Flaming cats. Let's go."

Nobody moved, then Suldon and Nina both raced for the half visible 'hole' at the same time.

"Flint," Scree said, grabbing Tasko by the collar and pulling him back when he started to crouch by the hole, "get down there and have a look." The other troll was into the hole and gone in an instant. Tasko grunted at the treatment, straightened his shirt and hurried after.

Only Kim was left, sitting on the lip, when Scree looked up again. The hurgon were closing quickly. They were in range and had their arms raised. Scree dived at Kim and knocked her aside. A burst of energy shattered the stone where she'd been. Someone down below grunted in pain.

Sandy's voice in Scree's head asked, <*You right, boss?*>

Scree was helping Kim to her feet and pulling her towards the minimal cover offered by a nest of pipes not far away. <We right, but we ain't going down the hole.>

<*Where you going?*>

<Don't know.> He ducked behind the pipes and looked around. The hurgon were still coming. <We gonna have to think of somewhere fast though.>

<*You want help?*>

<Too many of them. We'll find you.>

<*Right.*>

Flint joined in. <*Maybe not, Scree. Hundreds of the buggers down here. We got problems of our own.*>

<Keep in touch then.>

Scree had been examining his surroundings. One pipe, thirty centimeters in diameter, left the strange tangle and headed through the low wall that guarded the side of the building. He didn't know where it went once it got out the other side, but it looked like the best option.

"Come on." He took Kim's hand in his and pulled her along.

32: Easy

KIM WATCHED SCREE LEAN OVER THE EDGE of the wall and looked down. The pursuers had fallen behind. The robed ones seemed to be holding back, waiting for the protection of the others. A couple were visible, plodding along in their armor. They were moving slowly, as ever, but seemed much too close.

"Come on," Scree said as he climbed over the wall.

Kim took a look over the side of the building. It was too dark to see much but the pipe, which Scree was standing on, turned ninety degrees to go straight down

When Kim glanced at Scree he smiled, and she thought she knew exactly what he was thinking. But even if she'd had another option she wouldn't have refused to follow. His calm efficiency was a challenge she found hard to deny.

"Well, hurry up then," she said. "We don't have all day."

The troll's head disappeared and Kim followed. She put one foot on the pipe and hesitated. It was wide enough to stand on but... It was a pipe. She took a deep breath and carefully got her other leg over as well. She tried not to think about what she was doing as she carefully crouched down. Then she was straddling the pipe, sitting just a few centimeters from a very large drop. Her hands were sweating.

"There's a bracket about a meter down," Scree said.

"A meter?" They were a long way apart. Kim carefully slid around the curve of the pipe. She lowered herself further, sliding her feet along the wall as close to the pipe as she could.

She slid further. She was sure her feet had gone down a meter, but she still hadn't found the damn bracket. Her feet scrabbled against the wall, searching. Her hands were slipping.

"No," Scree said with infuriating calmness. "Down. A bit more down. You're almost there."

Kim stopped all movement and closed her eyes. She slid down the pipe with sweat-lubricated hands. Finally her feet found the bracket and she took a deep breath.

"Easy," Scree said.

Kim nodded. She didn't trust her voice.

"Course it is. Now, there's another bracket a meter and a half below you. If you slides your feet down the pipe to that you can transfer your hands to the top bracket, right."

"Right." Kim opened her eyes to look down, but changed her mind and stared at the cold grey bricks. With another deep breath she moved her feet off the bracket and started to slide again.

A lifetime passed before she was hanging grimly to the top bracket with her shaking feet planted firmly on the second.

With her more solid position, Kim risked a look down. Scree was another meter lower. One of his feet was planted solidly on the pipe where it turned ninety degrees to run along the wall, parallel to the ground. He was holding onto the bracket that supported Kim's feet. He was looking up at her.

"Come on bucko," Kim said with a slight smile that she wore over her unease like a mask, "keep your mind on the job."

"What?"

"Stop staring and move your arse." Arse might not have been the best word for her to use. Scree smiled. "Remember the bad guys," Kim said.

Kim watched as Scree nodded and spun around so both his feet were on the horizontal section of pipe and his back to the wall. It looked easy enough. Kim slid down to Scree's level as he edged along to give her room. But then she stopped. Scree made the spin look simple but, clinging to the pipe, waiting to do the same thing herself, Kim wasn't sure she could.

"You cans do it, Kim. This thing is plenty wide enough."

"Of course I can do it," Kim replied, taking another look. The pipe was wide enough and the fact that it was out from the wall a small way made it even easier. "I'm just catching my breath."

Scree nodded and leaned back against the bricks while Kim continued to cling to the vertical section of pipe. She may well have stayed there all day but the sound of the hurgon above startled her into life. With a quick, nervous movement she spun around to the left and leaned against the wall by Scree's side.

"That was easy," she said, with another glance down. She slowly took her left hand away from the bracket on the pipe.

Scree smiled. "Course it was. Now let's just hope this leads somewheres."

"Let's hope this leads somewhere? You don't know?" She leaned out slightly, trying to see along the wall, but Scree pushed her back with a large hand on her stomach.

"Looking won't helps. Let's just go."

"This is a great plan."

Scree smiled. He always seemed to be smiling when something dangerous was going on. "Well, if you likes we can go back up and see if we can come up with something else."

"Just move."

Kim sidled along the pipe after Scree. Examining her own feet, trying to ignore the space beyond, she kept going until she was pressed against Scree's side.

"Ummm... Why have we stopped?"

"We's all out of pipe."

Scree stopped her from leaning out to look again. "Just believe me."

Kim pressed against his hand, trying to see. The gentle pressure wouldn't let her move at all. "So what the hell are we going to do?"

"Stay calm. Let me thinks."

"I *am* calm." She licked her lips and took a deep breath. Calm. The pipe was plenty big enough. She could stand there all night.

Kim watched as Scree looked towards the ground. She looked as well. It was about fifteen meters away with its tall, tough looking grass and ubiquitous piles of rubble. It was way too far to be jumping, but Scree seemed to have other ideas.

With great care, the troll sat astraddle the pipe, squeezing his leg between it and the wall.

"What are you doing?"

He grabbed one of the brackets and leaned down until he was almost hanging upside down. "There's a window. If we sits on the pipe like this and grab the bracket we can lower ourselves down a bit and swing inside."

She knew what he meant but wasn't about to try it. Apparently there were limits to her acceptance of challenges. Her heart was racing. She tried to examine the window between the pipe and wall. She thought that maybe there was a drizzle of light but couldn't be certain. "I can't do it," she said. Thinking about it, she couldn't believe what she'd already done.

"You haven't even looked."

"I'm looking now."

"Sit down and have a look."

Kim did as she was told, slowly, carefully sitting then leaning all the way out and down to see. "I can't do it. I don't mind height too much—I *am* sitting here—but I'm not Lara Croft. I can't go hanging and swinging and jumping and... whatever." She had the feeling she was going to be doing it anyway. She couldn't see any other options and she was sure she'd let Scree convince her in the end.

"Take my hand then," Scree said, "and all you have to do is hang, I'll take care of everything else."

"What?"

"Take my hand."

She examined his hand for a moment then looked up at his face.

"Does you trust me?"

She took a deep breath and nodded.

"Take my hand."

She was an idiot. Her mother had been telling her that since she was a kid and Kim didn't really think she was in a position to argue.

With a sigh and one last look over the side she grabbed hold of Scree's wrist and he grabbed hers. She could feel his fingers lock around her and wondered what it would take to make him let go if he didn't want to. She licked her lips.

"You're sweating," Scree said.

"Well, duh."

He released her arm, wiped his hand on his trousers, then the wall and locked on again.

"Now all you have to do," he said, "is climb off the pipe."

"I knew you were going to say that."

But she couldn't move. She kept her legs wrapped around the pipe and, examining Scree's huge hand on her arm, wondered if the age-old question about the irresistible force and immovable object was finally going to be answered.

"Does you trust me?"

Idiot. With a deep breath she loosened her legs and leaned slowly sideways. Moments later she was hanging fifteen meters above the ground, swinging slightly and looking in through a window.

Hopefully nobody's in there, she thought. She couldn't see anything inside the room. For all she knew she might have been entering a room full of sleeping guard dogs.

"Ready?" Scree asked. He was already starting to swing her towards the wall.

"Not really." Her heart was racing faster than before, which she wouldn't have thought possible. Her mouth was dry.

"Well you better be ready by the time I count to three, 'cause I'll be letting go then."

"Shit."

She swung.

"One."

She dreaded the moment.

"Two."

What if...

"Three."

She sailed through the window. A table just inside caught her unexpectedly. She yelped with shock and pain, spun, clattered over onto the floor with the table coming behind. She hit the floor hard. The wind left her lungs in a rush. She rolled and came to rest on her back on a very comfortable, thick-piled rug. *Not a good sign*, she thought.

The squeak of a door opening to her right. To her left, a grunt as Scree hit the fallen table and knocked it completely upside down. He came to rest half on the table and half on her. His face was on her stomach, his hand on her face.

The wind knocked out of her again, Kim didn't move. She coughed and tried to draw in a breath. Scree was on his feet before the door across the other side of the room had opened all the way. He pulled a stunned hurgon into the room and knocked the alien unconscious. While Kim still struggled to breathe he poked his head outside to check, then closed the door.

"See, easy."

Kim groaned and nodded and wondered if the hurgon would mind her sleeping on the nice thick mat for a while. Scree was doing something by the door and moments later a slow bloom of light appeared overhead. It slowly became brighter until Kim decided that sitting up was preferable to looking at it. She heaved herself upright and rubbed at her back.

"Next time, you can go first."

"Can't hardly wait," Scree said as he quickly searched the room. There was no obvious weapon available so he picked up the table and ripped off two solid metal legs to use as clubs. "You right to go?" He opened the door a crack and peeked out.

"Where are we going?" She wasn't right. Any delay would help.

"The others are heading this way, but I think they's on the level below us. Looks like you was right about this being the border between two different families. There's guards everywhere, apparently."

Scree went through the door. With a sigh and a wince of discomfort, Kim stood and followed.

The next room was an office. There were a dozen desks. One whole wall was covered with pigeon holes and another with a long row of cabinets. A steam engine, with all sorts of pipes attached, chugged quietly in a corner. The pipes led to a range of machines. Some appeared to be computers, with rows of buttons and a furry, grey screen. Others were... Telephones? These latter were all lined up along the wall near another door. They had bits that might have been speaking tubes and other bits that... Hell, they could be coffee machines.

Steam spewed from one of the contraptions and set it to whistling. It was a sound that quickly got on Kim's nerves.

"There could be information here," Scree said, looking around as if wondering where to start his search.

"I think that whistling thing is a like a radio. Someone is supposed to be answering it about now. Either that or the coffee's ready."

"There's a map."

Scree hurried across to the other side of the room where a map several feet to a side hung from the wall.

The whistling machine suddenly fell silent.

"I think we should get out of here, Scree."

“Right then. Can’t follow this thing anyway.” He strode out through the room’s only other door as if he had every right to be there. Kim followed more cautiously.

They were in a wide, bare stone hallway that ended in a T-intersection ten meters to the left and seemed to open out into a large room thirty meters in the other direction.

Scree had gone a few steps towards the room but was now standing perfectly still, head cocked to one side. He spun around and headed the other way. “I think we should go this way,” he said.

“Why?” Kim peered down the passage for a moment. Then she heard it as well—the thumping feet on the floor. Lots of feet. Scree grabbed her arm and pulled her towards the intersection just as she saw a troop of hurgon, in formation, marching double time towards them.

Kim turned and ran.

33: New Shift

PING TOWELED HERSELF DRY and pulled on the new clothes she'd found in the hold. There was a whole container of clothes, sealed in airtight bags, to fit the diverse members of the crew. Unlike some of the others, she wasn't comfortable walking around in the EVA suites.

Once dressed, she stepped out of the cubicle into the main section of the bathroom and found a bare-breasted Crystal gazing at herself in a mirror.

"Hi, Ping."

"Crystal." Ping blushed and ducked her head.

"Them showers is good. Warm water and that soap stuff..."

Ping nodded. "They're wonderful."

There was a lift that came directly from the sleeping level above, and as Ping stood in the middle of the room, caught between stopping to brush her hair and hurrying down to her cabin on Level 6, the door screeched open.

Hoodek, with plaits in his long, red beard and hair, stepped into the room. The young dwarf looked at Ping and nodded. When he turned to Crystal he stared, looking slightly bemused, and blushed. Blinking rapidly, as if coming out of a trance, he put down his belongings and quickly turned to examine the noisy door.

Ping blushed harder, but Hoodek had accepted the situation and moved on. Well, perhaps he'd not accepted it, but realized that he wasn't going to be the person to change it.

Head down, Ping started for the bathroom's other door. It led directly to a hallway on Level 3. From there, she could catch a lift down to her cabin.

"Excuse me, Ping?"

She stopped to look at Hoodek. "Yes?"

"This door needs fixing. Looks like it might have some grit in the gears. But I don't have any tools or anything. I could go and get some and do it now. Or I could come back later if you want. Or..."

He was asking her? "Umm..."

"But I know there aren't any rosters or anything, or work gangs, so I'm not sure who should do it."

"Roster? Work gangs?"

"Yeah. If we knew that then we would know who would fix it. With all the commotion since we came on board I guess Keeble hasn't had time to organize anything."

Ping stood near the door holding her towel and hairbrush. "I..." According to the system used by the ship's clocks there were 1500 minutes in the day. If she divided that into 10 fifty minute hours. Three shifts daily. Surely she could work something out. "Ummm... Don't do anything yet."

"Oh. I just thought..."

"The engineering department will have a meeting and we can work that stuff out, okay?"

Hoodek nodded. "Thank you. It would be good to get organized properly. Everyone's just wandering around doing random things at the moment and it doesn't feel right." The dwarf smiled, collected his belongings and glanced at Crystal before heading quickly for the shower cubicles. Ping collected her thoughts and went the other way.

-oOo-

Ping put down her pad and pencil and sighed. She didn't know what she was doing. She wondered why she'd ever thought she'd be able to work the roster out. And even if she had everything perfect, the dwarves probably wouldn't listen. Deciding she needed help, Ping left her cabin and made her way the short distance to the engineering department.

Makar, Milo, Dogar and Kafin were there, engaged in various tasks. Ping hadn't spent a great deal of time with any of them.

"Does anyone know where Topper is?" she asked.

Makar shrugged without taking his eyes from the screen. "Saw him earlier."

That didn't help much. The ship had any number of places where a dwarf could find something to keep himself busy. Ping thought of asking Milo for help—he was the youngest and had once been Keeble's best friend. Instead, she crossed to a microphone and selected the setting that would page the entire ship. "Topper, please come to the engineering office. Topper to the engineering office." There was an alcove in the corner of the engineering room as well, but Dogar had commandeered the chair from there. He and Kafin should really have taken the pump they were repairing up to the workshop.

She thought of saying something but changed her mind. "We'll be having a meeting later," she said instead.

"Who says?" Kafin asked, running fingers through his long grey beard.

"I say." Ping's heart beat faster. It was all very well giving orders when Kim and Scree and even Keeble were there to back her up, but what would happen if the dwarves ignored her now? They were even less likely to listen to Meledrin—a woman and an elf all in one—though she'd been officially left in charge.

"And what if we don't want to go?"

Ping licked her lips. "Then you sit and watch while others do work."

"You can't stop us."

"The work gangs might if they see you doing work that they could be doing."

The old dwarf grunted and turned back to the pump.

Ping tuned and hurried back to her cabin to collect the half-completed list. She'd shifted her meager belongings from the small cabin beside Keeble's to the large one on the far side of the engineering department. The smaller cabin would probably have been plenty large enough in reality, but she was an officer so... She shook her head at the absurdity of it.

Ping quickly made her way through the engineering bay to the eastern side of the ship. The office there had three desks, each larger than the one before. Sitting down at the one closest to the door she took up her pen but didn't change the list at all before Topper arrived four minutes later.

"You wanted to see me?"

Ping jumped slightly and looked up. Topper was leaning in the door, hair upright and askew, breeches and shirt dirty. He was only slightly older than Ping and had been far more accepting of her and the dwives than almost any other dwarf. She hoped that would continue.

"Yes. I was talking to Hoodek and he suggested that all the dwarves might be more comfortable if there was a bit of a system in terms of shifts and work gangs. I was trying to work something out but..." She threw her piece of paper on the table. "I was wondering if you could help me."

"Sure. It does feel strange knowing there won't be a hooter to mark the end of the shift."

"Well, I can't work it out." She motioned to the list.

"Well," Topper said, ignoring the paper, "first you have to work out how many work gangs."

"Four."

"Why?"

"Because there are four Singers."

"Good, but what about you?" He tugged at his beard as he examined the names on the paper.

"What?"

"Well, the Singers will want to lead the groups, right?"

"Yes."

"So which group do you lead?"

"Umm... I thought I could work with your gang sometimes."

He didn't look disappointed at all when he nodded. "I'm the only choice. None of the others would like it much yet."

"You would still be in charge," Ping said. "If I don't officially put myself in a gang, then I can look in on anyone... Sort of keep an eye on things?" She didn't intend to go around shouting orders and criticizing, she just wanted to make sure the dwives were being treated fairly and that the different gangs were working together. It probably meant Keeble would be in charge of the actual work and she'd organize things, but that couldn't be helped.

Topper nodded slowly. "That's like what we call a Site Boss. You're job is to make sure everyone else is doing theirs... by working out rosters, for a start."

"Right."

"Sounds like a good idea."

Ping smiled at him. "Thanks, Topper."

"I think you chose the wrong desk, in that case." He pointed to the biggest desk. "The Site Boss is the one who does most of the office work.

Ping eyed the desk. It looked larger than anything she would ever need. "I think we can stay here for now."

"Right," Topper said, returning his attention to the partially completed list. "Next, you need at least one of your clock group in each gang. Ari, Dosa, Nina and Tess were the best of them, right? So spread them between the groups." He did that. "Then make sure there is an even spread of youngsters, old timers and dwives."

Ping watched as he wrote some more. "Are you sure that's right?"

"Yes." He wrote the last name with a flourish and laid the pencil down. Ping had agonized for an hour over what Topper had finished in a two and a half minutes.

"And the shifts?"

Topper shrugged. "Depends how you want to organize things."

"Well, I was thinking... The first thing we should do is give the ship some night and day. At the moment everything is the same. Sometimes I find that I am sleeping every five hours because I lose track of the time."

"Yeah, it's like that."

"I can program the lights to dim at a set time. Then we can have three shifts a day of five hundred minutes each. That is about 8 hours and twenty minutes."

"That could work. And the shifts just rotate. Three days on, one day off."

"Yes. But I was thinking that being on shift doesn't mean you work and nobody else does."

"So... what's the point, then?"

"Well, being on shift means you keep an eye on things. If we're on the ground, there is always at least one person on the bridge and one in the engineering bay. If we are flying, then there are two people in both those spots—except if we're in the other universe, because then it really doesn't matter."

"So what if something needs to be done then?"

"Then whoever's on shift asks for volunteers from amongst the others."

"What if nobody volunteers?"

Ping shook her head and laughed. After a second, Topper did as well.

"I don't think we have enough people to do it any other way." Ping thought Kim should have taken on a full crew. The ship could hold 85 people for a reason. If 50 people had been the optimal number then it would have been designed to have a crew of 50.

"All right then." Topper said, still trying to pick holes in her plan. "So, all the cleaning would be done by dwarves not on shift?"

"Yes, that way, there will always be somebody keeping an eye on things here and on the bridge."

"That could work."

Ping shrugged. "But will they listen?"

-oOo-

Ping found it strange that standing on a stage could make speaking all that much harder. She cleared her throat again but didn't know what else to say. She'd explained the roster and work gangs to all the dwarves, and of course they grumbled and cursed her for a stupid woman, but she thought they'd do as she said.

Milo put up his hand. "You aren't in a work gang, but Keeble is. Who's in charge of his gang when he's doing something else?"

Ping examined her list for a moment. She chewed on her thumbnail while she thought. She wanted to put Ari in charge though she knew the dwife was not the best choice. "Dogar," she said eventually. The dwarf seemed capable enough, but Ping wished she'd thought of that before getting on the stage so she could ask Topper. It would not matter all that much—Ping imagined she would be doing the 'something else' more often than Keeble.

"Who's on shift now?"

"Ummm... Tasko's gang is," Ping said. That would mean Hoodek was off shift—in Topper's gang—and he could fix the door in the shower's elevator. "Next will be Topper, Drago, then Keeble. All right?"

"Fine."

"Whatever."

"Typical."

It wasn't a rousing reception, but it could've been worse. Ping looked at Topper and he nodded slightly. She cleared her throat. "Tasko, one of the first things you have to do is organize for someone to see what's wrong with the bathroom on Level 6—there's no hot water." At least when that was fixed she wouldn't be bumping into naked trolls.

"The computer doesn't say anything about that."

"Well, maybe the computer is broken as well. All I know is that there's no hot water."

"All right then."

She was done but they all sat waiting for her to say something else. "That's all," she offered. It seemed it was enough. Several got up and wandered away. Topper crossed to stand near her when she made her way down from the stage. His gang crowded close by. There were two fifty minutes hours left before they got the boring job of keeping an eye on things.

"Can I fix that door?" Hoodek asked.

Ping pointed to Topper.

"What door?" Topper asked. But it didn't matter. "Yes, unless Tasko has something else for you."

"Ummm..." Ping said.

"Yes?"

"There's a pump sitting in the middle of the Engineering bay. I would rather that area was kept clear."

Topper nodded. "Right. Nina and Mintar can take it and all its parts up to the workshop. And I will..."

"You will come with me to see about the lighting. We'll be in Engineering."

Ping suspected that Topper wouldn't be needed for the task but she liked his company—he was not afraid to speak like the dwives sometimes were, and he was not rude to her all the time like a couple of the older dwarves."

Tasko and his gang were already on duty down stairs, apparently. Everyone else had found something to do. Soon only Topper remained, standing close by, waiting to get to work.

Captain Thorpe joined them after having watched the meeting from nearby. "Do you think they'll listen?"

"Perhaps," Topper replied. "If it suites them, certainly."

"We'll back you up if you need it, Ping, you know that." He motioned over his shoulder to two other humans—Paul, the junior SAS officer, and Airman Dongoske.

Ping shrugged. "The dwarves probably think you have even less right to be telling them what to do."

"Because we aren't 'full' members of the crew."

"Yes."

He shrugged. "We're still bigger and meaner than they are. And there are always the trolls."

"Thank you, Captain."

"Don't ever forget that you have the right to give those orders, Ping—it was one of the things they agreed to before being allowed to stay on the *Hakahei*." Ping nodded and Thorpe nodded in return. "Now, see those buttons over there—do you think one of them will make these seats disappear?"

Ping looked where he was pointing, to a small console by the wall near the front corner of the stage, then at the seats. She hadn't noticed before, but it looked as if they might retract into the floor to leave a large portion of the room totally uncluttered. "Perhaps," she said. "But why would they?"

"Keeble said that this is a scout ship and can go six months without stopping at a planet."

"So?"

"So, with eighty-whatever people stuck on here for six months the main problem would be boredom. The designers would have to do everything possible to avoid that. Movie theatre and assembly hall here, or take the chairs away for a sporting field."

"Sport?"

"Yes. We found a football." He smiled, though Ping had no idea what he was talking about. "If you don't mind, I'll press some buttons and see what happens."

"Very well. And if you discover something you can write some instructions."

Thorpe saluted, "Yes, ma'am," while he went to have a look. He chose a button, seemingly at random, and nothing obvious happened.

Ping turned away to leave him fiddling and headed towards the Engineering department.

34: The Gap

KEEBLE CONTINUED TO SING as he turned to look at Flint. "What do you mean they aren't coming?"

Flint shrugged and tugged at his moustache.

Sandy spoke. "They just got attacked. Couldn't get to the hole."

"But..."

"You might want to stop Singing before a hurgon falls down on top of us."

Keeble fell silent. It was so sudden it almost hurt. "So what's happening?"

"We're going that way," Flint said, pointing. "Hopefully they'll meet up with us."

"Hopefully?"

"There's lots of stuff going on around here—who knows what'll happen." Flint went to the door and looked out. "We've got Suldon and Tami," he said, "so our job is to find the P'targa family. Scree and Kim's job is to find us."

"But how'll we know what to do if we do the impossible thing and find the family?" Keeble wound the gears on his arm.

Flint shrugged. "Not my concern—you're in charge."

"Me?" He was in charge of the engineering department. That was all.

"Yep."

Keeble didn't like the idea much but after a moment of thought realized he had nothing to worry about. He could give all the orders he wanted but the two trolls would follow or not, and that would determine where everyone really went. And if they found the P'targa family then Flint would be able to talk to Scree in his head, and Scree would be able to talk to Kim. *Huh!* He didn't need Kim's help. "Let's go then. No time to waste."

But just when Keeble thought leadership would be easy, Flint quickly closed the door he'd just opened. "I was seen. You might want to start Singing again."

Keeble stared.

"Right now. They're only twenty meters away." While he was speaking, Flint motioned to Sandy and the two of them moved a large box to block the door.

Keeble launched straight into his Song without his usual slow build up. He tunneled through a wall and stuck his head through to check. He backed out in a hurry. "No good." He knew the wall to the north would lead to that huge hall and they'd still be a couple of levels above the floor. So down. He shifted the focus of his Song and motioned for the trolls to hold him.

Below was an empty room. As soon as Keeble said that he was dragged back up and Flint jumped down without even waiting for measurements. Tasko and Nina went next, one on either side of the hole, muttering under their breaths, lowering themselves carefully then letting go. Then the elves did the same. Keeble and Bargle followed with Sandy pushing on the wooden crate to hold the door closed. When Keeble hit the floor he moved quickly out of the way. Sandy hit the floor lightly, hair beads clattering like a rainstorm, an instant after he'd stepped clear. Flint was leading the way almost before the trollop had rolled to her feet. Keeble cut off his Song.

There was a knock at the door and everyone looked at each other.

After a moment, Keeble started to Sing again. He heard Tasko Singing as well and the other dwarf quickly molded the stone by the side of the door. He was flattening out a section, spreading it out past the timber and around the door handle. Seeing the door opened inwards, it would take axes or something similar to get past. Keeble sighed with relief and wound his Song down.

"Where we going?" Flint asked.

"What if we head back outside?" Keeble suggested. "We can't go forward anyway." The huge hall and all the guard made that impossible."

Flint nodded and motioned to one of the walls. "That way is one of those huge vacant blocks. The other way was that narrow gap between the buildings."

Keeble guessed he was supposed to pick a direction. He thought for a moment, giving each option careful thought. "The gap will be darker and give us another option if we're seen," he said eventually.

Flint nodded and Keeble smiled at the approval.

"Let's go then. You up to Singing us all the way through?"

"I'd rather not."

"Just one more then. We obviously can't use the door." Flint gestured to Tasko's handiwork. Whoever was outside was starting to get serious about getting in but it would still be a while. The timber wasn't giving up without a fight.

So after Singing through one more wall, Keeble was happy to fall in behind as Flint strode confidently along a hallway, heading in the wrong direction, until he came to the first intersection. The troll paused at the corner, peeking around, before he was off again.

"Shouldn't we be careful?" Keeble asked as they walked right down the center of the hall, past doors on either side.

"Am being careful. What do you think we going to do if someone walks out one of these doors? Where you think we going to hide?"

Keeble looked around though he already knew there was nowhere to hide. Sneaking furtively along, clinging to a wall wouldn't be much help at all. "We could go through one of the doors," he suggested.

"Yeah, but until we know where the bad guys are coming from how do we know which side is best?"

They reached another T-intersection and Flint examined the options again. He leaned against one of the stone walls and looked up and down the hall. "Is that the outside wall?" he asked, pointing to the wall opposite their passage. It didn't look any different to any other wall.

"No," Bargle said, saving Keeble the effort. All the dwarves would know the building's measurements from their time on the roof. "It's four meters beyond."

Flint nodded slowly as he continued to examine the passage. Eventually he shrugged and picked a direction. Keeble followed, looking around all the while. His companions were doing the same, though the trolls would probably pick up any danger long before anyone else. Thirty meters down was a door. Sandy raced to the front when Flint started to turn the handle. They burst through within moments of each other and Keeble trotted in behind.

It took Keeble a moment to react. During that time the two trolls knocked three hurgon unconscious. Then they started to pummel another couple. They seemed to be off duty guards who, somehow, hadn't been roused by the general emergency. Others were standing along the walls, blinking in astonishment as they woke.

When he had his bearings, Keeble chose one of these half-asleep figures. He charged forward. He might hinder the trolls more than he helped them, but the longer this took the more risk there was.

At the last moment, Keeble wondered if the hurgon had stomachs. He dropped his shoulder and barreled into the alien. He didn't know what his action did exactly, but it had a satisfyingly effect.

"There are too many," Tamidilin said. She was flailing about with her fists and feet in a graceful and effective manner. Suldon was no less aesthetically pleasing, but even more effective. Bargle and Tasko were working in tandem. Only Nina stood back and watched, probably never having said a harsh word to anyone in her life. The dwife wrung her hands and looked from combatant to combatant. Hurgon were coming through another door.

Flint stopped his pounding for a moment to point. "There, Keeble, let's go."

"I can't fight and Sing at the same time." Keeble wasn't much of a fighter at all, but neither were the hurgon, guards or not.

"Stinking cats."

The focus of the battle changed as Keeble's companions closed in around him. Nina made a mad, weaving dash across the room to join him in the center of the circle as Keeble caught his breath and started to Sing.

With the noise and the pressure it took him a few moments, but he stepped into the wall almost before the Song was focused. With hardly a look he jumped down to the packed earth of the gap. Nina crashed into his back and he almost lost concentration. He clamped onto his Song as more of his companions, the whole scrum of them, followed.

Flint and Sandy came last, but a few of the braver hurgon came as well. Three hit the ground hard, only to be thumped by the trolls before they had time to think. Another two were trapped in the wall when Keeble finished his Song. One was crushed instantly, fused with the stone, just its ugly, square-jawed face showing. The other was caught by the leg and flopped down to crash against the wall. It screamed and thrashed as it hung upside down by a twist of flesh and bone.

Keeble couldn't reach the alien to put it out of its misery. Those who *could* reach weren't inclined to do so. Tamidilin and Suldon watched in horror, as did almost everyone else. Flint and Sandy urged them all to get moving.

"Come on," Sandy said.

Keeble allowed himself to be dragged down the narrow alley between the towering buildings.

A hundred meters further down a kink in a wall offered a deeper patch of darkness. Flint crouched there and waited for everyone else to catch up.

"Flint," Keeble said when he was hidden away as well. He struggled to catch his breath. "I thought I was in charge."

"You is."

"Right. Then next time you want to do something trollish—like march into an unknown room—how about you ask me first."

"Sure thing, boss." He smiled. "I'm a troll. You got to point out things like that."

Keeble shook his head but smiled back. "Now what?"

Flint shrugged. "There won't be any doors into this alley—not near here anyway—so..."

"Why not?"

"No point having all that security in the big room if somebody can just go to one of the back doors and sneak in that way."

"Right. Of course."

"So we just decide which side we want to be on and you Sing us through."

"I think that side." Keeble pointed to the wall opposite the one they'd emerged through. "They probably have no idea about all the commotion. If they do, they still won't be expecting us."

"You're no fun."

Keeble smiled up at the older man. "It's the price of leadership, lad. You'll learn one day."

"Need to rest first?"

"For a moment, yes."

They sat quietly and rested. Back the way they'd come, the screaming hurgon finally fell silent. That made resting a whole lot easier.

Suldon pulled out the hurgon book Kim had given him and opened the cover. Keeble leaned back against the wall and rested while the elf strained to see the words on the page. Tamidilin looked over his shoulder and they were arguing about 'phonetics' and 'personal pronouns' in a matter of moments.

Keeble didn't know how long he sat there, listening to the elves, listening for sounds of pursuit. He may have dozed. The afterglow of his Singing lulled him.

"It'll be morning soon," Flint said. "We don't want to stay here all day. We should get going."

Keeble sighed and nodded. "All right." Pushing himself to his feet he crossed to the far side of the gap and laid his hand against the stone. He Sang, and stepped into the wall to see what was beyond.

The room was only two meters to a side, with thick carpet and some type of tapestry on the wall. The only light came through a partially open door. There was a hurgon standing against one of the walls, possibly asleep.

"There's someone in there," Keeble said around his Song once he was back out in the open again. "A small room. One person."

Flint cracked his knuckles. "No problem then. A good staging area. Won't be a moment."

"No, Flint."

"What?" He narrowed his eyes suspiciously, as if Keeble was deliberately taking away his fun.

"Sandy, go through and close the door. Flint, stop the hurgon from warning anyone else, but don't harm it."

"Don't harm it?"

"That's right. Instead of just thumping everyone, let's ask some questions."

Flint tugged on his moustache and smiled. "Huh. That's why you're the boss."

"Apparently."

The two trolls went through the wall. Keeble waited a few seconds then followed.

In the darkness, he could see that his orders had been obeyed. The hurgon, with yellow skin and dark eyes, was looking terrified but watched with obvious interest as people continued to come in through the wall.

"Suldon, tell it that we don't want to do it any harm. If it answers our questions we'll be on our way."

While Suldon translated Keeble tried to work out exactly what he was going to say. He needed to find out all he could without giving anything away.

Elves had a way with words. Grunting, he turned to Suldon and Tamidilin for advice.

35: Committees

IT WASN'T ENOUGH THAT TUKI had his own room for sleeping, he also discovered he had his own office. It had to be for him. He sat at the moai-sized desk for a long time, palms laid flat on the dusty surface, and wondered what he was supposed to do there.

Dozens of drawers lined one of the walls and when he got up to look, Tuki discovered files. He pulled one out and started to read slowly.

"'Calaneka. Phazer Prime 4. Calaneka was colonized by Dapudo immigrants in the year 4325. The mission was funded by a private corporation based in Old Hapagi which hired Juowopa IV, the largest colony transport available at that time.'"

Tuki skimmed through some more files, reading about different worlds and the people who lived there. Each file contained a few dozen pages and gave out information about religion, orbit patterns, alliances, revenue and a dozen other things he didn't understand.

Holding a file in his hand after reading about Yapin's Grin Wars, he ran his eyes over all the drawers.

"Are they all full of files?" he asked softly. But he could not understand why, when the computer could have held all the information quite easily. Although... The computers did not work in the other universe, so if you wanted to learn about your destination while you were travelling...

Tuki carefully put the file back in the drawer and sat back down at his desk. He had seen the desks in the other offices and each of those had a computer sitting on it. This one was just a large black surface. He opened the drawer in front of him and discovered a keyboard. The top drawer to his right hid a set of controls similar to those on his console in the bridge. Pressing the power button he watched as the top of his desk lit up like a computer screen.

"It is like the skyglass." Selecting a star, Tuki gently touched it with the tip of his finger. Information appeared in a box nearby. The coordinates. The type of star. Number of planets. Number of habitable planets. Number of inhabited planets. Number of space habitats. Population.

Another point of light and another list.

"I wonder if I can find Hulgorn," he muttered. He typed the name into the keyboard but no results were found. Perhaps the planet was known by a different name when the file was created. So he used the controls to center the image on the ship.

At one end of the desk was a bright yellow light the size of a pea. The word 'Tapalinda' hung in the air beside it. Halfway down was a tiny point of light called 'Kitawera'. Down the other end was 'Tapalinda Minor'.

Tuki touched his index finger to Kitawera then locked the new information.

"Kitawera is the home world of the alien race which calls itself hurgon. The planet and its people were discovered in 4189 by the UMEF Scout Ship Kitawera which was carrying out routine inspections of all G-type stars in the area. Being a race confined to one world and never having looked beyond themselves the hurgon had no name for their world and the Captain adopted the present nomenclature.

"Hakans and the hurgon have had little contact, with most experts believing that to interfere in their technological development may have disastrous long term effects. While others disagree with this view, there are not yet enough to effect a change in policy.

"The hurgon seem to be in the early stages of an industrial revolution. Most information about them has been gained through the interception of primitive radio signals."

"I will have to update the files," Tuki said. And he started using the keyboard, typing information into the keyboard one finger at a time. He did not know if all the information he was typing in was completely correct, and he did not know if he was spelling all the words correctly, but he would let Kim and the elves worry about that later. All he was worried about now was having something to do.

If only there was some information about the multeese, Tuki thought. And he wondered why there wouldn't be. It was possible such creatures had been around a long time and they had mentioned the word often enough. He found the search function on the computer and typed the word multeese with shaking fingers. The lights on the desk flashed. Information appeared on the screen.

"According to Hadrint Trycod Ti Delamanan of the Wanakama people, the multeese were created in a laboratory by an ancient race known only as Zo. *Trycod states that eese gas particles were treated (details of this are unclear) in an attempt to create energy. This experiment failed but when a certain critical mass was reached the gas cloud became a reasoning being. The difficulty for the multeese, lies in the fact that each particle remains self aware—with its own desires and agendas—but no ability to act without a general consensus from the cloud. What results is a being run by committee.*

"Trycod also suggests that the multeese lacks any gender at all and has no suggestion as to methods of reproduction.

"As ever, Trycod is reluctant to share his source material. This, added with his known loose handling of facts, has led many to doubt all of his conclusions."

The page ended and Tuki hit the button for more information. The notes continued. *"Things that are universally believed? The multeese think all other creatures are inferior and want them dead. The multeese may well be right, for they have technology far beyond anything we have ever seen. Many other species agree. The multeese never stay still—their ships (or perhaps it is just one ship) rove constantly around the known galaxy, turning up without warning and moving on as quickly, often leaving in the middle of battles for no apparent reason. (Some might conclude that this supports Trycod's assertion that it is a being run by committee.)*

"No matter the background or the reasons, in the end one thing is certain—all species, all races dread the arrival of the multeese ships." Tuki sat back. In fifty thousand years the multeese had not changed at all. And apparently, though everyone was against them, they still did as they pleased. He had hoped for information that would help defeat the aliens but it appeared that nobody could help.

He might have sat there all day, staring at the line of letters, trying to find something in them that would save everyone, but there was a knock at the door. "Ummm... Yes?" he said.

Stone entered the room and looked around, taking in everything. "We got problems."

"Pardon?" Why was Stone telling him?

"Problems. All them hurgon outside look like they're finally tired of sitting around. They're moving."

He thought for a moment, because that seemed the thing to do. "Where?"

"Don't know. Some are going, some are coming, some are just moving a bit. All looks very complicated."

"Where is Meledrin?"

"Sleeping."

"Oh. And Ping?"

"Sleeping."

"Oh."

"You're it for now, Tuki. We can wake one of them up if you want, but you got to tell us."

He scratched at his nose as he tried to work the problem through. Stone was examining his face as carefully as he had examined the room earlier. Tuki thought of telling him to go and rouse Meledrin—she had been left in charge, after all—but what could the elf do to help? She could talk to the hurgon, but if anything else was to be done there were people better suited to the task.

Tuki worked at the controls of his desk for a moment until he had a view of the outside of the ship. The hurgon were indeed moving, though it was all meaningless to him. After long seconds, he still had not come up with an answer.

He finally realized that he didn't need to come up with an answer. It was no point him asking Meledrin but, as he had already decided, there were others.

"Can we get Captain Thorpe and Sergeant McCree to help?" he thought for a moment more. "And Chasm and Cliff?"

Stone smiled and nodded, which made Tuki wonder if he was being tested. "I'll get Chasm to bring the humans with her when she comes up." The troll looked around again. "In here?"

"Umm..."

"How about the security office. It's made for this kind of stuff."

"Very well, then."

He and Stone met the others there to listen to what they had to say.

When Meledrin had first told Kim that the hurgon were surrounding the ship, the instructions had been to hold the ship. The ground party were not replying to radio signals, so Tuki and his security party decided that, without differing instruction, that was what they had to do.

Yellow troop were finished in the hold, so they would man the guns and fire on any hurgon taking decisive action against the ship. They would not fire indiscriminately and they would not kill more than was absolutely necessary.

Tuki walked out of Scree's office after the meeting to discover that the four weapons control chairs located there were already being manned. Trolls were strapping themselves in, talking all the while.

"Perhaps I should tell Meledrin before we do anything," Tuki said, looking over his shoulder at the others in the office.

Stone nodded. "If we're attacked we'll try to hold off until we get confirmation."

Out in the foyer, Tuki stopped and looked up at the lights. They did not seem very bright at all. Two dwarves, Milo and Dogar, were wandering past with toolkits.

"Is there something wrong with the lights?" Tuki asked.

Milo shook his head. "The lights are dim because it's night."

"Is it?"

"Yes. According to Ping. From now on the lights in the common areas of the ship will be dim for 500 hundred minutes between the hours of 2500 and 0500."

"Umm.. How long is the day?"

"1500 minutes. 30 fifty minute hours."

"All right." Tuki shrugged, though he thought it was strange that Ping would just decide to make it night-time. It could well be the middle of the day outside, though with the persistent smoke it was hard to tell. He headed down the stairs and left the dwarves to their work. On Level 2 he tried to remember which room was Meledrin's, then knocked quietly on the door.

The door slid open a small way and Meledrin stood peeking through the gap. Her hair was messed and it looked as if she had not been sleeping at all. Tuki could hear movement behind her.

"What is it, Tuki?"

"The hurgon in the square are doing something. They are all moving and... stuff."

"Give me a moment."

"There is no need..."

"Pardon?"

Tuki blushed and looked at his feet. "I talked to some of the soldiers and trolls. The guns are being manned. If the hurgon try anything the trolls will shoot them."

Meledrin raised an eyebrow. "You gave the trolls permission to shoot hurgon?"

"Only if the hurgon attacked us first. And they have to kill as few as possible. You are in charge though. Kim said. So I thought I would check with you first, so you can make another decision if you wish."

"You did not make those decisions on your own?"

Tuki shook his head.

"Captain Thorpe and Stone were involved?"

Tuki nodded. "And the last we heard from Kim was that we should hold the ship," he said.

"That is correct." Meledrin looked back over her shoulder for a moment. "You have done well. I am not needed. Good night." Then she was gone and Tuki was staring at the door.

And it *was* night. Tuki looked up at the ceiling lights and decided he should go to bed—he was tired and all the reading and typing had given him a headache. But it had also been hours since he had anything to eat. The dwives were going to be working out a roster for the cooking, but had not done anything yet so everyone was left to their own devices when it came to organizing food.

Tuki made his way to the stairs again and went down to the mess hall on Level 3. There were ten others at the tables, though there was nobody in the adjoining kitchen. Instead of going to the counter where meals would one day be collected, he went to one of the walls where there were machines that dispensed snacks. The dwarves had been restocking them earlier and anyone could take what they wanted.

Working his way from machine to machine, Tuki selected four silver packages that all looked the same apart from the labels on the outside. There was mango, apple, watermelon and something called muesli. When he opened the muesli he found that it consisted of a variety of grains glued together. It did not look very good, but tasted interesting. He also pushed a lever and was rewarded with a rich, dark drink of hot chocolate. He had tried the coffee and did not like that, but chocolate was another matter.

When he turned around, Tuki saw Ruby sitting at one of the tables watching him. He was surprised that he did not hesitate before going to sit across from her.

"You are not eating?" he asked.

"No. I was just about to leave."

"Oh."

She laughed. "Don't look so sad. I was about to leave before you sat down. Now I'm staying."

Tuki smiled, before realizing the first part of what she had said. Had he really been saddened by the thought of her leaving and had it really been so clear on his face.

Once again, sitting with Ruby, he thought of Keala. He had thought Keala beautiful and smart and interesting. Looking back, he knew that she had thought exactly the same things about herself. Ruby was all those things, and more, but did not seem to realize. He discovered he was staring at Ruby's face, at her sharp green eyes, and blushed. Lowering his gaze he concentrated on his meal.

"Hey, Rube?" Bones called from the door.

"Yeah, Bones."

Tuki had forgotten that Bones, his guard, was even there.

"You right to guard Tuki for a while?" the troll asked. "I don't think Kim'd mind if you took over."

Ruby eyed Tuki up and down—as much as was possible with the table between them—and smiled. "Yeah, I think I got it."

"Good. Crystal's got the skyglass up on the bridge."

Ruby waved him away and spoke to Tuki. "I hear you've been organizing the troops." She smiled again. "And Stone and Chasm and Cliff all listened to you."

"I listened to them more. They came up with plans and I just agreed."

"But Stone said it was your idea to get them all together. Them and the humans."

"I am sure he'd already thought of that."

"That isn't the point. It was a good idea. And Stone knew it was a good idea, and now he knows that you can come up with good ideas too. Come up with another couple and soon they will give *all* of your ideas some thought to see if they might be good too."

Tuki was sure he was blushing all the way to his bones. He crunched on his muesli and pushed the crumbs around on the table. "You wanted to play chess?" he asked, changing the subject. The game pieces were not exactly the same as chess pieces, but close enough.

She nodded, but she too dipped her head. "Well, you'll have to show me how."

"Would you like to?"

She nodded. "Now?"

"Umm..." He hadn't meant that but... "If you want."

"Here?"

There was no reason why they couldn't. "I have some of those music cubes in my cabin," he said, swallowing loudly. "We could listen to them if we played there."

"Okay. How about I get a board then and meet you there in a couple of minutes?" It appeared as if Ruby was ready to leap out of her chair and race out of the mess. Tuki nodded, and she did just that. Collecting his packets of food and his cup of chocolate, Tuki made his way to the lift.

-oOo-

The first cube Tuki put into the little machine was loud and clanging. He thought it would give him another headache. He removed that one and inserted another just as Ruby came through the door.

Tuki turned and saw Ruby carrying a chessboard and box of pieces. She had changed out of her EVA suit into a blue, sleeveless dress that came half way down her thighs.

"Do you like my dress?" She did a twirl.

Tuki nodded and swallowed.

"It's my first one. They never made a lot of sense to me before." She crossed the room and Tuki noticed that she was not wearing any shoes. She noticed him looking and wiggled her toes. "Barefoot never made much sense before either. And showers? Who'd have thought..."

Tuki nodded again. He had noticed the scent. He noticed the beating of his heart. He thought he should say something. "You smell like flowers," he said, then wished he hadn't.

But Ruby smiled. "Thank you." Head bowed, she hurried across to the table and put down the chessboard.

Tuki was glad he had mentioned the scent. It drifted around her like adoring children around a princess.

"Chip said I smelled like a cemetery," she said.

Tuki did not know what to say to that. He wanted to say something but he had used up all his courage.

"That's nice music," Ruby said into the lull.

Tuki turned to look at the music player, hearing it for the first time. The new cube had soft flowing music made with pipes and a fiddle. "I got it from the library," he said, though she already knew that. Where else would he have gotten if from?

They stopped speaking again. Music and the scent of flowers drifted around the room.

"Are we going to play?" Ruby sat down and started to take pieces from the box. She set them up randomly at either end of the board and Tuki had to gather his thoughts and try to remember the correct positions.

-oOo-

"You will be beating me soon." Tuki smiled when he said it, but he knew it was true. Not that it bothered him at all. He would let her beat him every day if it meant he could sit there and play against her.

Ruby shrugged and examined the pieces remaining on the board. "Maybe. You said you liked cards more, though."

It was Tuki's turn to shrug. "They are both good. It is what is happening other than the game that is more important. And tonight I like chess."

"I like chess too." Ruby played with her king and Tuki examined her hand. "I have to go and sleep now though," Ruby continued. "I have to sit in one of the guns tomorrow."

"When?"

A shrug. "Tomorrow."

She started to put the pieces back into the box and Tuki turned away from her hand to look at the bed. "You could sleep here," he said quietly.

The clatter of chess pieces into the container stopped. Tuki turned and saw Ruby with a knight held above the opening.

"Really?"

He had thought she would say no. Swallowing, he turned back to the bed. It was big enough for two. Tuki finally understood why some people wanted to share beds, if it meant that one or the other did not have to go home. He felt a stirring in his groin. "If you want."

Tuki and Ruby both stood up at the same time, then stayed where they were. Eventually, Ruby left the rest of the chess pieces on the table and went to lie on the bed and climbed beneath the covers. Tuki watched her go, then made his way slowly to the light switch by the door.

After turning off the light a dim grey remained—just enough to see. Ruby was lying on her side, facing the center of the bed. He wanted to stay where he was all night to make sure he could remember how she looked. The curve of her hip, hidden beneath the blanket but still beautiful. The way her red hair fell across the pillow.

But Ruby turned slightly to look at him and threw back the covers. He moved to the bed and carefully lay down. He clung to the edge of the bed, but Ruby moved closer.

He opened his mouth to speak, though he did not know what he intended to say. Ruby saved him the trouble of giving it thought when she leaned forward and touched her lips to his. It was not like his kisses with Keala had been—there were no tongues or coiled tension. It was gentle and brief and tasted that much sweeter.

Tuki did not want to think of Keala—he wanted her to go away—but... "When Keala kissed me," he said softly, not taking his eyes off Ruby's, "she said there was more."

"There is more, Tuki. A lot more. But not tonight."

Tuki sighed. "That is what she always said. But there was never any more."

She touched her finger to his lips. "There will be more, Tuki. I promise." She kissed him again, briefly, and Tuki discovered that he did not mind waiting. He did not mind at all.

36: Two Options

KEEBLE STARED AT SANDY. "What do you mean he isn't answering? He can't be that far away."

The trollop shrugged. "I'm calling in the right spot, he just ain't answering."

"So, he's sleeping?"

"Don't think so. You hear a voice in your head you usually wake up. I do anyway. Don't reckon Scree would be any different."

"Well..." Keeble didn't want to think about what that might mean. He sat on the floor and looked at the old hurgon. It squatted in the corner, looking warily at Flint, who stood guard. Suldon and Tami had talked the creature in circles for half an hour, trying to get it to say what they wanted without actually asking. In the end Keeble had decided it was easier to just ask outright.

They'd asked Penisari, back on the *Hakahei* to supply the names of a dozen hurgon families. And Suldon asked their prisoner for the location of them all, with the P'targa family thrown in the middle.

So now they knew. A hundred kilometers to the north. On the Gosen S'peka Railway line. But what were they to do? Keeble was wracked by indecision. Which fool had put him in charge? He tugged on his short beard while he tried to think.

If Kim and Scree had been captured did they need rescuing or would Scree work something out? If they needed rescuing could Keeble and his small group do the rescuing on their own or would they need back up? If they could not be rescued at all, would all of the convoluted plans in the world do those remaining on the *Hakahei* any good at all? If nothing else—who'd fly the ship?

"What's next then?" Bargle asked. He examined the lock on the door as if wanting to pull it apart.

Keeble was going to shrug but restrained himself. He looked at Flint. "Any suggestions?"

"What you thinking now?"

"Two options. Wait until we hear from Scree and let them worry about the decision. Or look for the..." He looked at the hurgon and decided against saying the word P'targa in case the alien recognized it amongst the rest of the babble, unlikely though it was. "Or head north now."

Flint nodded and gave the matter some thought though Keeble was pretty sure he knew what the troll would say. Flint obliged: "I say we start looking. We don't know how long we'll have to wait for Scree. We could spend the next day sitting here like a bunch of tree stumps."

"That's what I thought you'd say. Tasko?"

"He's right. We might find what we're after before we hear from Scree and Kim."

Keeble nodded slowly. "Suldon?" The elf looked surprised to be asked. Keeble was slightly surprised to be asking. *Just trying to spread the blame,* he thought.

"As Flint says, there is no point waiting. We may wait forever."

Forever? Keeble had been trying to avoid thinking about forever.

He looked at Tami and, after a moment, the elf nodded. Nina nodded as well.

Still, Keeble wasn't sure. What if they needed help? What if they were just a hundred meters away? Why had the two people in charge—the two best equipped to lead the *Hakahei* both left the ship? Who would lead them now. Not Meledrin. That was crazy—even she would admit that. Maybe Thorpe? Or Palsamon. Palsamon seemed like a sensible, intelligent person, especially for an elf. Or even Flint. Flint might well be the best option. No matter who it was, they would need the help of some of the hurgon. He sighed. "I guess we're going north then."

"A hundred kilometers though?" Flint said. "Long way to run."

Keeble smiled. "We will have to steal some form of transport." Tasko and Bargle were smiling with him.

"What about that?" Flint asked, pointing to the hurgon.

"Is there anything we can tie it up with? We only need half an hour start."

"Nothing in here," Sandy said. "Let me check." She opened the door, checked for activity, then slipped out. She returned a few minutes later with a large piece of cloth. She tore a strip off the side, but obviously wasn't happy about the strength.

"Let's plait them," Nina said.

"Yeah." Sandy smiled and the two of them started to work.

A few minutes later—far too quick for Keeble's liking—they were ready to go. Given a couple of more hours he might have been able to come up with a plan but...

"We need to find the Gosen S'peka Railway." He wound the gears on his hand for a moment. "Ask the hurgon, Suldon. That railway could go to a hundred places."

Flint removed the alien's gag and waited while Suldon asked the question. When the elf nodded, the gag was replaced.

"Two kilometers that way." Suldon pointed generally westwards with a long, pale finger.

"Let's do it," Flint said.

Keeble wished he'd said that. He nodded and rose to his feet. "Two kilometers through these buildings could take all day. Probably can't go a hundred meters in a straight line."

"We can always go through the walls."

Keeble shook his head. "You'd be carrying me before a kilometer was gone."

"Guess we go the long way then." Flint ducked out the door, turned to the right, and raced away. Sandy went next, following her companion's directions in her head and leading the group.

They moved quickly at first, jogging down the quiet passages, moving generally westward. Every now and then Keeble would see Flint race along a joining passage as he scouted the best route through the twists and turns. Once, they stopped in the middle of a T-intersection and, after several minutes, the troll raced through their midst.

"Dead end," he said as he passed. When he was gone around the next bend, Sandy followed again.

Then, seemingly between one moment and the next, between one passage and the next, something changed. Suddenly there were hurgon everywhere. The light didn't seem all that much different and there had been nothing to suggest a change of shift... They just stepped out of doors, wandered along passages, appeared as if by magic.

Keeble crouched near an intersection, looking over Sandy's shoulder at a closed wooden door. He wound the gears on his hand, clutching at nothing. Flint seemed to be taking forever.

Just when Keeble was ready to race across and burst through the door to see if Flint needed any help, the troll poked his head out and beckoned them across. Keeble was halfway across the hall before anyone else had moved.

The small room was decorated with a hurgon lying under the twisted remains of a wooden shelf. Another was reclining on what was now a three-legged, square table and a third was thrown in the corner like dirty washing.

Flint was bruised and bleeding from a cut above his eye.

"Are you all right?"

Flint nodded but touched the cut. "Bloody bastard snuck up behind me while I was busy with the other two. Hit me with that thing." He pointed to what looked a bit like a candelabrum.

"That cut doesn't look good," Keeble said, though he didn't know much about such things. Both the trolls would have more experience in such matters.

"I'll live."

But Nina seemed to have other ideas. "Here, it won't take a moment." After a lip-chewing, brow-wrinkling moment, she went collected a tablecloth and fashioned a bandage.

"So what's though the other door," Keeble said, motioning to the door the surprise hurgon had come through.

"Workshop," Flint said, touching the bandage as if it was a new invention.

A workshop? But Keeble kept himself thinking clearly. "Nobody else in there?" He saw Tasko sidling towards the door.

"What do you reckon?"

Keeble beat Tasko to the door and pulled it open. The next room was twenty meters long with all manner of machinery lined up along one of the walls. Three huge engines were chugging away. Curls of smoke escaped through two windows set up near the ceiling. Jobs had been left unfinished, though Keeble supposed that the three unconscious hurgon could be excused. Bargle pushed past and went to look.

Keeble wanted to join him, examining the strange tools and trying to work out what the engines were for. But he was in charge and had more important things to do. He took a deep breath to harden his resolve and crossed quickly to one of the idle the machines. He looked around the room—What was that over there? And that?—as he tested to see if the machine was hot. It wasn't, so he climbed up, using a loop of pipe, a bolt and a bent bracket as foot- and handholds. He reached the window and looked out.

There was another gap outside to divide the different families. Keeble sat on the wide stone sill and leaned out. He looked to the left and right. Fifty meters to the right, the gap turned.

"Anything interesting?" Sandy asked. She climbed up and leaned out to look as well.

"Down there," Keeble said, pointing to the turn. "It might almost run the right direction.

Sandy squinted in the half-light that posed as both day and night in Hulgorn. "Might do. Can't be any worse than dancing round in here."

"Me first then." Keeble turned around and prepared to lower himself to the ground. His mechanical arm scraped against the stone as he tried to keep his balance.

"Need a hand?" Sandy asked.

"Oh, very funny." But he took her offered hand and started over the edge. The trollop lowered him as far as possible then let go.

Keeble hit the ground awkwardly and fell. By the time he had climbed to his feet and dusted himself off, Nina was out the window and preparing to drop as well. While the rest of his companions exited the building, Keeble jogged down to the bend to see what he could see.

It wasn't as good as he'd hoped. The path between buildings only went for a hundred meters but, as Sandy had said, it was better than being inside. The others caught up and they all moved on together.

"No word from Scree?"

Flint shook his head.

"And the ship?"

"Talked to Meledrin a while ago. The hurgon are still outside the ship, but other than that..."

"And they haven't—"

"They haven't heard from Scree either."

They reached the end wall. Keeble craned his neck to look up. The roof was five stories above on either side and six at the end. There were no windows lower than the fourth floor. There was no way they were going anywhere except through the stone.

"I think we've come about a thousand meters," Keeble said, though he was far from sure. It was hard to keep track with all the twisting and turning they'd done. Tasko was nodding in agreement, but he didn't look sure either. "We might be half way."

Keeble took a deep breath, cleared his mind, and started to Sing. He did it slowly, building the layers, enjoying the power growing within him. He could feel the magic dancing along his skin, clearing his pores. He could feel the tingle in his fingers and toes.

When the Song was complete, filling him, he focused on the stone and stepped forward. The wall here was thicker than usual. He took one step, two. He was about to take a third when a big hand reached out from behind and pulled him back. A blast of air washed against the insubstantial stone. He could feel it thought he couldn't really because the stone was still there. A train rumbled past barely half a meter away.

Keeble stood, eyes wide, mouth continuing the Song through instinct alone. Flint, standing by his side in the center of the wall and still gripping his collar, must have known that he risked breaking his concentration.

"You didn't feel that shaking everything?" Flint shouted, watching the train rumble by.

Keeble shook his head. But he *had* felt it. He'd merely though it didn't concern him. He was expecting danger to come in the form of hurgon. He'd been reveling in the feel of his Song instead of concentrating.

The train went rumbling on. It was almost a shock when it was no longer there.

Taking a deep breath around his Song, Keeble stepped forward and into the clear. The train lines were just a step away. On the other side was a slightly raised path with regularly spaced gas lanterns above. Keeble looked both directions then hurried across. He sat down to calm his heart while he waited for the others.

"Are you sure the hurgon said two kilometers, Suldon?" he asked when he finally let his Song go.

Suldon nodded, then shook his head. "The hurgon do not have kilometers. They do not have any measurement that I have ever known. I thought... Perhaps I did not do the math correctly." He cleared his throat. "I was never very good at math."

"Never good at..." Keeble took a deep breath to calm himself again.

“Perhaps there are two train lines,” Tasko offered. “Perhaps we still have to go another kilometer to get to the right one.”

Keeble looked up and down the passage, as if a sign would appear to tell him what he wanted to know. He gave a bark of laughter—even if a sign did appear he wouldn’t be able to read it.

“So,” Flint said. “Where do we go now?”

Keeble shrugged. “I don’t know.”

“Don’t stop now.”

“Well, obviously we go north.”

“If it’s so obvious why didn’t you just say it?”

“I did.”

Flint shook his head and started up the tunnel. Keeble pushed himself to his feet to follow.

37: A Good Plan

KEEBLE WHISTLED AS HE STRODE along the walkway at the edge of the tunnel. A soft twilight marked the boundary between each of the gas lamps but everything was visible. It was almost a kilometer to the nearest station but, walking along the tunnel with no aliens to dodge or doors to check, it took barely fifteen minutes.

Once there, they hid in the shadows for a long time, looking for signs of life and hoping no trains were due.

Nothing moved.

A passage half way along the platform led away at right angles. Further along a huge wooden door, banded in studded iron, was closed. Flint was crouching by the tracks, one hand resting on the cold metal rail. Keeble stood behind him. They waited. Flint looked over his shoulder then turned to examine the station again.

"Are you waiting for me to say something?" Keeble asked after a while.

Flint grunted, straightened the bandage on his head, and stalked forward. He jumped up onto the platform and moved to stand behind a thick, ugly column. Keeble scanned the area. Nothing happened. Flint moved forward again to stand in front of the passage. He looked at the door.

Eventually he turned and beckoned the rest of them forward.

Keeble hauled himself up onto the huge tiles of the platform and jogged across to the troll. "It's very quiet," he said. "And dirty."

Flint nodded and stared down the passage as if he could hear something.

"That looks like a map," Sandy said, pointing to a mess of lines painted onto one of the walls.

Keeble went across for a closer look, as did Suldon and Tami. There were different colored lines coming and going and there were labeled boxes covering the lines at various points.

"Is she right?"

Sudlon shrugged, but Tami was shaking her head slowly. "It could be."

"How do we know where we are?"

Flint came to look as well. "We are somewhere on that line there," he said. "Either that square or that one. Maybe."

Keeble looked at him. "How do you know?"

"That has to be the hub where we started," he said, pointing to where all the lines seemed to meet. "We moved almost directly east from there and passed under two of the sky glide things." The troll tapped the wall where a red line—the only thing that went almost directly east—passed under first one blue line and then another. "This small junction here must be the T'loop compound, or near it, them being an important family and all."

Keeble was nodding. "And the line we're on now runs basically north south, so it must be that one."

Flint nodded.

"But that means it isn't the right line."

On the map, another line went almost directly north from the hub, swung east, then turned again to run parallel to their own for a long way. For a while, the two lines were so close they almost touched. They skipped away from each other, only to come back together and actually join further north.

"Suldon did the sums right after all," Sandy offered.

Keeble turned towards the elf to sneer, but wound the gears on his hand and nodded instead. Suldon nodded back.

"So," Keeble said, "how do we catch a train?"

As if to make a point, there was a rumbling in the distance and, a minute later, a train thundered through the station. And the point was—you don't catch a train. It didn't stop. It didn't slow. It went and went and went until Keeble wondered if it would ever end.

"We could jump on one as it goes past," Suldon shouted over the noise.

Keeble turned to look at him. Was the elf making a joke? On Suldon's other side, Flint was watching the train as if the plan had merit.

"We *won't* be jumping onto the train," Keeble shouted. He doubted the trolls would have a chance—it was certain nobody else would.

Eventually the train passed and the silence that remained was deafening. Keeble continued to stare and might have stayed there all day if Nina had not spoken.

"Look at this." She was pointing to a spot on the wall-map. "The boxes must be stations, I think. Most of them are centered over the line. But there's one between our line and the one next to it."

Keeble examined the picture. She was right. A short distance to the north—if all their guessing was correct—there was a station marked that seemed to hover between the two lines.

Nina turned to look at everyone. "Perhaps that means that the two lines share the station. Perhaps if we follow this line just a little further we'll be able to move to the other line with no problems at all."

Except that a station shared by two lines would probably be busy. He tugged on his beard and looked for other possibilities.

Tasko was shaking his head but Keeble ignored him. A week ago he'd been a Wanderer and less than a dwife. How could he suddenly become more worthy of respect while the dwives could not? Nina had come up with a good idea, why should it not be acknowledged? Ari used to have good ideas all the time, though he'd ignored them for the most part.

Keeble cleared his throat. "Sounds good, Nina. Let's go and have a look then, shall we?"

Nina smiled and nodded, blushing slightly. Keeble nodded back. He marched to the train line, checked for trains, and jumped down to the walkway.

"Do you think the hurgon have any food we can eat?" Bargle asked as he too checked for trains.

-oOo-

The station was even busier than Keeble expected. There were two lines with thirty meters of plain grey tiles between. But there were platforms on the outside of the two lines as well. It seemed as if the station was caught between two different family compounds. One side had guards in blue pantaloons and white shirts, the other in pink and black. On the middle platform it looked as if neither group knew who was in charge. They stared at each other across the tiles, constantly checking their weapons and all but ignoring the pandemonium around them.

The train that had passed through the deserted station was still here. The last three carriages were accessible. Steam trucks were sitting up on the platform, waiting while hurgon unloaded crates. They huffed and puffed, trucks and aliens both. Hundreds of other hurgon moved around them, coming and going from the train, unloading smaller cargoes, wandering around as if they had nothing better to do than look.

Keeble watched for a long time, but nothing seemed to change beyond the changes of the moment. The crowds did not thin. The guards did not wander off to walk a patrol.

Just as the train on their line left, another pulled in across the other side, disgorging passengers like a swarm of insects.

"So, there's a train," Flint said. "How do we get across there and get on it?"

Keeble watched some more. "I think your plan is perfect, Flint."

The troll eyed him suspiciously. "Which plan is that?"

"We run and we jump on it."

"We do?" He tugged at his moustache and looked across at the train.

"Yes."

"Not sure if I like that plan."

"Not urging me to be cautious, are you?"

"Well... Them guards *do* have weapons."

Keeble nodded. "Do you really think they'll shoot at us? I mean, even if they work out what's going on and don't stand there staring as they try to work out what we are? Do you think they'll fire their weapons with all these other hurgon around?

"Maybe."

"Who's the boss?"

"You are."

"Well, now is the time to prove that you really mean that. Right now. Look." Keeble pointed. The train across the other side of the platform was all but empty and the doors had closed. "Let's go."

Keeble jumped up onto the platform and started to run. He hoped everyone was following.

He'd gone almost five meters when the first of the hurgon reacted. An old one pointed in his direction and shouted. Keeble looked over his shoulder and saw his companions close behind. The trolls were leading the chase and would overtake him any moment. The elves weren't far behind.

Keeble turned, narrowly avoided an alien, dodged to the left and kept running. His arms pumped. His breath came in ragged bursts.

Flint sprinted by him and changed course slightly. He was heading for the rear of the train. Keeble kept on in the same direction. He sidestepped around a startled hurgon and slipped between two others who didn't even realize he was there. Halfway and the guards were starting to move. No two seemed to have the same plan in mind. Sandy wasn't far behind Flint. They were almost at the train when it started to move.

Flint threw himself at the rearmost door. Keeble could hear the impact, even through the growing noise of the crowd. The troll bounced off but it was as if that was exactly what he expected. He stayed on his feet and, with the train moving forward, watched with Keeble as Sandy had her turn. The door flew open and Sandy was on the train. Flint joined her a moment later and stood, leaning against the jamb, holding his shoulder and beckoning the rest of the group on.

Keeble looked back again. Suldon and Tamidilin were right there, and now that they knew exactly where they were going they increased their pace. Tasko and Bargle were not far behind but already moving as quick as they could. Nina was slowing.

Ahead, the train was gathering speed. Steam hissed, smoke billowed. Sparks flew as steel wheels slipped on steel rails.

Keeble let Tasko and Bargle slip by him and waited for Nina to catch up. The four of them headed for the northern end of the platform but it wasn't obvious if they'd make it. Keeble tried to calculate, but it was useless. He was tiring and the train driver, oblivious to all that was happening, continued to urge the train forward. Without knowing the rate of acceleration and the extent of Nina's exhaustion...

"Don't," Nina gasped, "Wait. For. Me."

Keeble barreled into a hurgon and barely stayed upright. He shouted an apology as he set off again and laughed at the absurdity of it. He was last now. The elves reached the edge of the platform and readied themselves to jump. Flint urged them on. Sandy was up the front of the carriage making sure nobody went forward to warn the driver.

A quarter of the train was out of the station and into the tunnel. Tasko and Bargle, realizing they were arriving ahead of schedule, changed course to meet the open door earlier. The elves were finally gone.

Keeble was at the back of the pack and decided to concentrate on running. He watched Nina's back as he gained on her.

Guards were finally starting to mobilize, converging on the quickly tiring dwife. Nina was starting to panic—Keeble could see it. She looked this way and that, as if seeking the right path when the right path was right there in front of her.

All her looking around meant she didn't see the luggage on the platform and went down in a pile of duffel bags and leather cases. Hurgon cursed. Nina cried. Keeble slid to a halt by her side and started to pull her to her feet.

"Don't wait for me," she said again. "I can't make it."

Keeble kept on tugging. "Nobody gets left behind," he said. That was Kim's rule—nobody gets left behind. Though Kim and Scree... "Get up or we'll both be caught."

Bargle and Tasko leapt onto the train. Only one and a half carriages remained. Guards were closing in.

"Get up now," Keeble shouted.

He got Nina onto her feet and pushed her forward. Taking her hand he started to run, dragging her behind. She resisted.

"You give up now," he shouted, looking back at her tear stained face, "and everything dwarves ever thought about dwives will be proven right."

Nina's eyes went wide. Her nostrils flared. She found a new reserve of energy and ran on her own.

They were almost there but train was slipping away. Keeble felt hands grasping at his shoulders and looked back. The guards were right there. One reached forward again and Keeble shrugged out of its grip. The train was almost gone, about to slip into the tunnel.

Nina leapt. She grazed her shoulder on the station's end wall. She was thrown off balance. She twisted, turned in mid air, landed inside the train and...

The door was gone from sight.

Keeble kept running. Two more steps. There was a door on the back of the train with a small landing on the outside.

He jumped.

One foot hit the landing, the other slipped off the edge. Keeble's whole body crashed against the wood and glass of the door and recoiled. His arms flailed as he struggled to keep his balance. He fell.

In one last act of desperation he reached out with his mechanical hand, grasping for something to hold onto. Anything. But there was nothing.

Until a huge troll fist smashed through the glass of the window. As he tumbled backwards, Keeble saw Flint lunge past the shards of broken glass and latch onto his arm.

Keeble looked at Flint's hand. Covered in blood. Gashed. He looked at his own hand, gears and leather and buckles.

Good workmanship, he thought. *Well done all round.*

Flint started to reel him in. The troll was smiling. "Good plan," he said. "That's why you's the boss."

38: Gone Quietly

KIM LEANED AGAINST THE WALL while Scree worked at the door. It was just a normal old timber thing that he probably could have broken in a moment if he'd been willing to make that much noise. But there were hurgon close by. There always were. Everywhere they turned there were aliens doing alien things. There was nowhere to hide. Not for more than a few minutes at any rate. If they could get outside... Every door was guarded. Every window they'd found so far was impossible—too narrow, too high above the ground, barred or right next to where the aliens seemed to congregate. There were hurgon everywhere.

Scree finally got the door open, splitting the timber and breaking the lock. They hurried through.

It felt like they'd been on the move for days and getting nowhere. In truth, it had only been a couple of hours since they split from the rest of the group and they'd been moving constantly since. Every step seemed to take them further away from their companions.

Kim was exhausted—from constant fear as much as the exertion. She knew she was slowing Scree down.

Beyond the door was a small, empty room. There were many of those, as if the hurgon built things, including buildings, for the sake of it and tried to work out what they might do with them later.

They paused again to listen. From beyond the next door came the sounds of a noisy old machine. Scree looked at Kim and she shrugged. What else was she supposed to do? One way was as dangerous as the next, as far as she could tell. They went through into a huge room that was almost completely filled by a monstrous engine. Hurgon swarmed all over it like flies on a dead horse. The machine clunked and rattled and shuddered and seemed to be in constant need of attention. To the left three hurgon, in dark clothes and breathing masks, shoveled coal into a furnace. Towards the back, twenty meters above the ground, another two heaved on a spanner, working at a bolt as big as a dinner plate. On the other side someone had removed an inspection panel and was watching a complex mesh of gears grind inexorably onwards.

Kim felt a touch on her shoulder. Scree pointed to another small door not far away. She nodded and they hurried across to it, dodging a puddle of oil on the floor and ducking beneath a knot of pipes that left a tank and headed out through the wall.

This door was locked as well, but Scree didn't worry about opening it quietly. He hit it with his shoulder once, twice, and almost fell though as it crashed open.

The room was empty of life. Kim might have thought it a waiting room, but there weren't any pot plants or five-year-old magazines. There was nobody waiting. Just a dozen seating perches around the walls and a 'coffee' table in the center.

There were three other doors, all of them the same. Kim picked the wooden one and pulled it open.

"Whoops."

A dozen hurgon, all genderless from what Kim could see, were taking showers. They turned to look at her and a dozen pairs of eyes, no two the same color, narrowed in unison.

Behind her, Kim heard Scree offer a trollish version of 'whoops'. She turned to look. Eight hurgon had come through one of the other doors. Kim guessed that this second group were guards. They paused for a couple of seconds then, as one, they rushed forward to attack.

Scree took two down easily in the first rush. The others immediately slowed and took more care. Scree finished another by darting forward and pounding his fist into its flat, purple face.

Five against Scree? Kim didn't think they had a hope. But apparently the bathers could see the action and came to the same conclusion. They quickly organized the cavalry and charged the door. Kim, being rushed by naked, dripping aliens, moved quickly to Scree's side.

"We've got problems, Scree."

The first time she hit a hurgon she realized she didn't have a chance. She'd hit some average human men in her time and knew she'd hurt them. Hitting the aliens was like hitting a brick wall. It was like hitting Scree. They hardly noticed at all.

One on one would have been an interesting fight. She couldn't hurt them, and they couldn't lay a hand on her. Unfortunately, she didn't have those odds.

It took the aliens about ten seconds to realize who the real danger was, and another thirty seconds to overwhelm him. Kim watched nine aliens rush forward as one, not worried for their own health. They piled on top of Scree, pounding and kicking. Kim was facing three of her own and didn't bother fighting. She was exhausted.

She dodged until the referee cleared the ruck.

The hurgon backed carefully away, revealing Scree lying bloody and bruised on the floor. Kim gasped and in that moment was hit. She would've gone quietly if they'd asked.

-oOo-

Kim didn't open her eyes. She was sure it would hurt if she did. She laid perfectly still, cheek pressed against cold stone, and took stock of her woe. Maybe her right foot was broken—it was swollen and painful. Her left knee wasn't much better—it felt like someone had stomped on it. Left hand, broken. She could hardly move her right shoulder. And an eye swollen so much that it wasn't going to open even when she got around to making the attempt.

Well, she thought, *at least I know I'm all here.* She finally opened her one good eye and looked at her surroundings. It was a cell, and not nearly as nice as the last. She could see some disgustingly dirty stone floor and a barred doorway. That was all. But she was willing to admit she was not in the best position to see much at all. With a deep breath she carefully sat up.

"Shit, that hurts." She added two broken ribs to her list of injuries. And a bleeding nose—which probably accounted for why there was no horrid smell. She wiped blood away as she took another look around. There wasn't a lot more to see. Disgustingly dirty stone floor. A barred door. Disgustingly dirty stone walls. And Scree lying on his back in a corner. He wasn't moving at all.

Kim wanted to rush over and see how he was, to see if he was breathing, but knew enough to give the matter some thought first. She could crawl across there, using her injured hand and knee. Or she could walk across on her injured foot. Either way her ribs were going to have their say. Eventually she crawled, simply because she didn't know if she had the energy to get to her feet. Her hand didn't hurt too bad, but her foot and knee screamed with pain at the slightest pressure. Her ribs just hurt all the time. And she'd forgotten about her shoulder. She held her arm to her body and crawled one handed, biting her lip and trying to think happy thoughts. She had trouble coming up with anything.

She was crying by the time she'd gone the two meters to Scree's side. His battered face didn't make her feel any better. She checked his breathing. It was shallow but constant. She touched at his cheek, wiping at a smudge of grease left by a hurgon. She checked him for obvious injuries, running her good hand over his body. Cuts and abrasions. A lump on the back of his head. No broken bones, though it was a bit hard to tell through the slabs of muscle. With a sigh of relief she gingerly leaned back against the wall by his side. Broken hand on her lap, the other on Scree's chest. The slow rise and fall told her there was still a chance. While the troll lived, there was always a chance.

-oOo-

Kim had no idea how long she sat, leaning against the wall. It seemed like hours. Nobody came to look in on them. Nobody even randomly walked past the door. The stone was hard and cold. The smell of damp and long-gone creatures seemed to grow. Her aches and pains subsided if she sat still, but as soon as she moved... So she tried not to move. Hand on Scree's chest, back against the wall.

It had been so quiet for so long that when Scree groaned and shifted slightly, Kim jumped. Pain lanced through her chest but she ignored it and concentrated on the troll.

"Lie still," she said softly.

He opened his eyes and stared at her. He stared for so long that she wondered if the lump on the back of his head was merely the external sign of internal damage.

"Can you hear me?" Kim asked, tears welling in her eyes.

Scree grunted. "Course I can hears you. I was just going to enjoy seeings you for a while though."

She slapped his shoulder and immediately regretted it. Her shoulder screamed at the treatment and the tears in her eyes found new purpose.

"You's hurt?"

Kim nodded. "A bit."

"Serious?"

Kim was going to shrug, but that probably would have hurt too much. "I don't know. I hurt is all I know."

"Wheres?"

"Shoulder, ribs, hand, knee, foot. And a splitting headache. I feel like I've been tumble dried."

Scree carefully sat up and started with her foot. He undid the fastener down the outside of the boot, holding her leg with surprising tenderness. All the tenderness in the world wouldn't have helped when it actually came to pulling the boot free. Kim bit her lip to stop herself from crying out. She gripped his wrist with her good hand. Scree winced as if he was the one hurting.

Kim examined her foot as Scree carefully manipulated it. There was swelling and bruising down near the toes. The troll poked and prodded.

"Brokens," was the verdict. "Not too bad though. Should heal as long as you stay off it for a while."

"Doubt I'll have much say in that."

Scree grunted and shook his head as he moved onto Kim's knee. He tried sliding her trouser leg up, but it was too tight to go beyond her calf. He looked at Kim, smiling slightly, as if considering the other option, but contented himself with leaving everything where it was and using his big strong fingers to examine from the outside. Kim watched his hands as he worked and wondered what sort of massage he could give.

"Nothing serious," he said. "Thinks you just jarred it. Will hurt like three angry cats in a sack for a while."

Ribs next. He knelt by Kim's side pushed her shirt up to examine the bruising. Kim hadn't seen it herself but from the look on the troll's face it wasn't pretty. He ran his fingers along the tender flesh just below her bra. She almost cried out when he pushed too hard. She tasted blood as she bit her lip.

"Not good," he said, "but what can ya do abouts broken ribs?" He shrugged then. "Maybe Thorpe could do something."

Scree continued with his examination, sliding one hand up to her shoulder. He stared into her one good eye the entire time and Kim wondered if he could feel the beating of her heart. He could probably hear it.

He was still looking at her face. "Dislocated shoulder," he said.

He put it back in with a quick, savage movement. This time Kim did scream. She swore at him and gasped for air all at once. She hurt her broken hand by grabbing at his arm. She swore at the world in general.

"Sorry 'bout that." Scree massaged at her shoulder but it wasn't quite the experience Kim had been thinking of.

She shook her head. It was the only coherent response she could make. Her chest ached from her ragged breathing.

One last injury to check. While Kim tried to gain control of her heart and lungs, Scree took up her left hand. He held it in both of his, prodding at the swelling over the fourth metacarpal, working his fingers against her palm.

"Clean break. Ends are lined up pretty good. Shouldn't be a problem."

Kim finally heard movement outside the cell. A hurgon, in the yellow uniform and red cross of the T'loop family, came into view. With Scree kneeling there in front of her, her left hand in his, Kim wouldn't have been surprised if her mother had turned up. She would have seen the tableau in the cell and jumped to all the wrong conclusions. She would have been planning the wedding before Kim could explain what was really going on.

The hurgon didn't look as happy as her mother might. It looked over its shoulder and beckoned to some companions, then started to open the door.

39: The Garden Option

MELEDRIN STAYED WHERE SHE WAS while Palsamon watered the stake marking the position of the seed. Though it had 'rained' in the garden for a good while earlier, the soil still accepted the water greedily. Grass was already starting to grow.

When Palsamon moved on, Meledrin climbed to her feet and looked around. This side of the garden, the eastern side, was going to be thick with vegetation, all carefully designed to appear natural. A lawn would dominate the other side with shade trees around the edge, as if shade was needed. Meledrin had a feeling the trolls would be down here playing their 'games' but that could not be helped. The small section of garden that overlooked the rest from the top of the cliff was going to offer strategic vantage points from which to see everything else.

"Do you like the design, Meledrin?" Lisarea asked. She and Hoodek were also watering.

Meledrin examined the layout as if she did not know exactly the name and position of every plant. She nodded. "Yes, Lisarea, I think we have done well with the limited resources." Though of course the elves could only rely on the human's descriptions of the plants the Americans had supplied at Nexis. "What do you think, Hoodek?"

The dwarf had worked as vigorously as anyone. He shrugged and looked around. "How would I know? It just looks like dirt to me at the moment."

"That is one of the many beauties of a garden—it is ever changing. Come down here in a week and it will be a different place. Even when completed, it will change from moment to moment."

Hoodek nodded but seemed unsure if constant change was a good thing.

"It will be wonderful to have a garden once again," Lisarea said into the silence.

"Yes." Meledrin felt that she had never agreed with anyone more wholeheartedly. The world outside the ship was harsh and dull. There was no hint of color, except in the clothes of the ever-milling hurgon and the hurgon themselves, and they represented bad things more than good.

The ship's PA system beeped, and everyone looked up expectantly. For a couple of seconds there was no other sound.

"Ah, Meledrin?" Bethalin's distorted voice said eventually. There was another pause, then the voice came again, clearer. "Meledrin could you come to the bridge please."

Meledrin dusted off her hands looked around as if there might be some last minute, vital order that needed to be given, then walked calmly towards the lift.

On the bridge, Bethalin, a young woman whose once-long hair had been cut and styled by one of the dwives, was manipulating the image in the dome.

"Yes, Bethalin," Meledrin said, starting up the stairs to the communications console.

"They are doing something. They may be preparing to attack."

Meledrin raised her eyebrow and the other woman blushed.

Bethalin nodded. "Cliff informed me."

"Ahhh... Very well then. And where has Cliff gone?" Meledrin would not have been confident of Bethalin's ability to predict an attack—it was not something she would feel confident of doing herself—but if one of the trolls had said so it was probably true.

"He went to the security office to speak with the other troop leaders."

Meledrin watched the movement in the dome, trying to work out what had given away the purpose behind the hurgon movements. They had been shifting position and marching around in the square for hours and, as far as Meledrin could tell, their present activities were simply more of the same.

"I shall go down and see what they have to say."

"Very well." Bethalin nodded. "And, Meledrin?"

"Yes?"

"I spoke with Flint a little while ago."

"Flint?" That did not sound good.

"Yes. Kim and Scree have been separated from the rest of the group. Flint has not heard from Scree either."

"It means nothing. Perhaps..." But Meledrin could not think of a single way in which Scree's silence might be a good thing. He would not turn his radio off, and he could not lose it. He could talk to the other trolls and carry on in the real world as if all was normal. "Maybe he is sleeping," she finished lamely. Scree woke up at the slightest noise. "I am going to the security office."

The office was filled with large people and seemed much smaller than it actually was. Ping and Topper were present as well, standing at the corner of the desk, struggling to hold their place against mass and numbers. Even Tuki was there, as if, because of his previous efforts, he was now a trusted adviser of the military men on board. He was a simple lad, not prone to speaking unless he was asked a direct question, but Meledrin sensed a difference in him. He was sitting up straighter than usual. He did not stare at his hands. Where before he has been focused inwards, now he was letting himself out.

They all fell silent when she entered the room.

"Meledrin."

"Captain Thorpe. What is happening outside?"

It was Stone who answered. "It looks like they're preparing for an assault. They've isolated one of their machines but moved their forces so they can support it or quickly access the ship near where it faces us."

"What sort of machine?"

Stone shrugged and pointed to Ping and Topper. They were squeezed between Cliff and Chasm. "Tuki suggested we bring in the experts, but they aren't telling us much at the moment either."

Tuki had suggested they ask the dwarves? It was not something Meledrin would have thought of herself. Though she had been working with Hoodek and seen how valuable his assistance could be, asking for the help of the dwarves still wasn't an idea that came naturally to her.

Meledrin hated that Palsamon had been proven right after all. When they had spoken for the first time after their argument, the two of them had carried on as if nothing had happened. Palsamon slept in her room and they made love and talked as they had twenty years ago. But all the while Meledrin had been thinking on what he had said. She had tried to change her attitude towards the other elves. All three women—Penisari, Lisarea and Bethalin—were speaking to her much more than they had in the past and were contributing strongly to the community.

But that had only been part of Palsamon's message, Meledrin thought, *telling me I was closed off from those around me.* The other part had been that she judged all people—elves and dwarves and men and all others—by standards that no longer mattered. On Sherindel, the dwarves had not been able to add anything to her life in the small village of Grovely, but that did not mean they might not be useful away from the village, or that the village was the perfect world.

Hoodek had assisted in the garden but she still thought of him as nothing more than a *dwarf*. He was a dwarf that she had allowed to assist them. He was not somebody who could contribute in his own right—as more than strong hands and back for digging.

Meledrin had often wondered why humans had been chosen to lead the hakans into space, but suddenly she knew. Humans had a little bit of all the other races in them—it meant they had a chance of seeing things from all the angles and could therefore come to a more informed opinion.

With a small shrug, Meledrin tried to move out of herself. She waved her fingers in a quick, perfunctory ceremony of *Beginning*—it felt like a lifetime since the last ceremony—and tried to think of the activities outside the ship from a different point of view.

"Is the machine outside a weapon or a tool?" she asked after a moment.

"There's a difference?" Cliff asked.

Meledrin nodded, though she realized the difference she had seen in her mind might not be immediately obvious. "I mean, is it going to explode or cut?"

Tuki hit some buttons and a picture of the machine was brought up onto the wall opposite the desk, right beside the door. Topper left his spot beside the table to go and have a closer look.

"This looks like it might be a coil for generating heat," Topper said, pointing to a part of the machine that looked basically the same as every other part to Meledrin. Topper continued. "But we can't be sure of course. The fact that the hurgon seem to have been in a steam age for millennia suggests the machine will cause explosions though. Using heat for cutting requires sustainable technology... I mean technology that can work continuously for long periods of time... which is very hard to do."

"What difference would either choice make to our plans?" Tuki asked.

Topper shrugged, but all of Meledrin's attention was on Tuki.

After a moment Ping spoke. "The hull is about a meter thick and designed to withstand entry into atmosphere," she said. "Surely that's more heat than they can generate."

"So we don't worry about cutting?" Tuki seemed to notice Meledrin watching him and looked at his hands for a moment, but he was not done. "So explosions?"

Ping and Topper both shrugged.

"From the outside," Ping said eventually, "most of the hull looks the same, but there are weak points—a dozen maintenance access panels and the doors."

"Can't we just shoot them?" Cliff asked. "We could clear the square in a couple of minutes, I reckon."

Meledrin shook her head. "That is not an option as long as we have people off the ship—and I have no doubt the hurgon are counting on that. The may be able to afford the losses, sending individuals against us until our batteries run out, but we have no such luxuries.

"Then we just shoot the machine and make it blow up or melt it down to slag—whichever comes first."

Topper shook his head. "What if it explodes? Could wipe out half the square anyway, plus a few buildings. And it might be *that* explosion that ruptures our hull—the machine isn't very far away at all."

Stone was examining the picture on the desk. "Can we disable it another way?"

"From here? No."

"What about from out there?"

"Without it blowing up?"

Stone grunted in disgust.

Tuki cleared his throat. Last time Meledrin had seen him, the moai would have waited for permission to speak after that, but now he ploughed straight into the question.

He still looked slightly nervous about it—his hands scratched reflexively at the tabletop. "You don't know what the machine does, but do you have any idea how it does it?"

"What?" Topper asked.

"We don't know what the machine is for, but you seem to know a bit about their technology so..."

"Right. Well, it's probably steam driven in some way," Topper said. He pointed to what appeared to be a tank. "Water in here gets heated and turns to steam, the pressure of the steam... does something. Turns a wheel or lifts a piston or... something."

"So we let out the water?"

Topper shook his head. "That would work short term, but they'd just fix the hole."

Ping grabbed his hand. "But... they *would* have to heat the water again, which would take a while. And we could put a hole somewhere else—attack the steam. Without pressure it will do nothing. Just slap a patch on the outside of that and it would soon be blown off."

"So all we need to do is put some holes in it?" Stone asked.

"It could buy us a couple of hours."

"Come on guys, let's see what we've got."

-oOo-

Meledrin watched from the bridge. She brought a picture of the machine up in the dome. On her main console screen she showed the freight door on Level 9. Five trolls were lined up with guns and a strange array of makeshift weapons that Meledrin did not entirely trust to work. Talus was standing by the button to open the door and looked ready to do so.

Meledrin quickly reached out and hit the button to turn on the intercom. "Wait."

Down in the hold the trolls looked up, grumbling and searching for a camera as if it would show what Meledrin was doing.

"I am coming down."

Meledrin took the lift, stopping at the gardens to collect the other elves and taking them the rest of the way with her.

In the hold, the trolls were standing around, edgy after being stopped on the brink of action.

"What's going on now?"

"Some recruits," Meledrin said. "Where are the bows my people brought on at Sherindel?"

Apparently the ones that had not been carried upstairs by the owners had been stowed in a crate. Bethalin, who had worked on the cargo computers earlier, led the way and had Chip open the lock.

"Topper," Meledrin said, as she took up a bow and collected five arrows. "Which is the most vital part of the machine? Which piece do we most want disabled?"

"Ummm... Do you remember the box on the top?" the dwarf asked.

"The one with the many pipes?"

"Yes."

"I think that's about the only thing your bows will work against."

"Very well. The trolls will do what they were going to do, the archers will follow my marker. If we break through, next in line chooses a likely target," she glanced at Topper, "even if it will not work."

The elves nodded and Meledrin nodded back. Soon everyone was lined up in firing positions, ready to go. Talus was by the door again, awaiting the order.

"And Talus..."

"Yeah, Mel?"

"Our survival is the most important thing. If you see the hurgon readying a response, close the door."

"You got it."

Meledrin waved her fingers in a ceremony of *Action*. "When you are ready."

When the door hissed open it took a moment for Meledrin to get her bearings. Several trolls had fired before she found her target and loosed. Almost before her arrow had shattered against the side of the machine, Palsamon fired as well. And the others. Five arrows smashed against the metal box in little more than two seconds. Meledrin fired again, hitting exactly the same place. At this range, barely fifty meters, the elvish long bow was a deadly, powerful weapon. The machine would not hold. And indeed Bethalin, firing third in the line, sent her third arrow into the interior of the machine. Lisarea had already fired and her arrow entered the same hole, stopping halfway. Penisari, next in line, chose another target in an instant and fired.

Meledrin shifted aim to match.

While the elves fired off a long stream of arrows, the trolls fired slower, heavier weapons. Some of their projectiles broke through on their own, others bounced harmlessly away. Barely thirty seconds after the start of the attack, Meledrin counted half a dozen holes.

Meledrin was about to fire her final arrow when she saw the hurgon, slow as ever, finally reacting. Orders were being shouted, weapons rose.

Talus hit the button and the door closed with a sigh.

Meledrin, smiling and taking a deep breath, danced her fingers. *Ending*. She felt no different after it was done and wondered why she had even bothered.

"Let us see what effect we have had." She handed her bow to Bethalin to put away and made her way to the lift. Then, she thought she might return to the garden.

40: A Bigger Room

KEEBLE QUICKLY GREW bored watching the driver. It wasn't as if he did much at all. The scenery wasn't all that exciting either—just more of the same buildings and empty lots.

So the train rushed on, adding to the density of the air, and Keeble just wanted to get there. Bargle seemed to have all sorts of questions for the driver and its two shoveling companions. He was fascinated by every little thing they did. At first they'd been reluctant to talk but as the journey stretched on, as they went thundering through more and more stations, as the hurgon realized they were probably safe, they started to talk.

Keeble reigned in his wandering thoughts to look at the driver. It was doing something. "What's happening?"

Tamidilin held a quick conversation with the driver. "Leeda says we are coming upon the P'targa family station."

"We are?" Keeble looked out the front window as the train started to slow.

Several minutes later they plunged into a building. The sound echoed enormously. Smoke gathered in the cabin. Keeble coughed and waved it away. The train continued to slow. And finally it stopped.

The station was the same as the last few had been. Small and brightly lit, with a platform on each side of the track. And also like the last few, a huge crowd had gathered to witness the excitement of the hijacked train flying through the station. When that didn't happen the crowds edged back. They looked to their companions, as if they might have an explanation for the strange turn of events. Guards stepped forward on both sides of the track.

"Which way?" Keeble asked.

"Tiv says the P'targa are that way." Tami gestured.

The crowd was larger on that side.

There were more guards, some armored, some not. Their uniforms were pale green with horizontal yellow stripes on the front. They all raised their weapons but didn't seem sure what to do after that.

"We doing this?" Sandy asked.

Keeble nodded slowly, as unsure as those outside. But the trolls had no room for doubt. They both stepped out onto the platform and stood near the door. After a few seconds they both took a step forward. The crowd edged away from them. They took another step and enlarged the beachhead. When they'd created a clear space around the door, with the guards watching silently, Keeble stepped out.

The quiet was eerie. Keeble quickly became the focus of attention—the colored eyes watched him suspiciously. He looked back at the train and in the carriages hurgon were pressed against the windows trying to see.

Just when Keeble's feeling of ridiculousness was starting to overtake his fear, Tami stepped to his side.

"What do you wish to say?"

"Errr... just hello and stuff, I suppose."

The elf took liberties with the translation. Arms waving, she talked back and forth with the leader of the guards for some time.

"Jisa greets us tentatively and wishes to know what we are doing."

"Well, tell Jisa we've come to talk to the Grandmother about an alliance between the P'targa Family and the Hakahei worlds."

That exchange took even longer and brought a lot of silent, arm-waving conversation from the onlookers. When they were done, Tami and Jisa stood staring at each other as if waiting for something to happen.

"Well?"

"Jisa said that the Grandmother is not presently in the compound and the Mother may not wish to speak with us. I replied that Jisa would not know without asking."

"And?"

"And Jisa is thinking about it."

Keeble thought he could see the thoughts turning over in the alien's head. Eventually it waved to one of its companions who raced away as best as the press and its hunched form would allow.

It was nearly half an hour before a response came—Keeble was starting to think it would never happen. Nina and Bargle were sitting on the train's step, chatting quietly, Tasko was Singing under his breath and using his boot to draw patterns on one of the slabs that tiled the floor. The trolls, elves and hurgon were standing silently, as if they were willing to wait all day.

When another troop of guards entered the station, barging their way through the crowd, it was a surprise to everyone.

Jisa spoke with the leader of the newcomers then turned to Tami and spoke in a loud voice for all the crowd to hear. The elf translated a couple of words behind.

"Jisa informs us that we are to be taken into custody."

Keeble swore. "Can't they see the advantages?"

"We can get back on the train," Flint said.

But they couldn't really and the troll knew it. The P'targa guards could shoot them before they got that far.

"What happens if we don't agree to this?"

Tami asked. "Apparently we will be killed."

"Tough choice," Keeble said bitterly. He sighed. They'd come so far. They were so close. "Come on then. We'll just have to escape later and find someone else to ask." Finding someone else would be the problem. He motioned his companions forward and the P'targa guards fell into step around them, guiding them towards the door. The train started to move off before they were off the platform.

-oOo-

Keeble looked around the room. It wasn't an official, overwhelming place like where they'd met the T'loop grandparents, but neither was it a cell.

An ancient hurgon, with pale brown skin and one drooping shoulder, entered the room. It tottered in with the help of a walking cane and surrounded by four guards. It looked at them with purple eyes but did not speak.

Suldon quickly composed himself and stepped out of the group and started to talk. Keeble watched the animated conversation and waited as patiently as he was able. He fidgeted and muttered to himself and tugged at his beard.

Eventually, Suldon turned to look at Keeble. "Mother Hupo apologizes for the charade, but it needed to be done in case there were spies present."

"What?" Keeble asked.

"It will not matter soon, but for now every little bit of extra time could be important."

"What?"

"We are not under arrest, Keeble. The Mother wishes to talk of an alliance."

"Oh." Keeble looked over his shoulder at his companions. "Very well. Ummm... Now what?"

"Now we talk, I would assume."

"Right. Of course."

Mother Hupo took up a position on a seating T, the guards stood close by.

"Tell her the story, Suldon."

"Which story?"

"About us not knowing about the war and them coming out of nowhere and attacking us. And tell her we don't want the war."

Apparently it was a long story. Keeble stood impatiently through the whole thing, winding the gears on his hand in and out. In and out. He watched the Mother, trying unsuccessfully to gauge her reactions—he still couldn't interpret hurgon body language. Even if he could, he couldn't understand what was being said to know what it was reacting *to*.

"The Mother wants to know what proof we have to back up our words."

"Proof? Well, we haven't attacked them in 500 of their cycles or whatever it is. And we're here."

That was quicker to translate.

"Are we official representatives of all the Hakahei worlds?"

"Umm..." Were they? Keeble wasn't exactly sure. And if the *Hakahei* was on 'official' business, did he have any right to do the talking? This should have been Kim's job. "Yes," he said eventually, simply because 'No' wouldn't be any help at all.

"What can we offer in terms of contracts?"

Keeble sighed but remembered how the last such conversation had progressed. "All we can offer at this stage is a verbal agreement to favor the P'targa family in all our dealings *after* the war is over."

"Mother Hupo will not like that."

"Well, Hupo doesn't have a choice. We still won't sign any contracts without being able to read what they say. Can you read their writing yet?"

"No."

"Well, there you go."

Suldon nodded unhappily, but translated what had been said. At least Keeble assumed he did. He wondered if the elf was really reciting love poems or trying to get the old hurgon to play chess.

"The Mother says such an agreement cannot be made."

"Why not? Did you explain the reasons? Ask if the P'targa family would sign a contract they'd not read."

"The P'targa would not but hakans cannot be trusted."

"The T'loop family entered into a verbal agreement with us," Keeble said through clenched teeth, "and then broke it within half an hour. Ask the Mother who it is that can't be trusted."

Keeble *really* wished he could recognize hurgon emotions. He watched the Mother's face as Suldon translated.

"It does not believe you," the elf said eventually.

"Of course not," Keeble muttered. He wondered what he was supposed to do. They couldn't offer anything more than a verbal agreement, but that wouldn't do. "How about we hold the Mother hostage until the P'targa family agrees to help us." He heard Flint and Sandy shifting their weight as if ready for the order, though they must have known he was joking. "Don't translate that, Suldon."

"I was not intending to."

"Good." But he didn't know what other options they had.

A knock at the door saved him from having to come up with something immediately. One of the guards answered and held a whispered conversation with someone outside. A moment later another old hurgon was ushered into the room.

Mother Hupo greeted the newcomer formally.

"Is that the Grandmother?" Keeble whispered.

Suldon shook his head. "It is Father Geena from the Di'linga family."

"Who are they?"

"I do not know? But it seems they are not friends of the P'targa. They are arguing."

"About what?"

"Hupo says that the Di'linga have never had anything to do with the business of the P'targa and that they never will. And Father Geena says the Di'linga don't want to be a part of the paltry deals organized by the P'targa, but that the safe return of the aliens—that is us—to the T'loop is a matter that concerns all hurgon." The conversation between the hurgon continued and Suldon cocked his head to listen. "The Mother says perhaps she was *not* going to return us to the T'loop because they obviously could not keep us locked safely away."

Keeble grunted. "I'd like to see them do better."

But the conversation had come to an end and the two hurgon were eying each other warily.

"What happened?"

"I believe they have reached an impasse. That is, both refuse to listen to the other."

"Ahhh..."

It seemed the hurgon would stand there all day, staring at each other, when there was another knock at the door. Keeble glanced at Suldon. The guards glanced at the Mother.

The process from earlier was repeated—the guard spoke with someone outside then ushered a hurgon into the room. This one was quite a bit younger than Hupo or Geena

"We'll need a bigger room soon," Bargle said.

"That is Father Kita," Suldon said softly as the greetings were made. "He is from the I'patin Family."

"Really. That's good to know." The conversation between the Mother and the new father seemed to be heading along the same path as the earlier one. "Suldon, tell the two fathers we're trying to make a deal with the P'targa that will make them rich and end the war. Tell them that the P'targa are not keen on this because all we can offer at the moment is a verbal agreement, but if they're interested..."

When Suldon started to speak the argument broke off as if a talking dog had surprised the newcomers. All three of the hurgon turned to look. When the elf was finished, a fresh argument broke out.

"Now they are arguing about what would happen if the T'loop family finds out what is happening. The Di'linga and I'patin had not thought of making a deal themselves. They wanted to get in good with the T'loop by returning us. They have found common ground and say that if the P'targa do not take us back then it could mean dire consequences."

Keeble sighed. "Ask them..." he said. But no, that wouldn't work. "What if..." He wound the gears on his hand and looked around at his companions as if they might help. Between them—dwarves, elves and trolls—surely they could come up with *one* idea that would work...

Keeble smiled—it was obvious. Dwarves, elves and trolls. "Ask them what they would prefer, a contact with the T'loop family, in which they would make money but lose a lot of other things, or an alliance of equals among minor families. The different strengths of their individual families could be used together to the advantage of all three families. It would be an alliance that promises them great advantages in their dealings with the Hakahei worlds after the war is over."

Suldon started to translate and the hurgon all fell silent again. "They do not understand," the elf said eventually.

"What bit?"

"The alliance among minor families."

"What?"

"I do not think they understand the idea of a business contract that has no immediate, obvious benefit. As far as they are concerned, what is the point of a contract that does not tell them how much money they are going to make?"

"Well, tell them that they'd just sign a contract that makes them into one large family with three Grandmothers in charge, each with an equal say. They could still run their own family businesses as usual, but just not in any way that detrimentally affects the other families. And they would also try to help the other families in terms of minor contracts because in doing so they would help themselves."

The translation followed. "They are intrigued by the idea, but wonder if three minor families will be enough to withstand the backlash from the major families."

There was a knock at the door.

41: A Good Guy

SCREE KNEW THEY WERE BACK where they'd started—the heart T'loop compound. He shook his head in disgust and let the guards herd him off the train. There were ten of them and they all had weapons. He probably could've escaped himself but Kim didn't have a chance.

They went between the squat columns then along the corridor to the lift. The lift shuddered and rumbled upwards and Scree wondered if they were going to go straight to the cell or back to the throne room first.

Neither, apparently. They were taken to a different floor where a narrow hall led between lichen-covered walls. There were no gas lamps, just torches, and they guttered fitfully. The sound of animal misery was everywhere. Scree took a quick look in the first door. The door was mainly wood, but through a small barred window he could see a hurgon shackled to the wall. It hung limply and might've been dead.

They weren't taken to a cell. At the very end of the hall, behind two large, iron-studded doors, was something far worse.

"Burnt cats."

The torture equipment had been made for hurgon but it was surprisingly similar to what hakans would've used. Sharp things everywhere with teeth and hooks and clamps. There was a stone table in the center of the room where the victim could be chained. Coals glowed dully in a small furnace in the corner. There were a dozen irons on the wall nearby.

"I think I like our last couple of cells better," Kim said quietly.

"I don't know," Scree replied. "At least there's something to look at here." It wasn't funny at all really. He didn't know why he'd said it. He didn't think Kim would be comforted if she thought about the things the hurgon might make her look at.

"Oh, yeah. Once they start I'm sure I'll be hooked."

Scree could hardly hear her. The worst bit was, Scree knew they'd start on Kim first. She was weaker, the one most likely to break, but Scree didn't know how long he'd be able to watch that.

Two hurgon held Kim with a weapon pointed at her back. She struggled for a moment, but soon gave up, which wasn't normal. Scree thought dying quickly may be better than the other options, especially for Kim, but did as he was told when another four motioned him towards some shackles fixed to the wall. They chained him there, hands and feet, and tested the locks. Scree tested them too but gave it up as useless. Kim was chained up as well and the hurgon filed out. The door slammed shut.

"Do we know where Flint is?" Kim said quietly. There was a quaver in her voice even then. "And the others?"

"No. Can't hear them." He was going to keep trying. They were the only hope of rescue.

"The ship?"

"They's talking." He shrugged. "What would I says? They don't know wheres we are or anything. Even on a train it would take thems a long time to get here."

"They have the Landers. And fighters."

"The hurgon know that too. I'm sure they gots it covered." Scree had considered all that already. Flint was their only hope.

"They would try."

Scree was sure they would. He knew *he* would. *Nobody stays behind,* he thought, examining Kim's face. She was about to cry. Her eyes were wide with fear.

The chain on Scree's wrist was thick and strong but he wrapped it around his hand anyway and pulled. He quivered with the effort. Veins stood out on his arm. Nothing. Not even a hint of weakness anywhere along the chain. He tried again. Then the other arm.

"What's that?" Kim asked.

Scree turned to see where she was looking. It was a circle of metal with a dozen little adjustable clamps and hooks facing inwards. It was used to peel flesh away from limbs in one piece.

"It's for making stockings," Scree said. "You wrap the wool around those little clamps, then you kinda wrap the next bit of wool around the first bits. Or something like that." He *had* seen a similar thing being done, but the equipment was different.

"Right," Kim said, nodding. "I think we call that *French* knitting."

Scree looked at her. She didn't believe him—the mention of making socks might have given away the contraption's real purpose—but she played along with the game.

"And that?"

It was a small cage with a hole in the bottom and blades facing inwards. It went over people's heads, cutting them whenever they moved.

"That," Scree said, "is for making patterns on the outside of watermelons for the Mid-summer Festival. You knows, you cut pictures on the skin so they looks good before you eats them."

"*Really*? Well, I'll be." She gave a slight smile. "I didn't know the hurgon had watermelons."

Scree shrugged. "I'm sure watermelons is a staple of every diet in the universe. How coulds any people live without watermelons?"

"And that thing?" She used her chin to point to a clamp that worked in reverse, the arms forcing apart instead of together. It was for separating ribs, probably, or whatever the hurgon had that was similar.

"That's for opening coconuts," Scree told her. "You use that drill there to put a hole in them, then..." But they'd carried the joke on too long. It wasn't funny any more, if it ever had been. Scree lapsed into silence and tried not to look any more.

-oOo-

"Scree?"

"Yeah." He'd been sleeping. It was obvious Kim hadn't. Her hair was everywhere, her eyes dark with exhaustion.

"You're a good guy, you know that?"

"No I ain't, Kim. Got a lot of things to make up for before that's true. I used to—"

"No. It doesn't matter what you used to do. None of the people on the ship, none of your friends, knew you before. What you did before doesn't matter."

"Ping knew me."

"Ping likes you though."

Scree didn't know if that was true. The little woman didn't go around saying she hated him, but there was something in her eyes. And who could blame her? The strangest thing was, he'd only had sex once since he tried to rape her—with Crystal near Danyon Ford—but felt no desperation at all. Well, there *was* a desperation, but of another kind.

He wanted Kim to accept him. He wanted all the people on the ship to accept him. His friends? He'd never had friends before. He grunted. That was all Ping's fault. Friends weren't worth the effort.

"You are a good man, Scree." Kim started crying. From the look on her face it wasn't the first time she'd done it recently.

Scree tried to pull the chains from the wall. He yanked and pulled and strained. He grunted and groaned with the effort. He cut his wrists on the manacles. He worked for almost a minute before stopping. He was breathing heavily and he thought that he'd cry too.

All Ping's fault. He cursed.

-oOo-

Two hurgon came in. They were wearing long green robes instead of the usual baggy pants and shirts. The guards looked around then pulled the door closed from the outside.

The hurgon didn't talk. One of them stoked up the furnace, the other arranged stuff neatly on a bench along the back wall.

Scree had imagined all sorts of things during the last hours. It had always involved Kim spread out on the table while he stayed chained to the wall. He didn't know if anything they actually did to him could be any worse.

As if to test the point, the alien by the furnace pulled the poker out and examined the tip. It was glowing hot. He moved to stand in front of Scree.

Scree stared at him. What else could he do?

When the hot iron was pressed against his shoulder he gritted his teeth against the pain and continued to stare. Beneath the hood, the hurgon's big, colored eyes widened. The alien stepped back and Scree smiled. He spat on the alien's face. A small victory, though would mean even less in a while.

Scree looked at Kim.

"I won't tell them anything, Scree," she said, staring at the burn on his shoulder.

Scree didn't know if she was joking. She could shout every secret she'd ever had at the top of her voice and it would make no difference—the hurgon couldn't understand her anyway.

The torture of waiting continued. Scree's tormentor went back to fiddling with the iron poker in the fire, twisting it and turning it as he examined the glowing tip. The other hurgon clanked and clatter at the rear of the room. Finally, when Scree thought maybe they were just cleaning up and weren't going to do anything more, they both walked to the center table as if on some unheard, unseen signal. They stared at their captives and Scree stared back.

It was all a foregone conclusion though. The hurgon crossed the room, slowly, and started to unchain Kim. Scree fought against his own bonds again. Straining and thrashing alternately, as if a sudden change of tactics might surprise the manacles and chains. He growled at the aliens. He would've bitten them if only he could have bent forward far enough.

Kim went without protest.

"Fight them, Kim," Scree urged her. "Kick them. Bite them." Scree knew it wouldn't do her any good. The hurgon weren't very good at fighting but they were strong and tough anyway. The torturers each had a good grip on one of Kim's wrists and she wouldn't be able to break free. But she didn't even try. That made Scree fight all the harder.

When Kim was lying on the table and the manacles had snapped into place around her wrists and ankles, the hurgon tore away her outer clothes. They left her lying there in her underwear as they went to play with their tools again, fiddling, picking them up and putting them down. But in the end they went with the hot poker again and it was a bit of an anti-climax.

Scree couldn't fight any more. He watched quietly as one of the hurgon held the tool close to Kim's face. But that was too much too soon. After a moment, it pressed the glowing metal against the tender flesh of her inner thigh.

It was obvious Kim wanted to grit her teeth and stare. She watched the hurgon coldly, not flinching until the metal touched her. Then she screamed and writhed in pain. The sounded goaded Scree into another few seconds of furious struggle.

The hurgon stepped away and went back to the furnace without saying anything.

Scree stared at the blistering wound on Kim's leg while she cried and moaned with pain. Her chest heaved. Then Kim was spitting curses at the hurgon for a whole minute. The aliens ignored her and the limits of her resistance showed when the hurgon eventually approached her with the iron again. She fell silent, staring at the tip of the poker. She held herself silent for a moment, during which time the sizzling of her flesh could be heard, but then screamed louder than the first time.

"Try thats on me you stinking, green bastard," Scree shouted. "Come over here and I'll shove that poker so far down your throat I'll cure your haemorrhoids."

Eventually Scree slumped forward and turned away. When he looked again there was a matching pair of wounds on Kim's leg, midway between groin and knee. She was crying again, shuddering, rubbing her wrists and ankles raw on the manacles. Scree wondered if her wounds from the fight were causing as much trouble as anything else.

Again, the two hurgon went back to what they were doing without speaking. The played with their toys and bided their time. Finally, one broke off what it was doing and approached Kim with something like a drill. Scree thought he recognized it as a thing used to cut muscle and tendon away from bone leaving hardly any external damage. The hurgon worked the machine as it motioned for its companion to hold Kim's wrist. Kim watched, eyes wide with horror though she probably didn't know the end result of the process.

Scree was horrified. He didn't look at the hurgon. He didn't look at the drill bit spinning in the end of the drill. He stared at Kim's eyes. The fear was obvious there, palpable, but so was her defiance, little good it would do her.

"Kim," Scree said softly, as the hurgon moved the drill towards her wrist. She turned to look at him but there was no recognition in her eyes. "I'm sorry." He saw her flinch as the drill bit at her flesh. She bit her tongue.

The door to the room creaked open.

The two hurgon looked up, their concentration broken. Scree stared into Kim's eyes for a moment longer before he turned to look as well. Standing in the door was another robed hurgon.

The newcomer said something, looking between the two prisoners. The reply was short. An animated discussion followed. The three hurgon almost growled at each other, and their arms waved wildly as they also spoke in the kil'ini sign language. They were going to quick for Scree to follow more than a couple of words.

Eventually the two original hurgon turned to face Kim so they could continue working. While they seemed to deliberately ignore the newcomer Scree studied it. The alternative viewing options weren't nice.

The newcomer went to the back of the room and picked up a knife, testing the blade on its thumb. It put that down and picked up the bladed head-cage weighing it in its hand.

Scree heard Kim gasp and turned to see that the drill had touched her skin again and sent out a small splatter of blood. She was shaking, shuddering.

Scree closed his eyes and took a deep breath. He should have fought earlier. He should have made sure Kim died before things went this far. They weren't after information—the T'loop family merely wanted revenge for being made to look like fools. He should have...

There was a gasp and a thump.

Scree opened his eyes and saw then the drill wielder collapse. The newcomer was standing close by with the head-cage in its hand. A ribbon of blood clung to the corner. The other hurgon, holding Kim's wrist, opened its mouth to shout but was thumped before it had a chance. The bars of the cage left a crosshatch of marks across its face. It stayed on his feet for a moment, then tumbled to the floor.

The hurgon with the cage dropped the makeshift weapon—as if unable to believe what had happened—then slowly pushed back its hood.

42: Things She'd Seen

PING LOOKED UP AS MELEDRIN'S VOICE came over the intercom system. "Captain Thorpe to the bridge, please."

She looked at Tess, but the dwife just shrugged. Bethalin had called Meledrin to the bridge not five minutes earlier.

"What's all the excitement, do you think?" Dido asked, taking another card from the deck.

"I'm going to find out," Ping said, throwing in her hand—which wasn't any good anyway—and heading for the door. She smiled as she heard Hoodek throw his cards down in disgust—like all dwarves, he wore his heart on his sleeve, only more so, and it was easy to see when he thought he had a good hand.

On the bridge she found that most of the current brains trust had gathered. Meledrin sat in her communications seat. Chasm and Cliff were leaning against the chairs of the gallery. Tuki and Thorpe were standing nearby. Bethalin was at the base of the stairs, as if she had not known where to go after being booted from the communications chair by Meledrin. Topper and Palsamon were on duty.

"Scree will be returning soon," Meledrin said. "Kim is in his company, apparently, but she is injured. Scree requests that you be ready to treat her, Captain Thorpe, and that the rest of us are ready to help him get her inside."

Ping gasped. If Scree was calling ahead to warn then Kim's injuries must be serious.

Thorpe nodded in his economical way. "I'll prepare. Does anyone know where Amy and Paul are?"

"Chasm'll get them to go to the medical bay," Chasm said, probably already asking the trolls to find the two humans in question.

"How is he getting here?" Ping asked. She wondered how many hurgon would have to die if he wanted to get through the square on foot.

Meledrin cleared her throat. "He is riding a small kidol. They should not be far away."

Ping went to the forward view port to look. She scanned the sky, but could see nothing. Unless... "Spin the bridge," she said, twirling her finger in the air.

"Pardon."

"Look out that way." The black dot was getting closer very quickly. Ping looked over her shoulder, but Meledrin didn't know how to spin the bridge.

"Three riders on the back," Cliff said, squinting. "Two more bats coming up behind. Stone knows," he said, nodding in satisfaction.

Ping could imagine the four weapons chairs on the floor below all shifting to face the oncoming bats.

Ping stared out the window, wondering exactly what had happened to Kim. The kidol came on like small, intense storm clouds, looming larger. Eventually, she turned and hurried from the bridge.

-oOo-

Ping's cabin seemed suddenly too small. She sat on the edge of the bed, hands clasped in her lap. There was a knock at the door but she didn't reply. She held her breath, as if that might help keep her hidden.

The silence that followed stretched on and on. Ten seconds. Twenty. Ping swallowed, took a breath, examined her hands.

The knock came again.

"Go away."

"Ping, it's Topper. I—"

"Go away."

"Scree and Kim are back. Kim's hurt pretty bad. She's got broken ribs and... other stuff. Scree did something to her shoulder, but I don't know what, exactly."

There were any number of things Scree could have done to her shoulder. Those around him seemed to get hurt all the time, and more often than not, he was the cause. Who could stop the troll if he really wanted to do something? She started to cry, not caring who heard.

Topper was the only one who could hear though, and he did. "Ping? Are you all right?"

"Go away."

But he didn't. "Ping?"

Ping looked up, ready to tell him to go away again, when the door slid open. Topper stood there, looking as if the last thing he wanted to do was step inside the room.

"Topper, I really..."

The dwarf stepped into the room. He stood just inside the door, shuffling his feet and examining the spanner in his hand.

"Why are you crying? Can I help?"

Ping almost laughed. Typical dwarf. There was a problem but he had a spanner—surely it could be fixed. Instead, she sniffed and wiped at her face.

"I'm fine, Topper. Just relieved that Scree and Kim are back home."

Home? Ping wanted to stand in the center of Shadon, in the park surrounding the Great Clock. She wanted to hear the midsummer chime and look up at the dozen towers on the hills around her, like a crown on the city. But the Great Clock was no more. Possibly Shadon was no more. And it certainly wasn't home, not after the places she'd been and the things she'd seen.

She sighed. She would have been dead, like so many of her countrymen, if it hadn't been for Scree. She hated the troll. She lay awake at night, remembering the look in his eyes as he tried to get into her armor. But that was a lifetime ago. On the ship he obeyed Kim and kept the peace. And that just made everything worse because she didn't know when the other Scree would return. If Kim was injured...

Topper cleared his throat but didn't question the poor excuse. "Keeble is coming back as well," he said.

"He is?" Ping smiled. It was strange how she was more comfortable with Keeble than with others. At least with him she knew what he was feeling. He didn't like women. He didn't try to pretend. He didn't try to make you like him by being nice. He didn't want to talk to women but he did when he needed to. There was no confusion at all.

There was a commotion outside the cabin as dwarves rushed past, heading for the stairs.

Ping wiped her eyes again and rose to her feet. "We'd better get going then," she said.

Topper opened his mouth to say something, then changed him mind and nodded. Ping, straightening her clothes.

On Level 3, almost everyone gathered on one side of the ship, staring out through the window.

"We might be able to get out of here," Kafin said to Hoodek.

Ping interrupted. "He found some rebels?"

Kafin nodded. "Apparently. Certainly some of the hurgon aren't too happy with him. It could get nasty around here soon."

"And who's supposed to be on engineering duty?"

"That would be Drago."

Ping looked around and found the dwarf trying to peer over Ari's shoulder to see outside. "Drago, what are you doing?"

"Trying to see."

"Are you supposed to be in engineering?"

"Yes, but—"

"No buts. We need somebody down there to monitor the systems."

"So why don't you go down there and monitor them yourself?"

Ping wasn't in the mood. "If you are not down there with your work gang in two minutes I'll ask Kim to drop you off on the next planet we find and get some replacements."

"Kim isn't likely to be listening to anything."

She was going to say she'd get whoever was in charge to do it, but that would be Scree. And Kim was going to be fine. *She was.*

"Then I'll do it myself." She remembered what Captain Thorpe had said and looked around for one of the humans. Brick Dunning was close by, gazing over the heads of a pair of dwarves. "Brick?"

"Yeah, Ping." He was almost as big as a troll.

"Drago, Makar, Tess and Dido are supposed to be in the engineering department and on the bridge."

"And they aren't there?"

"No."

"Maybe they don't know where the engineering department is," Brick said. "You want me to show them the way?"

"If you could."

Brick smiled at Drago. "You want to gather your friends." It wasn't a question.

A couple of minutes later Ping walked slowly out of the elevator and onto the bridge. Meledrin was there, and Tuki and Topper. But Scree wasn't. Stone was sitting in the weapons chair, looking very serious as he studied the pictures of outside.

"What are you doing here?" Ping asked the troll.

He looked up. "Somebody's got to do it."

"I meant, why isn't Scree here?"

Stone shrugged. "He's in medical."

"Is he sick too?"

"Nope. Watching Kim."

Did she need watching? And why would Scree want to do it? Perhaps he was worried. Perhaps people really *could* change. After all, Stone was in the chair because 'somebody has to do it'. It was doubtful those words had ever left his mouth in the past. And Topper? She did not look at the dwarf as she crossed to the second engineering seat and sat down. There was no doubt why he was on the bridge—because somebody had to do it—but why had he entered her cabin earlier?

A few minutes later, Drago and Tess entered the bridge. Apparently Brick's guidance had not been required.

"How are we supposed to be on duty when you two are sitting there," the dwarf asked. He stood with hands on hips. "Tess and I have work to do."

Ping nodded, wondering if Drago realized how he had included Tess in his comment. "Topper and I were about to move."

43: Thinking About It

SCREE STARED. "CUTO?"

The alien was babbling quietly, staring at the other two on the floor.

Scree got Cuto's attention by repeating his name over and over and when the alien looked up he used his chin to motion to the manacles. Cuto got the idea and continued with the rescue though he was shaking as badly as Kim and it took a while to get organized. He found the keys and put them to use while Scree waited impatiently.

Scree raced to Kim's side. She was conscious but didn't respond to anything he said. He shook her gently. She looked in his direction but no recognition showed in her eyes.

He didn't know what to do. He'd drawn Ping out of shock twice, but it had taken time. He didn't have time. With a curse Scree opened Kim's restraints and got her feet on the floor. She wouldn't stand on her own. He left her leaning against the table, wavering, while he collected her clothes. They were torn to pieces—worst than useless.

The hurgon robes. He stripped one of the aliens and slipped the robe over Kim's head. He noticed for the first time how badly her wrist was bleeding and used the remains of her shirt to make a bandage. He lifted her robe to examine the burns on her thigh as well. They were blistering and weeping but he knew there was nothing he could do. Bandages wouldn't help.

"We'll just have to see what happens, wont we?" Kim didn't reply and Scree let the robe fall back down. She leaned against the table and stared.

Cuto was watching distractedly.

Scree ignored the hurgon and collected a wicked looking curved knife so he could take care of the guards—there were only two and they weren't expecting trouble. He rammed the knife up into the first ones armpit. Blood sprayed as he pulled it free. He spun to the next and slashed it across the throat. The head almost came free. Both aliens toppled to the ground in a growing pool of blood.

"Bastards," Scree said, throwing the knife down. He thought of dragging them into the room, but there was enough blood on the floor and walls to alert even the dumbest guard. He wiped more blood from his face. Cuto was in the doorway, staring at the dead aliens as if having second thoughts. Scree ignored him again as he went to collect Kim. She limped slowly forward at his urging, offering neither resistance nor help.

"Flayed cats, this'll take all day." He scooped her up in his arms. "Where are we goings, Cuto?"

It didn't look as if they were going anywhere. The alien stood stupidly.

The elves could translate.

<Meledrin, you there?>

<*Scree? Is that you? This is Bethalin. Scree, we thought... That is...*>

<We ain't dead yet, Beth, but we was thinking about it. What about the others?>

<*We heard from them some time ago, but they are out of range now.*>

<How you know they ain't dead?>

<*Well... They said they were travelling north to the P'targa compound. They were stealing a train because it is a hundred kilometers to the north.*>

<They knows where it is?>

<*I believe so.*>

Scree needed to go after them—finding hurgon allies was the most important thing... He looked at Kim and muttered, "How could I help with the negotiations." But was Keeble a better choice? All he could do was hope the various hakans could balance each other out. Elves and dwarves and trolls—surely they made a sensible person between them.

<*Are you there?*> Beth asked.

<Yeah. How do you say 'take us to our ship' in hurgon?>

Bethalin was silent for a moment then grunted her way through the strange words. <*Do you have a hostage, Scree?*> she asked when she was done.

Scree didn't answer as he tried to remember the words. He transmitted in his mind while he spoke out loud so the elf could correct him if he was wrong.

Cuto replied, though it didn't look very enthusiastic about the idea.

<What does *pamghno kulth* mean?>

<*It means 'of course', or something similar. Although, with the hurgon language it can sometimes be—*>

<Yeah, that's great Beth. We're on our way back.>

<*Very well. I will inform Meledrin.*>

<Tell whoever you like.>

Scree motioned for Cuto to lead the way. As he followed, he spoke to Kim. "Cuto's taking us to the ship."

She stared at nothing. Scree spoke to her as he walked.

-oOo-

Scree didn't ask Cuto where they were going. He'd done it three times since they'd left the torture chamber for all the good it did. And it wouldn't matter if Cuto explained the exact route they were taking—he was hardly in a position to argue.

When the lift door opened, Scree looked out into a big empty room. He couldn't be sure, but he thought they were one level below the throne room where they'd met the Grandmother and Grandfather.

"Where are we going?" Scree whispered.

Cuto motioned like he was opening a door then strode out of the elevator. There was a small, timber door in the back corner of the room. It looked ancient, but most things on Hulgorn did.

As soon as they arrived, Cuto knocked and held a shouted conversation with someone beyond. And just when Scree thought the strangers had told Cuto to go kill a cat, the big old locks started to rattle and clank.

Scree carefully laid Kim on the floor and the moment the door started to open, he charged.

His shoulder hit the timber hard. Two hurgon were toppled backwards. There was another three meters beyond and two more to the right. All of them were armed.

Scree, staggering from the impact, kept his momentum going. He shifted course, put his shoulder into the chest of the next alien. None would stay down long, but it would give him time. While they struggled to catch their breath and rise, Scree turned to the last two guards.

They'd hardly moved. One was starting to raise a weapon, seemingly more through a very slow reflex than conscious choice. Scree danced forward, hitting it twice in the face. It staggered back and fell against the wall. Scree moved on, ducking down to sweep the final guard's legs from under it. Upright again a moment later, he kicked the prone alien in the head.

The first three guards were climbing to their feet. Scree moved quickly. He punched one in the stomach, spun, slammed his elbow into the head of another. Two down.

The hurgon Scree punched in the face was finally thinking clearly enough to raise its weapon. Scree took three steps. He jumped, aiming a kick at the alien's head. The creature moved quicker than expected. He had to content himself with kicking the weapon from its grasp.

Scree landed awkwardly and rolled to his feet.

The three aliens near the door were attacking. He dived toward them. Roll to his feet, hit one with a powerful uppercut to the chin.

Another gone.

Scree was pounded, a solid blow to the back of his neck. He stumbled forward into the path of the final hurgon's fist. Shifting slightly, the blow glanced off his jaw. It stunned him. Momentum carried him through and into the clear.

One of the creatures was picking up a dropped weapon. The other was stalking forward.

Scree tried to clear his head. He took a deep breath, darted forward. He lashed out at the nearest alien with his foot, but it shied away in an instinctive reaction that saved it from a broken arm. The weapon was knocked clear.

"Stinking cats."

The final hurgon, now on the far side of the room, had collected another weapon. It aimed and said something. Scree couldn't understand, but got the general idea. He just couldn't afford to give up. Scree dodged to the right, moved in. He probably wouldn't make it.

He was halfway to the armed alien when Cuto decided to help. He'd collected one of the weapons from the floor and moved unnoticed to a corner. Now, standing behind the armed guard, he said something that got the guard's attention. While he had the chance, Scree went quickly forward and snatched the weapon from the guard.

He stood back, weapon aimed, and watched while Cuto argued with the others. He breathed deeply and rubbed at the back of his neck. There was a big, tender lump there and his head pounded, but he'd live.

He smiled at the thought. *I'll lives.*

Eventually, Cuto convinced the three conscious guards to drag their companions into the other room. Scree bought Kim the other way and Cuto locked the door.

It wouldn't take long for the guards to raise the alarm, so Scree made his way to the next door and waited while Cuto composed himself. Then they set off, through the door and into a long hallway. Cuto took the first door on the left and climbed two floors to the roof. He muttered to himself the whole way.

<Beth, what's...> Scree listened for one of the regular lines in the hurgon's one sided argument and repeated it to the elf.

<It is something about a 'verbal agreement', I believe.>

They crossed a hundred meters of roof, skirting around pipes and ducts and skylights, before going down another set of stairs to the floor they'd started from. While they waited in the stairwell, Scree put Kim down and rubbed at his arms. He would have slung her over his shoulder, but wasn't sure how her broken ribs would react to the treatment. Six hurgon jogged along the hallway outside. They waited some more. And a couple of minutes later a pair of armored hurgon stomped by in the hall. Finally, Cuto opened the door fully and went out. With a sigh, Scree took up his burden again and followed.

They followed the hall, then went down further and across a circular room to wait for a lifetime near another door. Eventually, though nothing seemed to have changed, Cuto pulled a big, metal lever. A spurt of steam hissed out into the room and the door opened. Scree followed as the alien across a covered bridge. Vacant, rubble-strewn ground was below them. There were Guards on a balcony above but they were looking elsewhere, watching a line of kidol racing across the sky.

The next building was more opulent. The guards were more numerous. Scree had a feeling that being caught now would involve a quick death and lots of questions among the hurgon afterwards. He held onto Kim and followed.

The next time they reached a relatively secure area, Scree had to rest again. He carefully laid Kim down and tried to massage his arms and shoulders. He was hungry and tired and wanted to talk to someone.

<Beth?>

<*Yes, Scree?*>

<How's everything?>

<*Everything is fine, Scree. The hurgon seemed to be readying an attack some time ago, but we disabled a machine and now wait to see what they will do next. Is all well with you, Scree? Are you on your way back?*> Bethalin sounded concerned and Scree found he quite liked the idea.

<Maybe. Sorta. How can I tell? Cuto's leading and I'm following but...>

<*Cuto?*>

<Yeah.>

Scree glanced at the hurgon. Cuto, crouching nearby, stared silently, watching without emotion.

Before Scree was ready, the hurgon was on his feet again. He opened the door slightly, looked out, and froze.

<Gotta go,> Scree said silently. *Should've kept that damn knife.*

Cuto glanced back before slipping out into the passage. Scree listened as he talked to another hurgon, and when the door started to open again a minute later, he could see a set of reddish brown fingers on the edge of the timber. He charged into the door. He hurt his shoulder but the hurgon flew across the hall and crashed into the far wall. It didn't move. There was nobody else around. Cuto said something though Scree didn't know what. So he flexed his shoulder, collected Kim and stood waiting.

"Is this going to take much longer?" he asked, though he knew they weren't getting any closer to the ship at all.

<Beth?>

<*Yes?*>

<How does I ask where we're going?>

Scree repeated the words Beth gave him but he didn't need the elf's help with the reply. Cuto was taking them to a kidol—one of the giant bats that the hurgon used for transport. He used his chin to motion the alien onwards.

Cuto led a twisting journey. They stopped every few meters, it seemed, to hide and wait and watch hurgon stomp past. Scree's nerves were on edge. If they were spotted it would take a couple of seconds for him to put Kim down. It could be all over before he was ready to fight. Each time they stopped, each time a hurgon went past, he held his breath and waited silently.

Eventually Scree, on Cuto's heels, slipped though what appeared to be just another door. He stood silently and stared.

The room was fifty meters long and ten meters wide. There were five hurgon in the room besides Cuto. They were sweeping and scrubbing, cleaning up the mess left by ten kidol. The creatures were chained to perches and looking out an open wall at the grey, thick air of Hulgorn. Except these giant bats were about the size of a Lander when the ones Scree was used to were five times that size. Most stared out the window squawking quietly and clacking their huge, toothy beaks. The bat closest to Scree was pecking at the manacle around its ankle as if ready to rip it away and leap out the window to freedom.

Cuto ignored the hurgon, collected a stepladder, and stood it by the closest creature's side. He wordlessly urged Scree to climb.

One of the caretakers finally saw what was happening and shouted something. Scree couldn't understand, but the words spurred him into motion. With a sigh and a moment of worry he slung Kim over his shoulder. She gasped but made no other sound as Scree climbed. By the time he reached the top, Cuto had undone the chains and was scrambling up behind. The other hurgon were rushing around but not doing much at all. One finally went to look for help. The rest came to a halt nearby. They held tools as if they'd use them but didn't move.

At the top of the ladder, Scree stopped. He'd never even ridden a donkey so he certainly didn't know how to ride an alien bat. Cuto pushed him from below and he started to lose his balance. He had no choice but to throw his leg over and hope. When he was sitting, he carefully maneuvered Kim into a similar position in front of him. The creature looked back over its shoulder with dark unreadable eyes and clacked its beak.

Cuto shifted Scree, moving him forward, hooking his feet underneath the wing. While Cuto adjusted Scree, Scree adjusted Kim. Finally the hurgon seemed happy and pushed Scree so that he was lying on Kim's back. Then Cuto climbed on, laid behind Scree and shouted an order.

Guards burst into the room. Too late.

Scree felt the huge bat gather itself and leap into the nothing beyond the missing wall. His heart thumped in his chest and he felt a smile creeping onto his face. For the first few moments the kidol plummeted towards the ground. It snapped out its wings and the descent slowed. Then it started to fly. It beat at the air with powerful, easy strokes and gained altitude. Scree pushed Kim's hair away from his face and tried to see.

The square in which they flew had high buildings on all sides and the kidol continued to work until they topped a building and skimmed along its roof.

It seemed to rest slightly then, slowing its stroke, waiting. Cuto shouted and they banked to the left. They also started to climb.

Cuto shouted again. The kidol looked back as it flew, then screeched and halted its climb. It stayed close to the roof as it turned eastwards.

Scree looked back the way they'd come. He could just see the window over the edge of the roof and watched as five more kidol threw themselves into the open. They fell from sight, but Scree had no doubt they'd be visible in a moment. And there was probably only one rider on each, so they'd catch up soon enough. He didn't know what they'd do then.

-oOo-

When the kidol swerved, Scree could look back and see their pursuers. They were just meters behind but having trouble staying close. Scree decided the kidol weren't used to flying amongst the obstacles on the roofs. They seemed to be enjoying the game immensely, dodging and swerving, weaving between towers and protrusions. Scree might've enjoyed it himself, in other circumstances.

They broke from the cover offered by the rooftop and flew out over an empty, grassy block. The trailing kidol labored furiously, gaining ground. The first was right there.

The kidol Scree was riding screech furiously. There was a shadow. Scree looked up and saw a kidol diving towards them. So close. Cuto shouted and their own mount jinked immediately and severely. A wave of air washed over them as the attacker, wings folded back, flash by just meters to the left. Wing's touched in midair. Barely. Scree's kidol screeched again, lurched, lost its balance. It struggled for a moment, losing altitude, before regaining its rhythm.

Scree gripped furiously with his knees and held onto Kim, but he didn't close his eyes. The attacker flared its wings and tried to pull out of its dive. It was too late. It crashed into the ground with a sickening thud and terrified screech.

Scree heard another screech. There was a kidol just above them. Razor sharp claws extended, it snatched at the air as it tried to hold its position.

Cuto shouted. Their mount slowed suddenly and turned. Scree almost lost his balance but the bat swung back the other way and righted everything.

Cuto sent them curving away to the left with another bat snapping at their tail. They dipped down into a gap between two buildings, banked sharply around a corner then angled upwards to skim over a wall. They wove between antennae and machinery. The pursuers were closing again.

Scree cursed. Looking back, he could see Cuto's face as the hurgon concentrated on their path. He didn't look at all worried. They turned again, clearing the edge of the building by centimeters and dipping down into a square.

Now, Cuto shouted at the kidol constantly and slapped its side.

They were approaching another roost. Scree could see the kidol on their perches, all of them going wild. They were just a couple of meters away when one threw itself forward and broke its chain. Cuto directed their mount up over the wall and behind them the riderless bat flew headlong into one of the pursuers. Both creatures screeched and lashed out with their claws.

Moments later, a half dozen more uncontrolled bats came into sight and joined the fray.

Scree gave a cheer and turned his eyes forward. In the distance he could see the dome on the top of the *Hakahei.*

<Bethalin,> he said, <get ready. We's coming home. And make sure nobody shoots no bats.>

Scree hadn't really been directing the last statement at the elf, but she answered anyway. *<Very well, though I cannot understand why they would want to shoot bats.>*

Scree laughed. <Some little kidol is coming,> he said, <and we's riding the one out the front.>

<Oh.>

<And you gotta tell Thorpe to get ready with his medical stuff. Kim's got all sorts of problems.>

<I will let him know.>

<Good. We's coming.>

Scree saw a group of hurgon in a tower nearby. They were tracking the kidol with a weapon, keeping it in their sights the whole way. It was probably only the buildings and the hurgon within that stopped them from firing. He looked back over his shoulder as well. There were two bats back there again, gaining every second.

Cuto sent their mount around the edge of a huge empty square. The kidol rose and dipped over obstructions, shrieking all the way. Hurgon watched from windows.

The pursuers were only twenty meters behind when Cuto directed the kidol out over the square surrounding the *Hakahei.* Two guns fired and Scree almost thought he could feel the heat of the beams as they passed overhead.

<What you shooting at?> he said, but he glanced back and saw the other two kidol tumbling to the ground. They screeched as they went and landed in a thrashing heap amongst the hurgon in the square.

Hurgon were moving all around the square, though what they were actually doing was hard to work out. Either way, Scree didn't think it'd be easy to get from the bat's back in through one of the cargo doors.

<Get the hangar door open,> he said in his head. <And be quick about it.> While he talked, he motioned to Cuto to do a lap of the ship.

He wasn't sure the alien understood until it shouted an order. The kidol held its altitude and started to turn. When they sailed past the hangar door, Scree pointed. It had opened a crack and was quickly opening further still. Cuto nodded. They kept going around the ship and the hurgon on the ground started firing.

But Cuto shouted another order and the kidol gained some height. Then it folded its wings and ducked in through the hangar door with such ease and grace that it might have been doing it all its life.

It took a moment for it to find its balance on the hard floor, then it stood there, head bowed below the ceiling, and looked calmly around. By the time Scree passed Kim down to Peak and Gulch the door was already closing. Scree jumped down as Cuto chased the creature back out into the open.

44: Timely and Profitable

KEEBLE'S HEAD WAS SPINNING.

Before the I'patin, De'linga and P'targa families had got down to the serious business of negotiation, the representatives of two more families had arrived. The last two families, O'sabet and La'nesto, were the smallest of the lot. Apparently they were hardly families at all. Whatever they were, their arrival added a whole new layer of complexity to the negotiations.

Keeble grunted. "Can we hurry this up?" he said. "We need to get to the bit where we stop people from dying."

Suldon nodded, then rose to his feet and crossed to the table. Several guards shuffled forward, watching the elf carefully. Sandy stepped forward in response.

Suldon held a long conversation with the mother and all the fathers. Keeble almost fell asleep waiting for the outcome.

Eventually the elf turned back to look at Keeble.

"They say that stopping the war in not merely a matter of them asking for it to be done. Between these five families there are a total of thirty-seven kil'ini in the greater flock. It is hardly a speck in terms of voting. And seeing they are all minor families that only have one vote to the four of the Great families."

"Well, they need to get more minor families involved."

"How?"

"Umm... I don't suppose they are willing to give up some of their profits to others? No?" Keeble wound the gears on his hand. "Well, what else would the minor families like?"

Suldon asked then translated the reply. "Nobody was really sure, though Father Jorf of the La'nesta said his family would like more room. They cannot grow much more in term of population because there is no room for them to grow. Apparently that is one of the major hurdles facing smaller families—they could make more profits with higher numbers, but cannot get more numbers because they cannot afford to buy land."

Keeble nodded thoughtfully.

"I've seen Tuki's star-maps," Flint said after a while. "There's lots of stars out there."

"So?" Keeble asked.

“Well, there must be lots of planets as well. Why aren’t they moving to some of them? Some must have air and stuff.”

“Probably better air than here,” Sandy added under her breath.

“Good question,” Keeble said. “Ask them, Suldon.”

“The mother says they are not able, because the Great families will not allow it.”

Keeble sighed. “How many Great and minor families are there?”

“54 Great families and 207 minor.”

“Plus those that are less than minor? I reckon that if all the minor families got together, in this one thing at least, then who could stop them?”

Apparently, nobody could. But any minor family that became involved in rebellion would be breaking a 500-year-old contract. And the ‘Contract of Council’ had been set up so that it didn’t end until the war ended.

Keeble sighed—another one of those problems that fed back on itself. They could finish the war if they could break the contract, and they could break the contract if they could finish the war...

“There’s no other way?”

“No.”

“And they aren’t willing to just break it?”

“I do not believe so.”

“Why not?”

“It is what their society has been based on for so long.”

“What does the contract say exactly? It can’t still be relevant after 500 years.”

Suldon talked to the hurgon for a short while. Tami joined in. “They are not positive about what is in the contract. They have never actually seen it, and know of no one who has.”

Keeble was astounded. For people who put so much importance on contracts he would’ve thought they could recite it off the top of their heads. After a moment of staring, he suddenly thought he’d be able to recognize hurgon embarrassment in the future. Almost as one the fathers and mother shouted to their assistants. The assistants nearly knocked each over in their rush to get out the door.

-oOo-

“Wait a minute. What was that last bit.” Keeble laid his head on the table as Suldon asked the daughter to re-read the latest clause in the 125 page contract.

“If those participating in section (1), clause (a) should be—”

“Who are those?” Keeble asked. He shook his head, as if that might clear it. “Who are they? The ones participating?”

“They were the ‘Originals’. The eight Great families that were the principle signatories of the contract.”

"Right. Keep going."

"If those participating in section (1), clause (a) should be found to be negligent in their duties, as outlined in section (45) subsection (iv) clause (b), then a majority vote in either council shall be sufficient to see the contract ceased as outline in section (19)—"

"That'll do." Keeble had been listening to the clatter of numbers and sections and here-to-with for so long that he wasn't sure about anything any more. "What did that mean?"

Suldon gave it some thought. "It is obvious, I think—if the eight families in section (1)—"

Keeble gave the elf a look that stopped him in his tracks for a moment.

Suldon cleared his throat. "If they are not doing their job, the contract can be cancelled by a vote from 104 minor families who are up to date on the payments that keep them on the Lesser council."

"So, there's a way out then?"

"Well, yes, but only if they are not doing their job."

"And what is their job? Without all the sections and number and... whatever else."

Suldon got the hurgon who was doing the reading to find the relative page. The elf translated. "The... participants shall endeavor, with all care for the well being of the Great families, bring about a timely and profitable end to the conflict against the worlds of Hakahei."

For the first time in several hours, Keeble smiled. "I don't care how long you take to have breakfast in the morning, 500 years is not 'timely'." He sat back, almost tipping from his seating T, and smiled some more. He knew the next point was the clincher. "And how much money have all the families lost in that time as they geared up for this war? They could strip our seven worlds bare and they'd still be nowhere near making their money back."

Tami was translating this for the hurgon, and Keeble could see the moment they started to get excited as well.

Suldon whispered in Keeble's ear as Tami continued to speak with the hurgon. "They say that 'timely' may cause a problem, because others will be able to argue over that point for years. But they seem to think 'profitable' should do the trick."

"Good. Well, tell them to hurry up then. More people, ours and theirs, are dying by the moment."

"They must call an emergency session of the council. It may take a few days for everyone to arrive."

"A few days? We don't have that long."

"There are 207 members of the council from all around the world. They cannot arrive in an hour. And—"

"Well... can we go back to the ship? I'm starving."

"There is another problem, Keeble."

Keeble stared. The elf sounded serious. More serious than usual, even.

"The fathers can return to their compound with copies of the Hakahei Contract for their grandmothers to approve and sign but, as already stated by Jisa at the train station, Grandmother Donni of the P'targa is not on this world. If Donni does not sign, the contract is worthless."

"What? Nobody else can sign?"

"It is possible with some contracts," Suldon explained, "but not one of this magnitude."

"Well, they can call a council without the contract right?"

Tami stepped back from her conversation with the hurgon. "They can call the council but they will be going up against the great families, Keeble."

"In the Lessor Council?"

"Yes. The great families will simply buy votes," Tami said. "So the families here need to show strength and areas of possible profit for other minor families in order to set up a voting block they need."

"So all of this was for nothing?" Keeble stormed across the room towards the hurgon and found a guard in his face "We've been—"

But Flint grabbed his arm and pulled him back before he could do anything stupid. Keeble tried to calm down. He took a deep breath. He wound the gears on his mechanical hand. He took a deep breath.

"They are dying, Flint," Keeble said. "Dwarves and trolls and elves. They are dying while we sit here talking pointlessly."

"Not pointlessly, Keeble," Tamidilin said. "We have made progress."

"Progress?"

"This is a war, Keeble," Flint said. "You can't end normal ones overnight. And this one ain't anywhere near normal."

"But it could take a week. Thousands more could die in that time."

"It's the best we can do."

Keeble slumped back against a wall and closed his eyes. "Tell them to hurry up, Suldon. Tell them we'll take a copy of the contract to Grandmother Donni ourselves."

"Mother Hupo and all the fathers think that would be best—they still do not trust each other completely—but they each wish to send a representative with us."

"They want to put hurgon on the *Hakahei*?"

"They insist."

"Whatever. Just tell them to hurry."

-oOo-

The contract was difficult in the real world, but apparently simple on paper. Daughters from the five families had it organized in barely an hour. It was another three hours after that before the ten signed copies, one for each of the families and five for official records, were boxed on the desk and ready to go off-world for Donni's signature. Then they'd have to come back to get the others.

Keeble was ready to leave, but he and his companions were put through half an hour of official farewells that they couldn't understand anyway. Keeble thought that even Tamidilin wanted to say 'goodbye' and be done with it, but manners and tradition forced her to do the task properly. There was bowing—or what Keeble took for a hurgon form of a bow—and good wishes for the future and hopes that they'd return quickly so the contract could be officially registered and the war ended. And this and that and the other. Keeble tuned out half way through. When his turn came, he spoke to Tami at length about what he was going to have for lunch when he returned to the ship, then told her to come up with a suitable farewell. He was at the door before she was done.

"Mother Hupo suggests we return to the hub on a train—though one that stops at each station and does not draw attention to itself. And it wants us to wait for a signal from them before taking off."

"Why?"

"Mother Hupo thinks there may be trouble."

"The sooner we get to the *Hakahei* the better then. Let's go." Keeble could already taste the horrible mushy stuff in the shiny packets—and it tasted wonderful. Or maybe the dwives would have the kitchen set up and were cooking proper food.

They followed a small troop of guards, apparently heading towards the train station. Keeble had lost all track of direction but Sandy assured him they were heading the right way. She was bringing up the rear, hair beads clattering as she kept constant watch for trouble.

They stepped onto the platform several minutes later, just as a southbound train was pulling out.

"Is that our train?" Bargle asked.

"We must wait for the brothers, anyway," Suldon said.

"The who?"

"The brothers. They are the representatives from the five families."

Keeble looked around.

There were hardly any hurgon on the platform at all, nor on the other side of the track. There were a dozen civilians standing around plus as many guards.

A northbound train pulled in and Keeble wondered who controlled them all. There was only a single track here, so someone had to be switching them here and there and back again. That was the type of job that would be exciting for about five minutes, then extremely boring after that.

"Ask how long until the next train," Keeble said.

Tami answered without asking their escort. "Approximately five minutes."

"That's not too bad." In about two and a half hours they'd be back on the ship eating all they could eat.

Keeble was just starting to feel pleased with himself, having completed his first successful mission in charge, when things started to happen. He saw Flint and Sandy stiffen just as the latter said, "Trouble."

45: Remember

LOOKING UP, KEEBLE SAW A GROUP OF HURGON exiting the train. That was not strange in itself, a lot of others had done the same, but these ones were wearing the yellow and red uniform of the T'loop. They came out in a line before arraying themselves along the edge of the platform. They had weapons. Keeble didn't think they were going to ask nicely.

"Whenever you're ready, Flint," Keeble muttered.

"Ready for what? You want us to attack them?"

"No. Just get us out of here."

"You want me to come up with a plan to get us out of here?"

"Yes."

"Well..."

"Let's just run then?" Keeble liked simple plans—unlike the bloody hurgon. They couldn't go back the way they'd come. They were closer to a door on the other side of the platform. "Over there and up the stairs."

"On three then."

Keeble hadn't known Flint could count to three.

"One... Two... Three."

They turned and ran.

Behind them, the hurgon fired their weapons. Keeble felt a tickle against his shoulder. The hairs on his arm stood on end. He cursed as he bounded up the stairs behind Suldon.

There were shouted warnings and screams from behind. There were what could only be flung insults. But the firing of the weapons continued. Safely off the platform, Keeble stopped to look at his shoulder. The material of his shirt had been burned away. A ragged black hole showed red skin beneath.

"Whistler, that was close."

"So what do we do now?" Sandy asked. She had a burn on her hip. It didn't look good to Keeble but the trollop didn't seem worried.

Another troop of P'targa soldiers rushed past, weapons at the ready. They charged down into the train station, firing as they went. Two died before they'd gone more than a couple of steps.

Keeble swallowed. Nina moved up the stairs and leaned against the wall. She stared at her hands and didn't say anything. And Flint went the other way, taking a peek around the corner. And a second later the troll dashed out onto the platform, grabbed a weapon from a fallen P'targa and came back again.

"Don't do that, Flint," Keeble said. "That's an order."

The troll shrugged. "They was busy." He gave the weapon to Sandy. It was only a glove, not a whole sleeve, but looked to be the same as the weapons attached to the armor.

"They might have been busy, but I'm sure they'd stop what they were doing to shoot a hakan if they had the chance."

"Maybe."

"What *were* they doing?"

"Shooting. Dying."

"Who was doing which?"

"Everyone was doing both."

Keeble was forced to stand aside as more soldiers came.

"How many of the T'loop were out there?"

"The ones at the station ain't the problem. The one's in the train are."

"There's a whole train load of them?"

Flint nodded.

As the troop of P'targa ran out onto the platform, Flint darted out and collected the other weapon.

Keeble scowled at him. "I told you not to do that."

"I thought you were joking."

"Well, I wasn't."

"Right. Won't do it again then."

"Course you won't. We've got two trolls and two weapons."

Flint smiled.

"What actions do we take at this point in time?" Tami asked.

"I asked that before," Sandy pointed out, smiling at the elf. "Bet he doesn't answer you either."

"Why are we pretending I'm in charge, Flint?"

"Because you are."

"Then—"

"You's in charge of deciding what we do and where we go. I'm in charge of getting us there so we can do it."

"Told you he wouldn't answer."

"Let's finish this conversation away from here before—"

The few P'targa remaining on the train platform turned and fled.

"Run," Flint said. And the troll pushed Keeble up the stairs.

Sandy was leading this time. Up to the next level, turn left.

Keeble ducked around the corner not far behind Suldon. He felt a burst of energy crackle through the air close by.

"Too much straight line here," Flint muttered by his side. "Start Singing, Keeble."

"What?"

"Sing."

Keeble didn't know how successful he'd be, but he started working on his Song.

"Any door, Sandy," Flint shouted.

"Could be a dead end."

"Don't care."

Sandy picked a door as the T'loop clattered off the stairs and into the hallway. The trollop turned. She crouched down and fired her weapon.

Nina and Tami were through the door a second later. Everyone else followed. Keeble didn't think he'd make it. He was having trouble concentrating on where he was putting his feet and the Song wasn't even complete. But Flint was urging him on. He went through the door with the trolls on his heels.

He paused for breath and built the rest of the Song quickly.

There was a thump at the door.

They were in a storeroom with shelves lining most walls. There was one bare patch where a pair of mops stood in a bucket. "There," he said, pointing as he focused his Song on the wall. The mops tumbled to the floor. One second slower and Tasko would've been trying to run through solid stone.

The door burst open as everyone else surged forward.

Tami tripped on the bucket. Suldon and Bargle righted her.

Keeble almost fell as well and stumbled through. Weapons firing. Crackling energy. Flint looming over him.

"Close it," the troll shouted.

Keeble snapped off his Song. He gasped for breath.

"Where are we now?" Bargle asked.

"How would I know," Keeble replied.

"It seems to be sleeping quarters of some kind," Suldon said.

"It doesn't matter," Flint said. "We should keep moving." The troll was looking back the way they'd come. His fingers were pressed against the solid stone of the wall.

"Where is Sandy?" Tami asked.

"What?" Keeble looked around, as if he might miss seeing a black, 185 centimeter tall slab of muscle and attitude. "Where's Sandy?"

Flint shook his head. "They were coming too quick."

"We can't leave her there," Keeble said. *Nobody gets left behind.* "Why didn't you stop? Why didn't you—"

"I didn't know, Keeble. Not until it was too late." Flint spun around and headed for the door. "She was already dead."

"What?"

"She slowed them down, Keeble. Without her..." He pulled on the door handle, but apparently it was locked.

"She was a good trollop," Flint said quietly as he examined the door.

"I'm sorry, Flint," Keeble said. "I..."

"Weren't your fault—she was doing her job." He shrugged. "Anyways, we've had more fun since we been on the ship than we've had in a long time."

Keeble didn't think it was *all right.* He wasn't sure Flint really believed it either. "Just because she was having fun, and just because she was doing her job, that doesn't mean we can't be sorry she's gone. It doesn't mean we can't regret what happened. And it doesn't mean it's *all right.*"

Keeble turned when Nina moved to his side. She didn't do anything except wipe the tears from her own face and look at him.

Flint broke down the door. "Come on."

Keeble swallowed. "Where are we going?"

"That's for you to decide, remember."

"We can't leave her."

But the choice was taken away, if there had ever been a choice. They had barely walked out into the hall when a trio of guards found them. Weapons were raised. Warnings shouted. Explanations given.

Suldon, hands raised, did a *lot* of explaining. They took some convincing but Keeble really didn't care. One of the hurgon rushed away to find a superior officer. And they waited. Twenty minutes later, the hurgon returned and they were led into the maze of passages and hallways that crisscrossed the compound.

More than once, Keeble glanced back over his shoulder, each time expecting to see Sandy guarding his back. He would've felt safer if she'd been there. He didn't realize how comforting the sound of her hair beads had been, as if she'd worn them to let everyone know she was still there watching their backs. The silence left behind was painful.

They climbed more stairs, moving quickly, then rushed down a long, wide hallway. Hurgon in their loose, colorful clothes stepped aside to let them pass. It wasn't long before they were shown to something that looked a bit like a bus from Earth. It didn't touch the ground though, and an arm went out through a slot in the roof of the building. A skyrail, Keeble guessed.

Five hurgon were already inside, standing against the far wall. Each had a large pack on the floor near their feet.

Keeble turned as the leader of their escort said something.

"The brothers will escort us from here," Suldon said, motioning to the hurgon in the cabin. "These warriors are to return to the battle."

"They want you to give up your weapon, Flint," Tami added.

"What? Why? No."

"It is a P'targa weapon. If you were to be seen with it by the wrong hurgon it could be difficult for the family."

Flint looked the guards up and down, as if wondering if he could take them all, then grunted and handed the weapon over. "They got something else I can have?"

Apparently not.

They were herded onto the skyrail car. Before the door closed, Keeble grabbed one of the warriors by the arm.

"Suldon, find out this hurgon's name and tell it that I will hold it personally responsible for how Sandy is treated. We want her buried with a remembrance stone."

"I am not sure we should be making demands, Keeble. And burial might be inappropriate in hurgon society."

"Tell it."

"Very well."

Keeble didn't have the energy for anything else. When Suldon started to speak and it was obvious the hurgon was listening, he sat down on the floor and closed his eyes.

"That is, Biti, Keeble, and it says it will make sure our requests are met."

"Good." But it *didn't* sound good. Keeble sighed. He wasn't supposed to leave anyone behind. That was the rule.

-oOo-

The skyrail took them to the hub via a dozen compounds. They skimmed across the tops of buildings and flashed between towers. They leapt over vacant lots. Keeble saw none of it. He heard nothing of what his companions said—after the first few minutes he didn't know if they said anything at all. He didn't move until Flint nudged his shoulder three hours after they set out.

"What is it?"

"We've reached the hub."

All the others were already outside. Keeble joined them and the carriage continued on its journey. The five brothers, all wearing non-descript clothes, packs on their backs, stood calmly nearby. They appeared as calm as any hurgon Keeble had seen. He didn't think they were lawyers.

He tried to keep his mind on the job. "How far to the ship?"

Flint pointed.

Out a window, across the top of a gabled roof, Keeble could see the top of the *Hakahei*. It was barely two hundred meters away.

"Let's go then."

For a moment, Flint stood in indecision and Keeble knew what he was thinking. Sandy would've stayed with the group, watching for trouble coming up behind, while he led out. That wasn't possible.

"You watch the rear, Keeble," the troll said eventually.

Keeble found it strange to realize that he was about to admit there was a job that a woman could do better than he. "I'll do it," he said. "Take one of them with you?" He pointed to the hurgon.

"They won't be able to help," Flint said. But he looked them up and down and came to the same conclusion Keeble had reached earlier—the brothers weren't the type of hurgon who sat around in offices all day long. He nodded, found a volunteer and headed for the door. Keeble brought up the rear.

They found stairs and went all the way to the bottom. Keeble stopped at the top of each flight to look around and one of the hurgon stopped with him. If there was any danger, Keeble intended to shout a warning and run for cover. He didn't know what his silent companion would do. He didn't know if he'd see any trouble anyway. Tears blurred his vision. He couldn't concentrate. She was just a troll—a woman—and she was having fun...

He hurried to catch up to the others.

On the ground floor, he realized where they were. They were only fifty meters from the train station.

Flint was standing at the door to the long hall with the colonnades and historical clutter. He had his hand on the door handle. "Long hall through here," he said. "Guards at the end."

Keeble nodded. He could feel the others watching him.

Bargle cleared his throat. "Can we go another way?" he asked. "We could cut through some walls, maybe. That way we can come out in a place the hurgon don't expect."

Flint shook his head. "Chasm says the hurgon are everywhere. Wouldn't matter where we went out." He tugged on his moustache.

Keeble wasn't about to give the order to go through the door. The only plan he ever came up with was simply running, and it never really worked...

But Bargle was not done. "Could someone clear a landing zone with the ship's guns—don't even have to kill anyone. Then they can get a Lander onto the ground. We could go through the wall and straight into the back."

Flint was nodding, but Keeble didn't know if he was up to Singing.

"We'll do that," the troll said. "But we'll go through this door first. Will save us time and energy." He glanced at Keeble but didn't say anything more.

"But the guards..." Keeble said.

"There's only four and they ain't got any armor." Flint looked the hurgon up and down. "These brothers got weapons, Tami?"

"They do," Tami replied after asking, "but they are not willing to fire on other hurgon at this stage. That would be an act of war and would see the great families outlaw them. That would make all contracts void. It would make all arguments the families might present to the councils as irrelevant."

"But it's all right for us to kill hurgon?"

"Apparently."

"And what about all that shooting back at the train station?"

"I am unsure. Perhaps it has to do with who was in which compound."

Flint shook his head. "Just sounds like excuses to me." He sighed. "Well, we ready then?"

Keeble saw everyone else nod, but he just stared.

Flint pulled the door open and charged into the hall. Tasko, Bargle and Suldon followed. They raced across the inevitable grey tiles, heads down, arms pumping.

Keeble took three steps through the door then stopped. Nina and the brothers were just behind him, Tami to his left. They all watched silently.

The guards reacted slowly, their attention fixed on the noises beyond the door they were guarding.

Flint and Suldon led the race. The elf was lithe and graceful, hardly seeming to touch the floor. The troll powered along like a landslide.

Suldon slowed when he reached the first hurgon and lashed out with his leg to knock away the guard's weapon. Flint kicked as well. Leaping high into the air he smashed the heel of his heavy boot into a guard's face. They both fell to the floor and only Flint got up.

The dwarves arrived. Bargle launched himself into the air. He cannoned shoulder first into Suldon's opponent, knocked it to the ground. The elf finished things with a kick.

Tasko slid to halt and punched a hurgon in the stomach. He ripped the weapon from the alien's grasp and threw it away. He punched again and again before the hurgon thought to retaliate.

Flint was already onto the final guard. The hurgon didn't stand a chance. Keeble couldn't doubt that it had been hakans and not hurgon who had started the war all those years ago. Even after spending centuries getting ready, the hurgon weren't a warlike race.

Soon all four of the guards were on the floor. Keeble didn't really care. He watched the end of the fight with little enthusiasm. They still weren't back on the ship—anything could happen.

As if to prove the point, the hurgon Suldon and Bargle had first attacked moved. It pushed itself to its knees, weapon raised. It all seemed to happen in slow motion. Nina yelled a warning and Flint turned to look, first at Nina, then behind him. He started to move. Keeble could see that it was too late, even for a troll. There was ten meters between them and it was too late.

There was a soft hum. Keeble turned to his left to look. Tami was standing amidst the clutter beyond the row of columns, holding the huge, curling bow in her hands. She was standing perfectly still, staring at the far end of the room.

"Are you hurt, Bargle?" Tami asked after a moment of silence.

Keeble followed her gaze and saw the young dwarf holding his neck. Behind him, the hurgon had slumped to the floor with a long, fletched arrow protruding from its chest. Bargle must have been almost directly between the elf and her target.

Keeble walked slowly down to the other end of the hall. He pulled Bargle's hand away from his neck and examined the wound. It was a nick, bleeding freely.

"It's nothing," Keeble said. But he looked back at Tamidilin. She was using a strange bow with an unknown arrow. What she had done was either dangerous in the extreme or very brave. Actually, it was both. She was a woman. An elf. If she could do that...

The elf brought the bow and a quiver of arrows with her. The hurgon and Nina came along behind.

"Let's not worry about going anywhere else," Keeble said. He wanted to get back to the ship. He wanted to sit down. He wanted to sleep. Pointing to the wall beside the door he said, "I'll Sing through that—just tell me when."

Flint nodded and Keeble started to Sing softly. He built his Song carefully from the ground up, making sure every joint and seam was perfect. Time seemed to stretch. It took forever for Flint to give the signal. Keeble kept expecting the door to open, or for someone to come through from the station. All remained quiet inside, while outside the noise of the sieging hurgon washed over everything.

"Right," Flint said.

Keeble shifted his Song, focused it, and stepped through the wall. The Lander was just a meter away with the back door open. Keeble stepped forward and onto the Lander. He sat in a chair, keeping his Song going without thought. The brothers did not seem surprised when they joined him. They stood in the aisle and watched as everyone else came through.

Outside, hurgon were screaming and shouting. Flashes of energy lanced away from the *Hakabei*. More often than not they hit only ground, but occasionally one of the aliens decided to take the risk and was shot. There was a huge machine turning to face them.

"Where's Sandy?" someone shouted. Flint shook his head in reply and the Lander lurched away from the ground. Keeble stopped Singing and closed his eyes.

46: Different People

TUKI STOOD BY THE DOOR WITH RUBY. He watched the Lander dart into the hangar and smiled when his friends started to emerge. Ruby hit the button to close the door. She did not look very happy. Those climbing down did not look happy.

"What is wrong?" Tuki asked Ruby quietly.

She shook her head but answered anyway. "Sandy got dead."

"What?" Tuki turned back to the Lander and looked for Sandy. She wasn't there. The others milled about the back of the vessel as if they didn't quite know where they were supposed to go next.

There were two dozen people in the hangar and none spoke above a whisper.

Not until five hurgon climbed down from the Lander as well.

A flood of conversation broke out then, most of it angry, as if Flint would bring Sandy's killers onto the *Hakahei*.

Chasm stepped forward with her troop and led the new comers towards the stairs. Keeble, head down, walked silently in the middle of the group.

Soon, only Tuki and Ruby remained.

"Come on, Tuki." She took his hand. "Let's go and have something to eat. Somebody might be able to tell us what happened."

Tuki wasn't sure he wanted to know what had happened but he went anyway because he could never resist Ruby.

The dining hall was full for the first time since Sherindel. Half the people, including Keeble and companions, were eating. The others were watching expectantly.

The hurgon were nowhere to be seen.

Looking at Keeble, Tuki suddenly felt guilty. He had come here to hear the story of how Sandy had died with no thought to whether his friends wanted to tell the tale.

Tuki felt somebody behind him. Mintar and Dogar were waiting to get by.

Tuki decided it was time to put his officer title to use. "The dining hall is closed," he said.

"What do you mean? I can see it isn't closed. It's full."

"That's why it's closed. We cannot fit anyone else in here."

"But I want—"

"Come back later," Tuki said, staring at his feet.

It seemed Dogar would push his way past but Ruby cleared her throat as if the dwarf needed to be reminded that she was there as well. Dogar and Mintar grumbled but walked away down the hall.

Tuki turned back to the mess and cleared his throat as well. He didn't quite know what to say though. Perhaps Keeble and his companions would like to talk. Perhaps they wanted to be surrounded by others but... He cleared his throat again. "Everyone," he said, but of course nobody listened. "Hello."

"Hey," Ruby shouted. "Listen up."

The noise in the room died down slightly. Tuki stared at his shoes for a moment, then looked up. "Everyone who is not already eating food has to leave," he said. There were complaints from all around but Tuki didn't listen. "There are people here who are trying to eat and they should be allowed to do that in peace."

Everyone knew who he meant and at least some of them seemed willing to concede his point. They grumbled as they did so, but a large proportion of those who were not eating rose to their feet and filed from the room. Some stayed where they were. The line over by the vending machines did not break up either. Tuki turned to them.

"Lining up for food is not eating," he said to the people. "Come back later. And the rest of you."

There were more complaints. "And what if we don't go? What are you gunna do then?"

What was he going to do? That was a good question.

Chip, one of four trolls present besides Flint, was halfway to the door. He stopped and looked back. "He'll get some trolls to help get the message through is what he'll do."

"What are you going to do?" Milo shouted to Tuki. The young dwarf was near the front of the queue. "Are you going to have something to eat?"

If there was one thing Tuki knew from watching Kim, it was that leaders should not get special treatment. "I am not eating," he said, "so I will be leaving. And when others have finished eating they will leave too—they will not go back for seconds. There will still be plenty of food later."

Those still present and not eating headed for the door, walking slowly as if Tuki might change his mind or forget they were there.

Finally the room was only half full and Tuki retreated to the hall. Ruby closed the door behind her. "Let's go see Kim instead," she said.

Tuki nodded and started to push his way through the crowd.

"Get away from here," Ruby said as she followed in his wake. "There ain't nothing happening here. Go and do something."

Kim was stretched out on a bed in the medical bay. Thorpe had attached all sorts of things to her. There was a needle in her arm that went to a bag. There were wires that attached to a beeping machine. There were tubes and more wires. Scree sat in a chair nearby. He had been there since first carrying Kim in. He refused to go anywhere. He had not even helped with the rescue of Keeble and his companions though he was still the best driver.

Scree looked up as Tuki entered.

"Mo-boy. What ya doing?"

"I just came to see Kim," Tuki replied quietly.

Scree nodded. "Thorpe says it helps to talk to her, 'cause she can hear us even though she ain't responding."

Tuki had intended to tell Scree about Sandy, though he must have already known from the radio in his head. But if Kim could hear then talking of a dead companion might not be the best idea. "How is she?"

"Thorpe says she is healthy enough but she just moved her mind back from the edge so she couldn't notice nothing."

"When she was..."

Scree nodded again. "And now she still can't notice nothing."

"When... Will you come and talk to Keeble when he is ready?"

"What for? I can't help him."

Tuki almost didn't argue with the troll but Ruby gripped his hand and squeezed. Whether she was supporting this particular conversation or just supporting in general Tuki did not know. Staring at his feet he spoke again. "You can help, Scree. You are in charge while Kim is..." He gestured vaguely. "Until she is better. And Keeble is a dwarf, so I think the best thing for him is to do some work. I don't think he will do that unless someone tells him to."

"That's what you think is it? What if he doesn't need to work and I make him do it? What if all he needs is to be left alone?"

Tuki shrugged. "Then I suppose you make that decision. As long as you do make the decision and don't just..." he shrugged again.

"And don't just sit here doing nothing?"

"Yes. Maybe you need to do something as well. In Danyon Ford people were often given special duties to tune their mind back into the well being of the village."

"And Danyon Ford was perfect, weren't it?"

Danyon Ford had not been perfect, as Scree knew very well, but its problems were not in the day-to-day issues. They were larger than that.

Tuki tried another tack. "Kim left Meledrin in charge, Scree."

Scree grunted. "Won't get nothing done."

"That's right. Unless you go back up and take charge again."

Scree didn't say anything.

Ruby shifted her feet. "We's waiting for a signal from them P'targa to say we can leave the planet. When that happens..."

Scree turned to look at Kim, then did not move again.

-oOo-

Tuki turned off his music machine and sat back down. Ruby was lying on the big bed, staring at the ceiling.

"Is Flint talking on the radio?" Tuki asked Ruby. She nodded. "So he is all right?" Keeble and his companions still sat in the dining hall. They were on their own now and had been for some time.

"He ain't happy Sandy died—and he's having trouble getting used to the idea that he cared about her—but he's only there 'cause the others is."

"Are they talking?"

"No. Just sitting."

Tuki did not think that was good. From what he had seen it was Keeble who had been affected the most, which was strange in itself, but for them all to be just sitting there... The mood was hardly better in the rest of the ship. Everyone had survived being stuck in the other universe, where there was no hope. To lose Sandy now, like this, seemed impossible.

"We need to do something," Tuki said. Getting to his feet again, he paced the room. Ruby watched him. He wondered when he had become so comfortable with her presence. Eventually he spoke again. "In Danyon Ford we used to have a ceremony when someone died. The bodies were taken to a place down Dry River and buried so that their spirits could slowly return to the Earth. And then moai would get up and say things about the one who had died. We all knew the person had died, but we could remember the good things about them and warm the spirits with our friendship."

Ruby didn't say anything.

"Would the trolls be offended by that?"

Ruby shook her head. "It takes a lot to offend trolls, Tuki, though I ain't sure we'd feel the same way about it that you do."

"Should we do it, do you think?"

She shrugged.

-oOo-

Tuki took the small brass plaque from Milo an examined it. It was highly polished and the curving letters, in the language of Rongo, were beautifully formed. The words were:

Sandy
Watching our backs
Hulgorn
1AC

Tuki had thought for a long time about the last bit—the date. Which date did they go by? Kiva's or Earth's or Hulgorn's? In the end he had decided to make another date, so it was now the year 1AC—after contact. He wondered if anyone would mind. And he had wondered about what to say on it as well. Should they have just said her name? Flint had said how she had died when Ruby asked but...

He sighed. He could think about these things all day and still not know. The only way to find out was to show everyone else.

He found the microphone in the engineering bay. He had seen them used many times before but had never had the need or the courage to use one himself. Making sure it was on the right setting he pressed the button, which made speakers all over the ship beep, then cleared his throat. As soon as he did that he realized it would have been better to clear his throat first. He blushed.

"Umm..." he said into the microphone. He released the button and cleared his throat again. He looked to Milo and Ruby for support. Milo was shaking his head ruefully, which did not help at all, but Ruby smiled and motioned for him to try again. He did.

"Umm... Could everyone who is not on duty please report to the west garden." Report? He had heard Kim used that word. And most people, when they used the paging system also repeated themselves, to be sure nobody misheard. So Tuki said the sentence again. When he was done he left his finger on the button for a moment before thinking to release it.

"So, I can't go then?" Milo asked. "I liked Sandy, too."

"But somebody has to monitor the systems. And you can watch on a screen."

He grunted in disgust. "What's the chance something'll happen in the next half an hour?"

"I do not know," Tuki replied. "But would you forgive yourself if something happened on your shift and you were not here to fix it?"

Milo grunted again but didn't argue. Tuki smiled to himself—he was pleased to know that he had come up with the right argument. It was not hard when you knew a little bit about how people thought.

"You'll need this then," Milo said, rummaging through a wall cabinet. He eventually handed Tuki a tube.

"What is it?"

"Glue. Just put some on the back of the plaque and it should stick to just about anything. Just don't wait too long after squeezing it out."

"Thank you."

Tuki took the glue and the plaque and made his way to the gardens. Grass was already starting to grow there, tiny shoots poking above the soil. Dozens of other plants seemed to be flourishing as well. There were none near the western ducting though so the large black wall would still be in the clear when the elves had completed their work.

Some of the elves had obviously been working when Tuki made his announcement. Meledrin stood in the middle of the open space with Palsamon and Lisarea. Others started to arrive in ones and twos and threes. They all looked confused but Tuki did not explain anything just yet. Keeble was one of the last to arrive with Flint and Tamidilin just before him. When the trickle slowed and finally stopped, Tuki looked around.

He thought it strange that he felt closer to these people than he had to most of those in Danyon Ford where he had spent the first eighteen years of his life. Some he had hardly spoken to, like Hoodek and Penisari, Dosa and Gulch. Others he considered as family—the members of the Nav Department, with whom he spent so much time, and the members of the original crew. He looked around for Scree and Kim, but Kim was still sick and Scree most likely with her. Finally, he looked at Ruby for a moment. She was no longer by his side, going to stand with the spectators instead. These were people he would do anything for, he realized, and he held the memory of one in his hands.

He cleared his throat and pulled his eyes away from Ruby's face.

"I am not sure who believes in the gods," he said. He had given thought to what he was going to say but the words seemed to drift away from him. "And I am not sure what gods you might believe in."

He stalled but saw Ruby still smiling softly.

"The gods are there or they are not. Does it matter? No, because I realize now that religion has nothing to do with them. It is about what we believe in our hearts, and how we act on that belief. The gods are just the excuses we use to justify our actions." Tuki was not sure where he was going with the speech. He paused and examined his audience. None of them were moving.

"Trolls do not believe in any gods," he continued. "What they do they do for their own reasons and they make no excuses. So Sandy did not do the things that led to her death because of a threat or a promise, she did them because she wanted to. She did them because that was what was in her heart." He cleared his throat and ran his fingers along the lettering on the plaque. "Sandy went out onto a strange world to guard her friends and she died while those friends lived and made it home. Can there be any higher praise for a guard?"

There were rumblings of agreement from the audience.

Tuki nodded slowly. "I asked Milo to make this plaque," he said, examining it again. "I am going to put it on the wall here, so we will not forget."

He carefully squeezed some glue onto the back of the metal then lined it up on the wall. He was going to put it in the center but decided, no matter how much he wanted it to be otherwise, there might be more deaths before the war ended. Making sure it was straight, he pressed it against the cold metal of the wall over near the side. When he took his hands away, the plaque stayed in place.

He turned back to the rest of the crew. "If anyone else wants to say something..." He stepped aside to let someone else take his place. For a long time nobody moved. Finally, Ruby stepped forward.

"Sandy weren't much older than me," she said, "but she'd been with Cockroach Pack long time before I joined. It was my first pack, and I was scared in our first few raids 'cause I was only thirteen, but she looked out for me." It looked like that was all she was going to say. But she added, "She shared her loot with me."

When Ruby returned to the group, Tess stepped slowly forward. "Sandy was my friend too," the dwife said. "And she also showed me that I didn't have to be scared."

For a long while after Tess had finished nobody said anything. Tuki was about to suggest that they have a minute's silence to think about Sandy when Keeble cleared his throat and stepped forward.

The dwarf went to look at the plaque. He reached up and used his sleeve to polish away Tuki's fingerprints. When he was done, he turned to the audience. "I didn't know Sandy very well," he said. "She was a woman... why would I care?" The crowd muttered. "She couldn't build a chair. She couldn't fix an engine. But for everything she couldn't do, there was something she could do. She wasn't worse than me or better than me. She was different. And the universe needs as many different people as possible. It says on the plaque that she was watching our backs, and she was. And I'm sure that if heaven exists then she's watching them still."

Tuki watched Keeble. Everyone did. The dwarf stood perfect still for a long time, head bowed, as if saying a prayer, or remembering. Then he nodded and walked slowly back to the group.

Tuki went to stand in front of the wall again. "I think—"

The ship rocked. A harsh alarm sounded.

Bethalin's voice sounded over the speakers. *"We are under attack."* She was very calm. *"We are under attack."*

Tuki did not think *that* sentence needed to be repeated.

In the garden everyone stood in shock. The trolls were the first to react, heading for the stairs at a run. Before they had gone far another voice came over the speaker.

"Emergency situation in engineering," Milo said. *"Systems down everywhere."*

Tuki stared while everyone else started to move.

47: Red Flags

PING RACED INTO THE ENGINEERING BAY just behind Keeble. Milo was at one of the monitors, punching at the touch screen with one hand and using the keyboard with the other. Ari had a panel hinged open in the corner of the room and was trying to put out a small fire.

"What's going on?" Ping asked, wiping tears from her eyes. Keeble went to work on a separate computer.

"Some type of electrical pulse did something to Gravitic field generator number 1," Milo said, "and the heating circuits are out all over the place."

Keeble added some more. "We have a hull breach on Levels 3 and 4 at point 46."

Ping tried to think while Keeble and Milo searched. Dwarves were crowding into the room behind them. She turned to look and tried to prioritize tasks. If they had to take off, which seemed likely, then the hole came first. They could live without heating for a while if they had to.

"Topper, take your work gang, plus Drago and Tasko, and repair that hole, starting on Level 3. Just make us space worthy—don't worry about anything else." She rubbed at her temple. Who was on the bridge? Anyone? Seeing Milo and Ari were on shift that would mean... she tried to think of her roster. It was Keeble's shift so Dogar was on the bridge. But work gangs meant nothing now, besides a quick way to allocate jobs if needed. Did they need someone else up there? Not now, but they would if they got into the air. "Bargle, you're Dogar's right hand man on the bridge. Makar, Tess, Dido—Level 4. Get some EVA suits—everyone get EVA suits—and seal the storeroom doors. Then clear away the crap for when Topper is ready to repair the hole."

What else was there? She tried to think. The Gravitic Field Generator—one was still on line but...

Those who had been assigned jobs had already left.

"Keeble, the generator," Ping said.

"What?" He looked up from the monitor and seemed surprised to find the room half empty.

"One of the field generators is down. We need to fix it, especially since it may be upsetting the alignment again."

"Right."

"You do that. I can search the computer just as well as you."

"Right." He nodded and looked around to see who was still with them. "Ari, Kesi, Kafin—tools. And get the inspection panel off generator number 2." He turned back to the computer and began to look at the problem in detail. Two of his helpers were dwives, but he hardly seemed to notice. They ran to obey just as another blast rocked the ship.

Ping swore and went to work at another monitor. Milo was cataloguing problems and flagging them in order of importance. Drink dispenser on level 2 was malfunctioning. Lift 6, a freight elevator, was out of order. A clock was running at double time. The field generator. There were a dozen other flagged faults besides and a dozen more red flags waiting to be inspected.

"*Are we ready to fly?*" Bargle asked over the intercom. He must have only just arrived.

Ping hit the button. "Not yet." So Scree had decided to grace them with his presence.

"*How long?*"

"I don't know. We'll say when."

"*All right.*" It did not sound as if he was very keen to pass on that information.

"Right." Ping looked around. They were starting to run out of people. Keeble was gone. Only Dosa and Milo remained. She examined Milo's list once more, scrolling through it. The faulty clock was a higher priority than Milo thought—it should be right near the top. Who knew what a broken clock that was still connected to the system would do if they needed to go through an Ohoga Gate? "Dosa, change of plan. First, tell Topper he's to come back down here when he's done on 3. Forget the hole on 4—we're flying as soon as possible and we can seal the storeroom so it really doesn't matter. Then you get Makar, Tess and Dido and disconnect clock number 1 from the system. And do it quick. Then wait for more instructions."

The dwife looked very nervous but she nodded and hurried away.

Ping moved to the next flashing red flag to see what the problem was. The outer airlock door on level three was jammed. Good, as long as it was jammed shut. Damage to both air recyclers. Important. Ping put it below the repair of the clock. Water leak in the Level 6 bathroom. She thought about that one for a moment. It might be important, depending on what the computer meant by 'leak'. Was it dribbling or gushing? Get someone to check it out soon and let them decide on the priority. No power to the workshop or hangar—didn't matter just yet.

The ship shuddered again and more warning flags materialized on the screen.

There was a pressure build up in the fuel still. That couldn't have been a result of the last hit they'd taken, it must have been happening for some time.

"Milo?"

"Yes?" He looked up from the screen.

"Your turn."

"What?"

"Pressure build-up in the fuel still."

"But..." Milo looked around. There was nobody else. "Right."

"Do you need help?"

"Who?"

"I don't know."

"Maybe." He grabbed a toolbox from a locker and was gone.

Ping wondered what the others were doing. Seeing she didn't know how badly the hull was breached she didn't know how long Topper would be, and his party was the one upsetting the balance. Dosa would probably need about fifteen minutes to disconnect the clock. Not long now.

Another red light started flashing. At almost the same instant a discordant sounded echoed around the ship. The sound oscillated. It changed tone and pitch and frequency. It danced through registers. Ping blocked her ears but it didn't help.

"*What's that noise?*" Bargle asked over the intercom just as Keeble stuck he head out of the Gravitic field generator and shouted the same question.

"I'm not sure." She checked the latest problem. "It's the Ohoga engine."

"Whistler." Keeble came out into the room. Ari poked her head out behind him.

"What's that?"

"The Ohoga engine," Keeble was getting another tool kit. "You keep going on the generator."

"All right." The dwife disappeared.

The noise continued.

Finally, one of the problems was fixed, or at least postponed. On the screen the red symbol beside clock number one changed to yellow—still not working correctly, but no longer affecting any other system.

Ping hit the pager button. "Dosa, the Ohoga engine. Level 6, north west."

The sound from the Ohoga engine continued. Ping thought it was turning her brain to jelly. It seemed to shake her very bones.

Milo's voice erupted form the intercom. "*I need help. This could blow. Things are jammed—*"

"Okay. Give me a minute." But Ping needed more than a minute. She had nobody left. Topper on the hull, Ari on the generator, Keeble in the Ohoga engine. She couldn't go herself—somebody needed to stay in control. But with the noise and the fault reports on the screen Ping didn't know if she would be in control for much longer. She pushed the pager button and wondered who to send. Last resort. "Captain Thorpe can you take your men to Level 7 west. Captain Thorpe and troop to 7 west. And quick." They could unjam things and bash them if that was all that was needed, if not... it was Milo's problem now, she could do nothing more.

Ping realized she was standing in water. She started to follow a stream out the eastern door. It was running out of the bathroom. The leak was apparently a gush, or something close to one.

Topper's voice on the intercom next. "*We're done here, Ping.*"

Finally. Ping raced back inside. She switched the controls and stabbed at the button as she looked at her list. Hull, done. Clocks, done. The generator was all that stood between them and flight. Ari should not be far from finishing that. The flood had reached the far side of the room. "Two to the bathroom on 6. Three to the Ohoga engine and shut up the damn noise. Two to..." Help Milo or fix an air recycler? If they took a hull breach while in space... "Two to fix an air recycler. Number 1 should be the easiest, I think."

"Only six of us here, Ping."

"What? Oh... One to the bathroom."

"Right you are."

Ping felt a touch on her shoulder and jumped. Ari, Kafin and Kesi had emerged from the generator. "We're done in there."

Ping checked her monitor. Green for the generator. Not just disconnected but fixed. "Great." The fuel still was still flashing red. She sent the three dwarves down there. Hoodek stepped out of an elevator and into a puddle of water. He looked at Ping, raised his eyebrows and followed the trail.

Ping was trying to think of what she needed to do next. The ship rattled as it was hit again. Nothing else seemed to break.

"Scree," she said into the microphone, once she found the right setting. "Scree, let's get out of here."

There was no reply, but the Gravitic field generators started to hum and vibrate. Then there was a moment when Ping's weight doubled. Her knees buckled and she fell to the floor. Her head spun and she thought she'd throw up. Then the ship adjusted the internal gravity to counteract the powerful lift-off. If there was one thing you could predict about Scree, he'd be decisive.

The lessening of the weight coincided with the silencing of the faulty Ohoga engine. Ping breathed a sigh of relief as she climbed back to her feet. The engine still wasn't fixed though, and it wasn't disconnected.

Ping could feel the ship changing direction. Power readouts fluctuated as weapons fired. She tried not to think about what was happening outside.

"*Are we ready to jump?*" Bargle asked from upstairs.

Ping almost fell over herself in her rush to get to the microphone. "No. Definitely no." Keeble had said the Ohoga Gates were made of sound or by sound or... something. If that was true then who knew how out of tune the engines were at the moment?

As Ping scanned the computer, looking for further signs of trouble, the ship shook again. She immediately knew this was different to every other time. This had been an internal explosion. With a quick glance to make sure the only other problems remaining on her screen were minor ones, she hurried down stairs to the fuel still.

Smoke and steam billowed out the door. Kafin was lying on the floor in the hallway with blood streaming from a cut on his head.

"Kafin, what happened?" But she didn't wait to for an answer, rushing forward to look herself. Amy McCree, Brick and Milo were wreathed in smoke. The humans were struggling to lift a pipe while Milo waited to pull someone from underneath. Ping thought the gravity was messing up again—her knees felt weak and her stomach turned. After a moment, during which she clung to the door and tried to calm her racing heart, she skirted past where Milo was pulling Ari free from the rubble. She found the intercom.

"Scree we need some trolls down here now. 7 west." She went further in, back against the wall, edging past a still glowing heater. She emerged into an open space and discovered Captain Thorpe, shirtless, on his hands and knees. For a moment she thought he was injured, but Paul Manning, his SAS colleague, was lying before him.

The captain looked up. "He's losing a lot of blood. We need to get him up to medical."

Ping nodded, as she watched the pool of blood spreading across the floor like the water had spread across the floor earlier. Thorpe worked to stem the flow—most of it seemed to be coming from his leg. Ping removed her shirt and gave it to him.

"Trolls are coming to help," she said eventually. She tried to hide her underwear but Captain Thorpe hadn't even noticed. "When they get here, you go to medical and take charge there."

He nodded but said, "We can't get out of here. You're the only person who can fit through that gap."

"The trolls will get us out."

He nodded again and turned back to his patient. "Airman Dongoske is over there." He indicated with a momentary turn of his head. "He's..."

"Yo, Ping?"

"Stone?"

"Yeah."

"There's injured people in here but we can't get the out through the gap."

"We're on it."

Ping moved slowly across to Dongoske. He was half under the rubble. He had his own pool of blood. His eyes stared blankly.

"Where's Kesi?"

Thorpe shrugged without turning around. "She was further in."

Further in? Ping couldn't go further. Part of the roof had fallen in. A huge tank was leaking gas. Pipes and machinery everywhere. She laid down on her stomach and tried to look around the twists and turns of the obstructions.

"Kesi? Can you hear me? Kesi?"

There was no reply. Ping took a deep breath, wiped at her eyes with shaking fingers and turned back to help Captain Thorpe.

48: Not Dead Yet

MELEDRIN TRIED TO BLOCK OUT THE SOUND of the screaming Ohoga engine, but it was impossible. She needed to think.

"Cliff, who is attacking us?" It was a sensible question that should have been asked some time ago.

"Not sure, but they's in space."

"They are in space? Are they deliberately targeting us, do you think?"

The troll shrugged. "Think so. Hard to tell though." He checked a read-out. "Shields stopping a lot of the attacks but power's dropping."

"Should we take off, even without the—"

"Hakahei*?*" A voice erupted from the external radio. "*Can* Hakahei *hear? Mother Yuwi of the P'targa, with kil'ini Unias'a'ta speaks?*"

"*Yes, Yuwi. This is Meledrin of the* Hakahei."

"*Meledrin,* Hakahei *should leave. The P'targa were waiting for confirmation of legal delicacies but that will not be happening now. The T'loop have attacked our compound and kil'ini.*"

"*Meledrin thanks Yuwi. The* Hakahei *is having difficulties, but will fly as soon as possible.*"

"*Swift journey,* Hakahei. *Grandmother Donni has been sent an ans'ini message and awaits you on Lapenti.*"

The signal cut out and Meledrin looked up at the captain's chair. They would not be going anywhere without a driver. The noise from the Ohoga engine was still echoing around the ship making it difficult to think.

The trolls had experience driving the small vehicles on board the ship. Perhaps one of them could do the job. Or some of the human soldiers—their race had been made for the task, after all.

"*Captain Thorpe,*" Ping said over the intercom, "*take your men to Level 7 west. Captain Thorpe and troop to 7 west. And quick.*"

Meledrin sighed. There went the best of her options. She looked around the bridge. Only one option there, really, and he was as good as any other. If nothing else he had seen the schematics of the console and would know what a lot of the buttons did.

"Bargle."

"Yes?"

She pointed to the pilot's seat. "You have seen Kim flying?"

The dwarf swallowed and nodded. "Sort of."

"You know the basics?"

He nodded again.

"Good. You had better get ready then."

"But..."

"I shall help where I can."

For a moment it looked as if he would not move, then he was on his feet and racing up the stairs. He sat down on the edge of the seat and tried to get his bearings. Meledrin watched as he went about the task like a dwarf, starting at one side of the console and working his way across, looking at each control, probably cataloguing its use in his mind.

For a moment he chewed on his bottom lip, hands poised before the controls. He mumbled under his breath. Then he spun the steering ball and readied himself again. The wait seemed to last forever.

"Scree," Ping shouted over the intercom. *"Scree, let's get out of here."*

Meledrin nodded to Bargle and the dwarf took a deep breath. He turned on the engines then waited a moment before pushing the lever to thrust them skywards. Meledrin grunted as she was crushed back against the seat. Then the ship's systems adjusted and she was simply out of breath.

"Sorry about that," Bargle said, a surprised look on his face. At that moment the blaring noise of the Ohoga engine disappeared—the dwarf shouted into the silence. "Not quite used to the controls."

"That is quite all right, Bargle," Meledrin replied quietly. "I did not wish to remain there any longer than was necessary."

The dwarf nodded and smiled nervously.

The relative quite made Meledrin feel decidedly more confident. It made her feel as if she were in control again, which she doubted was actually true. "Perhaps you should watch where you are going, Bargle."

"Oh." He turned to look out the window.

But Meledrin looked up and all she could see was cloud beyond the blue glow of the shields. When they burst through into the clear a minute later, it seemed as if the sky was full of kil'ini. They were fighting against each other. There, one of the huge creatures was wallowing amidst a dozen of its smaller brethren, panicking apparently. Its eyestalks twisted this way and that as it tried to see all directions at once. It thrashed about with its tentacles and spat its missiles but there were too many against it. It did not stand a chance. Elsewhere two behemoths circled each other. Meledrin could not work out exactly what they were waiting for. And there, three grappled tentacle-to-tentacle, wrestling and spitting all at once.

There were thousands of the creatures and Meledrin knew of no way of identifying who was fighting for whom. There were a hundred radio conversations taking place all at once. She scanned frequencies.

Outside, three kil'ini simultaneously turned and spat projectiles at the *Hakahei.* The trolls had targets. Four in the weapons chairs down stairs and Cliff on the bridge all started firing in the same moment.

Mother Yuwi of the P'targa came back on the radio. "*The kil'ini firing at* Hakahei *have a contract with the A'nopo family, which has a contract with the T'loop.*" Four smaller kil'ini broke away from another battle to intercept.

Another hurgon joined the conversation. Meledrin knew enough to hear the mix of fear and anger in the voice. "*The P'targa are allowing prisoners to escape.*"

Yuwi was unperturbed. "*The hakans were not registered as prisoners.*"

"*Do you think the councils will care when they discover what has happened?*"

"*Do you think,*" Yuwi retorted, "*that the council will care about the prisoners when they learn that the T'loop invaded the P'targa compound?*"

"*The councils will—*"

"*Will decide for themselves. The Lesser Council has been called to session. There are many things to discuss, including the breaking of the War Contract.*"

"Where am I going?" Bargle asked quietly, dividing his glance between the controls and the view outside. The three T'loop kil'ini were still firing at the *Hakahei,* but were being harassed by the smaller creatures.

"Find the spot where the hurgon are thinnest and go," Meledrin said. But where were they going after that?

"Okay." Bargle spun the steering ball slightly and then a bit more, heading towards a pair of lifeless, floating kil'ini. He increased the thrust.

"Batteries at full charge," Dogar said.

"*The Lesser Council will never agree to the breaking of the War Contract.*"

"*The T'loop mother misunderstands. The P'targa and other minor families contend that the contract has been broken by the eight principles many years ago.*"

"*That is ridiculous.*"

"*Then the T'loop have nothing to fear.*"

Meledrin had heard enough. She wanted to get away from the fighting and bickering. The hurgon would obviously sort things out amongst themselves but it would not be a speedy process. And since it was impossible to tell who was on which side, the *Hakahei* could offer only minimal assistance.

"Tuki?"

"Yes?"

"You have the co-ordinates supplied by the P'targa?"

"Yes, Meledrin."

"Then please tell Bargle which direction we wish to travel."

"Meledrin?"

"Yes?"

"It can be done automatically. If I put the co-ordinates into my computer and then press this button..."

Meledrin raised her eyebrows, remembering all the time Kim had spent trying to point them in the right direction before jumping. "Very well, proceed."

"Meledrin?"

She sighed. "Yes Tuki."

"We should check with Ping before we do anything with the ohoga engines."

Meledrin nodded, pleased that someone had thought to suggest it. Bargle, relieved of any duties while Tuki worked on the co-ordinates, took it upon himself to do the checking.

"Are we ready to jump?" he asked into the microphone.

There was a moment before the reply. "*No. Definitely no.*"

"We aren't ready," Bargle said to Meledrin, who had heard perfectly well.

There was a beep from Tuki's console and Meledrin felt the ship's thrust change subtly.

"Alignment in five minutes," Tuki said.

"Thank you, Tuki."

While she waited Meledrin brought up different views of Hulgorn and the battle that raged around it. She scanned the radio frequencies. Another hurgon voice came from the radio.

"*Hakan vessel, this is Buni, of the great T'loop family. Buni orders the* Hakahei *to return to the planet. The hakans will not be harmed.*"

Meledrin sniffed and pressed the transmit button. "It has already been proven that the T'loop family cannot be trusted. The *Hakahei* will not make the same mistake twice."

"*No deal was brokered.*"

"We had a verbal agreement."

"*Verbal agreements mean nothing.*"

"Then a verbal agreement means nothing now as well. Buni of the T'loop should think before speaking. Besides, Cuto of the T'loop does not agree with Buni. Cuto helped the *Hakahei*'s grandmother and mother escape because when the T'loop broke the verbal agreement the T'loop also broke Cuto's heart."

"*Scree we need some trolls down here now.*" Ping said in the midst of the conversation. "Where are we? *Seven west.*"

"Cliff," Meledrin said, hoping the troll was not concentrating on shooting so much that he could not hear. He grunted in reply. "Can you ask Stone to go down and assist Ping. Level 7, on the western side."

He grunted again and continued firing.

Buni changed tack. "*The P'targa family started this war. The P'targa fired on a T'loop kil'ini. The councils will not stand for it.*"

"Buni, the legalities of the situation are being discussed on another frequency. Buni will not convince Meledrin to stop, so perhaps Buni should discuss this matter with Yuwi of the P'targa." She changed to another frequency.

"Alignment in one minute."

"We will reach top speed in three minutes," Barge said.

The *Hakahei* was still not clear of the confrontation but was being ignored for the most part. A half dozen kil'ini were following, but did not seem keen to come too close—perhaps they were there as protection.

"Aligned. Lapenti is thirty light years. That is one jump of 15 hours and twenty five minutes."

"Thank you, Tuki. Bargle?"

"Got it. Setting the timer for fifteen hours and twenty five minutes." The dwarf fiddled with the buttons. "Done. And we have top speed."

"Very well. Now we shall wait to hear from Ping."

"Right."

"The alien is jumping in, Meledrin."

"Pardon?" She looked around, thinking that one or all of the six hurgon on the *Hakahei* were storming the bridge.

"The multeese is leaving a jump."

"Ohhh..." She would have preferred the hurgon. The huge alien ship scared her immensely and she still did not understand how Kim intended to fight against it.

Tuki put the picture up in the dome. The ship was one thousand and seven kilometers away. For once, it did not immediately start firing.

A cold lifeless voice came over the radio, speaking in the hurgon language. "*Who would speak?*"

There was silence for long seconds. Meledrin was not about to reply and thought no one else was going to either. She rested her hands in her lap, keeping them well away from the transmit button.

"*This is Sister Liko of the En'kumo. Liko would speak with you.*"

"*Very well. Multeese will speak with Liko. Though there is one scuttle cockroach of a vessel that still requires attention.*"

The cold, passionless face appeared on all the *Hakahei*'s screens.

"*Still you run,*" the voice said in the language of Rongo. "*When will you learn that running will do you no good?*"

Keeble's voice came over the internal speaker. "*I'm not sure if you want to jump or not,*" he said, "*but you should be able to now.*"

Meledrin adjusted her controls with shaking fingers, glad of any excuse to look away from the screen. "Should be?" she asked Keeble.

"*One of the Ohoga engines has been disconnected.*" He sounded exhausted.

"Very well." Meledrin sat back and stared out the window. Keeble had not sounded very confident—which worried her—but the dwarf's confidence was the least of her worries.

"*If you wait but a moment I will kill you now. Otherwise, I can follow where ever you go.*" A volley of missiles streaked towards the *Hakahei*. "*Whenever. Wherever. I will find you when my crop is harvested. Go where you will.*"

"Forty two missiles," Cliff said. The trolls were firing all five guns but not meeting with any success. The missiles kept coming. "Impact in eight seconds."

"Bargle..."

But Bargle had already pressed the button to open the gate. "Prepare to jump," he said in to the intercom. "We're about to jump." He spun the bridge so they could watch the gate racing towards them.

"Impact in three seconds," Tuki said, wide eyed and staring.

Then the *Hakahei* was through the gate and the power shut down in the blink of an eye. Darkness.

There was a short, quick barrage against the hull. The ship shook and shuddered.

A whirring quiet. Fans approaching stillness. Motors winding down.

"Five missiles came through with us," Cliff said softly. "Obviously didn't work for some reason."

Meledrin didn't care. She breathed again and unclenched her fists.

"We should be dead," Bargle said.

"Maybe they had a mechanical ignition," Dogar replied.

"I thought we were dead."

Cliff lit a lantern and a soft, warm light started to spread around the bridge.

Meledrin looked at the faces of her companions. *We are not dead yet,* she thought and waved her fingers in a ceremony of *Beginning.*

49: All Over

SCREE LOOKED UP WHEN THE LIGHTS WENT OUT. There was a clatter of noise against the hull. "What's going on nows?"

But it was obvious enough— they'd gone through to the universe the ship used when travelling interstellar distances. No advanced machinery worked here, so the lights didn't work and lots of missiles weren't much better than rocks. Scree grunted. Rocks wouldn't have been surprising, either, seeing they'd put up with just about everything else.

And he still didn't know if it was worth it. Keeble had organized the contracts they needed to end the war with the hurgon, but if they couldn't get the last signature then it was all for nothing. They'd be back at the start, fighting two enemies they couldn't hope to beat. The hurgon would overwhelm them, eventually, with their endless hordes of living ships. And the single multeese ship would blow them into oblivion with technology.

Scree didn't even know who'd been throwing the most recent rocks, or the missiles that had come before, but he decided everyone on the *Hakahei* was probably lucky to be alive.

He turned to look back at Kim. She was only just visible in the murky half-light the universe offered. Long, dark hair framed her pale, slack face. Her skin was cold. She was breathing steadily but hadn't even stirred since passing out in the hurgon torture chamber. Some were luckier than others.

A moment later, Captain Dominic Thorpe stormed into the room carrying a lantern. The human hung the light on a hook in the center of the ceiling and threw his red SAS beret onto the bench. He started going through drawers and cupboards. The swinging lantern threw wild, dancing shadows on the walls, the furniture, stretched them all the way out the door. The squeaking of the handle quickly got on Scree's nerves but he didn't move, in case he broke the spell of studied concentration on the other man's face. Thorpe grabbed all sorts of things and put them on a small, wheeled table.

There was a commotion at the door. Trolls and humans were crowding outside. 'Brick' Dunning, an American Air Force Raven almost as big as a troll, was closest.

"Who have you got, Brick?" Thorpe asked.

"We've got Kafin, sir." Brick's dark face was splashed with light for a moment as the lantern continue to swing. A long smear of grease marked his cheek.

"Head wound, right?"

"Yes, sir."

"Put him there." He pointed to the bed beside Kim's, right near where Scree was sitting. It seemed Thorpe noticed Scree for the first time. He stared for a moment before going back to work.

Brick and Chip put Kafin on the bed. Blood poured from a gash across the dwarf's forehead and there was a lump the size of half a peach.

Talus and Stone brought in Paul Manning next. His left leg was a bloody pulp from the knee down. They laid the human on the main bed near the back of the medical bay. Crystal was with them, carrying the mangled, barely attached limb in one hand and a pair of pliers held close to the bloody knee in the other. All of them— patient and bearers— were covered in blood.

When the others cleared out, Crystal started to go with them.

"Not you, Crystal," Thorpe said sharply. "You stay there and keep hold of those pliers."

The trollop swallowed and nodded. Scree knew how she felt. Trolls knew better than anyone that death could be gruesome and bloody, but apparently life could be worse.

Ari was brought in next. There was only one bed left so she was put there. Her arm was swollen and bruised, obviously broken. She was hurting but she'd live. The other two probably wouldn't.

"What you gots there?" Scree asked Crystal, motioning to the pliers.

The trollop didn't even look up.

"What you gots there?" Scree asked again.

"Got got an artery," she replied eventually.

Scree grunted. "What happened?"

Thorpe answered. "What do you care?" He finished collecting his tools and wheeled the table over to Manning's side. "If you're just going to sit there, you do it and shut up."

Scree surged to his feet. He stared at Thorpe but the human didn't seem to notice. "I could kills you for that," Scree said. "I'm in charge on this ships while Kim's injured."

Thorpe spared him a glance. "Yeah, you could kill me, but you aren't in charge." He turned back to examine what was left of his countryman's leg. "We have to seal the artery," he said to Crystal. "I'm going to tie a bit of string around it. You just have to hold on until I'm done."

Crystal nodded. "All right right."

"What you means I ain't in charge?" Scree clenched his teeth, holding back more words. It was like he was a real troll again, like he'd been before he'd met Kim and his other strange, new companions.

"The hurgon were attacking from the ground and from space. Meledrin took charge on the bridge to get us off Hulgorn." Thorpe worked at Manning's leg while he talked. "We were seriously damaged. Keeble and Ping kept the workers from panicking. They got everything going enough for Meledrin to do her job, though, as you see, it wasn't easy."

The knot was tied. Crystal let go with the pliers and set the bloody tool down.

Blood was still seeping out of the leg but it was controllable. The knot was hidden in the pulp.

"Brick?"

"Sir," the American called from the hall.

"O-neg?"

"Not me, sir. I'll check with the others."

"Good." Thorpe rattled around on the little table. "Kesi's dead, Scree. At least we think she is. We haven't actually found her yet. Sandy? Now, Sandy's definitely dead."

Scree knew that. When Keeble and his party first came back to the ship with the contracts and the hurgon lawyers, Scree had listened to the other trolls talking in his head. They needed to take the damn things to another planet to get the final signature they needed.

Thorpe bent forward and poked in amongst the ruins of the leg. "Crystal, take his leg." He picked up a little knife and went in again. "Right, now twist a little bit."

The trollop did what she was asked, but didn't look happy about it. Scree agreed. It was strange doing that to save someone.

"Stop. Hold it there." Thorpe carefully cut something away. "And some more. Whoa." He cut again then stood up straight. "Okay, twist a bit more."

Crystal twisted the mangled bone. "It's tough tough," she said.

"Yeah, that's okay, just twist."

She did and there was a loud crack.

"Pull it out."

Scree watched as she pulled the shinbone and bloody flesh away.

"Right, now we're going to take these bits of skin and sew them over the end of the leg. Are you ready?"

"Umm... Yeah."

"Good."

She didn't look ready.

"Sandy died on Hulgorn, when Keeble was trying to return to the ship," Thorpe continued as he cut away hanging flesh to get some more spare skin. "Keeble isn't a soldier, Scree. He's just a young man, barely in his twenties. I imagine he's taking the loss of someone under his command pretty badly."

Scree grunted but wasn't sure what to say.

"He's out there working. He's doing his job. And who's doing your job while you sit in here and sulk?"

"I ain't sulking."

"Pining then— I don't give a shit what you call it. Meanwhile, who's doing your job? Meledrin's in overall charge and doing better than I would have expected. Bargle was driving— that's a scary thought as well, but he did well by all accounts. We aren't dead, after all. Everyone else— elves, trolls, dwarves, even the moai— is working under Keeble and Ping to get the ship working again."

"Sir?"

"Amy? Yes?"

The American Marine was in the doorway. "O-negative, sir." He red hair was dirty and singed. She had a cut on her cheek.

"Excellent." Thorpe pointed to a seat in the corner. "Bags in the locker above, I think. Can you do it yourself?"

"Yes, sir."

"Good."

Scree watched as the woman took a soft, clear bag down from the cupboard and found a hook for it on the wall. She tied a strap around her arm, pumped her hand a couple of times, and stuck a needle into a vein. Blood flowed into the bag. Scree saw Ari watching as well. Her arm looked terrible, but she didn't complain.

Thorpe was sewing strips of skin together, covering the stump of Manning's leg.

"One liter, Sir."

"Thanks, Amy."

"You want more?"

"Of course, but not from you. What about Tim? He's your brother."

"Already here, Dominic." Scree watched as the American sergeant strode into the room, already rolling up his sleeve. He was shorter than his sister, with a round face and crooked teeth.

"When you're done there, Amy, can you look at Ari's arm?"

"Sure."

Scree swallowed. He'd always laughed at human soldiers with all their orders and training. Why couldn't they just go and fight? But these ones moved calmly and surely, doing what they could and not giving up on anyone— including the living.

50: Assumptions

SCREE POINTED TO KAFIN. The dwarf hadn't moved since he'd been put there. "I'd looks at him first," he said. "That lump on his head don't look goods."

Thorpe looked at Scree for a moment, then across at the dwarf. "See what you can see, Amy. There has to be some type of scanning equipment in here."

"Won't work."

"What? Oh, damn." He looked over his shoulder at the lantern, then continued sewing. "Okay, give me a minute."

When they got out the hand drill, Scree had to leave. There were three trolls stationed around the outer, circular passage to keep watch, though what they'd do if they saw anything was anyone's guess.

"Where is everyone?" Scree asked Bones.

"All over. Here and there. Everywhere. Ping has some working on the clock. Something wrong with it. Too much tick and not enough tock maybe. Keeble's fixing a hole on Level 4. Level 4? Level 5? Yeah, I think it's level 4. Most of the rest are on Level 7 trying to clear the still. Went bang. Crap everywhere. Probably a hole in the wall there too."

"Right." Scree left before Bones could say anything else. In the semi-darkness, he took the stairs two at a time down to Level 7.

The hallway outside the fuel-still was full of wreckage. People were passing it out the door and piling it against the walls. Meledrin was there, tall and slim, and fidgeting like never before. Her copper colored hair was all over the place. The elf wasn't helping with the moving but stood watching as if every piece of broken machinery and every piece of twisted metal was her responsibility.

"What's going on?" Scree asked.

Meledrin turned to look. She stared for a moment and smoothed unconsciously at her hair. "We are attempting to reach Kesi."

"Is she dead?" A couple of the workers stop to look at him as if he'd broken a rule about asking that question.

Meledrin shrugged and waved her fingers in one of her small ceremonies. The lamp in the corner threw shadows of her dancing fingers onto the wall. "We are unable to ascertain with any certainty. We are not willing to make any assumptions, just in case."

"What you wants me to do?"

"There is insufficient room for more people in the still."

"Dwarves needed somewhere else?"

Meledrin nodded. "Perhaps. Topper?"

The dwarf stuck his head out of the room. "What?" His face was covered in soot and grease and there was a scrape on the side of his neck. The plaits in his long, sandy beard were unraveling. Weariness had settled on his shoulders as if he was trying to hold up a wall.

"Scree can assist in there if you wish to make use of dwarves elsewhere."

Topper looked at Scree with an expression the troll was starting to hate. It said exactly the same thing as Thorpe's 'What do you care?' from earlier. The dwarf tugged on his beard and killed off another plait. He looked at the leather thong in his hand for a moment, sighed, and put it in a pocket. "I'll send someone to help Mintar and Dosa with the air recyclers." He looked at the dwarves working outside. "Hoodek, Tess."

The two dwarves nodded and moved. They looked half defeated as well.

"You want me to pile stuff?" Scree asked.

Topper shook his head. "We need the muscle in here."

-oOo-

Scree was still there when most of the others had gone. There was only Topper and a couple of other dwarves left, trying to work out what needed to be done to get the still working again. They stood in the hall surveying the clutter.

Kesi's body had been carried away.

"Can I helps?" Scree asked. He'd worked for more than two hours and had forgotten about Kim and the world in general. He had forgotten about everything except the next piece of wreckage.

"I don't think so," Topper said, shaking his head slowly, still lost in thought. "Thanks for the help you did give though."

Scree grunted. "Weren't much help before that."

The dwarf shrugged. "We were all pissed off at you but I can kinda understand what was going on." He looked at the other dwarves for a moment. "This isn't vital," he said. "Why don't we have a break and get back to it later."

Makar, Dogar and Milo nodded and turned to walk slowly towards the stairs. Scree started to follow but Topper didn't move.

"You're friends with Ping, aren't you Scree?"

Scree thought about that as he went back to the dwarf. He and Ping had gotten along for the most part but 'friends' wasn't the right word. "Yeah, I suppose. Maybes."

"Do you know..?" He started to wander along a passage towards the back of the ship, absently working to tidy the plaits in his beard. Scree followed. "Well, in Tab Cavern if a dwife was living in the Hotel or the Maiden Bunker, you told her to move into your bunker and that was that. But with Ping I just don't know."

Scree laughed and Topper looked offended.

"It isn't funny," he said. "If you're just going to laugh—"

Scree held up his hand, still laughing. "It ain't funny, Topper. What's funny is that you thinks I can help. It wasn't exactly the same for me, but close enough." Scree had never really asked for anything in his life.

They stopped where the passage opened out near a door to a storeroom. Scree looked down at the young dwarf. Topper was being honest, opening himself up. Apparently, that was what friends did. Scree looked around. There was nobody else there. He cleared his throat. "If anything," he said, "I shoulds be the one asking for advice."

It was Topper's turn to laugh. "But Kim likes you. Everyone knows that."

"Could've told me." But maybe it *was* obvious. Maybe he'd known all along. So why didn't he do something? Because if he didn't act then he couldn't fail... Because if he didn't act then he wouldn't stop being a troll and become just another man...

Was there anything wrong with being a man? Keeble, Thorpe and Suldon were all men of different kinds. Were they so bad? Scree liked all of them, in one way or another. He *respected* them.

"You never look like you need any advice, Scree."

"Always do, Topper. Just don't know it most of the time." He smiled. "And Ping? I think she likes you too."

"You think?"

"Yeah. But..." Scree knew all too well why Ping might not trust men. He cleared his throat. "It mightn't be easy for her."

"Oh?"

"I reckon you should just take it slow. Hang around and be a nice guy. Make sure she knows what you want— and it better be more than sex or I'll rip your head off." He smiled as he said it, but he thought he might be serious. The look on Topper's face suggested he was thinking the same thing. "And then waits and see."

"Hello?" Inaki's voice echoed down the passage. "Is anyone down here?"

Scree looked at Topper and nodded. "Yo, Inaki-boy. We's here."

The moai poked his head around the corner. He was bigger than a troll but like Tuki, the other moai, was shy and quiet. When he'd first come aboard the *Hakahei* he wouldn't speak unless asked a question and almost blushed at the sight of a woman. "Everyone must come to the garden," he said quietly.

"Who says?"

"Tuki."

"Right then," Scree nodded.

Inaki disappeared, probably off to search for more people, and Scree looked at his companion. "You know what this is abouts?"

Topper nodded. "Come on."

Just about everyone was in the garden, a dozen lamps leached the color from their faces. Dust hung in the air.

"Shouldn't you be watching the patients?" Scree asked Thorpe when he saw the soldier amongst the crowd.

"Crystal's up there. She'll let us know."

51: Silence

SCREE GRUNTED AND TURNED TO LOOK at Tuki. He was standing at the front of the group. "What're we doing here?" Scree asked.

But Tuki started to speak. "We have lost more friends," he said. "Ben Dongoske and Kesi."

The moai was holding two metal plaques and there was another on the wall behind him. Scree tried to read the words but couldn't.

Tuki continued. "Wherever we go now, there seems to be danger. I lived a safe life before I came on this ship. I woke up each morning and could name those who might die that day— the old and the sick."

Scree listened to Tuki. The moai was still quiet— the crowd was hushed, leaning forward to hear— and he was still shy, but he was also confident. He studied the plaques in his hand while he spoke, but he said the words as if he expected people to listen. And they did. Trolls and elves, dwarves and humans, they all watched him and listened. Even the hurgon lawyers were there, diving their attention between Tuki and Meledrin. The elf was translating into the ini rituals. The aliens weren't showing any emotion, but they never did.

"But here..." Tuki said. "Here, we cannot know from one moment to the next what will happen and what friends we will lose. And yet..." He looked up and surveyed the faces. "I know I do not want to go back to my life in Danyon Ford though I know I might be the next to die. I would not exchange one day here for ten years there. Why? Because the people on this ship are my friends and the moai of Danyon Ford are just people I knew."

Scree examined the crowd as well. Ruby was crying. So were Tess and Bethalin. The elf and dwife were holding hands. Gulch and Flint were nodding their heads. Ping hooked a strand of her bobbed, brown hair behind her ear and bit her lip.

"We lost two more friends today. I wish they hadn't died but I know why they did. I know why they did, because I can feel in my heart that I would have done the same thing for them." Tuki held up the first plaque and read the words. "Kesi. A dwarf to the end."

'Dwarf' instead of 'dwife'. Scree wondered if Tuki had chosen it. The dwarves didn't seem to mind, either way.

Tuki squeezed glue onto the back of the brass plaque and carefully stuck it to the wall near the one that was already there for Sandy. Then he held up the next one. "Airman Ben Dongoske. United States Air Force. Above and beyond." That one was stuck to the wall as well.

After that, Scree listened as different people talked about those who'd died. They said good things. Scree smiled when Brick told the story about the scar on Dongoske's chest. And he was surprised when Keeble stepped forward and said that Kesi had lost a baby and had taken orphans into her home ever since.

When it appeared nobody else was going to say anything, Scree strode to the front of the group.

"Kesi and Ben both had good stories from before they came on this ship. I don't. I got bad stories. Nobody wants to hear them and Ping already knows too much." He saw the little woman shift nervously but ploughed on. "I never even understood what friends was for before I came here. But now... I've been born agains like somebody from one of Ben's religious stories— *re-incarnated.*

"The best things I can say about Kesi and Ben? All you people, from all different places, is willing to stand and hear stories about them and remember them. If I ever gets my name up on that wall," Scree said, pointing over his shoulder, "my best story will be if all you people is standing here thinking it was good to have known me too."

Scree wasn't sure if he was saying what he was supposed to be saying. It sounded like he was talking about himself, but he wasn't. "Their best stories are about having earned your respect and friendship," he added, hoping that was clearer. He shook his head and walked away from the wall. They all watched and he didn't know what they were thinking. But he looked at Ping and she turned away, tears running down her olive skinned face.

-oOo-

Ping fumbled for her lamp in the dark. When the light came it was blinding for three seconds and she blinked away tears. She turned to the clock beside her bed, but of course it wasn't working and she had lost track of the time. They were somewhere in the middle of the jump. She rubbed sleep from her eyes and stretched. She felt like she hadn't slept at all.

After pulling on her EVA suit and clothes, Ping went out into the hall then started up the stairs. She stopped on Level 3 to find some food.

There was a box of silver packets on a bench that offered dried fruit. The drink dispenser didn't work without power but a tap on the side gave her a cup of cool, flavored water. She took her breakfast and sat at one of the tables. There was nobody else there, which was unusual. Even if they weren't eating there were usually people there playing games or just chatting. Ping ate in silence.

When she was done Ping returned to the stairs and wondered where she would find some company. The elves, plus Hoodek, Makar and Dido who had, much to their embarrassment, taken a liking to gardening, would probably be in the gardens. Most of the dwarves would be in the workshop. The others... Ping didn't know. She decided to see who was on Level 2.

But she discovered that her guesses had been wrong. Almost everyone was on the habitation level. Meledrin and Chasm were sitting on the floor to the left of the stairs. It appeared as if the elf was trying to explain a poem to the troll and not having much luck.

"Allusion and metaphor are vying with each other in this stanza," the elf said.

"Chasm doesn't understand." The trollop shook her head. But she kept looking at the page, not giving in. "If they're vying with each other, Chasm just wishes one would deal a killing blow so there was only *one* riddle to solve."

Other small groups were spread around the main room, but the largest group was preparing to play some sort of game.

"What's going on?" Ping asked Meledrin.

Meledrin looked up from the book. "Captain Thorpe is attempting to explain a game he calls cricket."

Ping looked out at the game and tried to work out what was happening. As if reading her mind, Meledrin spoke again.

"I fail to see the point. The game that Keeble likes... Rugby? I can see the point of that, even if the rules escape me, but this one..." She shrugged her thin shoulders.

From the conversations going on amongst the players, Ping didn't think many of them got the point either. Even the Americans seemed to be at a loss.

"Who is watching Captain Thorpe's patients?" Ping asked.

"Scree."

"Oh. Is that..?"

Out on the field, Ruby shook her head in disbelief. "One game takes five days?" she asked.

"They can do," Thorpe replied. "But they can last one day as well."

"So you don't even know how long it'll take to play?"

"Well..."

Ruby shook her head again. "I don't think I'll ever understand this game."

Brick laughed. "Americans have been trying to understand it for a hundred years and still haven't had any luck."

"Let me know when you start playing that game Keeble keeps talking about. The one with the stomping and the thumping." Ruby waved away Thorpe's protests and walked past Ping with a smile of greeting. Ping was surprised when the trollop went straight to Tuki's cabin. She looked at Meledrin and Chasm. She looked at Amy and Tasko who were talking nearby. None of them seemed to notice Ruby's destination. Or if they did, they paid it no mind. Ping hated living on Level 6— it was close to the Engineering bay if there was an emergency, but there wasn't often an emergency so all it did was separate those living there from the rest of the crew.

"Hello, Ping."

"Hi, Topper."

"Come to play cricket, have you?"

Ping laughed. "No, I don't think so. I was just going to sit and watch."

"Oh."

"You can sit with me and tell me the rules though, so I know what I'm looking at."

52: Changes

PING SAT DOWN AND LEANED against the wall and Topper sat by her side. She hardly took any notice of his explanation of the rules and hardly saw the game, though she stared out at the players.

"How long to go in this jump?" she asked when the dwarf was done.

Topper shrugged. "About four hours, I think."

Ping sighed.

"You're bored?"

"A little. But in a good way. There are lots of things I could do if I wanted, but I just want to sit and complain and feel sorry for myself at the moment."

"Oh." He tapped the toes of his boots together and combed his fingers through his chin-beard. "What did Scree mean when he said you knew more of his stories than you wanted to know?"

Ping wasn't going to talk about that. "I just knew him before everyone else did. I saw him do some horrible things." But most of the things were not really horrible at all. There was just that once, but Ping had survived... "What happened to Kim?"

"Pardon?"

"What happened to Kim?"

Topper narrowed his eyes as he looked at her, as if trying to guess the link. "She was tortured by the hurgon."

Ping turned to look at Cuto. The T'loop was standing in a corner by himself, watching the cricket. "And Cuto rescued them?"

"Yeah, but only just. There are burn marks on Kim's legs and an injury on her wrist. Plus she had a few broken bones."

"Burn marks?"

"Yes."

Ping chewed on her thumbnail. Perhaps Scree had not had anything to do with Kim's current condition— he would not bother to burn her, after all. Perhaps he had meant those words he said in the garden.

"How come the dwarves were able to change so quickly?" Ping asked Topper.

"Change what?"

"Their views on women."

"Oh. I don't know. Perhaps we're too practical to argue with what's obvious. Some of the older dwarves still aren't completely comfortable with the idea, but they've seen the way the dwives worked."

Ping nodded.

"And you and Kim helped too. It's hard to say women are useless when the two of you are shouting the right orders as quick as any dwarf could and doing the right things." Topper tapped the toes of his boots together again, staring at them.

Ping sighed and rose to her feet again. "I think I am going to go downstairs."

"Oh. Do you want to play chess? Or something?"

"No. Thanks anyway. I think I'll just read for a while." She went through the hatch and down the stairs without looking back.

On Level 3, she headed for the library. The journey took her near the gym and the medical bay. Before she went in, she took a moment to look in at the patients lying on the beds. She stopped and leaned against the doorframe.

Kafin had bandages wrapped around his head. Paul's half-leg was swathed in bandages. Kim was on a third bed. Her wrist was bandaged, her foot was in a cast. Any other injuries were covered by her blanket or hidden in her mind. Scree was sitting by her side, hunched forward, quiet.

The troll glanced at the other patients, looking at each of them in turn. He saw Ping.

Ping could remember a time when she could not have walked down the stairs unnoticed. Now she could stand in the doorway.

Scree stared at her, none of the usual intensity in his eyes, until Ping turned and hurried the rest of the way to the library. She didn't know if reading would be enough to get her through the next four hours, but she needed something.

-oOo-

Meledrin breathed a sigh of relief. Despite the threats made by the multeese, there was nothing there to greet the Hakahei when they returned to the normal universe, just the blackness of space and the sharp pinpricks of the stars. Meledrin looked away from the window and examined her console, but there was nothing she could do— computers and systems had to restart, they had to realign themselves with their new reality. While that happened, Tuki and Keeble were the only ones performing any tasks, working with the scant information they were offered as the ship's momentum slowly recharged the batteries.

"All systems coming online in twenty seconds," Keeble said. "Everything seems to be fine, besides the bits that we know aren't. The repairs to Air Recycler 1 seem to have done the job. The hull repair on Level 4 is fine."

Meledrin waved her arms in the ini rituals for the benefit of Cuto and the five hurgon lawyers. She did not know if any of them cared what was being said, but if nothing else the translations might help the hakans learn.

"We are near Lapenti," Tuki said after a moment. "It looks like we have a few hours of travel before we get there."

Meledrin saw Scree nodded from his place in the weapons chair, but did not seem to be paying any attention. Perhaps he was saving his energy for something he could actually affect. "That the planet there, Tuki?" he asked.

It was obvious what he was talking about. There was a brown disk, barely the size of a pea, visible through the view port.

Tuki nodded.

"Good. Bargle?"

Bargle had tried to get Scree to take over the driving duties. Meledrin had been surprised when the troll refused. So now, Bargle sat in the seat, tugging his beard and studying the controls as if he had never previously seen them. But Scree trusted him to do the job and a newfound confidence was showing.

"Yes, Scree?"

"Take us to the planet."

"We don't have—"

"Yeah, I knows. As soon as we have power."

"Right. Of course."

The power returned just a moment later and Bargle pushed the button that brought the Gravitic field generators to life. After checking to make sure the steering ball was pointing in the right direction, he hit the thrust.

"One Ohoga engine and one clock still not working," Keeble continued with his report when the information came up. "The fuel still is not even registering. And nobody has bothered to fix the drink dispenser in the mess hall."

"At full speed it will take us approximately eight hours," Tuki said.

Meledrin sighed. After all the time spent in the other universe, she always though the journey on the far side felt like some kind of torture.

"Full charge in one hour at this speed." Keeble said.

Meledrin looked at those around her. Ping was working silently with Keeble checking the various systems to see what was functional and what was not, perhaps trying to work out what needed to be repaired first.

Tuki was working quietly as well. Once, it had almost seemed that he hesitated before even taking a breath, wondering if a woman would inform him that he was doing it incorrectly. At the funeral ceremony, he had shown he was still shy, but his confidence was obvious.

Looking at her companions, Meledrin considered the words the young moai had spoken at the ceremony and decided she agreed with some of it. She would not want to go back to Grovely to live as she once had, though a month ago she would not have though it possible to desire anything else. But she did not think of the people on the ship as her friends. They were more like her family. There were some of them she didn't really *like*— and she thought that liking was an important part of friendship— but she would still stand with any or all of these people, and face the wrath of the aliens.

She cleared her throat. "The multeese?" she said. "What actions are we going to take?"

Scree looked at her. "What about them?"

"They were present at Hulgorn. They stated that they were going to kill us."

"And you think they will?"

She nodded. "I cannot see how it can be otherwise, even if the Americans and all the hurgon assist us."

Scree was nodding slowly and turned to look out the window again.

Ping joined in. "I agree," she said. "With the weapons they have, how can we stop them? It might already be too late."

"Why's that?"

"Who knows how many people it has killed on the hakan worlds?"

Meledrin swallowed. It was quite possible the alien had killed every person on the seven hakan worlds. If it set its mind to it, it probably would not take long at all. But they did seem to be easily distracted. They flew from world to world, causing death and destruction wherever they went, without ever once completing a task.

"Their technology does make things difficult," Keeble said in what Meledrin thought was a major understatement. "How do we stop a weapon we don't understand? How do we beat shields we don't understand?"

Meledrin didn't reply— she didn't have an answer— and Scree continued to stare out the window.

"We need Kim," Ping said. Scree turned to look in her direction but didn't say anything before looking away again.

"Forty-five minutes until full power, " Keeble said quietly.

"Forty-seven," Ping said softly and Keeble shook his head.

Meledrin checked her radio, as if something she might hear on there would be good news.

53: A Straight Line

PING LOOKED UP AT THE PLANET OUTSIDE. If felt as if she had been staring at it for the last six hours. She was sure a lot of those in the viewing seats had been hadn't moved since leaving the other universe as well.

"Thirty-seven kil'ini visible," Tuki said softly. "There could be more around the far side of the world."

Scree was sitting in the gallery with his feet up on the back of another chair. He scratched his neck with a thumb. "Are they heading towards us?" He could see for himself.

"Some are," Tuki replied. "But it does not look as if they are attacking."

Ping watched a dozen kil'ini slowly coming closer. They scanned the region with the huge, stalked eyes, looking for signs of trouble. Tentacles trailed out behind them for hundreds of meters.

"Whose family is they?" Scree asked.

Ping turned to look at the hurgon brothers, present as ever, but they were giving nothing away. Perhaps they weren't yet sure themselves.

"I do not know," Tuki said.

The question obviously hadn't been for the moai. How was he to know? Each kil'ini was as individual as people but they didn't wear the colors of their aligned families as the hurgon did. Ping almost laughed but bit back the sound in case her nervousness came out at the same time and she couldn't stop. She chewed on her thumbnail instead and watched the kil'ini.

Meledrin had been translating everything, so the brothers were already discussing the problem, pointing and waving their arms in the ini rituals as if the kil'ini could already see them. From what Ping could tell, only one brother other than Koli of the P'targa had any family at all present in the area.

"Where's we going?" Scree asked.

Meledrin spoke with the hurgon. "The closest kil'ini is unknown," she said a minute later, "but the second one is Piti'ma'ningi, with Mother Duti of the P'targa in charge."

Ping sighed. An ally.

"That blue one?"

"That is correct," Meledrin replied.

"Well, get them on the radio and tells them we want to talk to the Grandmother."

"The Grandmother will not be on the kil'ini."

"I know that but they can tell us how to get to her."

"Scree—"

"If you's about to tell me that the hurgon don't have no men or women just shut up and get on the radio."

Ping smothered a smile. Meledrin sniffed and got to work.

"Brother Koli can talk from my console," Tuki said, moving out of the way.

Koli crossed to the console then stood looking until Tuki pointed to the relevant button and hesitantly waved his arms in explanation. The hurgon gave the alien version of a smile then set to work. Meledrin commentated as the conversation progressed.

"It appears as if a message has preceded us. Mother Duti welcomes us and informs us that the main P'targa compound is located around the far side of the world."

"Can we gets co-ordinates or something?"

"Directions are already being passed on. Hopefully Koli can remember them because I cannot."

While the conversation between the aliens continued Scree got Bargle to start taking the ship slowly around to the far side of the planet. The dwarf hardly hesitated at all and Ping thought he would find himself with a new job even after Kim had recovered from her injuries.

Ten minutes later Brother Koli pointed to a spot just coming into view on the skyglass and Tuki placed a marker for Bargle to see.

"So do we just fly down there now?" Bargle asked. "Or do we wait for permission or something?"

Nobody replied. It was unlikely even the hurgon would know, unless Mother Duti had passed the information on.

They continued to move slowly.

Ping looked up when Tuki nudged Koli out of the way a minute later. The moai worked for a few seconds, concentrating fiercely as if he still doubted his knowledge of the skyglass. Or as if he wanted to be wrong. "The multeese ship has just arrived," Tuki said a moment later.

Ping felt her heart skip a beat and turned back to the dome. The alien ship was thousands of kilometers away but there could be no doubt. It filled the view. Bargle quickly spun the bridge so they could see it out the viewport as well.

Stone was still slouching in the weapon's chair as if there was no problem at all. Ping did not know how he could be so calm. And Scree as well. Even Meledrin seemed to be sitting up straighter but the trolls were just looking at the image as if it were not a concern.

"What should we do, Scree?"

"Gets us down to the planet, Bargle." The troll swore. At least that was something. "Hopefully the bastard hasn't noticed us yet."

Bargle nodded as Ping strapped herself into her chair. The gravity waned momentarily as the *Hakahei* plunged towards the ground. Soon, the entire ship was shaking. It had never done that when Kim was in charge.

Keeble cleared his throat. "You may want to slow down, Bargle. I've got warning lights going off everywhere here."

Ping watched as Bargle glanced towards the image in the dome. A dozen kil'ini swarmed around the multeese ship, like flies around a donkey. It was terrible to watch the creatures die. Even more so when she thought of the hurgon who were inside each one.

"Theys distracted at the moment. Should be rights."

So Bargle slowed the ship, muttering to himself and trying to see everything at once.

"How's we going, Tuki?" Scree asked when they were finally nearing the ground.

Tuki checked his own readouts. "We are safe for now, I think."

"Goods." Scree picked at his teeth. "So where's we going?"

"Follow that valley." The moai pointed along a long narrow valley that had a sheer escarpment on one side and a long, wooded slope on the other. "That is pointing close to the right direction."

Bargle turned the ship one way then the other until they were finally heading in the right direction. Then he spun the bridge to face the right way as well.

"How far away are we," Ping asked.

"We are still more than twenty thousand kilometers from the Grandmother's location," Tuki said.

In space that would not take very long at all, but Ping didn't know how long it would take down near the planet.

When the valley wall started to curve away, Bargle lifted the ship up and kept them going.

A smudge of mountains marched by far to the south, barely visible. The ship crossed an ocean, diving into a storm that whipped up huge waves and sent sheets of rain against the viewport. Then they burst from the other side into bright sunlight. Half an hour later dusk had come and gone leaving a night alive with stars. And finally there were signs of life.

Stone towers surrounded by compounds with buildings squeezed between thick, hulking walls. Farmland stretching away as far as the eye could see. Dozens of machines, most as big as the *Hakahei*, worked in the darkness, belching out smoke as they moved like advancing armies through the crops. They could not be heard, but Ping could imagine a deafening rumble spreading ever outwards.

Keeble grunted. "They make farms the same way they make cities," he said.

Ping could only agree.

"Still goods, Tuki?"

Tuki nodded. "We are slightly off course but not much. We can realign when we get a bit closer."

The farms continued to pass beneath them. Rivers had been straightened out to allow the machines easier access. Roads and railway tracks between compounds ran almost exclusively in straight lines. And everywhere, the machines kept working.

"Ummm..." Keeble said a minute later.

Scree turned to look at him quickly. Ping as well. It didn't sound good.

"How far is it to the grandmother?"

Tuki checked. "It is not very far. Just over two thousand kilometers."

Ping examined the lights flashing on one of Keeble's screens. She worked out what he was going to say before he said it.

"That's..." He hit some buttons. He stopped, cocked his head to the side and hit some more. "We aren't going to make it."

"What?"

Ping wasn't sure who said it first. Bargle, Scree, or any of a half dozen other people who were on the bridge.

"We don't have enough fuel."

Scree's eyes narrowed. "Thought we had plenty."

Ping remembered something about that as well.

"We did. Until we started flying around down here."

"Right."

54: Whole Armies

PING DIDN'T KNOW HOW SCREE could still be so calm. They needed fuel to find the Grandmother but they also needed fuel to get back into space. Problem after problem and he just stood there and thought. She knew enough to know that Kim's indecision, her thoughts, would have shown on her face. Not so with the troll.

"So how long we gots?"

Keeble shrugged again. "Half an hour, maybe."

Scree grunted and examined the image shown by the skyglass. It was all fields now with an occasional compound like an island amidst the sea of grain, "Does we know who owns all this area?"

Brother Koli replied and Meledrin translated. "Koli states that the farms in this region are owned by the En'kumo, who are a highly placed minor family in the employ of the T'loop. They are worked by the P'targa."

"Right, where's the closest compound?"

"Slightly to our right," Tuki said after a moment.

Scree nodded. "And we'll makes it that far?"

"I think so."

"Bargle gets onto it then."

Bargle and Tuki worked together to get them moving in the right direction. Everyone else waited silently. Scree leaned against the wall, watching out the viewport.

Ping didn't know if it was a good idea going to one of the compounds— who knew how the hurgon living there would react?— but she wasn't in charge and didn't want to be.

They left the fields behind and moved into a barren, dry crumple of hills. The ship's lights revealed low cliffs with colorful stratum. Splintered rock covered the ground, as if it had fallen from the sky like sleet. Narrow, snaking gullies like veins in a hand. And all the while, Ping wondered if they were ever going to reach the compound. Eventually, after what seemed like half an hour, a soft glow of light came up over the horizon and raced towards them.

The compound was set down in a slight depression with a hundred meters of flat ground on the near side. Bargle gave a sigh of relief and slowed the ship so suddenly that Ping was slammed against her safety belts. Nonetheless they didn't stop completely until they'd almost reached the walls. A warning buzzer sounded.

"Out of fuel," Keeble said.

Ping wasn't sure if Bargle thumped them down onto the ground or if gravity was to blame. Her bones ached. She'd bitten her lip. And a cloud of dust and rock was raining down outside the ship.

There were ten seconds of relative silence.

"Now what, hey?" Gulch asked from the viewing gallery.

Scree scratched his cheek. "How fars to the Grandmother?"

Tuki swallowed noisily. "Two hundred and fifty kilometers in a straight line. There are some mountains in the way."

It was not far at all, really, if you had a starship to fly there.

"Chasm reckons we could fly there in one of those Landers quick enough," Chasm said.

Scree nodded but didn't look sure. "How far they flys, Keeble?"

The dwarf shrugged. "I don't know, but I don't think they're made for doing that."

Scree nodded again.

Ruby shook her head. "Bit of a target if you ask me. Nothing else like it around here— it's sure to get someone's attention sooner or later. At least in this thing we got some protection."

"Kim still sleepings? Anyone checked recently?" Scree got a far away look and Ping knew he was checking himself, using the radio in his mind to ask another troll. "Right," he said eventually. "Ain't no help there."

Cuto said something and Ping turned to watch the ini' rituals as the alien spoke with the five hurgon brothers. Ping could understand a lot now, but the aliens spoke so quickly between themselves that she could not keep up. Meledrin translated. "One of the brothers— I am unsure of its name— seems to think that trains can make the journey from here in approximately five hours."

"That ain't so bad. What about fuel? Where can we get some of that? What do we need, Keeble?"

"Hydrogen."

Another brother spoke.

"Brother Koli states that it may be possible to source hydrogen from the compound by which we are currently situated. Hydrogen is used for... Well, I am not aware of the word Koli uses but apparently it is unlikely a compound situated in this location has any other use."

Scree nodded for a third time, and this time it looked as if he meant it. "Heres it is then. Keeble is in charge of getting the fuel. Suldon is with you. Meledrin, you's going with the brothers."

"Scree, I do not think—"

"No, the problem is you think too much. Palsamon can go with you as back up. And there'll be some trolls, of course."

"Will Flint be among them?"

Scree looked at her. "If you wants."

And Meledrin looked unsure. Ping didn't think he'd ever seen that before. The elf cleared her throat. "I think it would be best."

-oOo-

Keeble started working on a final check of the systems. But they told him nothing he didn't already know, which was a good thing. He was about to turn his mind to the fuel, though he couldn't start to plan until he knew where it was and how it was stored and the transport options available. Before he could ask when they were going to get started Tuki, cleared his throat.

"The kil'ini are either dead or gone," he said. "It looks like..." He zoomed in on the multeese ship.

It was a bit blurry. Keeble squinted, trying to see. "Are they..."

"They Landers," Chasm said. "Chasm doesn't like the look of that."

Keeble grunted but another troll beat him to what he was going to say next as well.

"There's lot of 'em," Chip said.

"There are hundreds," Ping said. Keeble thought she sounded horrified.

"So whats does that mean, do you reckon?" Scree asked. He, on the other hand, didn't seem worried at all.

Keeble wasn't quite sure of the point of the question. Apparently Meledrin wasn't either and asked.

Flint answered from the viewing gallery. "They can probably kill everyone on the world from up there in their big ship. So why's they coming down here to do the killing in person? They doesn't seem like the kind who does stuff for fun."

"Does it matter?" Keeble asked. "It's good for us, surely, so let's not go asking them to explain."

"It might matters. If we knews the answer it might help us even more."

Keeble watched the images in the dome. Something about the scale worried him. His eyes narrowed. "The multeese ship is twenty kilometers long, isn't it?"

Tuki nodded. "A little bit over."

"Those Landers must be huge. They must be..."

Tuki hit some buttons and looked up suddenly. "They are each more than two hundred meters long."

Someone whistled.

Scree looked a bit concerned for the first time. "They could have whole armies in each one. How many hurgons are on this world?"

Meledrin translated for Brother Koli. "Koli is unsure exactly but a population of several million is suspected. There is a major city on the far side of the world plus five smaller cities and several hundred minor settlements such as the one here."

"Something going on, boss?" Flint asked. He took his feet down from the back of the chair in front and stood up to look out the view port, as if he could see something important.

Scree nodded. "The multeese have gots to know they don't need no huge army. The hurgon ain't much good as fighters anyways. So if they ain't bringing people down, maybe theys taking stuff back."

Keeble didn't know what that might be. Food? Slaves? Maybe their ship was fuelled by stone. "We could guess all day and still not be close," he said.

"So we don't knows shit, do we? As usual. All we cans do is work with what we know. Which is, we needs fuel and we needs to get them damn contracts signed. So nothing has changed, really."

"Except we try to do things quiet," Flint said.

"Except that," Scree agreed. "We's trolls. We should be good at that, right?"

Keeble laughed.

"Hurgon are gathering in the gateway," Tuki said as he zoomed in with a camera.

A gate in the compound wall had opened and a score of nervous looking hurgon were milling about in the stuttering yellow light offered by the lamps on the walls. It looked as if they were waiting for someone to make the first move. Keeble guessed that someone would be Scree.

"Come on," the troll said. "Let's get organized."

55: Before Breakfast

KEEBLE STOOD NEAR THE BACK of the group while all the introductions were done. He doubted his name was mentioned. Or most of the others. The Mother and Father of the compound wanted to have everyone arrested so they could be turned over to a Great Family. Then Koli gave them some codes and showed them the contract that needed to be signed. After that, as far as Keeble could tell, they were keen to help in any way they could. It probably made things a lot easier for the locals.

But could they help?

He stood quietly in the fitful light of the wall lamps and scratched at the ground with his boot. Just below the dust he found an old paving stone. It looked older than the compound. There was another beside it. An old road, maybe? Three and a half meters away, two bricks, edges worn away, poked their heads above the surface. So the compound had once been larger? He found it hard to believe that the population had dropped and the hurgon never seemed to move on...

Keeble sighed and turned his attention back to matters at hand. But Meledrin was still talking and waving her arms about as if it was the most important job in the world instead of something they had to get done so they could start the real job.

"What's going on?" he whispered to Suldon.

The elf kept one ear on the conversation and whispered a reply.

"Greetings have been exchanged. I think for a while the hurgon were wanting to find someone to write everything down so it could be signed."

Keeble wasn't sure if Suldon was serious, so said nothing.

"Now Meledrin is trying to establish just what assistance can be offered." A pause while Suldon listened. "There is a train station here, apparently, and a train that Meledrin and the brothers would be allowed to use. The journey to the Grandmother would take approximately four hours in each direction in normal circumstances. These, however, are not normal circumstances. As for our task..." Another pause. "Hydrogen is indeed used in this compound and is stored in underground chambers."

"Excellent. Should be done by breakfast then." It was the middle of the night, local time, but it was morning ship time and Keeble was ready to go.

"Perhaps not, Keeble. The gas is used for street lighting and several other functions but is not actually taken anywhere. There is no way to transport it, other than pipe work which has been in place underground for many years."

"Then we just make some more pipe."

"I dare say we will, but I don't imagine that will be something we can sort out *before breakfast*."

"Have some faith, Suldon. You're with dwarves now."

"I have *faith*, Keeble. What I don't have is some spare high pressure piping."

Keeble narrow his eyes. "Who have you been talking to? What do you know about gas work?"

Suldon shrugged his slim shoulders. "We have been in hyperspace for many hours and there are only so many books about fainting damsels and detectives and..." He waved a hand as if that explained all the other things he'd had to put up with. "There are many text books in the library as well, and in the engineering bay. And there are always dwarves willing to talk about such things for hours on end if one should be in the mood to listen."

"So you've been learning about gas work? Just in the off chance you might need to know?"

"I also learned of electricity, engines and physics." He sniffed and looked away for a moment. "To an extent. I must admit that gas works was one of the easier of the subjects I studied."

Keeble wound the gears on his hand. People astounded him every day and he wasn't sure he liked it. First there were dwarves working in the gardens and now this. Next thing you know there would be elves who could tell which end of a spanner was the business end and the difference between pishel and kalkal screwdrivers.

"And besides all that," Suldon concluded, "we might not have finished with all this talking before breakfast. I do believe the hurgon like formalities even more than elves."

"Huh. Never."

Ten minutes later Keeble was starting to think that Suldon might be right, on both counts, when Meledrin finally turned to look at Scree, who'd been standing waiting with the apparent patience of a mountain while the talk carried on around him.

"It is organized," Meledrin told him. "A train is being prepared at this moment and the foreman is on his way to the gas works."

Scree nodded. "Right. Goods. You lot know what you're about then so I'll get back to the ship and leaves you to it."

"You do not want to—"

"Nope. I'm hungry." Scree sniffed and scratched his crotch. "Flint's your second in command, Meledrin. Keeble..." Scree examined the group that would be working with him. "Gulch's your second, I suppose. Or Suldon. Whoever. Ask someone if there's any problems. And don't take too bloody long."

"Scree?"

"Tuki?" The troll looked around. Keeble did too and found the moai standing at the rear of the group. "What you doing heres?"

Tuki ducked his head. But quickly looked up again. "I was hoping to go with Meledrin."

"Why?"

Keeble thought Scree sounded incredulous and could understand why. Then he looked at the others who'd be accompanying the elf and understood. Ruby had been added to Blue Troop to bolster numbers for the mission. Scree worked it out as well but said nothing for the moment.

"Inaki knows all that needs to be known to work the skyglass," Tuki said.

"You can't go anyway. There's no reason to takes the risk."

And with that he turned and left.

"Right," Keeble said. Where Tuki went didn't concern him. He rubbed his hands together. "Right. Where's the gas works then?"

Cuto spoke to one of the locals then waved for him to follow. The fuel finding crew set off following one of the Mother's guards. There was Keeble's work gang— Milo, Ari and Dogar— plus Peak, Gulch and Suldon. More might be required at some stage but for the initial stages of the operation that would be more than enough. Though, if any trouble came it would take more than a two trolls to sort it out. Keeble looked up at the sky and the streaks of light from the multeese landing craft.

The wall of the compound was just short of two meters thick and beyond was a narrow warren of streets, some of which might never have seen the light of day. The buildings, crowding close, seemed newer here than on Hulgorn but were no better maintained. Chips had been taken from corners. Windows and doors had dried and cracked in the dry local air. The streets looked like they hadn't been repaired in decades.

"They just don't care, do they?" Dogar said from the middle of the group.

"They care," Peak replied, "they just care about other things." And it seemed the troll wasn't totally against their way of thinking. He ducked as they went through a low archway into a narrow alley that looked pretty much like the one they'd just left. His one eye blinked slowly as he looked around. "This is just stuff. Won't talk to you. Won't rut with you... Sorry Ari." He shrugged. "Don't mean much in the end."

The gas works was in the middle of the compound which, as far as Keeble was concerned, showed just how much the hurgon had to learn. The stone building was big and square and in need of repair. He hadn't expected otherwise. Big double doors, bolted together like the hurgon armor, opened up into an entrance hall 5.4

meters to a side. There was a mangled piece of machinery in the middle, testament to just how dangerous this sort of work could be.

"What does the plaque say?" Keeble asked Suldon. But reading hurgon was like learning a whole new language and even the elves were struggling with it. Suldon shook his head and asked Cuto.

"According to Cuto the plaque states, *For the P'targa lives lost beneath the marching feet of progress. The Haghar Chamber explosion. A sad end. A new beginning.* And then a date from thousands of years ago."

Keeble shook his head but someone else beat him to the punch line.

"There's a huge explosion in the first gas works, so they go and build the replacement in the middle of the city?" Milo said. "As dumb as elves..."

It was an old saying than had never offended anyone in the past. Nobody who'd heard it anyway. Milo cleared his throat and turned to examine the rest of the room.

There were three doors other than the one through which they'd entered. Around the far side of the memorial was a studded metal twin to the entrance door. To either side were smaller timber constructions, both open and showing offices beyond. A hurgon came from the one on the left talking quickly and waving his arms. Keeble could follow a lot of it but waited for Suldon to translate anyway, just in case.

"This is the foreman, Tasu. Tasu offers greetings and hope we can all work well together."

As Keeble listened it took him a moment to realize Suldon was paraphrasing. He narrowed his eyes, trying to see if there was a joke that he hadn't been let in on. "Right," he said eventually. "Sounds good. Cuto said something nice in reply, did he?"

"Yes, of course."

"Good, then let's get started."

"There is some type of contract to be signed first."

56: Different Paths

TUKI WATCHED AS SCREE WALKED AWAY. Then he turned and watched as Meledrin walked the other direction, through the gate, with Ruby guarding her side. They turned towards the north. When Tuki looked around a few seconds later he discovered he was all alone. Keeble and his work party were moving through the gate as well and Scree had disappeared long ago.

Scree is right, Tuki thought. *There is nothing I can do to assist Meledrin.* He looked around. *But there is nothing I can do while the ship is sitting on the ground.* After a moment of indecision he quickly followed Meledrin.

He looked over his shoulder as he moved beyond the wall. The guards watched but didn't try to stop him. Once inside the compound he paused again. But his companions were already out of view so he didn't have time. He hurried northwards, following the sound of Topper and the other dwarves as they filled the hissing, clattering silence with their voices. Not far along, he came to a small open space with the stone walls towering over his head on all sides. It made him nervous but the way ahead was obvious. Two of the exits were narrow passages, barely wide enough for Tuki to walk through. He would have to duck to avoid hitting his head on the lintels. The other passage, to the left, was a couple of meters across. He hurried on, glancing up at the sky. But when he reached the next intersection he had no idea where he should go next. He stood and looked one direction then the next. There were five choices available and nothing to help. He stood in the intersection, looking one direction and the next, spinning until he had to stop and think where it was he'd come from in the first place. And still he didn't know.

He was ready to turn around and go back to the ship when he saw a hurgon hiding in a doorway just down one of the streets. He drew in a deep breath and walked slowly forward. The alien backed further into the shadows. But once Tuki stopped he wasn't quite sure what to say.

"This one's name is Tuki."

The hurgon grunted. It was sweating and looked very uncomfortable.

"Tuki is looking for the train." He didn't even know what a train was, but he was sure that was the hand signal Meledrin had used.

"Tuki is hakan?"

"Yes."

"Is it true the hakans are signing a treaty with Grandmother Donni?"

"Yes."

"Hiklo will show Tuki to the train."

Tuki followed the hurgon as it made its way slowly down the street. It was limping, holding its stomach. The sweat dripping from its nose and elbow, chin and fingers, was like the patter of tiny footsteps in the stillness of the lane. They passed two more hurgon as they walked and both looked in as much distress as Hiklo. Others in the same predicament leaned from narrow windows overhead to watch them pass.

Tuki started to worry that there was a sickness spreading through the compound. He remembered what he had been told when he first travelled through the Ohoga Gate to Earth. Perhaps it would be a minor illness to the locals but deadly to the hakans. Or perhaps it was the hakans who had brought illness to the hurgon. He tapped the alien on the shoulder. *"Is Hiklo unwell?"*

"What does Tuki mean?" Hiklo did not stop walking and Tuki was having trouble reading the 'ini rituals correctly.

"Many hurgon here look unwell."

Hiklo gave an alien nod. *"This is the* hukarth *region of the compound."*

"Tuki does not know what that means."

"All hurgon here have chosen to be either symbo or givtar. Hurgon here are changing in preparation for the seeding."

Tuki didn't know what that meant either. *"What is symbo and givtar?"*

Hiklo stopped walking. *"Symbo are hurgon who choose to carry eggs and then care for the hatchlings. Givtar fertilize the eggs and provide nutrients for the hatchlings until they are old enough to eat properly. Both are grave responsibilities."*

"This is how hurgon have..." Tuki knew of no word for children. *"How hurgon breed?"*

"Correct. How do hakans breed?"

"Ummm..." Tuki blushed. Ruby had told him the purpose of sex but that wasn't really what Hiklo wanted to know anyway. *"Hakans cannot choose. Hakans are born Symbo or Givtar and remain that way for life."*

"Hiklo does not believe. How do hakans get anything done?"

"Well..."

"Though, perhaps, it is obvious. If hakans are constantly at war amongst hakans, why would hakans not be at war with others?"

Tuki did not think the hurgons were in a position to judge hakans— they had not made contact for many years after all— but he said nothing about that. *"Kim says that it is the diversity that hakans face in life that gives hakans strength. Perhaps it is also the diversity of the people that helps."*

"There is strength in stability."

"There is," Tuki agreed. *"Mountains are very stable, but mountains do not progress or advance. Mountains simply wear away."* Hiklo turned to look and Tuki was worried he had offended the alien. *"Must all hurgon choose?"* he asked, stumbling over the ini signals in his haste.

Hiklo paused. *"All hurgon must make a choice, though hurgon may choose to stay* yektil.*"* The hurgon said the last as if that was hardly a choice at all. This was confirmed a moment later. *"No hurgon remain* yektil, *especially now when hatchlings are required more than ever."*

"What happens if the war ends soon? Will there not be too many hatchlings?"

"The war will not end soon," Hiklo said. *"The Great Families do not want it to end."*

"The treaty Grandmother Donni is to sign could help end the war."

Hiklo gave a hurgon shrug. *"Hiklo will do what is best for the P'targa. Grandmother Donni will let Hiklo and all others know."*

-oOo-

Keeble sighed. Of course there was a contract. "What's it about? How much is it going to cost?"

"It will not cost us anything. It is more for their safety. We won't be using the gas in any way that goes against the interest of the P'targa. We won't be using it against the hurgon in general. And we won't sue if there are any problems."

"But you still can't read well enough to sign anything."

"What about Cuto?"

Keeble narrowed his eyes again and looked at the alien. "Do we trust him?"

Suldon turned to look as well. The elf nodded. "The greatest thing in any hurgon's life is family. Cuto gave that up for Scree and Kim, for all of us, believing that the T'loop family had behaved in a terrible manner. We are Cuto's family now."

"Are you sure?"

"Am I sure we are Cuto's family? No. I am unsure exactly how Cuto feels about us. Am I sure we can trust Cuto? Yes."

"Get him to read the contract then. Just be quick about it."

Keeble didn't know whether Suldon didn't pass on the message but either way it took well over an hour of haggling before Cuto was willing to sign the twenty-page document. The alien didn't appear to be happy about the outcome but Keeble really didn't care.

Eventually, Keeble and his work gang were shown to the plant room.

"Big bugger," Milo said.

Ari scratched her head. "But what does it do, exactly?" There was a hard cast on her broken arm but whatever drugs Thorpe had given her seemed to have taken away any pain.

Keeble couldn't answer her question. He asked Cuto who asked the foreman.

Suldon translated the reply. "There is a lake on the far side of the compound. Water is brought in here and a machine uses electricity to separate the hydrogen from the oxygen. The oxygen is released and the hydrogen is stored for later use."

"Right," said Dogar. "Electrolysis."

Ari shook her head. "But what do they do with the hydrogen?"

Keeble wasn't sure about that either.

"It can be used as a shielding gas for welding," Milo suggested.

"That's a lot of welding," Ari said.

"And it could be a reducing agent for smelting," Milo added.

Ari wrinkled her nose. "How much mining do they do around here?"

"Well I don't know," Milo said, obviously offended. "Why don't you ask?"

Keeble listened as Suldon did the asking. He also watched the ini' rituals as Tasu replied. He was pretty sure he understood most of them but just because he understood the words didn't mean he understood what was going on. "They don't know what the gas is for?"

Suldon nodded. "That is correct. There is a large refinery or factory in this compound that was constructed under supervision of the En'kumo family but it has never been used and the P'targa have not been told of its purpose."

"That's what I thought he said." It was all a bit strange, but in the end didn't concern him so he set about trying to get some information that *would* help.

But the details didn't help at all. That one factory, about a kilometer from the *Hakahei,* used the gas for purposes unknown. And the streets and buildings were lit with hydrogen lamps, but such a tiny trickle of gas was required that all except the main pipes were about the size of drinking straws. And that was that.

"What about the hydrogen collecting vehicle on the ship?" Milo asked. "Surely that's made for the job."

Gulch shook his head. "It ain't made for flying on planets. No chance, hey, unless you carries it around in something else."

"Can we do that? Carry it around, I mean?"

Gulch shrugged. "You tell me. I just point stuff in the right direction and tell it to go. And I can barely do that half the time, hey. I don't know what can carry what."

Keeble gave it some thought but decided it probably wouldn't work unless the hurgon had a vehicle that could do the job. The Lander wouldn't be powerful enough and it would take a couple of days to get everything ready to go anyway.

"We'll get someone to check with the hurgon about a vehicle, and in the meantime we'll work on the pipes," Keeble said eventually.

"Find a nice big main line," Dogar agreed. "Tap into that and we're set."

Tasu found a map so they could have a look.

Ari tried to scratch her broken arm as she examined the old, faded sheet of paper. "That is going to be twelve hundred meters, at least."

If they could go in a straight line it would be much easier.

"Can they supply enough pipe?"

"Who the hell knows?"

Keeble took the map with him.

57: Taramin's Blue

TUKI WONDERED WHAT IT WOULD BE like to live life without having to make any choices. He would not have been where he was, following a strange hurgon through the compound in pursuit of Ruby. And he would not be dreading what Scree would say when he returned.

He followed the hurgon, ducking through a low door and into a huge, dim bunkhouse. *"The hakans went this way?"*

"No. This way is quicker."

"Tuki thanks Hiklo." Though the hurgon's slow pace made Tuki wonder if they would ever reach the train at all.

The room was full of two dozen groans and moans that echoed back and back again to merge into something quite different. Though all the hurgon seemed to be in pain, sweating and squirming, they also seemed to be content with their misery, like Tuki felt after a long day of running.

"How long does this last?" he asked Hiklo.

"Several days. Changing back is painful but ends almost instantly."

"Must you change back?"

Hiklo stopped for a moment to think. *"Possibly not. Hiklo does not know if permanence has ever been attempted."*

"And how often does seeding occur?"

"It happens approximately once a century."

Tuki shook his head. The whole process seemed very strange to him but the whole idea of *hakan* sex still seemed very strange too.

There were many things he wanted to ask, but they came to another door and went through to a wide street with gas lamps flickering on the walls. A strip of star-speckled sky was barely visible through the glare.

"The train is in that building there," Hiklo said. *"The large door will take Tuki to Tuki's companions."*

Tuki nodded. *"Is there..."* He looked around. *"Is there another door Tuki can use?"*

Tuki thought Hiklo would comment on the odd request, but perhaps it was not possible for the alien to believe Tuki would do anything other than what was best for his family. So they went to a small door twenty meters from the larger one and went through into a storeroom. There was only one other exit.

"The train is through there?"

"Yes."

"Tuki thanks Hiklo."

"Tuki is welcome."

Tuki stood silently for a moment, hoping Hiklo would leave immediately, but the alien stayed put. So Tuki cleared his throat and opened the door a crack to peer out. He was just in time to see Palsamon and Ruby, the last of the hakans, climbing onto the train. So he glanced back at Hiklo, opened the door the rest of the way and slipped out onto the platform. He moved to his right and hid in the shadows beside a pile of large wooden crates. He was still standing there a few minutes later, wondering what he should do. A jet of steam hissed out from under the train and he jumped. Then the train lurched and, heart pounding, Tuki rushed forward. He went to the carriage behind the one his friends had used and tried the door. It opened easily and he jumped on just as the train started to move. Thankfully, there was nobody inside, just more wooden boxes.

It wasn't until a minute later, with the train moving between high, crowding walls, that Tuki wondered what he was doing.

-oOo-

Meledrin watched silently as the train pulled into the station, a long stream of smoke rising to fill the top half of the chamber. She had seen a chimney up there prior to the machine's arrival but as far as she could ascertain it was completely ineffective.

"Must we wait for much longer, do you think?" she asked Palsamon. They had been waiting for some time already. She thought it might almost be midnight. She should not have been surprised— the hurgon idea of time had already been witnessed.

The smoke was stinging her eyes and she also wished to be away from the confines of the compound. Hulgorn had made her feel trapped but the twisting, narrow streets of this compound, surrounded as it was by vast expanses of open land, was even worse.

Palsamon shrugged. "I do not know. I suspect they may need to take on fuel but I cannot be sure. And I am unsure how long that might take anyway."

Of course he could not know. He had been reading books from the library on the *Hakahei* voraciously, arguing and discussing the contents with Suldon and anyone else they could find, but the fifty thousand year old technology mentioned in the books were unlikely to relate in any way to what the hurgon used. Some of the dwarves might well know.

Topper and his work gang were waiting not far away. They were showing no interest at all in the train so they knew what it was and how it worked. That was reassuring, if nothing else. Meledrin was about to ask for details, though she knew most of them would be beyond her understanding anyway, but she was saved that slight indignity when they were motioned into a carriage by their escort. And almost before they had sat down the train sent out another belch of steam and lurched into motion.

Meledrin waved a *Beginning* as the train slowly gathered speed, moving between stone walls that were almost within reach outside the windows. The sound was terrible. The clatter of the wheels on the iron rails and the rhythmic thunder of the engine echoed and grew. Meledrin was unsure if the build up of pressure was entirely in her imagination or was actually happening.

Then they burst into the clear and the light of the falling multeese landers in the sky seemed to bring an early dawn. She blinked against the light and tried to calm her breathing. She waved a *Changing* but it did not help.

"How do we find ourselves here, Palsamon?" she asked after sitting for some time watching the walls of the narrow valley passing by outside the windows. And all around, like a storm of meteors, the multeese landing craft continued to fall. There seemed to be thousands, though there were probably nothing like those numbers. "At what point did we make the choice to be in this place?"

Palsamon was staring out the window as well, watching the multeese. "Every moment has brought us here," he said eventually. "Every choice we made from birth."

"You believe it was destiny?"

He laughed. "No. The opposite, I think. Every tiny choice we make has ramifications we cannot possibly know. Every moment and every choice matters."

Keeble had been the catalyst, really. If Meledrin had let him be cast out to die, as seemed to be the sensible option when she now gave the matter thought, he would not have been there to attack the Ohoga Tree and Meledrin would have died with most of the elves in Grovely. Sensible did not mean right. "Was it worth it?"

"Yes. We are more now than we ever were previously."

A landing craft was almost coming straight towards them, growing huge, seeming to fill the sky. The sound of its engines was astounding. It was a throbbing hum that filled her head as if it were a solid thing. Meledrin almost thought she could feel her head swelling with the physicality of it. The craft was huge, as Tuki had said though the numbers could never describe it accurately. It touched down in a cloud of dust not a kilometer from the train, just over the top of a small hill. And the train continued to race along the track like a herd of frightened horses.

"There is another compound over there," Brother Koli signed.

Meledrin nodded. What more could she do?

"How the hell do we fight *that*?" Topper asked. "Just that, I mean. Not even the mothership."

"There'll be a way," Flint said. The troll was sitting just behind Meledrin, as if he had appointed himself her shadow. "You just do your job, let other people do theirs."

"And it's your job to fight the multeese?" Nina asked.

Flint shrugged. "It's my job to do what I'm told."

"That's it?"

"Close enough. Course, if I've got any ideas, it's my job to pass them on as well. But it ain't my job to worry about it."

"So what's *our* job, exactly?" Topper asked.

Cliff scratched at the scar on his neck. "Right now, it's our job t' help get Meledrin and the brothers t' the Grandmother and back t' the ship."

"Sounds easy," Hoodek muttered.

But the trolls had settled down again to watch and the conversation died away. Meledrin didn't mind. She watched the rain of fire outside, trying to see the beauty and not the evil that was behind it.

A few minutes passed silently, except for the rattling of the train along the iron tracks. Eventually, Flint stood up and walked along the length of the carriage to the rear. Their escort, half a dozen bored looking hurgon in P'targa uniforms, watched as he went but they did not seem inclined to stop him. He reached the door and rattled the handle.

"Flint, I do not think—"

But the troll looked at the handle for a moment, found a lock and undid it. When he pulled the door open the P'targa stirred but said nothing.

Meledrin could see a small gap to the next carriage. Flint jumped across to a small landing. Once he had the second door open he stuck his head in, said something, then returned to his seat. Meledrin thought it all very strange until Tuki came into view a moment later. It took him a moment to work up the courage to jump across the gap, then he stood near the door, rubbing at the meteor tattoo on the back of his hand.

"We ain't sending you home, Tuki," Flint said as he tried to get comfortable on the wooden seat.

Finally, the moai moved forward. He looked at the seat beside Ruby, which was occupied by Nina, then sat down in the row behind.

"What are you doing here, Tuki?" Meledrin asked, though it was obvious enough. The lad did not bother answering anyway. "Does Scree know of this, Flint?"

"Course. Told him before the train left the station."

"And he does not mind?"

The troll shrugged. "Don't make that much difference. He ain't happy that Tuki didn't listen but he'll deal with that when we get back."

Meledrin saw Tuki swallow nervously and decided she did not want to be a part of that conversation either.

"Well, Tuki, now that you have your wish and are coming with us, I trust you will be more mindful of any orders you receive."

He nodded but didn't say anything. And Meledrin decided there wasn't a lot more she could say either, so she sat back and returned her attention to watch as the spectacular light show drew to a close.

"Do you remember that night long ago," Palsamon said quietly.

Meledrin turned to look at him.

"It was not long after I first went to your cabin. We went out after midnight, looking for sepamil flowers and—"

Meledrin smiled and nodded. "Yes." Then she blushed for she had interrupted. She carried on anyway. "There were hundreds of shooting stars. We lay on top of Taramin's Blue to watch."

Palsamon smiled as well. "I think that was the night I decided I loved you."

Meledrin returned her attention to the darkness outside the window. She pushed hair away from her face and tried to remember how she had felt on that night long ago. But she could remember nothing beyond the lights in the sky overhead.

The train plunged into a forest and started climbing towards the mountains. Meledrin sat back and closed her eyes.

58: A Small Group

SCREE SCANNED HIS SCREEN. There were a whole heap of multeese landing craft visible and a lot of those seemed to have landed within a couple of kilometers of the *Hakahei.* Maybe being quiet wasn't going to help. Maybe they'd already been spotted. He found that hard to believe though. He thought if they'd already been spotted they'd already be dead.

"Hey, boss, what we got?" Gulch was leaning in the doorway, packet of muesli in hand.

Scree shrugged. "I gots no idea." He leaned back in the chair. "One thing I thought earlier... We was wondering if the multeese were bringing down a huge army or if they was taking something back up to their ships. Well, what if they's huge. What if there's only one of thems squeezed into each of the ships?"

Gulch shrugged as well and scratched at his red hair with the stub of a finger. "Does it make any difference?"

"Maybe."

"Then, hey, let's go have a look."

Scree smiled. That was the type of plan Kim was likely to hate, but she still wasn't awake so she couldn't complain. "I suppose you wants to come?"

Gulch smiled.

"A small group, I reckons." They didn't have a lot of choice. They had to leave enough people behind to make sure the ship was safe. Scree called the senior marines to the office and, while he waited, picked up the food he'd forgotten about half an hour ago. It was past midnight local time, but that meant nothing to him.

"How far to the closest one, hey?" Gulch went to the desk to have a look at the images on the monitor.

The closest ship was barely two kilometers away. It had come down near the edge of the last of the fields and was now sitting silently, giving off waves of heat.

"Won't take long, hey."

Scree laughed around a mouthful of food. "Could be fighting our ways through an army of multeese in ten minutes, but no, won't takes long."

"They might be big, like you says. But, hey, maybe they're the size of rabbits too. Or maybe they has them huge ships cause everything else is little."

"So we should fights naked then, just to make them feel even worse?"

Gulch smiled. "Maybe me, hey, but Stone wouldn't impress anyone."

Stone stopped in the doorway. "You confused, Gulch. You just got small hands and I got big hands, you stupid bastard." He smiled as well. "Biggest hands you've ever seen."

"They must be huge, hey."

Stone went to stand by the desk as well. "You got a plan, Scree?"

"Well, Gulch suggested it, but it's the type of plan I like."

"This should be fun."

"Not so much funs for you, maybe."

"So I'm baby-sitting the ship? Burning cats, that'd be right."

"It was Gulch's idea."

"Who cares?"

Thorpe, Tim McCree, Chasm, Pool and Shardy all arrived together. Thorpe removed his red beret and took a seat, the others stayed on their feet.

"We're going for a frontal assault," Scree said, just to see how they reacted. Thorpe obviously thought it was a terrible idea but knew Scree wasn't completely serious. Tim didn't show anything and the trolls all liked the idea.

"What we got?"

"That's just it." Scree sighed. "We gots no idea. I'm going to go with Yellow Troop and have a look. There's one of the ships close by.

Tim looked at the monitor. "There are five of them close by."

"Aye." Pool leaned in closer to look as well. "Looks like they concentrated around our area."

"I'm not so sure," Thorpe said. "Are they focused on us, or the compound? Look over here." He pointed to another compound about halfway around the side of the world. "There's five around that compound as well."

It was obvious really. Scree nodded. "So we need to find out what's special about those compounds, then we might know where to starts."

"Exactly."

When Scree spoke to the bridge in his mind Tami replied and few minutes later, Bethalin arrived.

"You wished to speak with an elf, Scree?"

"Yeah, Beth. We needs to talk with one of the locals. We want some information about the compounds arounds about here."

"Very well. I shall see if I can find a hurgon who can assist."

"Right. Chip and Crystal'll meet you in the hold. They can tell you what questions we need answered." He looked at the computer. "Now, how does I get the computer to draw this picture for me?" He'd seen Keeble do it.

When Beth had gone, Scree turned back to his computer.

"So, no re-con mission," Thorpe said. "We'll have problems pretty soon anyway."

"How you figure that?"

"They're obviously going to attack all the compounds. And this one is more important than most of the others, for whatever reason."

Scree swore.

Chasm nodded slowly. "Chasm thinks we need to organize some defense. And quickly."

-oOo-

Keeble sighed. Of course they couldn't supply enough pipe.

He looked up at the racks in the storehouse and tried to calculate.

"Two hundred meters of the larger sized piping," Suldon said.

Keeble turned to look at him. "You're an expert on logistics now?" He shook his head. "That's just wonderful. I'll head back to the ship and leave you in charge, shall I?"

"He's right, Keeble," Milo said. "Well, I make it about one hundred and ninety." He shrugged. "But, you know."

Keeble looked at Suldon again. "Two hundred meters?"

Suldon nodded. "It says here." The elf held out a clipboard with a sheet of rough, ragged-edged paper on it.

"You *read* it? Give me that." He snatched the clipboard away.

"It is written in hurgon. I am unsure if it will do you any good."

And of course it didn't. "You can suddenly read hurgon? You couldn't back at the gas works."

"Numbers are relatively simple. There are not all that many of them, after all."

Keeble shook his head. "Two hundred meters? Where's the factory?"

It was Cuto who answered, using the ini rituals and no words. *"The pipes are manufactured in this compound, but only on a small scale. The plants are often left dormant."*

"How long to get them working?"

Cuto asked Tusa. *"Eight hours."*

That was better than he'd been expecting. But he guessed that was only half the problem. *"And how long to manufacture 800 meters of piping?"*

"Seven days."

Milo and the other dwarves groaned but Keeble had been expecting as much. And they only needed 800 meters of pipe if they could go in a straight line.

Cuto was signing some more. *"That might be halved if quality is not an issue."*

Normally the thought of doing a job half properly would have horrified Keeble but they didn't have that much time and the pipes only had to last for a couple of hours. He sighed. "Come on then, let's go see the plant. Maybe we can get it going quicker ourselves."

59: Peripheral Matters

"WE HAVE ALMOST STOPPED," Meledrin said. It was obvious and did not require pointing out, but she felt better having done it anyway. She examined the trees beyond the window.

Topper nodded. "This train hasn't got a lot of power. I'm not sure if something's wrong or this is just the way it is."

"Should you go to discover if there is a problem?"

The dwarf shrugged. "This lot here could probably tell us if this is normal," he said, indicating their silent hurgon escort. "What would I do anyway? It looks like we're getting close to the top of the hill so let's wait and see."

Meledrin nodded. "Very well."

She was about to resume her seat when she looked out the other window. Back near where they had started their journey, there were dozens of islands of light. The soft glow of the hurgon compounds contrasted clearly with the harsh white glare thrown by the alien landing craft.

"There are more ships than hurgon compounds," Meledrin said. "How can we hope to survive?"

Flint crossed to stand beside her. He had probably been examining the scene for some time. "We don't hope," he said, smoothing down his moustache. "Hope is for people who are sitting back waiting for others to do what needs to be done." He sniffed. "We don't hope. We plan and we think and we *do*."

"Then what do we *do*?"

"We're already doing it."

"But it seems to me that we are concentrating on peripheral matters."

"This is war, Mel. Most battles don't look important, until you realize they are. Or the other way around. You don't study the war until it's over."

"So we assume that what we are doing is of vital importance?"

"Yep."

"And if it is not? If we are wasting our time?"

"Then we try to waste the enemy's time as well."

The worldview of the trolls surprised Meledrin every time she conversed with one though each time she told herself not to be fooled by their blunt, simple exteriors. She regularly underestimated them, even Scree and Flint who were more intelligent than the others. The harsh lives they had lived left no room for affectation and they may well not live long enough to have second thoughts.

Meledrin returned to her seat. "How old are you, Flint?"

The troll looked a bit confused. "Not exactly sure. Seen about 30 summers, I think. Why?"

"You seem much older."

"Huh." He sat down as well. "I reckon a troll year might be longer than an elf year."

"I do not mean you look old. I mean—"

"I know what you mean, Mel. You lived in a nice cool forest with all your friends and the most you had to worry about was... Well, did you ever worry about anything?"

"We..." Meledrin looked the troll up and down and decided the concerns of her life in Grovely would pass unnoticed in the life of a troll. "I suppose we did not have a great many concerns."

He smiled. "Yeah. But I reckon a day of running in the desert, or a day running from soldiers, ages you real quick. Physically and emotionally. And you know what, you spend all day running and fighting and hiding, you got a lot of time to think about other things." Flint leaned back and closed his eyes. "Most trolls ain't big fans of thinking, but most of the time they ain't got any choice."

"And what thoughts have you thought, in all your running?"

"Don't waste time."

"I am sorry, I—"

Flint shook his head. "No, that's what I was thinking. Get the things you want. Do the things that need to be done. Eat and love and sing while you got the chance, 'cause you don't know if you will ever get the chance again." He smiled. "Don't waste time with *peripheral matters*."

Meledrin glanced at Palsamon but didn't say anything more.

The train labored up the final gasp of slope and entered a narrow cutting. Then it topped the hill and immediately began to accelerate.

"There we go," said Topper. "The worst part is over."

Meledrin was not so sure. "There seemed to be more of the multeese craft on this side than on the other. There are so many."

-oOo-

Keeble led his work crew down a narrow walkway between two machines. Hurgon were rushing around everywhere, stoking fires, oiling gears, adjusting wheels.

Every one of them was concentrating fiercely but still paused to watch the hakans go by. Then the activity broke out again, seemingly more urgent than before.

"Well?" Keeble asked, looking back.

Milo shook his head but Dogar nodded.

"I did some work in a foundry when I was younger. I reckon I could work this out if needed. Might be able to ask Makar too— he's had a bit to do with this kind of thing. I reckon the hurgon will be quicker though, either way."

"So what are *we* supposed to do then?" Milo asked. "Just stand around watching?"

Keeble wound the gears on his hand. Just the thought of standing around made his toes itch. "Let's see if we can help."

"I can thump some hurgon if them workin' too slow," Peak offered

Keeble laughed. "Not sure if that'd have the desired effect, Peak. I reckon the rest of the hurgon would head for the hills."

The troll shrugged. It probably didn't worry him either way— he'd just do what he was told.

Keeble looked around. Over the far side of the huge room hurgon were shoveling ingredients into barrows. "How about you and Gulch go over there and see if you can help with that. Maybe we can free up some skilled labor for elsewhere."

"Right."

The two trolls headed for the barrows, looking as if they meant business. Keeble imagined them pushing the aliens out of the way and going wild with the shovels. But when they arrived they waved their arms in the 'ini rituals— it didn't all make a lot of sense as far as Keeble could tell— then set to work once they'd deciphered the replies.

"Whistler, that could be interesting." Keeble looked around some more. "Looks like they're measuring over there." He pointed. "Ari, Milo, you two can handle that." They left to see what they could do. But there wasn't a lot else that looked like tasks anyone could complete.

"Let's go find out a bit more about the process," Dogar suggested.

"Right." *Of course.* If you don't know, ask. First thing every dwarf learnt on the job.

Keeble looked around and found the foreman. He was checking over some paperwork, talking to himself and making notes as he went. He wasn't looking happy.

"What's his problem, Suldon?"

Keeble didn't even bother trying to keep up with the hurgon's wild gesticulating.

"Uncle Habu is concerned about supplies, quotas and storage, not necessarily in that order. No production was scheduled for some time so raw materials are lacking and storage will be a concern when the job is completed."

Keeble thought about that for a second. "Couldn't give a stuff about the storage problems," he said, "but get a list of numbers for the quantities and the requirements translated for me."

"Very well." Suldon turned and spoke to the foreman for a minute. "This may take a little while he said eventually. "And I may need some assistance to work out what the ingredients actually are."

Keeble appointed Dogar and Cuto to be Suldon's assistants. "And is there someone who can show Dogar what some of these machines do. He might be able to speed them up or something." He wondered what they could get in return for showing the hurgon how to do things better. Or maybe that was all laid out in the contracts they were trying to get signed. Either way, the locals were probably going to learn a thing or two in the next few days.

Keeble looked around some more. There was nothing left there for him to do, as far as he could tell. Everyone seemed to be working as fast as they could. Although the only work they were really doing was getting ready to do the real work.

"I'm going back to the ship," he told Suldon. "Get Gulch or Peak to contact me if there's any problems."

On the way he stopped and looked up at the sky. It was well past midnight now and the multeese light show had finished, letting loose the stars again. Keeble breathed and tried to think. What was he missing? There was something he was overlooking. Pipe? Gas? "Whistler, it could be anything."

Connectors. That wasn't it, but he'd need them anyway. He started walking again, turning toward the storage facility so he could collect a couple of connectors for the end of the pipes.

-oOo-

Scree sat at the desk staring at the computer. There were too many things to think about. A few weeks ago all he had to think about was staying away from humans and finding one more meal. It was life and death stuff, but still not very complicated. Now it was fuel and contracts and the special compounds and trying to work out why the multeese suddenly didn't want to kill anyone.

"Why *don't* they wants to kill anyone?" It was just crazy. They were keen to do it every other time.

By the time Chip and Crystal got back from the compound, Scree was ready to get some sleep. The others had left a while ago, some to keep planning defenses, others to sleep. He could've used the radio, but they both came to the office and stood in the doorway.

"What we got?" Scree asked.

"We show the Mother a map," Crystal said, "and it took took about 2 seconds for her to work it out."

"And?"

"The only only thing all them places got got in common is some type of special factory."

"What sort of factory?"

Chip shrugged. "Mother don't know."

"She don't know? Ain't she in charge of the compound?"

"Kinda. But En'kumo tells P'targa what to do. And T'loop tell En'kumo what to do."

Scree grunted. "Bloody stupid peoples. This whole thing is stupid. I need to sleep."

"Get a dwarf to go look look."

Chip nodded. "Any of dwarves will think it's a great game."

"Good idea."

Scree followed the trolls to the elevator but when the others got off at Level 2 he continued all the way down to the Engineering Bay.

60: Too Far, Too Many

KEEBLE SAT DOWN at the second desk in the Engineering Office— the largest was Ping's— and examined the map. He used a pen to draw the position of the ship, making a mark eleven and a half meters from the wall. Then he examined the position of the gas works and the main pipelines radiating out from there. The closest any pipe came was seven hundred and seventy meters in a straight line. He spent ten minutes calculating different routes, winding through the narrow streets, and the best he could come up with was 1195 meters. It was too far. He went back and calculated again but couldn't improve on it.

"Damn." Keeble threw down his pen. That was going to take too long. But of course, it all depended on how long Meledrin took. As long as the fuel was in before she got back... He rubbed at his eyes and leaned back in his chair.

The longer he sat looking at the map, the more annoyed he was going to get, so he turned to the computer and examined the fuel tanks and the piping and the still, trying to work out how to get the pipes into the ship. The only options were the inlet valves but they were on the far side of the ship, adding an extra fifty-five meters to the length. He sighed, tapping his metal arm on the side of the desk.

Five minutes later, Keeble was still examining the schematics as if something might magically change. He was relieved when someone walked in the door.

"Scree, what can I do for you?" he said. "Please, let there be something for me to do."

"Having fun?"

"Of course. We're going to need nearly 1200 meters of pipe to weave through the damn streets. And there's only 200 meters in the warehouse." He pulled the map across to show him.

Scree grunted. "Take a while to make all that pipe?"

"In Tab Cavern we could have it done in about two days. Here it will be about a week, apparently."

Scree grunted again and looked at the map. "How high is them buildings?"

Keeble shrugged. "I think most of them are three stories high. Why?"

"Go over the roofs then."

Keeble looked at the map. He looked at Scree. He looked back at the map. "You may well be a genius. Have you been tested?"

"Whats?"

"Don't worry. I've got to go and..." But everyone was either sleeping or working. It could wait until morning. "Wait, you wanted me for something?"

"There's some types of factory here that the P'targa don't knows anything about."

"Yeah, it's the main factory, the one that uses all the hydrogen."

"Well, we needs to know what it does."

"Why?"

Scree shrugged. "They's gots something to do with why the multeese is here."

"You're kidding?" He wound the gears on his hand. "You're not kidding. So, do we need to look *now*?"

"Don't think it'll matters. Morning will do fines."

"Right. Good. I've got to do some calculations then." He didn't even notice Scree leaving the room.

-oOo-

Tuki looked up when the train came to a halt. Flint and Cliff were standing near the front of the carriage, leaning out the window to look in to the first hints of the morning. Ruby fell silent and watched as well.

"Don't look too bad from here," Flint said.

"Doesn't look like a whole army. Not from here. And they don't look much bigger than us. But there was a lot o' the landers," Cliff replied.

"Eight," Tuki told him.

"Eight?" Bones asked from his spot on the other side. "That's a lot. Them ships are big so it sounds like a lot to me." He turned to Quartz. "Sounds like a lot."

Cliff glanced at Bones then turned to Tuki. "You sure? Looked like more than that."

"I counted them when we were up higher." But Cliff was right— it had looked like there were a lot more than eight. In the night, the landers and the compounds were the only things that could be seen. And if they had all been full of people…

Flint nodded. "Eight's enough. If this is where Grandma Donni is, then stands to reason they'd concentrate the attack here."

"Not necessarily," Meledrin offered. "From the small amount we know of the situation I do not believe the multeese are concerned one way or the other about the Grandmother."

"I suppose this place is probably bigger than the other compounds?" Cliff said.

"Don't make much difference. Just got to get through them multeese to get to the compound. So, I say we listen to the great military mind we know as Keeble."

Tuki didn't know if Flint was serious. Meledrin obviously couldn't believe he was. "I beg your pardon?" the elf asked.

Flint smiled some more. "Keeble. He likes simple plans. Let's just go as fast as we can, drive this train right through them."

Tuki wasn't sure if that would work but he hardly thought it was his place to say.

Beside him, Ruby was shaking her head. "This is a bloody big target and it ain't as if we can duck and weave. They couldn't possibly miss."

"Maybe," Flint admitted. "But what're they gonna hit us with?" He gestured to the gun he'd left on his seat. "We could fire them things at the train all day and not do any good."

Topper interrupted. "Or you could get one lucky shot and blow the whole thing up."

"Really?"

Topper nodded. "Maybe. I don't know. At the very least we broke that weapon thing back on Hulgorn."

"And we already know they have better weapons than we do. Maybe they'll only need one shot."

"Any other suggestions then?"

"No."

"Anyone?"

Nobody said anything. Tuki didn't know that there were any other options. They could take the train or they could walk. And if they were taking the train, then the only thing they could control was the speed. That didn't mean he thought it was a good idea.

Flint turned to Meledrin. "You're in charge."

Meledrin looked from Flint to Palsamon and back. "I believe the plan sounds risky, Flint." She glanced at Palsamon again. "But if you can see no other alternative, then we obviously have no choice. We must get these contracts through as quickly as possible."

Tuki shifted on his seat and Cliff noticed. "What is it, Tuki?" he asked.

Tuki blushed. "It is as Meledrin says, we must get the contracts through, but if we die..."

"If we die then they won't get through at all," Ruby finished.

"And if we don't get there we die anyway," Flint said. "Maybe not today, but soon enough."

Meledrin nodded. "I shall inform the driver of the train of our desires. The decision may not be ours to make, ultimately."

She stood up but before she could move towards the door at the front of the carriage a hurgon came through the other way. Tuki watched the two of them wave their arms for a while with the brothers from Hulgorn watching on and adding their voices.

Eventually the hurgon turned and left and Meledrin resumed her seat. "Aunt Muti is not happy with our request but has been convinced. Muti suggests that we all find something to hold on to."

Tuki thought that sounded like a good idea but the seats were not much more than wooden boxes. They did not have safety belts like the seats on the *Hakahei.* They were not even attached to the floor. Apparently the trolls didn't want to sit anyway. They had all gone to stand by the windows so they could better see the action. Tuki looked around then went to the rear of the carriage to sit in the corner.

"Safer up the front, Tuki," Topper said. The dwarf was already heading in that direction. "If the train stops in a hurry you'll be thrown forward."

Tuki didn't care about the details. He trusted Topper, so he followed the dwarf and tried to find a spot amongst all the sensible people who were trying to find a safe place.

Amy smiled at him and moved aside slightly to make room. And as he sat down, Amy on one side and Nina on the other, Tuki wondered when he had become so comfortable around women. And how. Since leaving Danyon Ford he had discovered that women were less than he had been led to believe. But he turned to look at Ruby and knew that they were much more as well. They were people, and that was all. And every moment he spent with Ruby convinced him that men and women sharing their lives equally was the way it should be done, or at least the way he wanted it to be.

"How do you like taking orders from Kim?" Tuki asked Amy.

The American shrugged. "Not that much different to taking orders from the usual sources. She doesn't shout as much, I suppose. And it never really gets boring."

That was true. The Americans had been on the ship less time than Tuki and a lot had happened. There was always *something* happening.

"I think it might be nice to be bored occasionally."

Amy laughed. "I think I might be nearing that point myself, Tuki. Driving this train through the gauntlet doesn't strike me as a lot of fun."

"It is even better than that," Tuki said. "We don't even get to drive, we just sit here and hope."

"Don't remind me."

The train lurched into motion.

"Here we go."

They gathered speed and when they reached the valley floor the train was rattling and shaking as it raced along. Tuki knew they travelled much faster in the *Hakahei*, so much faster that is was really impossible to compare, but the train *seemed* to go much faster.

"Will we be able to stop?" Tuki asked.

Nobody answered.

He was about to ask again, though he supposed Aunt Muti knew what she was doing, when a window shattered and all the trolls dropped to the floor, almost as one.

"That was close," Bones said. A red welt marked his cheek. "Ouch. Did you see that? Huh. That hurt. It burned. A bit."

Quartz cleared her throat. "Maybe we should stay away from the windows for a while."

Flint raised his head just above the bottom of the window for another look. "You're no fun," he said. But he ducked back down and tried to get comfortable. "Don't think it's going to take long anyway."

More windows broke and Tuki covered his head with his arms. Glass rained down around him, catching the light like shooting stars, tinkling against the hard timber floor to become a new constellation. Strange marks, like burns, but not quite, appeared on the ceiling and the walls above the windows.

Soon, there were no windows left at all and glass covered the entire floor. The train thundered on, rattling and rolling, clattering noisily.

"Wish you'd stayed at home yet, Tuki?" Flint asked.

Tuki swallowed and shook his head. Ruby was smiling at the other end of the carriage.

Then the train lurched more than it had at any other time as it suddenly started to slow.

Bones risked another look out the window. "Not far, not far at all," he said. He cocked his head to one side. "Not sure if we'll stop in time." He sat back down and smiled. "This is fun. Lots of stuff happening. It's all happening. Maybe we should make Keeble the captain of the *Hakahei*. Now that would be fun."

Tuki thought that was a horrible idea, but he wasn't sure if the troll was serious.

Flint obviously didn't. "I think that would be a little too much fun, even for you, Bones."

61: Hallways

TUKI LEANED BACK AGAINST THE WALL, breathing deeply, as the train continued to slow. It still seemed to be going very fast when it plunged into the compound. Darkness engulfed them. The sound of the enemy weapons stopped suddenly but the sound of the train's passage seemed to double, triple, as the echoes came back from the thick stone walls. The screeching of brakes was like the cries of a hundred dragons.

Tuki got to his knees to look out the window and watched as they rushed through a brightly lit station. Then darkness again as the train continued to slow.

Finally, it stopped and the silence was a relief. Then a hiss of steam spurted out into the passage and the train started to go backwards. The journey back to the station seemed to take forever. Tuki sat silently and even the trolls seemed to feel the close crowding walls.

A few minutes later, light started to seep into the carriage again and Tuki breathed a sigh of relief.

Flint and Cliff went to look out the window. "That was easier than I thought," Flint said, straightening his uniform.

"Piece o' piss," Cliff agreed, scratching at the spot where his ear used to be. When the train stopped he opened the door. Half a dozen beams of energy hit him in the chest and he stumbled backwards. He fell to the floor and didn't move again.

Tuki gagged on the smell of burning flesh. He stood and stared until Ruby pulled him down to the floor. Everyone else was already taking cover while Flint quickly shut the door.

One of the hurgon Brothers said something. Meledrin was staring at Cliff's still form and didn't notice. The hurgon spoke again.

Tuki watched as Meledrin cleared her throat and visibly tried to collect her thoughts. "Brother Kalis..." She wiped a wisp of hair away from her face. "Ummm... Brother Kalis informs me that the guards waiting on the platform are not of the P'targa."

Flint grunted. "Really?"

"They are members of the En'kumo family."

"That doesn't tell us what their problem is."

"Why they shooting at us when there's a whole army of buggers out there?

Tuki tried not to look at Cliff and the hole that had been melted in the front of his EVA combat suit. "What do we do?" he asked, so quietly that he wasn't sure that anyone heard.

"Come on," Flint said.

Bones and Quartz had already opened a door on the far side of the carriage and were carefully looking out into the darkness of the tunnel.

"We gotta hurry," Flint said. He was herding the dwarves towards the door as he looked back over his shoulder.

"So we just run along the passage in the dark?" Tuki asked. It didn't sound like a lot of fun. And it didn't seem that it was a sound plan. "They'll know where we are going."

"Maybe," Flint said. But he turned to look at Topper. "You got a Song of Being, right?"

The dwarf nodded.

"What's with the wall out there?"

"It's just under a meter thick."

"Sing us through."

Topper nodded and started his Song. By the time Tuki climbed down to the ground half a minute later, last in line except for Bones and Quartz, the others had already climbed up into a refectory, much to the surprise of a dozen dining hurgon.

When he climbed up as well, Tuki nodded to the nearest alien and gave a greeting in the ini' rituals. The hurgon responded hesitantly.

But Tuki didn't notice anyway. His hands were covered in blood. There were dozens of pieces of glass in one. He hadn't noticed in all the confusion, but now the pain washed over him and all he could do was stare.

"Come on," Ruby grabbed his arm and pulled him towards the door on the far side of the room.

Flint nodded. "This gives us some time, but we don't want to waste it standing around here chatting."

Out in the hall, Ruby tugged Tuki's arm to make him stop. He looked around. Everyone else had stopped as well.

"What is our destination?" Meledrin asked.

Nobody answered for a moment.

Tuki turned to Flint. "Perhaps we should go back and chat with the hurgon in the refectory, to see if they can help." Ruby was working on his hands, gently picking out the pieces of glass. Tuki winced.

Flint grimaced. "Don't get smart with me, lad."

But Meledrin was already going back with Brother Koli to get some help. They emerged a couple of minutes later with what was obviously a reluctant guide and immediately headed down the hallway.

"What's happening around here?" Flint asked Meledrin.

The elf asked. "Apparently the En'kumo came yesterday and took over the compound. The action was not contested as the contracts stipulate that this can be done at any time. But the P'targa are starting to grow concerned as Grandmother Donni has not been seen since."

"The contract doesn't allow for that?"

"No. Family comes first, Flint. The contract exists for no reason other than to benefit both families. Any contract that threatens the Grandmother or any member of the P'targa family would not be allowed."

"But this guy don't know what's going on either?"

"Piko is unaware."

"Either way," Quartz said, "we got to find out where Donni is."

Tuki followed along silently, following close behind Ruby, trying to keep his eyes focused on where he was going, and not on his hands.

"Koli and I have explained the situation and Piko is concerned. Piko is leading us to the chambers where Grandmother Donni resides."

Flint nodded but did not look sure. "There's sure to be guards."

"If Donni's there at all," Dogar added. He was cleaning his teeth with his fingernail. "I'm not a troll but it doesn't seem like good strategy, for either side, for Donni to stay there."

Nina cleared her throat. "What are the rules of succession?" she asked. "What happens if Grandmother Donni has been killed?" She glanced at Piko as if the alien might understand.

"I do not know," Meledrin replied. "And I do not think now would be the best time to ask. Let us hope the question does not need to be answered."

Tuki looked at Piko as well, but the hurgon walked on, oblivious. Tuki wished he could do the same.

-oOo-

Meledrin glanced at Nina. She worried that, if Grandmother Donni had been killed as the dwife suggested, then all their efforts would have been for naught. Was the Grandfather on this world? Or would they have to take the brothers and all their contracts somewhere else? Back to Hulgorn, perhaps. Was the Grandfather next in line at all? She sighed. *We will just have to worry about that when the time comes.* She almost laughed at her repetition of Kim's favorite course of action. But she decided it was not necessarily a bad way to do things. She thought she might worry herself to a complete standstill were she to behave otherwise now.

Hurrying along the hall behind Piko, Meledrin tried to rein in her thoughts and concentrate. Despite her efforts she was surprised when Flint grasped the alien's arm and pulled it away from a cross passage. The troll leaned around the corner and fired his weapon. Bones and Quartz dashed forward to assist. Amy McCree stayed where she was, guarding the rear though she obviously wished to rush forward as well.

Meledrin listened to the clatter of the weapons, trying to shut from her mind what the sounds actually meant. Violence was not a common part of life in Grovely and she was unsure if she would ever become accustomed to it. She hoped not. She waved a ceremony of *Changing*, though it took her a moment to remember the exact movements required. *I am less and less an elf each day,* she thought. *Soon I will not remember the smell of the forest, or the sound of the trees whispering to the breeze.* She calmed her breathing and tried also to calm her racing heart. She looked at Palsamon, wondering if he felt the same fear as she. Not only the fear of the moment, of the death and destruction. But the fear of the future and what it would hold for themselves and all their people. She wasn't even sure who *their* people were any more.

No, she was sure of one person.

Hurgon shouts came from around the corner. Grunts of pain. A scream. Then nothing.

Meledrin discovered she was staring at Palsamon and quickly looked away as Flint motioned everyone forward. Meledrin didn't' move, but Piko edged towards the corner. The hurgon stopped after entering the cross passage and it seemed it would not move again.

The alien's stillness goaded Meledrin into motion. They did not have time to be shocked or to have doubts. All around this world, hurgon were dying. Possibly, hakans were dying as well. She glanced back the way they'd come, thinking of Cliff lying on the floor of the train amidst the glass.

"Come," she said. "We must hurry."

She walked forward and Flint started moving so she barely even had to look at the bodies of the aliens. Piko followed as well, then moved to the front to lead once more. The alien's pace quickened as if it too realized the consequences of delay.

"What were they guarding," Meledrin asked of nobody in particular.

Flint grunted and Palsamon was already asking Piko, obviously the only one who was likely to know an answer.

A guardroom? Meledrin informed Flint and the troll backtracked down the passage to the doorway. He lifted the latch and swung the big door inwards with a squeal of ancient, neglected hinges. Brother Koli nudged past him into the room and emerged a minute later with a dozen P'targa guards in his wake. The first five Cousins out stooped to collect weapons from the fallen En'kumo and stood ready for action. Piko said something and those with the weapons marched forward to take the lead.

Meledrin heard Palsamon thank Piko. The alien stood in the hallway and watched them move away behind the Cousins.

62: A Risky Plan

MELEDRIN STAYED IN THE MIDDLE of the group, with soldiers of one description or another all around. And each time they encountered another squad of En'kumo guards she tried to pretend the ensuing confrontation had nothing to do with her. In a way it didn't. The Brothers would be doing all the work once they found the Grandmother. Her presence was as much symbolic as anything else. She sighed. *I suppose it is required, nonetheless.* Though Palsamon could have taken the role as easily. She would not have like that either. To know he was in danger while she waited back at the ship seemed like a totally different kind of fear. And it was strange to realize that mere weeks ago she would not have wanted him to undertake the task simply because he was a man.

An hour later, they had lost most of the original P'targa but gained a dozen others from various sites. The element of surprise had allowed them to take care of nearly fifty of the enemy. Bones had been injured but refused all offers of assistance and limped painfully along with the rearguard, cheerfully complaining to anyone who would listen— even if they could not understand— with weapon ever at the ready. Dogar had been hurt as well. Nina had fashioned a bandage from a scrap of cloth found in a room and Hoodek supported him as he limped along. His complaints were not as good-natured as the troll's. His rough, weathered face was creased in a permanent scowl, but that was not far away from his usual expression.

The next battle, for a door at the end of a long, wide, colonnaded hallway, saw the death of three more P'targa guards. The P'targa did not seem overly concerned by the loss of their companions. They stepped over the bodies as if they were mere pieces of furniture. They showed no emotion at all.

"They do not even care," Meledrin said to Palsamon, who walked at her side. "They say family is important to them but it is obviously not in any emotional way."

Palsamon shook his head.

"What does that mean?"

"What do you think the dwarves have been saying about elves for the last thousand years, Meledrin?"

"I do not know. I am sure it was not flattering."

"They have said we are cold and emotionless." He gave a small smile. "And they were right. We guard our emotions from all but our closest friends. We are proud of that fact and you well know it."

"We control our emotions, Palsamon. The hurgon have none."

Palsamon shook his head again. "So you say. But even if you are correct, that does not make them less than us. Their civilization has lasted much longer than any hakan one. Who are we to argue with that?"

Perhaps he was right. He had been more often than not recently. Meledrin gave thought to the fact that she had dealt with Cliff's death and moved on. How was that different from the lack of emotion she had attributed to the hurgon? And just a couple of hours earlier, Palsamon had stated that he had loved Meledrin for more than twenty years though he had never said anything previously. She cleared her throat. "But is it worth it?"

"Do not ask me, Meledrin. Ask them."

But even if Meledrin had been so inclined, it seemed that they had reached their destination. The procession had come to a halt and Flint was using the ini rituals to slowly confer with Brother Kalis and the ranking officer among the locals.

"The Master Chambers are about 50 meters away, around a couple of corners," Flint reported to Meledrin eventually. "There are probably about a dozen guards—more in one group than we've faced so far."

"What is it that you propose?"

Flint smiled.

Meledrin sighed. "You are going to rush around the corner and attack?"

He shook his head and donned a worried expression. "It's a risky plan, Mel, but if that's what you want us to do..."

"Very amusing, Flint. You do as you see best but we have lost one too many people—" She looked at the hurgon. "We have lost far too many people already today."

"I know. It's not as if we have a lot of time though. Joku there says there's a back entrance, but it ain't a secret so the En'kumo will have guards there as well."

"Very well."

Flint nodded and went to organize the attack. A few minutes later he returned.

"We're going to leave you with Amy and—"

Amy McCree grunted. "Like hell you are." She bared her crooked teeth in a snarl. "I'm coming, too."

Flint looked at her, pursed his lips and looked around as if looking for other options.

Topper stepped forward. He had one of the hurgon weapons on his arm. "The brothers are staying here?"

"Yeah, can't risk them."

Topper nodded. “Me and the boys have got guns.” He turned and indicated the dwarves. Hoodek, Mintar and Dogar all had weapons as well, though none of them looked comfortable. Nina was unarmed and looked even more uncomfortable. “We can hold the bastards for a while if we have to while the brothers work something out.”

Flint gave a reluctant nod. “Right then. Come on Amy.” He looked at the dwarves before turning to look at Meledrin again. “This shouldn’t take long, one way or the other.”

-oOo-

Scree woke instantly but didn’t know why. He lay still, listening. Then there was a knock at his door.

“Yeah.”

The door slid open. Brick Dunning stood in the opening. “Thorpe sent me to get you.”

“What’s the time?”

The big man shrugged. “Early.”

“What’s happening?”

“Kim’s awake.”

Scree surged to his feet. He was ready to run from the room before he realized he was naked. “I’ll be there in a second.”

“Good idea,” Brick said, smiling and turning away. He never seemed to be in a hurry.

When he was dressed, Scree did hurry. He ignored the lifts and took the stairs three at a time. He almost knocked Thorpe from his feet when he entered the medical bay a minute later.

The soldier said something, but Scree didn’t even notice. Kim was sitting up, looking at the bandages on her hand. She looked up at the commotion.

“Scree.”

“Kim. You’re awake.” With an effort, Scree slowed his breathing. “You’re awake.” He wondered if his relief was visible to everyone else. It felt like it was leaking out his pores. Someone else to make the decisions. Someone else to think about all the problems he couldn’t get his head around. Kim awake— on it’s own, that was enough.

“I guess so.” She looked at herself as if listing her injuries. “What happened? I mean... I mean after...” She waved a bandaged arm.

“That don’t matter at the moment. Plenty of time for stories later. You’s all right?”

She nodded, though she didn't look sure. "I think so. I mean, it looks like nothing all that serious happened in the end. Did it?'

Scree shook his head. "Nothing too serious. Nothing permanent."

"That's good. I feel pretty good."

"Good." Scree didn't really know what to say. He nodded and looked at Kim's bandaged hand. "Cuto got to us just in time."

"Cuto?"

"Yeah. Cuto saved us. Broke us out then flew us back to the *Hakahei* on the back of a baby kidol."

"Seriously?"

"Yeah. Was kinda fun."

"Sorry I missed it then."

"Yeah, me too."

Nobody said anything for a while. Scree looked around and realized that both Thorpe and Brick had left the medical bay. Only Kafin and Paul Manning remained— either sleeping or unconscious.

"So what's going on? Where the hell are we?"

"We's messengers. Keeble organized a contract that could ends the war but we had to come to another planet to get it signed by a Grandmother. But nows the multeese is here and we don't knows why."

"Did they follow us?"

Scree shrugged. "Don't know. Maybe. We're still trying to figure everything outs." And now it was Kim's problem.

"So why aren't we dead? If the multeese are here, I mean?"

Scree shrugged. "We don't knows that either. The multeese is sending down ships but they don't seem keen on killing any ones. They's just hanging around at the moment."

"Really?"

"Yeah." And even standing there talking to Kim, it had him worried. As if maybe the aliens were working up to some amazing thing that would wipe out the whole planet in a single moment— a moment that he couldn't even fight, let alone win.

"So... Can I get up?"

"I don't know. I don't think you should—"

"Ask, Thorpe. Where's Captain Thorpe?"

Scree was going to tell her she wasn't going anywhere, but he needed her up and about. He needed her to work out what the hell was going on. So he went out into the hall looking for the soldier. And from there into the mess. Thorpe was sitting at a table cradling a cup of coffee.

"Kim wants to get up."

"I'm not sure." He sighed and, taking his mug with him, returned to the medical bay.

"Come on, Doc," Kim said before he was even in the door. "You know I'm fine."

Scree stayed near the door, leaning in the corner while Thorpe checked this and that and asked questions about a whole heap of stuff that didn't seem relevant.

Fifteen minutes later Thorpe sat down on the bench. "It isn't going to make any difference if I say no, is it?"

"It might. For a little while."

"Okay then. You can get out of bed, but only if you stay in a wheelchair."

"That'll just be a pain—"

"No, it won't. You have a broken foot, a bad knee, broken ribs, a recently dislocated shoulder and a broken hand. Walking will be a pain. Using crutches will be a pain."

"All right then. Just shut up and give me the damn wheelchair."

"We've got to find it."

Kim raised her eyebrow. "This is going to take a week to find, isn't it?"

"No. I've seen it somewhere."

"What's a wheelchair?" Scree asked.

"Just what it sounds like. A chair on wheels."

"Right." Scree checked with the trolls who were awake. "Chip says it's in the hold. He's going to bring it up."

"Thanks, Scree."

Scree smiled. "No worries."

Chip brought the wheelchair in a few minutes later and Scree watched as Thorpe helped Kim carefully out of bed. "Don't get up," he told her. "Not to look out of the window, not to climb up to your seat on the bridge. You can hop into bed, and that's it." It sounded as if he wasn't confident of being obeyed. "Is that clear?"

"Yes, Doctor."

"Shit. Bugger off then, I've got patients to look after."

63: Forgotten

TUKI FOLLOWED AS THE TROLLS aND HURGON went slowly around the first corner and down a short hallway. They paused for a moment at the next corner then rushed around as one, shouting as they went. Tuki followed a moment later, after the initial clatter of weapons, and saw Ruby clobber an En'kumo guard in the face. Her eyes were wild, her grin was fierce. First one down, she turned to another, knocking away its weapon and elbowing it in the stomach. Then she used her weapon the way it was intended and shot it in the face.

Blood sprayed and Tuki quickly ducked back behind the protection of the wall. He knew Ruby was a troll and he knew what trolls were like, but it was still a shock to know that Ruby was like that. It was a shock to see the violence in her eyes. It was a shock to see how easily the death and destruction came from her. He leaned back, breathing deeply and trying to stop his shaking hands. He pushed them against his legs but it didn't help. All it did was leave dark, bloody prints on his EVA suit.

Tuki heard Bones say, "That one spat at me. He spat. Probably should've tried using his gun. Might have done him more use."

Tuki stayed where he was until the noises died down then looked carefully around the corner again. There were a dozen bodies on the floor and Tuki was glad to see that none of the trolls nor Amy were among them. He hurried across to Ruby.

"Are..." He had intended to ask if she had been hurt, but the wild look was still in her eyes and his swallowed his words. "Ummm..." He looked around and for the first time thought to be sorry for the six P'targa guards who had fallen. "Do we know their names?" he asked.

Ruby turned to look and Tuki watched as the fire receded from her eyes. She drew in a deep breath. "No. It doesn't matter."

"It does matter," Tuki said.

"It doesn't matter to them, Tuki, why should it matter to us?"

And the surviving hurgon didn't care. "It doesn't matter what they think, Ruby. The multeese doesn't care what happens to *anybody*. Should we think like that as well?"

Ruby didn't reply. Brother Koli had been talking to somebody behind the door and latches and bars were being drawn. The door opened a crack, then further, and an ancient, stooped hurgon was revealed.

"Is that Grandmother Donni?" Tuki asked.

Meledrin's voice startled him. "It is not," the elf said from just behind him. "From the conversation Brother Koli just recently concluded, I gather it is merely a servant."

They were ushered into the room. It was a huge place filled with tall, book-covered tables and shelves that overflowed with more things than Tuki could imagine. The walls were carved with scenes of hurgon and kidol, as well as kil'ini orbiting worlds. There were no hurgon waiting.

Beyond was a much smaller room. Tables and shelves had been upended to form a barricade in the corner where five hurgon stood guard, weapons ready. Behind the scant protection they offered were another four aliens, though one of them was obviously not a guard at all. It was older than all the others, with grey, patchy skin and yellow teeth. It was sweating and appeared to be in pain, but the gaze was steady and clear.

Tuki watched Meledrin step forward with Brother Koli and wondered what there was to say. They had the contracts and they needed to be signed, but Grandmother Donni knew all about those already. So there were greetings, and perhaps introductions, though Tuki did not know if either of those were particularly important in the circumstances.

Apparently Meledrin and the hurgon thought otherwise. For the next ten minutes they talked back and forth, waving their arms quicker than he could follow. And when they were done there were drinks of some kind. Flint carefully sipped the bright green liquid, then nodded and downed the rest of his cup. Meledrin took a cautious sip as well but did not go any further. Then the Brothers drank, as if this was the final sealing of the friendship that had been agreed to in the contracts.

Not that they were signed yet. It was another half an hour before that was done and Tuki could see that even Flint was getting restless. But the Grandmother had to get a daughter from another room to read the contract quickly. They commented and chatted about various sections before the older hurgon finally dipped her pen into some ink and put her name on the bottom of each one in big, blocky writing.

Tuki sighed. It was done. Though, of course, the signing of the contract didn't mean all that much at all. It still had to be taken back to Hulgorn and entered into the... He didn't really know what had to be done with it, but he knew it had to be done on Hulgorn. And the contract might not be enough to stop the war anyway. And he knew that the war with the hurgon was not the real problem. As Kim had been saying for a long time, the multeese were the problem and he could see no solution to the threat they posed.

Hurgon were dying. Soon, hakans would probably be dying as well. The multeese had been threatening to kill them for so long that they would probably set their mind to the task soon enough. And he could not believe, that if they finally decided to do the job properly, that Kim or Scree or anybody else would come up with a way to save them. And he could not actually believe they were still alive. The multeese could kill everyone on Lapenti and chose not to, for some reason.

Nobody knew very much about the multeese at all. Just one small file...

Tuki swallowed. He suddenly realized he had not told anyone about the information he had discovered. He cleared his throat. "Flint?" he said softly, hoping Meledrin would not hear.

"Yeah, Tuki?"

"There is something I should have told someone before."

The troll narrowed his eyes. "What?"

Tuki swallowed again and told Flint about the files on the ship and the small amount they told about the multeese.

"So, they're made out of gas?"

Tuki nodded. "Or many tiny creatures join together to form a multeese." Tuki didn't really understand if they were one creature or many and it was obvious that nobody else did either.

Flint shook his head. "You really should've told someone about this, Tuki."

"A lot has been happening." Though he knew it was not a very good excuse.

"We need all the information we can get, Tuki. And I can't even tell Scree about it."

Tuki was saved from further admonishment when Grandmother Donni dropped a pile of papers.

"*Is Donni well?*" Meledrin asked, looking concerned.

"*Donni is well enough,*" the Grandmother signed, slow enough for Tuki to follow. It appeared as if she didn't have the energy for more.

"*What ails Donni?*" Meledrin asked.

"*It is no ailment at all, Meledrin. Donni is changing, becoming Givtar. It is many years since Donni last changed and it is having more of an effect than is common.*"

"*Changing?*" Meledrin asked.

But Donni did not have the energy to reply and the other hurgon did not have the desire. So Tuki explained what Hiklo had told him. Perhaps he should have passed this information on earlier as well.

"*Donni is preparing to breed?*" Meledrin asked the Grandmother when Tuki had finished.

"*That is correct. Donni is old and close to death and wished to produce one more hatchling to help bring P'targa greatness in this time of change.*"

"*Is there risk for Donni?*"

"Donni does not know. It is not often hurgon as old as Donni go through the change."

"You should not—"

Grandmother Donni waved away Meledrin's protest. *"It is done. If P'targa are to go on, there must be Givtar and Symbo. Donni will assist."*

Tuki shook his head. If the P'targa were to go on there must be an end to the war and an end to the multeese. Anything else, including standing in this room while the world continued to turn, was not helping.

64: Processing

KEEBLE WOKE WITH A START. He sat up and looked around. Ari was standing behind him with a cup of coffee held awkwardly in her broken hand and breakfast in the other.

"I brought you these."

Keeble rubbed at his face. "Thank you. Is the kitchen working now?"

Ari nodded. "What have you worked out?"

"Well, it was 770 meters in a straight line. But to get through the streets is about 1200 meters."

Air shrugged. "We will do what needs to be done. The factory is working at full speed now."

"Great, but Scree helped get it down to about 900 meters."

Ari looked at the map and the line Keeble had drawn there. "You're just going to knock some holes in the buildings?"

"No. Over the roofs." The coffee was fabulous. Strong, black coffee always made him feel better. "There's some bits that are higher so we can't go dead straight, but it's a lot better."

Ari nodded. "It's a great idea."

"I know. Isn't it?" And food. Proper food instead of the horrible stuff in the packets. He ate quickly for a while as he tried to think of all the things he needed to do. "Do you want to come for a walk with me this morning? I have to go have a look at the mysterious factory to see if I can work out what it does."

"Does it matter?"

"Apparently."

He had a quick shower, which did almost as much good as breakfast, and when he emerged Ari was waiting.

A few minutes later they were making their way through the gateway into the hurgon compound. There were now fifteen guards on the door. None of them said anything but they watched closely. Keeble signed a, "Good morning," but didn't slow.

Keeble had studied the map enough to know the factory was on the far side of the compound but it took him a while to find his way through the maze of streets and alleys. Hurgon were removing supplies from storage sheds in courtyards and taking them inside. Machinery was being locked down. Shutters were being pulled out to cover windows and doors. They were working slowly and calmly, as if it was something they did every other week.

The hurgon stood aside to watch them pass. Ari kept her eyes on her boots but Keeble waved ini' greetings. None of them replied. They all went back to work as soon as they had gone and not a word was spoken.

When they found the factory it was surrounded by a dozen hurgon who worked at getting it secured. Keeble found someone who looked like they were in charge.

"Keeble and Ari offer greetings."

The hurgon regarded them suspiciously. *"Uncle Gambo returns greetings."*

"Keeble and Ari would like to look at the factory."

The hurgon stared. *"Why? Gambo has been told of the hakan presence but has not been told if assistance should be given."*

"War is coming to this compound, Gambo. The factory is important to the enemy so Keeble wants to know what it's for."

"Gambo doesn't know the purpose of the factory."

"Keeble understands. That is why Keeble needs to look."

"Gambo doesn't think it would be allowed."

"Does Gambo wish for P'targa family members to die? Does Gambo wish for the P'targa to incur cost during repairs?"

The hurgon looked at Keeble then over his shoulder to the factory. He motioned to the group that had been securing the door and, without a word, they started undoing the work they'd already completed. A few minutes later, Keeble and Ari were taken inside.

"So, what have we got?" Keeble muttered.

He went from room to room, from machine to machine, and wasn't sure of much at all.

"It's for processing some type of crop, right?" Ari said.

Keeble nodded.

"And it obviously starts at this end."

Keeble nodded again.

The process started with crushing, but the press was huge. Twenty-four and a half meters to a side. Three meters, seventy centimeters high. The floor was a grate, so liquids could run through. The liquids went into the main piece of machinery and whatever happened in there involved the hydrogen. And the result was decanted into small metal barrels. The solid matter that couldn't fit through the grate was scraped into a furnace to be disposed of.

Keeble stood at the end of the production line and examined the barrels. They were bright and shiny, obviously brand new, and filled most of a large room, stacked on shelves and packing pallets. Something about them bothered him, but he couldn't put his finger on it. So he went back to examine the process again but it didn't help any more the second time.

"Where do the materials come from?" Ari asked.

"What?" But Keeble knew what she meant. There was one small door into the press. Other than that... He looked up. A trapdoor took up most of the roof. But that didn't tell them much. The materials came from a long way away, maybe, otherwise they wouldn't have to be flown in? "I don't know. I don't bloody know."

Keeble spent the next five minutes convincing Gambo to let him look at the workings of the main part of the machinery.

-oOo-

Meledrin looked around, as if the world would suddenly change now that the contracts were signed. As if all the problems would fade away. No such event occurred.

"Are you able to contact the ship, Flint?" Meledrin asked.

The troll shook his head and, for some reason, glanced at Tuki. "It's too far."

"What about you, Amy?"

The American had a mechanical radio attached to her head. "Like Flint says, too far. Or there's the mountain in the way. Either way, no."

Meledrin gave a small sigh before she could stop herself. She waved an Ending, followed quickly by a Beginning before wondering if there was really any difference.

At the table, Donni gave a tired hurgon nod and examined the piles of paper on the table as if wondering if there was anything else that needed to be done. It rested shaking fingers on the closest pile.

Flint cleared his throat and Meledrin turned to look. "What is it, Flint?"

"This guard here," he said, motioning to one of the hurgon, "Brother Kripo as far as I can tell, wants us to take Donni with us. He reckons it'll be safer. I could be wrong though, so can you find out if that's what's really going on?"

"Certainly."

Meledrin checked with the guard and discovered that Flint's interpretation had been correct. Before the guard had finished asking the question though, Grandmother Donni was complaining, saying she would not abandon any member of the P'targa family.

Meledrin thought it a strange sentiment. Surely the survival of the Grandmother was of vital importance. Donni could do nothing of value here, apart from die with all the others if the compound's defenses were to fail.

The guard was about to comply with her wishes but Amy McCree laughed. *"I suspect that's your hormones talking Grandmother Donni,"* she signed slowly. *"If your givtar are anything like ours, then Donni is thinking about saving everyone. That cannot be done. The best thing for the P'targa is to have Donni thinking about the fight that will follow this one. The En'kumo and the T'loop are back on Hulgorn and for the P'targa, winning this battle is pointless unless that one is won as well."*

Grandmother Donni did not seem convinced. Meledrin could understand the hurgon's sense of duty to assist all of the P'targa family, but she could also see the wisdom in what Amy was saying.

"If Grandmother Donni travels with the hakans to the Hakahei,*"* Meledrin signed, *"Donni will be under no obligation to travel further. If nothing else, the fact that you are mobile may confuse the En'kumo."*

Flint grunted. "I wanted to know if that's what the guard asked. I didn't want to invite her along."

"I am in charge, Flint," Meledrin said, before realizing that Flint probably didn't care one way or the other— about who was in charge or whether Grandmother Donni came with them.

While Meledrin had been speaking with the troll, Donni had been speaking with Brother Kripo.

"Donni will travel to the hakan construct," Donni signed. *"It will be a thing of great interest to see, if nothing else."*

Meledrin nodded. Flint grunted again.

Brother Kripo said, *"Guards will accompany Grandmother Donni, of course, and a diversion will be created."*

"Is that absolutely necessary?"

Quartz and Bones laughed, and Meledrin realized it was a ridiculous question. She glared at the two trolls anyway, until they had their mirth under control.

"Come one then," Flint said. "Let's get this over with." He started towards the door.

"Ummm..." Bones readied his weapon. "There's a back door right? I heard someone mention a back door. Sometime. I'm sure they did. A back door, right?"

Meledrin heard weapons being fired in the entrance chamber. Half a dozen hurgon rushed in through the door. Meledrin jumped, hand to her racing heart, but they turned to take up defensive positions. She belatedly noticed their P'targa uniforms.

Quartz laughed again. "If the back door was usable, do you think they would've been holed up in here?"

"Good point," Bones said. He jumped out from behind the wall and fired his weapon into the other room. A moment later he was protected again. "There's a lot of the buggers out there. Lot's of 'em. What does Kim say? Shit loads? Yeah, shit loads. That does sound like a lot, doesn't it?"

Meledrin swallowed. It certainly *did* sound like a lot. Especially when a troll said it.

65: The Front Door

TUKI FELT LIKE GOING TO HIDE behind the barricade where the grandmother had been, but he stayed where he was, wringing his hands and looking around as if another exit might present itself, seeing he *really* needed it. There was another door, but Bones and Quartz had already decided it would not be of any use.

Nothing else appeared, so Tuki crouched down and waited to be told what to do. Ruby was already over by the door. She and the other trolls were taking turns to pop out from behind the cover of the wall, each on a different side, each at a different height, to shoot at the attackers. As far as Tuki could tell, that would only work for so long. Soon, the hurgon would just be able to each aim at a likely spot and wait until someone appeared in their sights.

The trolls seemed to realize this too— of course they would— and as they continued with their tactics, Flint also started organizing the next stage of the fight. He shouted orders that the hurgon— neither those outside nor their allies waiting at their backs— could understand. But Meledrin translated as the troll spoke and they organized themselves as well. Tuki was not paying any attention. Nobody was telling him what to do, so he watched and waited silently and rubbed at the comet tattoo on the back of his hand.

A minute later Flint gave a signal and everyone just rushed out into the other room. It wasn't a very good plan as far as Tuki could tell. It seemed like one of the plans Flint joked about Keeble coming up with. But nonetheless it seemed to work.

Tuki watched Ruby rushing through the door, teeth bared in a snarl, guns shuddering in her hands. He barely recognized her, but hoped she was all right. A moment later there wasn't much to see— just one small section of room through the door— so he closed his eyes and listened. Weapons firing. Shouts and screams. Grunting. Clatters and crashing.

Another scream, louder than most. Tuki opened his eyes. And through the door, in that one small section of room, he could see bodies on the ground. Three hurgon, all wearing the uniform of the P'targa. Two had fallen awkwardly, one atop the other, blood dripping from a knee to a chin. Cold, dead eyes staring. The third hurgon was sitting, slumped forward like he had sat down to rest for a moment then nodded off. Perhaps he had— there were no visible injuries to suggest otherwise.

A moment later, when the silence came, it was a shock. Tuki stayed where he was, waiting for the fighting to start again, and only rose to his feet when he heard Flint's voice. He made his way slowly to the other room and looked around. There were twenty-three bodies, mainly En'kumo guards but there were also seven P'targa. And near the door, lying on her side, face twisted in a silent snarl, was Quartz. All Tuki could do was stare.

"Are you all right, Tuki?"

Tuki felt a hand on his shoulder and turned to see Ruby standing by his side. He shook his head. "No, I am not all right." There was the taste of vomit in his mouth. He shrugged off her hand and staggered to a wall so he could lean against it and make sure he stayed at least partially upright. His bloody hands were stinging. So were his eyes.

Ruby followed him. "Tuki, I—"

"Quartz has died. How can I be all right?" He glanced at the body before quickly looking away. "How can you just pretend it didn't happen?"

Ruby looked at the body too. "I ain't pretending it didn't happen. I don't have to because right now I'm not even thinking about it. Kim reckons trolls was bred to not think about that type of thing. If we think about it we won't do what needs to be done. But that ain't what you want to hear, is it? You just thinks I ain't crying cause I don't care."

Tuki didn't say anything, he didn't move, but something must have shown on his face.

Ruby grunted and shook her head. "Why don't you just count your bloody planets and stars and leave the hard stuff up to us? You just worry about your rocks and your fires and we'll deal with the people." She walked away, skirting around bodies as she made her way over to Bones, who was standing over Quartz's body, but not looking at it. The two of them stood together and for the first time ever, Bones stayed silent for a long time.

Across the other side of the room, near the door out into the hallway, Flint and Meledrin were talking with Grandmother Donni and the commander of her guards. Tuki had no idea what they were saying, but as before, he would be told what he needed to do. So he waited, back against the wall, hands shoved under his arms to stop them from shaking.

-oOo-

"You don't know what *what* is for?" Kim asked. She'd pushed one of the chairs away from the dining table and parked her wheelchair in its place. She wanted to get up and pace but stayed where she was, hands on the table, fiddling. She *had* tried getting up to change chairs, despite Thorpe's warnings, and discovered for herself that it really wasn't a good idea. Damn him.

Keeble sighed. "Ari and I went to have a look at the plant but we couldn't work out what it's for."

"What plant?" Kim asked. "Are they growing drugs or something? Is that what the multeese want?"

"Not that type of plant. A manufacturing plant. A processing plant."

"Oh, right."

Keeble tapped his metal arm on the table. "There something very strange about the whole thing but I just can't put my finger on it."

"Well, does it matter?" Kim asked. It probably did but Kim was having trouble keeping up with even the simplest conversation.

It was Scree who answered this time. "Maybe. Maybe not. If the plant's got somethings to do with why the multeese is here then knowing what it is might help." The troll glanced at Stone and Crystal sitting at a table on the far side of the mess hall. "And right now we needs all the help we can gets cause nobody's got any ideas." He obviously wasn't happy about that.

"At least it might protect us for now," Kim said.

"How's that?"

"If the multeese want those plants maybe they won't be willing to shoot us when we're so close."

"Or maybe they just wants them destroyed?"

"Well… couldn't they do that from space?"

Keeble interrupted. "It's no use worrying about it. We just have to work out how we defend the compound and the ship for the next couple of days."

"What, and then we just take off and leave them?" Nobody gets left behind.

Scree nodded. "We can't die here with the hurgon just because we feels guilty. We got to live so we can kill the bloody multeese. If that means we spend the next year running while we think of a plan then that's the way it is."

"*Everyone* could die in a year," Kim said.

Keeble was winding the gears on his hand.

"And how does we help that if we dies tomorrow?" Scree asked.

"Well..." Kim grabbed the wheels of her chair and moved back from the table with a violent jerk. She spun around awkwardly. She was about to head for the door but stopped and looked around instead. "Inaki," she called. The moai looked up from where he was talking with Peni. "Come here and push me."

Kim took a deep breath. Inaki didn't deserve that. "Sorry, Inaki," she said. Another deep breath. "Can you please push me?" She looked back over her shoulder. "I need the company of somebody nice for a while."

Inaki rushed over and pushed her from the room.

-oOo-

Tuki didn't know if he should keep his eyes ahead or watch his back. In the end he didn't really do either. He was so busy worrying and walking that he didn't see anything at all.

He was just starting to calm his racing heart when he bumped into the back of Palsamon as the elf came to a sudden stop.

"Careful, Tuki."

"Sorry. What is happening?"

Palsamon shook his head. "I am unsure. However, Flint has come to a halt at the intersection."

Tuki watched as Flint conferred with those closest to him. Then they called forward half the hurgon from the rear guard. A moment after they arrived, Bones darted across the adjoining hall. There was the crackle of hurgon weapons, shouts, but even limping, Bones was too quick. A moment later, En'kumo guards came into view, heading after the troll. Tuki closed his eyes and heard a rain of gunfire mingling with a couple of seconds of hurgon weapons. When he opened his eyes the En'kumo were dead. Eleven of the aliens were piled haphazardly, bleeding onto the stone floor.

Swallowing, Tuki took a step forward but Palsamon held his arm. Flint and the others had not moved either. Before Tuki could ask what was going on he heard a shout from around the corner. He was sure it was Bones, though the troll had not returned. And at that moment, Flint and his companions rushed around the corner. More gunfire, over as quickly as last time.

This time, Tuki moved with everyone else. Around the corner, Bones was talking with Flint, probably taking five minutes to say what could be said in a sentence. Then Flint and Brother Kripo started walking and everyone else had no choice but to follow.

Down one hallway that looked no different to the one before. And then another. Tuki never got lost, he knew directions and distances like Keeble knew machines, like Ping knew clocks, but the succession of passages was mind numbing. He'd heard trolls say that they never got lost either. He wondered if that was something to do with the 'engineering' Kim claimed had been done on the different hakan races, or was it something that had come to them at a later stage. Had science given them the ability, as it had been given to him, or was it life? And now, after all these years, did it matter? He looked back at Ruby where she walked with the rearguard. They were who they were, and no amount of explaining would change the fact, though it might change the reasons.

Tuki sighed and tried to concentrate. He might not get lost, but he could still get shot, or trip over. Any mistake here, in this crazy hostile place, could get him killed.

He looked back at Ruby again. The soft, smoldering embers of the fire were still in her eyes as she scanned their surroundings. She glanced at strange hurgon loitering in hallways, cocked her head at the slightest sound, taking everything in. The fire in her eyes might mean death for others, but meant life for her friends and her companions. Tuki knew that— and for her current task the reasons didn't matter— but wasn't sure if he could continue to see her as he had before.

66: A Green Ribbon

PING TRIED TO GATHER HER THOUGHTS as she turned her attention to Tess. "I'm not sure what's first on the list." She'd checked the computers the night before, prioritizing the faults on the ship, but the sight of Kim in the wheelchair had driven all thoughts from her head. "Ummm..."

"I'm glad Kim's awake," Dido said. She stopped playing with the green ribbon tied in her hair and took Ping's hand.

Ping was glad too, but Kim obviously wasn't her old self. When Inaki wheeled her out of the room, Ping took a deep breath. "Let's go take a look."

In the engineering bay, Mintar was already working on the computer. He looked up as Ping entered and snatched his hands away from the keyboard as if doing something he shouldn't.

"Sorry," he said. "I was just looking at the problems. Working out what we can do."

"Don't be sorry, Mintar," Ping replied. "We need to get this stuff fixed as quickly as we can."

"I'm not a Gang Leader though..."

"All that matters now is that we have work that needs doing."

"Right." He turned back to the screen. "You've already put this in order?"

"Yes."

"Right."

But she didn't know how many people Keeble needed, if any, for collecting the fuel. "The fuel still is really the only thing stopping us from flying now. Why don't we get Tasko, Bargle and Dosa to work on that?"

Mintar nodded. "Then the Ohoga engine and the air recycler. Do you want me to sort something out?"

"That would be great. Thanks. I'll take Tess, Dido and Ari to look at clock number 2." They were the four main things at the moment. Get them sorted out and she would feel a lot better.

"Ari's sleeping."

"What?"

"She was working at the foundry all night. Then she went to look at the stupid factory with Keeble."

Right. Tess and Dido would have to do then.

The two dwives had already found some tools and were waiting for Ping to join them by the door.

"Come on."

She led the way down to the clock and opened the access panel. Once inside, she stopped to stare. It looked as if there had been an explosion in here as well, though there was really nothing that could explode.

"What happened?" Dido asked.

Ping shook her head. "I don't know. Maybe... There must have been a loose cog or something and once it fell off things just kept going with it."

It was a mess. At least a tenth of the clock was lying on the floor. Some had actually broken and might be beyond repair. Everything was so mixed up it might take a week to sort out. Ping suddenly wasn't sure if she should bother. Perhaps it would be better to work on something they could actually get fixed in time and hope the other clock didn't malfunction as well.

"We won't do this now. Dido, you and I are going to check on the other clock to make sure it doesn't fall apart too. Tess, you go and see if Mintar needs your help, or needs you to do something. And tell him what we're doing, please."

"Very well."

"I could go and help Mintar," Dido offered, reaching for the ribbon in her hair again. But Tess was already heading out through the access panel.

"At least this should be an easy enough job."

Up above the engineering bay in Clock 1, Ping set down the toolbox and looked around. Everything appeared to be fine, but she intended to check every screw and every bolt she could get to without pulling things apart. She set to work and, after a moment of hesitation, Dido did as well. They worked in silence for three and a half minutes.

"Ping," Dido said. She stopped working and touched her green ribbon. "Why don't you like Topper?"

Ping thought it was a very strange question. "I *do* like Topper."

"But you don't *like* him."

"Well, no but..." Ping almost dropped her screwdriver. She sat down on the toolbox. "Topper..."

"You didn't know?" Dido asked.

Ping shook her head. But it was obvious when she thought about it. How could she not have noticed?

"Everyone else knows."

"Yes, thank you," Ping said. "That's very helpful."

Dido turned her concentration to her spanner and tightened a bolt holding a ratchet lever to the wall, though she didn't really look like she was interested. "How did things like that work on your world?" she asked eventually.

Ping shook her head to try to clear it. "How did what work?"

"Men and women? You know..."

"Relationships?" Ping said. "Courting?" Topper was with Meledrin. It was the most dangerous mission, if only because it took them away from any chance of help.

"Yes."

"I don't know. There weren't any *rules*. It worked however people wanted it to work. Somebody asked somebody else to have dinner with them. Or they went on a picnic, or they went dancing."

"Oh." Dido was playing with her hair again, twisting the strands between her fingers.

"How did it work for dwarves?"

"A dwarf went to the maiden bunker or a hotel and told a dwife to get her things. And they went to the dwarf's bunker and..."

"And that's it? You were told what you had to do?"

"Sometimes, if the dwarf didn't want the dwife to move into his bunker straight away, he would give her a ribbon so everyone knew she was spoken for." She seemed to notice the ribbon in her hair for the first time and quickly pushed the locks behind her ear. "Then he would come to visit when he wanted to see her."

"That's terrible."

Dido shrugged. "The only other choice was to stay in the maiden bunker and... Well, we did what we were told even if we weren't spoken for."

"Well, it won't be like that here. Kim won't allow it." Topper had never tried to tell her what to do. He was probably as confused as Dido was. All the dwarves probably were. "I guess it will work however you want it to work, Dido."

"So the dwives will have all the power?"

"Only if they want to." Ping didn't feel like she had any power at all. She examined the screwdriver in her hand, then sighed and got back to work. "Who is he?" she asked.

"Who is who?"

Ping looked up and Dido was playing with the ribbon once more. The dwife pushed her hair back over her shoulder and started working as well.

-oOo-

Tuki swallowed and edged back against the wall of the hallway. There were still En'kumo guards at the train station.

"There's ten of them," Flint said softly. "Not many."

Tuki nodded to himself and watched Meledrin translate for the hurgon. Ten really wasn't many. He took a deep breath and relaxed a little. Flint, Bones and Ruby could probably handle ten unarmored hurgon on their own.

"Do we want to kill them?" Bones asked. "I think we want to kill them but that might be dangerous." The troll divided his glance between Meledrin and Flint. "Maybe we want to sneak onto the train. Could we sneak onto the train, do you think?"

Tuki had no doubt that they would be able to sneak onto the train if they really wanted. But getting onto the train wasn't the hard bit. Keeping the En'kumo away long enough to get the train started was the problem. He didn't know much about trains, but he knew you couldn't just jump in one and leave immediately unless someone had prepared the train first.

Topper said as much. "The train is idle and cold," he said. "It's going to take a while to get it going."

"How long?" Flint asked.

Topper shrugged and looked at Hoodek. "Half an hour, Hoodek?"

The younger dwarf nodded, shrugged and nodded again. "Not sure. Sounds like it might be about right. Got to heat the water and..."

Meledrin had been translating into the ini' rituals and cleared her throat. "Brother Kripo is under the impression that there will be a preheated reservoir in this vicinity precisely for this application."

Topper nodded. "That'll help, obviously, but we'll still need to get rid of those hurgon, one way or the other. Where is this reservoir?"

Meledrin asked. "Brother Kripo is unsure. None of the others know either. They are guards, not train drivers."

"Right. Of course. So, none of them can drive?"

"No."

Topper smiled at Hoodek and Dogar. "That's a shame."

Flint grunted. "Come on then. Let's get this over with." He hefted his weapon and looked at those who would be fighting with him. "You dwarves better stay back here. The rest of you, let's just run out there and do it. We don't have time to find better positions."

Tuki sat down on the floor to wait. He glanced at Ruby. She didn't look scared, and perhaps had no reason to be. Hurgon were slow compared to trolls, and the En'kumo defending the train station were going to be surprised. They might well all be dead before they even raised their weapons. Tuki wondered if he should say something. *Be careful.* But then she was gone and it was too late.

The familiar sounds. The clatter of gunfire. Shouts and screams. The sizzle of hurgon weapons. And then silence.

Palsamon carefully poked his head around the corner to look.

"Be careful, Palsamon," Meledrin said. She half reached for him, then withdrew her hand.

"It is all clear."

Tuki followed the elf around onto the platform, trying not to look at the bodies. They all belonged to the En'kumo, but did that make it any better, really? Nui said that all lives were equal. But like the moai, perhaps all Nui knew was Danyon Ford. Perhaps Nui had never looked beyond the desert to see that there might be more out there. Or not beyond Kiva, or the seven linked worlds of the hakans.

Tuki made his way to the train behind Meledrin. Ruby stood with the other trolls near the door. She smiled at Tuki. He gave a small smile in return but climbed on board and found a spot to sit with his back against the wall. The dwarves, along with Brother Koli had gone to look at the engine.

A few minutes later, Topper came through the door at the front. "The hot water tank is just up ahead a bit. There's a hose so that won't take long. We'll have to heat it some more to get some pressure but it shouldn't take too long."

Tuki didn't really understand, but as long as Topper knew what was going on.

"Flint," the dwarf continued, "we should disconnect the other carriages. That'll give us a bit more speed. Don't know if it will be enough but..." He shrugged. "Can you do that?"

The trolls came onto the train and went to the rear door to see what they could see.

67: Left Behind

SCREE STOOD ON THE TOP OF THE WALL, hand flexing on the handle of his pistol. He could just see one of the multeese ships over the top of the hill. From where he was, it seemed that it alone would be enough to wipe out the hurgon compound. But he kept telling himself he didn't know that for sure. Maybe engines took up half the ship. Maybe everything was taken up by fuel tanks because *they* knew how dumb it was to run out. There were so many maybes that it was stupid to think about them. There were other ships, further away but on the tops of hills, sitting like wolves, patient and ready to attack when the moment was right.

There was a noise behind him and he turned to see Stone bounding up the stairs. "What we got?" Scree asked.

"Nothing."

"Nothin'?"

Stone nodded. "Pretty much." He looked out over the parapet to examine the ship as well. "Stinking cats."

"That's what I thoughts. But whats you mean by 'nothing'?"

"Well there's a small garrison here but it's next to pointless. Fifty hurgon with armor. And there's six of them kidol with the bits for riding in. Other than that there's four bigger guns— one on each wall."

"Range?"

"No."

"No?"

Stone shrugged. "Lethal to naked hurgon at about a hundred meters. Armor might get you to within fifty meters, long as you're walking forwards. And it takes a couple of minutes for them to recharge between shots, or something like that. "

"What's the use of them then?"

"There's some big animals round these parts. They still come out to play occasionally, when it's dry or whatever."

"Right. So how long to make some more?"

"It takes these stupid buggers all night to make one piece of pipe, remember? The cousin at the garrison reckons a couple of weeks at least."

"So we're screwed then?"

"Screwed like a whore at a love-god festival."

"What about the guns on the *Hakahei*?"

"Yeah, they might even hit that ship there. But they use battery power and it won't do us much good if Keeble comes up with the fuel and we got no batteries anyway."

Scree opened his mouth to speak but Stone continued.

"There's also the fact that using those guns would probably get the attention of the mothership up there."

Scree grunted. "Right. Last resort then."

"I'd still like to know what's going on with those bastards. Why ain't we dead yet? Why aren't the hurgon dead yet? I'm pretty sure when we find out the answer we're going to wish we was."

Scree wanted to know too. It didn't make any sense, any way he thought about it. And he'd been thinking about it a lot. "Any other options?"

"We could leave."

"If we could leaves, we wouldn't be having this conversation."

"I don't mean on the *Hakahei*. Reckon we could survive on this world real easy without anyone even knowing."

"I'm guessing you ain't talking about everyone? Just a few of the others?"

Stone nodded and Scree gave the idea some thought. He'd abandoned companions quickly enough in the past when it suited. But he'd only ever abandoned trolls, and they had never offered anything other than more of what he already had himself. They'd had different names and different weapons, but they'd really just been him. These companions did offer something different. Even the trolls had gone beyond what they had been before. They offered strength and skill and courage, but more importantly, they offered respect and friendship. Without them, he was just a troll.

Scree glanced at Stone and shook his head. "Nobody gets left behind," he said. And even as he said it, he realized it was the answer the other troll had been expecting. It was the answer he wanted to hear. "So, what else we gots? I know you is holding back something."

Stone turned to lean back against the dusty brown stones of the parapet. "Chasm went to have a look with Makar. Apparently they got enough stuff lying around to make a handful of catapults."

"How long for them?"

"Makar reckons he could have the first one ready in about two hours if he had a couple of other dwarves and a dozen hurgon. Range of a hundred meters or more."

"Burning cats. Catapults?" Scree looked at the pistol in his hand. "*Catapults*. Go on then, get them started."

"They're already been working for half an hour."

"And ammunition?"

"They convinced some hurgon to knock down a building or two to get some rocks."

"Catapults," Scree muttered. He looked at the ships again and wondered how long Keeble was going to take with the fuel.

He stood and looked out at the ships for a long time and eventually came to the conclusion he was going to have to revert to his original plan. Inaki was watching the multeese ships at the moment and the aliens seemed content to stay where they were, for a while at least. He was going to go and have a closer look while he had the chance.

-oOo-

Tuki sat on his own. Ruby looked his way, occasionally, but stayed with Amy and talked. Everyone else was either talking or sitting quietly.

When the train started to move, they all fell silent. A minute later, Hoodek came through the front door, rubbing a soot-stained hand through his spiky hair.

"We're going the wrong way," Flint said before the dwarf had a chance to say anything.

"We know that. Topper's taking us to the far side of the compound. At least that way we can have about two kilometers of run up before we get out in the open."

"Oh. Right. Good idea."

"We will not be turning around?" Meledrin asked.

Hoodek shook his head. "Well, maybe if there's somewhere to do it, but that's unlikely. Doesn't matter anyway— we can go just as fast backwards as forwards."

"If you are sure."

"We are. I reckon everyone should sit down and hang on." He looked around as if checking to see that everyone had taken his advice.

The hakans were already sitting and the ten hurgon who were coming along were holding onto the seating T's. That probably wouldn't be safe but who was going to order Grandmother Donni to sit down?

Tuki held on, though he supposed it would be a while before anything dangerous happened. They hardly moved above walking speed, but five minutes later the train came to a stop with a loud screech and a hiss of steam. And for a while they didn't move. Then the train lurched in the other direction. Paused and lurched again. This time it kept moving, slowly gathering speed. Tuki closed his eyes and listened.

He could understand something of the delight the dwarves took in machines. The *Hakabei* was cold and clean— at least the parts Tuki had anything to do with— but the train was a different thing. It was almost as if it were alive. When it was cold and silent or sitting still at the station, belching smoke out into the air, it was an ugly, brooding thing. But it had two lives. Once it was moving, it breathed and hissed and chugged and rattled as if it had made up it's mind and *wanted* something and would not stop until it got it. Even from inside the carriage it seemed to be all power and inevitability.

Tuki didn't want to know what was inevitable about this journey. He closed his eyes and hung on, waiting for whatever was to come.

Even with his eyes closed, Tuki knew when they had broken free of the compound and were out in the open air. The light on his eyes was almost painful after all the hours in the dim, gas-lit hallways. The sound of the train changed as well, the echoes left behind them and the open silence of the day welcoming them.

For a long time, Tuki stayed as he was, eyes closed, knees drawn up to his chest. Nobody else was saying anything so he had no idea what was happening. But the train was thundering on, pushing the carriage towards safety or towards death. And it was all out of Tuki's hands. He was doing all he could do; keeping out of the way and praying.

Eventually he opened his eyes. Everyone was where they had been last time he looked. The hurgon were still standing. Ruby was sitting with Amy. Meledrin and Palsamon together. Flint and Bones, next to each other but on two different worlds.

And above their heads, out the window, Tuki could see five kidol and each one was dropping their bombs almost as fast as they could. Normally the outer two of the three cylinders strapped to the creatures' bellies were full of soldiers, but Tuki thought they must have been left behind in favor of the weapons. He saw a dozen, two dozen bombs drop towards the ground. And more over there. From his spot on the floor he could feel the detonations, just, over the rumbling of the train, and he could see the plumes of smoke rising into the air, but he did not know if any of the multeese were dying. He hoped they were and the hope did not make him feel guilty. He glanced at Ruby.

Though he could not see them, he knew there were multeese on the ground for they were firing back at the kidol. Bones noticed the results as Tuki did. Or more likely, finally voiced the fact when Tuki noticed.

"Them multeese guns not doing much," he said.

Flint nodded.

"Maybe the guns aren't designed for killing," Ruby offered.

"The multeese do not want to kill the hurgon?" Tuki found that hard to believe. He knew the trolls thought it strange that the multeese did not simply kill everyone from space, but to have weapons that didn't even kill? That was crazy.

Flint nodded. "Maybe." But the look on his face suggested he thought the same as Tuki. "They haven't done much about killing anyone so far, have they?"

A kidol screeched, somehow heard above all the other noise, and plummeted to the ground. Apparently the guns could do enough.

The train thundered on.

-oOo-

Keeble stepped into the heat and noise of the workshop and immediately felt better. He knew that would only last until he found out how slow the work was going, so he stood near the door for a moment to enjoy the feeling.

It was almost like being back in Tab Cavern. Most of the factories there worked around the clock. And if what they normally made wasn't required, they'd quickly convert the machinery to making something else. That break in proceedings, the mad rush to work out the fastest, cheapest, best way to make the changes, was a process Keeble used to enjoy even more than the usual slow grind of production. But that was a lifetime ago and all he wanted now was a kilometer of piping to move some hydrogen. Was it too much to ask?

Makar emerged from a smoky corner. He was wiping his hands on an already oily rag and shouting at some unseen assistant. He saw Keeble and growled one last instruction before coming over to talk.

"That doesn't look good, Makar," Keeble said to the older dwarf.

"Nothing around here is good."

Keeble raised an eyebrow.

Makar sighed. "We were running ahead of schedule. We've got nearly 200 meters of pipe ready to go, but now the main furnace has got a two foot long crack."

"You're joking?"

Makar grunted. "No."

"So, how long?"

"I told you, two foot." He wiped his hands some more. "*That* was a joke."

Keeble raised an eyebrow.

Makar sighed. "Milo and Drago are discussing it with the foreman at the moment."

"And?"

"If the discussion finishes any time today I reckon it'll be at least eight hours after that until we can be up and running again."

"You're joking."

"Still no."

"So..."

"So, we've got 400 meters of pipe— that includes the 200 meters that was already here— that should be put in position as soon as possible. No use it sitting around here."

"Right. Of course. I'll get some people onto it straight away."

"Good. I'll keep hitting my head against the wall here." Makar shook his head. "We were doing so well."

"Is it possible—"

The older dwarf held up a hand and cut him off. "Don't even say it. We were running above capacity and that's what caused the failure. I knew it was a possibility but I thought it was worth the risk."

"It wasn't an accusation, Makar. Just a question. I would have done the same thing."

"Doesn't make me feel any better."

"Wouldn't help me either. Just see what you can do." Keeble looked around but there probably wasn't anything more he could do about the pipes. "How are the catapults coming along?"

"Two are being carried up onto the walls as we speak. It will still be an hour before they're set up, at best, but they're going better than expected."

"Good. Keep going. And let me know if you need more people."

68: Attack and Defense

PING SAT BACK AND WIPED SWEAT from her forehead. She wasn't sure what the day outside was like, but in the confines of the clock it was hot and humid. Dido was out of sight, working on the tangor assembly on the far side of the room. Ping was about to call out to see if she wanted a drink when Keeble stuck his head in through the access hatch.

"How's it going in here, Ping?"

"Not bad. We're just doing a check to hopefully stop anything from falling apart. We don't have time to fix the other clock yet."

"Oh, right."

"It all looks pretty good, so far." Ping let out a huff of breath and looked around. "Maybe we should go help with the Ohoga engine or something."

"I was just talking to Drago. I think he's got that under control. And the fuel still is just about done as well."

"So it's all under control then?"

"Pretty much. I was just talking to Makar about the catapults. He didn't mention needing help but..." The dwarf shrugged.

"All right, then."

When Keeble left, Ping rose to her feet and stretched. She packed away her tools, but left the toolbox on the floor. "Dido, I'm going to help with the catapults. You stay here and keep checking."

The dwife, mouth full of screwdriver, waved over her shoulder as she continued to work and Ping ducked out into the passageway. It was very quiet, but she supposed everyone was working somewhere, adding to the great machine that would let Keeble and Meledrin do the only two jobs that really mattered. Get the contracts and get the hydrogen. It felt strange that everything could come down to two such simple things. She sighed and headed down to the hold and from there to the compound.

The *Hakahei* was quiet but the compound was bustling with activity. Half the hurgon were wandering around in a daze, the other half all seemed to be doing something vitally important. Some were pulling wagons filled with what could only be ingredients for the pipe factory. Others had timber that could possibly be used for barricading windows and doors. They were all going somewhere.

It took a while for Ping to find out where the catapults were being made, and even then it was only because she bumped into Gulch heading the other way. He pointed her in the right direction then continued on, muttering to himself.

In a square, not far from the factory, the dwarves had set up a range of machines and jigs and were bustling around the bones of a catapult. Another was taking shape in an assembly area.

Ping looked around. "Milo, what can I do?"

Milo looked up for a moment then looked back to the task he'd been working on. He swung his mallet two more times, driving a wooden peg into a hole, joining two large sections of timber that would form part of a frame. When he was finished he wiped his hands on his trousers and looked around. "I'm not sure there's much you can do, Ping. Most of this isn't really skilled labor and the hurgon are handling it pretty well. They're just making pegs and fitting pieces together at the moment. The production line is running pretty smoothly."

Cuto had already taken up the mallet and was working on the next peg with the slow, steady determination shown by all hurgon.

"You could try Tasko," Milo continued. "He's building a crane on the wall near the *Hakahei*."

So Ping went back the way she'd come. She got turned around in the streets again but eventually found the outer wall and from there it wasn't hard to find the right gate. From down in the dust near the *Hakahei* she shaded her eyes and looked up at the top of the wall. Tasko was there, wide brimmed hat jammed down on his head, waving his arms as he tried to pass instructions to his hurgon work crew. Talus and Chip were there as well, but they probably didn't know any more than the hurgon.

"Do you need some help, Tasko?" Ping called.

"Ping?" He took off his hat and swatted it against his thigh, sending out a cloud of dust. "Not really. Once I get this lot to understand degobar pulleys it will pretty much be done. They'll probably be able to do the next one on their own."

Ping didn't know what a degobar pulley was. "Can I come up and have a look?" She had never given much thought to pulleys in the past, beyond the basics.

"Of course. If you want."

She crossed to the ladder and climbed slowly, gritting her teeth every time the ropes swung or she bashed her knuckles against the wall.

But it wasn't worth the effort. Not for the pulleys anyway. It was just a multiple pulley system that Tasko said was efficient and safe and had been used by the dwarves for centuries. But she listened to Tasko's explanation and nodded in all the right places and tried to remember, in case she needed it for something in the future. And when the lesson was over she watched the hurgon erecting the crane for a while then went to sit on the edge of the roof, feet dangling over nothing. From up there, the ruins surrounding the *Hakahei* were obvious. Straight, narrow streets that seemed no more deliberate than those in the current compound. And there was a crater about thirty meters to one side. It was about twenty meters across and ten deep and looked totally out of place amidst the flat dusty desert of the rest of the ruins.

"That must be where the old gas works were," Tasko said.

Ping jumped. She turned and saw the dwarf standing just behind her.

"There was an explosion. That's why the compound's in a different spot. The old one was almost completely destroyed."

"Wow."

"Yeah. Keeble was laughing about it because an explosion at the gas works destroyed one compound, so they went and built a new compound around the new gas works."

Ping gave a small laugh too. "It doesn't seem like the most sensible idea."

"The hurgon just can't seem to move forward."

"Maybe they will now. With us here and..." She gestured vaguely. "The multeese."

"Maybe."

Ping sighed. "I suppose I should go and do something. Sitting here isn't helping anyone."

-oOo-

Scree sat back and put his feet up on the desk.

"So, you're going to do this anyway?" Thorpe said. The human looked around at the others in the room, as if they might offer him support. They were trolls though, and the ones who weren't going wished that they were. "It's a worse idea now than it was before. You know that, right?"

Scree nodded. "I ain't doing it for fun. We know nothing about the multeese. This is probably the best chance we's going to get to find out."

"That doesn't mean it's the best option. And one way or another, you certainly shouldn't be going. What does Kim say?"

Scree shrugged.

"That's what I thought. You haven't told her."

"She's sleeping. I'd wakes her up but you said she needs to get lots of rest."

"That may be, but she's in charge and should have a say in a decision like this."

"You're right. You tell her about it when she wakes up."

"I'll tell her before you go."

Scree shrugged. He wasn't sure if Thorpe was serious and didn't care. "Whatever."

"So you're going?"

"Soon as we're ready."

"How many?"

"Me and Yellow Troop."

"That's it?"

"Got to make sure we can hold the ship and the compound."

"What about some dwarves, in case you need to work out how to fly the ship? And an elf, in case you decide to torture someone."

"Good idea. Elf will have to be Suldon, obviously. And... Mintar, maybe."

"I was joking."

"Really? Weren't funny." Scree smiled. "Thorpe, you and Stone is in charge. We'll need some of those explosives you got off the Americans."

Thorpe sighed. "Get one of the trolls to talk to Tim."

"Good."

"Go on, then. The sooner you go the better."

Scree rose to his feet and looked around at his companions. "Getting fuel is the priority. Make sure that happens. Come on Chasm, let's go." He called the rest of Yellow Troop in his head and asked them to find the two final members of the party. He wasn't sure what Suldon and Mintar would think of being volunteered but he didn't really care about that either.

He and Chasm stopped by the Weapons room to get body armor. By the time they made it down to the ground the others had already gathered. The trolls were checking their weapons and supplies. They were grim and focused. The other two were waiting silently, standing close and not looking all that comfortable.

"Peak informs us that we are going to look at one of the alien vessels."

Chasm nodded. "Don't want to come?"

Suldon shrugged.

Mintar said, "Suppose someone has to do it. Just hope I've been picked because you think I can do the job, not because I'm expendable."

"Ain't nobody's expendable, Mintar," Scree said. "You old enough to know how the world works and young enough to keep up, that's why you picked."

The dwarf laughed. He lifted the end of his long beard and kissed a green ribbon that had been tied there before pushing the hair back over his shoulder. "I won't be keeping up and you know it," he said.

69: Impossible to Kill

SCREE LOOKED OUT IN THE DIRECTION of the nearest ship, which he couldn't see from down on the ground. "I doubt we'll be running the whole way," he said. "That'd be too much to hopes for." He looked around to make sure everyone was ready. <Any action from the ships?> he asked in his mind.

Stone answered. <*Nothing.*>

<Right. Let me know if that changes.>

<*Course.*>

So they ran, following the rough, cobbled road that skirted along the bottom of the hill. After barely five hundred meters they swung around more to the west and climbed up through a shallow saddle. From there it was back down again, toward the next rough, gravel-strewn hill. They all looked pretty much the same.

<*I got movement,*> Stone said.

Scree pulled up in a hurry and looked around. <What's happening?>

<*Looks like a door opening but it's hard to be sure.*>

<That's it?>

<*At the moment.*>

"Come on," Scree said out loud. "If we take too long here we might be overrun."

Everyone started to run again. By the time they'd made it past the next hill even Scree was breathing heavily. Stopping for a rest he pulled the flask from the pouch on his belt and took a drink.

Mintar sat down and leaned against the carved cliff beside the road.

"Don't drink too much," Pool warned as she drank too. She poured a little into her hand and wiped it over her head.

Peak sat down as well and Scree shook his head. "Think we'll haves to see about doing some exercises on the ship. Should be able to run all the way to the damn multeese without stopping." He took another swig.

<*Aliens coming out, Scree. Shit load of them from three different doors. I got you over half way— about a kilometer out.*>

<Theys marching or forming up?>

<*Forming up.*>

One more hill then. "Come on. We gonna have company soon."

They turned aside from the road and climbed the side of the hill, sending down a small clattering landslide of stones with each step. Scree got down and crawled up to the crest. When he peered over the top he swore.

The ship was on the next hill. When Scree stood outside the *Hakahei* and looked up at it he found it hard to believe it could get off the ground. The multeese landing craft could have swallowed the *Hakahei* four times and still had room left for dessert. It looked like a strange insect with a dozen legs and long segmented tail. But if it was an insect it was blind for there was nothing that looked like a cockpit at the front, just a blank face with all sorts of equipment attached. There were all sorts of shapes stuck together with no purpose that Scree could see.

"What if it's automated?" Mintar asked when Scree voiced his thoughts.

"What?"

"What if whoever's in it doesn't actually fly it? The *Hakahei* can be programmed to do things on its own— like point towards a certain heading. What if the whole ship is like that?"

Peak shrugged. "Them ain't no windows in the kil'ini either, but the hurgon can see from inside."

"Well, yeah, I know, but..."

"Chasm saw a window on the front of the big ship," Chasm said.

"There you go, see," Mintar said. "If they need a window to fly the other ship then why don't they need one to fly this one?"

Peak shook his head. "That's the point, Mintar. We got no idea, so don't go making stuff up." He hefted his pack. "Come on, Scree, what we doing? Can't stand here all day."

"Maybe not, but we can't just go walking over there at the moment." Scree examined the closest of the aliens as the others lined up around it. It had three legs and three arms and each limb had three joints. The right arm didn't have a hand. It ended in a curved blade made from polished white bone. The left arm and hand looked like they were strong enough to crush rocks. The final arm, coming from the center of the chest— or what would be the chest if the alien was anything like a hakan— was small and delicate. It looked as if the whole body was covered in a hard shell, like a bug or a crab. The head was tall and tapered, ending in a crest of colored feathers, and could actually spin all the way around, like the bridge on top of the *Hakahei*. It was just about the weirdest thing Scree had ever seen and the others were basically the same. The feathers were different colors, but that was all. He figured there were about a thousand all up, but he didn't know how to guess something like that accurately. There were lots, which was all he really needed to know. <Can you see this, Stone?>

<Not great. More than I want to though, I suppose.>

<Tell me about it. All those landers... That's a damn lot of aliens.>

"What you thinking, hey, Scree?" Gulch asked.

Scree shook his head. "I'm thinking we got problems. Other than that..."

There was no signal, no order that Scree could hear, but as one the aliens started to move. They headed down towards the road in a column that kicked up a storm of dust in the still morning air. They marched in perfect unison, each arm held at a precise angle, each feathered crest fanned out brightly. The thudding of their feet set the ground to shaking.

"Hey, let's go," Gulch said.

"Where we going?" Mintar asked.

"Inside, of course. Where else, hey?"

Suldon shook his head. "I believe I can speak for Mintar as well when I say, I don't know if that is a sound course of action."

"What's the point of coming here if all we find out is that there's lots of them bastards, hey? We could've sat back on the *Hakahei* and worked that out."

"It ain't worth the risk," Scree said. "There's got to be some of them left on the ship. And if not, there's probably some type of automatic thing, even if the ships don't fly automatically."

Gulch stood up and hefted his pack. "Well, I'm going in there."

"No, you ain't."

But he was. Scree watched as the other troll jumped up and ran down the side of the hill, stooping low as if that might save him from the weapons that were probably already pointing in his direction. He was starting up the other side of the little valley before Scree thought to move.

"Flayed kittens. Come on then."

Suldon shook his head. "Just because Gulch disobeys your order and thus puts himself at risk does not mean the rest of us should do similarly."

But Scree was already following and he assumed the others, including the elf, would do the same. They made it all the way across the bare ground and up to the side of the ship. Gulch had already crept along to the nearest doorway and was sidling slowly up the ramp, weapon pointing into the brightly lit opening as he scanned for trouble. Scree swore again and raced to catch up.

They made it to the top of the ramp unscathed and stepped inside. The others came a moment later, spreading out slightly to cover all the angles.

<You still with me, Stone?>

<Yep. Can't see anything though.>

Scree didn't know what he was looking at anyway. There was row after row of holes in the ceiling, each one was about a meter across, hexagonal and penetrated more than two meters.

Pool pursed her lips and looked around. "What's all this about then, do you think?"

"I gots no idea. We should've brought Thorpe along."

"You want to listen to his complaining all day?" Peak asked, one eye scanning the room.

"He wouldn't haves complained. He would've done his job."

"I know that. Just saying."

"Right then." Scree looked around again too, but there was nothing new and none of what had been there before interested him. If he knew what it was it might make a difference. "What you think, Mintar?"

The dwarf tugged on his beard and fingered the ribbon. "Maybe the holes are just like seats."

"They ain't nothing like seats, hey," Gulch said. Peak agreed.

"But it might be hard to sit like we do with all those arms and legs." The dwarf was warming to his task. "See that bar at the end of each hole? Maybe they grab onto that with that strong hand of theirs and pull themselves up into the hole. That way the sides of the hole stops them from bouncing around too much."

"Seems a bit strange to me," Peak said, still not convinced.

"And them aliens seemed normal?" Scree asked. He wasn't sure Mintar was right, but he wasn't willing to rule anything out. "Whats if you's right, Mintar? What would that tell us about the aliens?"

The dwarf looked around some more. He nodded and continued to pull on his beard. "Well," he said. "I really don't have a clue."

Scree sighed. "That doesn't help."

"Well, obviously. How about this then— those strong arms must be *really* strong. I mean, could you hold yourself up in there for even five minutes." The dwarf looked Scree up and down. "Well, maybe *you* could, but I certainly couldn't."

Scree nodded. Seemed reasonable. But of course, the whole seat idea could be way off the mark anyway. "Come on, let's see what's through here."

He led the way through a large door on the far side of the room and found himself in hallway that seemed to run the length of the ship. There was another door on the far side of the hall and another room like the one he'd just left. And five meters away was a guard.

The creature was lightening fast. There was a weapon in its strong hand and it started to raise it almost instantly, as if it had been expecting hakans all along. But the trolls were quicker. While Suldon and Mintar darted back the way they'd come Scree opened fire and a moment later, the others did too. Bullets bounced away, clattering and rattling down the hall. A second longer and someone was going to get hurt, but an eye exploded in a spray of dark liquid and the alien finally stopped moving. It sank to the floor, still upright.

Scree moved carefully forward, not totally trusting that the creature was dead. "Tough bugger," he said as he prodded it with his gun. It still didn't move. He pushed harder, but it was like he was pushing against a tree trunk. "Don't know that you wants to try punching the thing. Just end up with a broken hand, I reckons."

The others finally came forward to examine the multeese as well.

Peak tapped at its arm and it sounded metallic.

"Aye, it's tough," Pool said. "And heavy. It's like it's armored." She went for a closer look. "Look here though. There's a gap at all the joints."

Scree figured it wouldn't be able to move otherwise. But he doubted anyone would be able to fire a bullet in there anyway. That left just the eyes, which weren't the biggest targets in the world either.

Peak grunted. "This has been a great mission," he said. "We've found out that there lot's of the aliens and them just about impossible to kill."

"Never thoughts it was going to be easy."

"Well, you been wrong before, Scree."

Scree shook his head. "No, I haven't. You thinking of Flint. Besides, we founds out that they *do* die, which is more than we knew before."

Chasm cleared her throat. "Might have to put that knowledge to use pretty soon."

Scree could hear it as well. Feet skittering on the hard floor. The trolls readied weapons. Mintar and Suldon tried to get out of the way.

"We ready?"

70: A Third Singer

KEEBLE WATCHED AS BRICK DUNNING and Talus dropped the first piece of pipe onto the ground at the base of the wall and sat down in the shade of the ship to rest for a minute.

"Where are the others?" Keeble asked.

But Crystal and Chip emerged from the gate a moment later. They dropped their pipe and went to rest as well.

"What took so long?"

Brick looked up at him. "We had to go the long way. You try getting a ten meter length of pipe through those streets."

"Oh. Right. Sorry."

He waved the apology aside. "Don't worry about it. We'd like to do it quicker, we'd like to go the short way. Those pipes are damn heavy."

"Only a hundred more lengths to go," Keeble said, trying to make it sound like it was going to be fun. Brick and Talus both muttered something he couldn't hear. "It won't all be this bad though."

"And why's that?"

"We've got this crane here and another is being built at the halfway point. That's barely a hundred meters from the factory."

"Yeah, in a straight line, maybe."

"Well, either way, it's closer than this."

"Fabulous." Brick sighed and climbed to his feet. He helped Talus up as well and the two of them headed back through the gate. Crystal and Chip followed not long after, leaving Keeble waiting for his construction crew. There was nothing he could do until they arrived.

When they did arrive Keeble had a plan of operation formed. He didn't waste any time. They didn't have any to waste.

"We're going to have to get this bit done as quickly as possible. There are multeese ships out there and who knows how long it will be before the bastards come looking for us in person." He looked around. "Shardy on the crane. It's geared so you should be able to handle it on your own easy enough."

The trollop started to scale the ladder to the top of the wall while Keeble worked with Cuto, Tasko, Bargle, Ari and Tim McCree to get a pipe beneath the crane and tied securely on.

A minute later, Shardy was working at the handle on the crane, reeling the heavy pipe in like a caught fish. The crew rushed up to help manhandle it over onto the roof. Then they were coming down again to get the next pipe ready to go.

"How we going to attach the pipe to the ship, Keeble?" Bargle asked.

Keeble swore. He had fittings to connect the pipes to each other, but they were of hurgon design and didn't match the valves on the ship. While the others worked on getting the pipe up the wall, he and Bargle went to the far side of the ship to look up at the valves.

"What's going on?" Tim asked. He shaded his eyes to look up as well.

Keeble told him.

The American nodded and continued to look. "Sing," he said eventually.

"Pardon."

"Sing a hole in the side of the ship and shove the pipe in there."

"Huh." Keeble looked back at the ship and tried to think of a reason why it wouldn't work. "The pipe will fill with stone when I stop Singing," he said. He hadn't given up on the idea but he had to think about it. If nothing else, it would save them having to get the pipe all the way around the other side of the ship.

Tasko joined them. They told him the problem and he had an answer straight away. "We block the end of the pipe," he said. "Then I Sing my Song of Doing the same time you Sing and the pipe will push the stone out of the way."

"That should work."

Tasko shook his head. "It does work. You obviously haven't had much to do with any plumbers."

"No."

"They've been doing it for years."

"Right then." Keeble swore. "Except we need three Singers to breach the hull. Where's Drago?"

"Not sure."

"Shardy," Keeble called. "Get someone to send Drago here as quickly as possible."

The trollop saluted as she continued to work the crane.

Keeble led the way and, without speaking, they started to get the two pieces of pipe connected. Keeble got in and worked with the wrench, tightening the clamps to join the pipes. Tasko and Bargle were sealing the joint with a sticky hurgon concoction that smelled terrible but dried hard in no time at all.

Keeble stood up when he was done and looked around on the roof. There was a piece of timber not far away. It was rotting on one end and likely to fall apart at any moment but it would stay together long enough to do the job. He scooped up the timber, broke it in half under his boot, then placed the two pieces side by side over the end of the pipe. But then he had to keep it in place.

Tasko was done with the joint. He saw what Keeble was doing and shook his head. "I wonder about you sometimes, Keeble." But he was smiling as he said it. He took a ball of string from one of the pouches on his belt and used it to tie the timber while Keeble held it.

Drago arrived before they'd finished, huffing up the ladder, beard thrown back over his shoulder. "What's going on?"

"We're putting this piece of pipe into the hull. Need a third Singer."

"Right you are then."

"Are we ready?" Shardy asked.

Keeble looked around, one final check. "Yes."

So they arranged themselves along either side of the pipe and started to push it out into the open air towards the ship. They were about halfway there when Tim asked, "Is this going to work?"

"Of course." But Keeble didn't know. The end was already starting to sag. The fuel tanks were lower than their current location so they'd just have to keep going and see what happened. "It'll have to." He didn't know if they'd be able to haul the pipes back in if it *didn't* work.

They kept pushing and it was going to be a close thing. Keeble tried to calculate the exact height of the floor on Level 8 fuel tanks.

"It's going to work." He started to Sing as they pushed some more. The weight was getting hard to hold. "Shardy, sit on the end." And they pushed some more.

Tasko and Drago were Singing, too.

When the pipe was almost touching the hull, Keeble concentrated on focusing his Song. He could feel the other Songs merging with his own, weaving melodies, Singing into the densely packed particles of the stone. They pushed the pipe into the magical opening and carefully lowered the end until it was resting on solid stone.

Keeble took a deep breath and let go of his song. He, Drago and Tasko stood side by side, looking at the ship.

"Too low," Tasko said.

"Too low," agree Drago.

"Yep." Keeble shook his head. "The damn thing will end up in the hold." He sucked on his teeth and wound the gears on his arm.

Tasko cocked his head to one side and ran his fingers through his red hair.

Ari stepped up beside them. "Could you Sing a ramp into the rock and just push the pipe up to the next level." She tried to scratch under the bandages on her arm.

Keeble shook his head. "Good idea, but no. It's hard enough pushing that damn thing as it is."

"Have we got a loop?" Bargle asked. The young dwarf was sitting on the edge of the roof, looking at the pipe as well.

"A loop of what?"

"Metal. An eyelet big enough for the crane's rope to go through."

"What for?"

"Have we got one?"

"No."

"A hook?"

"Yeah. Over there." Keeble had been intending to use it on the crane but didn't bother in the end.

Bargle went and picked up the hook. He examined it for a moment, gave a nod then went back to the edge of the roof. He took a deep breath, stepped up onto the pipe, and started to walk out towards the ship.

Keeble held his breath.

When Bargle reached the other side he leaned against the side of the ship for a moment before turning around to look back. "I need a little hole about here, Keeble. Just big enough to hold this." He pointed to a spot directly above the pipe.

And Keeble knew what the lad was talking about. "Good idea."

They Sang the hole so Bargle could set the hook into the stone up above his head. And Ari already had the end of the rope from the crane, ready to throw across. Bargle caught the rope and pushed it around behind the hook. Then, sitting down, he tied the end around the pipe just outside the wall. He tested the knot.

"Ready."

"Ready, Shardy," Keeble said. He, Drago and Tasko Sang again.

When they signaled, the trollop started to wind the handle on the crane and the end of the pipe lifted upwards through the stone while Bargle carefully hung on.

Keeble signaled again when it was high enough but didn't stop Singing.

"Ready, Bargle?" Tasko asked.

"Ready." Still straddling the pipe, Bargle moved backwards.

Keeble helped push the pipe further into the wall while Bargle shuffled backwards.

When they'd pushed far enough the young dwarf signaled. Keeble, Tasko and Drago reshaped their Songs so Bargle could climb through into the fuel tank and remove the timber from the end. Then he had to reshape the insubstantial stone on the way back out, molding it around the pipe and making it airtight.

Shardy cleared her throat. "You've got about five minutes."

71: The Other Side

TUKI HAD BEEN RELIEVED WHEN THE TRAIN was finally out of the open fields and under the trees. The sprint across the plain had seemed to take forever and every second they were there had brought another kidol closer to death. It had taken him some time to realize the creatures were only to draw attention away from the train and the Grandmother riding it. The distraction the hurgon had been talking about. Tuki felt guilty about each kidol that fell from the sky. Five. Five had died, along with the hurgon controlling them. He counted each one and said a small prayer.

But under the trees, finally, they started to climb, and even with just the one carriage for the train to push, they slowed. And each kilometer they slowed a little bit more. They were not being attacked under the trees, but Tuki figured it was only a matter of time.

The next minute passed, then the next until Tuki was unable to gauge the passing of time at all. He sat in the ever-moving patches of sunlight and shade, watching as the scatter of glass stars on the floor twinkled and flashed. The quiet talk of his companions filled his head. He wondered if his life had been paused, like one of the movies the humans and elves watched on the Hakahei.

And the train went slower and slower.

After a long time he rose to his feet and walked carefully to the back of the train, which was now the front. There was a glass window there, set in the top of a door, and he looked out to make sure the world outside the train still existed, that it was still moving forward like it should.

The trees were blowing in the breeze. Strange, ungainly birds burst into life as the train approached. The train was going so slow that the breeze overtook them, bringing with it the grey-white smoke from the engine.

The world moved on and the train labored up the hill.

Tuki jumped when somebody stepped up by his side. It was Topper, covered in soot and looking tired.

"How far to the top of this damn hill?" he asked softly, as if he too had been taken by the feeling of waiting.

Tuki shrugged. If he knew the exact speed of the train, and the total distances involved, he could have calculated...

"Seems much worse than it did last time."

Tuki could only agree. But even as they watched, the top of the hill came into view. And the narrow cutting where the train passed through to the other side.

"Huh." Topper gave him a pat on the back. "A couple of minutes then it's all down hill."

Tuki nodded. "But there is more open ground."

Topper didn't seem to care. "Flint," he said happily. "See if you can get Scree now. We're at the top. Or will be in a couple of minutes." The dwarf headed back towards the engine to tell his companions.

"Yeah, got him," Flint said a minute later. "Lucky bugger's been blowing stuff up. Kim isn't happy about that though."

Tuki stayed where he was, watching out the window as the cutting closed in around them, swallowed them, then spat them out the other side. And out in the open. Looking down the mountain, out across the forest -filled valley and the farmland, he gasped.

Someone heard him. "What is it, Tuki?"

He turned and saw that everyone was watching him. It was Flint who had spoken. The troll was already on his feet and heading towards the window as well.

"I have seen this valley before."

"Course you have. We came through it to get here."

"Yes, I know, but..." He shook his head. "I have seen it some other time as well."

"When."

"I do not know. I cannot remember."

"A picture?"

"I do not know."

Flint sighed. "Not really helpful then, is it."

"I guess not."

"Let me know if you remember."

Tuki nodded and watched out the window as time picked up speed and headed down the hill.

-oOo-

Keeble turned to look at the trollop. "What?" Keeble asked. "Five minutes?"

"Multeese is coming."

"Damn. Hurry it up there, Bargle."

Down below, Brick and Talus were back with another five meters of pipe. They dumped it on the ground and sat down to rest again. As had happened last time, Crystal and Chip emerged not long after.

"You'll have to take them back inside," Keeble called down.

"They can bloody well stay here," Brick said.

Keeble wondered if he'd have said something like that to one of his superior officers from the American Marines. "The multeese are coming."

"Shit. All right then."

The four members of the pipe-carrying squad climbed to their feet and got to work.

"How's that?" Bargle asked as the gate into the compound banged closed a minute later.

Keeble gathered his thoughts and tested the hull with his mind. He pointed out a split.

"Bargle," Shardy said. Keeble looked up at her. "Time to finish. Now."

"I'm not done yet."

"Now, Bargle."

Shardy pointed. Bargle wouldn't be able to see around the bulk of the ship but Keeble could. The multeese were approaching down the road. Strange white things with colorful feathers on their heads, scrabbling down the road like a long line of three legged cockroaches.

"I think you should get back here now, Bargle," Tasko said.

"We'll be finishing our Songs in about five seconds," Keeble said. He tried not to think about Sandy, but it was hard. Would it be worse this time? Did it get easier, each time you were responsible for a friends death? Or did the feelings merely accumulate, until it really was too much to bear? He didn't want to find out. "Get back here now. That's an order, Bargle."

Bargle shook his head. "None of this is any good if it isn't sealed properly." He kept working.

Twenty seconds later, Bargle sat back. "How is it?"

Sandy was a troll— it was her job to do dangerous things. Bargle was a dwarf… Keeble checked the hull with his mind. "It's great." There was a hollow spot about halfway through but it was sealed on either side, so it didn't really matter. And the multeese were down amid the ruins of the old compound. Keeble finished his Song as Bargle climbed to his feet.

"They're here?" Bargle asked.

"That's what we been saying," Shardy said. She had picked up her gun and was standing by the edge of the roof, though Keeble couldn't work out what she was going to do against... A thousand multeese?

The first aliens were almost at the wall. Bargle swore.

One of the creatures started to raise its weapon. Then another. Bargle swore again and started to walk along the pipe.

A weapon fired. It seemed to be an energy weapon, but the beam zinged off the pipe and whizzed away into nowhere.

Bargle started to run. Keeble watched, horrified. Another burst of energy passed behind Bargle. Then the aliens seemed to notice everyone else standing on the roof. More of the creatures started to raise their weapons and everyone moved back.

Keeble crouched down and stayed as close to the edge as he could. He wasn't willing to go too far. Shardy was by his side. Bargle was still running. It was barely more than ten meters but he seemed to take forever. Another weapon fired. Barge started to wobble. He had his arms out to keep his balance. It wasn't helping. He was only a couple of steps from the roof when he finally started to topple.

Keeble shouted. Bargle shouted. And with the last of his momentum threw himself towards the wall. He cartwheeled his arms. He thrashed at the air, trying to claw himself closer to the safety of the roof. He grabbed desperately at the wall. Missed.

But Shardy threw herself forward as well, sliding along the roof. Her hand shot out.

Bargle screamed. Shardy was almost hanging over the edge when she caught his wrist. She grunted, slid a bit further.

"A little help," she said, as if she was about to spill her cup of coffee.

But Tim was already there. He wedged his feet, grabbed her ankle and started to haul her back. After a moment, Keeble went to help as best he could with one hand, then Tasko was there and they were hauling the trollop back. Another weapon fired, but Bargle was slithering over the edge and onto the roof.

Keeble scrambled back and lay down out of sight. He watched the other dwarf and Bargle didn't move. Keeble licked his lips, heart racing. He reached forward, felt his throat constrict.

Then Bargle grunted and rolled over, spitting dust and testing to see if his nose was broken. "I think I knocked loose a tooth," he said.

Keeble slumped to the ground and drew in a dusty lungful of air. "Good work, everyone," he said between deep, ragged breaths. He wasn't sure if it had been worth it though. Bargle was right when he said that all the pipes in the world wouldn't help if it wasn't sealed at the ship, but they could've done that later.

"So we're stuck in the compound for a while now," Tim said. "Probably until this is sorted out."

Keeble grunted. At the speed the pipe was being made, that could be a while.

-oOo-

Scree dropped to one knee to give those behind him clear shots as half a dozen aliens stepped into the hall from the room they'd been in earlier. He aimed and fired, concentrating on the eyes.

But the multeese weren't stupid. After the first one went down, they held their bladed arms up to protect their faces and kept moving as they raised their weapons.

Scree swore. He charged forward, changing the angle of attack so he could get bullets in past their defenses. Pool and Gulch followed while the others kept the aliens busy.

Scree killed one, then another. When he turned to find another enemy he discovered they'd all been taken down.

"I think now might be a good time to leave," Mintar said.

Scree looked at the dwarf. He was holding his gun like he was ready to use it but really didn't look like he wanted to.

"You might be right." Scree cocked his head at the sound of more multeese getting closer. "Not quite yet though."

He got ready again and started firing before the multeese had a chance to think. They died quicker this time.

Scree motioned Pool forward. "Have a look for us."

Pool nodded. "Aye." She went forward to look into the room the creatures had come from. "Nobody in there," she said, beckoning the others forward.

Chasm went further in. "Chasm reckons they could be dangerous if they start thinking."

Scree agreed. "Just looks like they aren't used to any resistance at all. They arrives, others die."

"We'll have to show them otherwise, hey," Gulch said with a smile.

Peak nodded. "Right. We knows them can die, now let's set some of those explosive thingies and see if the ship can blow up. That sounds like much more fun than killing them buggers one at a time."

"It'll send a loud message, too, I reckon."

Pool removed her pack and took out the plastic bag that held the explosives. She held it up and examined the contents. "What we supposed to do with this stuff?" she asked.

"You got some plastic tube things in there, too, hey?" Gulch asked.

"Aye."

"That's a chemical fuse, hey. You break off a bit and shove it in the other bit. The longer the tube the longer its is until it goes bang."

Pool opened the plastic bag and took out the explosives for a closer look. She molded it in her hands. "And the more of this the bigger the bang?"

Gulch nodded. "That's what Tim said."

Scree picked up one of the multeese weapons and weighed it in his hand. It was heavy. Real heavy. He didn't know if he'd be able to carry it around for long. Not if he wanted to do anything.

"So how much do we want then?" Pool asked.

"Don't know. Tim didn't really say, hey."

Pool broke off a handful of the explosives then shrugged and took about half the entire amount. "So we stick it to a wall or something?" But she was already wedging it into the corner down near the floor, pushing it in to make sure it stayed.

Chasm had taken up the tube. "And how much of this?"

"A bit." Gulch broke off about ten centimeters. He held it up. "We ready? We have to run after I shoves this in, hey."

Scree nodded. "I'm ready."

Before Gulch could stick in the fuse the clatter of alien feet spun everyone around. A dozen aliens were standing in the hallway watching them.

"Who was supposed to be watching behind us?" Scree asked as he went the other way. But he'd been more interested in the explosives as well. Each and every day, the trolls were losing their edge. He grunted. It was probably his fault. Or at least, it was his job to make sure it didn't happen. He wasn't sure if those two things were the same or not and, as he skidded around a corner, he decided it was something he'd have to think about later.

He slowed down but could hear the skittering of the multeese close behind. So he ran some more, pulling Mintar with him up a set of broad, wide stairs. Three strides on each. Up four meters, five. The decor of the next floor didn't look all that different from the first. There were more doors and a T-intersection not far ahead. Scree headed that way. When they got there, half the trolls went one way, half the other. They stopped and turned to fight.

Four of the creatures died before they topped the stairs. The others came more slowly, arms up to protect their eyes.

72: Problems

SCREE CURSED. Without getting out into the open, there wasn't a lot they could do. "Any ideas?" he asked as another volley of bullets clattered harmlessly away. He looked around. The hall ended not far away in both directions. There was a door in the side wall.

"Through there," Mintar said.

"What the hell's in there?"

The dwarf sighed. "I don't know."

"Then why woulds we want to go in there?"

"Because there's just a single door."

Scree looked. Maybe there *was* only one door. Or there might be a door on the far side of wherever it led, meaning the multeese could attack from two directions. He sent Pool to look.

Around the corner, the multeese were getting closer. They were barely ten meters away now.

Pool came back. "No good. It's like a little control room."

"Control room?"

"Aye. They've got another ship in a hangar back there. 'Bout as big as the *Hakahei.*"

"Can we fly it?"

"No way down."

Scree looked around, trying to think. "Is that the outside wall?" He pointed to the wall at the end of the hall.

Mintar nodded. "I think so. It's about a meter thick if it is."

"And the other end?" Past the intersection where the others were hiding.

"Can't say, because I don't know how wide the ship actually is. I'd guess it was the outside though."

"Right. Gulch, use some of thats explosive on the wall there. Not too much though. Just enough to make a hole."

"We're about ten meters above the ground, hey," Gulch said.

"Twelve and a half," Mintar muttered.

"Whatever. The point is, we probably won't get down to the ground."

"You gots a better idea?"

Gulch stuck his head around the corner for another look. Then he pulled off a bit of the explosive and two centimeters of fuse. "We ready, hey?" Without waiting for an answer, Gulch stuck the fuse into the explosive.

"Ummm..." Mintar said.

Suldon took a step back.

Gulch watched the fuse intently.

"What are you doing, Gulch?" Chasm asked. She took a step back as well.

Scree stayed where he was. He didn't know what Gulch was doing, but he was willing to wait and see.

And right at the last second, just before it was too late, Gulch threw the explosives around the corner without even looking.

An explosion. The ship shook. Lights flickered. Part of the roof clattered down to the floor.

Scree tried to listen for the approach of the aliens, but his ears were ringing. After a few seconds he decided the fact they weren't yet being attacked was a good sign. He hefted his gun, and looked at his companions. Chasm gave him a nod. Across the other side of the connecting hall, Peak gave a nod as well. They ran out into the hall.

They needn't have bothered. The multeese were all dead, or so close that they weren't a threat to anyone.

"That worked better than expected, hey."

"Lucky for yous." Scree shot a squirming alien in the eye.

"Come on, it worked."

"Yeah, and a broken clock works twice a days."

"What?"

"It's one of Ping's sayings. Don't really understand it thoughs."

Suldon cleared his throat. "It means—"

But Scree turned to look at him and the elf fell silent. "I think we should get back to the place Pool left that other explosive stuff. We set that off then get the hell out of here."

"You might want to have a look at this first, Scree."

Scree went to stand by Mintar's side. The dwarf had pushed aside a piece of fallen ceiling panel and was looking at one of the multeese bodies. It took Scree a moment to work out what was so interesting.

"Scorched kittens."

"What is you looking at?" Peak asked.

Scree didn't say anything. He stared at the wires sticking out a hole in the chest of one of the dead multeese. There seemed to be a lot more wires beyond, with nothing that looked like an actual body part.

"They're robots," Mintar said when it became obvious Scree wouldn't.

"A what?"

"A robot."

Peak grunted. "Didn't understand you the first time, Mintar. What makes you think I would the second time?"

"A robot," Scree said. "Like a clockwork person. They ain't alive."

"Chasm doesn't understand either."

Scree sighed. "These things are just machines, like the *Hakahei*." But what did that mean? He didn't know and wasn't likely to work it out standing in the hallway of the alien ship. "Come on. Let's get out of here."

He led the way back down the wide, shallow stairs and stopped at the bottom to look around. After a moment, standing still in the silence, listening, he crept back to the explosives. He took the fuse off Gulch and broke away a long section.

"We ready?" He shoved the end into the explosives.

Back into the big room with the holes then out the door and down the ramp to the ground. None of the aliens could be seen. There were no more guards. They obviously thought they didn't need that many. That might all change very soon.

<What them multeese doing, Stone?> Scree asked as he ran.

<*They've all lined up out the front. Now they're waiting for something.*>

<They're in luck. Cause something's about to happen.>

<*That doesn't sound good.*>

<Course it's good. Just wait.>

Scree and his companions weren't waiting though. They ran down the first hill and up to the top of the second. They slid down behind the protection it offered.

"How long this gonna take?" Chasm asked.

Tim hadn't told Gulch, so how was Scree supposed to know?

They waited.

"Maybe—"

Then the multeese ship exploded. It was just one little explosion at first, but that explosion created another, then another. Parts of the ship were raining down around them, fizzing through the air, hissing quietly, sending up sprays of dirt when they hit.

A huge, buckled piece of hull, hit the ground not far away and Scree scuttled over to it with the others close behind. He slipped into the protective space beneath and made room. More explosions. Debris clattered against the metal. Something big hit— big enough to make a dent. Then there was quiet, apart from the crackle of a raging fire and the expansion of burning metals.

"Huh," Scree said. Another explosion shattered the day. He ducked down and covered his head, as if that might help. When the almost silence had returned he swallowed. He tried again, "Gulch, *that's* how you blows shit up."

Gulch didn't reply.

"Huh, you're just jealous," Scree said. "Gulch? Where's Gulch?"

He wasn't under the piece of hull. Scree climbed out and looked around. Gulch was lying on his side, halfway back to where they'd watched the first of the explosions. Scree swore. He made his way over to the other troll and rolled him onto his back. His head was caved in on one side. There were a dozen things nearby that might have done the damage.

"Flayed kittens."

Stone spoke in Scree's mind. *<That was pretty impressive, Scree, but you gots problems. Some of them multeese coming to have a look.>*

<Right then.>

<What's the problem?>

<Gulch didn't make it.>

<Dead?>

<Yeah.>

<Damn.>

<Yeah.>

<Well, you'd better leave him there. If you want to get back in you probably have to do it while they're still wondering what the hell's going on.>

Scree nodded, though obviously that wasn't going to help Stone. "Come on, we got to get back quick."

"So we're leaving Gulch?" Mintar asked.

"No choice."

"Kim won't be happy."

"She ain't going to be happy either way." Scree spat. All he could taste was smoke. The alien ship was still burning fiercely. "Come on." He spat again and started to run.

-oOo-

Kim watched on the camera as Bargle nearly got himself killed. Brave but stupid. Which normally amounted to the same thing anyway. She discovered she was standing up, and likely to get in trouble from Thorpe if he saw her, and lowered herself carefully back into her wheelchair.

She heard Inaki draw in a deep breath.

"That was a bit close, wasn't it?"

Inaki nodded in reply. "I did not think he was going to make it."

"Me either." Kim drew in some air as well.

Bargle *had* made it though, and now they had the first bit of pipe connected. There was still a long way to go, though, and the last Kim had heard there was a problem at the factory and no pipes at all were being made. They had about 400 meters— still a long way short of what was required.

She hit the button on the radio and adjusted it so she was talking to the security office. "Scree, why aren't we shooting at the multeese?"

"Scree ain't here," Stone replied. *"And we ain't shooting anyone cause they ain't shooting us. Our job is to survive long enough to get out of here, not start a fight."*

"Right. Fair enough." Kim sat back for a moment then asked, "Where's Scree?"

There was a slight pause. *"I'm not sure* exactly."

Kim grimaced. "You aren't very good at lying, Stone. I don't need to know *exactly* where he is. Approximate will do."

"Right. Well, at the moment he's lying on top of a hill a couple of kilometers from here."

That didn't sound good. "And why is he—"

There was an explosion. Not close by, but close enough to shake the ship and rattle her teeth. Kim stood up, hurt her knee, and quickly sat back down again. She was about to tell Inaki to find out what was going on, but he was already switching cameras. He probably didn't know what he was looking for.

It was obvious enough in the end. A huge cloud of smoke was rising into the sky in the direction of the closest multeese ship. Kim wanted to go up to her seat and spin the bridge. There were more explosions, as if one had set off the others. The clouds of smoke continued to rise.

Kim hit the button on the radio. "I'm guessing that was him."

"Yes."

"You weren't going to tell me this?"

There was a moment of silence. "*Well...*"

"Why didn't you tell me?" She drew in a breath. "And *don't* tell me I didn't ask."

"I didn't even know you were awake."

It was a fair enough point. And it wasn't Stone's job to tell her what Scree was doing. It was Scree's job.

"Well, I want to talk to him."

"Let's let him concentrate for a minute. He's on his way back anyway."

73: A Small Price

KIM WHEELED HER CHAIR BACKWARDS and forwards, going through all the things she was going to say to Scree when she had the chance. She could feel herself getting angrier by the moment. He shouldn't risk himself like that. Plus whoever he'd taken with him, of course. If he'd taken anyone at all. She wouldn't put it past him to go on his own. Did Thorpe know? She'd have to find him and ask.

She tried to calm down. Working herself into a spitting rage wasn't going to help anyone. Kim took a deep breath and looked around. Inaki was looking a bit worried, as if she was about to bite someone's head off, with him being the closest target. Another deep breath.

Kim was getting worse at waiting. In the past, as she backpacked around the world, waiting didn't really make all that much difference. The plane would leave eventually, the train would arrive, another lift would come along, someone would feed her before she starved. But now, every second seemed to count, so count them she did. Every single one.

Think about something else. "So, Inaki, are you angry with me? Do you wish you'd stayed back in Danyon Ford?"

The moai looked shocked to be asked, but gave the question some thought. "No, mo'shi. I think I feel as Tuki does— a life of risk is a small price to pay for doing deeds that matter."

Kim nodded. "So you don't hate me then? For lying to you?"

"You did not lie, mo'shi."

"I said we were going to heaven."

Inaki glanced at the aliens displayed above the skyglass and laughed. "Perhaps we are just going the long way."

Kim laughed as well and felt herself starting to relax. "Maybe we are." But Scree was out there still, coming back to a ship and compound that were under siege. "I think some of us are going a bit quicker than others."

A few minutes later, Stone was back on the radio. "*They're back.*"

Kim went to Inaki's radio and found the right frequency. She stabbed the button and almost shouted. "Scree."

"Hi, Kim. You're awake again."

"I've been awake for a while. But did you really think I was going to sleep through that damn earthquake anyway."

"You felt that?" Scree sounded amused.

"If you're going to do anything like that in the future— not just the explosion but the whole damn mission— you bloody tell me about it first or get back so quickly and so quietly that I never even know that you went."

"Course. I was going to—"

"Don't give me that shit."

There was a moment of silence. *"So why aren't you shooting at them, Stone?"*

"They weren't shooting at us, so we decided to wait and see what was happening with you."

"What's numbers like on the other sides?"

"Nothing like this side. Maybe a couple of hundred each side, but waiting in groups around the gates, not spread out."

Another voice joined the conversation. *"Hey, Scree. Kim. Stone."*

"Flint. Hows you going?" Scree asked.

"Yeah, you know. We got the contracts and we got Grandmother Donni."

"You got the Grandmother? We don't wants the bitch."

"Scree!" Kim said. Then she realized what else Flint had said. "The contracts are signed?" They were one step closer to getting out of there, though until everyone was on board, and they had fuel, the contracts didn't mean much at all.

"We's at the top of the mountains. Couple of hours away, hopefully."

"Good. That's great news." Things seemed to be going well. For a moment Kim thought that maybe she should put Scree in charge permanently. But she shook her head. That was just stupid. Scree was trying to get back after blowing up an alien spacecraft. And he'd probably pissed in the captain's seat for good measure. She was *not* going to leave him in charge.

"We'll let you know when we're getting close."

"Sounds, good. There's a bit of a siege going on here at the moment."

"Yeah, already run one of them twice today." As if it was something he did *every* day. *"Couple of other things. Far as we can work out, the aliens ain't the multeese."*

"What?" Kim said. She almost got up out of her chair again.

"Tuki found some stuff that suggests the multeese might be creatures made out of gas, or something. And these things obviously aren't made out of gas."

"They ain't actually aliens at all," Scree said. *"They're robots."*

Kim was having trouble keeping up. "The multeese are robots?" But no, they'd established that the multeese were gas creatures. However that worked. "So, the multeese have a robot army?"

"I'm just passin' on what Tuki told me."

"Don't matter at the moments," Scree said. *"Still gots to kill the buggers before they kill us."*

"Don't we always. Anyway, we's picking up speed now so we should see you soon."

"Good. See you soon, Flint. Be careful."

"Will do."

"And Scree, you'd better get back on this ship so I can tear shreds off you in person."

"Sounds like fun."

"We got four catapults and one big gun that can cover you on the way in, Scree," Stone offered.

"What about the Lander," Kim suggested.

"No way. Not yet, anyway. Gots to open the hangar doors. Who knows what the buggers might throws in there."

"Right."

Kim listened to the short conversation that followed but didn't really take part. Her military experience didn't involve catapults or sieges and she really didn't have anything to offer. Apart from telling people to be careful, as usual. And imagining all the horrible ways Scree could die. Scree and all the others. While the trolls talked, Kim asked Inaki to change the view in the dome. He showed the ground in front of the compound door and also showed the top of the wall in the smaller image above his console. By the time he was done, so were Scree and Stone.

"All right, here goes."

Kim leaned forward in her wheelchair to watch. She didn't want to watch, but couldn't turn away. Scree would get through. He always did.

-oOo-

Scree licked his lips.

There were a lot of aliens. A lot of robots. He wasn't sure that four catapults and one big gun were going to do much at all. Not much that would help, anyway. There were also a dozen P'targa guards and their energy weapons that were going to help. All of that might work as a diversion, but Scree and his companions were going to have to make their way through the middle of the enemy ranks. It would only take one second for them to be noticed and killed.

"That's why Kim's the boss," he muttered.

"Pardon?" Suldon asked.

"Nothing. You ready?"

"I am not."

"Let's go then."

The first catapult fired. It wasn't a very long shot— they could almost roll the rocks over the edge of the wall for the same effect. But it did do something. Some of the robots moved out of the way on quick, scuttling feet. Others died where they stood, some with a spectacular display of sparks, while others simply sank quietly to the ground, still upright.

Scree stood up and started to make his way slowly down the hill. Most of the enemy were around the main gate, obviously, which didn't help. But he headed in that direction because it was better than trying to climb the wall.

Another volley of stones and more of the robots scattered. And while they were moving, the big hurgon gun opened fire.

Half a dozen robots, all in one small area, exploded. Shrapnel whizzed past. Scree felt his arm cut, but didn't look. Another catapult, and a narrow avenue was starting to open up through the middle of the robots. They clambered over the first of the rocks. Mintar fell and Scree swore.

"Thought you dwarves loved this kind of stuff," Scree said as he stopped to help the dwarf to his feet.

"Running sieges?"

"No, clambering around on rocks and stuff."

"Only when I don't have to worry about other rocks landing on my head."

Scree smiled. Rocks landing on their heads were the least of their worries. "You right to walk?" He didn't want to have to carry him.

Mintar grunted in reply, as if the thought of doing anything other than walking was offensive. He started limping forward.

Nearby, one of the robots noticed their progress. Scree shot it in the eye just as Peak did the same thing. Then another robot.

Another explosion. More shrapnel. Scree's gun was almost knocked from his hand. A piece of metal was sticking from the side, just centimeters from his thumb. Sparks were biting at his fingers. He threw the weapon away and looked up in time to see a robot aiming in his direction. Suldon fired. He missed, but distracted the enemy long enough for Pool to get in a shot.

Big rocks rained down just meters away. Small pieces landed by their feet. Mintar went down again. Blood was streaming from a wound on his shoulder. Scree stopped again. He didn't have time to ask questions. He hauled the dwarf back to his feet. "Stop messing around and move."

Mintar winced with pain. "I apologize. I'll try to do better in the future."

"Good to hear."

The dwarf fingered the green ribbon tied in his beard, and started to walk. For a moment it looked like he wouldn't stay upright. Scree watched, saw he was going to be all right, for now at least, and turned his attention outwards again. He pulled the smaller, hand weapon from his belt and looked around. There was a fallen robot nearby. A stone had crushed one of its legs and it didn't seem to know how to handle the situation. Someone shot it.

There always seemed to be another robot. Amidst the rain of stone and occasional flying cloud of shrapnel there was always a robot ready to kill them. Scree and his companions tried to avoid attracting anyone's attention, but it wasn't easy. Scree shot another five, while he tried to keep an eye on Mintar. The dwarf stumbled along blindly, pain etched on his face.

Scree was just thinking they might make it when Pool stumbled as well. The trollop went down on all fours and before she had a chance to get even one foot under her, a beam of energy took her on the side of the face. It knocked her sideways, sent her tumbling onto her back. Scree swore. He grabbed Peak as the tall troll tried to go back for her.

"No, Peak," he shouted as another hail of stone smashed into the ground. "Suldon, keep moving." If they lost momentum they might never get going again.

Finally, the gates to the compound swung open and a dozen hurgon marched out. They started firing their weapons before the robots had a chance to react and cleared a small beachhead. Scree moved between the first of them. He looked back once, but Pool was lost from sight, hidden behind a mass of robots that now suddenly had targets they seemed to like.

The hurgon closed in behind Scree and his companions and the gates thudded shut behind them.

Scree sat down on the ground, throwing down his weapon. "Cats piss on them," he said. Kim's lecture would have to wait, but he thought it might be getting worse by the moment.

Mintar slumped to the ground and Suldon rushed to his side to see if he could help.

"Cat piss on them."

74: Visions

TUKI LOOKED UP FROM HIS SPOT ON THE FLOOR. "What did you say?" he asked.

Dogar pointed. "A meteor."

"Where."

"Out there. In the sky, obviously."

Tuki got to his feet and made his way to the dwarf's side.

"Over that way. Can't see it now. I didn't really see much of it before. Just a glimpse."

Tuki moved long the carriage, looking out the window, trying to see. And then he could see. A flaming ball was plummeting towards the ground from right up near the top of the sky. And as he watched, the meteor— though surely it was a spacecraft— broke into two pieces. Then both pieces were down behind the trees and lost from view.

"Stop the train," he said.

"What?"

"Stop the train."

"Why."

Tuki pushed past the dwarf and headed for the back of the carriage. He pulled the door open and jumped across to the engine without even thinking. He pulled open the next door and rushed through.

"You must stop the train, Topper."

"What? Why?"

Why did everyone ask questions all the time? Why did they not just listen? Perhaps it was because Tuki didn't usually give orders. He took a deep breath. "Stop the train now." He tried to sound like Kim did when she was giving an order that needed to be obeyed immediately. "That is an order."

There was an explosion somewhere, not far away. The ground shuddered and rumbled. Topper fell to the floor. Hoodek gripped a big, cast iron wheel. The train bounced and shook for a moment before settling down to clatter onwards.

On the floor, Topper had a wild look in his eyes. A moment later he was on his feet, pulling on a huge lever while he shouted at Hoodek and Nina.

The train lurched as the brakes engaged. The iron wheels screeched on the rails. The train started shaking all over again.

"What the hell is going on, Tuki?" Flint shouted from the carriage.

Tuki didn't answer. He jumped back to the carriage and rushed to the other end as best he could with the moving floor. It might not be the safest place but Tuki needed to see.

The train broke out into the clear. All around, trees had been flattened. Some were burning, others looked like they had dropped from the sky.

And not far ahead...

"What the hell is that?" Bones asked, rather succinctly.

"A spacecraft," Tuki replied.

"That was the meteor?" Dogar asked, holding a handle on the wall with one hand and pulling on his beard with the other.

Tuki nodded.

The train continued to screech and shake. It started to wobble as well. Tuki looked down and saw that the tracks were twisted and buckled.

When he looked up, the crashed ship was just in front of them, not far away at all. They weren't going to stop in time.

"Hang on," he shouted.

Just as he did, the train rolled to the right one more time, then hung on two wheels.

People screamed.

Without thinking, Tuki stepped towards the low side of the carriage, so when it finally toppled all the way, he hardly fell at all. The air was knocked from his lungs nonetheless. Glass stars rained down to inhabit a new universe on what had been the wall moments before.

There were shouts and groans.

"Are you all right?" someone asked. Tuki didn't know who had spoken. And if he was the target of the question, he wasn't sure he knew the answer.

Tuki rolled onto his back. He was lying on a small square of burnt grass and soil that had once been a window. He counted to ten. He moved his arms and legs, checking that it was still possible, then carefully sat up.

"Clear some space." Flint was hanging from the roof, strong fingers hooked onto a handle that ran along below a window, feet a meter above the ground. "Out of the way there, Meledrin."

The elf slowly moved out of the way, groaning as she did so, and Flint dropped down to the ground. "Everyone all right?" he asked.

"I will be all right," Tuki said. And he supposed that meant he should go and check on those who thought otherwise. Or those who could not answer. Palsamon was already bending over Dogar, helping the dwarf roll over. Bones was lifting some wooden seats off Grandmother Donni.

Tuki went to check on some of the hurgon guards who were not moving.

"Everyone all right down there?"

Tuki looked up again and saw Hoodek kneeling on top of the carriage, looking down through one of the windows.

"We are still endeavoring to find out, Hoodek," Meledrin replied. She had a cut on her arm and a large, purple bruise covered half of her face. "Are Topper and Nina well?"

"They'll live. Topper's already complaining."

"No point you gettin' down in here," Flint said. "You lot see if you can make us a door to get everyone out."

"Will do." And Hoodek hurried away. A minute later, there was a bang on the wall-that-was-the-roof that echoed around the carriage. A large section came loose and after a couple of more strikes a hole had been opened up.

Tuki helped carry Dogar out then clambered back in to help the others.

Fifteen minutes later, everyone was outside. One hurgon had hit its head and died, everyone else had sustained only minor injuries. Dogar was conscious, being tended to by Nina. Topper was near the front of the overturned carriage, looking at the remains of the railway tracks and the alien ship that had broken them. Everyone else was sitting quietly on the scorched earth.

Tuki pushed himself to his feet and went to crouch by Topper's side. The ship, or the half ship, seeing Tuki had watched it break apart, was about twenty meters away, half buried in the ground at the bottom of a crater. Despite being on fire in several places, sending up thick columns of black smoke, the ship was still mostly intact. It was a strange looking thing, all angles and protuberances and crazy tangles of equipment. Apart from the crackling of fires and the pinging of metal, all was quiet.

"How did you know?" the dwarf asked.

"I saw it in a vision," Tuki said.

"A vision?"

Tuki nodded. "I found a ewer in the desert. It showed me the valley and the meteor— the ship— destroying the tracks."

"You saw this valley in a vision shown to you by a bottle?"

"Yes. I think it has something to do with being able to link with the skyglass."

"When?"

"Back on Kiva." The same day he had seen the hurgon ships in the shy. So long ago, in another life.

"But... Visions aren't real," Topper said, throwing a stick at the side of the spaceship. It was still burning in a dozen different places that Tuki could see. Long tails of smoke were wagging in the sky.

Tuki raised his eyebrows. "You can tunnel through solid stone by singing but a vision surprises you?"

Topper shrugged. "It isn't *my* vision, though, is it?"

"I guess not."

"Either way, I'm not complaining. We'd be down in that crater with it if you hadn't told us to stop."

"Do you think that will make any difference with Scree?"

"What? Oh." Topper laughed. "I don't think it will. You're still going to be in trouble when we get back."

Flint joined them.

"What now?" Topper asked him.

"You tell me?"

"Me?" The dwarf laughed. "What, we fix the ship and fly it home? Or we move it out of the way and fix the rails?"

Flint gave a little smile. "I'm easy— you choose."

Topper shook his head. "Well, I've already driven a train, so I say we fix the ship."

"You won't get to drive," Flint told him. "Trolls drive that kind of thing."

"In that case, I absolutely refuse to do it."

"That's what I thought you'd say. I guess we have to walk then," Flint said. "How far to the compound, Tuki?"

"About forty kilometers." Looking at the sky, he guessed there were a couple of hours of light left, if they were lucky.

Flint examined the rest of the group, who had gathered near the train. "That's the rest of today and all of tomorrow with this lot, I reckon. Maybe old Donni can't make it at all. How long does this changing take them?" He grunted. "We could leave the hurgon behind. We could make it in about three hours." He looked at Topper then back at the others. "I could anyway."

"I could make it in an hour and a half," Tuki told him. "Maybe two."

"You're kidding?" Flint nodded, obviously impressed, and Tuki blushed. "Might have to see about that some time."

"If you wish."

And they all looked at the twisted tracks and the ship.

Tuki shifted and cleared his throat.

"What you got, Tuki?"

"There's ten kilometers of forest."

"Yeah. About that, I suppose."

"We could get everyone that far, couldn't we?"

Flint looked back again. "Maybe."

"Then we tell Scree to meet us there with another train."

"Do they have another train?" Topper asked.

"Not my problem now," Flint said a minute later. "I've told Scree the story. He's going to see what he can organize."

"And if he can't organize anything?" Tuki asked.

"Then we've already started walking. I'll go see what Meledrin thinks."

75: Different People

TUKI STAYED WHERE HE WAS while Flint rose to his feet and headed for the remains of the train. It was a formality because Meledrin would not be able to come up with an alternative plan. So, soon they would be running. Or at least walking.

But apparently Grandmother Donni wasn't walking anywhere. It took half an hour for the guards to build a stretcher she could sit on, then four of them took up the burden and started to skirt around the crater.

When Tuki climbed up onto the tracks on the far side of the ship, he stopped to look back. This side of the ship was in worse condition than the other. This was the side that had been attached to the other part. The interior was on display with all types of equipment spilling out onto the ground.

Ruby stopped close by, looking at the scene as well.

Tuki nodded as he started moving again, but did not stop to talk or even turn to look back. He jogged along the tracks until he caught up with Bones.

"What's with you and Ruby?" Bones asked. He was limping badly and there was pain in his eyes, but he scanned the surrounding forest as he talked. "What's going on there? Huh? What's happening?"

"Pardon? Nothing."

The troll gave a grunt of laugher. "I ain't had much to do with stuff like that— not many trolls have— but I ain't stupid. You fighting with her about something. Maybe not fighting. I don't know."

"We have not been fighting." And it was true. They hadn't been fighting at all. Tuki had hardly even talked to her, which might well be the same thing in this situation, he supposed. Bones seemed to think the same thing.

"Maybe not fighting, but there's something going on. No fighting?"

Tuki looked back at Ruby.

"Something, something, *something* going on. That's for sure and certain."

"It's just..." Tuki didn't know if he wanted to talk to Bones about it or not. If he was going to talk to anyone, would a troll be the best choice or would he only be able to see the situation from Ruby's perspective? He scratched at the meteor tattoo on the back of his hand. "It's just, she killed people today. She..."

"She killed people before. Yesterday. Well maybe not yesterday. We were flying yesterday. But probably lots of people. I don't know. She definitely killed some. Humans even, not just hurgon. Lots of people. Maybe a lot of them didn't deserve it."

"Yes, but..."

"But you ain't never seen her do it? She killed them though. You knew she had."

Tuki nodded.

"You knew she had. You had to have known. I mean, she's a troll. Did you think she was the one troll who was different? You think she was picking flowers? She was baking cakes?" He stopped and looked back at her. "You think she *can* bake cakes? Cakes is good."

Of course Tuki had suspected that Ruby had killed people before. He didn't think that was entirely the problem. "She becomes a different person when she does it. The look in her eyes—"

Bones laughed and shook his head.

"Why is that funny? It is true."

"No it ain't. You think there's some magic that turns her into a dragon when she picks up a gun?" Bones shook his head. "There ain't no magic. She don't become a different person. Put a gun in her hand and she's Ruby with a gun in her hand, that's all. Ruby with a job to do."

Tuki sighed.

"Do you think Meledrin is always like that?" Bones asked softly. "Even when she's alone with Palsamon?"

Tuki looked at the elf, pursing his lips. Bones looked as well and seemed to be having the same thought. "Perhaps she is."

"You're right. Maybe she is. Not a good example, but you know what I mean. I reckon we're all like them multeese. Lots of people inside each of us trying to take control at different times."

"But we aren't—"

Bones grabbed Tuki's arm and drew him to a halt. He cocked his head to listen. It seemed he was about to call out to Flint but, up at the front of the line, Flint had paused too. Tuki turned and saw Ruby looking back the way they'd come. She had her gun raised.

"Ruby?" Flint called, taking a few steps towards her.

She held up her hand. "Something's alive in that damn ship."

"Can't be," Bones said. He went to join her. "No. Nothing lived through that crash. Can't be."

Tuki stayed where he was, resisting the urge to turn and flee. He jumped when Flint stepped up beside him.

"There's something in there all right," Bones said. He raised his gun. "I can hear it. You hear it, Ruby?"

"Can't be," Flint said, echoing Bones' words of a minute earlier. Tuki was starting to think that there could be. He doubted both Bones and Ruby would be wrong about something like that. He doubted even one of them would be wrong.

Then the two of them started shooting. And they turned and ran along the track.

"Run," Ruby said. "There's dozens of them coming out."

"Them three legged bastards?"

"Yep."

Tuki took two steps along the track, but Ruby grabbed his arm and pulled him down the slope and into the trees.

A moment later, a multeese weapon fired and a hurgon tumbled to the ground. More weapons fired. Tuki heard something whiz past his head. He hunched his shoulders and changed direction, heading for a large tree.

Brother Koli was running right behind him, looking unconcerned.

Tuki reached the tree and slid to a halt. He looked back in time to see Koli struck down. The hurgon fell heavily, as if all his bones had suddenly turned to jelly. He hit the ground hard, bounced, rolled, and stopped right near the base of the tree in a tangle of limbs. He had a large, ugly mark in the middle of his back. Tuki stared for a moment, swallowed. He glanced out into the trees, then back at the hurgon. And it took a moment for him to realize Koli was still breathing.

Ruby was right. The multeese weapons were not made for killing. That was crazy, but now he had proof. Koli had been hit dead center but still lived. Tuki swallowed again, then darted out into the open and pulled Koli to safety. After a moment of indecision he hefted the alien onto his shoulder. He was big and heavy and Tuki didn't know how far he could go, but he went in search of Flint or Meledrin. He kept low, and wove from side to side.

Every moment, he expected the feel the heat of a weapon.

-oOo-

Ping watched as another section of pipe was swung around on the crane and lowered onto the roof. Tasko untied it, then Peak and Scree hoisted it up onto their shoulders and started to walk. Ping picked up the bucket of sealant she'd been sent to fetch and followed along behind. The roofs of most of the buildings in the compound were three stories, but that didn't mean they were exactly the same height. Some of the makeshift bridges that had been laid over the narrow streets climbed at alarming angles, or led on roundabout routes that skirted taller or shorter structures.

The trolls maneuvered the long pipe around tight corners and over gaps without slowing. They chatted and sang bawdy marching songs. Two men who knew how to find enjoyment in little things. Ping carried her bucket silently in their wake and couldn't help but smile. Behind her came two hurgon with another pipe, trudging along silently.

Shifting the bucket to another hand, Ping carefully negotiated a particularly steep bridge. Up ahead, Scree suddenly stopped singing. He stopped dead.

"Whats do you mean?" he shouted. "Cat piss on that."

Ping stopped as well.

"Are you sures?" Scree said, quietly this time, and Ping realized he was talking to someone in his head. He put the pipe down and sat on a strange piece of equipment. He rubbed his face. "Let me knows. I'll send the Lander."

A pause.

"I know, but what choice haves we gots? You're nowhere near the railway tracks." He seemed to realize he was talking out loud for the first time.

Ping watched as he continued silently. The hurgon went past with their pipe, edging past Peak, continuing forward as if they didn't realize what had just happened. As if they didn't realize that Scree losing control like that was a thing to cause concern.

"We couldn't know Scree," Peak said. He ran his fingers through his crazy tussock of hair. "Maybe we wouldn't have been able to do anything anyway."

"That ain't the points, Peak, and you know it. I told you not to go back."

Ping put her bucket down and cleared her throat. "What is it, Scree? What happened?"

Scree sighed. "Them multeese guns... The robot..." He kicked the pipe near his feet. "They don't kill. They just knocks you unconscious."

Ping licked her lips. "Surely that's a good thing."

Scree bent to pick up the pipe and surged to his feet with it on his shoulder. Peak looked at his end, where it still rested on the ground. "We left Pool out there," he said, his one eye blinking. "We left her outside the gate."

Ping opened her mouth. They'd thought Pool was dead, killed when they were trying to get back into the compound, and left her for the robots. She swallowed, blinked away tears. When she looked up, Peak and Scree had gone, around the next building and out of sight. She hurried to catch up.

At the work site, it was as if everything was normal, even if Scree wasn't singing and laughing as he had been a short while earlier. He was gruff and blustering and shouting orders, though Keeble had everything under control. He, Bargle and Mintar had already fitted the new pipe into the old and were tightening the clamps. Ping glanced at Scree, then rushed forward and started to apply the sealant. She hoped everything would hold together long enough.

76: Battles

PING JUMPED WHEN SOMETHING CRACKED and a piece of metal broke. Keeble swore. The clamp he'd been tightening had snapped, sending one piece rocketing into the side of a building.

"Useless crap," Keeble said. "The hurgon—"

"Not their fault, Keeble," Tasko said. "Makar's been making these as well and he's not taking the time to do quality checks."

"I know, but the hurgon can get into space and this is still the best metal they can come up with."

"They don't need metal in space. They have the kil'ini."

"I know, but dwarves weren't anywhere near space but still had better metal than this." He pulled the remains of the clamp off the pipe and went to get another from the pile. "And it's not as if all their metal is..."

Ping looked up from her work again as Keeble trailed away to silence. "What is it, Keeble?"

But the dwarf wasn't listening. He looked around, found the Uncle in charge of the hurgon and started waving his arms. Ping tried to follow.

"Are there any En'kumo in the compound?"

"There are approximately ten. En'kumo are here to deal with contractual matters and pass on orders."

"Where are the En'kumo?"

"The En'kumo live in a small unit near the south gate."

"Take Scree to them. Now."

"Uncle Taco does not—"

"Now." Keeble turned to Scree. "The En'kumo are working with the multeese," he said. "They're probably going to open the gates or something."

"What?" Ping said, but it could not be heard over Scree asking the same question.

"Just go." The dwarf pushed the hurgon towards the bridge. Scree and Peak followed.

"What's going on, Keeble?" Ping asked.

"I'm an idiot." He sat down on a waiting pipe. "There are barrels at the processing plant."

"So?"

"So, they were stainless steel. Bright, shiny, new stainless steel. Or something like it. The hurgon can't make anything like that."

Ping was feeling very stupid. "So?"

"So they had to get them from somewhere else. And now the multeese are here, attacking this compound in particular."

"So the En'kumo, or the T'loop really, have a contract with the multeese to..."

"To what? Yes, that would be the next question."

Ping stood up, looking at the spot where Scree had disappeared. Keeble sighed and did the same.

-oOo-

Meledrin crouched down behind the fallen log and tried to catch her breath. She touched at her aching cheek and turned to talk to Flint, but the troll was not there. He had been by her side for the last half an hour so it was quite a shock to discover otherwise. She looked around and saw he was barely ten meters away, taking cover behind a tree.

"How far to the edge of the forest?" she called to him.

"Tuki reckons about two kilometers but I ain't sure how accurate he can be with all this dodging and weaving."

Meledrin nodded and had a quick look up over the tree. She could see none of their pursuers so she darted across the open space to the troll. Bones was another twenty meters further on having taken over the point position after Flint decided she needed protection.

"What is the location of the brothers?" But they were close by as well, crouched behind a mound of dirt, trying to catch their breath.

The muffled bang of gunfire brought Meledrin's attention back to Flint. He was firing in the other direction.

"Come on, they're coming again."

Meledrin followed as he rushed on.

Three P'targa had gone down in the initial scramble, and been left behind. Another two had been rescued after Tuki's revelation that the enemy weapons did not kill. Meledrin sighed. Brother Koli may not be dead, but it was yet to be seen if the hurgon would ever wake.

Ever since the first attack, the multeese had been steadily pushing them north, though if that was a specific plan or mere coincidence, nobody could discern. So they continued to run, holding off the enemy attacks when they could, running when they couldn't. Another five hurgon had been hit and three left behind. So now all the brothers who remained were busy, four carrying Grandmother Donni on her stretcher, the others carrying their fallen companions.

Down into a gully that angled across their direction of travel, crouching as they ran along the bottom. Meledrin found herself beside Tuki. The lad had a gash on his cheek and was limping badly. He was still carrying Brother Koli over his shoulder, having taken him back from a hurgon after a short rest. But he looked exhausted again. Sweat was running down his face. It was doubtful he would be able to continue for much longer. It was hard to believe he had managed for as long as he had.

Meledrin stubbed her toe on a tree root and almost tripped. She caught herself before she used a trollish curse and turned her attention to what she was doing.

The sound of gunfire continued. Meledrin knew she should be afraid, but she was tired and sore and she knew it would take an hour of brushing to get the tangles from her hair. She was more angry than afraid. And she was tired. They had not run very far but they had been on the go for a long time and it didn't look like they would be able to rest any time soon.

She looked around for Palsamon and was relieved to see him not far away.

-oOo-

Scree didn't know how Keeble knew, but he wasn't about to argue. The dwarf wasn't the sort to say things if he wasn't sure. He wasn't the type who rushed into any type of commitment. So Scree followed the hurgon from one roof to the next, racing over the rickety bridge. On the next roof, Chip and Crystal were lugging a pipe around a mess of machinery.

"Drops that and come with me."

Scree didn't slow. He heard the pipe hit the floor and didn't even look back. Then it was Talus and Brick. They must've seen something in his eyes because they were lowering their burden before he even spoke.

"Come on."

They climbed down from the roofs then raced through the narrow, winding streets. Scree pushed past workers and stiff-legged, glassy-eyed hurgon. The complaints increased as the others came along behind.

Their guide finally stopped and pointed to the door of a tall, narrow building with bars on the windows and a big lock on the door. Scree didn't even slow. He hit the hinge side of the door with his shoulder, then kicked twice and was inside. Nothing. He paused for a moment, listening, before the others started to come in behind him.

"Talus," he waved the youngster up the stairs. Too late though. He knew it.

<*Clear,*> Talus said a second later. Then twice more as he checked each floor.

"Where's the nearest gate?" Scree asked the hurgon. Then he had to slow down and get his brain moving so he could use the ini rituals.

When he got the idea, the hurgon led the way.

It wasn't far. Around one corner, two, and they found a fight. Two P'targa guards were dead. Another dozen were trying to hold the gates closed and fight off the En'kumo at the same time. Scree didn't have a weapon, but that would be easy enough to fix. He threw himself into the fight, punching and kicking, before he pulled a gun away from a stunned hurgon. He started firing and a second later, Brick and Crystal were doing the same. Peak was clubbing at the hurgon with a lump of wood he'd found on the ground. His one eye was wide and wild.

The tide of the battle inside the walls changed quickly, but the pressure on the gate was increasing. Scree fired his gun again and again then threw it on the ground and put his shoulder against the ancient, grey wood to help push. A beam of energy burst through the gap and took down an En'kumo. Scree grunted and strained, pushing, trying to find purchase for his feet. A clawed, white arm slithered through the gap, waving, thrashing, looking for something to hit. Anything. Peak was there then, attacking the arm with his lump of wood, beating and pounding for what seemed like forever.

Then the arm broke, snapped at the elbow. Blue and red sparks spat and the robot withdrew. Peak leant his strength to the door and they started to make progress. Slow, sweating progress.

The battle inside the gate quietened. Scree looked back and saw that there was only one En'kumo remaining. It didn't last long. Then Brick and the other trolls hit the door like the men in one of Keeble's rugby games. The door started to move faster. More bolts of energy found a way through the closing gap, but nobody was hurt. Scree pushed and heaved until the door thudded home, then spun around and stood with his back against it, heels wedged into a join in the cobbles, while a huge bar was lowered.

Finally, he slid down to the ground, breathing deeply. "Is that all of them?" he asked, gesturing to the En'kumo. Then he swore and used the ini' rituals.

There were definitely supposed to be ten, and there were definitely ten. Scree drew in a ragged breath and sighed. That was done.

Now, pipes.

"Come on." He pushed himself to his feet and started heading back towards the work site.

77: Time

MELEDRIN DUCKED BEHIND A ROCK and leaned back to rest. She closed her eyes— one was barely open now anyway— and tried to breathe. A touch on her shoulder brought her back to the present.

"What is it, Palsamon?"

"Are you well? Your face looks…"

For a moment she did not answer. She closed her eyes again and breathed some more. "Yes. Thank you. I merely need to rest."

"Soon, hopefully. Where is Flint?"

At that moment the troll came and slumped down by their side. He'd been helping the remaining hurgon carry their unconscious companions and trying to keep everyone moving. It looked as if he had run five times as far as anyone else and it was quite possible.

"How far away is Scree?"

"Scree ain't driving. Shardy is."

"I am unconcerned about the identity of the driver."

"Right. She won't be long. Five minutes, maybe."

"Can we wait that long?"

Flint nodded but checked over the top of the rock, as if wondering if they *could* wait. He ducked back down quickly and Meledrin started to worry. The troll signaled to Ruby, Bones and Amy McCree. Then he tried some of the ini rituals to the hurgon. And he sat down to wait while the others spread out. Another signal and those on one side of the line jumped out from behind their cover and fired. Seconds later they ducked back out of sight. Then the other side. Then the middle. Palsamon jumped up as well, though Meledrin tried to stop him. He fired his weapon several times then dropped to the ground.

"I do not know if that is wise, Palsamon. You could be injured."

Palsamon was fiddling with his gun. "So only trolls and hurgon should take risks?"

"It is their role." That was true enough, but Meledrin discovered that her concerns were more personal, and more selfish.

"We are fighting this war together. I might not be as skilled as they, but I can assist. Topper and the dwarves are helping."

Palsamon looked around when Flint jumped up again and a moment later did the same. He fired. Hid.

"Palsamon, please stay hidden." She was still unsure that she really knew what love was, but she admitted to herself that her life would be a much darker and colder place without Palsamon in it. She waved a *Greater Changing*. "If you were to be hurt, I am not sure what I would do."

Palsamon was staring at her. Meledrin blushed and ducked her head.

"Shardy's here." Flint was looking out towards the open ground beyond the edge of the trees. "There." He pointed.

Meledrin tried to see the Lander. She could see nothing until she shifted and finally saw the craft coming in from behind a tree. It was already being fired upon. It took a moment for Meledrin to realize that it was being targeted from the sides. She thought of pointing out the fact to Flint— it might be important— but decided he would already know.

"Come on you lot. That rock over there." He ran and Meledrin had no choice but to follow. She leapt over a fallen branch, wove, slipped between two trees and stopped behind the rock Flint had indicated. The troll was running backwards, firing into the trees. The other wings of the defensive line were coming as well, heading for the same hiding place.

It was crowded behind the rock and Meledrin was unsure of the strategic sense of grouping everyone together, but she had not noticed any other options as she ran so could not really complain.

The clear ground was only a few meters away, but with the trees thinning it was possible to see the multeese warriors closing in from all around.

"Where is Shardy?" Meledrin asked, pushing hair away from her face.

But she located the Lander again as it dropped below the height of the trees, humming and clattering as if something were wrong. The multeese weapons were constantly hitting it. Clouds of dust billowed into the air.

"Are we to go?" Meledrin asked.

"Not yet. Wait."

The Lander thumped down onto the ground and Chasm jumped down from the back. She had a weapon in each hand, larger than the ones usually used by the trolls, and started to fire.

"Now." Flint shouted and waved his arms at the same time. Hakans and hurgon moved as one, heading for the Lander. Meledrin stumbled and someone held her upright. She didn't know who. The weapons kept firing around her. Dosa was hit. She flopped to the ground right in front of Meledrin. Meledrin almost fell over her. She stopped, reached down and grabbed the dwife's arm. Someone else grabbed another arm.

Dogar looked up at Meledrin. "Don't just stand there."

They dragged Dosa towards the Lander. Meledrin concentrated on the back door, willing it closer. Her hand was slippery with sweat but she tightened her grip, holding on. And between one moment and the next Dosa seemed to double in weight. She looked back and Dogar was lying on the ground, limp and motionless. Meledrin kept moving mindlessly for seconds.

"Dogar!" But obviously he didn't reply.

The multeese were coming, streaming from the trees, closing on the Lander from all sides. Hurgon and trolls were climbing up. Grandmother Donni was handed inside. Topper and Hoodek climbed up. Tuki. Hurgon were scrambling up. One fell. Another.

The multeese were getting closer.

Then Meledrin was at the back of the Lander and hands were pulling her inside. And Dosa too.

Flint, Ruby, and Chasm were the only ones left outside. Meledrin saw Flint take a step towards Dogar. But the multeese were almost there and Ruby pulled him back. She pulled him into the Lander and the others were onboard a moment later.

Meledrin watched as the multeese warriors swarmed over the still form of Dogar as the Lander leapt into the air. She was crying, but didn't even notice.

-oOo-

Kim froze.

"Greetings, scuttle bug. Multeese sees you there. Did you think we would not?"

She turned to look at the screen on the back wall of the bridge. The old, inhuman, humanoid face of the multeese was there. Or not the multeese. No more than the robots surrounding the *Hakahei* were.

Kim swallowed. "Well, we were hoping." It was barely audible.

"Well, you have annoyed multeese one time too many now. Multeese has plans, schedules, and you are in the way. Once multeese have finished collection in this region, multeese will go to your region, to clean up the mess."

What would Scree do? What would he say? He'd insult the bastard, or he'd try to get every advantage he could. "Ummm... How long?" It was probably arrogant enough to answer.

"Two hours until we arrive, but multeese roboids..." A flicker on the screen. *"Multeese robots have been reprogrammed. Hakans were unexpected. That will no longer be the case. The battle will be over before multeese arrives."*

And it was gone. Kim could breathe again. She turned to look at Inaki. The lad was sitting, mouth open, eyes wide. Lisarea was there as well, standing near the lift. The elf looked as scared as Inaki.

"What do we do, mo'shi?"

Kim had no idea but didn't say so. It wasn't what the moai wanted to hear.

Lisarea cleared her throat. "Perhaps you should alert Stone," she suggested.

Good idea. But not just Stone. She got on the radio. "Thorpe, Chasm, Tasko and Stone come to the security office please. Now." She hoped somebody had an idea.

She rolled herself over to the lift and went down. When she arrived, Stone was already there. Thorpe arrived a minute later, then Dido.

"Dido?"

"Tasko isn't here, Kim. I'm not sure who is."

"Right. You're up then. What about Chasm?"

"She's off getting Meledrin and the others," Stone said.

"Right." Kim looked at the others. Not the sort of brain trust she'd been hoping for.

But Stone was fiddling with his radio. "Scree, you there? Flint?"

"Yeah."

"Yeah, got ya."

"Everyone all right with you, Flint?" Kim asked.

A second of silence. *"We lost Dogar and Quartz."*

Kim sat back.

Stone said, "What about you, Scree?"

"We're all fine. Bloody bastards."

"What happened?" Kim hadn't known there was any reason to worry.

Stone explained. "The En'kumo delegation in the compound tried to open a gate for the multeese."

"What?"

"Exactly. Keeble worked out that the processing plant in there—"

"The one we know nothing about?"

"Yeah. That's built for the multeese."

"So the En'kumo have a contract with them? And were trying to let them in?"

"That's about it."

"Shit. Christ." Kim rubbed her face as if that might erase the past few weeks of her life. "It does explain one thing."

"What's that?"

"Just had a call from the multeese. Seems we've pissed them off."

"We pissed thems off?"

"Yep. I imagine they were supposed to be in and using the plant by now. Whatever the hell it's for."

"You must be right," Stone said. "Lisarea's up on the bridge. She reckons there's a whole heap of multeese ships landing around the compound. Smaller than them other ones though. Maybe they're the ones that were inside."

"What?"

"There was a smaller ships inside the big ship that we blews up."

"Right. You didn't think to tell me this?" Not that it made any difference, really, seeing she didn't know what they were for.

Nobody said anything for a while, then Flint asked. *"So what happens now?"*

"The multeese reckons we've got about two hours until it arrives here personally. But in the mean time the robots have been reprogrammed."

Stone winced.

"You know what that means?"

Stone shrugged. "For an enemy with technological superiority the multeese have been a bit tentative. They could've wiped out most of the planet by now if they wanted. But their weapons weren't even killing us, apparently, just knocking us out."

"But..." Kim pictured Pool being shot outside the compound door. "Pool." She closed her eyes in the silence.

Flint spoke first. *"So now we've got two hours against a more determined enemy, until the real problems arrive?"*

"Sounds like abouts it," Scree replied.

"Well, we should be back in a few minutes."

"Keeble ain't anywhere near ready, Flint."

"Well, he'd better work something out. You want us in the ship or the compound?"

Kim couldn't stop thinking about Pool. They'd left her behind.

Thorpe said, "But they probably wouldn't do much from in the ship. So the compound would probably be best."

Kim nodded mutely.

"All right, then."

"See you soon, Flint," Stone said.

Kim sat back in her seat and rubbed her face. She needed to think. "Do you know anything about what's going on with Keeble, Dido?"

The dwife shook her head.

"Can he do it?"

Another shake of the head. "They still wouldn't even have enough pipe."

Kim swore. "Well, you guys work on that. I'll see if I can find out what Tuki was reading about the multeese." She should have checked earlier— she'd known for hours— but the damn T'loop must have hit hear on the head, because she couldn't think straight. *Creatures made out of gas?* Maybe the bump on the head was making her hear things as well.

78: Gas

PING PUT DOWN HER BRUSH. "Stop, Keeble."

"We've got two hours. We can't just give up."

Ping sighed. "I know that, but we don't have enough pipe, even if we could put it together quick enough."

"So we just sit here and wait to die?"

"No. We think."

"Right, because we haven't tried that before. And it might just find us another 300 meters of pipe."

"It's no use doing pointless work."

Keeble obviously didn't agree, but he threw down his tools and sat on the now useless piece of pipe.

Ping stayed where she was, eyes closed. Everyone else was silent as well.

"How much do we needs to get us into space?" Scree asked.

Keeble shrugged. "Not that much. A couple of thousand liters if we can go straight up."

"Can we turn the Lander into a tanker?" Tasko asked. "We could seal it with the pipe sealant and..."

"If we had more time, then yes. But we'd have to seal everything. Every piece of equipment that might cause a spark. And that means building a wall to separate the cockpit and—"

"All right. We get it."

"Good idea, though."

"Yeah, great."

Ping couldn't think. She wasn't like the dwarves. She didn't think better amidst the clatter of activity and life. Rising to her feet, she moved away from the others. She crossed a bridge to the next roof and, with the others still arguing behind her, across to the next. This was the last one. The *Hakahei* was just beyond, rising high above the compound. Ping stopped where she was for a moment to look and think. She could hear the sounds of the multeese robots as they moved. They were trying to get in all around the compound, though they had not come equipped, seeing they expected to be let through the gate.

After three and a half minutes of standing, Ping got down and crawled to the edge of the roof. She found a spot between a bucket and pipe-fitting where, she hoped, she could remain hidden. And she lay there. She could still hear the others, but now the sound of voices was a comforting presence, not a distraction. Some robots were pounding on the gates with the largest of their three hands while others were shooting the timber and the rest milled about, waiting. They did not appear to be having any luck, but that could change at any moment. She looked further afield. And as if to confirm her suspicions, a troop of robots was coming down out of the hills with a tree held between them. A battering ram.

Ping thought of going to tell Scree, but they would find out soon enough, if Inaki or Peni or whoever was on the bridge hadn't already informed them.

And the *Hakahei*. Home. Apparently it was immune to the alien attacks as well, or they hadn't bothered trying. From what she understood of things like robots, they only did what they were programmed to do. If these had been told to take the compound, they might well try to do that to the exclusion of all else. They had been reprogrammed, but in how much detail? Would they attack the ship, or had the multeese not even given thought to the possibility. So perhaps the *Hakahei* was safe for the moment. For another two hours, hopefully.

The ruins of the old compound spread around the ship. The crater where the gas had exploded. The hills beyond.

Ping sat up. She sat down again very quickly when she realized she was exposed to the robots below. But... Ping slid back from the edge and raced back across the roof. She clattered across the bridge, around the high part of the next roof, across the next bridge. The others were quiet now, lost in their own thoughts. Perhaps they were trying to come up with a plan. Perhaps they were thinking of their deaths. Ping skidded to a stop, breathless and trying to talk.

"Keeble."

"What?" he hardly roused.

Deep breath. Calm. "We don't need a kilometer of pipe. We need... A hundred meters. At most. Maybe."

That got his attention. Everyone sat up straighter. Everyone leaned forward.

"The old compound. The old gas works. They're right out there." Ping pointed, as if they might not know. "The reservoir must still be under there as well. Right under the ship, maybe."

Ping followed Keeble as he raced back the way she had come. The others thumped across the bridge behind them.

-oOo-

Kim made her way into Tuki's office. She sat in her wheelchair in the middle of the room and slowly spun around. There was one big, empty desk— no computer, no coffee cup, no pen holder— and one wall full of what looked like filing cabinets. That made the first decision easy. She rolled over to the first cabinet and had a look inside. It was full of files. The first she pulled out seemed to contain information about a planet and its inhabitants.

"Right then," she said, "where the hell are the multeese then?" She didn't really know what order the Rongo alphabet was in, so she started at one end and worked her way towards the other, looking in each drawer. Halfway along, she found the right letter near the front of the drawer and she found the file on the multeese. It wasn't very big. Over at the desk she opened the file and read from the single sheet of paper.

"According to Hadrint Trycod Ti Delamanan of the Wanakama people, the multeese were created in a laboratory by an ancient race known only as Zo. *Trycod states that Eese gas particles were treated (details of this are unclear) in an attempt to create energy. This experiment failed but when a certain critical mass was reached the gas cloud became a reasoning being. The difficulty for the multeese lies in the fact that each particle remains self aware— with its own desires and agendas— but no ability to act without a general consensus from the cloud. What results is a being run by committee.*

'Trycod also suggests that the multeese is exclusively male and has no suggestion as to methods of reproduction.

"As ever, Trycod is reluctant to share his source material. This, added with his known loose handling of facts, has led many to doubt all his conclusions."

'Things that are universally believed? The multeese think all other creatures are inferior and want them dead. The multeese may well be right, for they have technology far beyond anything we have ever seen. Many other species agree. The multeese never stay still— their ships (or perhaps it is just one ship) rove constantly around the known galaxy, turning up without warning and moving on as quickly, often leaving in the middle of battles for no apparent reason. (Some might conclude that this supports Trycod's assertion that it is a being run by committee.)

'No matter the background or the reasons, in the end one thing is certain— all species, all races, dread the arrival of a multeese ship."

That was it? That was all the information hakans had been able to gather on the multeese? A lot of guesswork and... And not much else, really.

None of it helped. Kim pushed the file away and watched it slide across the glass top of the desk and onto the floor.

"Damn it." She left the paper where it was and wheeled herself out of the office.

She wheeled to the lift, then changed her mind and went to her cabin. She lay down on the bed, arms across her face, and tried to think.

"We've got homicidal maniacs made out of gas," she said softly. "They killed hundreds of the hurgon before without batting an eye. Now, suddenly, they've set their phasers to stun. Why would they do that?

"Because deep down they're actually nice guys and they just want the universe to like them?

"No? The multeese haven't changed. They, it, whatever, are still doing what's best for them. So the hurgon have changed?" *Have they changed?* Cuto still seemed like the solid, dependable guy he had been. Kim hadn't seen him much recently but...

"I should find Cuto and talk to him, actually. I haven't even thanked him for saving my life." But that didn't matter now. Everyone was busy.

"Right, so have the hurgon changed?" She hadn't really seen any of them recently to know, locked up in the ship like she was. She stood up, ignored the wheelchair, and went out into her office. She sat down, found the radio, and turned it on.

79: Knowledge

"SCREE, ARE YOU THERE?" Kim said into the radio.

"Yeah, what's going on?"

"Have the hurgon changed?"

"What?"

"Have the hurgon changed."

"What are you talking abouts? No. Theys still the same dopey buggers they ever were."

"No, I mean—"

Flint joined the conversation. *"Some have changed,"* he said, *"but not all of them. They got a choice and most of them do what's best for the family."*

Now Kim was confused. "What are you talking about?"

"The change thing they do. They just do what the Grandmother wants them to do."

"What change thing?"

"What are you talking about?" Flint asked. Apparently the confusion was infectious.

"What are *you* talking about?"

"The change thing, where they have to choose if they're male or female. Or something like that."

"The hurgon are choosing if they're male of female?"

"Well, like I said, the Grandmother and her assistants do the choosing, but yeah, basically."

"They're doing this now?"

"Yep. Apparently it's breeding season or something. Some choose to be male, some choose to be female. They got different words for it though. Then they mate and lay eggs or.. I don't know. Tuki didn't give me the details. Knowing Tuki he probably didn't get the details about something like that."

"They're breeding?"

"Not yet, I don't think. Just getting ready."

"Reproducing?"

"Yeah—"

But Kim was already out the door and heading back to Tuki's office. Her foot hurt. Her knee and ribs hurt but she hardly noticed. She almost threw herself onto the floor, scrabbling for the piece of paper she'd thrown there earlier. She found the line she was after and read again. "Trycod also suggests that the multeese is exclusively male and has no suggestion as to methods of reproduction."

She sat on the floor and stared at the paper.

"Shit." She found Tuki's radio and turned it on. "Flint?"

"Where'd you go," Scree asked. *"You all right?"*

"I'm fine. Flint, how often do the hurgon breed?"

There was a moment of silence before Flint came back on. *"Tuki says about once every century. I reckon that'd be a hurgon century though, so how long was that?"*

Kim couldn't remember exactly what Cuto had said, back in the old days when they were escaping from Area 51. But... "A few hundred. I'm pretty sure it's a few hundred."

"Why?" Scree asked. *"Whats you got?"*

"The multeese are exclusively male and so they can't reproduce naturally. They have factories here and they turn up just as the hurgon are starting to breed. And they don't want to kill the hurgon where a couple of weeks ago they were blowing them out of the sky everywhere."

"So... Whats?" Scree asked.

Flint answered. *"So they only knock the hurgon out because they want them to be fresh when they put them through those damn processing plants."*

"They need hormones or... Estrogen... Or whatever, to reproduce."

Kim thought of all the ships that were lining up outside. Bringing in the hurgon to be 'processed'. All of them still alive.

-oOo-

Keeble stopped when he was well short of the edge, but he was already questing forward with is mind, feeling the stone under the *Hakahei* and around close by. He heard everyone else behind him, breathing, waiting.

"The stone is deep beneath the ship," Tasko said.

Keeble nodded. "Not where the crater is though. It's thirteen meters thick there." He turned to look at Ping and smiled. "Well done, Ping."

"Thirteen meters," Ari said. "That's just two pipes."

"Plus the depth of the crater," Bargle said. "Then to the ship. Ten sections of pipe all up."

"We've got plenty," Peak said.

"Yeah, but have you noticed all the damn killer robots down there?"

"You worry abouts the pipe," Scree said. "We'll worry abouts the robots."

Keeble shook his head. "Right, of course, we'll worry about the pipe."

Down below, he could hear the robots becoming more active. There was a long boom and a rapid volley of gunfire.

"What was that?" Ari asked, scratching at her broken arm and looking nervous.

"They gots a ram," Scree said.

"Great."

"And there's that as well." The troll pointed to the sky. The Lander was flying in. Shardy was coming almost straight down. The robots were firing upwards, but it didn't look as if they were going to have any luck.

"Huh. The Lander," Bargle said. "We set the pipe up in two sections and carry them in with the Lander. Then all we have to do is join them."

Keeble nodded. There was no time to waste. "Tasko, you're in charge of getting from the reservoir to beneath the ship. I'll get up to the ship from the ground."

"Right." Tasko said. A second later he was shouting orders and looking at the pipes lying across the roof.

"I'll need these two as is," Keeble said. The one that was partly in the ship and the one attached to it. He'd put a elbow join on the end, then two pipes to get them to the ground then just push the whole thing further into the ship. He explained to Tasko.

The other dwarf nodded. "Why don't we do that, but just drop it over the edge. That'll save us the trouble of using the Lander to slide it all the way in. We can bring the other pipes here as easily as to the ship. It'll be one extra bit at most."

Keeble gave it a second's thought. "Right." He'd be done in about ten minutes. He started working on the clamp at the end of the pipe. "Ping, I need—" But Peak had already brought an elbow.

Before he had attached the elbow, the Lander touched down on an adjoining roof and everyone piled out. Keeble didn't have time to pay any attention. Trolls and hurgon rushed to pick up two sections of pipe. Bargle had already disconnected the other end. They wove around obstacles then set it down in place. They slipped it into the elbow. Keeble started on the clamp and Ping worked with the sealant. A well-oiled machine.

"Now what?" Ari asked.

"Everyone on this pipe," he said.

Those who'd been in the Lander had come across the roofs to look. Meledrin was there, the whole side of her face covered with an ugly bruise, and a whole bunch of hurgon, including an old one on a stretcher.

The trolls and dwarves came to help.

Keeble examined the line of them, ready to go beside the pipe.

Topper was lined up next to Ping. Keeble saw her take the other dwarf's hand for a moment.

"Hello, Topper," she said.

Topper reacted to the momentary contact and Keeble couldn't help but smile. He glanced at Ari and the dwife was looking at him. He gave a quick nod, then looked away.

"We ready?" Keeble asked Tasko and Drago and they started to Sing, focusing on the point where the pipe entered the ship. Everyone pushed. For a moment it looked as if nothing was going to happen. Then the pipe started to slide. Five seconds later it had fallen over the edge and everyone cheered. Keeble risked a look. The end of the pipe had embedded in the ground, but it was nothing that a good lever wouldn't fix.

"Thirty degrees," Bargle said.

"What?"

"We'll need a thirty degree elbow."

"Whistler. Course we will. Off you go then."

Ten minutes and one part of the operation was complete. The easiest part, obviously. Tasko was arranging his sections of pipe, getting the pieces in place. Four lengths attached to three. One of the ends was blocked by a leather cuff so the Sung stone wouldn't go up inside. Trolls and hurgon were rushing to do as they were told. But it didn't fit on the roof properly. Tasko should've checked. Keeble should've checked. They changed the angles, shifted pipes, cursed and swore until it finally fit, lying across three roofs, hanging out into thin air at one end. The clamps were going on. Ping ran from join to join with her bucket of sealant, slopping it on with no care for being tidy.

Half an hour and they were done. Keeble stood up, worked the muscles in his back. He looked at Tasko. He looked at Bargle and Drago.

"Are we ready?"

Tasko nodded.

"How's the length?"

"A bit longer than I would have liked, but it'll do."

Keeble nodded. "Damn. Have we got ropes that will hold this much weight? Seven sections of pipe?" They only had one bit of rope and it was attached to the crane.

"Whistler. No."

"Chains. There must be some somewhere."

They sent the hurgon to get some. And they waited. And waited. It was half an hour before they returned, six of them lugging two huge chains between them. They'd hold. So they shackled the chains to the pipes, then Shardy brought the Lander over, setting it down carefully on the roof, and they shackled them there as well.

"We'll need someone to undo the shackles," Keeble said.

Scree nodded but didn't say anything.

Peak stepped up. "I'll do it."

Scree nodded again.

"A dwarf will have to go too," Keeble said. "So you know where the hole is."

After another moment of silence, Hoodek cleared his throat. "Guess that would be me then."

"Just remember," Flint said, "you'll get dead if you're shot now."

"Yeah. I know." Peak climbed into the back of the Lander as Shardy started the engine.

"I'd rather you didn't remind me," Hoodek muttered as he followed.

Keeble swore. "And we need to get the cover off the end somehow. Otherwise the gas won't get through anyway."

"Rope," Ari said. "Tie a rope to the knot and just pull the rope when the end of the pipe is through."

"We need rope."

The rope on the crane wasn't long enough so a hurgon went to get another. It was attached to the cuff so it could be released and Peak was told what he had to do.

Time ticked away.

"We ready, dwarves?" Getting the pipes joined wouldn't be easy.

Tasko, Bargle, Drago and Ari nodded. So did Ping.

"We'll need some muscle too, Scree."

Tim McCree had been working on the pipes from the start. He volunteered. And Chasm, Flint, Brick and Cuto.

Keeble gave them all a nod of thanks. "We'll go straight down here, then out through the wall. They probably won't even know we're there with all the commotion. He Sang them a hole down to the top floor of the building, jumping down onto some tables. Then down again, and they found a long section of small gauge metal pipe in a storeroom. Down the stairs to ground level.

Keeble took a deep breath and reshaped his Song. "This is us right here," he said. "We ready."

"We better be," Chasm said. "Shardy just took off."

80: Throwing Stones

KEEBLE NODDED AND THREW his Song at the wall. Catapults were lobbing stones close by, shattering against the ground and against the robots. Then the area was all but clear and Keeble stepped through the wall. And when they were all out he shifted the focus of his Song, sliding it down into the ground and then out towards the crater. While he Sang, the others worked on getting the pipe out of the ground. They used the smaller pipe they'd found and used Bargle's thirty-degree elbow as a fulcrum. They heaved and pushed as Keeble searched for the thin piece of rock in the crater. He found it, expanded his Song, concentrating on the musical flows as things continued to happen around him.

Rocks fell from the sky. The guns of the *Hakahei* were being used as well— it was no use hiding any more. And if this didn't work, then all the battery power in the world wouldn't make any difference. Robots died, spitting sparks and exploding or simply ceasing to function. Chasm, Flint and Cuto put their weight onto the lever. More rocks. And the big hurgon gun shattered multeese robots, sending out showers of shrapnel.

Shardy flew lower, positioning the pipe over the crater, then slowly took it down. Peak was hanging out the door, firing madly. Hoodek must have been hiding.

Keeble hardly noticed any of it. His Song was stretched. It was stretching him. He was focused a long way from his body and it was a big hole. It was all he could do to keep the edges of his thoughts from unraveling and spinning away into the stone. He clung to his Song, fluttering at the seams to keep it all together.

Finally, they levered the end of the pipe out of the ground. Flint and Chasm took up their weapons, checked their surroundings, then headed towards Shardy and the Lander. Cuto went with them. Brick and Tim stayed where they were, keeping watch on the work party. The catapults and hurgon guns up on the walls were firing constantly.

One end of Shardy's pipe had already sunk into Keeble's hole. Keeble narrowed the hole and the whole assembly started to change orientation, one side shifting towards perpendicular, the other towards horizontal. All the way down. Flint and his followers reached the horizontal section of pipe just as it came within reach of the ground. Cuto and Chasm grabbed on and started swinging it around to where it needed to be. Flint kept watch.

Bargle, Tasko, Ari were fitting the elbow to the bottom of the pipe that came from the *Hakahei.* They worked quickly, tightening the clamp. Ping slopped on the sealant. They all concentrated fiercely on their tasks.

Rocks rained down from above. The pipe came around.

Keeble adjusted his hole. He brought it closer so Flint could bring the pipe closer. The pressure in his mind eased slightly.

A robot fell at Keeble's feet, almost breaking his concentration. A cold, dead eye stared. The bladed arm waved dangerously until Brick shot the machine again.

Then the end of the pipe was right there and Keeble jumped. It was gaping at him like the mouth of some strange beast. The trolls and humans manhandled it into position as Shardy carefully lowered it to the ground. The end slipped into the elbow.

They clamped it, sealed it, in record time and Tasko gave a signal. Peak released the chains and pulled on the rope to release the cover. He was back in the Lander in less than twenty seconds and the craft shot up into the air.

Something exploded. Something whizzed past Keeble's face. He clung to his Song. A pair of robots were burning with fierce blue flames.

Keeble felt a touch on his arm and turned to see Tasko give the thumbs up. So he reeled in his Song with an effort, and pushed it into the wall at his back. He felt hands pulling him through the stone, stumbled, then lost consciousness.

-oOo-

Kim was sitting in the gallery when a group of people came through the door a few minutes later. There were dwarves, trolls, humans and hurgon.

"Is Keeble all right?" she asked. She thought she should probably greet Grandmother Donni or something but stayed where she was.

Brick found a seat close by. "Passed out for a second, that's all. He's down there shouting at people now."

"Good."

"Those catapults worked pretty well," Tasko said taking a seat as well.

Kim nodded. "Thank God."

Scree grunted. "Better than expected. Maybe we can makes one that'll knock downs that mothership?"

Tasko smiled. "I'll talk to Makar but I don't think we can make one big enough."

Kim grunted. "Unfortunately."

"Bit of a worry if we have to resort to throwing stones, I reckon."

"It worked heres."

"Yeah, but on the ship they've got shields," Tasko said, "and guns that can shoot our rocks out of the sky."

Kim sighed and sat back in her seat. Was that the only thing that made the rocks a bad idea? Shields and guns? Was that the only thing that stood between them and victory? When you said it like that, it didn't seem like much at all.

Kim turned her attention back out the window. Flint was in the weapons chair, working to thin out the robots, and other trolls were helping from the weapons room below. The hurgon were going to need all the help they could get.

"How's the batteries going with all this shooting?" Scree asked.

"We're doing all right," Kim said. "Hopefully we can kill all of them before we go."

"Won't do any good. There's lots more where them came from."

"Shut up, Scree."

Scree waved the comment away. "Best things we can do for the hurgon is draw the multeese mothership after us."

"You're kidding right?"

"Didn't say I wanted to do it. Just said it was the best things for the hurgon."

Tasko smiled. "We can't throw rocks at them if they're too far away."

-oOo-

Kim shook her head. "One thing we're definitely going to do on the way out is blow up that damn processing plant. I don't care if we do it with a rock, just make sure we do it."

Tasko cleared his throat.

"What?" Kim snapped. She didn't want anyone telling her it couldn't be done.

Tasko pulled on his beard. "That plant uses a lot of hydrogen. A *lot* of hydrogen. And it's stored underground everywhere around here. It should be easy enough to blow up, I just suggest you make sure we're a few kilometers up when you decide to do it."

"A few kilometers?"

Tasko nodded. "On the bright side, when you blow up the compound you should also blow up every one of those multeese ships that are sitting around waiting to get in."

"Shit." Kim shook her head. *Was it worth killing all the hurgon to get a few of the robots as well? Would the hurgon be conscious when they went into the processing plant?* She glanced at Grandmother Donni, sweating silently in one of the gallery chairs. The alien saw her watching.

"Donni would appreciate it if Kim did not kill the P'targa," Donni signed. *"The P'targa may well die soon, but at least there is a chance."*

Kim nodded. "*Of course.*" But none of it would really matter if the *Hakahei* didn't get off the ground pretty soon. "Scree?"

But Scree wasn't paying any attention. He was staring out the window. Kim followed his gaze. All she saw was one of the catapults, being manned by some hurgon.

"Scree?"

The troll rose to his feet. "I gots to think." He headed for the lift.

"Shit." Kim was tired of thinking. That was all she'd been doing, stuck in her stupid wheelchair, and she wanted to *do* something. If she thought throwing rocks might help in anyway, she would've been willing to give it a try.

But they couldn't do anything. Not until someone down below told them they could leave. And even then, all they could do was run away, as usual.

Kim sat back and closed her eyes.

"How can we beat the ship?" she muttered. She didn't think she said it loud enough for anyone else to hear.

But Brick answered. "We can't."

"Don't talk unless you are going to say something interesting." Kim said, opening her eyes again. "The multeese aren't gods, I don't think, so there must be a way to beat them."

Brick nodded. "But that's an entirely different question."

Kim narrowed her eyes. "What?"

"First you asked how to beat the ship. Then you asked how to beat the multeese. Two different questions."

Kim nodded slowly. "Right." She was thinking herself in knots. "But surely we have to beat the ship to beat the multeese."

Brick just shrugged.

Kim turned to look out the window. Brick was right, even if it didn't help. She stared out the window while she imagined a hundred ways to beat a vastly superior spacecraft. And the catapult outside threw another rock, crushing a robot below.

Eventually, hours later, it seemed, Ping's voice came over the intercom. "We're ready to go, Bargle. Just be careful at first— Keeble and the others are Singing so the pipes can come out."

Bargle was ready and had them moving in an instant. He lifted them gently off the ground while he spoke into his microphone. "Strap yourselves in," he said, "we're about to take off." Ten meters up, twenty.

Kim gripped the side of her seat and bit her lip.

Then Ping came over the intercom again. "Good to go."

Bargle pushed the thrust lever and threw the *Hakahei* into the sky.

Kim held on while the internal gravity caught up then tried to relax as she looked out the window. As they got higher, relaxing became impossible. The multeese mothership was rising like a new moon, coming around the side of the planet. Any second now...

"Run, scuttle bug. Multeese is coming now."

And there it was.

"Batteries charging," Bargle said.

If Kim remembered correctly, they charged quickly in atmosphere.

"We should be able to jump as soon as we get out of the gravity well. A few minutes."

"You will not escape."

Kim stared, imagining the catapult throwing rocks at the multeese ship, wiping the stupid smile off the pristine white face.

And…

"What are you smiling at?" Brick asked. "Have you got a plan?"

She hadn't realized she was smiling. And there wasn't really anything to smile about. Kim nodded, shook her head. "Not so much a plan as an idea, but… It's crazy. Suicidal."

Brick nodded. "Life's suicidal at the moment. And, anyway, just because you haven't yet worked out how you'll live through the plan doesn't mean it's suicidal. Suicide is a conscious choice, it isn't a lack of options. There's a big difference."

"Really? And if you never work out a viable option for survival?"

The big man shrugged. "Then you die. It happens. And sometimes it's the only way. Even an actual suicidal plan would be better than sitting around waiting to die."

"You really think that?"

He nodded again. "You come up with a half reasonable plan, or even an idea, I'll be at the front of the line to help."

"But…" Kim took a deep breath. "But sending people to their deaths, Brick. I don't know if I can do that."

"You did it before. At Sherindel, apparently. At Hulgorn."

"Only one person died." Just Sandy, and she was one too many.

Brick shrugged. "We were lucky. And if everyone on this ship dies but we manage to kill the multeese? Well, that will be lucky too."

"I can't…"

"Think of it this way. We'll all be dead very soon, one way or the other. We can die running, or we can die fighting."

Kim knew he was right. She knew there really wasn't any choice. "All right."

"So we're going to do it? Whatever it is?"

Kim nodded. "I guess so."

"And what's the plan?"

"Stones, Brick."

"Stones?"

"We're going to throw stones." Kim rose to her feet, ignoring all her pains. "Where's Scree?"

Brick didn't know, but Flint answered between bursts of gunfire from the weapons chair. Kim didn't know what he was shooting at.

"In the security office."

"Right." Kim started to hobble out as fast as she could. She paused before she got to the lift and looked up at the pilot's seat. "Bargle, set up for a jump of... Two hours. But don't do anything else."

"What heading?"

"Couldn't care less."

Flint stopped his shooting for a moment. "What are you up to?"

But Kim just smiled some more and left.

81: Instinct

TUKI LEFT THE BRIDGE AND WENT LOOKING FOR RUBY. He had seen her leave with the other warriors but had no idea where she might have gone. He went down the lift to Level 3. Some of the others were there— Thorpe and Scree and Stone— but he could not see Ruby.

"You looking for Ruby, Tuki?" Bones asked.

"Yes."

"Think she went upstairs. To your cabin. I think so, anyway. Could have gone to have a shower, I suppose. Don't know though. You could check the showers."

"Oh. Thank you. I will look in my cabin first."

He used the stairs then wandered through the hallways to his cabin. He stood where he was for a long time, looking at the door, wondering if he should go in. He started to turn away, to go back to the bridge, when the door opened.

Ruby was standing there. She was holding a piece of metal pipe, thick and strong and as long as Tuki's arm. "Oh. Hello, Tuki."

"Hello, Ruby."

"Were you coming in?"

"No. Yes."

"Were you looking for me?"

"Yes."

She stepped aside and motioned him in.

"What is happening? What are you doing here?"

"I came to get this." She held up a pendent Tuki had given her. It had a red glass bead on the end that looked a bit like a ruby.

"Oh."

They stood in silence for a few seconds.

"What is the pipe for?"

"It's part of Kim's plan."

"Kim's plan involves plumbing?"

"Apparently."

"But she won't tell you what it is?"

Ruby shook her head. "Scree knows, and he'll tell us what we need to know.

Trolls work better without planning. Think about something too much and all those thoughts just get in the way. Much better to do things by instinct."

"And what if you don't have the right instincts?"

"You worry about that when the time comes."

Another silence that stretched on.

"Have I done something wrong, Tuki. I ain't used to this, so I don't know if I should've..."

Tuki shook his head. "You know more about these things than I do," he said. He was starting to think he didn't know very much at all. "It's just..."

"Yes?"

"When you..."

"When I kill people?"

"Yes. It isn't something I like to think about."

Ruby shook her head and sat down on the bed. "It ain't something *I* like. Not any more. I don't know if I ever did."

"But you *look* like you enjoy it."

She shook her head. "I don't. Maybe... Well, maybe I do like it in a way. I like helping my friends and that's the best way I can do it. I like being good at a job that I've got to do."

"You are good at other things."

Ruby laughed. "But nothing like that, Tuki. If I lived on Earth, maybe I could play some of their sports, but I'm not good at thinking or... Or anything like that."

"You are not stupid, Ruby."

"I didn't say I was." She sighed. "Tuki, this is who I am. If you can't handle that, then maybe I should move my stuff out of your cabin."

He didn't know what to say so he didn't say anything. And there was no way that could be the right thing to do. The time had come and his instincts failed him. He should say something...

"All right. I'll get my stuff as—"

An alarm sounded, a harsh, screeching buzz that could not be ignored.

"Come on. We've got to go."

"Where?"

"To the places where we're supposed to be. Instinct, Tuki," she said. "Is your instinct telling you to stand there like that?"

Tuki's instincts were telling him to stop Ruby from leaving the room. They were saying they should both stay in there and wait for Scree and Kim to sort everything out. Except Scree and Kim would need all the help they could get.

He watched Ruby as she grabbed her metal bar and headed out the door. After a moment he followed, rushing to the lift and pressing the button for Level 1. From there he took the next lift to the bridge. Palsamon was there, but only just. The elf was half in the navigation chair and half out. One leg had already started to creep towards the door.

He looked up and jumped up from the chair. "Come on, lad, no time to waste." He adjusted a couple of controls and then was gone, running towards the lift. Tuki took his place and strapped himself in.

"What's going on?" Though he knew what was going on. The multeese ship was there. It was a hundred kilometers behind them but it looked as if it was hanging just outside the window.

Bargle was looking at his controls as if trying to find the button that would save them all. "What do we do now?"

"We wait for Kim," Meledrin said. She was still calm, or at least looked it. "She told us to accelerate, and that is all."

There was nobody in the weapons chair.

Tuki thought he was going to be sick. He wondered where Ruby was. He wondered if it was too late to go and talk to Kim and get her to change her mind. Tuki did not know what the plan was, but surely they could just run away instead.

He sighed.

He really didn't believe that it would be possible to run away. And how far would they have to run?

"It is gaining on us," Tuki said. "A hundred kilometers away."

Kim returned to the bridge. "Are we ready?"

Meledrin nodded, but Kim probably didn't care. Tuki supposed that it would not make any difference. *Ready or not, here they come.*

"Kim, are you going to tell us what is happening?" Meledrin asked.

"We're going to throw rocks at this damn alien. Get it on the radio." Kim climbed the stairs to stand beside Meledrin's chair. "And let's hope it's as arrogant as it seems."

"It should be able to hear us," Meledrin said a moment later.

"Good." Kim pressed the button. "Hello."

"*You run and you run but you get nowhere.*" The white face appeared on the screen on the back wall of the bridge. "*There will be no more running after this.*"

"But running is what we do best," Kim replied.

Tuki thought she looked very confident, more confident that she had for a long time, but he did not know how that was possible.

"And yet multeese catches you time and again."

Kim shrugged. "Well, all we can do is keep trying. I mean. It isn't as if we could beat you in a fight."

"It is inconceivable."

"Right. But like you said, it isn't really much use running either, is it?"

Tuki thought of telling Kim how far the alien ship was— barely fifty kilometers— but at that range, it really didn't make any difference.

"I mean, I bet you could fly that ship right up here beside us, if you wanted. You seem to be able to do whatever you want with it."

"Of course. Multeese are in perfect control."

"Show me then."

"Multeese are going to kill you."

Tuki was surprised it hadn't already done so. Maybe it liked showing off.

"I know you're going to kill us. But just show me how great your ship is first. Driving something that big with any precision must take a lot of skill."

What was Kim doing? Did she really think the aliens would let them live simply because he was nice to them?

"We have been travelling the galaxy for a millennia killing the lesser races— you are the first to acknowledge us for what we truly are."

"Come on then, fly that mountain right along beside us."

The ship was pulling up alongside them. Tuki looked out the window and saw the shining bulk of it. It was just fifty meters away and there was almost twenty kilometers of it stretched out behind them. He swallowed.

"We can do whatever we wish. We are all powerful."

"I know. And if we went to that other universe, the one where we go to travel, you could follow us, right? So we wouldn't be able to get away. You've been there before."

"You cannot escape."

Tuki saw Kim took a deep breath and glance around the bridge. "So you are really going to kills us this time. I mean, all those other times you just got distracted and took off. You didn't have the perseverance to finish us off. We ran away, and you were just too lazy to chase us."

Tuki could not tell if the alien was annoyed. The expression on the white face did not change. He really didn't know that it was a good idea to *try* to annoy it though. He looked away from the ship— still only the front end was visible, as if the alien had slowed to match their speed.

"It is not a matter of perseverance. Do you swat at every fly that buzzes around your head?"

"Admit it, you're just lazy."

"We can kill you any time. We merely wait to educate you, as you wished."

"Well, I've changed my mind." Kim said. "I reckon we'll show you a thing or two instead."

"Impossible."

"How about this for a start," Kim said. "We'll show you how to go to another universe. Bet you'll see something shiny and take off somewhere else instead of following."

"We will kill you."

"Yeah? We'll see." She signaled and, before her hand finished moving, Bargle hit the button to open the Ohoga Gate and start the timer. He spoke a warning into the pager.

"*Do you think that will save you?*" the alien asked. Two weapons fired, missiles zeroing in on the *Hakahei.* A warning alarm sounded. They were so close there was no way they could avoid being hit.

Stone, in the weapons chair, had the shields up in an instant. Why wasn't he shooting? Maybe they could hit it. Maybe... Maybe they would be lucky.

The first projectile exploded against the shields. The second…

The lights went out as the ship passed through the gate into the other universe. The alarm fell silent.

Tuki breathed a sigh of relief though the silver alien had come with them. It seemed larger in the shifting, sickening colors of the other universe. "We will be dead in two hours," he said to nobody in particular.

"Two hours," Bargle agreed. "Two hours."

Tuki wondered if it had really been worth it. All that just for a couple of hours of life. As the alien said, they could not run forever. They were as good as dead already.

Kim had slumped down onto the floor. There were tears running down her face.

"What is happening, Kim?" Tuki asked.

She looked up. "As usual, I got us into trouble, and now Scree has to save us all."

Tuki shook his head. "It is your plan, Kim. If Scree saves us it will be because of you." Tuki didn't understand the plan, but that didn't make any difference. As long as someone did.

82: Into the Mist

SCREE STRODE ALONG THE PASSAGE with everyone closing in behind. He knew he was going to die one day but he'd always thought it would happen on the day he gave up. "I ain't giving up today," he said.

"Pardon?" Tim asked.

"Nothin'. We ready for this?" Not many people had officially been told the plan, but they would've worked it out by now.

"We're ready," Thorpe replied quietly. Scree looked back at the human. He had a shovel handle, sharpened at one end and held it like he knew what he was doing. He also had metal pipe, about ten centimeters across, strapped to his back. The other humans had backpacks that rattled and clanked when they walked. They wore looks of determination that matched the look on every other face. Scree smiled and continued walking.

If the aliens is as smart as they thinks they are they should be getting worried about now, he thought.

"You sure these explosives will work?"

Thorpe nodded. "Stuff burns slower in this universe than our own. Gunpowder burns so slowly that it doesn't create an explosion at all, but this stuff burns much quicker than gunpowder. The explosions won't be as large as normal but they'll do the job."

Scree grunted and gave a curt nod. He didn't really want the details. He just wanted to know it would work.

At the airlock Scree swung the pack onto his back and picked up his sword. He'd never thought to use the weapon again but it felt good in his hand now. It had come a long way from Kiva, but not nearly as far as he'd come himself.

Twenty-two hakans and half a dozen hurgon entered the airlock behind him. Each had a club or bow or weapon of some kind and looked ready to use them.

"Get that door closed."

Scree fitted the breather and mask over his face. Topper and Hoodek were closing the inner door, winding the handles steadily. As soon as they were done, Talus and Dido started getting the outer door open. Scree felt the gentle pull of exiting air, but ignored it. He watched the doors slowly opening. It was a minute before they were wide enough.

"Hold this for me." He handed his sword to Chip and tightened the straps on his pack.

The alien ship was so close. It looked like he could almost reach out and touch it. He wished he could. He examined the outer surface of the ship. There were lumps and equipment and all sorts of handholds. And there, near what looked like an antenna...

"Low south," Scree said, taking a deep breath. There were lines that might be the outline of a separate panel. Or it could have been anything.

"Got it." Bone's voice was muffled by the mask but audible.

"Let's do this." Scree said. *We're going faster than it looks,* he added to himself. With another deep breath he ran and dived into the sickening, swirling colors.

As soon as he left the protection of the ship, Scree could feel the wind of their passage buffeting him. He'd aimed himself towards the very front of the alien craft, but wasn't sure if it had been enough. The journey seemed to take forever. His target didn't seem to be getting any bigger, but seeing it was all he could see— it filled his vision completely— he was willing to admit that it might be hard to judge. He wanted to look back at the *Hakahei* to see how close it was— how far it was— but didn't want to upset his momentum or aim.

Away from the lanterns on the *Hakahei* it was still possible to see, though only just. The mist clung to his face, ran down his arms and leapt off his fingers into the swirling nothingness. And Scree continued forward, seemingly forever.

When he hit the alien ship he almost knocked himself out. He clung to the cold metal as the mist tried to rip him free.

He would've liked to hang there all day, one hand on a silvered, shadowed lump, one foot in a circular hole, but he knew he had a time limit.

He flexed his shoulders, then turned to look back at the *Hakahei.* He seemed to be about fifty yards south of where he needed to be, and too high. He could see Thorpe pointing and started to move.

It took five minutes to get to the spot he'd been aiming for. He wasn't sure it was a door, but there seemed to be some type of join and that was enough.

He took one of the explosive packages out of his pack and stuck it to the side of the ship and then one of the chemical fuses was stuck in the side of that. He scampered away as quickly as he could and waited for it to go boom. With a strange piece of equipment protecting him he was hardly even aware of the bomb going off, but the result was certainly visible.

There was a hole in the side of the ship large enough to drive a Lander though. He turned towards the Hakahei to call them across but Bones was already on his way, sailing silently across the gap. A piece of grappling cable trailed behind him. He must have learned from Scree for he hit the side of the ship not three yards from the hole.

<Ready?> Scree asked as soon it was obvious he wasn't going to bounce off into the nothing.

<*Yep.*>

They swung around and went through the hole together. There was nobody waiting for them. Wires and cables and pipes were all around, filling the cramped space. While Bones unclipped the cable from his belt and attached it to a pipe, Scree flailed around, pulling on and breaking everything he could get his hands on.

<Go.> Scree said in his mind and he knew his companions were coming across behind with a small piece of wire hooked over the cable to make sure they flew true. Chip flew in through the hole a minute later, trailing mist behind him. He rolled and came to his feet amongst the mess. Scree took his sword.

"Let's see if we can find a proper passage."

They went to the inner wall and Chip used his makeshift club as a ram, pounding on the wall with the end.

The space behind them was starting to fill by the time they broke through. The thumping revealed a small join and Scree was able to push near that to fold back a large section of wall. He stepped through into... a passage.

Scree looked one direction then the next. The passage, silver and circular, seemed to go on forever in both directions though he wasn't really sure how far he could see.

"Talus. Peak," Scree called.

The two trolls climbed into the passage and looked as well. Then they started running toward the front of the ship. It was two minutes before Scree heard from them.

<Dead end. > Scree heard in his head. <Might be a hatch.>

He looked in the direction they'd gone. If it was a dead end, did they really want to go that way?

Thorpe stepped through the hole and, raising one of the lanterns above his head, walked to the base of the passage. His eyes were cold and hard behind his mask. "What's going on?"

"Dead end that way. Maybe a hatch, apparently."

Thorpe shrugged. "Who says the other way will be better. And the front is that way."

"Right. We ready?"

He led the way quickly down the passage. After about two hundred meters it started to curve to the left, towards the top/bottom axis of the ship. Another five hundred meters after that and they came to the two trolls. They were sitting on the floor near a metal grille that filled the entire passage.

"Dead end," Talus repeated. But he pointed at a circular panel in the ceiling.

"Yeah. Topper?"

The dwarf had a look, holding his lantern up to see it better. “Shouldn’t be too hard.” He pulled a tool from a pouch on his belt and two trolls boosted him up so he could work.

Scree was aware of every minute ticking by— it seemed to take forever to get through. Finally, Topper pushed the circle and it hinged upwards. He kept pushing and it fell back with a clatter loud enough to wake the dead. Scree wasn’t going to wait to see what happened though. He strode up to the hole. Before he could jump up and grab the edge, Shardy grabbed his arm.

“You ain’t going first.” She pulled him back and went herself, jumping up and puling herself up through the hole. <All clear,> she said a moment later. <And we got air in here too.>

Scree didn’t know how she’d checked.

He went through the hole and took off his mask as he looked around. “Think we should blow this up, Topper?”

He waited while the dwarf clambered through the hole.

“That’s the biggest engine I’ve ever seen.”

Scree laughed. “A couple of weeks ago you were living in a cave.”

“Yeah, but still...”

They were in a spaceship that was twenty kilometers long so it was obvious the thing would have a large engine, but Scree was still amazed. It went up for a couple of hundred meters. He couldn’t see the other end through the mess of machinery.

“Pick a spot,” Scree said. The rest of the pack came through the hatch and spread out. The door banged shut behind the last of them and Hoodek turned a wheel to seal it.

“That bit looks important.”

The glowing box Topper pointed to was about twenty meters to a side with cables and pipes and clear glass tubes coming and going. Scree shrugged and started towards it, weaving his way through lesser things to get there. Topper went with him while some of the others explored the room.

Scree knelt and let Topper take some explosive and a length of fuse from his pack. There was whole coil of the fuse— it was probably supposed to last them years. The dwarf grabbed a big wad of the former and, taking it out of its protective wrapping, molded it around where one of the glass tubes joined the box.

“Two minutes for every centimeter of starter, right?” Topper asked, before shoving the tube into the explosive. Then he pulled the string that started the process. “We’ve got about an hour.”

“Come on then,” Scree said. <Where to?>

<Northwest corner.>

<Right.> Scree waved for those who had waited with him to follow.

The door Chasm had found led out the western wall.

"Fifty yards of passage, and it's a normal old square passage, not like the last one," she said. "Branch leading to the right at the halfway point."

Scree nodded, but she wasn't finished.

"Around the corner is aliens. Six of 'em."

"Aliens? Or them robots?"

She shrugged. "Robots, I suppose."

83: A Long Way

SCREE MARCHED DOWN THE HALL and stuck his head around the corner. Six of the three-legged robots were in the middle of the passage. "Hello," Scree said. None of them moved. He went out into the hall. They still didn't move, so he went forward and stabbed the closest one in the eye. He twisted his sword as he pulled it out. He did the same to the others then went back to the intersection.

"What's at the far end of the passage?" Topper asked.

"Door like this one," Chasm said.

"What if they have backup for everything as well, like on our ship?" Hoodek said.

"What?"

"What if the door at the other end of the passage leads to another engine like the last one?"

Scree nodded. "Right. Take some more explosive. Stone, you and your guys go with him."

"How about you just give me the pack?" Topper said.

"What?"

"You might have to fight. I can carry the stupid pack as well as you."

"But the robots don't work in this place."

"What about the multeese?"

"Right." Though he wasn't sure he could fight gas anyway. He shrugged out of the pack and gave it to the dwarf. "Makar and Hoodek, you two stick with Topper no matter what. Just in case. The rest of you," he hefted his sword, "let's scout ahead a bit."

They ran down the passage, around a corner, then stopped. There were stairs. The window on the front of the ship had been near the top, so Scree started to climb. "Chasm, wait here for the others."

At the next floor, he stopped. "We'll wait here." No use splitting the group up too much. Probably stupid coming as far ahead as he had.

A couple of minutes later, the others climbed the stairs.

"Topper?"

"Here."

"Come on then. We're running out of time."

"Where are we going?" Topper asked.

"What do you mean?"

"Where are we going?"

"To the front of the ship."

Suldon cleared his throat. "Scree, Brother Koli would like to point out that we are are quite some distance from the front of the ship."

"Approximately five kilometers," Palsamon agreed.

"Yeah, but..." Where else were they supposed to go?

"And who says the front is where we really want to be?"

"Well..." Scree looked around but all he could see was empty, white passage. He didn't want to be talked out of killing the multeese by hand.

Topper joined in. "We just want to blow up as much of this ship as possible and hopefully stop it from going back to the other universe, right?"

"Right?"

"How do we know the best bits to blow up aren't around here somewhere? Or the other way?"

"Well..."

"Who says we didn't just attach some explosives to their coffee machine?" Topper asked.

"You're the one who wanted to do it."

"I know, but my point is, we have no idea what's important and the ship's so big we could spend a week wandering around in here and walk right past the self-destruct button."

"The what?"

"It was in a book I read."

"So tell me the point again."

"We have to set the explosives somewhere near here and hope that we make a big enough explosion to do something." He lifted the pack higher on his back. "And then we have to get back to the cable and get the hell out of here."

Scree tried to think. Topper was right, of course, but that didn't help a whole lot because he was also wrong. They couldn't just stick the explosives to the wall here and hope the passage was important. This might be the only chance they got to finish the job properly. He'd have thought a dwarf would understand that.

"Who's up for some running?"

"What? Why?"

"We can't be sure of anything around here. There might be ten of those machines that we just set to blow. But at the front of this ship, there's a big window, so that's where the important people sit. That's where the whole thing is run from. That's the only way we can be sure."

"We've got about an hour, Scree," Thorpe said. "If those five kilometers Palsamon mentioned were in a straight line you might have a shot, it could be closer to ten. Then we have to get out of here."

"We jumped across, we can jump back." Scree knew it wasn't that simple. The alien ship was a hard target to miss but their own ship was tiny in comparison.

"I'm up for it," Brick said. Scree could see in the human's eyes that he knew the odds. Amy and Tim volunteered as well.

Scree could see the moment that Thorpe was going to point out the flaw of the plan and held up a stalling hand. "Don't. We gotta kill these bastards, plain and simple. We got to make sure."

Thorpe shook his head and sighed. "I'm coming."

All the trolls wanted to come as well, but Scree told Stone that their troop was staying with Topper. The dwarf had a better chance of succeeding and had to be given all the help possible.

So Scree took a third of the remaining explosives and passed them out amongst the humans and Yellow troop. Then he handed around the long coils of chemical fuse.

"We will be coming as well," Palsamon said. Suldon and Bethalin nodded their agreement.

"And me," Dido said.

"There's ain't no reason."

"I am coming."

Scree looked at Amy, Chasm and Shardy and new there really wasn't any reason Dido shouldn't be allowed to come. He gave a curt nod, knowing he would regret it.

"Me too," Mintar said, glancing at Dido.

When they were ready to go Scree gripped Stone's arm.

"Why you always pick me for the babysitting?" Stone asked, half-serious. "You want me sitting back on the ship watching while you have all the fun?"

"Don't care about you, Stone," Scree replied with a smile. "It's Ruby I'm worried about."

"Ruby?"

"Well, Ruby and Tuki."

Stone shook his head and grunted.

"You might miss out on the fun today, Stone, but Kim's bound to find some more for you tomorrow." Scree gave a nod. "See you back there, anyway."

"Course. Kill some of them bastards for me."

"I'll let some get past, just so you can do it yourself." Scree turned to his smaller group when Stone started to head back the way they'd come. "We ready?" nobody said otherwise.

-oOo-

Scree ran quickly, never pausing for thought. There wasn't any point— he didn't know exactly where he was, where he was going, or how to get there. He'd climb towards the front of the ship and worry about anything else when the time came. If he wasn't going to make it all the way to the bridge, he'd find something else to blow up. The others followed him with only Bones' conversation to break the silence.

The first living, breathing creature he saw was three meters tall and thinner than an elf. It turned and ran, though not very convincingly. It ran like a four year old girl, all knees and elbows and wobbling head. It rushed around a corner and Scree followed slowly. And almost lost his head.

He ducked as a huge club whistled towards him. Rolled and slashed at a knee before realizing there was no knee. The creature looked like a two-meter high solid block of stone with four arms and one heavy-lidded eye on the front face.

Scree came to his feet and examined the edge of his sword.

"What the hell is that?" Flint asked.

Scree looked at him. "Its name is Gimbald," he said.

"What?"

"Well hows am I supposed to know?"

"Right. Sorry."

The thing, whatever it was, was covered in a clear goo that was slowly dripping onto the floor.

"Can't be too quick can it?" Bones said. "Thing like that? Have to be pretty slow, I reckon."

"Why? Because it looks like a rock and rocks don't move quick?"

"Well, yeah."

"Nearly took my head off," Scree said. "Seemed plenty quick enough to me."

"Well, we can't just stand here," Bones said. And he charged forward. Flint, Chip and Talus went as well.

Scree swore but hung back for a second. When he thought the rock was distracted he darted around the side. And found himself looking at another cold, slow-blinking eye.

"Cat piss on you." He attacked, feinting one direction, knocking aside a blow that nearly broke his arm and stabbed at the eye. Some type of orange liquid gushed out onto the floor, making footing treacherous, but that was about it. Scree swore again as he gave himself some room.

The rock rose slightly, shuffled backwards, then sank back to the floor.

Scree looked up in time to see Peak leap up onto the top of the creature. He had a sledgehammer he'd taken from the garden on the *Hakahei* and put it to use. For a whole minute he pounded on the thing's flat head, sending out sparks and chips of stone. Scree and his companions tried to keep the arms busy.

Finally, with one final, mighty blow, Peak split the stone block in two, right down the middle. He bellowed triumphantly, then leapt down to the floor. The effect was lost when he slipped in the goo but he righted himself quickly and smiled.

"A hammer's the right weapon for this quarry," he said. He looked around. "You know, a quarry where them get rocks."

"That's terrible," Flint said. "Were you up there pounding on that thing trying to think of that line?"

"Maybe."

"Well, you should've stayed up there a bit longer."

"You're just jealous."

Flint shook his head. "Come on."

But they didn't get far. At the next corner, there was a dragon. It writhed in the air, long tail flicking. And like the stone creature, it was covered in goo.

84: Stupid Things

KIM COULDN'T STAND THE WAITING, though Scree had led the boarding party across barely ten minutes earlier. She took a deep breath and looked around. Everyone had gathered by the long, curved window on Level 3 and stood watching the multeese ship as if expecting it to explode, or disappear, or do something totally unexpected at any moment. Grandmother Donni was surrounded by the last of her guards.

"Will the contracts really help the P'targa?" Kim asked in the ini rituals.

Donni gave a hurgon nod. *"They would have helped immensely, but Donni is not sure if they are required any longer."*

"They aren't? Why is that?"

"The T'loop were killing the P'targa for the benefit of all the other families but there was no benefit for the P'targa. If there had been a contract..."

Kim couldn't believe what the Grandmother was saying. *"The P'targa would have signed a contract to sacrifice P'targa to the multeese if the price was right?"*

"There is always a bargaining point, tough the P'targa price would have been high in this case. But P'targa were not given a choice. So, the T'loop will help finish the war with the hakans or the P'targa will inform the councils what was happening and the T'loop will no longer exist. The P'targa will become a great family instead."

Kim cleared her throat, though the conversation was in sign language. *"What if all the great families already know about the T'loop deal with the multeese? What if they were party to it?"*

Apparently Donni hadn't considered that possibility. *"Then we will inform the minor families and the minor families will rise up and the* hurgon *will be no more. The hurgon will become something else, for the great shall fall and no hurgon will desire to be great at all. Donni says that the P'targa do not want to be 'great' if that is greatness."*

"In that case, Kim believes Donni should avoid threatening the T'loop in private."

"Why?"

"Because T'loop will be given warning and will be able to formulate plans and call on allies. The P'targa should go directly to the councils."

"Kim might be correct."

"Will the minor families win?"

"Without doubt, because all minor families will join together for the first time. The Great Families will relent, or there will be a change of wars— a minor rebellion like there has never been. It will be a war the great families cannot win."

Kim nodded. Without doubt? Sounded easy. If it came to war, the hakans could probably help. A few trolls and dwarves would make a lot of difference. Probably just some different points of view were all that was needed. Though, for all of Donni's plans to be put into action, Kim's plan had to work first. And what chance was there of that? She looked back at the multeese ship, a mountain flying beside them— a heavily armed mountain— and wondered what she could have done differently. What other options had there been?

Half an hour later Kim was still sitting, staring across at the other ship but hardly taking any notice, when she saw a subtle shift in the crowd. They leaned forward slightly. They hushed. Kim sat up straighter, hurting her ribs in the process, and tried to see what they were looking at.

There was a... something... floating between the two ships. She followed the white thing as it tumbled and twisted. "Is that one of the aliens?" she asked.

Meledrin shrugged. "A multeese? I could not say." Her bruised face was disconcerting.

It probably wasn't. It didn't look like it was made out of gas. It was like a two-legged snake with a dozen tiny arms. It seemed to be dead.

Kim heard others gasp, but remained silent herself. A troll had tumbled out into the open. Whoever it was left a trail of blood in the swirling mist and showed no signs of life.

Kim stared at the rent torn in the other ship's hull but there was no other sign of action until another body came through a few minutes later. It was another alien. This one was huge, with four legs, two massive arms and a long, barbed tail. It wasn't quite dead. It thrashed feebly, as if it might find something to grip. Kim almost felt sorry for it— almost. But then it *did* find something to grab and the audience gasped again. It grabbed onto the cable linking the ships. Kim thought it would use it to climb back to the vessel, but apparently it knew what the outcome of that would be. Instead, it gripped the cable with its powerful hands and hung there as if catching its breath. Then it jack-knifed around and used the barb on its tail to cut at the cable. It chopped and it sawed.

Kim knew how strong the cable was but she had no doubt that the creature would succeed. How could it not? How could it not?

Then the cable parted, and the released tension flung the alien out into the nothing of the universe. It thrashed and kicked as it went, but that didn't make Kim feel better at all.

The shoulders of the audience visibly slumped. Ari started to cry.

"They jumped across there," Kim said, "they can jump back, right?"

Keeble stared at the trailing end of the cable. "You may have noticed the difference in the size of the targets," he said quietly. "We are travelling at just under 10 kilometers a second..."

"Scree can make it." But even Kim had her doubts.

There was movement in the hole on the side of the enemy ship. Kim stood to get a closer look. She could see a troll there, hanging out the side, examining the remains of the cable.

"Why didn't they leave someone on here so we could communicate with them?"

Ping shrugged. "There was no point. If they do not succeed then we will all be dead the moment the alien gets power back. Everyone was needed." She touched at the window. "Topper is there as well. And Hoodek and Mintar. And some of the elves."

"Yes, but..."

"Ruby is over there," Tuki said softly, hands pressed against the glass as well. "I was silly. I did not understand. I..."

Kim shook her head. "Tuki, I'm sorry." She had sent them out to die. All of them. It was a good plan— the only one that had any hope of succeeding, but it was still a suicide mission…

Kim saw the muscles in the lad's arm bunching under his EVA suit. He surged away from the wall and headed for... the airlock.

"No, Tuki. Wait?"

He did stop. He turned back, his face hard like Kim had never seen before. "At Ben Dongoske's funeral, I said that the people on the ship were my friends and that I would risk my life for them. I would do that. But nobody ever told me I would ever have to risk something worth much more."

Kim didn't know what to say. Tuki had changed and Ruby had a lot to do with that. She could not imagine how hard it must be for him.

Tuki turned and started to walk towards the airlock.

"What do you intend to do, Tuki?" Keeble asked. "The outer door is still open, so if you go in there you will release a lot of our air. And then what? There is only one cable in there, and it's broken. It's useless to you."

Kim wanted to say something as well. That Ruby had died trying to save her friends. That she wouldn't want him to do anything stupid. But the only things left to any of them now were the stupid things. Before she had a chance to say anything, before she could bring forth some platitude she would immediately regret, Tuki turned and ran towards the center of the ship. Kim went to follow, though she didn't know what she'd say, but he was already disappearing through the door into the stairwell.

Still, she considered following him, but the minutes ticked by and she stayed where she was, watching the occasional flashes of movement in the hole in the side of the alien ship. The trolls wouldn't give up. If there was a slim chance of success, they would jump out into the nothing, only to float around until they ran out of air.

-oOo-

As Scree sighed and readied himself he heard the soft cold voice of the dragon whispering in his mind. *"I have slept for millennia. Now I feed."*

"You ain't the multeese?" Scree asked.

There was a pause. *"I am Vazakainar. First Wyrm of Hugafalar."*

"Whatever. If you don't want to die, you'd better get out of my way."

The wyrm darted forward, fast as lightning, and it was all Scree could do to get his sword up. The creature stopped instantly, a hair's breadth from the blade.

"You have iron," it said, slowly backing up.

"Yeah."

"Here's some more," Suldon said from behind Scree.

Three arrows scratched through the air. One sank into the wyrm's eye. The others entered its mouth and disappeared. A second later, so did the wyrm itself. All that was left behind was a mist of dust that fell to the floor.

Scree turned to look at the elves. "Iron arrow heads?"

"Yes," Bethalin said.

"Wish we could gets them back."

"We have dozens, Scree," Palsamon told him. "Now that we know they work, we will be able to prevail against many more of these wyrms yet."

Thorpe joined them. "I don't think that'll be necessary."

"Why nots?"

"Have a look at this."

Scree followed the soldier through one of the doors that led off the passageway. Beyond was a small room and three glass tanks. And in each tank was a creature. These matched neither the stone thing nor the wyrm. They were green, with eyes on stalks and webbed feet. There were a couple of differences between each one, but they were obviously of the same species.

"So?"

"Now look at this."

Thorpe led the way back out into the hall and then into the next room .

This time there were two cases with another two creatures that were obviously related.

"Again, so?"

"One more."

In the third room, the case was horizontal, rather than vertical. It was long and thin. It was broken. It was empty. The floor was covered in the clear goo that had covered the wyrm and there was some still in the bottom of the case.

Scree looked. "So, the wyrm was in this case?"

"That's my guess."

"And that first guy we saw, that silly tall guy, broke the case to let it out?"

Thorpe nodded.

Scree tried to think. It wasn't working. "So, the multeese..."

Thorpe sighed. "I'm not sure. It's obvious these cases aren't made to be opened, otherwise they wouldn't need to be broken. So maybe this is like a collection, like a zoo. The multeese goes around collecting specimens to put in the display cases. But instead of killing them it keeps them alive because it's a sick bastard."

"So how many specimens are there?" Flint asked. He was pulling on his moustache, like a dwarf working at a problem.

Thorpe shrugged. "The multeese has been around for at least fifty thousand years, remember. Probably a lot longer. There could be thousands of these things."

"And that guy is just going to release every one until it finds one that can kill us?"

"Not *every* one, obviously. Those others are still in the cases after all. But that first alien must be a servant of the multeese. Or something. I don't know."

"So?"

"So, if you knew who was who in all these cases, would you stop to release Tuki, or would you head straight for the trolls?"

"So we gots to catch it." It wasn't a question.

Thorpe nodded.

Flint grunted. "But we'll have to fight our way through a heap of aliens to get to it." That wasn't a question either.

There was a commotion out in the hall. Grunts. The clash of weapons.

Scree shrugged. "What are we waiting for then?" He rushed out into the hall to help.

Outside were two dog-like creatures that walked on two legs. Well, they normally did. One was already dead. The second was about to be overwhelmed. Amy cracked its skull with her hoe and before the body had hit the ground Scree was running.

"We've got to catch that tall skinny alien. Before it lets out too many of these damn things."

He heard the others following.

Scree turned down another passage and kept running. He found another flight of stairs and started to climb.

"Take it steady, Scree," Thorpe told him. "We don't want to be too buggered to do anything the next time we run into trouble."

Scree grunted but slowed slightly. At the top of the stairs he ran straight across the hall and up the next flight. One full step on each tread. Sweat was running into his eyes.

The stairs ended but the passage kept going, long and straight and wide. Scree kept going too. A hundred meters on, there was a branching passage to the right, and he was forced to slow.

Long, tall shadows were stretching out from the side passage. Judging by what had come before they shouldn't have been there.

Scree cocked his head to listen but couldn't hear anything. He looked around. Thorpe nodded. So did a couple of others. So Scree charged around the corner. And stopped.

There were half a dozen things that looked like... Scree didn't know what they looked like. They were soft, liquid masses and seemed to be able to form themselves into any shape they wanted. Scree rushed forward, hoping someone would go with him. His target bent away from his first strike. But it wasn't quick enough the second time. And arm fell to the floor with a splash. Scree watched as the limb ran along the floor to rejoin the main body.

"Stinking cats. We got problems."

85: Aliens

SCREE WENT FORWARD AGAIN, though he didn't know if there was any point. Mintar, Chasm, Bones and two hurgon went with him. The dwarf and hurgon attacked low, the others went high. The first creature broke apart completely this time and splashed all over the floor.

They went for the next, Chasm at the front. Her mattock passed harmlessly through empty air as the thing twisted away, but she punched before the shape reformed. Her fist sank into the water and the trollop screamed. She shook her hand, trying to pull it free, but she was sucked further in, fighting all the way. She screamed until her face was completely submerged. Then her whole body was pulled inside the water. For a second more she continued to struggle, then she was gone. Dissolved away to nothing.

Scree swore as he started to back away. His sword was up, ready, but he didn't know if he'd be able to do anything with it.

"Clear the way," Thorpe shouted, his voice hoarse. He had the metal pipe down from his back and was wedging the closed end into the corner where the floor met the wall. Tim shoved some explosives down the other end and Amy followed that with bits of scrap metal from Brick's pack. "Clear," Thorpe shouted again as he broke off a tiny bit of chemical fuse.

Scree and the others got out of the way and a second later, Thorpe poured the chemical directly into a hole drilled near the base of the pipe.

The explosion made Scree's ears ring. He couldn't hear anything else. He looked around and saw the water creatures spread all over the floor, as if someone had dropped a tank out of the sky. But even as he watched, they were quickly reforming.

"Can we run?" asked Dido. It looked like she was ready to give it a try.

Scree doubted it.

All the little puddles started to join. There weren't going to be six creatures, there was going to be one huge one. Scree swallowed and started to back away.

Something stepped into the hall beyond the creature. A tree, leaves still dripping goo onto the floor. It bellowed, almost as loud as Thorpe's makeshift cannon, and charged forward, swinging mighty branch arms. The water creature shattered again and the tree dipped its root toes into each of the puddles.

Scree didn't want to hang around to see what was going to happen next. He turned and ran, continuing on the way he'd been going.

There was a voice in his head. <*How's it going, Scree?*>

<Stone. We got problems.>

<*Us too. You expected otherwise?*>

<I thought it'd be fun.>

They passed another knot of frozen, three legged robots.

"Scree, slow down. We could run into anything."

Scree gave a nod and slowed to a walk. Behind him, Flint, Bones and Shardy were taking the backpacks to give the humans a break.

<*You going to make it?*> Stone asked.

<Should do, I think. We must be close. How about you?>

<*We're almost there. But weird stinking things keep attacking us. We lost Chip and Makar.*>

<Damn.> If they'd missed some of the aliens there could be any number of deadly things wandering around the ship.

<*Yeah. Talus hurt pretty bad too.*>

<Just get everyone home.> Scree slowed as he approached another intersection. He thought he could hear something and stopped completely. <And Stone. Not sure if you wants to tell Kim, but looks like the multeese got a zoo on this ships. That's what Thorpe says anyway. Those things attacking you are somes of the dangerous specimens, but there's heaps of others still locked up.>

<*Reckon Kim'll want to know something like that.*>

<Maybe, but could be dangerous. You decide.>

<*Will do. See you on the other side, Scree.*>

<Yeah, see you there. Been nice knowing you.>

Scree readied his sword.

Shardy stepped up beside him, adjusting her pack and shifting her grip on her metal bar. "We killing things other trolls ain't even dreamed about, Scree," she said softly.

Scree gave a snort of laughter.

Tim McCree and Brick came up to the front line as well. The others got ready behind them.

"These things might be the last of their kind, Shardy," Tim said with a crooked smile. "We might be wiping out entire species."

They all laughed and charged around the corner.

An arrow the length of a pike took Shardy in the throat and knocked her a meter backwards. After a moment of shocked silence Beth, Suldon and Palsamon returned fire.

Their enemy was a huge shaggy beast about ten feet tall with leather armor and boots like drinking troughs. It hunched in the passageway like an unhappy wall.

The elves had fired three volleys and it hadn't even thought of reloading. Keeping to the side of the passage, Scree moved quickly forward. The creature swatted at him with a club the size of a small tree. The weapon knocked a hole in the wall and smashed through a glass case beyond. It reefed the club free and swung again. Scree ducked and there was a hole on the other side of the passage. Before the goo had splashed out onto the floor, before the alien could pull the tree trunk free again, Brick and Tim ran the creature through. It collapsed with a gurgle of breath and a sad look on its face.

Thorpe bent over Shardy but Scree didn't wait for the confirmation of what was obvious. He kicked the alien's sad face and started to walk.

"Ah, Scree?" Dido said.

He turned around. "What?"

The dwife was pointing through the hole in the first wall. There was creature lying on the floor. It looked like a turtle with a bright shell and long, pointed ears. It squirmed as they watched, coughing and shuddering.

"Burning cats." Scree turned to look at the other wall. The tree trunk club was still there, half in the room beyond, half out. And on the floor was... "What the hell?"

Dido went to look too.

There were what looked like a dozen or more arms, none of them attached to anything, with hands on both ends. There were also four donuts of two different sizes, and six balls about the size of one of Thorpe's cricket balls.

The arms started to move, and Scree raised his sword. Dido scurried back out of the way. Scree readied himself, turning to examine the turtle for a moment, wondering which creature would attack first. He had just come to the conclusion that *he* would attack first when...

"Wait, Scree." Thorpe held his arm. "The servant didn't release these ones. Let's just leave them and go."

Scree gave a small nod but didn't like the idea of leaving anything at his back. "How we going for time?"

Thorpe checked his watch— it was a mechanical thing from earth. "We've got about three quarters of an hour."

"All right." Scree nodded, turned and walked away. He glanced at Shardy once, then started to run.

-oOo-

Kim looked back out the window and saw Tuki, sailing across the empty space with a cable trailing behind.

"The other airlock," Dosa said. "On Level 6."

It hadn't looked quite the same as when Scree did it— the lad wobbled and twisted and squirmed— but it was a sight to see nonetheless.

On the other ship, someone had spotted Tuki, and apparently they could see where he was going to end up. There was a troll scrambling along the side of the ship, heading aft, trying to meet up with him. It was Scree, it had to be. Kim's heart was racing but she wasn't sure if she wanted to watch. She closed one eye, as if that would make a difference.

Tuki had only worked in zero gravity one other time, inside the kil'ini. That experiment hadn't been very successful. And like last time, he was going too fast. It was obvious to everyone, possibly even Tuki. The troll on the intercept mission was flying along now, letting go completely and letting the ship, at almost 10 kilometers per second, slowly overtake him. It was going to be close.

Tuki hit the ship and bounced. Kim winced as he started to float back the other way. He flailed his arms trying to grab something, anything.

And he grabbed the troll's hand. The two of them jerked to a halt and swung around onto the side of the ship with a thump that Kim almost thought she could hear.

"Time," Kim asked.

"Fifteen minutes."

It would be close. By the time the two of them got back to the hole... But they weren't going back to the hole. Kim saw the troll unclip the cable from Tuki's belt and attach it to the side of the ship.

"Too hard to move with that cable," Keeble said. He wound the gears on his hand. In and out. In and out. It annoyed the shit out of Kim and she turned back to the window.

People were exiting the hole, moving quickly along the side of the ship. Two trolls went first, then dwarves and an elf, then another two trolls. That was all.

"Where are the rest?" Kim said. "Where the hell are the rest?"

Tuki was already coming back across the cable, pulling himself along hand over hand. By the time the first troll started along the lad was halfway back. He was caught not long after. The troll used the same technique, but flew solo a lot of the time, merely using the cable to stay heading in the right direction.

"The elf is slowing them down," Keeble said.

Kim looked at the line moving along the side of the ship. It was true. The dwarves had grown up in the mountains and the trolls could do anything physical. The elf, it looked like a female, was the weak link when it came to climbing. She picked her way along carefully.

Scree must be at the back of the line, Kim thought. He won't leave them behind. She had thought the opposite a minute ago, but that didn't matter. She held her breath and watched.

Tuki and the troll were out of sight around the curve of the ship. The next two started across.

"Time?"

"Ten minutes."

The next bit wasn't so easy for the dwarves. They were hardly more confident than Tuki had been, pulling themselves along slowly. Finally, the elf reached the cable and immediately started to pull herself out into the nothing.

Kim opened her mouth to ask—

"Four minutes," Ping said.

"Shit."

The last troll in line unclipped the cable from the side of the ship before starting off.

"What's he doing?"

Those already on the *Hakahei* started to pull the cable, reeling in the stragglers like hooked fish.

"Two minutes."

The troll hanging onto the end of the cable was in the middle of nowhere. It seemed to be taking forever. He sliced through the mist as the others continued to pull him in.

"The gate's open," Tasko shouted.

86: Honor

KIM TURNED TO LOOK towards the front of the ship. The shifting glow of the gate was visible. "Shit. Shit, shit, shit."

The last troll moved out of sight around the curve of the ship.

"We should be on the bridge," Kim said, but they couldn't do anything anyway and the only enemy who could really hurt them was out there. They stood and watched.

Explosions erupted. In four places, all close to the hole in the side by the alien ship's standards. Blooms of fire flared momentarily. Huge holes appeared. Chunks of hull flew across the gap and clattered horribly against the *Hakahei.*

The ship disappeared. The universe disappeared.

Here and there, lights flickered on.

Kim took a deep breath. Empty space, real space, filled the window.

"Three minutes until all systems are back online," Keeble said. "Come on Inaki." He beckoned to the moai and the two of them hurried up to the bridge.

Kim wanted to go the other direction. She wanted to make sure everyone was all right. She wanted to find out who wasn't. Instead, she wheeled herself to the stair-hatch and stayed there. She took a deep breath and hurt her ribs.

Stone was the first person through the door. He looked exhausted. He was cut and bruised.

"Stone," Kim said. "Where's everyone else?"

"They're comin'."

"And... everyone else? Scree? And Thorpe and..."

Stone shrugged, then stepped out of the way as someone else came through the door behind him. Topper nudged his way past and threw himself down onto the floor.

"We can't just leave them back there. The whole ship didn't blow up. Just little bits. They might still be alive."

Kim forgot her knee and her foot and her ribs. She pushed herself upright and hobbled to the bridge as fast as she could. "Keeble, we've got to go back."

"Why?"

"Because we have to. They might be alive."

Keeble looked at his controls. “We can’t.”

“Why not?”

“We don’t have enough power. It’ll be two hours at this speed. Half an hour once we get going.”

“So...”

“And when we do have enough power, we have to locate the ship in the other universe, which will be next to impossible.” He glanced at Inaki, as if wondering if it could actually be done. “Then, if the ship’s still moving, we have to match speed and—”

Kim shouted. “I don’t care. Work something out.”

But surviving all the other million-to-one chances couldn’t help them with this one.

-oOo-

Scree was exhausted.

They crushed a thousand bugs under their boots, cracking the shells with a little pop and sending out sprays of black juice. Suldon got bitten and his ankle doubled in size in a matter of minutes. He didn’t complain and they kept walking.

Two hurgon were sprayed with acid when a snake lost its head. They died, screaming in agony. Another hurgon was torn in half by a shaggy, four armed creature that talked almost as much as Bones in a strange, singing language.

They used Thorpe’s cannon to blast their way through a plant that stumped along in a pot like a one legged monkey. Leaves drifted around as if autumn had come to the hallway.

Bethalin died when a huge, spiked creature rolled over the top of her. The elf didn’t make a sound.

They sliced open a giant purple frog and left its stinking corpse in the hall as its blood bubbled and popped.

Thorpe killed Peak with the cannon when bats swarmed all over the troll. When the creatures fell away he was half eaten, face twisted in a rictus of pain. Scree plunged forward with Talus, Mintar and Bones to hack and beat the last bats out of the air with grim, cold determination.

When they were done, Scree glanced at Peak’s body. “Time,” he asked.

“Half an hour.”

Around the next corner...

Scree stopped. Lying in the middle of the passage was the three-meter high alien who’d run from them back at the start. The one who’d been releasing all the others. It was dead. It was half eaten. The creatures that had done the eating were still there.

They looked up, blood dripping from their faces, and looked pleased at the idea of dessert. Scree crouched and readied his sword.

"Come on, you bastards." But he edged towards the wall as he said it.

The creatures, six of them, all different but unmistakably related, arranged themselves across the hall. They stalked forward, low to the ground, clawed feet clicking on the floor, red eyes dark with hatred.

The cannon took down two and injured a third. It pissed the rest off and they leapt forward. One attacked Scree and it was all he could do to stay alive for the first few seconds. He had one hand around the creature's neck, holding it off. He dropped his sword, used his other hand as well. The creature was snapping at him. The smell of blood and death washed over Scree's face and he almost vomited.

Then a moment of rest.

Amy was there, attacking with her hoe. Scree couldn't keep his grip when the creature suddenly changed its point of attack. It lashed out at the American with claws and teeth. It grabbed her hand, pulled her close. She screamed when it took her hand in its mouth and bit. She held up the stump, spraying blood, and screamed some more.

Scree scrabbled on the floor for his sword, couldn't find it. Then he kicked it away and scrambled after it on his hands and knees.

Finally, he grabbed it and rose to his feet. Tim raced forward to help his sister. He beat at the alien, pummeling its back and legs, mad with rage. The creature pulled Amy close again, silenced her screams with one jaw stretching bite. Tim was screaming and crying. He swung harder as his sister's body fell to the floor. The creature batted away his club, grabbed his arm, pulled him towards those blood soaked teeth.

A second after reclaiming his sword, Scree attacked too. He hacked at a leg, ran the creature through. He twisted the sword as the alien turned back to him. It spat out Tim's arm, lunged, but Scree twisted the sword again, used it to keep his distance.

And the alien died on the end of his sword, still slavering after his throat, still struggling to have one more bite.

Pulling his blade free, Scree turned to face the next fight. But it was done. Numbers had prevailed. Flint took Scree's sword from his hand and used it to finish the alien that had been injured in the initial cannon blast. He hacked the heads off all of them to make sure there'd be no surprises.

Scree drew in a deep breath. There was blood everywhere. Red blood and the dark, thick blood of the aliens. Everyone was covered in it. He wiped his face as he looked around. Tim and Amy were lying together and that seemed right. They'd never spoke much to each other, but Scree had seen them communicating in other ways. They'd left notes for the other to find, played games of hide and seek that could last hours, threw things at each other as they passed in the *Hakahei*'s narrow halls.

They'd continued to play the games they'd played as kids.

Another hurgon was dead too. Scree didn't even know its name. He hadn't really talked to any of them.

And...

"Dido?" Scree went to stand by the fallen dwife. Mintar was already there, crouched by her side. The green ribbon in the dwife's hair had come loose and Mintar took it out, wiped the blood away, and retied it. He smoothed her hair.

"I'm sorry, Mintar," Scree said. "She shouldn't have been here. I shouldn't have let her come."

But Mintar shook his head. "She wanted to be here. She wanted to help. We needed people, Scree, and dwives are people too."

"Yes, but..."

"Should we have stopped Amy from coming?"

Scree wasn't going to argue with him. "I'm sorry, Mintar."

Palsamon cleared his throat. "If we are to do this we should run. The servant is dead, we can hope these are the last creatures he released."

Scree looked around again. But if he stopped to look he would stay there until the world ended, which might not be all that far away. So he ran, and the others ran with him.

Twenty minutes later, Scree rounded a corner and slowed to a walk, sucking in deep breaths.

"Getting soft," he mumbled.

"Pardon?"

"Nothing." A few months ago he'd have fought his way from one end of the ship to the other without difficulty. Now? All he wanted to do was sit down to rest. But a few months ago he wouldn't have been fighting this fight at all. A lifetime ago he'd told Nemucca that trolls avoided any fight they couldn't win, and yet here he was. The lad had replied that he'd change his mind when he found someone whose honor he craved. Scree had probably called him an idiot, and yet here he was...

Just down the hall was a door. A bloody big door, with reinforcing panels seamlessly joined to what already appeared to be impervious material. There were no other passages. There were no other doors.

"What do you think?" Thorpe asked.

"How much time we got?"

"About fifteen minutes."

"Then I reckon we've found what we've been searching for."

Thorpe nodded and looked around. He went to Flint and took the pack of explosives.

"You want some of this," Bones said. He took off his pack and handed over the fusing. "I reckon you will. Don't want too much though. Haven't got all day, do we.

Not all day. Not long at all." He rubbed his injured leg. "I reckon I've had enough running for today."

Thorpe and Brick set the explosives, jamming some into each corner of the door and saving the biggest piece for the middle. Then they broke off five even lengths of fuse. Bones went forward to take one of the fuses. Mintar took another and Brother Kalis took the last one. They stood near the explosives, looking at each other. Looking at Scree.

"Ready," said Thorpe. "One, two... Three."

They stuck the fuses into the explosives and ran. Scree waited until they had passed him, then he ran as well.

From around the corner the blast was powerful enough to make his ears hurt. He didn't wait to recover. He raced around the corner and ran through the smoke.

The door was a twisted, red-hot wreck. He went through the gap, sword ready. Hakans and hurgon crowded his back.

87: Multeese

SCREE STALKED THROUGH THE SMOKE, ready to do violence. He could see three figures standing motionless near the front of the room.

They still didn't move as Scree got closer. Eventually, he could see why. They were robots. Three legged, like the army on Lapenti, but with shining bodies and clear glass bulbs for heads.

The robots weren't a threat, so Scree turned to examine the rest of the room.

Lying on the floor in the corner was another of the tall, skinny servants. The creature's head was holding on with one thin, bloody bit of flesh. An arm was missing. It was cut and bleeding from a dozen other wounds. A piece of shrapnel was lodged in its chest. Scree wanted to kill it again anyway.

But he continued to look around.

The one huge window went down low to the ground. The controls seemed to be nothing more than different colored panels on the floor with levers and switches on the walls.

The only movement came from the bulbs on top of the robots. Green gases swirled around a mess of wires— copper, silver, and gold.

"Is that the multeese?" Scree asked.

Thorpe was already looking. "I'm not sure?" he said. He tapped on the bulb and the gas swirled and danced. "I think it must be." He pursed his lips. "I suppose this might be the only way they could think to actually be able to *do* anything."

"Ten minutes," Brick said, checking his watch.

Scree shrugged. "Don't think it matters. Lets blow things up then get out of here."

"Get out of here?" Mintar said. "And go where?"

"Home."

Bones was already getting to work, sticking explosives to the robots and preparing small fuses.

"We can't jump back," Mintar said. "We'll never make it."

Scree shrugged. "I'd rather die slow out there than in here not trying."

"Save some for that wall there," Scree told Bones, pointing to the side wall facing out towards the *Hakahei.* At least the bridge was on the right side of the ship instead of being in the center.

When the explosives were set, they put on their breather masks and blew out the wall. Scree went to stand in the hole. If he leaned out he thought he could see the ship, a spot of blackness about five kilometers behind.

Thorpe leaned out to look as well. “Easy.”

“I thinks I notice your sarcasm.” Scree said. Thorpe was right though. It was so impossible there wasn’t even any point trying.

“Let’s kill these suckers, then do nothing,” Brick said from beside one of the robots. “Let’s just sit here and wait to be rescued.”

“By who?”

“Kim’ll give it a shot.”

Mintar shook his head. “It won’t work, no matter how much Kim wants it to.”

“Why not?” Brick asked.

Mintar explained. Scree couldn’t fault the explanation.

Thorpe sighed. “See if Stone has made it back to the *Hakahei*.”

“Five minutes.”

Scree didn’t like sitting around doing nothing, but he nodded. <Yo Stone, you there?>

<*Yo, Scree.*>

<Where you at?>

<*Climbing.*>

<You gonna make it back to the *Hakahei*?>

<*Doing it now.*>

<We thought we might hang around here. You know, see what happens.>

<*Right. See you ‘round then, Scree.*>

Other trolls said their farewells too, and Scree finally knew for sure that none of them were trolls any more. <Say good-bye to Kim for me.> He gave a little smile. <It was an honor...>

“The *Hakahei* has gone,” Mintar said.

“I knows.”

-oOo-

Scree looked around, adjusted his mask and cleared his throat. “So we need to blow these things up then?”

“I guess so,” Thorpe replied. “Might as well use all the explosives. Make sure we do it properly.”

Scree was about to agree when he saw a flash of movement out of the corner of his eye. He leapt back, sword raised, and watched as a strange creature climbed up the first of the robots. It was the thing they had left lying on the floor after the giant’s club broke the glass box. Not the turtle, the other thing. Or part of it. Or some of them. Eight hands had grabbed onto one of the big donuts. Three of those arms had also grabbed some of the other bits— the balls and the smaller donut— with the hands on the other end of the arms.

"What the hell?"

Two of the balls had eyes on them, blinking slowly, separately. One of the hands held a piece of metal.

Another flash of movement and the rest of the body parts from down below came to a halt in the middle of the room. The parts quickly rearranged themselves into an approximation of a hakan body. Two 'legs', beneath the larger donut. Three arms holding onto the top of that— two as actual arms, the last as a neck holding the smaller donut. There were three more arms, two holding eyeballs and the last holding a ball that had a mouth. The mouth was smiling.

"Bloody hell." Thorpe said.

The second creature sidled toward the soldier. It wasn't threatening. It was testing Thorpe's reaction. "Let's see what it wants," he said, though he didn't sound confident.

The thing came closer and Thorpe still didn't move, so it reached out one of its hands.

Thorpe looked at Scree. He looked around. "Nice knowing you all," he said, and he reached out and took the hand.

The creature shuddered and shook for a moment, then let go.

"That's it?" Brick asked. "It just wanted to hold hands?"

The creature shook again, like a dog drying off. One eye blinked, the other. A long tongue came out of the mouth, wiggled, rolled, went back in. It licked its lips. "Hello."

Scree almost dropped his sword.

"Hello," Palsamon said calmly. "My name is Palsamon."

"My name is," it glanced at Thorpe, "William."

Thorpe raised his eyebrows. "William? That's my father's name."

"I apologies if I offended you. My real name would be unpronounceable for you. This way is easier."

"No, that's all right." Thorpe rubbed at the hand that had held the hand of the alien.

The creature nodded. "I am William, then. I have been imprisoned for... A long time. I do not know how you would measure the time. A long time. My people were once called tokken."

"Perhaps your people yet live," Palsamon said.

"Perhaps," William said. "But I would like revenge, just in case."

"We were going to blow the bastards up," Scree said.

William nodded. "We would prefer something a bit more personal," he said. "If you don't mind."

Scree nodded. "Whatever. Long as they die."

"We wanted to let them live."

Scree narrowed his eyes. "How's that revenge?"

"If we throw them out into this strange universe the gas particles will be separated. They will still be able to think, to a degree, but will not be able to actually *do* anything."

"Are you sure?"

"There needs to be a certain amount of the gas in one place, interacting, for them to be able to act."

Thorpe smiled. "So they'll have an eternity to think about what they're missing."

William nodded his upper donut.

"Sounds good then," Scree said.

Some of hakans pushed the multeese robot towards the hole in the wall.

The second tokken clung to its head all the while. When they got close, it started to bash on the glass bulb with its piece of metal. The glass cracked and the creature paused. And when the robot was at the wall, starting to lean out, it bashed again. The glass smashed and the tokken stuck its hand into the gas as it streamed out through the hole. The robot tipped further and the alien leapt clear before it finally tumbled into the nothing of the universe. And the gas disappeared, separated, blown away by the wind of their passage.

The next two robots went the same way, lost in moments in the horrible, swirling mist.

When they were done, the two creatures touched each other. The second one shook, like William had, and tested its lips and tongue. "Hello."

Scree nodded. "Hi."

"My name is," this one looked at Thorpe as well, considered... "My name is Molly."

Thorpe laughed. "My dog when I was a boy."

"Thank you," Molly said. It rearranged itself into almost-humanoid form.

"You're welcome." Scree was slightly bemused. "I suppose."

"Can we leave this universe now, please? I don't like it very much."

"No, actually," Scree said.

"We don't really know how," Thorpe added. "So we're going to wait here to be rescued."

"You don't know how?" William asked. "This was part of your plan?"

"You sound a bit too much like Thorpe," Scree said. "But how many multeese have been killed in the past?"

"None that I know of," William conceded.

"Right, then don't points out the one little thing we did wrong."

The one little thing.

88: One Button

KIM SAT IN THE CAPTAIN'S chair and stared out the window, trying to think. Thinking wasn't actually the problem— not thinking about Scree and Brick and Thorpe and all the others, that was the problem. How far had the alien ship drifted in the other universe? How long until it stopped? Impossible to know. Maybe impossible to work out.

She turned her attention to her console, as if she would find the one button to fix all her problems.

"Hurgon," Inaki said.

"What?" Of course, he was right. The hurgon were the only people who could really help them now. The kil'ini could maneuver in the other universe and, maybe, bring the ship back.

"There are kil'ini back at Lapenti. Not many, but if we can get them a message, they may help."

Kim hit the buttons for the intercom and called for Cuto to come to the bridge. Then she sat impatiently, waiting for him to arrive.

"Cuto, we need help. How long will it take kil'ini to get here from Lapenti?"

"Not very long. Only minutes, I suspect."

"Get them then, quickly. Use the ansible."

"Why are they needed?"

"Because Scree and the others might still be alive."

"Cuto will call. Though it might be half an hour by the time any rescue is complete."

"What? Why?"

"It is not just getting here. Kil'ini will have to chase the multeese ship. And then get everyone out. Then get oxygen into the rescue chamber. Half an hour might be a conservative estimate. They may run out of air in the meantime."

"Don't..." She held up a hand. *"Just do it."*

Inaki cleared his throat. "Kim?"

"What is it, Inaki? I'm busy."

She turned and looked at the moai. He was pointing out the window. And the multeese ship was there, racing along a couple of hundred kilometers in front of the *Hakahei.*

Kim swallowed. "I thought Stone said it was all under control." She waited for the face on the screen behind her. She waited for the missiles.

A voice came over the radio. *"You goings to send someone to gt us or nots?"* Scree asked.

"What? Yes. We're on our way. Yes."

She was wondering what to do, trying to get her head working. She was looking at all the buttons, looking for the magical one again.

"Get us closer," Stone said over the radio.

Kim had accelerated a while ago, trying to charge the batteries, so they were already gaining on the larger ship. *Done then.* As much as it could be. She had everything under control. Apart from her hands. Her hands were shaking.

And her heart.

When they finally got within range she tried to match speeds. By the time she was done, she noticed the Lander crossing to the gap. She sat back and closed her eyes and prayed that Scree and the rest of her crew would get back alive.

She didn't know how long she sat like that, breathing, tapping strange, meaningless rhythms on the arm of her chair, but she didn't open her eyes until there was a commotion down on the floor of the bridge.

Scree was standing there with a group of hakans and a hurgon behind him. She stood up, staring at Scree. It was long seconds before she turned her attention to the others. Thorpe, Brick, Flint and Bones. Suldon, Palsamon and Mintar. That was all? Where were the others who had gone across and not come back with the first group? The McCrees. Chasm, Peak and Shardy. Beth. Dido. Where was Dido? She sat back down in her chair, rubbing at her eyes. How could Dido have died? Kim knew the dwife was no more worthy of life than any of the others, but she was the one who seemed to symbolize all those who had been lost.

Those who were still alive deserved something, but Kim didn't think she could do it. Dido?

"What are you doing?" Thorpe asked. "I told you to stay in the wheelchair."

Kim opened her eyes. She stared at the soldier and thanked him silently. "You mind your own business, Thorpe." She gave a small smile. "I'm the Captain and I'll do as I please."

"Of course." He nodded. "I apologize."

Kim could see that they were all exhausted, even the trolls, but they had the look of people who'd done great things and would do them again when the time came. She smiled for them all. "I'm glad you're home," she said. "But how did you do it?" How did they do it? How did any of them get back alive. She had sent them out expecting they would all die, perhaps for nothing. To have any of them back alive was more than she had hoped for. She tried to concentrate on the positives, but it was hard. Dido…

Scree shrugged. "There was a button. We pressed it."

"There was just one button?"

"No, there were lots."

"And you just happened to press the right one?"

"No. William pressed it."

Kim didn't say anything for a moment. "Who's William?"

"My father," Thorpe said. "And also an alien we met."

"You met an alien?"

"We mets a few. Buts William and Molly were the only friendly ones."

"Right. And you talked to William and Molly?" The odds of that were unbelievable.

"Yes. But more importantly," Thorpe said, "Molly talked to a multeese for a moment as it was leaving the ship."

Kim couldn't think. She needed sleep. But she supposed Scree and Thorpe were being deliberately difficult. The multeese left the ship? "What?"

"Molly talked to the multeese and, amongst other things, found out where the button was. Not that she knew it was important at the time."

"Right." She wouldn't worry about it now. She'd ask them later, when they weren't being so obtuse and she wasn't being so stupid.

"Would you like to meet William and Molly?" Scree asked. "They're down stairs. If they decide to hang around they might do Meledrin out of a job." He seemed pleased by the thought.

"Yes, of course. But I think you should all go and rest. Go to medical. And, Scree."

"Kim?"

"Don't you ever do something like that again. You're a bloody idiot."

He smiled. "You told me to."

Kim smiled back. "Well, I'm a idiot too."

"By the way," Thorpe said, "there's thousands of other aliens across in the multeese ship. It's like a zoo."

"What?"

Kim listened as Thorpe explained. And when he'd finished, she sat silently for a long time. "Ahhh... So we have to rescue them before they run out of oxygen?" What were the odds that they all breathed oxygen?

"They should be fine for a while," Thorpe said. "Power is probably a bigger issue, to run the life support things they were in."

Good. She had a minute to think. "Go to medical, then. Rest. I'll see what I can organize." Calling Earth would probably be a good start. Then organizing for the hurgon to get their contracts back to Hulgorn. And...

But Scree and his companions hadn't moved.

Flint, standing by Scree's side, suddenly stood to attention and saluted. Others started to do the same.

Kim blushed and quickly sat back down. "Well, if none of you are going to medical or to rest then I'll find jobs for you," she said in her best serious voice.

But there was an alien down stairs, and more across in the multeese ship. She'd have to think about them sooner or later.

Endings

KIM STOOD TO THE SIDE, listening as Tuki spoke. His confidence was there for all to see.

He spoke of the sacrifices made and the great deed of defeating the multeese.

And he was right, but just now, Kim still thought the price they paid was too high. She wanted to go up the front and add her voice to the memories, but she couldn't. She stayed where she was, tears running down her cheeks, and listened.

When the ceremony was over, people drifted away. Suldon and Thorpe were talking to William, a strange conglomeration of body parts that seemed to come and go as they pleased. The other one was nearby, talking with Lisarea.

"Kim?"

Kim watched Keeble, Topper, Ari and Ping for a moment as they wandered away. She reined in her attention. "Yes, Mel?"

"Palsamon and I were hoping you would be able to take us to Sherindel."

"What? Why?"

"We believe we know the location of a lost city and we wish to investigate."

"You've found a lost city since leaving Sherindel?"

"Yes. Palsamon was reading a book and it mentioned a name. I am not really sure I am interested in digging up the past when the future seems much more interesting but..." She glanced at Palsamon and blushed. "It seems my future lies with Palsamon, one way or the other."

Mel was giving up what she wanted to be with a man? Kim smiled but decided to keep quite on that subject. "So you're going to set up camp at this city and study it? Dig stuff up and whatever?"

"It would seem so. We are going to see if we can convince some dwarves to assist us."

Kim raised an eyebrow.

"It was Palsamon's idea."

"What about the *Hakahei*? Who'll run the communications department?"

"Tami is more than capable."

"Tami?"

Meledrin blushed. "Tamidilin."

"Of course, Mel."

The elf walked away and Kim smiled as, over near the wall, Topper tentatively took Ping's hand.

Hoodek and Bargle were laughing about something. The two young dwarves cut off, as if feeling guilty.

Mintar was talking with Tuki and Ruby. The dwarf had a green ribbon in his hand. When Tuki and Ruby left, he tied it into his beard and went to look at the newest memorial plaque on the wall.

A knot of trolls were nearby.

Standing in the dirt, watching the swirl of people around her, Kim felt alone. She didn't know if it was because she was the captain or because she had hardly taken any part at all in the events of the last few days. She'd been unconscious or injured through most of them. And when she woke up she sent everyone out to die.

Kim watched as Scree and Thorpe came to stand with her.

"William and Molly are fascinating people," Thorpe said. "They can feel their limbs from about a hundred meters away, but if they are separated for too long the parts will die. The small circle bit holds the brain. The large one has most of the other bits they need. But energy and... whatever... can be passed from one bit to the other, just through contact." He shook his head. "They can also take stuff from other beings— like information from me, for instance. Very interesting."

Kim shook her head. "Amazing."

Scree nodded, "They are. But I reckon there's a lot of interesting and amazing hakans around here as well." He ran his hand over his bald head. "Anyway, I thinks I'm going to go and rest." He nodded to Thorpe and Kim and left.

Kim stood for a moment, blinking. "Ummm... You'll be pleased to know, Doctor Thorpe, that I'm going to rest too. Let me know if we hear any updates from Captain Fallon and the *Amelia*." The American ship could arrive any time.

"Of course."

She nodded and hurried away, the momentary touch of Scree's hand on hers singing in her mind. Hakans could pass information through contacts as well, apparently. She didn't feel so alone after all.

-oOo-

KIM WATCHED AS WILLIAM searched through the files.

"The multeese computers are vast and complicated," the alien said.

Kim could believe that.

"If Molly had not touched the multeese I would not be able to find anything." He sent one of his spare hands crawling off to push some of the buttons on the other side of the room. "There are one hundred and twenty seven thousand intelligent species stored on this ship, with one of each gender for each. Some have only one gender, but others have as many as five."

Kim raised her eyebrows. "That's a lot of aliens." It was a lot of people to get to know. The *Amelia* was just a few hours away now, racing through real space after a few long jumps. The Americans were going to be busy helping very soon.

"A lot, yes," William agree. "They have been collected over nearly two hundred thousand years from across three galaxies."

"How do they all fit?"

"Many are hardly the size of..." He held his fingers a couple of centimeters apart. "Some are very small."

"Yeah, but some must be huge."

"I would shrug, but I do not have shoulders." He tapped at a few more buttons. "There are hakans in here as well, twelve in all?"

"Twelve?"

"Yes. It seems that the genetic codes of the six peoples were altered slightly— do you know what that means?— so the multeese could not decide if the six different peoples were truly the same species."

"Where are they? We should release them."

"There is no hurry. All of this will be very shocking for them and you should make sure you are prepared to help them adjust."

Kim looked at William and swallowed. For the first time, she wondered how well he and Molly were really coping. Perhaps his contact with both Thorpe and the multeese was helping. She cleared her throat. "Does it say where your home is?"

"Yes. The hurgon home world— there are three hurgon stored in the ship somewhere— is here." He pointed to one side of the room. "And my home is over there." He pointed to the other side of the room. There is almost half a galaxy between."

Kim looked from one point to the next, as if she could see the distance between them. "After we drop off Grandmother Donni and the damn contracts, we're going to start heading in that direction." She figured it was the least they could do. "We'll get you and Molly back home."

"We are not going to stay to help the P'targa?"

Kim shrugged. "I don't want to be involved in that mess. I'm sure the Americans will do what they can."

"But the outcome…"

"Isn't really important. The hurgon will probably take a few decades to sort themselves out and hakans will have all that time to get organized as well." She sighed and sat back. "Donni says the minor families won't lose, but we'll be well and truly ready if they do."

"If you say so."

"If nothing else, we've got the multeese technology. We can use it to bargain or to threaten." She shrugged. "Either way, the hurgon aren't an issue. So, we'll concentrate on getting you home. A worthy cause, I think."

"We have been gone a long time. It might not even exist anymore."

He didn't sound sad. Maybe it was too big a thing to truly understand.

"We'll get you home," Kim repeated.

"It is a long way." He looked back at the computer. "It could take a thousand years to get there. On the way we could pass a thousand of the other civilizations mentioned in these computers. Or their remains."

Kim nodded. "It should be an interesting journey."

Other Books
By Scott J Robinson

The Last Great Hero:
The Age of Heroes
A History of Magic
An Army of Heroes

Rawk is one of the great Heroes. He has travelled the world for forty years, hunting exotic creatures, battling magic and fighting evil wherever he found it. But he has been fighting mostly mundane battles since Prince Weaver outlawed magic. And with no great deeds left to be done, Rawk is afraid he'll soon be the old man in the corner of the tavern, dreaming of the good old days and telling tales for anyone who will buy him a drink.

But when a huge wolden wolf is spied from the walls of Katamood it signals a return to a time when magic and monsters prevailed. And, as always, the city turns to Rawk to save them.

Rawk will fight to ensure the Age of Heroes doesn't slip away into history, but what if the good old days aren't quite as good as he remembers?

The Brightest Light

Kade was once the up and coming star of The Skyway Men, a ruthless criminal organization. Then he made one mistake. The another. Then one too many. Lucky to be left alive, he was banished to a backwoods skyland that flew the quietest wind-lanes.

When he's finally offered another chance Kade can't believe his luck. But ten years working a smithy and fixing crystal engines is a long time, and with a weapon like none other up for grabs, the stakes are higher than ever.

In a world of death and corruption, shady deals and dirty deeds Kade doesn't know who to trust. He doesn't know who's on which side. He doesn't even know which side *he's* on any more.

All he knows is that murder and mayhem aren't what they used to be.

About the Author

Scott J. Robinson has been writing fantasy and Science Fiction for as long as he can remember. He's had short stories and poetry published in various publications over the last 25 years.

When he isn't writing, Scott wastes too much time on Facebook. He also likes photography and recently retired from a very mediocre cricket career.

Scott lives in Woodford, a small town near Brisbane in Queensland, Australia with his wife and 3 children.

For more information visit www.tengama.com

www.ingramcontent.com/pod-product-compliance
Lightning Source LLC
Chambersburg PA
CBHW030643120726
47905CB00001B/31
9780994335531